PARA HANDY

PARA HANDY

The collected stories from 'The *Vital Spark*',
'In Highland Harbours with Para Handy' and
'Hurricane Jack of the *Vital Spark*'
by

NEIL MUNRO
(HUGH FOULIS)

With eighteen previously uncollected stories

Introduced and Annotated
by

BRIAN D. OSBORNE
&
RONALD ARMSTRONG

Birlinn

This edition first published in 1992 by
Birlinn Limited
West Newington House
10 Newington Road
Edinburgh
EH9 1QS

www.birlinn.co.uk

Reprinted 1993, 1995
Revised editions 1997 and 2002

Introductory material
copyright © Brian D. Osborne and
Ronald Armstrong 1992 and 2002

ISBN 1 84158 227 1

British Library Cataloguing-in-Publication Data
A catalogue record for this book is available
from the British Library

Cover images reproduced by courtesy of
Dan McDonald and Mrs Annie McMillan

Printed and bound by
Cox & Wyman Ltd, Reading

Contents

In Highland Harbours with Para Handy

Hurricane Jack of the Vital Spark

Uncollected Stories 1905–1924

Foreword

The remarkable endurance of the "Para Handy" stories, which still attract a wide audience over ninety years after their first appearance in the *Glasgow Evening News*, is testified to by the collected stories remaining in print throughout this period. Apart from the continuing popularity of the stories, however, there are two reasons for suggesting that readers will find this volume useful.

Firstly we hope to rehabilitate some of Munro's literary reputation, once considerable and largely based on his historical novels, but we believe properly owing as much to these shorter pieces.

Along with the reading public's appetite for the West Highland tales goes a wider celebrity, amounting almost to notoriety, which owes much to the television adaptations of recent years. At any rate the man in the street has an image of Para Handy and a range of quotations and anecdote based on the character or its televised representation even if he has never read the stories. We are unaware of any other collection of Scots comic prose which enjoys such a lasting and secure place in the affections of the public.

Paradoxically, though, Munro's creation can be termed neglected, since few critics have taken the stories seriously. The only Munro with an entry in Margaret Drabble's *Oxford Companion to English Literature* is H.H. Munro ("Saki"). Furthermore Munro seems to have set the tone for the undervaluing of these stories by his publishing them under the pen-name of "Hugh Foulis".

As importantly, we feel that present day readers, while relishing the vivid and highly accessible comedy of character and dialogue, will appreciate the stories more fully with an understanding of the background and an explanation of the many specific references to contemporary people and events. These tales have a richly observed setting, rooted in time and place and the largely vanished Glasgow,

Clyde and West Highland world of the *Vital Spark* needs and deserves describing and illustrating.

The explanatory notes also look at such intriguing questions as: where was Para Handy born; what were his religious views; what did he think of international affairs; what did he do before becoming skipper of the *Vital Spark*?

Also included are eighteen stories, rescued from the pages of the *Glasgow Evening News*, which were never included in the three original separate volumes of stories or any of the complete editions published in the last fifty years.

Para's World

No one surely, reads these stories for the social history, when there are so many other good reasons, yet a clear picture emerges of a lost world of West Highland villages bound together by the sea and the vessels on it. In late Victorian or Edwardian times (the period covered by the stories is roughly 1900-1920) these communities were enjoying a golden age of water transport. Along Munro's native Loch Fyneside alone there were seven piers and yet other places where a boat came out to meet the steamer.

A winter service was kept up but it was the holiday trade which made the steamers profitable. Munro's description of a typical July Saturday which appears in "Wee Teeny" is worth quoting here for its characteristically colourful account of a scene which could be repeated at anyone of scores of piers from Craigendoran to Campbeltown.

"The last passenger steamer to sail that day from Ardrishaig was a trip from Rothesay. It was Glasgow Fair Saturday and Ardrishaig Quay was black with people. There was a marvellously stimulating odour of dulse, herring and shell-fish, for everybody carried away in a handkerchief a few samples of these marine products that are now the only sea-side souvenirs not made in Germany. The *Vital Spark* in ballast, Clydeward bound, lay inside the passenger steamer, ready to start when the latter had got under weigh, and Para Handy and his mate meanwhile sat on the fo'c'sle-head of "the smertest boat in the tred" watching the frantic efforts of lady excursionists to get their husbands on the steamer before it was too late, and the deliberate efforts of the said husbands to slink away up the village again just for one more drink. Wildly the steamer hooted from her siren, fiercely clanged her bell, vociferously the Captain roared upon his bridge, people aboard yelled eagerly to friends ashore to hurry up, and the people ashore as eagerly demanded to know what all the hurry was about, and where the bleezes was Wull. Women loudly defied the purser to let the ship go away without their John, for he had paid his money for his ticket, and though he was only a working-man his money was as good as anybody else's; and John, on the quay, with his hat thrust back on his head, his thumbs in the armhole of his waistcoat and a red handkerchief full of dulse at his feet, gave display of step-dancing that was responsible for a great deal of the congestion of traffic at the shore end of the gangway."

This description, with its colour, vitality and shrewd observation could almost be from the "Pickwick Papers".

At the same time the gabbarts, and later the steam puffers, were attending to the more essential needs of these coastal communities. The puffer was generally thought of as a coal boat, but could also be pressed into carrying a tremendous variety of goods. If we are to believe her skipper the *Vital Spark* was suited to carrying "nice genteel luggage for the shooting lodges" as did the doyenne of steamers, the *Columba,* but in practice the cargoes were more likely to be "coals and whunstone, and oak bark, and timber, and trash like that". She did take a farmer's flitting on at least one occasion, though, and her mixed cargo included everything " from bird cages to cottage pianos".

A life in the "coastin' tred" was hard and dirty no doubt, but you might not suppose so from a quick glance at these stories. Para, Dougie and the rest of the crew, "Brutain's hardy sons" each and every one, certainly are seen now and then battling against a gale but usually the picture is of a leisurely life — "we went into Greenock for some marmalade, and did we no' stay three days". In harbour there was from time to time some conflict between the skipper and the crew. Para, with an eye to enhancing the ship's reputation as the "smertest boat in the tred", would often wish some painting to be done, while the crew, if in funds, would rather go ashore and relax in a harbour-side inn.

When the crew were at their ease, they would sit in the fo'c'sle, a small triangular space in the bows of the ship which acted as cabin, galley and mess-room for the four man crew, and tell a baur or two of "All the seas that lie between Bowling and Stornoway".

Para's Places

Turn to the section on "Para in Print" to discover that Munro's stories, appearing as they did in an evening newspaper, were written with an eye to topical events and personalities; very much of their time. They were, however, even more firmly rooted in a sense of place.

Just how deep were Munro's knowledge and affection for "Para's Places" we can guess from a glimpse of his 1907 publication *The Clyde, River and Firth*. This popular account, perhaps rather over-written to modern taste, gives a lyrical description of the river from its source to Ailsa Craig. A few extracts from its pages provide an interesting commentary on the setting in which Munro placed the Captain and his crew. And firstly...

GLASGOW

"A mighty place for trade...; with a stern and arid Sabbath; and a preposterous early hour for the closing of public houses".

In the stories, Glasgow is where Para goes to get his orders from the *Vital Spark*'s owner; it is also home for the crew who seldom venture out of the relatively circumscribed area of the harbour and the housing areas nearby like Gorbals, Plantation & Finnieston.

On either side of

" a fairway of 620 feet at its widest and 362 at its narrowest point" ..."the harbour life slops over its actual precincts, and the neighbouring streets...bear a marine impress. Their tall "lands" of flats fed from a common stair are the homes of folk whose men are on the quays."

In "Dougie's Family" Munro informs us that the mate, and his wife and ten children, live up one of these common stairs in the Plantation area, and in the very next tenement lives Dan Macphail and his family. Even the Captain goes to live in Glasgow after his marriage to the baker's little widow. At other times we hear of "baals" and similar "high jeenks" at, presumably, the Highlanders' Institute; a canary is purchased at the Bird Market; and of course the "Highlandman's Umbrella" is used as a meeting place for exiles from the North. As Para says "its Gleska for gaiety, if you have the money".

Neil Munro was a working journalist before anything else and his Glasgow and its river are seen from the perspective which comes from first-hand experience. Undoubtedly he haunted the ferries, lingered on the quays among sailors of all nations and gazed at the cargoes loading and unloading in the harbour of what was then the second city of the Empire.

Yet perhaps more than just a working journalist, even in the cub reporter days; a poet perhaps, a Conrad or an Orwell before his time? (Though not exactly "Down and Out in Glasgow".) Examine this characteristic passage from *The Clyde* and speculate.

"Nor even then can one rightly comprehend the harbour who has not brooded beside sheer-leg and crane-jib that are mightily moving enormous weights as if they had been toys; swallowed the coal-dust of the docks, dodged traction engines, eaten Irish stew for breakfast in the Sailors' Home, watched Geordie Geddes trawl for corpses, sat in the fo'c'sles of "tramps", stood in a fog by the pilot on the bridge, heard the sorrows of a Shore Superintendent and the loyal lies of witnesses in a Board of Trade examination, who feel bound to "stick by the owners" and swear their engines backed ten minutes before the accident; or sat on a cask in the Prince's Dock on peaceful Sabbath mornings when the shipping seemed asleep, or an unseen concertina played some sailor's jig for canticle."

Did the memory of the "unseen concertina" provide an inspiration for our jaunty character Sunny Jim? It is a jig-tune he plays on his "bonny wee melodeon" to accompany the dancing sausages in the story "A New Cook" which first appeared a few months after the publication of *The Clyde, River and Firth*.

THE UPPER RIVER

The stretch of the river from Bowling to Greenock features in several of the tales. Although never stated, the *Vital Spark*'s home port would seem to have been Bowling, although she frequently called in at Greenock for orders and cargoes. Although the puffer design was based on the necessity to pass through the 70 foot locks on the Forth and Clyde Canal the *Vital Spark* was an "outside boat" and we have but one record of the crew negotiating the Forth and Clyde Canal.

THE FIRTH OF CLYDE

The wider Firth was where the courses of the elegant passenger steamers of Messrs. Macbrayne and the railway companies crossed that of the workaday *Vital Spark*. The great *fin de siècle* holiday boom had led to the expansion of resorts such as Largs, Millport and Rothesay. Newer watering places had grown up alongside older communities and the steam puffer came into its own as a workhorse to bring in the building materials and fuel. Neil Munro described all this in *The Clyde, River and Firth* while in his fictional recreation of this world Para Handy is to be found ploughing all the waters of the estuary.

Down to ARRAN for example; Para has a wager with a Brodick man about a singing canary and returns with a "cargo of grevel" to collect his bet. It is also in Arran that we first hear of Hurricane Jack, that larger than life character, "as weel kent in Calcutta as if he wass in the Coocaddens", stealing "wan smaal wee sheep" from the shore on the island's west coast at Catacol.

Elsewhere, at the head of LOCH LONG the Arrochar midges are so fierce one night that they provoke the Captain to such hyperbole as to make "Mudges" a favourite tale with anyone who has visited the West Coast in high summer.

LOCH FYNE

The Clyde's longest sea-loch is the real centre of Para Handy's world. About one half of the stories have a connection with this area and Para himself may have been born there. However, for a fuller discussion of this point, see the notes to "In Search of a Wife".

Go to Loch Fyne now and to the uninitiated it may seem like a sleepy backwater, but to the devoted readers of these tales almost every placename has its delightful associations:

busy TARBERT — where Para met the spae-wife at the Fair and where he fell foul of the law for sounding the ship's whistle at 2.00 a.m.

quiet CAIRNDOW — where "they keep the two New Years"

and perhaps most magical of all, FURNACE — "where you don't need tickets for a baal as long as you ken the man at the door and taalk the Gaalic at him."

You might, today, follow the "Royal Route" from the Clyde to Ardrishaig, through the Crinan Canal and out into West Highland waters through the Dorus Mor, the "Great Gate", sailing perhaps as far as Mull, where at Tobermory the enterprising crew sold tickets to look at the whale. There is indeed much charm in the descriptions of these more distant scenes; however in reading this book you must, above all, know your Loch Fyne as it was in the heyday of the herring fishing, that legendary time of "high jeenks and big hauls; you werena very smert if you werena into both of them."

...many generations of Loch Fyneside men have followed a vocation which has much of the uncertainty of backing horses without so much amusement. Towns like Inveraray, Lochgilphead, and Tarbert grew up, as it were, round the fishing smacks that in old days ran into their bays for shelter, and Minard, Crarae, Lochgair, Castle Lachlan, Strachur, and other villages on either side of the Loch depend to some extent for their existence on the silver harvest of the sea

The Humour of "Para Handy"

Almost all of the comic flavour of these stories is to be found in the dialogue rather than in the narrative, and no part of the dialogue is more important than Para Handy's own contribution. Into the mouth of his skipper Munro has put any amount of humorous anecdotes and reflections, so much so that some of the stories are virtually monologues. For example, although it may be a matter of taste, to many readers the semi-mythical Hurricane Jack as described by Para with a "back on him like a shipping box" is preferable to the Jack who later makes a personal appearance in the stories.

Para's speech is of course given a fine exotic touch by the fact that he, and Dougie the Mate, have "the Gaalic". (No lover of these stories could, with the wealth of examples provided, commit the solecism of pronouncing Gaelic as "Gaylic"!)

While there may be a touch of the stage Highlander about such "Handyisms" as "chust sublime" and "high jeenks", that is really only another way of saying that the Captain is a larger-than-life character. He is an original, curiously reminiscent of a Dickensian character such as Sam Weller or one of Sir Walter Scott's Doric speakers. In a more far-fetched way Para also has a certain resemblance to "the wily Odysseus", another sea-farer who roamed among sea-girt islands, had an adventure with sheep and who "had rather a gallant way with the sex, generally said 'mem' to them all..."

Para too, is no stranger to exaggeration, but more often it is an appreciative "baur" of epic proportions about the mighty Hurricane Jack who

> "...iss a man that can sail anything and go anywhere, and aalways be the perfect chentleman. A millionaire's yat or a washinboyne — it's aal the same to Jeck...And never anything else but 'lastic sided boots, even in the coorsest weather... "

Much of the humour of the stories lies in the juxtaposition of the Highland characters, Para and Dougie, and the Lowland figures, The Tar, Sunny Jim and, particularly, Macphail the Engineer (who, despite his Highland surname, is a low country man, from Motherwell in industrial Lanarkshire). Hugh MacDiarmid (C.M.Grieve) has written of the "Caledonian antizyzygy" – the contrast or conflict between the two competing strains within the Scottish personality. In the tensions between the romantic, generous, imaginative Highland skipper and the thrawn, prosaic Lowland engineer we see a fine example of the contrast between the two races.

> "Do you know the way it iss that steamboat encheneers is alwaays doon in the mooth like that? It's the want of nature. They never let themselves go. Poor duvvles, workin' away among their bits o' enchines, they never get the wind and sun aboot them right the same ass us seamen."

Additional piquancy is given to the situation by Macphail, the severely practical engineer, having a none too secret passion for the most lurid penny novelettes.

A new dimension comes into the stories with the arrival of the Glaswegian Sunny Jim. As The Tar's replacement, Davie Green, to give him his full name for once, is more than good value. He it is who devises the Tobermory whale exhibition and starts the persecution of the Captain after the death of the cockatoo in "An Ocean Tragedy" –

> "If it's no' murder, it's manslaughter; monkeys, cockatoos, and parrots a' come under the Act o' Parliament. A cockatoo's no' like a canary; it's able to speak the language and give an opeenion, and the man that wad kill a cockatoo wad kill a wean."

The persecution or "roasting" of Para by his crew is a most amusing example of a traditional kind of Scottish humour; something kindlier than satire and more subtle than ridicule. It may be descended from the ancient Scottish literary custom of "flyting" as found in the poems of Dunbar and his contemporaries and survives to this day in the innocent sport found in every workplace of "taking a loan of" someone and in its latest form "winding someone up". To wind a workmate up , as his shipmates do to Dougie in "Dougie's Family" is to lead him on to make statements or commit indiscretions which will provide further scope for innocent amusement.

Curiously enough Para Handy has not himself had many imitators, except perhaps in a coincidental way in Sean O'Casey's Captain Jack Boyle, who actually was "only wanst on the watter, on an old collier from here to Liverpool."

Para in Print

Every Monday "The Looker-On" column in the *Glasgow Evening News* gave Neil Munro the chance to reflect on current events, to air his views or to entertain with a short story. On Monday 16th January 1905 a new and enduring character in Scottish fiction was launched on the public:

"A short, thick-set man, with a red beard, a hard round felt hat ridiculously out of harmony with a blue pilot jacket and trousers and a seaman's jersey..."

In short, Para Handy, Master Mariner, had arrived.

At intervals of two or three weeks during 1905 and the early months of 1906 a further instalment in the saga of the *Vital Spark* and her crew appeared to brighten the Glaswegians' Mondays. How quickly Para and the *Vital Spark* became an accepted part of Glasgow life, of local folklore almost, may be judged from a cartoon which appeared in the *News* on 9th August 1905. Headlined "The Next Tramway Extension" it was a comment on the recent gift of the Ardgoil Estate to the City of Glasgow and shows a Glasgow Corporation tramcar mounted on a ship named *Vital Spark* and headed down river to the new Argyllshire property. In less than eight months and after only thirteen stories Munro's creation had so completely come to life that the *Vital Spark* had become a name that a cartoonist could use without explanation or sub-title.

By the Spring of 1906 William Blackwood & Sons were arranging for the publication of the first anthology of Para stories — twenty-two tales which originally appeared in the *News* and three stories: "Lodgers on a Houseboat", "The Disappointment of Erchie's Niece" and "Para Handy's Wedding", written especially for the book.

One other *News* story from this period, "The Maids of Bute", was held over and appeared in the second anthology *In Highland Harbours with Para Handy, s.s. Vital Spark* in 1911. The final anthology *Hurricane Jack of the Vital Spark* did not appear until 1923. The omnibus edition of the Para stories, the Erchie stories and the tales of Jimmy Swan; which was the first to formally link Munro, rather than "Hugh Foulis", with these stories; appeared in 1931, the year after Munro's death.

The order of stories in the 1906 anthology bore little relationship to the original order of newspaper publication — except that "Para Handy Master Mariner" — the first story in the book was also the first story to appear in the *News*. Some stories had obvious topicality, for example "Three Dry Days", which is set in February, that odd month when as Dougie says "...the New Year's no' right bye, and the Gleska Fair's chust comin' on..." appeared on 5th February 1906 and its companion piece "The Valentine That Misfired" came out on 19th February, as close to St.

Valentine's Day as the Monday publication schedule for the "Looker-On" column would allow.

Two of the extra stories written for the anthology would seem to have had particular aims. "The Disappointment of Erchie's Niece" reintroduces the reader to Erchie Macpherson from the "Erchie, My Droll Friend" series. Munro had published an anthology of Erchie stories in 1904 and this was perhaps an attempt to link the two sets of stories with benefit to the sales of both volumes.

Another of the new stories written for book publication, "Para Handy's Wedding" is clearly an extremely appropriate way to round off the volume. It perhaps, in view of Munro's very limited interest in these humorous sketches, was also meant to end the career of Peter Macfarlane.

However like another contemporary writer, Sir Arthur Conan Doyle, who also considered that his historical novels were his most important work and his short stories of lesser worth, the character refused to be killed. Just as Holmes survived the Reichenbach Falls, so Para survives marriage to the Widow Crawford and to our delight continues to sail the west coast for many years.

If the newspaper publication of the stories had been an obvious success, so too was their appearance in book form. The *News* in a regular weekly book feature, the "In the Bookshop" column, noted on 12th April 1906

"Among the shilling books specially suited for reading on the Spring Holiday, I must note "The Vital Spark" which is just being published by Messrs. Blackwood. It would seem that the success of Erchie has given the booksellers confidence in anything bearing the signature of "Hugh Foulis", as the orders for "The Vital Spark" are much larger than for the former book. London orders are particularly large. As most Glasgow people know, the sketches, which originally appeared in the *News*, of the exploits of Para Handy and his crew are intensely funny, without degenerating into caricature, and it is safe to predict a very large sale for the book when it is placed before the public."

After what must have been a long wait for admirers of Para the *Vital Spark* sailed again on 10th February 1908 when Sunny Jim appeared as "A New Cook". Over the next three years the bulk of the stories which were to feature in the second anthology *In High-land Harbours with Para Handy, s.s. Vital Spark* appeared at irregular intervals in the *News*.

The return of Para was welcomed in an enthusiastic letter to the editor and after a few weeks Munro's two humorous series — Para and Erchie — were moved from the Monday "Looker-On" spot to the Saturday edition with its week-end reading section. In the announcement of this change both series were, for the first time, announced as being written by Neil Munro. However by the end of the year Para was back as an irregular feature in the "Looker-On" column.

Many of the stories of this period are very closely linked to and inspired by contemporary events and it would seem that Munro increasingly waited for topical inspiration before turning out a Para story. For example "To Campbeltown by Sea" is set in a heat wave and published in July 1908 when Scotland was suffering a remark-able spell of heat and drought and "Pension Farms", originally published in December 1908 relates to the introduction of old age pensions in that year. The collection which appeared in July 1911 was enthusiastically welcomed — the *News* reviewer noting "they sparkle with a humour that is ever fresh".

A third collection appeared in 1923. Fourteen tales which ap-peared in the *News* after 1912 were omitted from this collection; most of these were inspired by the World War and, although Munro used a number of war-time stories in the 1923 edition, he presumab-ly chose to reduce the number of references to war-time events. These must have seemed a little dated just a few years after the events although the passage of seventy years has given considerable interest and charm to these once-rejected stories. However apart from the novelty value of these fourteen stories, and another written after *Hurricane Jack of the Vital Spark* appeared in 1923, many of them are tales of the highest quality.

These "minor pieces" which Munro turned out as part of his regular journalistic work and which he thought of so little worth have been his most lasting works. They were transferred into successful television series which brought the *Vital Spark* and her crew to an audience far beyond Munro's Glasgow.

The omnibus edition reprinted regularly for twenty years, being replaced in Blackwood's list by a collection of the three volumes of the Para stories in 1955, the Erchie and Jimmy Swan stories going out of print at this time. Paperback editions of the Para Handy stories have been available since 1969. Ironically, the historical novels, which Munro valued so highly and which he published under his own name unlike the short stories issued under a pseudonym, had by the 1980s all gone out of print.

Neil Munro

"My goodness!...and you'll be writing things for the papers? Cot bless me!...and do you tell me you can be makin' a living off that? I'm not asking you, mind, hoo mich you'll be makin', don't tell me; not a cheep! not a cheep! But I'll wudger it's more than Maclean the munister."

Neil Munro was born in Inveraray on Loch Fyneside, in the building known as Crombie's Land on 3rd June 1864. Generations of his family had lived and worked as farmers and shepherds at the village of Carnus, now disappeared, in Glen Aray — or so at least goes the version printed in all the standard sources.

In fact the truth is slightly different. Munro was in fact born on 3rd June 1863 — exactly one year earlier than the "official" date. The birth certificate shows him to have been the illegitimate son of Ann Munro, Kitchen Maid. A twin sister was still-born. There is no record of a marriage of this Ann Munro to the James Thompson Munro who was later represented as Neil Munro's father on, among other sources, his death certificate. The 1871 census returns for Inveraray record a family living in a one-roomed dwelling at McVicar's Land, Ark Lane, consisting of Angus McArthur Munro, aged 66, formerly a crofter; his daughter, Agnes Munro, unmarried domestic servant aged 38 and Neil, his grandson, aged 7. (It is noteworthy that the correct date of birth had been supplied to the census enumerator.) It would thus seem that Munro, like his hero Para Handy, was "....brocht up wi' an auntie..."

He attended a village school at Glencaldine near Inveraray and

later Church Square Public School in Inveraray. When he left school
he was at the age of fourteen –

> "...insinuated, without any regard for my own desires, into a
> country lawyer's office, wherefrom I withdrew myself as soon as
> I arrived at years of discretion and revolt." (*The Brave Days*)

The country lawyer's office was in fact the office of the Sheriff
Clerk of Argyll and one may speculate as to the influence which
placed a poor boy with no obvious family influence in such a sought
after and prestigious post. During his five years there he countered
the boredom of office routine by reading and developed his flair for
writing by contributing short articles for local newspapers.

His youthful boredom was coupled with a realisation that the
future for the small communities of Loch Fyneside was bleak. Years
later in his *The Clyde, River and Firth* he wrote:

> "In 1750 the Duke of Argyll could raise if necessary 10,000 men
> able to bear arms. The bulk of them must have been found
> between the shores of Loch Fyne and Loch Awe; single glens of
> Loch Fyne could turn out over two hundred swords; now they
> are desolate."

In May 1881 like many ambitious young men before him, and
even more since, he took the sea-road south to Glasgow and, while
learning shorthand, earned his living in the cashier's office of an
ironmonger's shop in the Trongate. Before long however he found a
post on a small local newspaper, spending ten years there before
moving on to a newspaper of some significance *The Greenock
Advertiser*. He next worked for *The Glasgow News* where he
remained until it closed, when he was offered a post with the much
larger *Glasgow Evening News*. He soon became chief reporter as well
as Art, Drama and Literary Critic. He semi-retired from journalism
around 1902 to devote himself to his novels. During the War he
returned to full time work and was made editor in 1918, a position
which he held until his — reluctant — retirement in 1927.

While engaged on his journalistic work Munro began writing
short stories, novels and poetry. His shorter work appeared in a
number of the flourishing literary periodicals of the period and a
collection of stories *The Lost Pibroch* was published by Blackwoods
in 1896.

The theme of much of Munro's fiction was the decline of the old order in the Highlands, a theme he had tackled in his 1898 novel *Gillian the Dreamer*. His reputation as a novelist largely rests on the historical adventure novels *John Splendid, Doom Castle* and *The New Road*. Munro became seen, particularly after the publication of *The New Road* in 1914, as the heir to the Robert Louis Stevenson tradition and *The New Road* — based on the impact of General Wade's military road and the inevitable changes it would bring to Highland ways and the local balance of power — is certainly worthy to be considered in the same league as Stevenson's *Kidnapped*. Sadly his output, particularly after his early retirement, was not large.

Two collections of essays and journalism were published after his death *The Brave Days* and *The Looker-On*. *The Brave Days* being a series of autobiographical sketches he contributed to the *News* after his retirement, while the other collection gathered together some of the splendidly characteristic pieces from his literary journalism, some special reports and the regular "Looker-On" column from earlier in the century.

After his final retirement from the *News* he moved in 1927 to a beautiful Regency villa in Helensburgh overlooking his beloved Firth of Clyde. He named the house "Cromalt" after a stream in his native Inveraray.

On 27th December 1930 the Dumbartonshire local paper the *Lennox Herald* noted:

"The death has occurred at his residence, "Cromalt", of Mr Neil Munro, LL.D., the Scottish novelist and journalist. He was in his 67th year and had been in failing health for some time. Of a reticent and unassuming nature, he never sought public favour, but as long ago as 1908 he was honoured with the degree of LL.D by Glasgow University and, only two months ago, a similar compliment was paid him by Edinburgh University. He received the freedom of his native town of Inveraray in 1909."

Munro was buried at Kilmalieu, in Inveraray, and later a memorial service was held in Glasgow Cathedral, attended by his Glasgow friends, representatives of the University and the Church. The *Glasgow Herald* obituary observed that although in latter years he had published but little "he had already accomplished his life's work — of taking up and wearing the mantle of R.L.S. ..." The Rev. Lauchlan MacLean Watt, an authority on the works of Stevenson, went further and described Munro as the "greatest Scottish novelist since Sir Walter Scott, and in the matter of Celtic story and character he excelled Sir Walter because of his more deeply intimate knowledge of that elusive mystery." The novelist Hugh Walpole lamented the death of "one of Scotland's few great novelists".

One of his great advocates was a friend and former *News* colleague, the novelist George Blake, who edited and introduced the two posthumous collections *The Brave Days* and *The Looker-On*. In his introduction to the former volume Blake speaks of Munro's reticent nature and of the contrast between his two personalities and two fields of writing — the Neil Munro of the novels and the "Hugh Foulis" of the lighter writing and the journalism. There was also certainly an evident tension manifest in much of his work between the Glasgow journalist, working in a city which he knew well and loved deeply and the Highland exile, forever homesick for the Argyllshire of his childhood.

Five years after his death a monument was erected to him on a bleak hillside in Glen Aray, facing the vanished home of his ancestors. The intiative to commemorate him was taken by An Comunn Gaidhealach. Speaking at the unveiling Robert Bontine Cunningham-Graham described Munro as "the apostolic successor of Sir Walter Scott". The monument is a pyramid of local stone crowned by a Celtic book-shrine, and, unlike the tombstone in Kilmalieu cemetery and all the public and published biographical sources, bears Munro's true birth date of 1863.

ACKNOWLEDGEMENTS

The authors are grateful to Graham Hopner of West Dunbartonshire Libraries for his help with Neil Munro's biography. Our thanks are also due to David Harvie for his contribution to this section and for other advice and encouragement and to Jessie MacLeod for her help and advice on matters Gaelic.

The Vital Spark

1. *Para Handy, Master Mariner*

A SHORT, thick-set man, with a red beard, a hard round felt hat, ridiculously out of harmony with a blue pilot jacket and trousers and a seaman's jersey, his hands immersed deeply in those pockets our fathers (and the heroes of Rabelais) used to wear behind a front flap, he would have attracted my notice even if he had not, unaware of my presence so close behind him, been humming to himself the chorus of a song that used to be very popular on gabbarts[1], but is now gone out of date, like "The Captain with the Whiskers took a Sly Glance at Me". You may have heard it thirty years ago, before the steam puffer[2] came in to sweep the sailing smack from all the seas that lie between Bowling and Stornoway. It runs—

"Young Munro he took a notion
  For to sail across the sea,
  And he left his true love weeping,
  All alone on Greenock Quay,"

and by that sign, and by his red beard, and by a curious gesture he had, as if he were now and then going to scratch his ear and only determined not to do it when his hand was up, I knew he was one of the Macfarlanes. There were ten Macfarlanes, all men, except one, and he was a valet, but the family did their best to conceal the fact, and said he was away on the yachts, and making that much money he had not time to write a scrape home.

"I think I ought to know you," I said to the vocalist with the hard hat. "You are a Macfarlane: either the Beekan, or Kail, or the Nipper, or Keep Dark, or Para Handy — "

"As sure as daith," said he, "I'm chust Para Handy, and I ken your name fine, but I cannot chust mind your face." He had turned round on the pawl[3] he sat on, without taking his hands from his pockets, and looked up at me where I stood beside him, watching a river steamer being warped into the pier.

"My goodness!" he said about ten minutes later, when he had wormed my whole history out of me; "and you'll be writing things for the papers? Cot bless me! and do you tell me you can be makin' a living off that? I'm not asking you, mind, hoo mich you'll be makin', don't tell me; not a cheep! not a cheep! But I'll wudger it's more than Maclean the munister. But och! I'm not saying: it iss not my business. The munister has two hundred in the year and a coo's gress[4]; he iss aye the big man up yonder, but it iss me would like to show him he wass not so big a man as yourself. Eh? But not a cheep! not a cheep! A Macfarlane would never put his nose into another man's oar."

"And where have you been this long while?" I asked, having let it sink into his mind that there was no chance to-day of his learning my exact income, expenditure, and how much I had in the bank.

"Me!" said he; "I am going up and down like yon fellow in the Scruptures — what wass his name? Sampson — seeking what I may devour.[5] I am out of a chob. Chust that: out of a chob. You'll not be hearin' of anybody in your line that iss in want of a skipper?"

Skippers, I said, were in rare demand in my line of business. We hadn't used a skipper for years.

"Chust that! chust that! I only mentioned it in case. You are making things for newspapers, my Cot! what will they not do now for the penny? Well, that is it; I am out of a chob; chust putting bye the time. I'm not vexed for myself, so mich as for poor Dougie. Dougie wass mate, and I wass skipper. I don't know if you kent the *Fital Spark*?"

The *Vital Spark*, I confessed, was well known to me as the most uncertain puffer that ever kept the Old New-Year[6] in Upper Loch-fyne.

"That wass her!" said Macfarlane, almost weeping. "There was never the bate of her, and I have sailed in her four years over twenty with my hert in my mooth for fear of her boiler. If you never saw the *Fital Spark*, she is aal hold, with the boiler behind, four men and a derrick, and a watter-butt and a pan loaf[7] in the fo'c'sle. Oh man! she wass the beauty! She was chust sublime! She should be carryin' nothing but gentry for passengers, or nice genteel luggage for the shooting-lodges, but there they would be spoilin' her and rubbin' all the pent off her with their coals, and sand, and whunstone, and oak bark, and timber, and trash like that."

"I understood she had one weakness at least, that her boiler was apt to prime."

"It's a — lie," cried Macfarlane, quite furious; "her boiler never primed more than wance a month, and that wass not with fair play. If Dougie wass here he would tell you.

"I wass ass prood of that boat ass the Duke of Argyll, ay, or Lord Breadalbane. If you would see me waalkin' aboot on her dake when we wass lyin' at the quay! There wasna the like of it in the West Hielan's. I wass chust sublime! She had a gold bead aboot her; it's no lie I am tellin' you, and I would be pentin' her oot of my own pocket every time we went to Arran for gravel. She drawed four feet forrit and nine aft, and she could go like the duvvle."

"I have heard it put at five knots," I said maliciously.

Macfarlane bounded from his seat. "Five knots!" he cried. "Show me the man that says five knots, and I will make him swallow the hatchet. Six knots, ass sure ass my name iss Macfarlane; many a time between the Skate and Otter.[8] If Dougie wass here he would tell you. But I am not braggin' aboot her sailin'; it wass her looks. Man, she was smert, smert! Every time she wass new pented I would be puttin' on my Sunday clothes. There wass a time yonder they would be callin' me Two-flag Peter in Loch Fyne. It wass wance the Queen had a jubilee, and we had but the wan flag, but a Macfarlane never wass bate, and I put up the wan flag and a regatta shirt, and I'm telling you she looked chust sublime!"

"I forget who it was once told me she was very wet," I cooed blandly; "that with a head wind the *Vital Spark* nearly went out altogether. Of course, people will say nasty things about these hookers. They say she was very ill to trim, too."

Macfarlane jumped up again, grinding his teeth, and his face purple. He could hardly speak with indignation. "Trum!" he shouted. "Did you say 'trum'? You could trum her with the wan hand behind your back and you lookin' the other way. To the duvvle

with your trum! And they would be sayin' she wass wet! If Dougie
wass here he would tell you. She would not take in wan cup of watter
unless it wass for synin'[9] oot the dishes. She wass that dry she would
not wet a postage stamp unless we slung it over the side in a pail. She
wass sublime, chust sublime!

"I am telling you there iss not many men following the sea that
could sail the *Fital Spark* the way I could. There iss not a rock, no,
nor a chuckie stone inside the Cumbrie Heid that I do not have a
name for. I would ken them fine in the dark by the smell, and that iss
not easy, I'm telling you. And I am not wan of your dry-land sailors.
I wass wance at Londonderry with her. We went at night, and did
Dougie no' go away and forget oil, so that we had no lamps, and
chust had to sail in the dark with our ears wide open. If Dougie wass
here he would tell you. Now and then Dougie would be striking a
match for fear of a collusion."

"Where did he show it?" I asked innocently. "Forward or aft?"

"Aft," said the mariner suspiciously. "What for would it be aft? Do
you mean to say there could be a collusion aft? I am telling you she
could do her six knots before she cracked her shaft. It wass in the bow,
of course; Dougie had the matches. She wass chust sublime. A gold
bead oot of my own pocket, four men and a derrick, and a watter-butt
and a pan loaf in the fo'c'sle. My bonnie wee *Fital Spark*!"

He began to show symptoms of tears, and I hate to see an ancient
mariner's tears, so I hurriedly asked him how he had lost the
command.

"I will tell you that," said he. "It was Dougie's fault. We had yonder
a cargo of coals for Tarbert, and we got doon the length of Greenock,
going fine, fine. It wass the day after the New Year, and I wass in fine
trum, and Dougie said, 'Wull we stand in here for orders?' and so we
went into Greenock for some marmalade, and did we no' stay three
days? Dougie and me wass going about Greenock looking for
signboards with Hielan' names on them, and every signboard we
could see with Campbell, or Macintyre, on it, or Morrison, Dougie
would go in and ask if the man came from Kilmartin or anyway
roond aboot there, and if the man said no, Dougie would say, 'It's a
great peety, for I have cousins of the same name, but maybe you'll
have time to come oot for a dram?'[10] Dougie was chust sublime!

"Every day we would be getting sixpenny telegrams from the man the coals was for at Tarbert, but och! we did not think he wass in such an aawful hurry, and then he came himself to Greenock with the *Grenadier*[11], and the only wans that wass not in the polis-office wass myself and the derrick. He bailed the laads out of the polis-office, and 'Now,' he said, 'you will chust sail her up as fast as you can, like smert laads, for my customers iss waiting for their coals, and I will go over and see my good-sister[12] at Helensburgh, and go back to Tarbert the day efter to-morrow.' 'Hoo can we be going and us with no money?' said Dougie — man, he wass sublime! So the man gave me a paper pound of money, and went away to Helensburgh, and Dougie wass coilin' up a hawser forrit ready to start from the quay. When he wass away, Dougie said we would maybe chust be as weel to wait another tide, and I said I didna know, but what did he think, and he said, 'Ach, of course!' and we went aal back into Greenock. 'Let me see that pound!' said Dougie, and did I not give it to him? and then he rang the bell of the public hoose we were in, and asked for four tacks and a wee hammer. When he got the four tacks and the wee hammer he nailed the pound note on the door, and said to the man, 'Chust come in with a dram every time we ring the bell till that's done!' If Dougie wass here he would tell you. Two days efter that the owner of the Fital Spark came doon from Gleska and five men with him, and they went away with her to Tarbert."

"And so you lost the old command," I said, preparing to go off. "Well, I hope something will turn up soon."

"There wass some talk aboot a dram," said the mariner. "I thought you said something aboot a dram, but och! there's no occasion!"

A week later, I am glad to say, the Captain and his old crew were reinstated on the Vital Spark.

2. *The Prize Canary*

"CANARIES!" said Para Handy contemptuously, "I have a canary yonder at home that would give you a sore heid to hear him singing. He's chust sublime. Have I no', Dougie?"

It was the first time the mate had ever heard of the Captain as a bird-fancier, but he was a loyal friend, and at Para Handy's wink he said promptly, "You have that, Peter. Wan of the finest ever stepped. Many a sore heid I had wi't."

"What kind of a canary is it?" asked the Brodick man jealously. "Is it a Norwich?"

Para Handy put up his hand as usual to scratch his ear, and checked the act half way. "No, nor a Sandwich; it's chust a plain yellow wan," he said coolly. "I'll wudger ye a pound it could sing the best you have blin'. It whustles even-on[1], night and day, till I have to put it under a bowl o' watter if I'm wantin' my night's sleep."

The competitive passions of the Brodick man were roused. He considered that among his dozen prize canaries he had at least one that could beat anything likely to be in the possession of the Captain of the *Vital Spark*, which was lying at Brodick when this conversation took place. He produced it — an emaciated, sickle-shaped, small-headed, bead-eyed, business-looking bird, which he called the Wee Free[2]. He was prepared to put up the pound for a singing contest anywhere in Arran, date hereafter to be arranged.

"That's all right," said Para Handy, "I'll take you on. We'll be doon this way for a cargo of grevel in a week, and if the money's wi' the man in the shippin'-box at the quay, my canary 'll lift it."

"But what aboot your pound?" asked the Brodick man. "You must wudger a pound too."

"Is that the way o't?" said the Captain. "I wass never up to the gemblin', but I'll risk the pound," and so the contest was arranged.

"But you havena a canary at aal, have you?" said Dougie, later in the day, as the *Vital Spark* was puffing on her deliberate way to Glasgow.

"Me?" said Para Handy, "I would as soon think of keepin' a hoolet.[3] But och, there's plenty in Gleska if you have the money. From the needle to the anchor. Forbye, I ken a gentleman that breeds canaries; he's a riveter, and if I wass gettin' him in good trum he would maybe give me a lend o' wan. If no', we'll take a dander[4] up to the Bird Market, and pick up a smert wan that'll put the hems[5] on Sandy Kerr's Wee Free. No man wi' any releegion aboot him would caal his canary a Wee Free."

The Captain and the mate of the *Vital Spark* left their noble ship at the wharf that evening — it was a Saturday — and went in quest of the gentleman who bred canaries. He was discovered in the midst of an altercation with his wife which involved the total destruction of all the dishes on the kitchen-dresser, and, with a shrewdness and consideration that were never absent in the Captain, he apologised for the untimely intrusion and prepared to go away. "I see you're busy," he said, looking in on a floor covered with the debris of the delf[6] which this ardent lover of bird life was smashing in order to impress his wife with the fact that he was really annoyed about something — "I see you're busy. Fine, man, fine! A wife need never weary in this hoose — it's that cheery. Dougie and me wass chust wantin' a wee lend of a canary for a day or two, but och, it doesna matter, seein' ye're so throng; we'll chust try the shops."

It was indicative of the fine kindly humanity of the riveter who loved canaries that this one unhesitatingly stopped his labours, having disposed of the last plate, and said, "I couldna dae't, chaps; I wadna trust a canary oot o' the hoose; there's nae sayin' the ill-usage it micht get. It would break my he'rt to ha'e onything gang wrang wi' ony o' my birds."

"Chust that, Wull, chust that!" said Para Handy agreeably. "Your feelings does you credit. I would be awful vexed if you broke your he'rt; it'll soon be the only hale thing left in the hoose. If I wass you, and had such a spite at the delf, I would use dunnymite," and Dougie and he departed.

"That's the sort of thing that keeps me from gettin' merrit," the Captain, with a sigh, confided to his mate, when they got down the stair "Look at the money it costs for dishes every Setturday night."

"Them riveters iss awfu' chaps for sport," said Dougie irrelevantly.

"There's nothing for't now but the Bird Market," said the Captain, leading the way east along Argyle Street. They had no clear idea where that institution was, but at the corner of Jamaica Street[7] consulted several Celtic compatriots, who put them on the right track. Having reached the Bird Market[8], the Captain explained his wants to a party who had "Guaranteed A1 Songsters" to sell at two shillings. This person was particularly enthusiastic about one bird which in the meantime was as silent as "the harp that once through Tara's halls". He gave them his solemn assurance it was a genuine prize roller canary; that when it started whistling, as it generally did at breakfast time, it sang till the gas was lit, with not even a pause for refreshment. For that reason it was an economical canary to keep; it practically cost nothing for seed for this canary. If it was a songster suitable for use on a ship that was wanted, he went on, with a rapid assumption that his customers were of a maritime profession, this bird was peculiarly adapted for the post. It was a genuine imported bird, and had already made a sea voyage. To sell a bird of such exquisite parts for two shillings was sheer commercial suicide; he admitted it, but he was anxious that it should have a good home.

"I wish I could hear it whustlin'," said the Captain, peering through the spars at the very dejected bird, which was a moulting hen.

"It never sings efter the gas is lighted," said the vendor regretfully, "that's the only thing that's wrang wi't. If that bird wad sing at nicht when the gas was lit, it wad solve the problem o' perpetual motion."

Para Handy, considerably impressed by this high warrandice[9], bought the canary, which was removed from the cage and placed in a brown paper sugar-bag, ventilated by holes which the bird-seller made in it with the stub of a lead pencil.

"Will you no' need a cage?" asked Dougie.

"Not at aal, not at aal!" the Captain protested; "wance we get him doon to Brodick we'll get plenty o' cages," and away they went with their purchase, Para Handy elate at the imminent prospect of his prize canary winning an easy pound. Dougie carefully carried the bag containing the bird.

Some days after, the *Vital Spark* arrived at Brodick, but the Captain, who had not yet staked his pound with the man in the shipping-box as agreed on, curiously enough showed no disposition to bring off the challenge meeting between the birds. It was by accident he met the Brodick man one day on the quay.

"Talking about birds," said Para Handy, with some diffidence, "Dougie and me had a canary yonder — "

"That's aal off," said the Brodick man hurriedly, getting very red in the face, showing so much embarrassment, indeed, that the Captain of the *Vital Spark* smelt a rat.

"What way off?" he asked. "It sticks in my mind that there wass a kind of a wudger, and that there's a pound note in the shupping-box for the best canary."

"Did you bring your canary?" asked the Brodick man anxiously.

"It's doon there in the vessel singin' like to take the rivets oot o' her," said Para Handy. "It's chust sublime to listen to."

"Weel, the fact iss, I'm not goin' to challenge," said the Brodick man. "I have a wife yonder, and she's sore against bettin' and wudgerin' and gemblin', and she'll no let me take my champion bird Wee Free over the door."

"Chust that!" said Para Handy. "That's a peety. Weel, weel, the pund'll come in handy. I'll chust go away down to the shupping-box and lift it. Seeing I won, I'll stand you a drink."

The Brodick man maintained with warmth that as Para Handy had not yet lodged his stake of a pound the match was off; an excited discussion followed, and the upshot was a compromise. The Brodick man, having failed to produce his bird, was to forfeit ten shillings, and treat the crew of the *Vital Spark*.

They were being treated, and the ten shillings were in Para Handy's possession, when the Brodick sportsman rose to make some disconcerting remark.

"You think you are very smert, Macfarlane," he said, addressing the Captain. "You are thinkin' you did a good stroke to get the ten shullin's, but if you wass smerter it iss not the ten shullin's you would have at aal, but the pound. I had you fine, Macfarlane. My wife never said a word aboot the wudger, but my bird is in the pook[10], and couldna sing a note this week. That's the way I backed oot."

Para Handy displayed neither resentment nor surprise. He took a deep draught of beer out of a quart pot, and then smiled with mingled tolerance and pity on the Brodick man.

"Ay, ay!" he said, "and you think you have done a smert thing. You have mich caause to be ashamed of yourself. You are nothing better than a common swundler. But och, it doesna matter; the fact iss, oor bird's deid."

"Deid!" cried the Brodick man. "What do you mean by deid?"

"Chust that it's no' livin'," said Para Handy coolly. "Dougie and me bought wan in the Bird Market, and Dougie was carryin' it doon to the vessel in a sugar-poke when he met some fellows he kent in Chamaica Street, and went for a dram, or maybe two. Efter a while he didna mind what he had in the poke, and he put it in his troosers pockets, thinkin' it wass something extra for the Sunday's dinner. When he brought the poor wee bird oot of his pocket in the mornin', it wass chust a' remains."

3. *The Malingerer*

THE crew of the *Vital Spark* were all willing workers, except The
Tar, who was usually as tired when he rose in the morning as when
he went to bed. He said himself it was his health, and that he had
never got his strength right back since he had the whooping-cough
twice when he was a boy. The Captain was generally sympathetic,
and was inclined to believe The Tar was destined to have a short life
unless he got married and had a wife to look after him. "A wife's the
very thing for you," he would urge; "it's no' canny[I], a man as
delicate as you to be having nobody to depend on."

"I couldna afford a wife," The Tar always maintained. "They're all
too grand for the like of me."

"Och ay! but you might look aboot you and find a wee, no' aawfu'
bonny wan," said Para Handy.

"If she was blin', or the like of that, you would have a better chance
of gettin' her," chimed in Dougie, who always scoffed at The Tar's
periodical illnesses, and cruelly ascribed his lack of energy to sheer
laziness.

The unfortunate Tar's weaknesses always seemed to come on
him when there was most to do. It generally took the form of
sleepiness, so that sometimes when he was supposed to be preparing the dinner he would be found sound asleep on the head of a
bucket, with a half-peeled potato in his hand. He once crept out of
the fo'c'sle rubbing his eyes after a twelve-hours' sleep, saying,
"Tell me this and tell me no more, am I going to my bed or comin'
from it?"

But there was something unusual and alarming about the illness
which overtook The Tar on their way up Loch Fyne to lift a cargo
of timber. First he had shivers all down his back; then he got so stiff
that he could not bend to lift a bucket, but had to kick it along the
deck in front of him, which made Dougie admiringly say, "Man!
you are an aawful handy man with your feet, Colin"; his appetite,
he declared, totally disappeared immediately after an unusually
hearty breakfast composed of six herrings and two eggs; and
finally he expressed his belief that there was nothing for it but his
bed.

"I'll maybe no trouble you long, boys," he moaned lugubriously. "My heid's birling roond that fast that I canna even mind my own name two meenutes."

"You should write it on a wee bit paper," said Dougie unfeelingly, "and keep it inside your bonnet, so that you could look it up at any time you were needin'."

Para Handy had kinder feelings, and told The Tar to go and lie down for an hour or two and take a wee drop of something.

"Maybe a drop of brandy would help me," said The Tar, promptly preparing to avail himself of the Captain's advice.

"No, not brandy; a drop of good Brutish spurits will suit you better, Colin," said the Captain, and went below to dispense the prescription himself.

The gusto with which The Tar swallowed the prescribed dram of British spirits and took a chew of tobacco after it to enhance the effect, made Para Handy somewhat suspicious, and he said so to Dougie when he got on deck, leaving The Tar already in a gentle slumber.

"The rascal's chust scheming," said Dougie emphatically. "There iss nothing in the world wrong with him but the laziness. If you'll notice, he aalways gets no weel when we're going to lift timber, because it iss harder on him at the winch."

The Captain was indignant, and was for going down there and then with a rope's-end to rouse the patient, but Dougie confided to him a method of punishing the malingerer and at the same time getting some innocent amusement for themselves.

Dinner-time came round. The Tar instinctively wakened and lay wondering what they would take down to him to eat. The *Vital Spark* was puff-puffing her deliberate way up the loch, and there was an unusual stillness on deck. It seemed to The Tar that the Captain and Dougie were moving about on tiptoe and speaking in whispers. The uncomfortable feeling this created in his mind was increased when his two shipmates came down with slippers on instead of their ordinary sea-boots, creeping down the companion with great caution, carrying a bowl of gruel.

"What's that for?" asked The Tar sharply. "Are you going to paste up any bills?"

"Wheest, Colin," said Para Handy, in a sick-room whisper. "You must not excite yourself, but take this gruel. It'll do you no herm. Poor fellow, you're looking aawful bad." They hung over his bunk with an attitude of chastened grief, and Dougie made to help him to the gruel with a spoon as if he were unable to feed himself.

"Have you no beef?" asked The Tar, looking at the gruel with disgust. "I'll need to keep up my strength with something more than gruel."

"You daurna for your life take anything but gruel," said the Captain sorrowfully. "It would be the daith of you at wance to take beef, though there's plenty in the pot. Chust take this, like a good laad, and don't speak. My Chove! you are looking far through."

"You're nose is as sherp as a preen,"[2] said Dougie in an awed whisper, and with a piece of engine-room waste wiped the brow of The Tar, who was beginning to perspire with alarm.

"I don't think I'm so bad ass aal that," said the patient. "It wass chust a turn; a day in my bed 'll put me aal right — or maybe two."

They shook their heads sorrowfully, and the Captain turned away as if to hide a tear. Dougie blew his nose with much ostentation and stifled a sob.

"What's the metter wi' you?" asked The Tar, looking at them in amazement and fear.

"Nothing, nothing, Colin," said the Captain. "Don't say a word. Iss there anything we could get for you?"

"My heid's bad yet," the patient replied. "Perhaps a drop of spurits — "

"There's no' another drop in the ship," said the Captain.

The patient moaned. "And I don't suppose there's any beer either?" he said hopelessly.

He was told there was no beer, and instructed to cry if he was requiring any one to come to his assistance, after which the two nurses crept quietly on deck again, leaving him in a very uneasy frame of mind.

They got into the quay late in the afternoon, and the Captain and mate came down again quietly, with their caps in their hands, to discover The Tar surreptitiously smoking in his bunk to dull the pangs of hunger that now beset him, for they had given him nothing since the gruel.

"It's not for you, it's not for you at aal, smokin'!" cried Para Handy in horror, taking the pipe out of his hand. "With the trouble you have, smoking drives it in to the hert and kills you at wance."

"What trouble do you think it iss?" asked the patient seriously.

"Dougie says it's — it's — what did you say it wass, Dougie?"

"It's convolvulus in the inside," said Dougie solemnly; "I had two aunties that died of it in their unfancy."

"I'm going to get up at wance!" said The Tar, making to rise, but they thrust him back in his blankets, saying the convolvulus would burst at the first effort of the kind he made.

He began to weep. "Fancy a trouble like that coming on me, and me quite young!" he said, pitying himself seriously. "There wass never wan in oor femily had it."

"It's sleep brings it on," said Dougie, with the air of a specialist who would ordinarily charge a fee of ten guineas — "sleep and sitting doon. There iss nothing to keep off convolvulus but exercise and rising early in the morning. Poor fellow! But you'll maybe get better; when there's hope there's life. The Captain and me wass wondering if there wass anything we could buy ashore for you — some grapes, maybe, or a shullin' bottle of sherry wine."

"Mercy on me! am I ass far through ass that?" said The Tar.

"Or maybe you would like Macphail, the enchineer, to come doon and read the Scruptures a while to you," said Para Handy.

"Macphail!" cried the poor Tar; "I wudna let a man like that read a song-book to me."

They clapped him affectionately on the shoulders; Dougie made as if to shake his hand, and checked himself; then the Captain and mate went softly on deck again, and the patient was left with his fears. He felt utterly incapable of getting up.

Para Handy and his mate went up the town and had a dram with the local joiner, who was also undertaker. With this functionary in their company they were moving towards the quay when Dougie saw in a grocer's shop-door a pictorial card bearing the well-known monkey portrait[3] advertising a certain soap that won't wash clothes. He went chuckling into the shop, made some small purchase, and came out the possessor of the picture. Half an hour later, when it was dark, and The Tar was lying in an agony of hunger which he took to be the pains of internal convolvulus, Para Handy, Dougie, and the joiner came quietly down to the fo'c'sle, where he lay. They had no lamp, but they struck matches and looked at him in his bunk with countenances full of pity.

"A nose as sherp as a preen," said Dougie; "it must be the galloping kind of convolvulus."

"Here's Macintyre the joiner would like to see you, Colin," said Para Handy, and in the light of a match the patient saw the joiner cast a rapid professional eye over his proportions.

"What's the joiner wantin' here?" said The Tar with a frightful suspicion.

"Nothing, Colin, nothing — six by two — I wass chust passing — six by two — chust passing, and the Captain asked me in to see you. It's — six by two, six by two — it's no' very healthy weather we're havin'. Chust that!"

The fo'c'sle was in darkness and The Tar felt already as if he was dead and buried. "Am I lookin' very bad?" he ventured to ask Dougie.

"Bad's no' the name for it," said Dougie. "Chust look at yourself in the enchineer's looking-gless." He produced from under his arm the engineer's little mirror, on the face of which he had gummed the portrait of the monkey cut out from the soap advertisement, which fitted neatly into the frame. The Captain struck a match, and in its brief and insufficient light The Tar looked at himself, as he thought, reflected in the glass.

"Man, I'm no' that awful changed either; if I had a shave and my face washed. I don't believe it's convolvulus at aal," said he, quite hopefully, and jumped from his bunk.

For the rest of the week he put in the work of two men.

4. *Wee Teeny*

THE last passenger steamer to sail that day from Ardrishaig was a trip from Rothesay. It was Glasgow Fair Saturday[1], and Ardrishaig Quay was black with people. There was a marvellously stimulating odour of dulse[2], herring, and shell-fish, for everybody carried away in a handkerchief a few samples of these marine products that are now the only seaside souvenirs not made in Germany.[3] The *Vital*

Spark, in ballast, Clydeward bound, lay inside the passenger steamer, ready to start when the latter had got under weigh, and Para Handy and his mate meanwhile sat on the fo'c'sle-head of "the smertest boat in the tred" watching the frantic efforts of lady excursionists to get their husbands on the steamer before it was too late, and the deliberate efforts of the said husbands to slink away up the village again just for one more drink. Wildly the steamer hooted from her siren, fiercely clanged her bell, vociferously the Captain roared upon his bridge, people aboard yelled eagerly to friends ashore to hurry up, and the people ashore as eagerly demanded to know what all the hurry was about, and where the bleezes was Wull. Women loudly defied the purser to let the ship go away without their John, for he had paid his money for his ticket, and though he was only a working man his money was as good as anybody else's; and John, on the quay, with his hat thrust back on his head, his thumbs in the armholes of his waistcoat and a red handkerchief full of dulse at his feet, gave a display of step-dancing that was responsible for a great deal of the congestion of traffic at the shore end of the gangway.

Among the crowd who had got on board was a woman with eleven children. She was standing on the paddle-box counting them to make sure — five attached to the basket that had contained their food for the day, other four clinging to her gown, and one in her arms. "Yin, twa, three, fower, and fower's eight, and twa's ten, and then there's Wee Teeny wi' her faither doon the caibin." She was quite serene. If she could have seen that the father — at that moment in the fore-saloon singing

"In the guid auld summer time,
   In the guid auld summer time,
   She'll be your tootsy-wootsy
   In the guid auld summer time."

had no Wee Teeny with him, she would have been distracted. As it was, however, the steamer was miles on her way when a frantic woman with ten crying children all in a row behind her, and a husband miraculously sobered, made a vain appeal to the Captain to go back to Ardrishaig for her lost child.

The child was discovered on the quay by the local police ten minutes after the excursion steamer had started, and just when Para

Handy was about to cast off the pawls. She was somewhere about three years old, and the only fact that could be extracted from her was that her name was Teeny. There had probably not been a more contented and self-possessed person on Ardrishaig Quay that day: she sucked her thumb with an air of positive relish, smiled on the slightest provocation, and showed the utmost willingness to go anywhere with anybody.

"The poor wee cratur!" said Para Handy sympathetically. "She minds me fearfully of my brother Cherlie's twuns. I wudna wonder but she'a twuns too; that would be the way the mistake would be made in leavin' her; it's such a terrible thing drink. I'm no' goin' to ask you, Dougie, to do anything you wudna like, but what would you be sayin' to us takin' the wean wi' us and puttin' her ashore at Rothesay? Mind you, chust if you like yoursel'."

"It's your own vessel, you're the skipper of her, and I'm sure and I have no objections, at aal at aal," said Dougie quite heartily, and it was speedily arranged with the police that a telegram should be sent to wait the Captain of the excursion steamer at Rothesay, telling him the lost child was following in the steam-lighter *Vital Spark*.

Macphail the engineer, and The Tar, kept the child in amusement with pocket-knives, oil-cans, cotton-waste, and other maritime toys, while the Captain and Dougie went hurriedly up the village for stores for the unexpected passenger.

"You'll not need that mich," was Dougie's opinion; "she'll fall asleep as soon as it's dark, and no' wake till we put her ashore at Rothesay."

"Ah, but you canna be sure o' them at that age," said the Captain. "My brother Cherlie wass merrit on a low-country woman, and the twuns used to sit up at night and greet in the two languages, Gaalic and Gleska, till he had to put plugs[4] in them."

"God bless me! plugs?" said Dougie astonished.

"Ay, chust plugs," said the Captain emphatically. "You'll see them often. They're made of kahouchy[5], with a bone ring on them for screwing them on and off. It's the only thing for stopping them greetin'."

The adventures of Wee Teeny from this stage may be better told as Para Handy told it to me some time afterwards.

"To let you ken," he said, "I wass feared the wean would sterve.

Nothing in the ship but sea biscuits and salt beef. I went into wan shop and got a quart of milk on draught, half a pound of boiled ham the same as they have at funerals, and a tin tinny For a Good Girl. Dougie wasna slack either; he went into another shop and got thruppence worth of sweeties and a jumpin'-jeck. It wass as nice a thing ass ever you saw to see the wee cratur sittin' on the hatches eatin' away and drinkin' wi' the wan hand, and laughing like anything at the jumpin'-jeck wi' the other. I never saw the ship cheerier; it wass chust sublime. If Dougie wass here himsel' he would tell you. Everything wass going first-rate, and I wass doon below washing my face and puttin' on my other jecket and my watchchain oot o' respect for the passenger, when Dougie came doon in a hurry wi' a long face on him, and says —

" 'She's wantin' ta-ta.'

" 'Mercy on us, she canna be more ta-ta than she iss unless we throw her over the side,' I says to Dougie. But I went up on dake and told her she would be ta-ta in no time becaase the ship was loggin' six knots and the wind wi' us.

" 'Ta-ta,' says she, tuggin' my whuskers the same as if I wass merrit on her — ah, man! she wass a nice wee thing. And that good-natured! The best I could do wass to make The Tar show her the tattoo marks on his legs, and Dougie play the trump (Jew's harp), and when she wass tired o' that I carried her up and doon the dake singin' 'Auld Lang Syne' till she was doverin' over.

" 'She's goin' to sleep noo,' I says to Dougie, and we put her in my bunk wi' her clothes on. She wanted her clothes off, but I said, 'Och! never mind puttin' them off, Teeny; it's only a habit.' Dougie said, if he minded right, they always put up a kind of prayer at that age. 'Give her a start,' I says to Dougie, and he said the 23rd Psalm in Gaalic, but she didn't understand wan word of it, and went to sleep wi' a poke o' sweeties in her hand.

"We were off Ardlamont, and Macphail wass keepin' the boat bangin' at it to get to Rothesay before the mother went oot of her wuts, when I heard a noise doon below where Teeny wass. I ran doon and found her sittin' up chokin' wi' a sweetie that wass a size too lerge for her. She wass black in the face.

" 'Hut her on the back, Peter!' said Dougie.

" 'Hut her yoursel'; I wudna hurt her for the world,' I says, and

Dougie said he wudna do it either, but he ran up for The Tar, that hasna mich feelin's, and The Tar saved her life. I'm tellin' you it wass a start! We wouldna trust her below, herself, efter that, so we took her on dake again. In ten meenutes she fell down among Macphail's engines, and nearly spoiled them. She wasna hurt a bit, but Macphail's feelin's wass, for she wass wantin' the engines to her bed wi' her. She thought they were a kind of a toy. We aye keep that up on him yet.

" 'My Chove! this wean's no' canny,' said Dougie, and we took her up on dake again, and put up the sail to get as mich speed oot of the vessel as we could for Rothesay. Dougie played the trump even-on to her, and The Tar walked on his hands till she was sore laughing at him. Efter a bit we took oor eyes off her for maybe two meenutes, and when we turned roond again Teeny wass fallin' doon into the fo'c'sle.

" 'This iss the worst cargo ever we had,' I says, takin' her up again no' a bit the worse. 'If we don't watch her like a hawk aal the time she'll do something desperate before we reach Rothesay. She'll jump over the side or crawl doon the funnel, and we'll be black affronted.'

" 'I wudna say but you're right,' said Dougie. We put her sittin' on the hatch wi' the jumpin'-jeck, and the tin tinny For a Good Girl, and my watch and chain, Dougie's trump, the photygraph of The Tar's lass, and Macphail's new carpet sluppers to play wi', and the three of us sat roond her watchin' she didna swallow the watch and chain.

"When I handed her over to her mother and father on Rothesay Quay, I says to them, 'I'm gled I'm no' a mother; I would a hunder times sooner be a sailor.'

"But it's a nice thing a wean, too; for a week efter that we missed her awful," concluded the Captain pensively.

5. The Mate's Wife

THAT the Captain of the *Vital Spark* should so persistently remain a bachelor surprised many people. He was just the sort of man, in many respects, who would fall an easy prey to the first woman on the look-out for a good home. He had rather a gallant way with the sex, generally said "mem" to them all, regardless of class; liked their society when he had his Sunday clothes on, and never contradicted them. If he had pursued any other calling than that of mariner I think he would have been captured long ago; his escape doubtless lay in the fact that sailing about from place to place, only briefly touching at West-Coast quays, and then being usually grimed with coal-dust, he had never properly roused their interest and natural sporting instincts. They never knew what a grand opportunity they were losing.

"I'm astonished you never got married, Captain," I said to him recently.

"Ach, I couldn't be bothered," he replied, like a man who had given the matter his consideration before now. "I'm that busy wi' the ship I havena time. There's an aawful lot of bother aboot a wife. Forbye, my hert's in the *Fital Spark* — there's no' a smarter boat in the tred. Wait you till I get her pented!"

"But a ship's not a wife, Captain," I protested.

"No," said he, "but it's a responsibulity. You can get a wife any time that'll stick to you the same as if she wass riveted as long's you draw your pay, but it takes a man with aal his senses aboot him to get a ship and keep her. And chust think on the expense! Oh, I'm not sayin', mind you, that I'll not try wan some day, but there's no hurry, no, not a bit."

"But perhaps you'll put it off too long," I said, "and when you're in the humour to have them they won't have you."

He laughed at the very idea.

"Man!" he said, "it's easy seen you have not studied them. I ken them like the Kyles of Bute. The captain of a steamer iss the most popular man in the wide world — popularer than the munisters themselves, and the munisters iss that popular the weemen put bird-lime in front of the Manses to catch them, the same ass if they were green-linties[1]. It's worse with sea-captains — they're that dashing, and they're not aalways hinging aboot the hoose wi' their sluppers on."

"There's another thing," he added, after a little pause, "I couldna put up with a woman comin' aboot the vessel every pay-day. No, no, I'm for none o' that. Dougie's wife's plenty."

"But surely she does not invade you weekly?" I said, surprised.

"If the *Fital Spark's* anywhere inside Ardlamont on a Setturday," said Para Handy, "she's doon wi' the first steamer from Gleska[2], and her door-key in her hand, the same ass if it wass a pistol to put to his heid. If Dougie was here himsel' he would tell you. She's a low-country woman, wi' no' a word o' Gaalic, so that she canna understand Dougie at his best. When it comes to bein' angry in English, she can easy bate him. Oh, a cluvver woman: she made Dougie a Rechabite[3], and he's aalways wan when he's at home, and at keepin' him trum and tidy in his clothes she's chust sublime. But she's no' canny aboot a ship. The first week efter she merried him we were lyin' at Innellan, and doon she came on the Setturday wi' her door-key at full cock. When Dougie saw her comin' doon the quay he got white, and turned to me, sayin', 'Peter, here's the Mustress; I wish I hadna touched that dram, she'll can tell it on me, and I'm no' feared for her, but it would hurt her feelings.'

" 'Man!' I said, 'you're an aawful tumid man for a sailor; but haste you doon the fo'c'sle and you'll get a poke of peppermint sweeties in my other pocket I had for the church to-morrow. Chust you go like the duvvle, and I'll keep her in conversation till you get your breath shifted.'

"Dougie bolted doon below, and wass up in a shot. 'I got the sweeties, Peter,' he said, 'but, oh! she's as cunning as a jyler, and she'll chalouse something if she smells the peppermints. What would you say to the whole of us takin' wan or two sweeties so that we would be aal the same, and she wouldna suspect me?' 'Very weel,' I said, 'anything to obleege a mate,' and when the good leddy reached the side of the vessel the enchineer and The Tar and me and Dougie wass standin' in a row eating peppermints till you would think it wass the front sate of the Tobermory Free Church.

" 'It's a fine day and an awfu' smell o' losengers,' was the first words she said when she put her two feet on the deck. And she looked very keen at her man.

" 'It is that, mem,' I said. 'It's the cargo.'

" 'What cargo?' said she, looking at Dougie harder than ever. 'I'll cargo him!'

" 'I mean the cargo of the boat, mem,' I said quite smert. 'It's a cheneral cargo, and there's six ton of peppermint sweeties for the Tarbert fishermen.'

" 'What in the wide world dae the Tarbert fishermen dae wi' sae mony sweeties?' said she.

" 'Och, it's chust to keep them from frightening away the herrin' when they're oot at the fishin',' I said. Man! I'm tellin' you I had aal my wuts aboot me that day! It wass lucky for us the hatches wass doon, so that she couldna see the cargo we had in the hold. There wasna wan sweetie in it.

"I couldna but be nice to the woman, for she wasna my wife, so I turned a bucket upside doon and gave her a sate, and let on that Dougie was chust ass mich a man of consequence on the *Fital Spark* as myself. It does not do to let a wife see wi' her own eyes that her man iss under you in your chob, for when she'll get him at home she'll egg him on to work harder and get your place, and where are you then, eh! where are you then, I'm asking? She wass a cluvver woman but she had no sense. 'Weel,' said she, 'I don't think muckle o' yer boat. I thocht it was a great big boat, wi' a cabin in it. Instead o' that, it's jist a wee coal yin.'

"Man! do you know that vexed me; I say she wasna the kind of woman Dougie should have married at aal, at aal. Dougie's a chentleman like mysel'; he would never hurt your feelings unless he wass tryin'.[4]

" 'There's nothing wrong with the *Fital Spark*, mem,' I said to her. 'She's the most namely ship in the tred; they'll be writing things aboot her in the papers, and men often come to take photographs of her.'

"She chust sniffed her nose at that, the way merrit women have, and said, 'Jist fancy that!'

" 'Yes; chust fancy it!' I said to her. 'Six knots in a gale of wind if Macphail the enchineer is in good trum, and maybe seven if it's Setturday, and him in a hurry to get home. She has the finest lines of any steamboat of her size coming oot of Clyde; if her lum wass pented yellow and she had a bottom strake or two of green, you would take her for a yat. Perhaps you would be thinkin' we should have a German band[5] on board of her, with the heid fuddler goin' aboot gaitherin' pennies in a shell, and the others keekin' over the ends of their flutes and cornucopias for fear he'll pocket some. What? H'm! Chust that!'

"Efter a bit she said she would like to see what sort of place her man and the rest of us slept in, so there was nothing for it but to take her doon to the fo'c'sle, though it wass mich against my will. When she saw the fo'c'sle she wass nestier than ever. She said 'Surely this iss not a place for Christian men'; and I said, 'No, mem, but we're chust sailors.'

" 'There's nae richt furniture in't,' she said.

" 'Not at present, mem,' I said. 'Perhaps you were expectin' a piano,' but, och! she wass chust wan of them Gleska women, she didna know life. She went away up the toon there and then, and came back wi' a bit of waxcloth, a tin of black soap, a grocer's calendar, and a wee lookin'-gless, hung her bonnet and the door-key on a cleat, and started scrubbin' oot the fo'c'sle. Man, it wass chust peetiful! There wass a damp smell in the fo'c'sle I could feel for months efter, and I had a cold in my heid for a fortnight. When she had the floor of the fo'c'sle scrubbed, she laid the bit of waxcloth, got two nails from The Tar, and looked for a place to hang up the calendar and the wee lookin'-gless, though there wass not mich room for ornaments of the kind. 'That's a little mair tidy-like' she said when she was feenished, and she came up lookin' for something else to wash. The Tar saw the danger and went ashore in a hurry.

" 'Are ye merrit?' she asked me before she left the vessel wi' Dougie's pay.

" 'No, mem,' I said, 'I'm not merrit yet.'

" 'I could easy see that,' she said, sniffin' her nose again, the same ass if I wass not a captain at aal, but chust before the mast. 'I could easy see that. It's time you were hurryin' up. I ken the very wife wad suit you; she's a kizzen[6] o' my ain, a weedow wumman no' a bit the worse o' the wear.'

" 'Chust that!' said I, 'but I'm engaged.'

" 'Wha to?' she asked quite sherp, no' very sure o' me.

" 'To wan of the Maids of Bute, mem,' I told her, meanin' yon two pented stones you see from the steamer in the Kyles of Bute; and her bein' a Gleska woman, and not traivelled mich, she thocht I wass in earnest.

" 'I don't ken the faimily,' she said, 'but it's my opeenion you wad be better wi' a sensible weedow.'

" 'Not at aal, mem,' I said, 'a sailor couldna have a better wife nor wan of the Maids of Bute; he'll maybe no' get mich tocher with her, but she'll no' come huntin' the quays for him or his wages on the Setturday.' "

6. *Para Handy — Poacher*

THE *Vital Spark* was lying at Greenock with a cargo of scrap-iron, on the top of which was stowed loosely an extraordinary variety of domestic furniture, from bird cages to cottage pianos. Para Handy had just had the hatches off when I came to the quay-side, and he was contemplating the contents of his hold with no very pleasant aspect.

"Rather a mixed cargo!" I ventured to say.

"Muxed's no' the word for't," he said bitterly. "It puts me in mind of an explosion. It's a flittin'[1] from Dunoon. There would be no flittin's in the *Fital Spark* if she wass my boat. But I'm only the captain, och aye! I'm only the captain, thirty-five shullin's a-week and liberty to put on a pea-jecket. To be puttin' scrap-iron and flittin's in a fine smert boat like this iss carryin' coals aboot in a coach and twice. It would make any man use Abyssinian language."

"Abyssinian language?" I repeated, wondering.

"Chust that, Abyssinian language — swearing, and the like of that, you ken fine, yoursel', withoot me tellin' you. Fancy puttin' a flittin' in the *Fital Spark*! You would think she wass a coal-laary, and her with two new coats of pent out of my own pocket since the New Year."

"Have you been fishing?" I asked, desirous to change the subject, which was, plainly, a sore one with the Captain. And I indicated a small fishing-net which was lying in the bows.

"Chust the least wee bit touch," he said, with a very profound wink. "I have a bit of a net there no' the size of a pocket-naipkin, that I use noo and then at the river-mooths. I chust put it doon — me and Dougie — and whiles a salmon or a sea-troot meets wi' an accident and gets into't. Chust a small bit of a net, no' worth speakin' aboot, no' mich bigger nor a pocket-naipkin. They'll be calling it a splash-net, you ken yoursel' withoot me tellin' you." And he winked knowingly again.

"Ah, Captain!" I said, "that's bad! Poaching with a splash-net! I didn't think you would have done it."

"It's no' me; it's Dougie," he retorted promptly. "A fair duvvle for high jeenks, you canna keep him from it. I told him many a time that it wasna right, becaause we might be found oot and get the jyle for't, but he says they do it on aal the smertest yats. Yes, that iss what he said to me — 'They do it on aal the first-cless yats; you'll be bragging the *Fital Spark* iss chust ass good ass any yat, and what for would you grudge a splash-net?' "

"Still it's theft, Captain," I insisted. "And it's very, very bad for the rivers."

"Chust that!" he said complacently. "You'll likely be wan of them fellows that goes to the hotels for the fushing in the rivers. There's more sport aboot a splash-net; if Dougie wass here he would tell you."

"I don't see where the sport comes in," I remarked, and he laughed contemptuously.

"Sport!" he exclaimed. "The best going. There wass wan time yonder we were up Loch Fyne on a Fast Day[2], and no' a shop open in the place to buy onything for the next mornin's breakfast. Dougie says to me, 'What do you think yoursel' aboot takin' the punt and the small bit of net no' worth mentionin', and going doon to the river mooth when it's dark and seeing if we'll no' get a fush?'

" 'It's a peety to be poaching on the Fast Day,' I said to him.

" 'But it's no' the Fast Day in oor parish,' he said. 'We'll chust give it a trial, and if there's no fush at the start we'll come away back again.' Oh! a consuderate fellow, Dougie; he saw my poseetion at wance, and that I wasna awfu' keen to be fushin' wi' a splash-net on the Fast Day. The end and the short of it wass that when it wass dark we took the net and the punt and rowed doon to the river and began to splash. We had got a fine haul at wance of six great big salmon, and every salmon Dougie would be takin' oot of the net he would be feeling it all over in a droll way, till I said to him, 'What are you feel-feelin' for, Dougie, the same ass if they had pockets on them? I'm sure they're all right.'

" 'Oh, yes,' he says, 'right enough, but I wass frightened they might be the laird's[3] salmon, and I wass lookin' for the luggage label on them. There's none. It's all right; they're chust wild salmon that nobody planted.'[4]

"Weel, we had got chust ass many salmon ass we had any need for when somebody birled a whustle[5], and the river watchers put off in a small boat from a point outside of us to catch us. There wass no gettin' oot of the river mooth, so we left the boat and the net and the fush and ran ashore, and by-and-by we got up to the quay and on board the *Fital Spark*, and paaused and consudered things.

" 'They'll ken it's oor boat,' said Dougie, and his clothes wass up to the eyes in salmon scales.

" 'There's no doo't aboot that,' I says. 'If it wassna the Fast Day I wouldna be so vexed; it'll be an awful disgrace to be found oot workin' a splash-net on the Fast Day. And it's a peety aboot the boat, it wass a good boat, I wish we could get her back.'

" 'Ay, it's a peety we lost her,' said Dougie; 'I wonder in the wide world who could have stole her when we were doon the fo'c'sle at oor supper?' Oh, a smert fellow, Dougie! when he said that I saw at wance what he meant.

" 'I'll go up this meenute and report it to the polis office,' I said quite firm, and Dougie said he would go with me too, but that we would need to change oor clothes, for they were covered with fush-scales. We changed oor clothes and went up to the sercheant of polis, and reported that somebody had stolen oor boat.

He wass sittin' readin' his Bible, it bein' the Fast Day, wi' specs on, and he keeked up at us, and said, 'You are very spruce, boys, with your good clothes on at this time of the night.'

" 'We aalways put on oor good clothes on the *Fital Spark* on a Fast Day,' I says to him; 'it's as little as we can do, though we don't belong to the parish.'

"Next day there wass a great commotion in the place aboot some blackguards doon at the river mooth poachin' with a splash-net. The Factor[6] wass busy, and the heid gamekeeper wass busy, and the polis wass busy. We could see them from the dake of the *Fital Spark* goin' aboot buzzin' like bum-bees.

" 'Stop you!' said Dougie to me aal of a sudden. 'They'll be doon here in a chiffy, and findin' us with them scales on oor clothes — we'll have to put on the Sunday wans again.'

" 'But they'll smell something if they see us in oor Sunday clothes,' I said. 'It's no' the Fast Day the day.'

" 'Maybe no' here,' said Dougie, 'but what's to hinder it bein' the Fast Day in oor own parish?'

"We put on oor Sunday clothes again, and looked the Almanac to see if there wass any word in it of a Fast Day any place that day, but there wass nothing in the Almanac but tides, and the Battle of Waterloo, and the weather for next winter. That's the worst of Almanacs; there's nothing in them you want. We were fair bate for a Fast Day any place, when The Tar came up and asked me if he could get to the funeral of a cousin of his in the place at two o'clock.

" 'A funeral!' said Dougie. 'The very thing. The Captain and me'll go to the funeral too. That's the way we have on oor Sunday clothes.' Oh, a smert, smert fellow, Dougie!

"We had chust made up oor mind it wass the funeral we were dressed for, and no' a Fast Day any place, when the polisman and the heid gamekeeper came doon very suspeecious, and said they had oor boat. 'And what's more,' said the gamekeeper, 'there's a splash-net and five stone of salmon in it. It hass been used, your boat, for poaching.'

" 'Iss that a fact?' I says. 'I hope you'll find the blackguards,' and the gamekeeper gave a grunt, and said somebody would suffer for it, and went away busier than ever. But the polis sercheant stopped behind. 'You're still in your Sunday clothes, boys,' said he; 'what iss the occasion to-day?'

" 'We're going to the funeral,' I said.

" 'Chust that! I did not know you were untimate with the diseased,' said the sercheant.

" 'Neither we were,' I said, 'but we are going oot of respect for Colin.' And we went to the funeral, and nobody suspected nothin', but we never got back the boat, for the gamekeeper wass chust needin' wan for a brother o' his own. Och, ay! there's wonderful sport in a splash-net."

7. *The Sea Cook*

THE TAR's duties included cooking for the ship's company. He was not exactly a chef who would bring credit to a first-class club or restaurant, but for some time after he joined the *Vital Spark* there was no occasion to complain of him. Quite often he would wash the breakfast-cups to have them clean for tea in the evening, and it was only when in a great hurry he dried plates with the ship's towel. But as time passed, and he found his shipmates not very particular about what they ate, he grew a little careless. For instance, Para Handy was one day very much annoyed to see The Tar carry forward the potatoes for dinner in his cap.

"That's a droll way to carry potatoes, Colin," he said mildly.

"Och! they'll do no herm; it's only an old kep anyway," said The Tar. "Catch me usin' my other kep for potatoes!"

"It wass not exactly your kep I wass put aboot for," said the Captain. "It wass chust running in my mind that maybe some sort of a dish would be nater and genteeler.[1] I'm no' compleenin', mind you, I'm chust mentioning it."

"Holy smoke!" said The Tar. "You're getting to be aawful polite wi' your plates for potatoes, and them no peeled!"

But the want of variety in The Tar's cooking grew worse and worse each voyage, and finally created a feeling of great annoyance to the crew. It was always essence of coffee, and herring — fresh, salt, kippered, or red — for breakfast, sausages or stewed steak and potatoes for dinner, and a special treat in the shape of ham and eggs for Sundays. One unlucky day for the others of the crew, however, he discovered the convenience of tinned corned beef, and would feed them on that for dinner three or four days a week. Of course they commented on this prevalence of tinned food, which the engineer with some humour always called "malleable mule", but The Tar had any number of reasons ready for its presence on the midday board.

"Sorry, boys," he would say affably, "but this is the duvvle of a place; no' a bit of butcher meat to be got in't till Wednesday, when it comes wi' the boat from Gleska." Or "The fire went oot on me, chaps, chust when I wass making a fine thing. Wait you till Setturday, and we'll have something rare!"

"Ay, ay; live, old horse, and you'll get corn," the Captain would say under these circumstances, as he artistically carved the wedge of American meat. "It's a mercy to get anything; back in your plate, Dougie."

It became at last unbearable, and while The Tar was ashore one day in Tarbert, buying bottled coffee and tinned meat in bulk, a conference between the captain, the engineer, and the mate took place.

"I'm no' going to put up wi't any longer," said the engineer emphatically. "It's all very well for them that has no thinking to do wi' their heids to eat tinned mule even on, but an engineer that's thinking aboot his engines all the time, and sweatin' doon in a temperature o' 120, needs to keep his strength up."

"What sort o' heid-work are you talking aboot?" said the Captain. "Iss it readin' your penny novelles? Hoo's Lady Fitzgerald's man gettin' on?" This last allusion was to Macphail's passion for penny fiction, and particularly to a novelette story over which the engineer had once been foolish enough some years before to show great emotion.

"I move," said Dougie, breaking in on what promised to be an unprofitable altercation, — "I move that The Tar be concurred."

"Concurred!" said the engineer, with a contemptuous snort. "I suppose you mean censured?"

"It's the same thing, only spelled different," said the mate.

"What's censured?" asked the Captain.

"It's giving a fellow a duvvle of a clourin'²," answered Dougie promptly.

"No, no, I wouldna care to do that to The Tar. Maybe he's doin' the best he can, poor chap. The Tar never saw mich high life before he came on my boat, and we'll have to make an allowance for that."

"Herrin' for breakfast seven days a week! it's a fair scandal," said the engineer. "If you were maister in your own boat, Macfarlane, you would have a very different kind of man makin' your meat for you."

"There's not mich that iss wholesomer than a good herrin'," said Para Handy. "It's a fush that's chust sublime. But I'll not deny it would be good to have a change noo and then, if it wass only a finnen haddie³."

"I have a cookery book o' the wife's yonder at home I'll bring wi' me the next time we're in Gleska, and it'll maybe give him a tip or two," said the engineer, and this was, in the meantime, considered the most expedient thing to do.

Next trip, on the way to Brodick on a Saturday with a cargo of bricks, The Tar was delicately approached by the Captain, who had the cookery book in his hand. "That wass a nice tender bit of tinned beef we had the day, Colin," he said graciously. "Capital, aaltogether! I could live myself on tinned beef from wan end of the year to the other, but Dougie and the enchineer there's compleenin' that you're givin' it to them too often. You would think they were lords! But perhaps I shouldna blame them, for the doctor told the enchineer he should take something tasty every day, and Dougie's aye frightened for tinned meat since ever he heard that the enchineer wance killed a man in the Australian bush.[4] What do you say yoursel' to tryin' something fancy in the cookery line?"

"There's some people hard to please," said The Tar; "I'm sure I'm doin' the best I can to satisfy you aal. Look at them red herrin's I made this mornin'!"

"They were chust sublime!" said the Captain, clapping him on the back. "But chust try a change to keep their mooths shut. It'll only need to be for a little, for they'll soon tire o' fancy things. I have a kind of a cookery book here you might get some tips in. It's no' mine, mind you, it's Macphail's."

The Tar took the cookery book and turned over some pages with contemptuous and horny fingers.

"A lot o' nonsense!" he said. "Listen to this: 'Take the remains of any cold chicken, mix with the potatoes, put in a pie-dish, and brown with a salamander.' Where are you to get the cold chucken? and where are you to take it? Fancy callin' it a remains; it would be enough to keep you from eatin' chucken. And what's a salamander? There's no' wan on this vessel, at any rate."

"It's chust another name for cinnamon, but you could leave it oot," said the Captain.

"Holy smoke! listen to this," proceeded The Tar: " 'How to make clear stock. Take six or seven pounds of knuckle of beef or veal, half a pound of ham or bacon, a quarter of a pound of butter, two onions, one carrot, one turnip, half a head of celery, and two gallons of water.' You couldna sup that in a week."

"Smaal quantities, smaal quantities, Colin," explained the Captain. "I'm sorry to put you to bother, but there's no other way of pleasin' them other fellows."

"There's no' a thing in this book I would eat except a fowl that's described here," said The Tar, after a further glance through the volume.

"The very thing!" cried the Captain, delighted. "Try a fowl for Sunday," and The Tar said he would do his best.

"I soon showed him who wass skipper on this boat," said the Captain going aft to Dougie and the engineer. "It's to be fowl on Sunday."

There was an old-fashioned cutter yacht at anchor in Brodick Bay with a leg of mutton and two plucked fowls hanging openly under the overhang of her stern, which is sometimes even yet the only pantry a yacht of that type has, though the result is not very decorative.

"Look at that!" said the engineer to The Tar as the *Vital Spark* puffed past the yacht. "There's sensible meat for sailors; no malleable mule. I'll bate you them fellows has a cook wi' aal his wuts aboot him."

"It's aal right, Macphail," said The Tar; "chust you wait till to-morrow and I'll give you fancy cookin'."

And sure enough on Sunday he had two boiled fowls for dinner. It was such an excellent dinner that even the engineer was delighted.

"I'll bate you that you made them hens ready oot o' the wife's cookery book," he said. "There's no' a better cookery book on the South-side of Gleska; the genuine Aunt Kate's. People come far and near for the lend o' that when they're havin' anything extra."

"Where did you buy the hens?" inquired the Captain, nibbling contentedly at the last bone left after the repast.

"I didna buy them at aal," said The Tar. "I couldna be expected to buy chuckens on the money you alloo me. Forbye, it doesna say anything aboot buying in Macphail's cookery book. It says, 'Take two chickens and boil slowly.' So I chust had to take them."

"What do you mean by that?" asked Para Handy, with great apprehension.

"I chust went oot in a wee boat late last night and took them from the stern o' yon wee yacht," said The Tar coolly; and a great silence fell upon the crew of the *Vital Spark*.

"To-morrow," said the Captain emphatically at last — "to-morrow you'll have tinned meat; do you know that, Colin? And you'll never have chucken on the boat again, not if Macphail was breakin' his he'rt for it."

8. *Lodgers on a House-Boat*

A MAN and his wife came down Crarae Quay from the village. The man carried a spotted yellow tin box in one hand and a bottle of milk in the other. He looked annoyed at something. His wife had one child in her arms, and another walked weeping behind her, occasionally stopping the weeping to suck a stalk of The Original Crarae Rock. There was a chilly air of separation about the little procession that made it plain there had been an awful row. At the quay the *Vital Spark* lay with her hold half covered by the hatches, after discharging a cargo. Her gallant commander, with Dougie, stood beside the winch and watched the family coming down the quay.

"Take my word for it, Dougie," said Para Handy, "that man's no' in very good trum; you can see by the way he's banging the box against his legs and speaking to himsel'. It's no' a hymn he's going over I'll bate you. And hersel's no' much better, or she wouldna be lettin' the poor fellow carry the box."

The man came forward to the edge of the quay, looked at the newly painted red funnel of the *Vital Spark*, and seemed, from his countenance, to have been seized by some bright idea.

"Hey! you with the skipped kep," he cried down eagerly to Dougie, "when does this steamer start?"

Para Handy looked at his mate with a pride there was no concealing. "My Chove! Dougie," he said in a low tone to him. "My Chove! he thinks we're opposeetion to the *Lord of the Isles*[1] or the *King Edward*[2]. I'm aye tellin' you this boat iss built on smert lines; if you and me had brass buttons we could make money carryin' passengers."

"Are ye deaf?" cried the man on the quay impatiently, putting down the tin box, and rubbing the sweat from his brow. "When does this boat start?"

"This iss not a boat that starts at aal," said the Captain. "It's a — it's a kind of a yat."

"Dalmighty!" exclaimed the man, greatly crestfallen, "that settles it. I thocht we could get back to Gleska wi' ye. We canna get ludgin's[3] in this place, and whit the bleezes are we to dae when we canna get ludgin's?"

"That's a peety," said the Captain. "It's no' a very nice thing to happen on a Setturday, and there's no way you can get oot of Crarae till Monday unless you have wan of them motor cars."

"We havena oors wi' us," said the wife, taking up a position beside her husband and the tin box. "I'm vexed the only thing o' the kind I ha'e 's a cuddy[4], and if it wasna for him we would ha'e stayed at Rothesay, whaur you can aye get ludgin's o' some kind. Do ye no' think ye could gie us twa nicht's ludgin's on your boat? I'm shair there's plenty o' room."

"Bless my sowl, where's the plenty o' room?" asked the Captain. "This boat cairries three men and an enchineer, and we're crooded enough in the fo'c'sle."

"Where's that?" she asked, taking all the negotiations out of the hands of her husband, who sat down on the spotted tin box and began to cut tobacco.

"Yonder it is," said Para Handy, indicating the place with a lazy, inelegant, but eloquent gesture of his leg.

"Weel, there's plenty o' room," persisted the woman, — "ye can surely see for yersel' there's plenty o' room; you and your men could sleep at the — at the — the stroup[5] o' the boat there, and ye could mak' us ony kind o' a shake-down doon the stair there" – and she pointed at the hold.

"My coodness! the stroup o' the boat!" exclaimed Para Handy; "you would think it wass a teapot you were taalkin' aboot. And that's no' a doon-stairs at aal, it's the howld. We're no' in the habit of takin' in ludgers in the coastin' tred; I never had wan in the Fital Spark in aal my life except the time I cairried Wee Teeny. We havena right accommodation for ludgers; we have no napery, nor enough knives and forks — "

"Onything wad dae for a shove-bye," said the woman. "I'm shair ye wouldna see a dacent man and his wife and twa wee hameless lambs sleepin' in the quarry[6] as lang as ye could gie them a corner to sit doon in on that nice clean boat o' yours."

She was a shrewd woman; her compliment to the Vital Spark found the soft side of its captain's nature, and, to the disgust of Macphail the engineer and the annoyance of The Tar — though with the hearty consent of the mate — Jack Flood and his family, with the tin box and the bottle of milk, were ten minutes later installed in the fo'c'sle of the *Vital Spark* as paying guests. The terms arranged were two shillings a night. "You couldna get ludgin's in a good hotel for much less," said the Captain, and Mrs Flood agreed that that was reasonable.

The crew slept somewhat uncomfortably in the hold, and in the middle watches of the night the Captain wakened at the sound of an infant crying. He sat up, nudged Dougie awake, and moralised.

"Chust listen to that, Dougie," he said, "the wee cratur's greetin' ass naitural ass anything, the same ass if it wass a rale ludgin's or on board wan of them ships that carries passengers to America. It's me that likes to hear it; it's ass homely a thing ass ever happened on this vessel. I wouldna say but maybe it'll be good luck. I'm tellin' you what, Dougie, we'll no' cherge them a d — ha'penny; what do you think, mate?"

"Whatever you say yoursel'," said Dougie.

The wail of the infant continued; they heard Jack Flood get up at the request of his wife and sing. He sang "Rocked in the Cradle of the Deep" — at least he sang two lines of it over and over again, taking liberties with the air that would have much annoyed the original composer if he could have heard him.

"It's chust sublime!" said Para Handy, stretched on a rolled-up sail. "You're a lucky man, Dougie, that iss mairried and has a hoose of your own. Oor two ludgers iss maybe pretty cross when it comes to the quarrelling, but they have no spite at the weans. You would not think that man Flood had the sense to rise up in the muddle of the night and sing 'Rocked in the Cradle of the Deep' at his child. It chust shows you us workin'-men have good he'rts."

"Jeck may have a cood enough he'rt," said Dougie, "but, man! he has a poor, poor ear for music! I wish he would stop it and no' be frightenin' the wean. I'm sure it never did him any herm."

By-and-by the crying and the music ceased, and the only sound to be heard was the snore of The Tar and the lapping of the tide against the run of the vessel.

Sunday was calm and bright, but there was no sign of the lodgers coming on deck till late in the forenoon, much to the surprise of the Captain. At last he heard a loud peremptory whistle from the fo'c'sle, and went forward to see what was wanted. Flood threw up four pairs of boots at him. "Gie them a bit polish," he said airily. "Ye

needna be awfu' parteecular," he added, "but they're a' glaur[7], and
we like to be dacent on Sunday."

The Captain, in a daze, lifted the boots and told The Tar to oil
them, saying emphatically at the same time to Dougie, "Efter aal,
we'll no' let them off with the two shillin's. They're too dirty
parteecular."

There was another whistle ten minutes later, and Dougie went to
see what was wanted.

"I say, my lad," remarked Mr Flood calmly, "look slippy with the
breakfast; we cannae sterve here ony langer."

"Are you no' comin' up for't?" asked Dougie in amazement. "It's
a fine dry day."

"Dry my auntie!" said Mr Flood. "The wife aye gets her breakfast
in her bed on Sundays whether it's wet or dry. Ye'll get the kippered
herrin' and the loaf she brung last nicht beside the lum."

The Tar cooked the lodgers' breakfast under protest, saying he
was not paid wages for being a saloon steward, and he passed it
down to the fo'c'sle.

"Two shilling's a night!" said the Captain. "If I had known what it
wass to keep ludgers, it wouldna be two shillin's a night I would be
cherging them."

He was even more emphatic on this point when a third whistle
came from the fo'c'sle, and The Tar, on going to see what was
wanted now, was informed by Mrs Flood that the cooking was not
what she was accustomed to. "I never saw a steamer like this in my
life," she said, "first cless, as ye micht say, and no' a table to tak' yer
meat aff, and only shelfs to sleep on, and sea-sick nearly the hale
nicht to the bargain! Send us doon a pail o' water to clean oor faces."

Para Handy could stand no more. He washed himself carefully,
put on his Sunday clothes and his watch chain, which always gave
him great confidence and courage, and went to the fo'c'sle-head. He
addressed the lodgers from above.

"Leezy," he said ingratiatingly (for so he had heard Mr Flood
designate his wife), "Leezy, you're missing aal the fun doon there;
you should come up and see the folk goin' to the church; you never
saw such style among the women in aal your days."

"I'll be up in a meenute," she replied quickly; "Jeck, hurry up and
hook this."

On the whole, the lodgers and the crew of the *Vital Spark* spent a fairly pleasant Sunday. When the Flood family was not ashore walking in the neighbourhood, it was lying about the deck eating dulse and picking whelks culled from the shore by Jack. The mother kindly supplied the infant with as much dulse and shell-fish as it wanted, and it had for these a most insatiable appetite.

"You shouldnae eat any wulks or things of that sort when there's no 'r's' in the month," Para Handy advised her. "They're no' very wholesome then."

"Fiddlesticks!" said Mrs Flood. "I've ett wulks every Fair since I was a wee lassie, and look at me noo! Besides, there's an 'r' in Fair, that puts it a' richt."

That night the infant wailed from the moment they went to bed till it was time to rise in the morning; Jack Flood sang "Rocked in the Cradle of the Deep" till he was hoarse, and the crew in the hold got up next morning very sorry for themselves.

"You'll be takin' the early steamer?" said Para Handy at the first opportunity.

"Och! we're gettin' on fine," said Jack cheerfully; "Leezy and me thinks we'll just put in the week wi' ye," and the wife indicated her hearty concurrence.

"You canna stay here," said the Captain firmly.

"Weel, we're no' goin' to leave, onywye," said Mr Flood, lighting his clay pipe. "We took the ludgin's, and though they're no' as nice as we would like, we're wullin' to put up with them, and ye canna put us oot withoot a week's warnin'."

"My Chove! do you say that?" said Para Handy in amazement. "You're the first and last ludger I'll have on this vessel!"

"A week's notice; it's the law o' the land," said the admirable Mr Flood, "isn't that so, Leezy?"

"Everybody that has sense kens that that's richt," said Mrs Flood. And the Flood family retired *en masse* to the fo'c'sle.

Ten minutes later the *Vital Spark* was getting up steam, and soon there were signs of her immediate departure from the quay.

"Whaur are ye gaun?" cried Jack, coming hurriedly on deck.

"Outward bound," said Para Handy with indifference. "That's a sailor's life for you, here the day and away yesterday."

"To Gleska?" said Mr Flood hopefully.

"Gleska!" said Para Handy. "We'll no' see it for ten months; we're bound for the Rio Grande."

"Whaur's that in a' the warld?" asked Mrs Flood, who had joined her husband on deck.

"Oh! chust in foreign perts," said Para Handy. "Away past the Bay of Biscay, and the first place on your left-hand side after you pass New Zealand. It's where the beasts for the Zoo comes from."

In four minutes the Flood family were off the ship, and struggling up the quay with the spotted tin trunk, and the *Vital Spark* was starting for Bowling.[8]

"I'm a stupid man," said Para Handy in a few minutes after leaving the quay. "Here we're away and forgot aal aboot the money for the ludgin's."

9. *A Lost Man*

IT WAS a dirty evening, coming on to dusk, and the *Vital Spark* went walloping drunkenly down Loch Fyne with a cargo of oak bark[1], badly trimmed. She staggered to every shock of the sea; the waves came combing over her quarter, and Dougie the mate began to wish they had never sailed that day from Kilcatrine. They had struggled round the point of Pennymore, the prospect looking every moment blacker, and he turned a dozen projects over in his mind for inducing Para Handy to anchor somewhere till the morning. At last he remembered Para's partiality for anything in the way of long-shore gaiety, and the lights of the village of Furnace gave him an idea.

"Ach! man, Peter," said he, "did we no' go away and forget this wass the night of the baal at Furnace? What do you say to going in and joining the spree?"

"You're feared, Dougie," said the Captain; "you're scaared to daith for your life, in case you'll have to die and leave your money. You're thinkin' you'll be drooned, and that's the way you want to put her into Furnace. Man! but you're tumid, tumid! Chust look at me — no' the least put aboot. That's becaause I'm a Macfarlane, and a Macfarlane never wass bate yet, never in this world! I'm no' goin' to stop the night for any baal — we must be in Clyde on Friday; besides, we havena the clothes wi' us for a baal. Forbye, who'll buy the tickets? Eh? Tell me that! Who'll buy the tickets?"

"Ach! you don't need tickets for a Furnace baal" said Dougie, flicking the spray from his ear, and looking longingly at the village they were nearing. "You don't need tickets for a Furnace baal as long as you ken the man at the door and taalk the Gaalic at him. And your clothes 'll do fine if you oil your boots and put on a kind of a collar. What's the hurry for Clyde? It'll no' run dry. In weather like this, too! It's chust a temptin' of Providence. I had a dream yonder last night that wasna canny. Chust a temptin' of Providence."

"I wudna say but it is," agreed the Captain weakly, putting the vessel a little to starboard; "it's many a day since I was at a spree in Furnace. Are you sure the baal's the night?"

"Of course I am," said Dougie emphatically; "it only started yesterday."

"Weel, if you're that keen on't, we'll maybe be chust as weel to put her in till the mornin'," said Para Handy, steering hard for Furnace Bay; and in a little he knocked down to the engines with the usual, "Stop her, Macphail, when you're ready."

All the crew of the *Vital Spark* went to the ball, but they did not dance much, though it was the boast of Para Handy that he was "a fine strong dancer". The last to come down to the vessel in the morning when the ball stopped, because the paraffin-oil was done, was the Captain, walking on his heels, with his pea-jacket tightly buttoned on his chest, and his round, go-ashore pot hat, as he used to say himself, "on three hairs". It was a sign that he felt intensely satisfied with everything.

"I'm feeling chust sublime," he said to Dougie, smacking his lips and thumping himself on the chest as he took his place at the wheel, and the *Vital Spark* resumed her voyage down the loch. "I am chust like the eagle that knew the youth[2] in the Scruptures. It's a fine, fine thing a spree, though I wass not in the trum for dancing. I met sixteen cousins yonder, and them all in the committee. They were the proud men last night to be having a captain for a cousin, and them only quarry-men. It's the educaation, Dougie; educaation gives you the nerve, and if you have the nerve you can go round the world."

"You werena very far roond the world, whatever o't," unkindly interjected the engineer, who stuck up his head at the moment.

The Captain made a push at him angrily with his foot. "Go down, Macphail," he said, "and do not be making a display of your ignorance on this ship. Stop you till I get you at Bowling! Not round the world! Man, I wass twice at Ullapool, and took the *Fital Spark* to Ireland wance, without a light on her. There iss not a port I am not acquent with from the Tail of the Bank to Cairndow, where they keep the two New Years.[3] And Campbeltown, ay, or Barra, or Tobermory. I'm telling you when I am in them places it's Captain Peter Macfarlane iss the mich-respected man. If you were a rale enchineer and not chust a fireman, I would be asking you to my ludgings to let you see the things I brought from my voyages."

The engineer drew in his head and resumed the perusal of a penny novelette.

"He thinks I'm frightened for him," said the Captain, winking darkly to his mate. "It iss because I am too cuvil to him : if he angers me, I'll show him. It is chust spoiling the boat having a man like that in cherge of her enchines, and her such a fine smert boat, with me, and a man like me, in command of her."

"And there's mysel', too, the mate," said Dougie; "I'm no' bad mysel'."

Below Minard rocks the weather grew worse again: the same old seas smashed over the *Vital Spark*. "She's pitching aboot chust like a washin'-boyne[4]," said Dougie apprehensively. "That's the worst of them oak-bark cargoes."

"Like a washin'-boyne!" cried Para Handy indignantly; "she's chust doing sublime. I wass in boats in my time where you would need to be bailing the watter out of your top-boots every here and there. The smertest boat in the tred; stop you till I have a pound of my own, and I will paint her till you'll take her for a yat if it wasna for the lum. You and your washin'-boyne! A washin'-boyne wudna do you any herm, my laad, and that's telling you."

They were passing Lochgair; the steamer *Cygnet*[5] overtook and passed them as if they had been standing, somebody shouting to them from her deck.

Para Handy refrained from looking. It always annoyed him to be passed this way by other craft; and in summer time, when the turbine *King Edward* or the *Lord of the Isles* went past him like a streak of lightning, he always retired below to hide his feelings. He did not look at the *Cygnet*. "Ay, ay," he said to Dougie, "if I was telling Mr MacBrayne[6] the umpudence of them fellows, he would put a stop to it in a meenute, but I will not lose them their chobs; poor sowls! maybe they have wifes and femilies. That'll be Chonny Mactavish takin' his fun of me; you would think he wass a wean. Chust like them brats of boys that come to the riverside when we'll be going up the Clyde at Yoker and cry, '*Columbia*[7], ahoy!' at us — the duvvle's own!"

As the Cygnet disappeared in the distance, with a figure waving at her stern, a huge sea struck the *Vital Spark* and swept her from stem to stern, almost washing the mate, who was hanging on to a stay, overboard.

"Tar! Tar!" cried the Captain. "Go and get a ha'ad o' that bucket or it'll be over the side."

There was no response. The Tar was not visible, and a wild dread took possession of Para Handy.

"Let us pause and consider," said he to himself, "was The Tar on board when we left Furnace?"

They searched the vessel high and low for the missing member of the crew, who was sometimes given to fall asleep in the fo'c'sle at the time he was most needed. But there was no sign of him. "I ken fine he wass on board when we started," said the Captain, distracted, "for I heard him sputtin'. Look again, Dougie, like a good laad." Dougie looked again, for he, too, was sure The Tar had returned from the ball with him. "I saw him with my own eyes," he said, "two of him, the same as if he was a twins; that iss the curse of drink in a place like Furance." But the search was in vain, even though the engineer said he had seen The Tar an hour ago.

"Weel, there's a good man gone!" said Para Handy. "Och! poor Tar! It was yon last smasher of a sea. He's over the side. Poor laad! poor laad! Cot bless me, dyin' without a word of Gaalic in his mooth! It's a chudgment on us for the way we were carryin' on, chust a chudgment; not another drop of drink will I drink, except maybe beer. Or at a New Year time. I'm blaming you, Dougie, for making us stop at Furnace for a baal I wudna give a snuff for. You are chust a disgrace to the vessel, with your smokin' and your drinkin', and your

ignorance. It iss time you were livin' a better life for the sake of your
wife and femily. If it wass not for you makin' me go into Furnace last
night, The Tar would be to the fore yet, and I would not need to be
sending a telegram to his folk from Ardrishaig. If I wass not steering
the boat, I would break my he'rt greetin' for the poor laad that never
did anybody any herm. Get oot the flag from below my bunk, give it
a syne in the pail, and put it at half mast, and we'll go into Ardrishaig
and send a telegram — it'll be a sixpence. It'll be a telegram with a
sore he'rt, I'll assure you. I do not know what I will say in it, Dougie.
It will not do to break it too much to them; maybe we will send the
two telegrams — that'll be a shilling. We'll say in the first wan 'Your
son, Colin, left the boat to-day': and in the next wan we will say —
'He iss not coming back, he iss drooned.' Och! och! poor Tar, amn't
I sorry for him? I was chust going to put up his wages a shillin' on
Setturday."

The *Vital Spark* went in close to Ardrishaig pier just as the *Cygnet*
was leaving after taking in a cargo of herring boxes. Para Handy and
Dougie went ashore in the punt, the Captain with his hands washed
and his watch-chain on as a tribute of respect for the deceased.
Before they could send off the telegram it was necessary that they
should brace themselves for the melancholy occasion. "No drinking, chust wan gless of beer," said Para Handy, and they entered a
discreet contiguous public-house for this purpose.

The Tar himself was standing at the counter having a refreshment,
with one eye wrapped up in a handkerchief.

"Dalmighty!" cried the Captain, staggered at the sight, and
turning pale. "What are you doing here with your eye in a sling?"

"What's your business?" retorted The Tar coolly "I'm no' in your
employ anyway."

"What way that?" asked Para Handy sharply.

"Did you no' give me this black eye and the sack last night at the
baal, and tell me I wass never to set foot on the *Vital Spark* again? It
was gey mean o' you to go away withoot lettin' me get my dunnage
oot, and that's the way I came here with the *Cygnet* to meet you. Did
you no' hear me roarin' on you when we passed?"

"Weel done! weel done!" said Para Handy soothingly, with a wink
at his mate. "But ach! I wass only in fun, Colin; it wass a jeenk; it wass
chust a baur aalthegither. Come away back to the boat like a smert

laad. I have a shilling here I wass going to spend anyway. Colin, what'll you take? We thought you were over the side and drooned, and you are here, quite dry as usual."

10. *Hurricane Jack*

I VERY often hear my friend the Captain speak of Hurricane Jack in terms of admiration and devotion, which would suggest that Jack is a sort of demigod. The Captain always refers to Hurricane Jack as the most experienced seaman of modern times, as the most fearless soul that ever wore oilskins, the handsomest man in Britain, so free with his money he would fling it at the birds, so generally accomplished that it would be a treat to be left a month on a desert island alone with him.

"Why is he called Hurricane Jack?" I asked the Captain once.

"What the duvvle else would you caal him?" asked Para Handy. "Nobody ever caals him anything else than Hurricane Jeck."

"Quite so, but why?" I persisted.

Para Handy scratched the back of his neck, made the usual gesture as if he were going to scratch his ear, and then checked himself in the usual way to survey his hand as if it were a beautiful example of Greek sculpture. His hand, I may say, is almost as large as a Belfast ham.

"What way wass he called Hurricane Jeck?" said he. "Well, I'll soon tell you that. He wass not always known by that name; that wass a name he got for the time he stole the sheep."

"Stole the sheep!" I said, a little bewildered, for I failed to see how an incident of that kind would give rise to such a name.

"Yes; what you might call stole," said Para Handy hastily; "but, och! it wass only wan smaal wee sheep he lifted on a man that never went to the church, and chust let him take it! Hurricane Jeck would not steal a fly — no, nor two flies, from a Chrustian; he's the perfect chentleman in that."

"Tell me all about it," I said.

"I'll soon do that," said he, putting out his hand to admire it again, and in doing so upsetting his glass. "Tut, tut!" he said. "Look what I have done — knocked doon my gless; it wass a good thing there wass nothing in it.

"Hurricane Jeck," said the Captain, when I had taken the hint and put something in it, "iss a man that can sail anything and go anywhere, and aalways be the perfect chentleman. A millionaire's yat or a washing-boyne — it's aal the same to Jeck; he would sail the wan chust as smert as the other, and land on the quay as spruce ass if he wass newly come from a baal. Oh, man! the cut of his jeckets! And never anything else but 'lastic-sided boots, even in the coorsest weather! If you would see him, you would see a man that's chust sublime, and that careful about his 'lastic sided boots he would never stand at the wheel unless there wass a bass[1] below his feet. He'll aye be oil-oiling at his hair, and buying hard hats for going ashore with: I never saw a man wi' a finer heid for the hat, and in some of the vessels he wass in he would have the full of a bunker of hats. Hurricane Jeck wass brought up in the China clipper tred, only he wassna called Hurricane Jeck then, for he hadna stole the sheep till efter that. He wass captain of the *Dora Young*, wan of them clippers; he's a hand on a gaabert the now, but aalways the perfect chentleman."

"It seems a sad downcome for a man to be a gabbart hand after having commanded a China clipper," I ventured to remark. "What was the reason of his change?"

"Bad luck," said Para Handy. "Chust bad luck. The fellow never got fair-play. He would aye be somewhere takin' a gless of something wi' somebody, for he's a fine big cheery chap. I mind splendid when he wass captain on the clipper, he had a fine hoose of three rooms and a big decanter, wi' hot and cold watter oot at Pollokshaws[2]. When you went oot to the hoose to see Hurricane Jeck in them days, time slupped bye. But he wassna known as Hurricane Jeck then, for it wass before he stole the sheep."

"You were just going to tell me something about that," I said.

"Jeck iss wan man in a hundred, and ass good ass two if there wass anything in the way of trouble, for, man! he's strong, strong! He has a back on him like a shipping-box, and when he will come down Tarbert quay on a Friday night after a good fishing, and the trawlers are arguing, it's two yerds to the step with him and a bash in the side of his hat for fair defiance. But he never hit a man twice, for he's aye the perfect chentleman iss Hurricane Jeck. Of course, you must understand, he wass not known as Hurricane Jeck till the time I'm going to tell you of, when he stole the sheep.

"I have not trevelled far mysel' yet, except Ullapool and the time I wass at Ireland; but Hurricane Jeck in his time has been at every place on the map, and some that's no'. Chust wan of Brutain's hardy sons — that's what he iss. As weel kent in Calcutta as if he wass in the Coocaddens[3], and he could taalk a dozen of their foreign kinds of languages if he cared to take the bother. When he would be leaving a port, there wassna a leddy in the place but what would be doon on the quay wi' her Sunday clothes on and a bunch o' floo'ers for his cabin. And when he would be sayin' good-bye to them from the brudge, he would chust take off his hat and give it a shoogle[4], and put it on again; his manners wass complete. The first thing he would do when he reached any place wass to go ashore and get his boots brushed, and then sing 'Rule Britannia' roond aboot the docks. It wass a sure way to get freend or foe aboot you, he said, and he wass aye as ready for the wan as for the other. Brutain's hardy son!

"He made the fastest passages in his time that wass ever made in the tea trade, and still and on he would meet you like a common working-man. There wass no pride or nonsense of that sort aboot Hurricane Jeck; but, mind you, though I'm callin' him Hurricane Jeck, he wasna Hurricane Jeck till the time he stole the sheep."

"I don't like to press you, Captain, but I'm anxious to hear about that sheep," I said patiently.

"I'm comin' to't," said Para Handy. "Jeck had the duvvle's own bad luck; he couldna take a gless by-ordinar' but the ship went wrong on him, and he lost wan job efter the other, but he wass never anything else but the perfect chentleman. When he had not a penny in his pocket, he would borrow a shilling from you, and buy you a stick pipe for yourself chust for good nature — "

"A stick pipe?" I repeated interrogatively. "Chust a stick pipe — or a wudden pipe, or whatever you like to call it. He had three medals and a clock that wouldna go for saving life at sea, but that wass before he wass Hurricane Jeck, mind you; for at that time he hadna stole the sheep."

"I'm dying to hear about that sheep," I said.

"I'll soon tell you about the sheep," said Para Handy. "It wass a thing that happened when him and me wass sailing on the *Elizabeth Ann*, a boat that belonged to Girvan, and a smert wan too, if she wass in any kind of trum at aal. We would be going here and there aboot the West Coast with wan thing and another, and not costing the owners mich for coals if coals wass our cargo. It wass wan Sunday we were passing Caticol in Arran, and in a place yonder where there wass not a hoose in sight we saw a herd of sheep eating gress near the shore. As luck would have it, there wass not a bit of butcher-meat on board the *Elizabeth Ann* for the Sunday dinner, and Jeck cocked his eye at the sheep and says to me, 'Yonder's some sheep lost, poor things; what do you say to taking the punt and going ashore to see if there's anybody's address on them?

" 'Whatever you say yoursel',' I said to Jeck, and we stopped the vessel and went ashore, the two of us, and looked the sheep high and low, but there wass no address on them. 'They're lost, sure enough,' said Jeck, pulling some heather and putting it in his pocket — he wassna Hurricane Jeck then — 'they're lost, sure enough, Peter. Here's a nice wee wan nobody would ever miss, that chust the very thing for a coal vessel,' and before you could say 'knife' he had it killed and carried to the punt. Oh, he iss a smert, smert fellow with his hands; he could do anything.

"We rowed ass caalm ass we could oot to the vessel and we had chust got the deid sheep on board when we heard a roarin' and whustling.

" 'Taalk about Arran being releegious!" said Jeck. 'Who's that whustling on the Lord's day?'

" The man that wass whustling wass away up on the hill, and we could see him coming running doon the hill the same ass if he would break every leg he had on him.

" 'I'll bate you he'll say it's his sheep,' said Jeck. 'Weel, we'll chust anchor the vessel here till we hear what he hass to say, for if we go away and never mind the cratur he'll find oot somewhere else it's the *Elizabeth Ann*.'

"When the fermer and two shepherds came oot to the *Elizabeth Ann* in a boat, she wass lying at anchor, and we were all on deck, every man wi' a piece o' heather in his jecket.

" 'I saw you stealing my sheep,' said the fermer coming on deck, furious. 'I'll have every man of you jiled for this.'

" 'Iss the man oot of his wuts?' said Jeck. 'Drink — chust drink! Nothing else but drink! If you were a sober Christian man, you would be in the church at this 'oor in Arran, and not oot on the hill recovering from last night's carry-on in Loch Ranza, and imagining you are seeing things that's not there at aal, at aal.'

" 'I saw you with my own eyes steal the sheep and take it on board,' said the fermer, nearly choking with rage.

" 'What you saw was my freend and me gathering a puckle heather for oor jeckets,' said Jeck, 'and if ye don't believe me you can search the ship from stem to stern.'

" 'I'll soon do that,' said the fermer, and him and his shepherds went over every bit of the *Elizabeth Ann*. They never missed a corner you could hide a moose in, but there wass no sheep nor sign of sheep anywhere.

" 'Look at that, Macalpine,' said Jeck. 'I have a good mind to have you up for inflammation of character. But what could you expect from a man that would be whustling on the hill like a peesweep[5] on a Sabbath when he should be in the church. It iss a good thing for you, Macalpine, it iss a Sabbath, and I can keep my temper.'

" 'I could swear I saw you lift the sheep,' said the fermer, quite vexed.

" 'Saw your auntie! Drink; nothing but the cursed drink!' said Jeck, and the fermer and his shepherds went away with their tails behind their legs.

"We lay at anchor till it was getting dark, and then we lifted the anchor and took off the sheep that wass tied to it when we put it oot. 'It's a good thing salt mutton,' said Hurricane Jeck as we sailed away from Caticol, and efter that the name he always got wass Hurricane Jeck."

"But why 'Hurricane Jack'?" I asked, more bewildered than ever.

"Holy smoke! am I no' tellin' ye?" said Para Handy. "It wass because he stole the sheep."

But I don't understand it yet.

11. *Para Handy's Apprentice*

THE OWNER of the *Vital Spark* one day sent for her Captain, who oiled his hair, washed himself with hot water and a scrubbing-brush, got The Tar to put three coats of blacking on his boots, attired himself in his good clothes, and went up to the office in a state of some anxiety. "It's either a rise in pay," he said to himself, "or he's heard aboot the night we had in Campbeltown. That's the worst of high jeenks; they're aye stottin' back and hittin' you on the nose; if it's no' a sore heid, you've lost a pound-note, and if it's nothing you lost, it's somebody clypin' on you." But when he got to the office and was shown into the owner's room, he was agreeably enough surprised to find that though there was at first no talk about a rise of pay, there was, on the other hand, no complaint.

"What I wanted to see you about, Peter," said the owner, "is my oldest boy Alick. He's tired of school and wants to go to sea."

"Does he, does he? Poor fellow!" said Para Handy. "Och, he's but young yet, he'll maybe get better. Hoo's the mustress keepin'?"

"She's very well, thank you, Peter," said the owner. "But I'm anxious about that boy of mine. I feel sure that he'll run away some day on a ship; he's just the very sort to do it and I want you to help me. I'm going to send him one trip with you, and I want you to see that he's put off the notion of being a sailor — you understand? I don't care what you do to him so long as you don't break a leg on him, or let him fall over the side. Give him it stiff."

"Chust that!" said the Captain. "Iss he a boy that reads novelles?"

"Fair daft for them!" said the owner. "That's the cause of the whole thing."

"Then I think I can cure him in wan trip, and it'll no' hurt him either."

"I'll send him down to the *Vital Spark* on Wednesday, just before you start," said the owner. "And, by the way, if you manage to sicken him of the idea I wouldn't say but there might be a small increase in your wages."

"Och, there's no occasion for that" said Para Handy.

On the Wednesday a boy about twelve years of age, with an Eton suit and a Saturday-to-Monday hand-bag, came down to the wharf in a cab alone, opened the door of the cab hurriedly, and almost fell into the arms of Para Handy, who was on shore to meet him.

"Are you the apprentice for the *Fital Spark*?" asked the Captain affably. "Your name'll be Alick?"

"Yes," said the boy. "Are you the Captain?"

"That's me," said the Captain. "Gie me a haad o' your portman-ta," and taking it out of Alick's hand he led the way to the side of the wharf, where the *Vital Spark* was lying, with a cargo of coals that left her very little free-board, and all her crew on deck awaiting develop-ments. "I'm sorry," he said, "we havena any gangway, but I'll hand you doon to Dougie, and you'll be aal right if your gallowses[1] 'll no' give way."

"What! is THAT the boat I'm to go on?" cried the boy, astounded.

"Yes," said the Captain, with a little natural irritation. "And what's wrong with her? The smertest boat in the tred. Stop you till you see her goin' roond Ardlamont!"

"But she's only a coal boat; she's very wee," said Alick. "I never thought my father would apprentice me on a boat like that."

"But it's aye a beginnin'," explained the Captain, with remarkable patience. "You must aye start sailorin' some way, and there's many a man on the brudge of Atlantic liners the day that began on boats no bigger than the *Fital Spark*. If you don't believe me, Dougie 'll tell you himsel'. Here, Dougie, catch a haad o' oor new apprentice, and watch you don't dirty his clean collar wi' your hands." So saying, he slung Alick down to the mate, and ten minutes later the *Vital Spark*, with her new apprentice on board, was coughing her asthmatic way down the river outward bound for Tarbert. The boy watched the receding wharf with mixed feelings.

"What do you say to something to eat?" asked the Captain, as soon as his command was under way. "I'll tell The Tar to boil you an egg, and you'll have a cup of tea. You're a fine high-spurited boy, and a growin' boy needs aal the meat he can get. Watch that rope; see and no' dirty your collar; it would never do to see an apprentice wi' a dirty collar."

Alick took the tea and the boiled egg, and thought regretfully that life at sea, so far, was proving very different from what he had expected.

"Where are we bound for?" he asked.

"Oh! a good long trup," said the Captain. "As far as Tarbert and back again. You'll be an AB by the time you come back."

"And will I get wearing brass buttons?" inquired Alick.

"Brass buttons!" exclaimed Para Handy. "Man they're oot o' date at sea aalthegither; it's nothing but hooks and eyes, and far less trouble to keep them clean."

"Can I start learning to climb the mast now?" asked Alick, who was naturally impatient to acquire the elements of his new profession.

"Climb the mast!" cried Para Handy, horrified. "There wass never an apprentice did that on my vessel, and never will; it would dirty aal your hands! I see a shoo'er o' rain comin'; there's nothing worse for the young sailor than gettin' damp; away doon below like a good boy, and rest you, and I'll give you a roar when the rain's past."

Alick went below bewildered. In all the books he had read there had been nothing to prepare him for such coddling on a first trip to sea; so far, there was less romance about the business than he could have found at home in Athole Gardens. It rained all afternoon, and he was not permitted on deck; jelly "pieces"[2] were sent down to him at intervals. The Tar was continually boiling him eggs; he vaguely felt some dreadful indignity in eating them, but his appetite compelled him, and the climax of the most hum-drum day he had ever spent came at night when the Captain insisted on his taking gruel to keep off the cold, and on his fastening his stocking round his neck.

Alick was wakened next morning by The Tar standing at the side of his bunk with tea on a tray.

"Apprentices aye get their breakfast in their bed," said The Tar, who had been carefully coached by the Captain what he was to do. "Sit up and take this, and then have a nice sleep to yoursel', for it's like to be rainin' aal day, and you canna get on deck."

"Surely I can't melt," said the boy, exasperated. "I'll not learn much seamanship lying here."

"You would maybe get your daith o' cold," said The Tar, "and a nice-like job we would have nursin' you." He turned to go on deck when an idea that Para Handy had not given him came into his head, and with great solemnity he said to the boy, "Perhaps you would like to see a newspaper; we could put ashore and buy wan for you to keep you from wearyin'."

"I wouldn't object to 'Comic Cuts'," said Alick finding the whole illusion of life on the deep slipping from him.

But "Comic Cuts" did not come down. Instead, there came the Captain with a frightful and familiar thing — the strapful of school-books to escape from which Alick had first proposed a sailor's life. Para Handy had sent to Athole Gardens for them the previous day.

"Shipmate ahoy!" he cried, cheerily stumping down to the fo'c'sle. "You'll be frightened you left your books behind, but I sent The Tar for them, and here they are," and, unbuckling the strap, he poured the unwelcome volumes on the apprentice's lap.

"Who ever heard of an apprentice sailor taking his school-books to sea with him?" said Alick, greatly disgusted.

"Who ever heard a' anything else?" retorted the Captain. "Do you think a sailor doesna need any educaation? Every apprentice has to keep going at us Latin and Greek, and Bills of Parcels, and the height of Ben Nevis, and Grammar, and aal the rest of it. That's what they call navigation, and if you havena the navigation, where are you? Chust that, where are you?"

"Do you meant to tell me that when you were an apprentice you learned Latin and Greek, and all the rest of that rot?" asked Alick, amazed.

"Of course I did," said the Captain unblushingly. "Every day till my heid wass sore!"

"Nature Knowledge, too?" asked Alick.

"Nature Knowledge!" cried Para Handy. "At Nature Knowledge I wass chust sublime! I could do it with my eyes shut. Chust you take your books, Alick, like a sailor, and wire into your navigation, and it'll be the brudge for you aal the sooner."

There were several days of this unromantic life for the boy, who had confidently expected to find the career of a sea apprentice something very different. He had to wash and dress himself every morning as scrupulously as ever he did at home for Kelvinside Academy[3]; Para Handy said that was a thing that was always expected from apprentices, and he even went further and sent Alick back to the water-bucket on the ground that his neck and ears required a little more attention. A certain number of hours each day, at least, were ostensibly devoted to the study of "Navigation", which, the boy was disgusted to find, was only another name for the lessons he had had at the Academy. He was not allowed on deck when it was wet without an umbrella, which the Captain had unearthed from somewhere; it was in vain he rebelled against breakfast in bed, gruel, and jelly "pieces".

"If this is being a sailor, I would sooner be in a Sunday School," said Alick finally.

"Och! you're doin' splendid," said Para Handy. "A fine high-spurited laad! We'll make a sailor of you by the time we're back at Bowling if you keep your health. It's pretty cold the night; away doon to your bunk like a smert laad, and The Tar'll take doon a hot-watter bottle for your feet in a meenute or two."

When the *Vital Spark* got back to the Clyde, she was not three minutes at the wharf when her apprentice deserted her.

Para Handy went up to the owner's office in the afternoon with the boy's school-books and the Saturday-to-Monday bag.

"I don't know how you managed it," said Alick's father, quite pleased; "but he's back yonder this morning saying a sailor's life's a fraud, and that he wouldn't be a sailor for any money. And by the fatness of him, I should say you fed him pretty well."

"Chust that!" said Para Handy. "The Tar would be aye boilin' an egg for him noo and then. Advice to a boy iss not much use; the only thing for it iss kindness, chust kindness. If I wass wantin' to keep that boy at the sailin', I would have taken the rope's-end to him, and he would be a sailor chust to spite me. There wass some taalk aboot a small rise in the pay, but och — "

"That's all right, Peter; I've told the cashier," said the owner, and the Captain of the *Vital Spark* went down the stair beaming.

12. *Queer Cargoes*

"THE WORST cargo ever I sailed wi'," said Macphail the engineer, "was a wheen o' thae Mahommedan pilgrims: it wasna Eau de Colong they had on their hankies."

"Mahommedans!" said Para Handy, with his usual suspicions of the engineer's foreign experience — "Mahommedans! Where were they bound for? Was't Kirkintilloch?"[1]

"Kirkintilloch's no' in Mahommeda," said Macphail nastily. "I'm talkin' aboot rale sailin', no' wyding in dubs[2], the way some folk does a' their days."

"Chust that! chust that!" retorted the Captain, sniffing. "I thought it wass maybe on the Port Dundas Canal[3] ye had them."

"There was ten or eleeven o' them died every nicht," proceeded Macphail, contemptuous of these interruptions. "We just gied them the heave over the side, and then full speed aheid to make up for the seven meenutes."

"Like enough you would ripe their pockets first," chimed in Dougie. "The worst cargo ever I sailed with wass leemonade bottles; you could hear them clinking aal night, and not wan drop of stumulents on board! It wass duvilish vexing."

"The worst cargo ever I set eyes on," ventured The Tar timidly, in presence of these hardened mariners, "wass sawdust for stuffing dolls."

"Sawdust would suit you fine, Colin," said the Captain. "I'll warrant you got plenty of sleep that trup.

"You're there and you're taalking about cargoes," proceeded Para Handy, "but there's not wan of you had the experience I had, and that wass with a cargo of shows for Tarbert Fair. They were to go with a luggage-steamer, but the luggage-steamer met with a kind of an accident, and wass late of getting to the Broomielaw: she twisted wan of her port-holes or something like that, and we got the chob. It's me that wassna wantin' it, for it wass no credit to a smert boat like the *Fital Spark*, but you ken yoursel' what owners iss; they would carry coal tar made up in delf crates[4] if they get the freight for it."

"I wouldna say but what you're right," remarked Dougie agreeably.

"A stevedore would go wrong in the mind if he saw the hold of the vessel efter them showmen got their stuff on board. You would think it wass a pawnshop struck wi' a sheet o' lightning. There wass everything ever you saw at a show except the coconuts and the comic polisman. We started at three o'clock in the mornin', and a lot of the show people made a bargain to come wi' us to look efter their stuff. There wass the Fattest Woman in the World, No-Boned Billy or the Boy Serpent, the Mesmerising Man, another man very namely among the Crowned Heads for walkin' on stilts, and the heid man o' the shows, a chap they called Mr Archer. At the last meenute they put on a wee piebald pony that could pick oot any card you asked from a pack. If you don't believe me Macphail, there's Dougie; you can ask him yoursel'."

"You're quite right, Peter," said Dougie emphatically. "I'll never forget it. What are you goin' to tell them aboot the Fair?" he added suspiciously.

"It's a terrible life them show folk has!" resumed the Captain, without heeding the question. "Only English people would put up with it; poor craturs, I wass sorry for them! Fancy them goin' aboot from place to place aal the year roond, wi' no homes! I would a hundred times sooner be a sailor the way I am. But they were nice enough to us, and we got on fine, and before you could say 'knife' Dougie wass flirtin' wi' the Fattest Woman in the World."

"Don't believe him, boys," said the mate, greatly embarrassed. "I never even kent her Chrustian name."

"When we got the shows discherged at Tarbert, Mr Archer came and presented us aal with a free pass for everything except the stilts. 'You'll no' need to put on your dress clothes,' says he. He wass a cheery wee chap, though he wass chust an Englishman. Dougie and me went ashore and had a royal night of it. I don't know if ever you wass at a Tarbert Fair, Macphail — you were aye that busy learnin' the names of the foreign places you say you traivelled to, that you wouldn't have the time; but I'll warrant you it's worth while seein'. There's things to be seen there you couldna see the like of in London. Dougie made for the tent of the mesmeriser and the Fattest Woman in the World whenever we got there: he thought she would maybe be dancin' or something of that sort, but aal she did was to sit on a chair and look fat. There wass a crood roond her nippin' her to make sure she wasna padded, and when we got in she cried, 'Here's my intended man, Mr Dugald; stand aside and let him to the front to see his bonny wee rosebud. Dugald, darling, you see I'm true to you and wearin' your ring yet,' and she showed the crood a brass ring you could tie boats to."

"She wass a caaution!" said Dougie. "But what's the use of rakin' up them old stories?"

"Then we went to the place where No-Boned Billy or the Boy Serpent wass tying himself in knots and jumpin' through girrs. It was truly sublime! It bates me to know hoo they do it, but I suppose it's chust educaation."

"It's nothing else," said the mate. "Educaation 'll do anything for you if you take it when you're young, and have the money as weel."

"Every noo and then we would be takin' a gless of yon red lemonade they sell at aal the Fairs, till Dougie got dizzy and had to go to a public-house for beer."

"Don't say a word aboot yon," interrupted the mate anxiously.

"It's aal right, Dougie, we're among oorsel's. Weel, as I wass sayin', when he got the beer, Dougie, right or wrong, wass for goin' to see the fortune-teller. She wass an Italian-lookin' body that did the spaein'[5] and for a sixpence she gave Dougie the finest fortune ever you heard of. He wass to be left a lot of money when he wass fifty-two, and mairry the dochter of a landed chentleman. But he wass to watch a man wi' curly hair that would cross his path, and he wass to mind and never go a voyage abroad in the month o' September. Dougie came out of the Italian spaewife's in fine trum wi' himsel', and nothing would do him but another vusit to the Fattest Woman in the World."

"Noo, chust you be canny what you're at next!" again broke in the mate. "You said you would never tell anybody."

"Who's tellin' anybody?" asked Para Handy impatiently. "I'm only mentionin' it to Macphail and Colin here. The mesmeriser wass readin' bumps when we got into the tent, and Dougie wass that full o' the fine fortune the Italian promised him that he must be up to have his bumps read. The mesmeriser felt aal the bumps on Dougie's heid, no' forgettin' the wan he got on the old New-Year at Cairndow, and he said it wass wan of the sublimest heids he ever passed under his hands. 'You are a sailor,' he said to Dougie, 'but accordin' to your bumps you should have been a munister. You had a fine, fine heid for waggin'. There's great strength of will behind the ears, and the back of the foreheid's packed wi' animosity.'

"When the readin' of the bumps wass done, and Dougie wass nearly greetin' because his mother didna send him to the College in time, the mesmeriser said he would put him in a trance, and then he would see fine fun."

"Stop it, Peter," protested the mate. "If you tell them, I'll never speak to you again."

Para Handy paid no attention, but went on with his narrative. "He got Dougie to stare him in the eye the time he wass working his hands like anything, and Dougie was in a trance in five meenutes. Then the man made him think he wass a railway train, and Dougie went on his hands and knees up and doon the pletform whustlin' for tunnels. Efter that he made him think he wass a singer — and a plank of wud — and a soger — and a hen. I wass black affronted to see the mate of the *Fital Spark* a hen. But the best of the baur was when he took the Fattest Woman in the World up on the pletform and mairried her to Dougie in front of the whole of Tarbert."

"You gave me your word you would never mention it," interrupted the mate, perspiring with annoyance.

"Then the mesmeriser made Dougie promise he would come back at twelve o'clock the next day and take his new wife on the honeymoon. When Dougie wass wakened oot of the trance, he didn't mind onything aboot it."

"Neither I did," said the mate.

"Next day, at ten meenutes to twelve, when we were makin' ready to start for the Clyde, my mate here took a kind of a tirrivee[6], and wass for the shows again. I saw the dregs of the mesmerisin' wass on the poor laad, so I took him and gave him a gill of whisky with sulphur in it, and whipped him on board the boat and off to the Clyde before the trance came on at its worst. It never came back."

"Iss that true?" asked The Tar.

"If Dougie wass here — Of course it iss true," said the Captain.

"All I can mind aboot it is the whisky and sulphur," said Dougie. "That's true enough."

The Birth Place of Para Handy

One of the major unsolved problems in Para Handy scholarship is the vexed question of our hero's birth place. As a larger than life character it is hardly surprising that he cannot easily be tied down to one place or time. In the next story he tells The Tar that he knows Loch Fyne well "I ken every bit of it...I wass born aal along this loch-side and brocht up wi an auntie." In "The Goat" he reveals that he was at school in Tarbert, Loch Fyne and throughout the stories we read of his numerous relatives on Loch Fyne-side — not least of the sixteen cousins he met at the Furnace baal "...the proud men last night to be having a captain for a cousin and them only quarry-men..."

However in "Para Handy has an Eye to Business" we learn from Para's own lips of a totally different place of origin. Modestly he tells Sunny Jim (who has fanciful ideas about a puffer skipper's powers) "...its no' the way we're brought up on Loch Long; us Arrochar folk, when we're Captains believe in a bit o' compromise wi' the crews..." and later in the same tale says "...we're no' that daft, us folk from Arrochar..."

Arrochar is, of course, at the very heart of the Clan Macfarlane lands and there is nothing inherently improbable in a Dumbartonshire, rather than an Argyllshire origin for Para.

We are however confronted with two contradictory and equally authoritative accounts of the birth of Para. It may be that no firm conclusion can be reached, although careful study of the registrations of birth for the counties of Argyll and Dumbarton in the 1860s might be instructive.

The statement that he "wass born aal along this loch-side" is suspiciously vague and coupled with the statement that he was reared by an aunt may lead some to suspect some family tragedy or scandal.

13. *In Search of a Wife*

THE TAR had only got his first week's wages after they were raised a shilling, when the sense of boundless wealth took possession of him, and went to his head like glory. He wondered how on earth he could spend a pound a week. Nineteen shillings were only some loose coins in your pocket, that always fell through as if they were red-hot: a pound-note was different, the pleasure of not changing it till maybe to-morrow was like a wage in itself. He kept the pound-note untouched for three days, and then dreamed one night that he lost it through a hole in his pocket. There were really holes in his pockets, a fact that had never troubled him before; so the idea of getting a wife to mend them flashed on him. He was alarmed at the notion at first — it was so much out of his daily routine of getting up and putting on the fire, and cooking for the crew, and working the winch, and eating and sleeping — so he put it out of his head; but it always came back when he thought of the responsibility of a pound a week, so at last he went up to Para Handy and said to him sheepishly, "I wass thinking to mysel' yonder that maybe it wouldna be a bad plan for me to be takin' a kind of a wife."

"Capital! First-rate! Good for you, Colin!" said the Captain. "A wife's chust the very thing you're needing. Your guernsays iss no credit to the *Fital Spark* — indeed they'll be giving the boat a bad name; and I aalways like to see everything in nice trum aboot her. I would maybe try wan mysel', but I'm that busy on the boat with wan thing and another me being Captain of her, I havena mich time for keeping a hoose. But och! there's no hurry for me; I am chust nine and two-twenties of years old, no' countin' the year I wass workin' in the sawmull. What wass the gyurl you were thinkin' on?"

"Och, I didna get that length," said The Tar, getting very red in the face at having the business rushed like that.

"Weel, you would need to look slippy," said Para Handy. "There's fellows on shore with white collars on aal the time going aboot picking up the smert wans."

"I wass chust thinkin' maybe you would hear of somebody aboot Loch Fyne that would be suitable: you ken the place better nor me."

"I ken every bit of it," said Para Handy, throwing out his chest. "I wass born aal along this loch-side and brocht up wi' an auntie. What kind of a wan would you be wantin'?"

"Och, I would chust leave that to yoursel'," said The Tar. "Maybe if she had a puckle money it wouldna be any herm."

"Money!" cried the Captain. "You canna be expectin' money wi' the first. But we'll consuder Colin. We'll paause and consuder."

Two days later the *Vital Spark* was going up to Inveraray for a cargo of timber, Para Handy steering, and singing softly to himself –
"As I gaed up yon Hieland hill
   I met a bonny lassie;
   She looked at me and I at her,

And oh, but she was saucy.
With my rolling eye,
Fal tee diddle dye,
Rolling eye dum derry,
With my rolling eye."

The Tar stood by him peeling potatoes, and the charming domestic sentiment of the song could not fail to suggest the subject of his recent thoughts. "Did you have time to consuder yon?" he asked the Captain, looking up at him with comical coyness.

"Am I no' consudering it as hard as I'm able?" said Para Handy. "Chust you swept aal them peelin's over the side and no' be spoiling the boat, my good laad."

"I wass mindin', mysel', of a femily of gyurls called Macphail up in Easdale, or maybe it wass Luing," said The Tar.

"Macphails!" cried Para Handy. "I never hear the name of Macphail but I need to scratch mysel'. I wouldna alloo any man on the *Fital Spark* to mairry a Macphail, even if she wass the Prunce of Wales. Look at that man of oors that caals himsel' an enchineer; he's a Macphail, that's the way he canna help it."

"Och, I wass chust in fun," The Tar hastened to say soothingly. "I don't think I would care for any of them Macphail gyurls whatever. Maybe you'll mind of something suitable before long."

Para Handy slapped himself on the knee. "My Chove!" said he, "I have the very article that would fit you."

"What's — what's her name?" asked The Tar alarmed at the way destiny seemed to be rushing him into matrimony.

"Man, I don't know," said the Captain, "but she's the laandry-maid up here in the Shurriff's[1] — chust a regular beauty. I'll take you up and show her you to-morrow."

"Will we no' be awfu' busy to-morrow?" said The Tar hastily. "Maybe it would be better to wait till we come back again. There's no' an awfu' hurry."

"No hurry" cried the Captain. "It's the poor heid for business you have, Colin; a gyurl the same as I'm thinkin' on for you will be snapped up whenever she gets her Mertinmas wages.[2]"

"I'm afraid she'll be too cluver for me, her being a laandry-maid," said The Tar. "They're aawfu' highsteppers, laandry-maids, and aawfu' stiff."

"That's wi' working among starch," explained Para Handy. "It'll aal come oot in the washin'. Not another word, Colin; leave it to me. And maybe Dougie, och ay, Dougie and me 'll see you right."

So keenly did the Captain and Dougie enter into the matrimonial projects of The Tar that they did not even wait till the morrow, but set out to interview the young lady that evening. "I'll no' put on my pea jecket or my watch-chain in case she might take a fancy to mysel'," the Captain said to his mate. "A man in a good poseetion like me canna be too caautious." The Tar at the critical moment, showed the utmost reluctance to join the expedition. He hummed and hawed, protested he "didna like," and would prefer that they settled the business without him; but this was not according to Para Handy's ideas of business, and ultimately the three set out together with an arrangement that The Tar was to wait out in the Sheriff's garden while his ambassadors laid his suit in a preliminary form before a lady he had never set eyes on and who had never seen him.

There was a shower of rain, and the Captain and his mate had scarcely been ushered into the kitchen on a plea of "important business" by the Captain, than The Tar took shelter in a large wooden larder at the back of the house.

Para Handy and Dougie took a seat in the kitchen at the invitation of its single occupant, a stout cook with a humorous eye.

"It was the laandry-maid we were wantin' to see, mem," said the Captain, ducking his head forward several times and grinning widely to inspire confidence and create a genial atmosphere without any loss of time. "We were chust passing the door, and we thought we would give her a roar in the by-going."

"You mean Kate?" asked the cook.

"Ay! chust that, chust that — Kate," said the Captain, beaming warmly till his whiskers curled. "Hoo's the Shurriff keeping himsel'?" he added as an afterthought. "Iss he in good trum them days?" And he winked expansively at the cook.

"Kate's not in," said the domestic. "She'll be back in a while if you wait."

The Captain's face fell for a moment. "Och perhaps you'll do fine yoursel'," said he cordially, at last. "We have a fellow yonder on my boat that's come into some money, and what iss he determined on but to get mairried? He's aawfu' backward, for he never saw much

Life except the Tarbert Fair, and he asked us to come up here and put in a word for him."

"Is that the way you do your courtin' on the coal-gabbarts?" said the cook, greatly amused.

"Coal-gaabert!" cried Para Handy, indignant. "There iss no coal-gaabert in the business; I am the Captain of the *Fital Spark*, the smertest steamboat in the coastin' tred – "

"And I'm no' slack mysel'; I'm the mate," said Dougie, wishing he had brought his trump.

"He must be a soft creature not to speak for himself," said the cook.

"Never mind that," said the Captain; "are you game to take him?"

The cook laughed. "What about yoursel'?" she asked chaffingly, and the Captain blenched.

"Me!" he cried. "I peety the wumman that would mairry me. If I wass not here, Dougie would tell you — would you no', Dougie? — I'm a fair duvvle for high jeenks. Forbye, I'm sometimes frightened for my health."

"And what is he like, this awfu' blate[3] chap?" asked the cook.

"As smert a laad as ever stepped," protested Para Handy. "Us sailors iss sometimes pretty wild; it's wi' followin' the sea and fightin' hurricanes, here the day and away yesterday; but Colin iss ass dacent a laad ass ever came oot of Knapdale[4] if he wass chust letting himself go. Dougie himsel' will tell you."

"There's nothing wrong wi' the fellow," said Dougie. "A fine riser in the mornin'."

"And for cookin', there's no' his equal," added the Captain.

"It seems to me it's my mistress you should have asked for," said the cook; "she's advertising for a scullery-maid." But this sarcasm passed over the heads of the eager ambassadors.

"Stop you!" said the Captain, "and I'll take him in himsel'; he's oot in the garden waiting on us." And he and the mate went outside.

"Colin!" cried Para Handy, "come away and be engaged, like a smert laad." But there was no answer and it was after considerable searching they discovered the ardent suitor sound asleep in the larder.

"It's no' the laandry-maid; but it's a far bigger wan," explained the Captain. "She's chust sublime. Aal you have to do now is to come in and taalk nice to her."

The Tar protested he couldn't talk to her unless he had some conversation lozenges[5]. Besides, it was the laundry-maid he had arranged for, not the cook.

"She'll do fine for a start; a fine gyurl," the Captain assured him, and with some difficulty they induced The Tar to go with them to the back-door, only to find it emphatically shut in their faces.

"Let us paause and consuder, what day iss this?" asked the Captain, when the emphasis of the rebuff had got time to sink into his understanding.

"Friday," said Dougie.

"Tuts! wass I not sure of it? It's no' a lucky day for this kind of business. Never mind, Colin, we'll come to-morrow when the laandry-maid's in, and you'll bring a poke of conversation lozenges. You mustna be so stupid, man; you were awfu' tumid!"

"I wasna a bit tumid, but I wasna in trum," said The Tar, who was walking down to the quay with a curious and unusual straddle.

"And what for would you not come at wance when I cried you in?" asked the Captain.

"Because," said The Tar pathetically, "I had a kind of an accident yonder in the larder: I sat doon on a basket of country eggs."

14. *Para Handy's Piper*

IF YOU haven't been at your favourite coast resort except at the time of summer holidays, you don't know much about it. At other seasons of the year it looks different, smells different, and sounds different — that is, when there's any sound at all in it. In those dozing, dreamy days before you come down with your yellow tin trunk or your kit-bag, there's only one sound in the morning in the coast resort — the sizzling of frying herring. If it is an extra lively day, you may also hear the baker's van-driver telling a dead secret to the deaf bellman at the other end of the village, and the cry of sea-gulls. Peace broods on that place then like a benediction, and (by the odour) some one is having a sheep's head singed at the smithy.[1]

I was standing one day on Brodick quay with Para Handy when the place looked so vacant, and was so quiet we unconsciously talked in whispers for fear of wakening somebody. The *Vital Spark* shared the peace of that benign hour: she nodded idly at the quay, her engineer half asleep with a penny novelette in his hands; The Tar, sound asleep and snoring, unashamed, with his back against the winch; Dougie, the mate, smoking in silent solemnity, and occasionally scratching his nose, otherwise you would have taken him for an ingenious automatic smoking-machine, set agoing by putting a penny in the slot. If anybody had dropped a postage-stamp in Brodick that day, it would have sounded like a dynamite explosion. It was the breakfast hour.

Suddenly a thing happened that seemed to rend the very heavens : it was the unexpected outburst of a tinker piper, who came into sight round the corner of a house, with his instrument in the preliminary stages of the attack.

"My Chove!" said Para Handy, "isn't that fine? Splendid aal-thegither!"

"What's your favourite instrument?" I asked.

"When Dougie's in trum it's the trump," said he in a low voice, lest the mate (who was certainly very vain of his skill on the trump — that is to say, the Jew's harp) should hear him; "but, man! for gaiety, the pipes. They're truly sublime! A trump's fine for small occasions, but for style you need the pipes. And good pipers iss difficult nooadays to get; there's not many in it. You'll maybe can get a kind of a plain piper going aboot the streets of Gleska noo and then, but they're like the herrin', and the turnips, and rhubarb, and things like that — you don't get them fresh in Gleska; if you want them at their best, you have to go up to the right Hielands and pull them off the tree. You ken what I mean yoursel'."

And the Captain of the *Vital Spark* widely opened his mouth and inhaled the sound of the bagpipe with an air of great refreshment.

"That's 'The Barren Rocks of Aden'[2] he iss on now," he informed me by and by. "I can tell by the sound of it. Oh, music! music! it's me that's fond of it. It makes me feel that droll I could bound over the mountains, if you understand. Do you know that I wance had a piper of my own?"

"A piper of your own!"

"Ay, chust that, a piper of my own, the same ass if I wass the Marquis of Bute. You'll be thinkin' I couldna afford it," Para Handy went on, smiling slyly, "but a Macfarlane never wass bate. Aal the fine gentry hass their piper that plays to them in the mornin' to put them up, and goes playin' roond the table at dinner-time when there's any English vusitors there, and let them chust take it! It serves them right; they should stay in their own country. My piper wass a Macdonald."

"You mean one of the tinker pipers?" I said mischievously, for I knew a tribe of tinker pipers of that name.

Para Handy was a little annoyed. "Well," he said, "I wouldna deny but he wass a kind of a tinker, but he wass in the Militia when he wass workin', and looked quite smert when he wass sober."

"How long did you keep the piper?" I asked, really curious about this unexpected incident in the Captain's career.

"Nearly a whole day," he answered. "Whiles I kept him and whiles he wass going ashore for a dram.

"To let you understand, it wass the time of the fine fushin's in Loch Fyne, and I had a cousin yonder that wass gettin' mairried at Kilfinan. The weddin' wass to be on a Friday, and I wass passin' up the loch with a cargo of salt, when my cousin hailed me from the shore, and came oot in a small boat to speak to me.

" 'Peter,' he said to me, quite bashful, 'they're sayin' I'm goin' to get mairried on Friday, and I'm lookin' for you to be at the thing.'

" 'You can depend on me bein' there, Dougald,' I assured him. 'It would be a poor thing if the Macfarlanes would not stick by wan another at a time of trial.'

" 'Chust that!' said my cousin; 'there's to be sixteen hens on the table and plenty of refreshment. What's botherin' me iss that there's not a piper in Kilfinan. I wass thinkin' that maybe between this and Friday you would meet wan on your trevels, and take him back with you on your shup.'

" 'Mercy on us! You would think it wass a parrot from foreign perts I wass to get for you,' I said. 'But I'll do my best,' and off we went. I watched the hillsides aal the way up the loch to see if I could see a piper; but it wass the time of the year when there's lots of work at the hay, and the pipers wass keepin' oot of sight, till I came to Cairndow. Dougie and me wass ashore at Cairndow in the mornin', when we saw this Macdonald I'm telling you aboot standin' in front of the Inns with pipes under his oxter[3]. He wass not playin' them at the time. I said to him, 'There's a weddin' yonder at Kilfinan to-morrow, that they're wantin' a piper for. What would you take to come away doon on my vessel and play for them?'

" 'Ten shillin's and my drink,' he said, as quick as anything.

" 'Say five and it's a bargain,' I said; and he engaged himself on the spot. He wass a great big fellow with a tartan trooser and a cocketty bonnet, and oh, my goodness! but his hair wass rud! I couldna but offer him a dram before we left Cairndow for we were startin' there and then, but he wouldna set foot in the Inns, and we went on board the *Fital Spark* withoot anything at all, and started doon the loch. I thought it wass a droll kind of a piper I had that would lose a chance.

"When we would be a mile or two on the passage, I said to him, 'Macdonald, tune up your pipes and give us the Macfarlanes' Merch.'

"He said he didna kriow the Macfarlanes had a Merch, but would do the best he could by the ear, and he began to screw the bits of his pipes together. It took him aboot an hour, and by that time we were off Strachur.

" 'Stop you the boat,' he said, 'I'll need to get ashore a meenute to get something to soften the bag of this pipes; it's ass hard ass a bit of stick.'

" 'You can get oil from the enchineer,' I said to him.

" 'Oil!' said he; 'do you think it's a clock I'm mendin'? No, no; there's nothing will put a pipe bag in trum but some treacle poured in by the stock.'

"Well, we went ashore and up to the Inns, and he asked if they could give him treacle for his bagpipes. They said they had none. 'Weel,' said he, 'next to that the best thing for it iss whusky — give me a gill of the best, and the Captain here will pay for it; I'm his piper.' He got the gill, and what did he do but pour a small sensation of it into the inside of his pipes and drink the rest? 'It comes to the same thing in the long run,' said he, and we got aboard again, and away we started.

" 'There's another tune I am very fond of,' I said to him, watchin' him workin' away puttin' his drones in order. 'It's "The 93rd's Farewell to Gibraltar".'[4]

" 'I ken it fine,' he said, 'but I don't ken the tune. Stop you, and I'll give you a trate if I could get this cursed pipe in order. What aboot the dinner?'

"The dinner wass nearly ready, so he put the pipes past till he wass done eatin', and then he had a smoke, and by the time that wass done we were off Lochgair. 'That puts me in mind,' said he; 'I wonder if I could get a chanter reed from Maclachlan the innkeeper? He plays the pipes himself. The chanter reed I have iss bad, and I would like to do the best I could at your cousin's weddin'.'

"We stopped, and Dougie went ashore in the smaal boat with him, and when they came back in half-an-hour the piper said it wass a peety, but the innkeeper wasna a piper efter aal, and didna have a reed, but maybe we would get wan in Ardrishaig.

" 'We're no' goin' to Ardrishaig, we're goin' to Kilfinan,' I told him, and he said he couldna help it, but we must make for Ardrishaig, right or wrong, for he couldna play the pipes right withoot a new reed. 'When you hear me playing,' he said, 'you will be glad you took the trouble. There iss not my equal in the three parishes,' and, man, but his hair wass rud, rud!

"We wouldna be half-an-oor oot from Lochgair when he asked if the tea would soon be ready. He wass that busy puttin' his pipes in order, he said, he was quite fatigued. Pipers iss like canaries, you have to keep them going weel with meat and drink if you want music from them. We gave him his tea, and by the time it wass finished we were off Ardrishaig, and he made me put her in there to see if he could get a reed for his chanter. Him and Dougie went ashore in the smaal boat. Dougie came back in an oor wi' his hair awfu' tousy and nobody wi' him.

" 'Where's my piper?' I said to him.

" 'Man, it's terrible!' said Dougie; 'the man's no a piper at aal, and he's away on the road to Kilmertin. When he wass standin' at Cairndow Inns yonder, he was chust holdin' the pipes for a man that wass inside for his mornin', and you and me 'll maybe get into trouble for helpin' him to steal a pair o' pipes.'

"That wass the time I kept a piper of my own," said Para Handy, in conclusion. "And Dougie had to play the trump to the dancin' at my cousin's weddin'."

15. *The Sailors and the Sale*

PARA HANDY's great delight was to attend farm sales. "A sale's a sublime thing," he said, "for if you don't like a thing you don't need to buy it. It's at the sales a good many of the other vessels in the tred get their sailors." This passion for sales was so strong in him that if there was one anywhere within twelve miles of any port the *Vital Spark* was lying at, he would lose a tide or risk demurrage[1] rather than miss it. By working most part of a night he got a cargo of coals discharged at Lochgoilhead one day in time to permit of his attending a displenishing sale[2] ten miles away. He and the mate, Dougie, started in a brake that was conveying people to the sale; they were scarcely half-way there when the Captain sniffed.

"Hold on a meenute and listen, Dougie," said he. "Do you no' smell anything?"

Dougie sniffed too, and his face was lit up by a beautiful smile as of one who recognises a friend. "It's not lemon kali[3] at any rate," he said knowingly, and chuckled in his beard.

"Boys!" said the Captain, turning round to address the other passengers in the brake, who were mainly cattle dealers and farriers — "Boys! this iss going to be a majestic sale; we're five miles from the place and I can smell the whisky already."

At that moment the driver of the brake bent to look under his seat, and looked up again with great vexation written on his countenance. "Isn't it not chust duvvelish?" he said. "Have I not gone away and put my left foot through a bottle of good spurits I wass bringing up wi' me in case anybody would take ill through the night."

"Through the night!" exclaimed one of the farmers, who was plainly not long at the business. "What night are you taalking aboot?"

"This night," replied the driver promptly.

"But surely we'll be back at Lochgoilhead before night?" said the farmer, and all the others in the coach looked at him with mingled pity and surprise.

"It's a ferm sale we're going to, and not a rent collection," said the driver. "And there's thirty-six gallons of ale ordered for it, no' to speak of refreshments[4]. If we're home in time for breakfast from this sale it's me that'll be the bonny surprised man, I'm telling you."

At these farm sales old custom demands that food and drink should be supplied "ad lib." by the outgoing tenant. It costs money, but it is a courtesy that pays in the long-run, for if the bidding hangs fire a brisk circulation of the refreshments stimulates competition among the buyers, and adds twenty per cent to the price of stots[5]. It would be an injustice to Para Handy and Dougie to say they attended sales from any consideration of this sort; they went because of the high jeenks. At the close of the day sometimes they found that they had purchased a variety of things not likely to be of much use on board a steam-lighter, as on the occasion when Dougie bought the rotary churn.

"Keep away from the hoosehold furniture aaltogither!" said the Captain, this day. "We have too mich money in oor pockets between us, and it'll be safer no' to be in sight of the unctioneer till the beasts iss on, for we'll no' be tempted to buy beasts."

"I would buy an elephant for the fun of the thing, let alone a coo or two," said Dougie.

"That's put me in mind," said the Captain, "there's a cousin of my own yonder in Kilfinan wantin' a milk coo for the last twelve month; if I saw a bargain maybe I would take it. But we'll do nothing rash, Dougie, nothing rash; maybe we're chust sailors, but we're no' daft aalthegither."

By this time they were standing on the outside of a crowd of prospective purchasers interested in a collection of farm utensils and household sundries, the disposal of which preceded the rouping[6] of the beasts. The forenoon was chilly; the chill appeared to affect the mood of the crowd, who looked coldly on the chain harrows, turnip-cutters, and other articles offered to them at prices which the auctioneer said it broke his heart to mention, and it was to instil a little warmth into the proceedings that a handy man with red whiskers went round with refreshments on a tray.

"Streetch your hand and take a gless," he said to the Captain. "It'll do you no herm."

"Man, I'm not mich caring for it," drawled the Captain. "I had wan yesterday. What do you think, Dougie? Would it do any herm chust to take wan gless to show we're freendly to the sale of impliments and things?"

"Whatever you say yoursel'," replied Dougie diffidently, but at the same time grasping the glass nearest him with no uncertain hand.

"Weel, here's good prices!" said the Captain, fixing to another glass, and after that the sun seemed to come out with a genial glow.

The lamentable fact must be recorded that before the beasts came up to the hammer the mate of the *Vital Spark* had become possessor of a pair of curling-stones — one of them badly chipped — a Dutch hoe, and a baking-board.

"What in the world are you going to do with that trash?" asked the Captain, returning from a visit to the outhouse where the ale was, to find his mate with the purchases at his feet.

"Och! it's aal right," said Dougie, cocking his eye at him. "I wassna giving a docken[7] for the things mysel', but I saw the unctioneer aye look-looking at me, and I didna like no' to take nothing. It's chust, as you might say, for the good of the hoose. Stop you and you'll see some fun."

"But it's a rideeculous thing buying curling-stones at this time of the year, and you no' a curler. What?"

Dougie scratched his neck and looked at his purchases. "They didn't cost mich," he said; "and they're aye handy to have aboot you."

When the cattle came under the hammer it was discovered that prices were going to be very low. All the likely buyers seemed to be concentrated round the beer-barrel in the barn, with the result that stots, queys[8], cows, and calves were going at prices that brought the tears to the auctioneer's eyes. He hung so long on the sale of one particular cow for which he could only squeeze out offers up to five pounds that Para Handy took pity on him, and could not resist giving a nod that put ten shillings on to its price and secured the animal.

"Name, please?" said the auctioneer, cheering up wonderfully.

"Captain Macfarlane," said Para Handy, and, very much distressed at his own impetuosity, took his mate aside. "There you are, I bought your coo for you," he said to Dougie.

"For me!" exclaimed his mate. "What in the world would I be doing with a coo?

"You said yoursel' you would take a coo or two for the fun o' the thing," said Para Handy.

"When I'm buying coos I'm buying them by my own word o' mooth; you can chust keep it for your cousin in Kilfinan. If I wass buyin' a coo it wouldna be wan you could hang your hat on in fifty places. No, no, Peter, I'm Hielan', but I'm no' so Hielan' ass aal that."

"My goodness!" said Para Handy, "this iss the scrape! I will have to be taking her to Lochgoilhead, and hoisting her on the vessel, and milking her, and keeping her goodness knows what time till I'll have a cargo the length of Kilfinan. Forbye, my cousin and me's no' speakin' since Whitsunday last."

"Go up to the unctioneer and tell him you didna buy it at aal, that you were only noddin' because you had a tight collar," suggested the mate, and the Captain acted on the suggestion; but the auctioneer was not to be taken in by any such story, and Para Handy and his mate were accordingly seen on the road to Lochgoil late that night with a cow, the possession of which took all the pleasure out of their day's outing. Dougie's curling-stones, hoe, and baking-board were to follow in a cart.

It was a long time after this before the *Vital Spark* had any occasion to go to Lochgoilhead. Macphail the engineer had only to mention the name of the place and allude casually to the price of beef or winter feeding, and the Captain would show the most extraordinary ill-temper. The fact was he had left his purchase at a farmer's at Lochgoil to keep for him till called for, and he never liked to think upon the day of reckoning. But the *Vital Spark* had to go to Lochgoilhead sooner or later, and the first time she did so the Captain went somewhat mournfully up to the farm where his cow was being kept for him.

"It's a fine day; hoo's the mustress?" he said to the farmer, who showed some irritation at never having heard from the owner of the cow for months.

"Fine, but what aboot your coo, Peter?"

"My Chove! iss she living yet?" said the Captain. "I'll be due you a penny or two."

"Five pounds, to be exact; and it'll be five pounds ten at the end of next month."

"Chust the money I paid for her," said Para Handy. "Chust you keep her for me till the end of next month and then pay yoursel' with her when my account iss up to the five pound ten," a bargain which was agreed on; and so ended Para Handy's most expensive high jeenk.

The Career of Captain Peter Macfarlane

WHEN we first meet Para Handy he had been sailing in the *Vital Spark* "...four years over twenty with my hert in my mooth for the fear of the boiler." In these twenty-four years he had travelled widely – twice at Ullapool and "... wance at Londonderry...". We may well believe that he is not one of "your dry-land sailors", he has been "...twice wrecked in the North at places that's not on the maps."

However his whole career was not spent on the *Vital Spark*, after all he confides to The Tar in "In Search of a Wife" that he is "...chust nine and two twenties of years old, no' countin' the year I wass workin' in the sawmull." We know from his tale of how he painted the Maids of Bute that he spent time as a deck hand on MacBrayne's *Inveraray Castle*. Above all he served with the redoubtable Hurricane Jack (who came from Kinlochaline) "...and that iss ass good ass a Board of Tred certuficate..." on, amongst other ships, the gabbart *Margaret Ann*, the *Julia*, the *Aggie*, the *Mary Jane* as well as on the *Elizabeth Ann*. It was while serving on the latter ship that Hurricane Jack stole the sheep at Catacol and won his somewhat obscure nickname.

In addition to his long and varied service in the coasting trade which enabled him to boast, "There iss not a port I am not acquent with from the Tail of the Bank to Cairndow, where they keep the two New Years" he also served "... a season or two in the yats mysel' — the good old *Marjory*...". However, despite the attractions of the yachts he concludes "...there's nothing bates the mercantile marine for makin' sailors. Brutain's hardy sons! We could do withoot yats, but where would we be withoot oor coal-boats?"

16. *A Night Alarm*

THE wheel of the *Vital Spark* was so close to the engines that the Captain could have given his orders in a whisper, but he was so proud of the boat that he liked to sail her with all the honours, so he always used the knocker. He would catch the brass knob and give one, two, or three knocks as the circumstances demanded, and then put his mouth to the speaking-tube and cry coaxingly down to the engineer, "Stop her, Dan, when you're ready." That would be when she was a few lengths off the quay. Dan, the engineer, never let on he heard the bell; he was very fond of reading penny novelettes, and it was only when he was spoken to soothingly down the tube that he would put aside 'Lady Winifred's Legacy', give a sigh, and stop his engine. Then he would stand upright — which brought his head over the level of the deck, and beside the Captain's top-boots — wiping his brow with a piece of waste the way real engineers do on the steamers that go to America. His great aim in taking a quay was to suggest to anybody hanging about it that it was frightfully hot in the engine-room — just like the Red Sea — while the fact was that most of the time there was a draught in the engine-room of the *Vital Spark* that would keep a cold store going without ice.

When he stuck up his head he always said to the Captain,"You're aye wantin' something or other; fancy goin' awa' and spoilin' me in the middle o' a fine baur.[1]"

"I'm sorry, Dan," Para Handy would say to him in an agony of remorse, for he was afraid of the engineer because that functionary had once been on a ship that made a voyage to Australia, and used to say he had killed a man in the Bush. When he was not sober it was two men, and he would weep. "I'm sorry, Dan, but I did not know you would be busy." Then he would knock formally to reverse the engine, and cry down the tube, "Back her, Dan, when you're ready; there's no hurry," though the engineer was, as I have said, so close that he could have put his hand on his head.

Dan drew in his head, did a bit of juggling with the machinery, and resumed his novelette at the place where Lady Winifred lost her jewels at the ball. There was something breezy in the way he pulled in his head and moved in the engine-room that disturbed the Captain. "Dan's no' in good trum the day," he would say, in a hoarse whisper to the mate Dougie under these circumstances. "You daurna say wan word to him but he flies in a tiravee."

"It's them cursed novelles," was always Dougie's explanation; "they would put any man wrong in the heid, let alone an enchineer.

If it wass me wass skipper of this boat, I wadna be so soft with him, I'll assure you."

"Ach, you couldna be hard on the chap and him a Macphail," said the Captain. "There wass never any holdin' o' them in. He's an aawful fellow for high jeenks; he killed a man in the Bush."

One afternoon the *Vital Spark* came into Tarbert with a cargo of coals that could not be discharged till the morning, for Sandy Sinclair's horse and cart were engaged at a country funeral. The Captain hinted at repainting a strake[2] or two of the vessel, but his crew said they couldn't be bothered, forbye Dougie had three shillings; so they washed their faces after tea and went up the town. Peace brooded on the *Vital Spark*, though by some overlook Macphail had left her with almost a full head of steam. Sergeant Macleod, of the constabulary, came down when she lay deserted. "By Cheorge!" said he to himself, "them fellows iss coing to get into trouble this night, I'm tellin' you," for he knew the *Vital Spark* of old. He drew his tippit[3] more closely about him, breathed hard, and went up the town to survey the front of all the public-houses. Peace brooded on the *Vital Spark* — a benign and beautiful calm.

It was ten o'clock at night when her crew returned. They came down the quay in a condition which the most rigid moralist could only have described as jovial, and went to their bunk in the fo'c'sle. A drizzling rain was falling. That day the Captain had mounted a new cord on the steam whistle, so that he could blow it by a jerk from his position at the wheel. It was drawn back taut, and the free end of it was fastened to a stanchion. As the night passed and the rain continued falling, the cord contracted till at last it acted on the whistle, which opened with a loud and croupy[4] hoot that rang through the harbour and over the town. Otherwise peace still brooded on the *Vital Spark*. It took fifteen minutes to waken the Captain, and he started up in wild alarm. His crew were snoring in the light of a small globe lamp, and the engineer had a 'Family Herald Supplement' on his chest.

"That's either some duvvlement of somebody's or a warnin'," said Para Handy, half irritated, half in superstitious alarm. "Dougie, are you sleepin'?"

"What would I be here for if I wass not sleepin'?" said Dougie.

"Go up like a smert laad and see who's meddlin' my whustle."

"I canna," said Dougie; "I havena but the wan o' my boots on. Send up The Tar." The Tar was so plainly asleep from his snoring that it seemed no use to tackle him. The Captain looked at him. "Man!" he said, "he hass a nose that minds me o' a winter day, it's so short and dirty. He would be no use any way. It's the enchineer's chob, but I daurna waken him, he's such a man for high jeenks." And still the whistle waked the echoes of Tarbert.

"If I wass skipper of this boat I would show him," said Dougie, turning in his bunk, but showing no sign of any willingness to turn out. "Give him a roar Peter, or throw the heel of yon pan loaf at him."

"I would do it in a meenute if he wasna a Macphail," said the Captain, distracted. "He wance killed a man in the Bush. But he's the enchineer; the whustle's in his depairtment. Maybe if I spoke nice to him he would see aboot it. Dan!" he cried softly across the fo'c'sle to the man with the 'Family Herald Supplement' on his chest — "Dan, show a leg, like a good laad, and go up and stop that cursed whustle."

"Are you speakin' to me?" said the engineer, who was awake all the time.

"I was chust makin' a remark," explained the Captain hurriedly. "It's not of any great importance, but there's a whustle there, and it's wakin' the whole toon of Tarbert. If you werena awfu' throng[5] sleepin', you might take a bit turn on dake and see what is't. Chust when you're ready, Dan, chust when you're ready."

Dan ostentatiously turned on his side and loudly went to sleep again. And the whistle roared louder than ever.

The Captain began to lose his temper. "Stop you till I get back to Bowling," he said, "and I'll give every man of you the whole jeeng-bang[6], and get rale men for the *Fital Spark*. Not a wan of you iss worth a spittle in the hour of dancher and trial. Look at Macphail there tryin' to snore like an enchineer with a certeeficate, and him only a fireman! I am not a bit frightened for him; I do not believe he ever killed a man in the Bush at aal — he hass not the game for it; I'll bate you he never wass near Australia — and what wass his mother but wan of the Macleans of Kenmore?[7] Chust that; wan of the Macleans of Kenmore! Him and his pride! If I had my Sunday clothes on I would give him my opeenion. And there you are,

Dougie! I thocht you were a man and not a mice. You are lying there in your ignorance, and never wass the length of Ullapool. Look at me — on the vessels three over twenty years, and twice wrecked in the North at places that's not on the maps."

The two worthies thus addressed paid no attention and snored with suspicious steadiness, and the Captain turned his attention to The Tar.

"Colin!" he said more quietly, "show a leg, like a cluvver fellow, and go up and put on the fire for the breakfast." But The Tar made no response, and in the depth of the fo'c'sle Para Handy's angry voice rose up again, as he got out of his bunk and prepared to pull on some clothes and go up on deck himself.

"Tar by by-name and Tar by nature!" said he. "You will stick to your bed that hard they could not take you off without half-a-pound of saalt butter. My goodness! have I not a bonny crew? You are chust a wheen of crofters. When the owners of vessels wass wantin' men like you, they go to the Kilmichael cattlemarket and drag you down with a rope to the seaside. You will not do the wan word I tell you. I'll wudger I'll not hammer down to you again, Dan, or use the speakin'-tube, the same ass if you were a rale enchineer — I'll chust touch you with the toe of my boot when I want you to back her, mind that! There iss not a finer nor a faster vessel than the *Fital Spark* in the tred; she iss chust sublime, and you go and make a fool of her with your drinking and your laziness and your ignorance."

He got up on deck in a passion, to find a great many Tarbert people running down the quay to see what was wrong, and Sergeant Macleod at the head of them.

"Come! come! Peter, what iss this whustlin' for on a wet night like this at two o'clock in the mornin'?" asked the sergeant, with a foot on the bulwark. "What are you blow-blow-blowin' at your whustle like that for?"

"Chust for fun," said the Captain. "I'm a terrible fellow for high jeenks. I have three fine stots from the Kilmichael market down below here, and they canna sleep unless they hear a whustle."

"The man's in the horrors!"[8] said the sergeant in a whisper to some townsmen beside him on the quay. "I must take him to the lock-up and make a case of him, and it's no' a very nice chob, for he's ass strong ass a horse. Wass I not sure there would be trouble when I saw the *Fital Spark* the day? It must be the lock-up for him, and maybe Lochgilphead, but it iss a case for deleeberation and caaution — great caaution.

"Captain Macfarlane," he said in a bland voice to the Captain, who stood defiant on the deck, making no attempt to stop the whistling. "Mr Campbell the banker wass wantin' to see you for a meenute up the toon. Chust a meenute! He asked me to come doon and tell you."

"What will the banker be wantin' wi' me?" said the Captain, cooling down and suspecting nothing. "It's a droll time o' night to be sendin' for onybody."

"So it is, Captain Macfarlane," admitted the constable mildly. "I do not know exactly what he wants, but it iss in a great hurry. He said he would not keep you wan meenute. I think it will be to taalk about your cousin Cherlie's money."

"I'll go wi' you whenever I get on my bonnet," said the Captain, preparing to go below.

"Never mind your bonnet; it iss chust a step or two, and you'll be back in five meenutes," said the sergeant; and, thus cajoled, the Captain of the *Vital Spark*, having cut the cord and stopped the whistle, went lamb-like to the police office.

Peace fell again upon the *Vital Spark*.

17. *A Desperate Character*

THOUGH Para Handy went, like a lamb, with Sergeant Macleod, he had not to suffer the ignominy of the police office, for the sergeant found out on the way that the Captain belonged to the Wee Free, and that made a great deal of difference. Instead of putting the mariner into a cell, he took him into his own house, made a summary investigation into the cause of the whistling of the *Vital Spark*, found the whole thing was an accident, dismissed the accused without a stain on his character, gave him a dram, and promised to take him down a pair of white hares for a present before the vessel left Tarbert.

"I am glad to see you belong to the right Church, Peter," he said.

"Did I not think you were chust wan of them unfuduls that carries the rud-edged hime- books[1] and sits at the prayer[2], and here you are chust a dacent Christian like mysel'. My goodness! It shows you a man cannot be too caautious. Last year there wass but a small remnant of us Christians to the fore here — myself and Macdougall the merchant, and myself and the Campbells up in Clonary Farm, and myself and the steamboat aagent, and myself and my cousins at Dunmore; but it'll be changed days when we get a ha'ad o' the church. They'll be sayin' there's no hell; we'll show them, I'll assure you! We are few, but firm — firm; there's no bowin'[3] of the knee with us, and many a pair of white hares I'll be gettin' from the Campbells up in Clonary. I have chust got to say the word that wan of the rale old Frees iss in a vessel at the quay, and there will be a pair of white hares doon for you to-morrow."

"I'm a staunch Free," said Para Handy, upsetting his glass, which by this time had hardly a drop left in it. "Tut! tut!" he exclaimed apologetically, "it's a good thing I never broke the gless. Stop! stop! stop in a meenute; I'm sure I'm no needin' any more. But it's a cold wet nicht, whatever. I'm a staunch Free. I never had a hime-book on board my boat; if Dougie wass here he would tell you."

"You'll no' get very often to the church, wi' you goin' about from place to place followin' the sea?" said the sergeant.

"That's the worst of it," said Para Handy, heaving a tremendous sigh. "There's no mich fun on a coal vessel; if it wasna the *Fital Spark* wass the smertest in the tred, and me the skipper of her, I would mairry a fine strong wife and start a business. There wass wan time yonder, when I wass younger, I wass very keen to be a polisman."

"The last chob!" cried the sergeant. "The very last chob on earth! You would be better to be trapping rabbits. It iss not an occupation for any man that has a kind he'rt, and I have a he'rt mysel' that's no slack in that direction, I'm tellin' you. Many a time I'll have to take a poor laad in and cherge him and he'll be fined, and it's mysel' that's the first to get the money for his fine."

"Do you tell me you pay the fine oot of your own pocket?" asked Para Handy, astonished.

"Not a bit of it; I have aal my faculties about me. I go roond and raise a subscruption," explained the sergeant. "I chust go roond and say the poor laad didna mean any herm, and his mother wass a weedow, and it iss aal right, och aye! it iss aal right at wance wi' the folk in Tarbert. Kind, kind he'rts in Tarbert — if there's any fushing. But the polis iss no chob for a man like me. Still and on it's a good pay, and the uniform, and a fine pair of boots, and an honour, so I'm no' complaining. Not a bit!"

Para Handy put up his hand with his customary gesture to scratch his ear, but as usual thought better of it, and sheered off — "Do you ken oor Dougie?" he asked.

"Iss it your mate?" replied the constable. "They're telling me aboot him, but I never had him in my hands."

"It's easy seen you're no' long in Tarbert," said the Captain. "He wass wan time namely here for makin' trouble; but that wass before he wass a kind of a Rechabite. Did you hear aboot him up in Castlebay in Barra?"

"No," said the sergeant.

"Dougie will be aye bouncin' he wass wan time on the yats, and wearing a red night-kep aal the time, and whitening on his boots, the same ass if he wass a doorstep[4], but, man! he's tumid, tumid! If there's a touch of a gale he starts at his prayers, and says he'll throw his trump over the side. He can play the trump sublime — reels and things you never heard the like of; and if he wass here, and him in trum, it's himself would show you. But when the weather's scoury[5], and the *Fital Spark* not at the quay, he'll make up his mind to live a better life, and the first thing that he's going to stop 's the trump. 'Hold you on, Dougie,' I'll be sayin' to him; 'don't do anything desperate till we see if the weather'll no lift on the other side of Minard.' It's a long way from Oban out to Barra; many a man that hass gold braid on his kep in the Clyde never went so far, but it's nothing at aal to the *Fital Spark*. But Dougie does not like that trup at aal, at aal. Give him Bowling to Blairmore in the month of Aagust, and there's no' a finer sailor ever put on oilskins."

"Och, the poor fellow!" said the sergeant, with true sympathy.

"Stop you!" proceeded Para Handy. "When we would be crossing the Munch, Dougie would be going to sacrifice his trump, and start releegion every noo and then; but when we had the vessel tied to the quay at Castlebay, the merchants had to shut their shops and make a holiday."

"My Chove! do you tell me?" cried the sergeant.

"If Dougie was here himsel' he would tell you," said the Captain. "It needed but the wan or two drams, and Dougie would start walkin' on his heels to put an end to Castlebay. There iss not many shops in the place aaltogither, and the shopkeepers are aal Mac-Neils, and cousins to wan another; so when Dougie was waalkin' on his heels and in trum for high jeenks, they had a taalk together, and agreed it would be better chust to put on the shutters."

"Isn't he the desperate character!" said the constable. "Could they no' have got the polis?"

"There's no a polisman in the island of Barra," said Para Handy. "If there wass any need for polismen they would have to send to Lochmaddy, and it would be two or three days before they could put Dougie on his trial. Forbye, they kent Dougie fine; they hadna any ill-wull to the laad, and maybe it wass a time there wasna very mich business doin' anyway. When Dougie would find the shops shut he would be as vexed as anything, and make for the school. He would go into the school and give the children a lecture on music and the curse of drink, with illustrations on the trump. At last they used to shut the school, too, and give the weans a holiday, whenever the *Fital Spark* was seen off Castle Kismul[6]. He wass awfu' popular Dougie, wi' the weans in Castlebay."

"A man like that should not be at lerge," said the constable emphatically.

"Och! he wass only in fun; there wass no more herm in Dougie than a fly. Chust fond of high jeenks and recreation; many a place in the Highlands would be gled to get the lend of him to keep them cheery in the winter-time. There's no herm in Dougie, not at aal, chust a love of sport and recreation. If he wass here himsel' he would tell you."

"It iss a good thing for him he does not come to Tarbert for his recreation," said the constable sternly, "we're no' so Hielan' in Tarbert ass to shut the shops when a man iss makin' himsel' a nuisance. By Cheorge! if he starts any of his high jeenks in Tarbert he'll suffer the Laaw."

"There iss no fear of Tarbert nowadays," said the Captain, "for Dougie iss a changed man. He mairried a kind of a wife yonder at Greenock, and she made him a Good Templar[7], or a Rechabite, or something of the sort where you get ten shillin's a week if your leg's broken fallin' doon the stair, and nobody saw you. Dougie's noo a staunch teetotaller except aboot the time of the old New Year, or when he'll maybe be takin' a dram for medicine. It iss a good thing for his wife, but it leaves an awfu' want in Barra and them other places where they kent him in his best trum."

18. *The Tar's Wedding*

IT WAS months after The Tar's consultation with Para Handy about a wife: The Tar seemed to have given up the idea of indulgence in any such extravagance, and Para Handy had ceased to recommend various "smert, muddle-aged ones wi' a puckle[1] money" to the consideration of the young man, when the latter one day sheepishly approached him, spat awkwardly through the clefts of his teeth at a patch in the funnel of the *Vital Spark*, and remarked, "I wass thinkin' to mysel' yonder, Captain, that if there wass nothing parteecular doing next Setturday, I would maybe get mairried."

"Holy smoke!" said the Captain; "you canna expect me to get a wife suitable for you in that time. It's no reasonable. Man, you're gettin' droll — chust droll!"

"Och, I needn't be puttin' you to any trouble" said The Tar, rubbing the back of his neck with a hand as rough as a rasp. "I wass lookin' aboot mysel' and there's wan yonder in Campbeltown 'll have me. In fact, it's settled. I thocht that when we were in Campbeltown next Setturday, we could do the chob and be dune wi't. We were roared[2] last Sunday – "

"Roared!" said the Captain. "Iss it cried, you mean?"

"Yes, chust cried," said The Tar, "but the gyurl's kind of dull in the hearing, and it would likely need to be a roar. You'll maybe ken her — she's wan of the MacCallums."

"A fine gyurl," said the Captain, who had not the faintest idea of her identity, and had never set eyes on her, but could always be depended on for politeness. "A fine gyurl! Truly sublime! I'm not askin' if there's any money; eh? — not a word! It's none of my business, but, tuts! what's the money anyway, when there's love?"

"Shut up aboot that!" said the scandalised Tar getting very red. "If you're goin' to speak aboot love, be dacent and speak aboot it in the Gaelic. But we're no' taalkin' aboot love; we're taalkin' aboot my merrage. Is it aal right for Setturday?"

"You're a cunning man to keep it dark till this," said the Captain, "but I'll put nothing in the way, seein' it's your first caper of the kind. We'll have high jeenks at Campbeltown."

The marriage took place in the bride's mother's house, up a stair that was greatly impeded by festoons of fishing-nets, old oars, and net-bows on the walls, and the presence of six stalwart Tarbert trawlers, cousins of The Tar's, who were asked to the wedding, but were so large and had so many guernseys on, they would of themselves have filled the room in which the ceremony took place; so they had agreed, while the minister was there at all events, to take turn about of going in to countenance the proceedings. What space there was within was monopolised by the relatives of the bride, by Para Handy and Dougie, The Tar in a new slop-shop³ serge suit, apparently cut out by means of a hatchet, the bride — a good deal prettier than a Goth like The Tar deserved — and the minister. The wedding-supper was laid out in a neighbour's house on the same stair-landing.

A solemn hush marked the early part of the proceedings, marred only by the sound of something frying in the other house and the shouts of children crying for bowl-money⁴ in the street. The minister was a teetotaller, an unfortunate circumstance which the Captain had discovered very early, and he was very pleased with the decorum of the company. The MacCallums were not church-goers in any satisfactory sense, but they and their company seemed to understand what was due to a Saturday night marriage and the presence of "the cloth". The clergyman had hardly finished the ceremony when the Captain began manoeuvring for his removal. He had possessed himself of a bottle of ginger cordial and a plate of cake.

"You must drink the young couple's health, Mr Grant," he said. "We ken it's you that's the busy man on the Setturday night, and indeed it's a night for the whole of us goin' home early. I have a ship yonder, the *Fital Spark*, that I left in cherge of an enchineer by the name of Macphail, no' to be trusted with such a responsibility."

The minister drank the cheerful potion, nibbled the corner of a piece of cake, and squeezed his way downstairs between the Tarbert trawlers.

"We're chust goin' away oorsel's in ten meenutes," said the Captain after him.

"Noo that's aal right," said Para Handy, who in virtue of his office had constituted himself master of ceremonies. "He's a nice man, Mr Grant, but he's not strong, and it would be a peety to be keeping him late out of his bed on a Setturday night. I like, mysel', yon old-fashioned munisters that had nothing wrong wi' them, and took a Chrustian dram. Pass oot that bottle of chinger cordial to the laads from Tarbert and you'll see fine fun."

He was the life and soul of the evening after that. It was he who pulled the corks, who cut the cold ham, who kissed the bride first, who sang the first song, and danced with the new mother-in-law. "You're an aawful man, Captain Macfarlane," she said in fits of laughter at his fun.

"Not me!" said he, lumberingly dragging her round in a polka to the strains of Dougie's trump. "I'm a quate fellow, but when I'm in trum I like a high jeenk noo and then. Excuse my feet. It's no' every day we're merryin' The Tar. A fine, smert, handy fellow, Mrs MacCallum; you didn't make a bad bargain of it with your son-in-law. Excuse my feet. A sailor every inch of him, once you get him wakened. A pound a-week of wages an' no incumbrance. My feet again, excuse them!"

"It's little enough for two," said Mrs MacCallum; "but a man's aye a man," and she looked the Captain in the eye with disconcerting admiration.

"My Chove! she's a weedow wuman," thought the Captain; "I'll have to ca' canny, or I'll be in for an engagement."

"I aye liked sailors," said Mrs MacCallum; "John — that's the depairted, I'm his relic[5] — was wan."

"A poor life, though," said the Captain, "especially on the steamers, like us. But your man, maybe, was sailin' foreign, an' made money? It's always a consuderation for a weedow."

"Not a penny," said the indiscreet Mrs MacCallum, as Para Handy wheeled her into a chair.

At eleven o'clock The Tar was missing. He had last been seen pulling off his new boots, which were too small for him, on the stair-head; and it was only after considerable searching the Captain and one of the Tarbert cousins found him sound asleep on the top of a chest in the neighbour's house.

"Colin," said the Captain, shaking him awake, "sit up and try and take something. See at the rest of us, as jovial as anything, and no' a mau hit yet. Sit up and be smert for the credit of the *Fital Spark*."

"Are you angry wi' me, Captain?" asked The Tar.

"Not a bit of it, Colin! But you have the corkscrew in your pocket. I'm no' caring myself, but the Tarbert gentlemen will take it amiss. Forbye, there's your wife; you'll maybe have mind of her — wan Lucy MacCallum? She's in yonder, fine and cheery, wi' two of your Tarbert cousins holding her hand."

"Stop you! I'll hand them!" cried the exasperated bridegroom, and bounded into the presence of the marriage-party in the house opposite, with a demonstration that finally led to the breaking-up of the party.

Next day took place The Tar's curious kirking[6]. The MacCallums, as has been said, were not very regular churchgoers; in fact, they had overlooked the ordinances since the departed John died, and forgot that the church bell rang for the Sabbath-school an hour before it rang for the ordinary forenoon service.

Campbeltown itself witnessed the bewildering spectacle of The Tar and his bride, followed by the mother and Para Handy, marching deliberately up the street and into the church among the children. Five minutes later they emerged, looking very red and ashamed of themselves.

"If I knew there wass so much bother to mind things I would never have got married at all," said the bridegroom.

19. *A Stroke of Luck*

IT WAS a night of harmony on the good ship *Vital Spark*. She was fast in the mud at Colintraive quay, and, in the den of her, Para Handy was giving his song, "The Dancing Master" —
    "Set to Jeanie Mertin, tee-teedalum, tee-tadulam,
    Up the back and doon the muddle, tee-tadalum, tee-tadulam.
    Ye're wrong, Jeck, I'm certain; tee-tadalum, tee-tadulam,"

while the mate played an accompaniment on the trump — that is to say, the Jew's harp, a favourite instrument on steam-lighters where the melodeon has not intruded. The Captain knew only two verses, but he sang them over several times. "You're getting better and better at it every time," The Tar assured him, for The Tar had got the promise of a rise that day of a shilling a week on his pay. "If I had chust on my other boots," said the Captain, delighted at this appreciation. "This ones iss too light for singin' with — " and he stamped harder than ever as he went on with the song, for it was his idea that the singing of a song was a very ineffective and uninteresting performance unless you beat time with your foot on the floor.

The reason for the harmony on the vessel was that Dougie the mate had had a stroke of luck that evening. He had picked up at the quay-side a large and very coarse fish called a stenlock, or coal-fish[1], and had succeeded, by sheer effrontery, in passing it off as a cod worth two shillings on a guileless Glasgow woman who had come for the week to one of the Colintraive cottages.

"I'm only vexed I didna say it wass a salmon," said Dougie, when he came back to the vessel with his ill-got florin. "I could have got twice ass much for't."

"She would ken fine it wasna a salmon when it wasna in a tin," said the Captain.

"There's many a salmon that iss not in a canister," said the mate.

"Och ay, but she's from Gleska; they're awfu' Hielan'[2] in Gleska aboot fush and things like that," said the Captain. "But it's maybe a peety you didn't say it wass a salmon, for two shullin's iss not mich among four of us."

"Among four of us!" repeated Dougie emphatically. "It's little enough among wan, let alone four; I'm going to keep her to mysel'."

"If that iss your opeenion, Dougie, you are maakin' a great mistake, and it'll maybe be better for you to shift your mind," the Captain said meaningly. "It iss the jyle you could be getting for swundling a poor cratur from Gleska that thinks a stenlock iss a cod. Forbye, it iss a tremendous risk, for you might be found oot, and it would be a disgrace to the *Fital Spark*."

Dougie was impressed by the possibility of trouble with the law as a result of his fish transaction, which, to do him justice, he had gone about more as a practical joke than anything else. "I'm vexed I did it, Peter," he said, turning the two shillings over in his hand. "I have a good mind to go up and tell the woman it wass chust a baur."

"Not at aal! not at aal!" cried Para Handy. "It wass a fine cod right enough; we'll chust send The Tar up to the Inn with the two shullin's and the jar, and we'll drink the Gleska woman's health that does not ken wan fish from another. It will be a lesson to her to be careful; chust that, to be careful."

So The Tar had gone to the Inn for the ale, and thus it was that harmony prevailed in the fo'c'sle of the *Vital Spark*.

"Iss that a song of your own doing?" asked Dougie, when the Captain was done.

"No," said Para Handy, "it iss a low-country song I heard wance in the Broomielaw. Yon iss the place for seeing life. I'm telling you it is Gleska for gaiety if you have the money. There iss more life in wan day in the Broomielaw of Gleska than there iss in a fortnight on Loch Fyne."

"I daarsay there iss," said Dougie; "no' coontin' the herring."

"Och! life, life!" said the Captain, with a pensive air of ancient memory; "Gleska's the place for it. And the fellows iss there that iss not frightened, I'm telling you."

"I learned my tred there," mentioned the engineer, who had no accomplishments, and had not contributed anything to the evening's entertainment, and felt that it was time he was shining somehow.

"Iss that a fact, Macphail? I thocht it wass in a coal-ree[3] in the country," said Para Handy. "I wass chust sayin', when Macphail put in his oar, that yon's the place for life. If I had my way of it, the *Fital Spark* would be going up every day to the Chamaica Brudge the same as the *Columba*[4], and I would be stepping ashore quite spruce with my Sunday clothes on, and no' lying here in a place like Colintraive, where there's no' even a polisman, with people that swundle a Gleska woman oot of only two shullin's. It wass not hardly worth your while, Dougie." The ale was now finished.

The mate contributed a reel and strathspey on the trump to the evening's programme, during which The Tar fell fast asleep, from which he wakened to suggest that he should give them a guess.

"Weel done, Colin!" said the Captain, who had never before seen such enterprise on the part of The Tar. "Tell us the guess if you can mind it."

"It begins something like this," said The Tar nervously: " 'Whether would you raither — ' That's the start of it."

"Fine, Colin, fine!" said the Captain encouragingly. "Take your breath and start again."

" 'Whether would you raither,' " proceeded The Tar — " 'whether would you raither or walk there?' "

"Say 't again, slow," said Dougie, and The Tar repeated his extraordinary conundrum.

"If I had a piece of keelivine (lead pencil) and a lump of paper I could soon answer that guess," said the engineer, and the Captain laughed.

"Man Colin," he said, "you're missing half of the guess oot. There's no sense at aal in 'Whether would you raither or walk there?' "

"That's the way I heard it, anyway," said The Tar, sorry he had volunteered. " 'Whether would you raither or walk there?' I mind fine it wass that."

"Weel, we give it up anyway; what's the answer?" said the Captain.

"Man, I don't mind whether there wass an answer or no'," confessed The Tar, scratching his head; and the Captain irritably hit him with a cap on the ear, after which the entertainment terminated, and the crew of the Vital Spark went to bed.

Next forenoon a very irate-looking Glasgow woman was to be observed coming down the quay, and Dougie promptly retired into the hold of the *Vital Spark*, leaving the lady's reception to the Captain.

"Where's that man away to?" she asked Para Handy. "I want to speak to him."

"He's engaged, mem," said the Captain.

"I don't care if he's married," said the Glasgow woman; "I'm no' wantin' him. I jist wanted to say yon was a bonny-like cod he sell't me yesterday. I biled it three oors this mornin', and it was like leather when a' was done."

"That's droll," said the Captain. "It wass a fine fush, I'll assure you; if Dougie was here himsel' he would tell you. Maybe you didna boil it right. Cods iss curious that way. What did you use?"

"Watter!" snapped the Glasgow woman; "did you think I would use sand?"

"Chust that! chust that! Watter? Weel, you couldna use anything better for boilin' with than chust watter. What kind of coals did you use?"

"Jist plain black yins," said the woman. "I bocht them frae Cameron along the road there," referring to a coal agent who was a trade rival to the local charterer of the *Vital Spark*.

"Cameron!" cried Para Handy. "Wass I not sure there wass something or other wrong? Cameron's coals wouldna boil a wulk, let alone a fine cod. If Dougie wass here he would tell you that himsel'."

Para's Opinions

A man of firm views, Para has expressed himself on a wide variety of topics including: —

BOWMORE

"...iss namely for its mudges" [Mudges]

CAPTAINS

"The Captain of a steamer iss the most popular man in the wide world – popularer than the munisters themselves, and the munisters iss that popular the women pit bird-lime in front of the manses to catch them...It's worse with sea-captains - they're that dashing, and they're not aalways hinging aboot the hoose wi' their sluppers on." [The Mate's Wife]

CREW OF THE *VITAL SPARK*

"...four men and a derrick" [Para Handy, Master Mariner]

DOUGIE

"...ass cheery a man ass ever you met across a dram" [An Ocean Tragedy]

HURRICANE JACK

"A night wi' Jeck iss ass good as a college education" [Hurricane Jack]

MACPHAIL

"The want o' the hair's an aawful depredaation" [Mudges]
"I wouldna alloo any man on the Fital Spark to mairry a
Macphail even if she wass the Prunce of Wales" [In Search of a
Wife]

SUNNY JIM

"He's chust sublime...If he wass managed right there would be
money in him" [Treasure Trove]

THE TAR

"A sailor every inch of him, once you get him wakened" [The
Tar's Wedding]

DANCING

"I'm kind of oot o' the dancin', except La Va and Petronella I
don't mind one step" [The Disappointment of Erchie's Niece]
but see also
"I can stot through the middle o' a dance like a tuppeny
kahoochy ball" [The Leap-Year Ball]

DRINK

"A drop of good Brutish spurits will suit you better" [The
Malingerer]
"I hate them tea-pairties — chust a way of wasting the New
Year" [The Baker's Little Widow]

EDUCATION

"It's the educaation, Dougie; educaation gives you the nerve and
if you have the nerve you can go round the world" [A Lost Man]

THE ENGLISH

"...poor craturs, I wass sorry for them" [Queer Cargoes]

GLASGOW

"...it is Gleska for gaiety if you have the money. There iss more
life in wan day in the Broomielaw of Gleska than there iss in a
fortnight on Loch Fyne" [A Stroke of Luck]

HERRING

"It's a fush that's chust sublime" [The Sea Cook]

HIGH JEENKS

"...they're aye stottin' back and hittin' you on the nose..." [Para Handy's Apprentice]

LOCH FYNE

"...wass the place for Life in them days - high jeenks and big hauls..." [Herring: A Gossip]

LOVE

"...what's the money anyway, when there's love" [The Tar's Wedding]

MINISTERS

"I like, mysel', yon old-fashioned munisters that had nothing wrong wi' them, and took a Chrustian dram." [The Tar's Wedding]

MUSIC

"If I had chust on my other boots. This ones iss too light for singin' with – " [A Stroke of Luck]

SHIPOWNERS

"...they would carry coal tar made up in delf crates if they get the freight for it" [Queer Cargoes]

SMOKING

"With the trouble you have, smoking drives it in to the hert and kills you at wance" [The Malingerer]

THE *VITAL SPARK*

"...nothing bates the mercantile marine...Brutain's hardy sons! We could do withoot yats, but where would we be withoot oor coal- boats?" [Among the Yachts]
"The smertest boat in the tred" [Sources Various!]
"She would not take in wan cup of watter unless it wass for synin' oot the dishes" [Para Handy, Master Mariner]

WOMEN

"I ken them like the Kyles of Bute" [The Mate's Wife]
"A fine gyurl! Truly sublime!" [The Tar's Wedding]

20. *Dougie's Family*

THE SIZE of Dougie the mate's family might be considered a matter which was of importance to himself alone, but it was astonishing how much interest his shipmates took in it. When there was nothing else funny to talk about on the *Vital Spark*, they would turn their attention to the father of ten, and cunningly extract information from him about the frightful cost of boys' boots and the small measure of milk to be got for sixpence at Dwight's dairy in Plantation.[1]

They would listen sympathetically, and later on roast him unmercifully with comments upon the domestic facts he had innocently revealed to them.

It might happen that the vessel would be lying at a West Highland quay, and the Captain sitting on deck reading a week-old newspaper, when he would wink at Macphail and The Tar, and say, "Cot bless me! boys, here's the price of boots goin' up; peety the poor faithers of big families." Or, "I see there's to be a new school started up Partick[2], Dougie; did you flit[3] again?"

"You think you're smert, Peter," the mate would retort lugubriously. "Fun's fun, but I'll no' stand fun aboot my femily."

"Och! no offence, Dougald, no offence," Para Handy would say soothingly. "Hoo's the mustress keepin'?" and then ask a fill of tobacco to show his feelings were quite friendly.

In an ill-advised moment of parental pride and joy the mate brought on board one day a cabinet photograph[4] of himself and his wife and the ten children.

"What do you think of that?" he said to Para Handy, who took the extreme tip of one corner of the card between the finger and thumb of a hand black with coal-grime, glanced at the group, and said —

"Whatna Sunday School trup's this?"

"It's no' a trup at aal," said Dougie with annoyance.

"Beg pardon, beg pardon," said the Captain, "I see noo I wass wrong; it's Quarrier's Homes[5]. Who's the chap wi' the whuskers in the muddle, that's greetin'?"

"Where's your eyes?" said Dougie. "It's no' a Homes at aal; that's me, and I'm no' greetin'. What would I greet for?"

"Faith, I believe you're right," said the Captain. "It's yoursel' plain enough, when I shut wan eye to look at it; but the collar and a clean face make a terrible dufference. Well, well, allooin' that it's you, and you're no greetin', it's rideeculous for you to be goin' to a dancin'-school."

"It's no' a dancin'-school, it's the femily," said the mate, losing his temper. "Fun's fun, but if you think I'll stand — "

"Keep caalm, keep caalm!" interrupted the Captain hurriedly, realising that he had carried the joke far enough. "I might have kent fine it wass the femily, they're aal ass like you both ass anything, and that'll be Susan the eldest."

"That!" said Dougie, quite mollified – "that's the mustress hersel'."

"Well, I'm jeegered," said the Captain, with well-acted amazement. "She's younger-looking than ever; that's a woman that's chust sublime."

The mate was so pleased he made him a present of the photograph.

But it always had been, and always would be, a distressing task to Dougie to have to intimate to the crew (as he had to do once a year) that there was a new addition to the family, for it was on these occasions that the chaff of his shipmates was most ingenious and galling. Only once, by a trick, had he got the better of them and evaded his annual roastings. On that occasion he came to the *Vital Spark* with a black muffler on, and a sad countenance.

"I've lost my best freend," said he, rubbing his eyes to make them red.

"Holy smoke!" said Para Handy, "is Macmillan the pawnbroker deid?"

"It's no' him," said Dougie, manfully restraining a sob, and he went on to tell them that it was his favourite uncle, Jamie. He put so much pathos into his description of Uncle Jamie's last hours, that when he wound up by mentioning, in an off hand way, that his worries were complicated by the arrival of another daughter that morning, the crew had, naturally, not the heart to say anything about it.

Some weeks afterwards they discovered by accident that he never had an Uncle Jamie.

"Man! he's cunning!" said Para Handy, when this black evidence of Dougie's astuteness came out. "Stop you till the next time, and we'll make him pay for it."

The suitable occasion for making the mate smart doubly for his deceit came in due course. Macphail the engineer lived in the next tenement to Dougie's family in Plantation, and he came down to the quay one morning before the mate, with the important intelligence for the Captain that the portrait group was now incomplete.

"Poor Dugald!" said the Captain sympathetically. "Iss it a child or a lassie?"

"I don't ken," said the engineer. "I just got a rumour frae the night polisman, and he said the wife was fine."

"Stop you and you'll see some fun with Dougie," said the Captain. "I'm mich mistaken if he'll swundle us this twict."

Para Handy had gone ashore for something, and was back before his mate appeared on board the *Vital Spark*, which was just starting for Campbeltown with a cargo of bricks. The mate took the wheel, smoked ceaselessly at a short cutty pipe[6], and said nothing; and nobody said anything to him.

"He's plannin' some other way oot of the scrape," whispered the Captain once to the engineer; "but he'll not get off so easy this time. Hold you on!"

It was dinner-time, and the captain, mate and engineer were round the pot on deck aft, with The Tar at the wheel, within comfortable hearing distance, when Para Handy slyly broached the topic.

"Man, Dougie," he said, "what wass I doin' yonder last night but dreamin' in the Gaalic aboot you? I wass dreamin' you took a charter of the *Fital Spark* doon to Ardkinglas with a picnic, and there wass not a park[7] in the place would hold the company."

Dougie simply grunted.

"It wass a droll dream," continued the Captain, diving for another potato. "I wass chust wonderin' hoo you found them aal at home. Hoo's the mustress keepin'?"

The mate got very red. "I wass chust goin' to tell you aboot her," he said with considerable embarrassment.

"A curious dream it wass," said Para Handy, postponing his pleasure, like the shrewd man he is, that he might enjoy it all the more when it came. "I saw you ass plain ass anything, and The *Fital Spark* crooded high and low with the picnic, and you in the muddle playing your trump. The mustress wass there, too, quite spruce, and — But you were goin' to say something aboot the mustress, Dougie. I hope she's in her usual?"

"That's chust it," said Dougie, more and more embarrassed as he saw his news had to be given now, if ever. "You would be thinkin' to yourself I wass late this mornin', but the fact iss we were in an aawful habble[8] in oor hoose — "

"Bless me! I hope the lum[9] didn't take fire nor nothing like that?" said Para Handy anxiously; and The Tar, at the wheel behind, was almost in a fit with suppressed laughter.

"Not at aal! worse nor that!" said Dougie in melancholy tones. "There's — there's — dash it! there's more boots than ever needed yonder!"

"Man, you're gettin' quite droll," said Para Handy. "Do you no' mind you told me aboot that wan chust three or four months ago?"

"You're a liar!" said Dougie, exasperated; "it's a twelvemonth since I told you aboot the last."

"Not at aal! not at aal! your mind's failin'," protested the Captain. "Five months ago at the most; you told me aboot it at the time. Surely there's some mistake?"

"No mistake at aal aboot it," said the mate, shaking his head so sadly that the Captain's heart was melted.

"Never mind, Dougald," he said, taking a little parcel out of his pocket. "I'm only in fun. I heard aboot it this mornin' from Macphail, and here's a wee bit peeny[10] and a pair o' sluppers that I bought for't."

"To the muschief! It's no' an 'it'," said Dougie; "it's — it's — it's a twuns!"

"Holy smoke!" exclaimed Para Handy. "Iss that no chust desperate?" And the mate was so much moved that he left half his dinner and went forward towards the bow.

Para Handy went forward to him in a little and said, "Cheer up, Dougie; hoo wass I to ken it wass a twins? If I had kent, it wouldna be the wan peeny and the wan sluppers; but I have two or three shillin's here, and I'll buy something else in Campbeltown."

"I can only — I can only say thankye the noo, Peter; it wass very good of you," said the mate, deeply touched, and attempting to shake the Captain's hand.

"Away! away!" said Para Handy, getting very red himself; "none of your chat! I'll buy peenies and sluppers if I like."

21. *The Baker's Little Widow*

ON THE night after New Year's Day the Captain did a high-spirited thing he had done on the corresponding day for the previous six years; he had his hair cut and his beard trimmed by Dougie the mate, made a specially careful toilet — taking all the tar out of his hands by copious applications of salt butter — wound up his watch (which was never honoured in this way more than once or twice a twelvemonth), and went up the quay to propose to Mrs Crawford. It was one of the rare occasions upon which he wore a topcoat, and envied Macphail his Cairngorm scarfpin. There was little otherwise to suggest the ardent wooer, for ardent wooers do not look as solemn as Para Handy looked. The truth, is, he was becoming afraid that his persistency might wear down a heart of granite, and that this time the lady might accept him.

The crew of the *Vital Spark*, whom he thought quite ignorant of his tender passion for the baker's widow, took a secret but intense interest in this annual enterprise. He was supposed to be going to take tea with a cousin (as if captains took the tar off their hands to visit their own cousins!), and in order to make the deception more complete and allay any suspicions on the part, especially, of Macphail, who, as a great student of penny novelettes, was up to all the intrigues of love, the Captain casually mentioned that if it wasn't that it would vex his cousin he would sooner stay on the vessel and play Catch the Ten[1] with them.

"I hate them tea-pairties," he said; "chust a way of wasting the

New Year. But stay you here, boys, and I'll come back ass soon ass ever I can."

"Bring back some buns, or cookies, or buscuits wi' you," cried Dougie, as the Captain stepped on to the quay.

"What do you mean?" said Para Handy sharply, afraid he was discovered.

"Nothing, Peter, nothing at aal," the mate assured him, nudging The Tar in the dark. "Only it's likely you'll have more of them than you can eat at your cousin's tea-pairty."

Reassured thus that his secret was still safe, Para Handy went slowly up the quay. As he went he stopped a moment to exchange a genial word with everybody he met, as if time was of no importance, and he was only ashore for a daunder. This was because, dressed as he was, if he walked quickly and was not particularly civil to everybody, the whole of Campbeltown (which is a very observant place) would suspect he was up to something and watch him.

The widow's shop was at a conveniently quiet corner. He tacked back and forward off it in the darkness several times till a customer, who was being served, as he could see through the glass door, had come out, and a number of boys playing at "guesses" at the window had passed on, and then he cleared his throat, unbuttoned his topcoat and jacket to show his watch-chain, and slid as gently as he could in at the glass door.

"Dear me, fancy seeing you, Captain Macfarlane!" said the widow Crawford, coming from the room at the back of the shop. "Is it really yourself?"

"A good New Year to you," said the Captain, hurried and confused. "I wass chust goin' up the toon, and I thought I would give you a roar in the by-going. Are you keeping tip-top, Mery?"

His heart beat wildly; he looked at her sideways with a timid eye, for, hang it! she was more irresistible than ever. She was little, plump, smiling, rosy-cheeked, neat in dress, and just the exact age to make the Captain think he was young again.

"Will you not come ben and warm yourself? It's a nasty, damp night," said Mrs Crawford, pushing the back door, so that he got the most tempting vision of an interior with firelight dancing in it, a genial lamp, and a tea-table set.

"I'll chust sit doon and draw my breath for a meenute or two. You'll be busy?" said the Captain, rolling into the back room with an elephantine attempt (which she skilfully evaded) at playfully putting his arm round the widow's waist as he did so.

"You're as daft as ever, I see, Captain," said the lady. "I was just making myself a cup of tea; will you take one?"

"Och, it's puttin' you to bother," said the Captain.

"Not a bit of it," said the widow, and she whipped out a cup, which was suspiciously handy in a cupboard, and told the Captain to take off his coat and he would get the good of it when he went out.

People talk about young girls as entrancing. To men of experience like the Captain girls are insipid. The prime of life in the other sex is something under fifty; and the widow, briskly making tea, smiling on him, shaking her head at him, pushing him on the shoulder when he was impudent, chaffing him, surrounding him with an intoxicating atmosphere of homeliness, comfort, and cuddleability, seemed to Para Handy there and then the most angelic creature on earth. The rain could be heard falling heavily outside, no customers were coming in, and the back room of the baker's shop was, under the circumstances, as fine an earthly makeshift for Paradise as man could ask for.

Para Handy dived his hand into his coat pocket. "That minds me," said he; "I have a kind of a bottle of scent here a friend o' mine, by the name of Hurricane Jeck, took home for me from America last week. It's the rale Florida Water; no' the like o't to be got here, and if you put the least sensation on your hanky you'll feel the smell of it a mile away. It's chust sublime."

"Oh! it's so kind of you!" said the widow, beaming on him with the merriest, brownest, deepest, meltingest of eyes, and letting her plump little fingers linger a moment on his as she took the perfume bottle. The Captain felt as if golden harps were singing in the air, and fairies were tickling him down the back with peacocks' feathers.

"Mery," he said in a little, "this iss splendid tea. Capital, aal-thegither!"

"Tuts! Captain," said she, "is it only my tea you come to pay compliments to once a year? Good tea's common enough if you're willing to pay for it. What do you think of myself?"

The Captain neatly edged his chair round the corner of the table to get it close beside hers, and she just as neatly edged her chair round the other corner, leaving their relative positions exactly as they had been.

"No, no, Captain," said she, twinkling; "hands off the widow. I'm a done old woman, and it's very good of you to come and have tea with me; but I always thought sailors, with a sweetheart, as they say, in every port, could say nice things to cheer up a lonely female heart. What we women need, Captain — the real necessity of our lives — is some one to love us. Even if he's at the other end of the world, and unlikely ever to be any nearer, it makes the work of the day cheery. But what am I haverin'² about?" she added, with a delicious, cosy, melting, musical sigh that bewitchingly heaved her blouse. "Nobody cares for me, I'm too old."

"Too old!" exclaimed the Captain, amused at the very idea. "You're not a day over fifty. You're chust sublime."

"Forty-nine past, to be particular," said the widow, "and feel like twenty. Oh! Captain, Captain! you men!"

"Mery," entreated Para Handy, putting his head to one side, "caal me Peter, and gie me a haad o' your hand." This time he edged his chair round quicker than she did hers, and captured her fingers. Now that he had them he didn't know very well what to do with them, but he decided after a little that a cute thing to do was to pull them one by one and try to make them crack. He did so, and got slapped on the ear for his pains.

"What do you mean by that?" said she.

"Och, it was chust a baur, Mery," said Para Handy. "Man, you're strong, strong! You would make a sublime wife for any sober, decent, good-looking, capable man. You would make a fine wife for a sailor, and I'm naming no names, mind ye; but" — here he winked in a manner that seemed to obliterate one complete side of his face — "they caal him Peter. Eh? What?"

"Nobody would have me," said the widow, quite cheerfully, enjoying herself immensely. "I'm old — well, kind of old, and plain, and I have no money."

"Money!" said Para Handy contemptuously; "the man I'm thinking of does not give wan docken for money. And you're no more old than I am mysel' and as for bein' plain, chust look at the lovely polka you have on and the rudeness of your face. If Dougie was here he would tell — no, no, don't mention a cheep[3] to Dougie — not a cheep; he would maybe jalouse[4] something."

"This is the sixth time of asking, Captain," said the widow. "You must have your mind dreadful firm made up. But it's only at the New Year I see you; I'm afraid you're like all sailors — when you're away you forget all about me. Stretch your hand and have another London bun."

"London buns iss no cure for my case," said the Captain, taking one, however. "I hope you'll say yes this time."

"I'll — I'll think about it," said the widow, still smiling; "and if you're passing this way next New Year and call in, I'll let you know."

The crew of the *Vital Spark* waited on deck for the return of the skipper. Long before he came in sight they heard him clamping down the quay singing cheerfully to himself —

"Rolling home to bonnie Scotland
Rolling home, dear land, to thee;
Rolling home to bonnie Scotland,
Rolling home across the sea."

"Iss your cousin's tea-pairty over already?" said Dougie innocently. "Wass there many at it?"

"Seven or eight," said Para Handy promptly. "I chust came away. And I'm feeling chust sublime. Wan of Brutain's hardy sons."

He went down below, and hung up his topcoat and his watch and took off his collar, which uncomfortably rasped his neck. "Mery's the right sort," said he to himself; "she's no' going ram-stam[5] into the business. She's caautious like mysel'. Maybe next New Year she'll make her mind up."

And the widow, putting up her shutters that night, hummed cheerfully to herself, and looked quite happy. "I wish I HAD called him Peter," she thought; "next year I'll not be so blate."

22. *Three Dry Days*

ON THE first day of February the Captain of the *Vital Spark* made an amazing resolution. Life in the leisure hours of himself and his crew had been rather strenuous during the whole of January, for

Dougie had broken the Rechabites. When Dougie was not a Rechabite, he always carried about with him an infectious atmosphere of gaiety and a half-crown, and the whole ship's company took its tone from him. This is a great moral lesson. It shows how powerful for good or evil is the influence and example of One Strong Man. If Dougie had been more at home that month, instead of trading up the West Coast, his wife would have easily dispelled his spirit of gaiety by making him nurse the twins, and she would have taken him herself to be reinstalled in the Rechabites, for she was "a fine, smert, managin' woman", as he admitted himself; but when sailors are so often and so far away from the benign influences of home, with nobody to search their pockets, it is little wonder they should sometimes be foolish.

So the Captain rose on the first day of the month with a frightful headache, and emphatically refused to adopt the customary method of curing it. "No," he said to his astonished mates, "I'm no' goin' up to the Ferry Hoose nor anywhere else; I'm teetotal."

"Teetotal!" exclaimed Dougie, much shocked. "You shouldna make a joke aboot things like that, and you no' feelin' very weel; come on up and take your mornin'."

"Not a drop!" said Para Handy firmly.

"Tut, tut, Peter; chust wan beer," persisted the mate patiently.

"Not even if it wass jampaigne," said the Captain, drying his head, which he had been treating to a cold douche. "My mind's made up. Drink's a curse, and I'm done wi't, for I canna stand it."

"There's nobody askin' you to stand it," explained the mate. "I have a half-croon o' my own here."

"It's no odds," said the Captain. "I'm on the teetotal tack. Not another drop will I taste — "

"Stop, stop!" interrupted Dougie, more shocked than ever. "Don't do anything rash. You might be struck doon deid, and then you would be sorry for what you said. Do you mean to tell us that you're goin' to be teetotal aalthegether?"

"No," said the Captain, "I'm no' that desperate. I wouldna care chust to go aal that length, but I'm goin' to be teetotal for the month o' February."

"Man, I think you're daft, Peter," said the mate. "February, of aal months! In February the New Year's no' right bye, and the Gleska Fair's chust comin' on; could you no' put it off for a more sensible time?"

"No," said the Captain firmly, "February's the month for me; there's two or three days less in't than any other month in the year."

So the crew filed ashore almost speechless with astonishment — annoyed and depressed to some extent by this inflexible virtue on the part of Para Handy.

"He's gettin' quite droll in his old age," was Dougie's explanation.

"Fancy him goin' away and spoilin' the fun like that!" said The Tar incredulously.

"I aye said he hadna the game in him," was the comment of Macphail the engineer.

Para Handy watched them going up to the Ferry House, and wished it was the month of March.

The first day of his abstinence would have passed without much more inclination on his part to repent his new resolution were it not for the fact that half a score of circumstances conspired to make it a day of unusual trial. He met friends that day he had not met for months, all with plenty of time on their hands; Hurricane Jack, the irresistible, came alongside in another vessel, and was immediately for celebrating this coincidence by having half a day off, a proposal the Captain evaded for a while only by pretending to be seriously ill and under medical treatment; the coal merchant, whose cargo they had just discharged, presented the crew with a bottle of whisky; there was a ball at the George Hotel; there was a travelling piper on the streets, with most inspiring melodies; the headache was away by noon — only a giant will-power could resist so many circumstances conducive to gaiety. But Para Handy never swerved in his resolution. He compromised with the friends who had plenty of time and the inclination for merriment by taking fills of tobacco from them; confiscated the bottle of whisky as Captain, and locked it past with the assurance to his crew that it would be very much the more matured if kept till March; and the second time Hurricane Jack came along the quay to see if the Captain of the *Vital Spark* was not better yet, he accompanied him to the Ferry House, and startled him by saying he would have "Wan small half of lime-juice on draught."

"What's that, Peter?" said Hurricane Jack. "Did I hear you say something aboot lime-juice, or does my ears deceive me?"

"It's chust for a bate[1], Jeck — no offence," explained the Captain hurriedly. "I have a bate on wi' a chap that I'll no' drink anything stronger this month; but och! next month, if we're spared, wait you and you'll see some fine fun."

Hurricane Jack looked at him with great disapproval. "Macfarlane," he said solemnly, "you're goin' far, far wrong, and mind you I'm watchin' you. A gembler iss an abomination, and gemblin' at the expense of your inside iss worse than gemblin' on horses. Us workin' men have nothing but oor strength to go on, and if we do not keep up oor strength noo and then, where are we? You will chust have a smaal gill, and the man that made the bate wi' you 'll never be any the wiser."

"No, Jeck, thank you aal the same," said the Captain, "but I'll chust take the lime-juice. Where'll you be on the first o' Merch?"

Hurricane Jack grudgingly ordered the lime-juice, and asked the landlady to give the Captain a sweetie with it to put away the taste, then looked on with an aspect of mingled incredulity and disgust as Para Handy hurriedly gulped the unaccustomed beverage and chased it down with a drink of water.

"It's a fine thing a drap watter," said Para Handy, gasping.

"No' a worse thing you could drink," said Hurricane Jack. "It rots your boots; what'll it no' do on your inside? Watter's fine for sailin' on — there's nothing better — but it's no' drink for sailors."

On the second day of the great reform Para Handy spent his leisure hours fishing for saithe from the side of the vessel, and was, to all appearance, firmer than ever. He was threatened for a while by a good deal of interference from his crew, who resented the confiscation of the presentation bottle, but he turned the tables on them by coming out in the *rôle* of temperance lecturer. When they approached him, he sniffed suspiciously, and stared at their faces in a way that was simply galling — to Dougie particularly, who was naturally of a rubicund countenance. Then he sighed deeply, shook his head solemnly, and put on a fresh bait.

"Are you no' better yet?" Dougie asked. "You're looking ass dull ass if the shup wass tied up to a heidstone in the Necropolis o' Gleska[2]. None o' your didoes[3], Peter; give us oot the spurits we got the present o'. It's Candlemas."[4]

Para Handy stared at his fishing-line, and said gently, as if he were speaking to himself, "Poor sowls! poor sowls! Nothing in their heids but drink. It wass a happy day for me the day I gave it up, or I might be like the rest o' them. There's poor Dougald lettin' it get a terrible grup o' him; and The Tar chust driftin', driftin' to the poor's-hoose, and Macphail iss sure to be in the horrors before Setturday, for he hasna the heid for drink, him no' bein' right Hielan'."

"Don't be rash; don't do anything you would be vexed for, but come on away up the toon and have a pant,"[5] said Dougie coaxingly. "Man, you have only to make up your mind and shake it off, and you'll be ass cheery ass ever you were."

"He's chust takin' a rise oot o' us; are you no', Captain?" said The Tar, anxious to leave his commander an honourable way of retreat from his preposterous position.

Para Handy went on fishing as if they were not present.

"Married men, too, with wifes and femilies," he said musingly. "If they chust knew what it wass, like me, to be risin' in the mornin' wi' a clear heid, and a good conscience, they would never touch it again. I never knew what happiness wass till I joined the teetotal, and it'll be money in my pocket forbye."

"You'll go on, and you'll go on with them expuriments too far till you'll be a vegetarian next," said Dougie, turning away. "Chust a vegetarian, tryin' to live on turnips and gress, the same ass a coo. If I was a Macfarlane I wouldna care to be a coo."

Then they left him with an aspect more of sorrow than of anger, and he went on fishing.

The third day of the month was Saturday; there was nothing to do on the *Vital Spark*, which was waiting on a cargo of timber, so all the crew except the Captain spent the time ashore. Him they left severely alone, and the joys of fishing saithe and reading a week-old newspaper palled.

"The worst of bein' good iss that it leaves you duvelish lonely," said the Captain to himself.

An hour later, he discovered that he had a touch of toothache, and, strongly inclined for a temporary suspension of the new rules for February, he went to the locker for the presentation bottle.

It was gone!

23. *The Valentine That Missed Fire*[1]

A FORTNIGHT of strict teetotalism on the part of the Captain was too much of a joke for his crew. "It's just bounce," said the mate; "he's showin' off. I'm a Rechabite for six years, every time I'm in Gleska; but I never let it put between me and a gless of good Brutish spurits wi' a shipmate in any port, Loch Fyne or foreign."

"It's most annoyin'," said The Tar. "He asked me yesterday if my health wassna breakin' doon wi' drink, the same ass it would break doon wi' aal I take."

"Chust what I told you; nothing but bounce!" said Dougie gloomily. "Stop you! Next time he's in trum, I'll no' be so handy at pullin' corks for him. If I wass losin' my temper wi' him, I would give him a bit o' my mind."

The engineer, wiping his brow with a wad of oily waste, put down the penny novelette he was reading and gave a contemptuous snort. "I wonder to hear the two o' ye talkin'," said he. "Ye're baith feared for him. I could soon fix him."

"Could you, Macphail?" said Dougie. "You're aawful game: what would you do?"

"I would send him a valentine that would vex him," replied the engineer promptly; "a fizzer o' a valentine that would mak' his hair curl for him."

The mate impulsively smacked his thigh. "My Chove! Macphail," said he, "it's the very ticket! What do you say to a valentine for the Captain, Colin?"

"Whatever you think yersel'," said The Tar.

That night Dougie and The Tar went ashore at Tarbert for a valentine. There was one shop-window up the town with a gorgeous display of penny "mocks" designed and composed to give the recipient in every instance a dull, sickening thud on the bump of his self esteem. The two mariners saw no valentine, however, that quite met the Captain's case.

"There'll be plenty o' other wans inside on the coonter," said Dougie diplomatically. "Away you in, Colin, and pick wan suitable, and I'll stand here and watch."

"Watch what?" inquired The Tar suspiciously. "It would be more like the thing if you went in and bought it yoursel'; I'll maybe no' get wan that'll please you."

"Aal you need to ask for iss a mock valentine, lerge size, and pretty broad, for a skipper wi' big feet. I would go in mysel' in a meenute if it wassna that — if it wassna that it would look droll, and me a muddle-aged man wi' whuskers."

The Tar went into the shop reluctantly, and was horrified to find a rather pretty girl behind the counter. He couldn't for his life suggest mock valentines to her, and he could not with decency back out without explanation.

"Have you any — have you any nice unvelopes?" he inquired bashfully, as she stood waiting his order.

"What size?" she asked.

"Lerge size, and pretty broad, for a skipper wi' big feet," said The Tar in his confusion. Then he corrected himself, adding, "Any size, muss, suitable for holdin' letters."

"There's a great run on that kind of envelope this winter," the lady remarked, being a humorist. "How many?"

"A ha'pennyworth," said The Tar. "I'll chust take them wi' me."

When The Tar came out of the shop the mate was invisible, and it was only after some search he found him in a neighbouring public-house.

"I chust came in here to put by the time," said Dougie; "but seein' you're here, what am I for?"

The Tar, realising that there must be an unpleasant revelation immediately, produced the essential threepence and paid for beer.

"I hope you got yon?" said the mate anxiously.

"Ass sure ass daith, Dougie, I didna like to ask for it," explained the young man pathetically. "There's a gasalier[2] and two paraffin lamps bleezin' in the shop and it would gie me a rud face to ask for a mock valentine in such an illumination. Iss there no other wee dark shop in the toon we could get what we want in?"

The mate surveyed him with a disgusted countenance. "Man, you're a coward, Colin," he said. "The best in the land goes in and buys mock valentines, and it's no disgrace to nobody so long ass he has the money in his hand. If I had another gless o' beer I would go in mysel'."

"You'll get that!" said The Tar gladly, and produced another threepence, after which they returned to the shop-window, where Dougie's courage apparently failed him, in spite of the extra glass of beer. "It's no' that I give a docken for anybody," he explained, "but you see I'm that weel kent in Tarbert. What sort o' body keeps the shop?"

"Ooh, it's chust an old done man wi' a sore hand and wan eye no' neebours," replied The Tar strategically. "Ye needna be frightened for him; he'll no' say a cheep. To bleezes wi' him!"

Dougie was greatly relieved at this intelligence. "Toots!" he said. "Iss that aal? Watch me!" and he went banging in at the door in three strides.

The lady of the shop was in a room behind. To call her attention Dougie cried, "Shop!" and kicked the front of the counter, with his eyes already on a pile of valentines ready for a rush of business in that elegant form of billet-doux. When the pretty girl came skipping out of the back room, he was even more astounded and alarmed than The Tar had been.

"A fine night," he remarked affably: "iss your faither at the back?"

"I think you must have made a mistake in the shop," said the lady. "Who do you want?"

"Him with the sore hand and the wan eye no' right neebours," said the mate, not for a moment suspecting that The Tar had misled him. "It's parteecular business; I'll no' keep him wan meenute."

"There's nobody here but myself," the girl informed him, and then he saw he had been deceived by his shipmate.

"Stop you till I get that Tar!" he exclaimed with natural exasperation, and was on the point of leaving when the pile of valentines met his eye again, and he decided to brazen it out.

"Maybe you'll do yoursel'," said he, with an insinuating leer at the shopkeeper. "There iss a shipmate o' mine standin' oot there took a kind o' notion o' a mock valentine and doesna like to ask for't. He wass in a meenute or two ago — you would know him by the warts on his hand — but he hadna the nerve to ask for it."

"There you are, all kinds," said the lady, indicating the pile on the counter, with a smile of comprehension. "A penny each."

Dougie wet his thumb and clumsily turned over the valentines, seeking for one appropriate to a sea captain silly enough to be teetotal. "It's chust for a baur, mind you," he explained to the lady.

"No herm at aal, at aal; chust a bit of a high jeenk. Forbye, it's no' for me: it's for the other fellow, and his name's Colin Turner, but he's blate, blate." He raised his voice so that The Tar, standing outside the window, could hear him quite plainly; with the result that The Tar was so ashamed, he pulled down his cap on his face and hurriedly walked off to the quay.

"There's an awful lot o' them valentines for governesses and tylers[3] and polismen," said Dougie; "the merchant service doesna get mich of a chance. Have you nothing smert and nippy that'll fit a sea captain, and him teetotal?"

The shopkeeper hurriedly went over her stock, and discovered that teetotalism was the one eccentricity valentines never dealt with; on the contrary, they were all for people with red noses and bibulous propensities.

"There's none for teetotal captains," said she; "but here's one for a captain that's not teetotal," and she shoved a valentine with a most unpleasant-looking seaman, in a state of intoxication, walking arm-in-arm with a respectable-looking young woman.

"Man, that's the very tup!" said Dougie, delighted. "It's ass clever a thing ass ever I seen. I wonder the way they can put them valentines thegather. Read what it says below, I havena my specs."

The shopkeeper read the verse on the valentine:

"The girl that would marry a man like you
Would have all the rest of her life to rue;
A sailor soaked in salt water and rum
Could never provide a happy home."

"Capital!" exclaimed the mate, highly delighted. "Ass smert ass anything in the works of Burns. That wan'll do splendid."

"I thought it was for a teetotal captain you wanted one," said the lady, as she folded up the valentine.

"He's only teetotal to spite us," said Dougie. "And that valentine fits him fine, for he's coortin' a baker's weedow, and he thinks we don't know. Mind you, it's no' me that's goin' to send the valentine, it's Colin Turner; but there's no herm, chust a bit of a baur. You ken yoursel'."

Then an embarrassing idea occurred to him — Who was to address the envelope?

"Do you keep mournin' unvelopes?" he asked.

"Black-edged envelopes — yes," said the shopkeeper.

"Wan," said Dougie; and when he got it he put the valentine inside and ventured to propose to the lady that, seeing she had pen and ink handy, she might address the envelope for him, otherwise the recipient would recognise Colin Turner's hand-of-write.

The lady obliged, and addressed the document to

CAPTAIN PETER MACFARLANE,

 S.S. VITAL SPARK,

  TARBERT.

Dougie thanked her effusively on behalf of The Tar, paid for his purchases and a penny stamp, and went out. As he found his shipmate gone, he sealed the envelope and posted it.

When the letter-carrier came down Tarbert quay next morning, all the crew of the *Vital Spark* were on deck — the Captain in blissful unconsciousness of what was in store for him, the others anxious not to lose the expression of his countenance when he should open his valentine.

It was a busy day on the *Vital Spark*; all hands had to help to get in a cargo of wood.

"A mournin' letter for you, Captain," said the letter-carrier, handing down the missive.

Para Handy looked startled, and walked aft to open it. He took one short but sufficient glimpse at the valentine, with a suspicious glance at the crew, who were apparently engrossed in admiration of the scenery round Tarbert. Then he went down the fo'c'sle, to come up a quarter of an hour later with his good clothes on, his hat, and a black tie.

"What the duvvle game iss he up to noo?" said Dougie, greatly astonished.

"I hope it didna turn his brain," said The Tar. "A fright sometimes does it. Wass it a very wild valentine, Dougie?"

Para Handy moved aft with a sad, resigned aspect, the mourning envelope in his hand. "I'm sorry I'll have to go away till the efternoon, boys," he said softly. "See and get in that wud nice and smert before I come back."

"What's wrong?" asked Dougie, mystified.

The Captain ostentatiously blew his nose, and explained that they might have noticed he had just got a mourning letter.

"Was't a mournin' wan? I never noticed," said Dougie.

"Neither did I," added The Tar hurriedly.

"Yes," said the Captain sadly, showing them the envelope; "my poor cousin Cherlie over in Dunmore iss no more; he just slipped away yesterday, and I'm goin' to take the day off and make arrangements."

"Well, I'm jiggered!" exclaimed Dougie, as they watched Para Handy walking off on what they realised was to be a nice holiday at their expense, for they would now have his share of the day's work to do as well as their own.

"Did ye ever see such a nate liar?" said The Tar, lost in admiration at the cunning of the Captain.

And then they fell upon the engineer, and abused him for suggesting the valentine.

24. *The Disappointment of Erchie's Niece*

PARA HANDY never had been at a Glasgow ball till he went to the Knapdale Natives', and he went there simply to please Hurricane Jack. That gallant and dashing mariner came to him one day at Bowling, treated him to three substantial refreshments in an incredibly short space of time, and then delivered a brilliant lecture on the duty of being patriotic to one's native place, "backing up the boys", and buying a ticket for the assembly in question.

"But I'm not a native of Knapdale," said the Captain. "Forbye, I'm kind of oot o' the dancin'; except La Va and Petronella I don't mind wan step."

"That's aal right, Peter," said Hurricane Jack encouragingly; "there's nobody 'll make you dance at a Knapdale ball if you're no' in trum for dancin'. I can get you on the committee, and aal you'll have to do will be to stand at the door of the committee room and keep the crood back from the beer-bottles. I'm no' there mysel' for amusement: do you ken Jean Mactaggart?"

"Not me," said Para Handy. "What Mactaggarts iss she off[1], Jeck?"

"Carradale," said Hurricane Jack modestly. "A perfect beauty! We're engaged."

The Captain shook hands mournfully with his friend and cheerlessly congratulated him. "It's a responsibulity, Jeck," he said, "there's no doot it's a responsibulity, but you ken yoursel' best."

"She's a nice enough gyurl so far ass I know," said Hurricane Jack. "Her brother's in the Western Ocean tred. What I'm wantin' you on the committee for iss to keep me back from the committee room, so that I'll not take a drop too much and affront the lassie. If you see me desperate keen on takin' more than would be dacent, take a dozen strong smert fellows in wi' you at my expense and barricade the door. I'll maybe taalk aboot tearin' the hoose doon, but och, that'll only be my nonsense."

The Captain accepted the office, not without reluctance, and went to the ball, but Hurricane Jack failed to put in any appearance all night, and Para Handy considered himself the victim of a very stupid practical joke on the part of his friend.

Early next forenoon Hurricane Jack presented himself on board the *Vital Spark* and made an explanation. "I'm black affronted[2], Peter," he said, "but I couldna help it. I had a bit of an accident. You see it wass this way, Peter. Miss Mactaggart wass comin' special up from Carradale and stayin' with her uncle, old Macpherson. She wass to put her clothes on there, and I wass to caal for her in wan of them cabs at seven o'clock. I wass ready at five, all spruce from clew to earing[3], and my heid wass that sore wi' wearin' a hat for baals that I got hold of a couple of men I knew in the China tred and went for chust wan small wee gless. What happened efter that for an oor or two's a mystery, but I think I wass drugged. When I got my senses I wass in a cab, and the driver roarin' doon the hatch to me askin' the address.

" 'What street iss it you're for?" said he.

" 'What streets have you?' I asked.

" 'Aal you told me wass Macfarlane's shup,' he said; 'do you think we're anyway near it?'

"When he said that I put my heid oot by the gless and took an observation.

" 'Iss this Carrick Street or Monday mornin'?' says I to him, and then he put me oot of his cab. The poor sowl had no fear in him; he must have been Irish. It wass not much of a cab; here's the door handles, a piece of the wud, and the man's brass number; I chust took them with me for identification, and went home to my bed. When I wakened this mornin' and thought of Jean sittin' up aal night waitin' on me, I wass clean demented."

"It's a kind of a peety, too, the way it happened," said Para Handy sympathetically. "It would put herself a bit aboot sittin' aal night wi' her sluppers on."

"And a full set o' new sails," said Hurricane Jack pathetically. "She was sparin' no expense. This'll be a lesson to me. It'll do me good; I wish it hadna happened. What I called for wass to see if you'll be kind enough, seein' you were on the committee, to go up to 191 Barr Street, where she's stayin' wi' Macpherson, and put the thing as; nicely for me ass you can."

Para Handy was naturally shy of the proposal. "I never saw the lassie," said he. "Would it no' look droll for me to go instead of yoursel'?"

"It would look droll if you didna," said Hurricane Jack emphatically. "What are you on the committee for, and in cherge of aal the beer, unless you're to explain things? I'll show you the close, and you'll go up and ask for two meenutes' private conversation with Miss Mactaggart, and you'll tell her that I'm far from weel. Say I wass on my way up last night in fine time and the cab collided with a tramway car. Break it nice, and no' frighten the poor gyurl oot of her senses. Say I was oot of my conscience for seven oors, but that I'm gettin' the turn, and I'm no' a bit disfigured."

Para Handy was still irresolute. "She'll maybe want to nurse you, the way they do in Macphail's novelles," said he, "and what'll I tell her then?"

This was a staggerer for Hurricane Jack. He recognised the danger of arousing the womanly sympathies of Miss Mactaggart. But he was equal to all difficulties of this kind. "Tell her," said he, "there's nobody to get speakin' to me for forty-eight 'oors, but that I'll likely be oot on Monday."

The Captain agreed to undertake this delicate mission, but only on condition that Dougie the mate should accompany him to back him up in case his own resourcefulness as a liar should fail him at the critical moment.

"Very well," said Hurricane Jack, "take Dougie wi' you, but watch her uncle; I'm told he's cunning, cunning, though I never met him

— a man Macpherson, by the name of Erchie[4]. Whatever you tell her, if he's there at the time, tell it to her in the Gaalic."

Para Handy and his mate that evening left Hurricane Jack at a discreet public bar called the "Hot Blast", and went up to the house of Erchie Macpherson. It was himself who came to answer their knock at his door, for he was alone in the house.

"We're no' for ony strings o' onions, or parrots, or onything o' that sort," he said, keeping one foot against the door and peering at them in the dim light of the rat-tail burner[5] on the stair-landing. "And if it's the stair windows ye want to clean, they were done yesterday."

"You should buy specs," said the Captain promptly — "they're no' that dear. Iss Miss Mactaggart in?"

Erchie opened the door widely, and gave his visitors admission to the kitchen.

"She's no' in the noo," said he. "Which o' ye happens to be the sailor chap that was to tak' her to the ball last nicht?"

"It wasna any o' us," said Para Handy. "It wass another gentleman aalthegither."

"I micht hae kent that," said Erchie. "Whit lock-up is he in? If it's his bail ye're here for, ye needna bother. I aye tell't my guid-sister's dochter she wasna ill to please when she took up wi' a sailor. I had a son that was yince a sailor himself, but thank the Lord he's better, and he's in the Corporation noo[6]. Were ye wantin' to see Jean?"

"Chust for a meenute," said Para Handy, quietly taking a seat on the jawbox[7]. "Will she be long?"

"Five feet three," said Erchie, "and broad in proportion. She hasna come doon sae much as ye wad think at her disappointment."

"That's nice," said Para Handy. "A thing o' the kind would tell terribly on some weemen. You're no' in the shuppin' tred yoursel', I suppose? I ken a lot o' Macphersons in the coast line. But I'm no' askin', mind ye; it's chust for conversation. There wass a femily of Macphersons came from the same place ass mysel' on Lochfyne-side[8]; fine smert fellows they were but I daresay no relation. Most respectable. Perhaps you ken the Gaalic?"

"Not me!" said Erchie frankly — "jist plain Gleska. If I'm Hielan' I canna help it; my faither took the boat to the Broomielaw as soon as he got his senses."

The conversation would have languished here if Dougie had not come to the rescue. "What's your tred?" he asked bluntly.

"Whiles I beadle[9] and whiles I wait," replied Erchie, who was not the man to be ashamed of his calling. "At ither times I jist mind my ain affairs; ye should gie 't a trial — it'll no hurt ye."

The seamen laughed at this sally: it was always a virtue of both of them that they could appreciate a joke at their own expense.

"No offence, no offence, Mr Macpherson," said Para Handy. "I wish your niece would look slippy. You'll be sorry to hear aboot what happened to poor Jeck."

Erchie turned quite serious. "What's the maitter wi' him?" he said.

"The cab broke doon last night," said the Captain solemnly, "and he got a duvvle of a smash."

"Puir sowl!" said Erchie, honestly distressed. "This'll be a sair blow for Jeanie."

"He lost his conscience[10] for 'oors, but there's no disfeegurement, and he'll be speechless till Monday mornin'. It's a great peety. Such a splendid voice ass he had, too; it wass truly sublime. He's lyin' yonder wi' his heid in a sling and not wan word in him. He tell't me I was to say to — "

Here Dougie, seeing an inconsistency in the report, slyly nudged his captain, who stopped short and made a very good effort at a sigh of deep regret.

"I thocht ye said he couldna speak," said Erchie suspiciously.

"My mistake, my mistake," said the Captain. "What I meant wass that he could only speak in the Gaalic; the man's fair off his usual. Dougie 'll tell you himsel'."

Dougie shook his head lugubriously. "Ay," said he, "he's yonder wi' fifteen doctors roond him waitin' for the turn."

"What time did it happen?" inquired Erchie. "Was it efter he was here?"

"He wass on his way here," said Para Handy. "It was exactly half past seven, for his watch stopped in the smash."

At this Erchie sat back in his chair and gave a disconcerting laugh. "Man," he said, "ye're no' bad at a baur, but ye've baith put yer feet in't this time. Will ye tak' a refreshment? There's a drop speerits in the hoose and a bottle or two o' porter."

"I'm teetotal mysel' at present," said Para Handy, "but I have a nesty cold. I'll chust take the spurits while you're pullin' the porter. We'll drink a quick recovery to Jeck."

"Wi' a' my he'rt," said Erchie agreeably. "I hope he'll be oot again afore Monday. Do ye no' ken he came here last nicht wi' the cab a' richt, but was that dazed Jeanie wadna gang wi' him. But she got to the ball a' the same, for she went wi' Mackay the polisman."

"My Chove!" said the Captain, quite dumbfoundered. "He doesna mind, himself, a thing aboot it."

"I daresay no'," said Erchie, "that's the warst o' trevellin' in cabs; he should hae come in a motor-caur."

When the Captain and Dougie came down Macpherson's stair, they considered the situation in the close.

"I think mysel'," said the Captain, "it wouldna be salubrious for neither o' the two of us to go to the 'Hot Blast' and break the news to Jeck the night."

"Whatever ye think yoursel'," said Dougie, and they headed straight for home.

25. *Para Handy's Wedding*

IT IS possible that Para Handy might still have been a bachelor if Calum Cameron had not been jilted. Three days before Calum was to have been married, the girl exercised a girl's privilege and changed her mind. She explained her sad inconstancy by saying she had never cared for him, and only said "yes" to get him off her face. It was an awkward business, because it left the baker's widow, Mrs Crawford, with a large bride's-cake[1] on her hands. It is true the bride's-cake had been paid for, but in the painful circumstances neither of the parties to the broken contract would have anything to do with it, and it continued to lie in the baker's window, a pathetic evidence of woman's perfidy. All Campbeltown talked about it; people came five and six miles in from the country to look at it. When they saw what a handsome example of the confectioner's art it was, they shook their heads and said the lassie could have no heart, let alone good taste.

Mrs Crawford, being a smart business woman, put a bill in the window with the legend —

EXCELLENT BRIDE'S-CAKE

SECOND-HAND

17/6

But there were no offers, and she was on the point of disposing of it on the Art Union principle[2], when, by one of those providential accidents that are very hard on the sufferer but lead by a myriad consequent circumstances to the most beneficent ends, a man in Carrick Street, Glasgow, broke his leg. The man never heard of Para Handy in all his life, nor of the *Vital Spark*; he had never been in Campbeltown, and if he had not kept a pet tortoise he would never have figured in this book, and Para Handy might not have been married, even though Calum Cameron's girl had been a jilt.

The Carrick Street man's tortoise had wandered out into the close in the evening; the owner, rushing out hurriedly at three minutes to ten to do some shopping, tripped over it, and was not prevented by the agony of his injured limb from seizing the offending animal and throwing it into the street, where it fell at the feet of Para Handy, who was passing at the time.

"A tortoise!" said the Captain, picking it up. "The first time ever I kent they flew. I'll take it to Macphail — he's keen on birds anyway," and down he took it to the engineer of the *Vital Spark*.

But Macphail refused to interest himself in a pet which commended itself neither by beauty of plumage nor sweetness of song, and for several days the unhappy tortoise took a deck passage on the *Vital Spark*, its constitution apparently little impaired by the fact that at times The Tar used it as a coal-hammer.

"I'll no' see the poor tortoise abused this way," said Para Handy, when they got to Campbeltown one day; "I'll take it up and give it to a friend o' mine," and, putting it into his pocket in the evening, he went up to the baker's shop.

The widow was at the moment fixing a card on the bride's-cake intimating that tickets for the raffle of it would cost sixpence each, and that the drawing would take place on the following Saturday. Her plump form was revealed in the small shop-window; the flush of exertion charmingly irradiated her countenance as she bent among her penny buns and bottles of fancy biscuits; Para Handy, gazing at her from the outside, thought he had never seen her look more attractive. She blushed more deeply when she saw him looking in at her, and retired from the window with some embarrassment as he entered the shop.

"Fine night, Mery," said the Captain. "You're pushin' business desperate, surely, when you're raffling bride's-cakes."

"Will you not buy a ticket?" said the lady, smiling. "You might be the lucky man to get the prize."

"And what in the world would I do wi' a bride's-cake?" asked the Captain, his manly sailor's heart in a gentle palpitation. "Where would I get a bride to — to — to fit it?"

"I'm sure and I don't know," said the widow hurriedly, and she went on to explain the circumstances that had left it on her hands. The Captain listened attentively, eyed the elegant proportions of the cake in the window, and was seized by a desperate resolve.

"I never saw a finer bride's-cake," he said; "it's chust sublime! Do you think it would keep till the Gleska Fair?"

"It would keep a year for that part o't," said the widow. "What are you askin' that for?"

"If it'll keep to the Fair, and the Fair suits yoursel'," said Para Handy boldly, "we'll have it between us. What do you say to that, Mery?" and he leaned amorously over the counter.

"Mercy on me! this is no' the New Year time" exclaimed the widow; "I thought you never had any mind of me except at the New Year. Is this a proposal, Captain?"

"Don't caal me, Captain, caal me Peter, and gie me a haad o' your hand," entreated Para Handy languishingly.

"Well, then — Peter," murmured the widow, and the Captain went back to the *Vital Spark* that night an engaged man: the bride's-cake was withdrawn from the window, and the tortoise took up its quarters in the back shop.

Of all the ordeals Para Handy had to pass through before his marriage, there was none that troubled him more than his introduction to her relatives, and the worst of them was Uncle Alick, who was very old, very deaf, and very averse to his niece marrying again. The Captain and his "fiancée" visited him as in duty bound, and found him in a decidedly unfavourable temper.

"This is Peter," said the widow by way of introduction; and the Captain stood awkwardly by her side, with his pea-jacket tightly buttoned to give him an appearance of slim, sprightly, and dashing youthfulness.

"What Peter?" asked the uncle, not taking his pipe out of his mouth, and looking with a cold, indifferent eye upon his prospective relative.

"You know fine," said the lady, flushing. "It's my lad."

"What did you say?" inquired Uncle Alick, with a hand behind his ear.

"My lad," she cried. "Peter Macfarlane — him that's Captain on the *Vital Spark*."

"Catched him in a park," said Uncle Alick. "I'll wudger you didna need to run fast to catch him. Whatna park was it?"

"The *Fital Spark*," roared the Captain, coming to Mary's assistance. "I'm captain on her."

"Are you, are you?" said Uncle Alick querulously. "Weel, you needna roar at me like that; I'm no' that deaf. You'll be wan o' the Macfarlanes from Achnatra; they were aal kind of droll in the mind, but hermless."

The Captain explained that he was a member of a different family altogether, but Uncle Alick displayed no interest in the explanation. "It's none of my business," said he.

"Mery thinks it is," rejoined the Captain. "That's the reason we're here."

"Beer!" said Uncle Alick. "No, no, I have no beer for you. I never keep drink of any sort in the hoose."

"I never said beer," exclaimed Para Handy.

"I'll be tellin' a lie then," said Uncle Alick. "The same ass if I didn't hear you with my own ears. You'll be the man that Mery's goin' to merry. I canna understand her; I'm sure she had plenty of trouble wi' Donald Crawford before he went and died on her. But it's none o' my business: I'm only an old done man, no' long for this world, and I'm not goin' to interfere wi' her if she wass to merry a bleck. She never consulted me, though I'm the only uncle she has. You shouldna put yoursel's to bother tellin' me anything aboot it; I'm sure I would have heard aboot it from some o' the neebours. The neebours iss very good to me. They're sayin' it's a droll-like thing

Mery merryin' again, and her wi' a nice wee shop o' her own. What I says to them iss, 'It's her own business: perhaps she sees something takin' in the man that nobody else does. Maybe,' I says to them, 'he'll give up his vessel and help her in the shop.' "

"Och, you're chust an old haiver!"[3] remarked the Captain *sotto voce*, and of course the deaf man heard him.

"A haiver!" said he. "A nice-like thing to say aboot the only uncle Mery has, and him over eighty-six. But you're no' young yoursel'. Maybe it wass time for you to be givin' up the boats."

"I'm no' thinkin' o' givin' them up, Uncle," said Para Handy cheerfully. "The *Vital Spark*'s the smertest boat in the tred. A bonny-like hand I would be in a shop. No, no, herself here — Mery, can keep the shop or leave it, chust ass it pleases hersel', it's aal wan to me; I'm quite joco.[4] I hope you'll turn up at the weddin' on the fufteenth, for aal langsyne."

"What's your wull?" inquired Uncle Alick.

"I hope you'll turn up at the weddin' and give us support," bellowed the Captain.

"Give you sport," said the old man indignantly. "You'll surely get plenty of sport withoot takin' it off a poor old man like me."

"Och! to the muschief!" exclaimed the Captain somewhat impatiently. "Here's a half pound o' tobacco me and Mery brought you, and surely that'll put you in better trum."

"What wey did you no' say that at first?" said Uncle Alick. "Hoo wass I to know you werena wantin' the lend o' money for the weddin'? Stop you and I'll see if there's any spurits handy."

I was not at the wedding, but the Captain told me all about it some days afterwards. "It would be worth a bit in the papers," he said with considerable elation. "I'll wudger there wasna another weddin' like it in Kintyre for chenerations. The herrin' trawlers iss not back at their work yet, and herrin's up ten shullin's a box in Gleska. Dougie and The Tar and their wifes wass there, quite nate and tidy, and every noo and then Macphail would be comin' doon to the boat and blowin' her whustle. Och, he's not a bad chap Macphail, either, but chust stupid with readin' them novelles.

"I never saw Mery lookin' more majestic; she wass chust sublime! Some of them said I wassna lookin' slack mysel', and I daarsay no', for I wass in splendid trum. When the knot was tied, and we sat doon to a bite, I found it wass a different bride's-cake aalthegither from the wan that julted Cameron.

" 'What's the meanin' of that?' I whuspered to the mustress. 'That's no' the bride's-cake you had in the window.'

" 'No,' says she, 'but it's a far better one, isn't it?"

" 'It's a better-lookin' wan,' I says, 'but the other wan might have done the business.'

" 'Maybe it would,' she said, 'but I have all my wuts aboot me, and I wasna goin' to have the neighbours say that both the bride and bride's-cake were second-hand.' Oh! I'm tellin' you she's a smert wan the mustress!"

"Well, I wish you and your good lady long life and happiness, Captain," I said.

"Thanky, thanky," said he. "I'll tell the mustress. Could you no put a bit in the papers sayin', 'The rale and only belle o' Captain Macfarlane's weddin' wass the young lady first in the grand merch, dressed in broon silk.' "

"Who was the young lady dressed in brown?" I asked.

"What need you ask for?" he replied. "Who would it be but the mustress?"

In Highland Harbours
with Para Handy

26. *A New Cook*[1]

THE S.S. *Texa*[2] made a triumphal entry to the harbour by steaming in between two square-rigged schooners, the *Volant* and *Jehu,* of Wick, and slid silently, with the exactitude of long experience, against the piles of Rothesay quay, where Para Handy sat on a log of wood. The throb of her engine, the wash of her propeller, gave place to the strains of a melodeon, which was playing "Stop yer ticklin Jock", and Para Handy felt some sense of gaiety suffuse him, but business was business, and it was only for a moment he permitted himself to be carried away on the divine wings of music.

"Have you anything for me, M'Kay?" he hailed the *Texa*'s clerk.

The purser cast a rapid glance over the deck, encumbered with planks, crates, casks of paraffin oil, and herring-boxes, and seeing nothing there that looked like a consignment for the questioner, leaned across the rail, and made a rapid survey of the open hold. It held nothing maritime — only hay-bales, flour-bags, soap-boxes, shrouded mutton carcases, rolls of plumbers' lead, two head-stones for Ardrishaig, and the dismantled slates, cushions, and legs of a billiard-table for Strachur.

"Naething the day for you, Peter," said the clerk; "unless it's yin o' the heid-stanes," and he ran his eye down the manifest which he held in his hand.

"Ye're aawful smert, M'Kay," said Para Handy. "If ye wass a rale purser wi' brass buttons and a yellow-and-black strippit tie on your

neck, there would be no haadin' ye in! It's no' luggage I'm lookin' for;
it's a kind o' a man I'm expectin'. Maybe he's no' in your depairtment; he'll be traivellin' saloon. Look behind wan o' them herring-
boxes, Lachie, and see if ye canna see a sailor."

His intuition was right; the *Texa*'s only passenger that afternoon
was discovered sitting behind the herring-boxes playing a
melodeon, and smiling beatifically to himself, with blissful unconsciousness that he had arrived at his destination. He came to himself
with a start when the purser asked him if he was going off here;
terminated the melody of his instrument in a melancholy squawk,
picked up a carelessly tied canvas bag that lay at his feet, and hurried
over the plank to the quay, shedding from the bag as he went a trail
of socks, shoes, collars, penny ballads, and seamen's biscuits, whose
exposure in this awkward fashion seemed to cause him no distress
of mind, for he only laughed when Para Handy called them to his
attention, and left to one of the *Texa*'s hands the trouble of collecting
them, though he obligingly held the mouth of the sack open himself
while the other restored the dunnage. He was a round, short,
red-faced, cleanshaven fellow of five-and-twenty, with a thin serge
suit, well polished at all the bulgy parts, and a laugh that sprang from
a merry heart.

"Are you The Tar's kizzen? Are you Davie Green?" asked Para
Handy.

"Right-oh! The very chap," said the stranger. "And you'll be
Peter? Haud my melodeon, will ye, till I draw my breath. Right-oh!"

"Are ye sure there's no mistake?" asked Para Handy as they
moved along to the other end of the quay where the *Vital Spark* was
lying. "You're the new hand I wass expectin', and you name's
Davie?"

"My name's Davie, richt enough," said the stranger, "but I
seldom got it; when I was on the Cluthas[3] they always ca'd me Sunny
Jim."

"Sunny Jum!" said the Captain. "Man! I've often heard aboot ye;
you were namely for chumpin' fences?"[4]

"Not me!" said Davie. "Catch me jumpin' onything if there was a
hole to get through. Is that your vessel? She's a tipper! You and me 'll
get on A1. Wait you till ye see the fun I'll gie ye! That was the worst
o' the Cluthas — awfu' short trips, and every noo and then a quay;

ye hadn't a meenute to yerself for a baur at all. Whit sort o' chaps hae ye for a crew?"

"The very pick!" said Para Handy, as they came alongside the *Vital Spark*, whose crew, as a matter of fact, were all on deck to see the new hand. "That's Macphail, the chief enchineer, wan of Brutain's hardy sons, wi' the wan gallows; and the other chap's Dougie, the first mate, a Cowal laad; you'll see him plainer efter his face iss washed for the tea. Then there's me, mysel', the Captain. Laads, this iss Colin's kizzen, Sunny Jum."

Sunny Jim stood on the edge of the quay, and smiled like a sunset on his future shipmates. "Hoo are yez, chaps?" he cried genially, waving his hand.

"We canna compleen," said Dougie solemnly. "Are ye in good trum yersel'? See's a grup o' your hold-aal, and excuse the gangway."

Sunny Jim jumped on board, throwing his dunnage-bag before him, and his feet had no sooner touched the deck than he indulged in a step or two of the sailor's hornpipe with that proficiency which only years of practice in a close-mouth[5] in Crown Street s.s.[6], could confer. The Captain looked a little embarrassed; such conduct was hardly business-like, but it was a relief to find that The Tar's nominee and successor was a cheery chap at any rate. Dougie looked on with no disapproval, but Macphail grunted and turned his gaze to sea, disgusted at such free-and-easy informality.

"I hope ye can cook as weel's ye can dance," he remarked coldly.

Sunny Jim stopped immediately. "Am I supposed to cook?" he asked, concealing his surprise as he best could.

"Ye are that!" said Macphail. "Did ye think ye were to be the German band on board, and go roon' liftin' pennies? Cookin's the main thing wi' the second mate o' the *Vital Spark*, and I can tell ye we're gey particular; are we no', Dougie?"

"Aawful!" said Dougie sadly. "Macphail here hass been cookin' since The Tar left; he'll gie ye his receipt for haddies made wi' enchine-oil."

The *Vital Spark* cast off from Rothesay quay on her way for Bowling, and Sunny Jim was introduced to several pounds of sausages to be fried for dinner, a bag of potatoes, and a jar of salt, with which he was left to juggle as he could, while the others, with expectant appetites, performed their respective duties. Life on the open sea, he found, was likely to be as humdrum as it used to be on the Cluthas, and he determined to initiate a little harmless gaiety. With some difficulty he extracted all the meat from the uncooked sausages, and substituted salt. Then he put them on the frying-pan. They had no sooner heated than they began to dance in the pan with curious little crackling explosions. He started playing his melodeon, and cried on the crew, who hurried to see this unusual phenomenon.

"Well, I'm jeegered," said the Captain; "what in aal the world iss the matter wi' them?"

"It's a waarnin'," said Dougie lugubriously, with wide-staring eyes.

"Warnin', my auntie!" said Sunny Jim, playing a jig-tune. "They started jumpin' like that whenever I begood to play my bonnie wee melodeon."

"I daarsay that," said Para Handy; "for you're a fine, fine player, Jum, but — but it wassna any invitation to a baal I gave them when I paid for them in Ro'sa'."

"I aye said sausages werena meat for sailors" remarked the engineer, with bitterness, for he was very hungry. "Ye'll notice it's an Irish jig they're dancin' to," he added with dark significance.

"I don't see mysel'," said the Captain, "that it maitters whether it iss an Irish jeeg or the Gourock Waltz and Circassian Circle."

"Does it no'?" retorted Macphail. "I suppose ye'll never hae heard o' Irish terrier dugs? I've ett my last sausage onywye! Sling us ower that pan-loaf" and seizing the bread for himself he proceeded to make a spartan meal.

Sunny Jim laughed till the tears ran down his jovial countenance. "Chaps," he exclaimed, with firm conviction, "this is the cheeriest ship ever I was on; I'm awful gled I brung my music."

Dougie took a fork and gingerly investigated. "As hard ass whun-stanes!" he proclaimed; "they'll no' be ready by the time we're at the Tail o' the Bank. Did you ever in your mortal life see the like of it?" and he jabbed ferociously with the fork at the bewitched sausages.

"That's richt!" said Macphail. "Put them oot o' pain."

"Stop you!" said Para Handy. "Let us pause and consuder. It iss the first time ever I saw sassages with such a desperate fine ear for music. If they'll no' fry, they'll maybe boil. Put them in a pot, Jum."

"Right-oh!" said Sunny Jim, delighted at the prospect of a second scene to his farce, and the terpsichorean sausages were consigned to the pot of water which had boiled the potatoes. The crew sat round, staving off the acuter pangs of hunger with potatoes and bread.

"You never told us what for they called you Sunny Jum, Davie," remarked the Captain. "Do you think it would be for your complexion?"

"I couldna say," replied the new hand, "but I think mysel' it was because I was aye such a cheery wee chap. The favourite Clutha on the Clyde, when the Cluthas was rinnin', was the yin I was on; hunners o' trips used to come wi' her on the Setturdays on the aff-chance that I wad maybe gie them a baur. Mony a pant we had! I could hae got a job at the Finnieston Ferry[7] richt enough, chaps, but they wouldna alloo the melodeon, and I wad sooner want my wages."

"A fine, fine unstrument!" said Para Handy agreeably. "Wi' it and Dougie's trump we'll no' be slack in passin' the time."

"Be happy! — that's my motto," said Sunny Jim, beaming upon his auditors like one who brings a new and glorious evangel. "Whatever happens, be happy, and then ye can defy onything. It's a' in the wye ye look at things. See?"

"That's what I aalways say mysel' to the wife," said Dougie in heart-broken tones, and his eye on the pot, which was beginning to boil briskly.

"As shair as daith, chaps, I canna stand the Jock o' Hazeldean[8] kind o' thing at a' — folk gaun aboot lettin' the tear doon-fa a' the time. Gie me a hearty laugh and it's right-oh! BE HAPPY! — that's the Golden Text for the day, as we used to say in the Sunday School."

"I could be happy easy enough if it wassna that I wass so desperate hungry," said Dougie in melancholy accents, lifting the lid to look into the pot. He could see no sign of sausages, and with new forebodings he began to feel for them with a stick. They had disappeared! "I said from the very first it wass a waarnin'!" he exclaimed, resigning the stick to the incredulous engineer.

"This boat's haunted," said Macphail, who also failed to find anything in the pot. "I saw ye puttin' them in wi' my ain eyes, and noo they're no' there."

Para Handy grabbed the spirtle[9], and feverishly explored on his own account, with the same extraordinary results.

"My Chove!" he exclaimed, "did you ever see the like of that, and I havena tasted wan drop of stimulants since last Monday. Laads! I don't know what you think aboot it, but it's the church twice for me to-morrow!"

Sunny Jim quite justified his nickname by giving a pleasant surprise to his shipmates in the shape of a meat-tea later in the afternoon.

27. *Pension Farms*

THE *Vital Spark* was making for Lochgoilhead, Dougie at the wheel, and the Captain straddled on a waterbreaker, humming Gaelic songs, because he felt magnificent after his weekly shave. The chug-chug-chug of the engines was the only other sound that broke the silence of the afternoon, and Sunny Jim deplored the fact that in the hurry of embarking early in the morning he had quite forgotten his melodeon – those peaceful days at sea hung heavy on his urban spirit.

"That's Ardgoil," remarked Macphail, pointing with the stroup of an oil-can at the Glasgow promontory[1], and Para Handy gazed at the land with affected interest.

"So it iss, Macphail," he said ironically. "That wass it the last time we were here, and the time before, and the time before that again. You would think it would be shifted. It's wan of them guides for towerists you should be, Macphail, you're such a splendid hand for information. What way do you spell it?"

"Oh, shut up!" said the engineer with petulance; "ye think ye're awfu' clever. I mind when that wee hoose at the p'int was a hen farm, and there's no' a road to't. Ye could only get near the place wi' a boat."

"If that wass the way of it," said Dougie, "ducks would suit them better; they could swim. It's a fine thing a duck."

"But a goose is more extraordinar'," said Macphail with meaning. "Anyway it was hens, and mony a time I wished I had a ferm for hens."

"You're better where you are," said the Captain, "oilin' engines like a chentleman. A hen ferm iss an aawful speculation, and you need your wuts aboot you if you start wan. All your relations expect their eggs for nothing, and the very time o' the year when eggs iss dearest, hens takes a tirrievee[2] and stop the layin'. Am I no' tellin' the truth, Dougie?"

"You are that!" said the mate agreeably; "I have noticed it mysel'."

"If ye didna get eggs ye could live aff the chickens," suggested Sunny Jim. "I think a hen ferm would be top, richt enough!"

"It's not the kind o' ferm I would have mysel whatever o't," said Para Handy; "there's far more chance o' a dacent livin' oot o' rearin' pensioners."

"Rearin pensioners?" remarked Macphail; "ye would lie oot o' your money a lang while rearin pensioners; ye micht as weel start growin' trees."

"Not at aal! not at aal!" said Para Handy; "there's quick returns in pensioners if you put your mind to the thing and use a little caation. Up in the Islands, now, the folks iss givin' up their crofts[3] and makin' a kind o' ferm o' their aged relations. I have a cousin yonder oot in Gigha wi' a stock o' five fine healthy uncles — no' a man o' them under seventy. There's another frien' o' my own in Mull wi' thirteen heid o' chenuine old Macleans. He gaithered them aboot the islands wi' a boat whenever the rumours o' the pensions started[4]. Their frien's had no idea what he wanted wi' them, and were glad to get them off their hands. 'It's chust a notion that I took,' he said, 'for company; they're great amusement on a winter night,' and he got his pick o' the best o' them. It wassna every wan he would take; they must be aal Macleans, for the Mull Macleans never die till they're centurions, and he wouldna take a man that wass over five and seventy. They're yonder, noo, in Loch Scridain, kept like fightin' cocks; he puts them oot on the hill each day for exercise, and if wan o' them takes a cough they dry his clothes and give him something from a bottle."

"Holy smoke!" said Dougie; "where's the profits comin' from?"

"From the Government," said Para Handy. "Nothing simpler! He gets five shillings a heid in the week for them, and that's £169 in the year for the whole thirteen — enough to feed a regiment! Wan pensioner maybe wadna pay you, but if you have a herd like my

frien' in Mull, there's money in it. He buys their meal in bulk from
Oban, and they'll grow their own potatoes; the only thing he's vexed
for iss that they havena wool, and he canna clip them. If he keeps his
health himsel', and doesna lose his heid for a year or twa, he'll have
the lergest pension ferm in Scotland, and be able to keep a gig. I'm
no' a bit feared for Donald, though; he's a man o' business chust ass
good ass you'll get on the streets o' Gleska."

"Thirteen auld chaps like that aboot a hoose wad be an awfu'
handful," suggested Sunny Jim.

"Not if it's at Loch Scridain," answered Para Handy; "half the
time they're on the gress, and there's any amount o' fanks⁵. They're
quite delighted swappin' baurs wi' wan another aboot the way they
could throw the hammer fifty years ago, and they feel they're more
important noo than ever they were in a' their lives afore. When my
frien' collected them, they hadna what you would caal an object for
to live for except it wass their own funerals; noo they're daaft for
almanacs, and makin' plans for living to a hundred, when the fermer
tells them that he'll gie them each a medal and a uniform. Oh! a
smert, smert laad, Donal'. Wan o' Brutain's hardy sons! Nobody
could be kinder!"

"It's a fine way o' makin' a livin'," said Macphail. "I hope they'll
no' go wrang wi' him."

"Fine enough," said Para Handy, "but the chob iss not withoot
responsibilities. Yonder's my cousin in Gigha wi' his stock o' five, and
a nice bit ground for them, and you wouldna believe what it needs in
management. He got two of them pretty cheap in Salen, wan o' them
over ninety, and the other eighty-six; you wouldna believe it, but
they're worse to manage than the other three that's ten years
younger. The wan over ninety's very cocky of his age, and thinks the
other wans iss chust a lot o' boys. He says it's a scandal givin' them a
pension; pensions should be kept for men that's up in years, and
then it should be something sensible — something like a pound.
The wan that iss eighty-six iss desperate dour, and if my cousin
doesna please him, stays in his bed and says he'll die for spite."

"That's gey mean, richt enough!" said Sunny Jim; "efter your
kizzen takin' a' that trouble!"

"But the worst o' the lot's an uncle that he got in Eigg; he's
seventy-six, and talkin' aboot a wife!"

"Holy smoke!" said Dougie; "isn't that chust desperate!"

"Ay; he hass a terrible conceity notion o' his five shillin's a-week; you would think he wass a millionaire. 'I could keep a wife on it if she wass young and strong,' he tells my cousin, and it takes my cousin and the mustress aal their time to keep him oot o' the way o' likely girls. They don't ken the day they'll lose him."

"Could they no put a brand on him?" asked Dougie.

"Ye daurna brand them," said the Captain, "nor keel⁶ them either. The law 'll no allo' it. So you see yersel's there's aye risk, and it needs a little capital. My cousin had a bit of a shop, and he gave it up to start the pension ferm; he'll be sayin' sometimes it wass a happier man he wass when he wass a merchant, but he's awfu' prood that noo he hass a chob, as you might say, wi' the Brutish Government."

28. *Para Handy's Pup*

ONE NIGHT when the *Vital Spark* lay at Port Ellen¹ quay, and all the crew were up the village at a shinty concert, some one got on board the vessel and stole her best chronometer. It was the property of Macphail, had cost exactly 1s. 11d., and kept approximate time for hours on end if laid upon its side. Macphail at frequent intervals repaired it with pieces of lemonade wire, the selvedges of postage stamps, and a tube of seccotine.

"Holy smoke!" said the Captain, when the loss was discovered; "we'll be sleepin' in in the efternoons as sure as anything. Isn't this the depredation!"

"The champion wee nock!" said Macphail, on the verge of tears. "Set it to the time fornenst yon nock o' Singerses at Kilbowie², and it would tick as nate as onything to the Cloch."³

"Right enough!" said Sunny Jim impressively; "I've biled eggs wi't. There's the very nail it hung on!"

"It's the first time I ever knew that nock to go without Macphail doin' something to it wi' the stroup o' an oil-can," said Dougie.

It was decided that no more risks of quay-head burglary were to be run, and that when evening entertainments called the rest of the crew ashore, the charge of the ship should depend on Sunny Jim.

"I couldna tak' it in haund, chaps!" he protested feelingly. "Ye've nae idea hoo silly I am at nicht when I'm my lane; I cod mysel' I'm seein' ghosts till every hair on my heid's on end.'

"I'm like that mysel'!" confessed Para Handy. "I can gie mysel' a duvvle o' a fright, but it's only nonsense, chust fair nonsense! there's no' a ghost this side o' the Sound o' Sleat; nothing but imagination."

"Ye shouldna be tumid!" counselled Dougie, who never could stay in the fo'c'sle alone at night himself for fear of spirits.

"Ye'll can play your melodeon," said Macphail, "if there's onything to scare the life oot o' ghosts it's that."

But Sunny Jim was not to be induced to run the risk, and the Captain wasn't the sort of man to compel a body to do a thing he didn't like to do, against his will. Evening entertainments at the ports of call were on the point of being regretfully foresworn, when Sunny Jim proposed the purchase of a watch-dog. "A watchdug's the very ticket," he exclaimed. "It's an awfu' cheery thing on a boat. We can gie't the rin o' the deck when we're ashore at nicht, and naebody 'll come near't. I ken the very dug-it belangs to a chap up Fairfield[4], a rale Pompanion, and he ca's it Biler. It has a pedigree and a brass-mounted collar, and a' its P's and Q's."

"Faith! there's worse things than a good dog; there's some o' them chust sublime!" said Para Handy, quite enamoured of the notion. "Iss it well trained your frien's Pompanion?"

"Top!" Sunny Jim assured him. "If ye jist seen it! It would face a regiment o' sodgers, and has a bark ye could hear from here to Campbeltown. It's no awfu' fancy-lookin', mind; it's no' the kind ye'll see the women carrying doon Buchanan Street[5] in their oxters; but if ye want sagaciosity — !" and Sunny Jim held up his hands in speechless admiration of the animal's intelligence. "It belangs to a riveter ca'd Willie Stevenson, and it's jist a pup. There's only the wan fau't wi't, or Willie could live aff the prizes it wad lift at shows — it's deaf."

"That's the very sort o' dug we wad need for a boat like this," said Macphail, with his usual cynicism. "Could ye no' get yin that was blin' too?" But nobody paid any attention to him; there were moments when silent contempt was the obvious attitude to the engineer.

"The worst about a fine, fine dog like that," said Para Handy reflectively, "iss that it would cost a lot o' money, and aal we want iss a dog to watch the boat and bark daily or hourly ass required."

"Cost!" retorted Sunny Jim; "it wad cost naething! I wad ask Willie Stevenson for the len' o't and then say we lost it ower the side. It has far mair sense than Willie himsel'. It goes aboot Govan wi' him on pay Setturdays, and sleeps between his feet when he's sittin' in the public-hooses backin' up the Celts[6]. Sometimes Willie forget's it's wi' him, and gangs awa' without waukenin 't, but when Biler waukens up and sees its maister's no there, it stands on its hind legs and looks at the gless that Willie was drinkin' frae. If there's ony drink left in't it kens he'll be back, and it waits for him."

"Capital!" said Para Handy. "There's dogs like that. It's born in them. It's chust a gift!"

The dog Biler was duly borrowed by Sunny Jim on the next run to Glasgow, and formally installed as watch of the *Vital Spark*. It was distinctly not the sort of dog to make a lady's pet; its lines were generously large, but crude and erratic; its coat was hopelessly unkempt and ragged, its head incredibly massive, and its face undeniably villainous. Even Sunny Jim was apologetic when he produced it on a chain. "Mind, I never said he was onything awfu' fancy," he pleaded. "But he's a dug that grows on ye."

"He's no' like what I thocht he would be like at aal, at aal," admitted the Captain, somewhat disappointed. "Iss he a rale Pompanion?"

"Pure bred!" said Sunny Jim; "never lets go the grip. Examine his jaw."

"Look you at his jaw, Dougie, and see if he's the rale Pompanion," said the Captain; but Dougie declined. "I'll wait till we're better acquent," he said. "Man! doesn't he look desperate dour?"

"Oor new nock's a' richt wi' a dug like that to watch it," said Macphail; "he's as guid as a guardship."

Biler surveyed them curiously, not very favourably impressed, and deaf, of course, to all blandishments. For a day or two the slightest hasty inovement on the part of any of his new companions made him growl ferociously and display an appalling arsenal of teeth. As a watch-dog he was perfect; nobody dared come down a quay within a hundred yards of the *Vital Spark* without his loud, alarming bay. Biler spoiled the quay-head angling all along Loch Fyne.

In a week or two Para Handy got to love him, and bragged incessantly of his remarkable intelligence. "Chust a pup!" he would say, "but as long in the heid as a weedow woman. If he had aal his faculties he would not be canny, and indeed he doesna seem to want his hearin' much; he's ass sharp in the eye ass a polisman. A dog like that should have a Board of Tred certuficate."

Dougie, however, was always dubious of the pet. "Take my word, Peter," he would say solemnly, "there's muschief in him; he's no a dog you can take to your he'rt at aal, at aal, and he barks himsel' black in the face wi' animosity at Macphail."

"Didn't I tell you?" would the Captain cry, exultant. "Ass deaf ass a door, and still he can take the measure o' Macphail! I hope, Jum, your frien' in Fairfield's no' in a hurry to get him back."

"Not him," said Sunny Jim. "He's no expectin' him back at a'. I tell't him Biler was drooned at Colintraive, and a' he said was 'ye might hae tried to save his collar.'"

And Dougie's doubts were fully justified in course of time. The *Vital Spark* was up with coals at Skipness, at a pier a mile away from the village, and Para Handy had an invitation to a party. He dressed himself in his Sunday clothes, and, redolent of scented soap, was confessed the lion of the evening, though Biler unaccountably refused to accompany him. At midnight he came back along the shore, to the ship, walking airily on his heels, with his hat at a dashing angle. The crew of the *Vital Spark* were all asleep, but the faithful Biler held the deck, and the Captain heard his bark.

"Pure Pompanion bred!" he said to himself. "As wise as a weedow woman! For the rale sagacity give me a dog!"

He made to step from the quay to the vessel's gunnel but a rush and a growl from the dog restrained him; Biler's celebrated grip was almost on his leg.

"Tuts, man," said the Captain, "I'm sure you can see it's me; it's Peter. Good old Biler; stop you and I'll give you a buscuit!"

He ventured a foot on the gunnel again, and this time Biler sampled the tweed of his trousers. Nothing else was stirring in the *Vital Spark*. The Captain hailed his shipmates for assistance; if they heard, they never heeded, and the situation was sufficiently un-pleasant to annoy a man of better temper even than Para Handy. No matter how he tried to get on board, the trusty watch-dog kept him back. In one attempt his hat fell off, and Biler tore it into the most impressive fragments.

"My Cot," said the Captain, "issn't this the happy evenin'? Stop you till I'll be pickin' a dog again, and it'll be wan wi' aal his faculties."

He had to walk back to the village and take shelter ashore for the night; in the morning Biler received him with the friendliest overtures, and was apparently astonished at the way they were received.

"Jum," said the Captain firmly, "you'll take back that dog to your frien' in Fairfield, and tell him there's no' a bit o' the rale Pompanion in him. He's chust a common Gleska dog, and he doesna know a skipper when he sees him, if he's in his Sunday clothes."

29. *Treasure Trove*

SUNNY JIM proved a most valuable acquisition to the *Vital Spark*. He was a person of humour and resource, and though they were sometimes the victims of his practical jokes, the others of the crew forgave him readily because of the fun he made. It is true that when they were getting the greatest entertainment from him they were, without thinking it, generally doing his work for him — for indeed he was no sailor, only a Clutha mariner — but at least he was better value for his wages than The Tar, who could neither take his fair share of the work nor tell a baur. Sunny Jim's finest gift was imagination; the most wonderful things in the world had happened to him when he was on the Cluthas — all intensely interesting, if incredible: and Para Handy, looking at him with admiration and even envy, after a narrative more extraordinary than usual, would remark, "Man! it's a peety listenin' to such d — d lies iss a sin, for there iss no doobt it iss a most pleeasant amuusement!"

Macphail the engineer, the misanthrope, could not stand the new hand. "He's no' a sailor at a'!" he protested; "he's a clown; I've see'd better men jumpin' through girrs[1] at a penny show."

"Weel, he's maybe no' aawful steady at the wheel, but he hass a kyind, kyind he'rt!" Dougie said.

"He's chust sublime!" said Para Handy. "If he wass managed right there would be money in him!"

Para Handy's conviction that there was money to be made out of Sunny Jim was confirmed by an episode at Tobermory, of which the memory will be redolent in Mull for years to come.

The *Vital Spark*, having discharged a cargo of coal at Oban, went up the Sound to load with timber, and on Calve Island, which forms a natural breakwater for Tobermory harbour, Dougie spied a stranded whale. He was not very much of a whale as whales go in Greenland, being merely a tiny fellow of about five-and-twenty tons, but as dead whales here are as rarely to be seen as dead donkeys, the *Vital Spark* was steered close in to afford a better view, and even stopped for a while that Para Handy and his mate might land with the punt on the islet and examine the unfortunate cetacean.

"My Chove! he's a whupper!" was Dougie's comment, as he reached up and clapped the huge mountain of sea-flesh on its ponderous side. "It wass right enough, I can see, Peter, aboot yon fellow Jonah[2]; chust look at the accommodation!"

"Chust waste, pure waste," said the skipper; "you can make a meal off a herrin', but whales iss only lumber, goin' aboot ass big as a land o' hooses, blowin' aal the time, and puttin' the fear o' daith on aal the other fushes. I never had mich respect for them."

"If they had a whale like that aground on Clyde," said Dougie, as they returned to the vessel, "they would stick bills on't; it's chust thrown away on the Tobermory folk."

Sunny Jim was enchanted when he heard the whale's dimensions. "Chaps," he said with enthusiasm, "there's a fortune in't; right-oh! I've see'd them chargin' tuppence to get into a tent at Vinegar Hill[3], whaur they had naethin' fancier nor a sea-lion or a seal."

"But they wouldna be deid," said Para Handy; "and there's no' mich fun aboot a whale's remains. Even if there was, we couldna tow him up to Gleska, and if we could, he wouldna keep."

"Jim'll be goin' to embalm him, rig up a mast on him, and sail him up the river; are ye no', Jim?" said Macphail with irony.

"I've a faur better idea than that," said Sunny Jim. "Whit's to hinder us clappin' them tarpaulins roon' the whale whaur it's lyin', and showin' 't at a sixpence a heid to the Tobermory folk? Man! ye'll see them rowin' across in hunners, for I'll bate ye there's no much fun in Tobermory in the summer time unless it's a Band o' Hope[4] soiree[5]. Give it a fancy name-the 'Tobermory Treasure'; send the bellman roond the toon, sayin' it's on view to-morrow from ten till five and then goin' on to Oban; Dougie'll lift the money, and the skipper and me'll tell the audience a' aboot the customs o' the whale when he's in life. Macphail can stand by the ship at Tobermory quay."

"Jist what I said a' alang," remarked Macphail darkly. "Jumpin' through girrs! Ye'll need a big drum and a naphtha lamp."

"Let us first paause and consider," remarked Para Handy, with his usual caution; "iss the whale oors?"

"Wha's else wad it be?" retorted Sunny Jim. "It was us that fun' it, and naebody seen it afore us, for it's no' mony oors ashore."

"Everything cast up on the shore belangs to the Crown; it's the King's whale," said Macphail.

"Weel, let him come for 't," said Sunny Jim; "by the time he's here we'll be done wi 't."

The presumption that Tobermory could be interested in a dead whale proved quite right; it was the Glasgow Fair week, and the local boat-hirers did good business taking parties over to the island where an improvised enclosure of oars, spars, and tarpaulin and dry sails concealed the "Tobermory Treasure" from all but those who were prepared to pay for admission. Para Handy, with his hands in his pockets and a studied air of indifference, as if the enterprise was none of his, chimed in at intervals with facts in the natural history of the whale, which Sunny Jim might overlook in the course of his introductory lecture.

"The biggest whale by three feet that's ever been seen in Scotland," Sunny Jim announced. "Lots o' folk thinks a whale's a fish, but it's naething o' the kind; it's a hot-blooded mammoth, and couldna live in the watter mair nor a wee while at a time withoot comin' up to draw its breath. This is no' yin of thae common whales that chases herrin', and goes pechin'[6] up and doon Kilbrannan Sound[7]; it's the kind that's catched wi' the harpoons and lives on naething but roary borealises and icebergs."

"They used to make umbrella-rubs wi' this parteecular kind," chimed in the skipper diffidently; "forbye, they're full o' blubber. It's an aawful useful thing a whale, chentlemen." He had apparently changed his mind about the animal, for which the previous day he had said he had no respect.

"Be shair and tell a' your friends when ye get ashore that it's maybe gaun on to Oban to-morrow," requested Sunny Jim. "We'll hae it up on the Esplanade there and chairge a shillin' a heid; if we get it the length o' Gleska, the price 'll be up to hauf a-croon."

"Is it a 'right' whale?" asked one of the audience in the interests of exact science.

"Right enough, as shair's onything; isn't it, Captain?" said Sunny Jim.

"What else would it be?" said Para Handy indignantly. "Does the chentleman think there iss onything wrong with it? Perhaps he would like to take a look through it; eh, Jum? Or mayhe he would want a doctor's certeeficate that it's no a dromedary."

The exhibition of the "Tobermory Treasure" proved so popular that its discoverers determined to run their entertainment for about a week. On the third day passengers coming into Tobermory with the steamer *Claymore*[8] sniffed with appreciation, and talked about the beneficial influence of ozone; the English tourists debated whether it was due to peat or heather. In the afternoon several yachts in the bay hurriedly got up their anchors and went up Loch Sunart, where the air seemed fresher. On the fourth day the residents of Tobermory overwhelmed the local chemist with demands for camphor, carbolic powder, permanganate of potash, and other deodorants and disinfectants; and several plumbers were telegraphed for to Oban. The public patronage of the exbibition on Calve Island fell off.

"If there's ony mair o' them wantin' to see this whale," said Sunny Jim, "they'll hae to look slippy."

"It's no' that bad to windward," said Para Handy. "What would you say to coverin' it up wi' more tarpaulins?"

"You might as weel cover't up wi' crape or muslin," was Dougie's verdict. "What you would need iss armour-plate, the same ass they have roond the cannons in the man-o'-wars. If this wind doesn't change to the west, half the folk in Tobermory 'll be goin' to live in the cellar o' the Mishnish Hotel."

Suspicion fell on the "Tobermory Treasure" on the following day, and an influential deputation waited on the police sergeant, while the crew of the Vital Spark, with much discretion, abandoned their whale, and kept to their vessel's fo'c'sle. The sergeant informed the deputation that he had a valuable clue to the source of these extraordinary odours, but that unfortunately he could take no steps without a warrant from the Sheriff, and the Sheriff was in Oban. The deputation pointed out that the circumstances were too serious to perrnit of any protracted legal forms and ceremonies; the whale must be removed from Calve Island by its owners unmediately, otherwise there would be a plague. With regret the police sergeant repeated that he could do nothing without authority, but he added casually that if the deputation visited the owners of the whale and scared the life out of them, he would be the last man to interfere.

"Hullo, chaps! pull the hatch efter yez, and keep oot the cold air!" said Sunny Jim, as the spokesman of the deputation came seeking for the crew in the fo'c'sle. "Ye'd be the better o' some odecolong on your hankies."

"We thought you were going to remove your whale to Oban before this," said the deputation sadly.

"I'm afraid," said Para Handy, "that whale hass seen its best days, and wouldna be at aal popular in Oban."

"Well, you'll have to take it out of here immediately anyway," said the deputation. "It appears to be your property."

"Not at aal, not at aal!" Para Handy assured him; "it belongs by right to His Majesty, and we were chust takin' care of it for him till he would turn up, chairgin' a trifle for the use o' the tarpaulins and the management. It iss too great a responsibility now, and we've given up the job; aren't we, Jum?"

"Right-oh!" said Sunny Jim, reaching for his melodeon; "and it's time you Tobermory folk were shiftin' that whale."

"It's impossible," said the deputation, "a carcase weighing nearly thirty tons — and in such a condition!"

"Indeed it is pretty bad," said Para Handy, "perhaps it would be easier to shift the toon o' Tobermory."

But that was, luckily, not necessary, as a high tide restored the "Tobermory Treasure" to its natural element that very afternoon.

30. *Luck*

PARA HANDY, gossiping with his crew, and speaking generally of "luck" and the rewards of industry and intelligence, always counted luck the strongest agent in the destiny of man. "Since ever I wass a skipper," he said, "I had nobody in my crew that was not lucky; I would sooner have lucky chaps on board wi' me than tip-top sailors that had a great experience o' wrecks. If the *Fital Spark* hass the reputation o' bein' the smertest vessel in the coastin' tred, it's no' aalthegither wi' navigation; it's chust because I had luck mysel', and aalways had a lot o' lucky laads aboot me. Dougie himsel' 'll tell you that."

"We have plenty o' luck," admitted Dougie, nursing a wounded head he had got that day by carelessly using it as a fender to keep the side of the ship from the piles of Tarbert quay. "We have plenty of luck, but there must be a lot o' cluver people never mindin' mich aboot their luck, and gettin' aal the money."

"Money!" said the Captain with contempt; "there's other things to think aboot than money. If I had as mich money ass I needed, I wouldna ask for a penny more. There's nothing bates contentment and a pleesant way o' speakin' to the owners. You needna empty aal the jar o' jam, Macphail; give him a rap on the knuckles, Jum, and tak' it from him."

Macphail relinquished the jam-jar readily, because he had finished all that was in it. "If ye had mair luck and less jaw aboot it," said he snappishly, "ye wadna hae to wait so lang on the money ye're expectin' frae your cousin Cherlie in Dunmore[1]. Is he no deid yet?"

"No," said Para Handy dolefully; "he's still hangin' on; I never heard o' a man o' ninety-three so desperate deleeberate aboot dyin', and it the winter-time. Last Friday week wass the fifth time they sent to Tarbert for the munister, and he wasna needed."

"That was your cousin Cherlie's luck," said the engineer, who was not without logic.

"I don't caal that luck at aal," retorted Para Handy; "I call it just manoeuvrin'. Forbye, it wasna very lucky for the munister."

Cousin Cherlie's deliberation terminated a week later, when the

MR NEIL MUNRO.

Neil Munro *c* 1907 *(The Baillie)*

Puffer Saxon (East Dunbartonshire Libraries)

T.S.S. King Edward (Argyll & Bute Libraries)

Launch of Puffer *Briton* at Kirkintilloch (East Dunbartonshire Libraries)

Steamers leaving Broomielaw Glasgow (Authors' collection)

Steamers leaving Bridge Wharf, Broomielaw, Glasgow

Cargo steamer in Loch Fyne (Argyll & Bute Libraries)

Arrochar, Loch Long (West Dunbartonshire Libraries)

Among the Yachts (Argyll & Bute Libraries)

The Kyles of Bute (Argyll & Bute Libraries)

Tarbert, Loch Fyne (Argyll & Bute Libraries)

To Campbeltown by Sea (Argyll & Bute Libraries)

Carradale, Kintyre (Argyll & Bute Libraries)

Gabbarts at Bowling Harbour (West Dunbartonshire Libraries)

Gourock Harbour (Argyll & Bute Libraries)

The Clyde at Glasgow (Argyll & Bute Libraries)

Vital Spark was in Loch Fyne, and the Captain borrowed a hat and went to the funeral. "My own roond hat iss a good enough hat and quite respectable," he said, "but someway it doesna fit for funerals since I canna wear it on my heid except it's cocked a little to the side. You see, I have been at so many Tarbert Fairs with it, and high jeenks chenerally."

The crew helped to make his toilet. Macphail, with a piece of oily engine-room waste, imparted a resplendent polish to the borrowed hat, which belonged to a Tarbert citizen, and had lost a good deal of its original lustre. Dougie contributed a waistcoat, and Sunny Jim cheerfully sacrificed his thumb-nails in fastening the essential, but unaccustomed, collar on his Captain's neck. "There ye are, skipper," he said; "ye look A1 if ye only had a clean hanky."

"I'm no feelin' in very good trum, though," said the Captain, who seemed to be almost throttled by the collar; "there's no' mich fun for us sailor chaps in bein' chentlemen. But of course it's no' every day we're buryin' Cherlie, and I'm his only cousin, no' coontin' them MacNeills."

"Hoo much did ye say he had?" asked Macphail. "Was it a hunder pounds and a free hoose? or a hunder free hooses and a pound?"

"Do you know, laads," said the Captain, "his money wasna in my mind!"

"That's wi' the ticht collar," said the engineer unfeelingly; "lowse yer collar and mak' up yer mind whit yer gaun to dae wi' the hunder pounds. That's to say, if the MacNeills don't get it."

The Captain's heart, at the very thought of such disaster, came to his throat, and burst the fastenings of his collar, which had to be rigged up anew by Sunny Jim.

"The MacNeills," he said, "'ll no' touch a penny. Cherlie couldna stand them, and I wass aye his favourite, me bein' a captain. Money would be wasted on the MacNeills; they wouldna know what to do wi't."

"I ken whit I wad dae wi' a hunder pound if I had it," said Macphail emphatically.

"You would likely gie up the sea and retire to the free hoose wi' a ton or two o' your penny novelles," suggested the Captain.

"I wad trevel," said the engineer, heedless of the unpleasant innuendo. "There's naething like trevel for widenin' the mind. When

I was sailin' foreign I saw a lot o' life, but I didna see near sae much as I wad hae seen if I had the money."

"Fancy a sailor traivellin'!" remarked Sunny Jim. "There's no much fun in that."

"I don't mean traivellin' in boats," explained Macphail. "Ye never see onything trevellin' in boats; I mean trains. The only places abroad worth seein' 's no' to be seen at the heid o' a quay; ye must tak' a train to them. Rome, and Paris, and the Eyetalian Lakes — that sort o' thing. Ye live in hotels and any amount o' men's ready to carry yer bag. Wi' a hunder pound a man could trevel the world."

"Never heed him, Peter," said Dougie; "trevellin's an anxious business; you're aye losin' your tickets, and the tips you have to give folk 's a fair ruination. If I had a hunder pound and a free hoose, I would let the hoose and tak' a ferm."

"A ferm's no' bad," admitted Para Handy, "but there's a desperate lot o' work aboot a ferm."

"There's a desperate lot o' work aboot anything ye can put your hand to, except enchineerin'," said Dougie sadly, "but you can do wonders if you have a good horse and a fine strong wife. You wouldna need to be a rale fermer, but chust wan o' them chentleman fermers that wears knickerbockers and yellow leggin's."

"There's a good dale in what you say, Dougie," admitted the Captain, who saw a pleasing vision of himself in yellow leggings, "It's no' a bad tred, chentleman fermin'."

"Tred!" said Dougie; "it's no a tred — it's a recreation, like sailin' a yat. Plooin'-matches and 'oolmarkets every other day; your own eggs and all the mutton and milk you need for nothing. Buy you a ferm, Peter, I'm tellin' you!"

"Chust that!" said the Captain cunningly. "And then maybe you would be skipper of the *Fital Spark*, Dougie."

"I wasna thinkin' aboot that at aal!" protested the mate.

"I wasna sayin' you were," said the Captain, "but the mustress would give you the notion."

"If I was you I wad tak' a shop in Gleska," said Sunny Jim. "No' an awfu' big shop, but a handy wee wan ye could shut when there was any sport on withoot mony people noticin'."

Para Handy buttoned his coat, and prepared to set out for the funeral. "Whether it wass trevellin', or a ferm, or a shop, I would get on sublime, for I'm a lucky, lucky man, laads; but I'm no lettin' my mind dwell on Cherlie's money, oot o' respect for my relative. I'll see you aal when I come back, and maybe it might be an Occasion."

Dougie cried after him when he was a little up the quay, "Captain, your hat's chust a little to the side."

Para Handy was back from the funeral much sooner than was expected, his collar in his pocket, and the borrowed hat in his hand. He went below to resume his ordinary habiliments without a word to the crew, who concluded that he was discreetly concealing the legacy. When he came up, they asked no questions, from a sense of proper decorum, but the Captain seemed surcharged with great emotion.

"Dougie," he said to the mate, "what would be the cost o' a pair o' yellow leggin's?"

"Aboot a pound," said the mate, with some exultation. "Have you made up your mind for fermin'?"

"No," said the Captain bitterly; "but I might afford the leggin's off my cousin Cherlie's legacy, but it wouldna go the length o' knicker-bockers."

31. *Salvage for the Vital Spark*

THE VESSEL was rounding Ardlamont in a sou'-wester that set her all awash like an empty herring-box. Over her snub nose combed appalling sprays; green seas swept her fore and aft; she was glucking with internal waters, and her squat red funnel whooped dolorously with wind. "Holy smoke!" gasped Para Handy "isn't this the hammerin'!"

"A sailor's life!" said Dougie bitterly, drawing a soaking sleeve across his nose; "I would sooner be a linen-draper."

In flaws of the wind they could hear Macphail break coals in the engine-room, and the wheezy tones of Sunny Jim's melodeon as he lay on his bunk in the fo'c'sle quelling his apprehensions to the air of "The Good Old Summer-Time". Together at the wheel the Captain and his mate were dismal objects, drenched to the hide, even below their oil-skins, which gave them the glistening look of walruses or seals. They had rigged a piece of jib up for a dodger; it poorly served its purpose, and seemed as inefficient as a handkerchief as they raised their blinking eyes above it and longingly looked for the sheltering arms of the Kyles.

"I wish to the Lord it wass Bowlin' quay and me sound sleepin'," said the mate. "Yonder's the mustress in Plantation snug and cosy on't, and I'll wager she's no' a bit put aboot for her man on the heavin' bullow. It makes me quite angry to think of it. Eggs for her tea and all her orders, and me with not a bite since breakfast-time but biscuits."

"Holy smoke! you surely wouldna like her to be wi' you here," said Para Handy, shocked.

"No," said Dougie, "but I wish she could see me noo, and I wish I could get her and her high tea at the fireside oot on' my heid; it's bad enough to be standing here like a flag-pole thinkin' every meenute'll be my next."

"Toot! man, Dougie, you're tumid, tumid," said the Captain. "Draw your braith as deep's you can, throw oot your chest, and be a hero. Look at me! my name's Macfarlane and I'm wan of Brutain's hardy sons!"

The *Vital Spark* got round the Point, and met a wave that smashed across her counter and struck full in the face the mariners at the wheel. Dougie, with his mouth inelegantly open, swallowed a pint or two, and spluttered. Para Handy shook the water from his beard like a spaniel, and looking more anxiously than before through smarting eyes, saw a gabbart labouring awkwardly close on the shore of Ettrick Bay.

"Dougie," said he, "stop giggling a bit, and throw your eye to starboard — is yon no' the *Katherine-Anne*?"

"It wassna giggling I wass," said Dougie irritably, coughing brine, "but I nearly spoiled the Kyles o' Bute. It's the *Katherine-Anne* right enough, and they've lost command o' her; stop you a meenute and you'll hear an awfu' dunt."

"She'll be ashore in a juffy," said the Captain tragically. "Man! iss it no' chust desperate! I'm no' makin' a proposeetion, mind, but what would you say to givin' a slant across and throwin' a bit o' a rope to her?"

Dougie looked wistfully at Tighnabruaich ahead of them, and

now to be reached in comfort, and another at the welter of waves between them and the struggling gabbart. "Whatever you say yoursel', Peter," he replied, and for twenty minutes more they risked disaster. At one wild moment Para Handy made his way to the fo'c'sle hatch and bellowed down to Sunny Jim, "You there wi' your melodeon — it would fit you better if you tried to mind your Psalms."

When they reached the *Katherine-Anne*, and found she had been abandoned, Para Handy cursed at first his own soft heart that had been moved to the distress of a crew who were comfortably on their way to Rothesay. He was for leaving the gabbart to her fate, but Macphail, the engineer, and Sunny Jim remarked that a quite good gabbart lacking any obvious owners wasn't to be picked up every day. If they towed her up to Tighnabruaich they would have a very pretty claim for salvage.

"Fifty pounds at least for ship and cargo," said Macphail; "my share 'll pay for my flittin' at the term, jist nate."

"Fifty pounds!" said Para Handy. "It's a tidy sum, and there might be more than fifty in't when it came to the bit, for fifty pounds iss not an aawful lot when the owner gets his wheck of it. What do you think yoursel', Dougie?"

"I wass chust thinkin'," said Dougie, "that fifty pounds would be a terrible lot for poor MacCallum, him that owns the *Katherine-Anne*; he hasna been very lucky wi' her."

"If we're no' gaun to get the fifty pound then, we can just tow her up to Tighnabruaich for a baur'" said Sunny Jim. "It doesna dae to be stickin'. If there's naething else in't, we'll get a' oor names in the papers for a darin' deed at sea. Come on, chaps, be game!"

"I wish to peace the *Katherine-Anne* belonged to any other man than John MacCallum," said the skipper. "You're an aawful cluver laad, Macphail; what iss the law aboot salvage?"

"Under the Merchant Shippin' Act," said Macphail glibly, "ye're bound to get your salvage; if ye divna claim't, it goes to the King the same as whales or onything that's cast up by the sea."

"Ach! it disna maitter a docken aboot the salvage," said Sunny Jim. "Look at the fun we'll hae comin' into Tighnabruaich wi' a boat we fun' the same as it was a kitlin[I]. See's a rope, and I'll go on board and mak' her fast."

When they had towed the *Katherine-Anne* to Tighnabruaich, Dougie was sent ashore with a telegram for the owner of the *Vital Spark*, suggesting his immediate appearance on the scene. Later in the afternoon the crew of the *Katherine-Anne* came by steamer to Tighnabruaich, to which port she and they belonged, and the captain and owner ruefully surveyed the vessel he had abandoned, now lying safe and sound at his native quay. He sat on a barrel of paraffin-oil and looked at Para Handy in possession.

"Where did you pick her up?" said MacCallum sadly.

"Oh, chust doon the road a bit," said Para Handy. "It's clearin' up a nice day."

"It's a terrible business this," said MacCallum, nervously wiping his forehead with his handkerchief.

"Bless me! what is't?" exclaimed Para Handy. "I havena seen the paper this week yet."

"I mean about havin' to leave the *Katie-Anne* almost at our own door, and you finding her."

"Chust that; it wass Providence," remarked Para Handy piously, "chust Providence."

"I'll hae to gie you something for your bother" said MacCallum.

"I wouldna say but you would," replied the skipper. "It's a mercy your lifes wass saved. Hoo are they keepin', aal, in Ro'sa'?"

"Are ye no' comin' ashore for a dram?" remarked MacCallum, and Para cocked at him a cunning eye.

"No, John," he said; "I'm no' carin' mich aboot a dram the day; I had wan yesterday."

But he succumbed to the genial impulse an hour later, and leaving his mate in possession of the *Katherine-Anne*, went up the village with the owner of that unhappy craft. MacCallum took him to his home, where Para Handy found himself in the uncomfortable presence of a wife and three daughters dressmaking. The four women sewed so assiduously, and were so moist about the eyes with weeping, that he was sorry he came.

"This is the gentleman that found the *Katie-Anne*" remarked MacCallum by way of introduction, and the eldest daughter sobbed.

"Ye're aal busy!" said Para Handy, with a desperate air of cheerfulness.

"Indeed, aye! we're busy enough," said the mother bitterly.

"We're workin' oor fingers to the bane, but we're no' makin' much o't; it's come wi' the wind and gang wi' the water," and the second daughter sobbed in unison with her sister as they furiously plied their needles.

"By Chove!" thought Para Handy, "a man would need to have the he'rt o' a hoose-factor[2] on a chob like this; it puts me aal oot o' trum," and he drank his glass uncomfortably.

"I think ye mentioned aboot fifty pounds?" said MacCallum mournfully, and at these words all the four women laid their sewing on their knees and wept without restraint. "Fi-fi-fifty p-p-pounds!" exclaimed the mother, "where in the wide world is John MacCallum to get fifty pounds?"

Para Handy came hurriedly down the quay and called Dougie ashore from the *Katherine-Anne*.

"Somebody must stay on board of her, or we'll have trouble wi' the salvage," said the mate.

"Come ashore this meenute," commanded the Captain, "for I'm needin' some refreshment. There's four women yonder greetin' their eyes oot at the loss o' fifty pounds."

"Chust that!" said Dougie sympathetically. "Poor things!"

"I would see the salvage to the duvvle," said the Captain warmly, "if we hadna sent that telegram to oor owner. Four o' them sew-sew-sewing yonder. And dreepin', like the fountain oot in Kelvingrove!"[3]

"Man, it wass lucky, too, aboot the telegram," said Dougie, "for I didna like to send it and it's no' away."

Para Handy slapped him on the shoulder. "Man!" he said, "that's capital! To the muschief with their fifty pounds! Believe you me, I'm feelin' quite sublime!"

32. *Para Handy has an Eye to Business*

It was a lovely day, and the *Vital Spark*, without a cargo, lay at the pier of Ormidale[1], her newly painted under-strakes reflected in a loch like a mirror, making a crimson blotch in a scene that was otherwise winter-brown. For a day and a half more there was nothing to be done. "It's the life of a Perfect Chentleman" said

Dougie. The engineer, with a novelette he had bought in Glasgow, was lost in the love affairs of a girl called Gladys, who was excessively poor, but looked, at Chapter Five, like marrying a Colonel of Hussars who seemed to have no suspicion of the fate in store for him; and Sunny Jim, with the back of his head showing at the fo'c'sle scuttle, was making with his melodeon what sounded like a dastardly attack on "The Merry Widow".

"I wass thinkin', seein' we're here and nothing else doin', we might be givin' her the least wee bit touch o' the tar-brush," remarked Para Handy, who never cared to lose a chance of beautifying his vessel.

"There it is again!" exclaimed Macphail, laying down his novelette in exasperation. "A chap canna get sittin' doon five meenutes in this boat for a read to himsel' withoot somebody breakin' their legs to find him a job. Ye micht as weel be in a man-o'-war." Even Dougie looked reproachfully at the Captain; he had just been about to pull his cap down over his eyes and have a little sleep before his tea.

"It wass only a proposeetion," said the Captain soothingly. "No offence! Maybe it'll do fine when we get to Tarbert. It's an awfu' peety they're no' buildin' boats o' this size wi' a kind of a study in them for the use o' the enchineers," and he turned for sympathy to the mate, who was usually in the mood to rag Macphail. But this time Dougie was on Macphail's side.

"There's some o' your jokes like the Carradale funerals — there's no' much fun in them," he remarked. "Ye think it's great sport to be tar-tar-tarring away at the ship; ye never consult either oor healths or oor inclinations. Am I right, Macphail?"

"Slave-drivin'! that's whit I ca't," said Macphail emphatically. "If Lloyd George kent aboot it, he would bring it before the Board o' Tred."[2]

The Captain withdrew, moodily, from his crew, and ostentatiously scraped old varnish off the mast. This business engaged him only for a little; the weather was so plainly made for idleness that he speedily put the scraper aside and entered into discourse with Sunny Jim.

"Whatever you do, don't you be a Captain, Jum," he advised him.

"I wisht I got the chance!" said Sunny Jim.

"There's nothing in't but the honour o' the thing, and a shilling or two extra; no' enough to pay the drinks to keep up the poseetion.

Here am I, and I'm anxious to be frien'ly wi' the chaps, trate them
the same's I wass their equal, and aalways ready to come-and-go a
bit, and they go and give me the name o' a slave-driver! Iss it no'
chust desperate?"

"If I was a Captain," said Sunny Jim philosophically, "I wad dae
the comin' and mak' the ither chaps dae the goin', and d — d smert
aboot it."

"That's aal right for a Gleska man, but it's no' the way we're brocht
up on Loch Long; us Arrochar folk, when we're Captains, believe in
a bit o' compromise wi' the crews. If they don't do a thing when we
ask them cuvilly, we do't oorsel's, and that's the way to vex them."

"Did ye never think ye wad like to change your job and try
something ashore?" asked Sunny Jim.

"Many a time!" confessed the Captain. "There's yonder jobs that
would suit me fine. I wass nearly, once, an innkeeper. It wass at a
place called Cladich[3]; the man came into a puckle money wi' his
wife, and advertised the goodwull at a great reduction. I left the boat
for a day and walked across to see him. He wass a man they caalled
MacDiarmid, and he wass yonder wi' his sleeves up puttin' corks in
bottles wi' a wonderful machine. Did you ever see them corkin'
bottles, Jum?"

"I never noticed if I did," said Sunny Jim; "but I've seen them
takin' them oot."

"Chust that! This innkeeper wass corkin' away like hey-my-
nanny.

" 'You're sellin' the business?' says I.

" 'I am,' says he; and him throng corkin' away at the bottles.

" 'What's your price?' says I.

" 'A hundred and fifty pounds for the goodwull and the stock the
way it stands,' says he.

" 'What aboot the fixtures?' then says I.

" 'Oh, they're aal right!" said the innkeeper, cork cork-corkin'
away at the bottles; 'the fixtures goes along with the goodwull.'

" 'What fixtures iss there?' says I.

" 'There's three sheep fermers, the shoemaker doon the road, and
Macintyre the mail-driver, and that's no' coontin' a lot o' my Sunday
customers[4],' said the innkeeper."

"You didna tak' the business, then?" said Sunny Jim.

"Not me!" said Para Handy. "To be corkin' away at bottles aal my lone yonder would put me crazy. Forbye, I hadna the half o' the hunder-and-fifty. There wass another time I went kind o' into a business buyin' eggs — "

"Eggs!" exclaimed Sunny Jim with some astonishment — 'whit kin' o' eggs?"

"Och! chust egg eggs," said the Captain. "It wass a man in Arran said there wass a heap o' money in them if you had the talent and a wee bit powney[5] to go roond the countryside. To let you ken: it wass before the Fital Spark changed owners; the chentleman that had her then wass a wee bit foolish; nothing at aal against his moral and releegious reputaation, mind, but apt to go over the score with it, and forget whereaboots the vessel would be lying. This time we were for a week or more doin' nothin' in Loch Ranza, and waitin' for his orders. He couldna mind for the life o' him where he sent us, and wass telegraphin' aal the harbour-masters aboot the coast to see if they kent the whereaboots o' the *Fital Spark*, but it never came into his heid that we might be near Loch Ranza, and there we were wi' the best o' times doin' nothing."

"Could ye no' hae sent him a telegraph tellin' him where ye wiz?" asked Sunny Jim.

"That's what he said himsel', but we're no' that daft, us folk from Arrochar; I can tell you we have aal oor faculties. Dougie did better than that; he put a bit o' paper in a bottle efter writin' on't a message from the sea – 's.s. *Fital Spark* stranded for a fortnight in a fit o' absent-mind; aal hands quite joco, but the owner lost'.

"We might have been lyin' in Loch Ranza yet if it wassna that I tried Peter Carmichael's business. 'When you're doin' nothing better here,' he said to me, 'you micht be makin' your fortune buyin' and sellin' eggs, for Arran's fair hotchin' wi' them.'

" 'What way do you do it?' says I.

" 'You need a wee cairt and a powney,' said Peter Carmichael, 'and I've the very cairt and powney that would suit you. You go roond the island gatherin' eggs from aal the hooses, and pay them sixpence a dozen — champion eggs ass fresh ass the mornin' breeze. Then you pack them in boxes and send them to Gleska and sell them at a profit.'

" 'What profit do you chenerally allow yoursel'?' I asked Peter.

" 'Oh! chust nate wan per cent,' said Peter; 'you chairge a shillin' in Gleska for the eggs; rale Arran eggs, no' foreign rubbadge. Folk 'll tell you to put your money in stone and lime; believe me, nothing bates the Arran egg for quick returns. If the people in Gleska have a guarantee that any parteecular egg wass made in Arran, they'll pay any money for it; it's ass good ass a day at the coast for them, poor craturs!'

"Seein' there wass no prospeck o' the owner findin' where we were unless he sent a bloodhound oot to look for us, I asked Carmichael hoo long it would take to learn the business, and he said I could pick it up in a week. I agreed to buy the cairt and powney and the goodwull o' the business if the chob at the end o' the week wass like to bring in a pleasin' wage, and Dougie himsel' looked efter the shup. You never went roond the country buyin' eggs? It's a chob you need a lot o' skill for. Yonder wass Peter Carmichael and me goin' roond by Pirnmill, Machrie, and Blackwaterfoot, Sliddery, and Shiskine — "

"Ach! ye're coddin'!" exclaimed Sunny Jim; "there's no such places."

"It's easy seen you were a' your days on the Clutha steamers," said the Captain patiently; "I'll assure you that there's Slidderys and Shiskines oot in Arran. Full o' eggs! The hens oot yonder's no' puttin' bye their time!

"Three days runnin' Peter and me and the powney scoured the country and gaithered so many eggs that I begun to get rud in the face whenever I passed the least wee hen. We couldna get boxes enough to hold them in Loch Ranza, so we got some bales o' hay and packed them in the hold of the *Fital Spark*, and then consudered. 'There's nothing to do noo but to take them to the Broomielaw and sell them quick at a shillin',' said Carmichael. 'The great thing iss to keep them on the move, and off your hands before they change their minds and start for to be chuckens. Up steam, smert, and off wi' ye! And here's the cairt and powney — fifteen pounds.'

" 'Not at aal, Carmichael!' I said to him; 'I'll wait till I'll see if you wass right aboot the wan per cent of profits. Stop you here till I'll come back.'

"I telegraphed that day to the owner o' the vessel, sayin' I was comin' into the Clyde wi' a cargo, and when we got to Gleska he wass standin' on the quay, and not in the best o' trum.

" 'Where in a' the world were you?' says he; 'and me lookin' high and low for you! What's your cargo?'

" 'Eggs from Arran, Mr Smuth,' says I, 'and a bonny job I had gettin' them at sixpence the dozen.'

" 'Who are they from?' he asked, glowerin' under the hatches.

" 'Chust the cheneral population, Mr Smuth,' says I.

" 'Who are they consigned to?' he asked then — and man he wassna in trum at aal, at aal!

" 'Anybody that'll buy them, sir,' said I; 'it's a bit of a speculation.'

"He scratched his heid and looked at me. 'I mind o' orderin' eggs,' says he, 'but I never dreamt I wass daft enough to send for a boat-load o' them. But noo they're here I suppose we'll have to make the best o' them.' So he sold the eggs, and kept the wan p·r cent for freight and responsibeelity, and I made nothin' of it except that I shifted my mind aboot takin' a chob ashore, and didn't buy Carmichael's cairt and powney."

33. *A Vegetarian Experiment*

THE *Vital Spark* had been lying for some time in the Clyde getting in a new boiler, and her crew, who had been dispersed about the city in their respective homes, returned to the wharf on a Monday morning to make ready for a trip to Tobermory.

"She's a better boat than ever she was," said Macphail with satisfaction, having made a casual survey. "Built like a lever watch! We'll can get the speed oot o' her noo. There's boats gaun up and doon the river wi' red funnels, saloon caibins, and German bands in them, that havena finer engines. When I get that crank and crossheid tightened, thae glands packed and nuts slacked, she'll be the gem o' the sea."

"She's chust sublime!" said Para Handy, patting the tarred old hull as if he were caressing a kitten; "it's no' coals and timber she should be carryin' at aal, but towrist passengers. Man! if we chust had the accommodation!"

"Ye should hae seen the engines we had on the Cluthas!" remarked Sunny Jim, who had no illusions about the *Vital Spark* in that respect. "They were that shiney I could see my face in them."

"Could ye, 'faith?" said Macphail; "a sicht like that must have put ye aff yer work. We're no' that fond o' polish in the coastin' tred that we mak' oor engines shine like an Eyetalian ice-cream shop[1]; it's only vanity. Wi' us it's speed — "

"Eight knots," murmured Sunny Jim, who was in a nasty Monday-morning humour. "Eight knots, and the chance o' nine wi' wind and tide."

"You're a liar!" said the Captain irritably, "and that's my advice to you. Ten knots many a time between the Cloch and the Holy Isle,"[2] and an argument ensued which it took Dougie all his tact to put an end to short of bloodshed.

"It's me that's gled to be back on board of her anyway," remarked Para Handy later; "I suppose you'll soon be gettin' the dinner ready, Jum? See and have something nice, for I'm tired o' sago puddin'."

"Capital stuff for pastin' up bills," said Dougie; "I've seen it often in the cookin'-depots. Wass the wife plyin' ye wi' sago?"

"Sago, and apples, potatoes, cabbage, cheese, and a new kind o' patent coffee that agrees wi' the indigestion; I havena put my two eyes on a bit of Christian beef since I went ashore; the wife's in wan of her tirravees, and she's turned to be a vegetarian."

"My Chove!" said Dougie incredulously; "are you sure, Peter?"

"Sure enough! I told her this mornin' when I left I would bring her home a bale of hay from Mull, and it would keep her goin' for a month or two. Women's a curious article!"

"You should get the munister to speak to her," said Dougie sympathetically. "When a wife goes wrong like that, there's nothing bates the munister. She'll no' be goin' to the church; it's aalways the way wi' them fancy new releegions. Put you her at wance in the hands o' a dacent munister."

"I canna be harsh wi' her, or she'll greet," said Para Handy sadly.

"It's no harshness that's wanted," counselled the mate, speaking from years of personal experience; "what you need is to be firm. What way did this calamity come on her? Don't be standin' there, Jum, like a soda-water bottle, but hurry and make a bit of steak for the Captain; man! I noticed you werena in trum whenever I saw you come on board. I saw at wance you hadn't the agility. What way did the trouble come on her?"

"She took it off a neighbour woman," explained the Captain. "She wass aal right on the Sunday, and on the Monday mornin' she couldna bear to look at ham and eggs. It might happen to anybody. The thing was at its heid when I got home, and the only thing on the table wass a plate of maccaroni."

"Eyetalian!" chimed in the engineer. "I've seen them makin' it in Genoa and hingin' it up to bleach on the washin'-greens. It's no' meat for men; it's only for passin' the time o' organ-grinders and shipriggers."

" 'Mery,' I said to her, 'I never saw nicer decorations, but hurry up like a darlin' wi' the meat.' 'There'll be no more meat in this hoose, Peter,' she said, aal trumblin'; 'if you saw them busy in a slaughter-hoose you wadna eat a chop. Forbye, there's uric acid in butcher meat, and there's more nourishment in half a pound o' beans than there iss in half a bullock.' 'That's three beans for a sailor's dinner; it's no' for nourishment a man eats always; half the time it's only for amusement, Mery,' said I to her, but it wass not the time for argyment. 'You'll be a better man in every way if you're a vegetarian,' she said to me. 'If it iss a better man you are wantin',' I says to her, wonderful caalm in my temper, 'you are on the right tack, sure enough; you have only to go on with them expuriments wi' my meat and you'll soon be a weedow woman.'

"But she wouldna listen to reason, Mery, and for a fortnight back I have been feedin' like the Scribes and Sadducees[3] in the Scruptures."

"Man! iss it no chust desperate?" said Dougie compassionately, and he admiringly watched his Captain a little later make the first hearty meal for a fortnight. "You're lookin' a dufferent man already," he told him; "what's for the tea, Jum?"

"I kent a vegetarian yince," said Sunny Jim, "and he lived maist o' the time on chuckie soup."

"Chucken soup?" repeated Dougie interrogatively.

"No; chuckie soup. There was nae meat o' ony kind in't. A' ye needed was some vegetables, a pot o' hot water, and a parteecular kind o' chuckie-stane. It was fine and strengthenin'."

"You would need good teeth for't, I'm thinkin'," remarked the Captain dubiously.

"Of course ye didna eat the chuckie-stane," Sunny Jim explained;

"it made the stock; it was instead o' a bane, and it did ower and ower again."

"It would be a great savin'," said Dougie, fascinated with the idea. "Where do you get them parteecular kinds of chuckies?"

"Onywhere under high water," replied Sunny Jim, who saw prospects of a little innocent entertainment.

"We'll get them the first time we're ashore, then," said the mate, "and if they're ass good ass what you say, the Captain could take home a lot of them for his vegetarian mustress."

At the first opportunity, when he got ashore, Sunny Jim perambulated the beach and selected a couple of substantial pieces of quartz, and elsewhere bought a pound of margarine which he put in his pocket. "Here yez are, chaps — the very chuckie! I'll soon show ye soup," he said, coming aboard with the stones in which the crew showed no little interest. "A' ye have to do is to scrub them weel, and put them in wi' the vegetables when the pot's boilin'."

They watched his culinary preparations closely. He prepared the water and vegetables, cleaned the stones, and solemnly popped them in the pot when the water boiled. At a moment when their eyes were off him he dexterously added the unsuspected pound of margarine. By and by the soup was ready, and when dished, had all the aspect of the ordinary article. Sunny Jim himself was the first to taste it *pour encourager les autres*.

"Fair champion!" he exclaimed.

The engineer could not be prevailed to try the soup on any consideration, but the Captain and the mate had a plate apiece, and voted it extraordinary.

"It's a genius you are, Jum!" said the delighted Captain; "if the folk in Gleska knew that soup like this was to be made from chuckiestanes they wouldna waste their time at the Fair wi' gaitherin' cockles."

And the next time Para Handy reached the Clyde he had on board in all good faith a basket-load of stones culled from the beach at Tobermory for his vegetarian mistress.

34. *The Complete Gentleman*

"THE finest chentleman I ever knew was Hurricane Jeck," said Para Handy. "His manners wass complete. Dougie himsel' will tell you."

"A nice laad," said the mate agreeably; "he had a great, great facility."

"Whaur did he mak' his money?" asked Sunny Jim, and they looked at him with compassion.

"There iss men that iss chentlemen, and there iss men that hass a puckle money," said the Captain impressively; "Hurricane Jeck wass seldom very rife with money, but he came from Kinlochaline[1], and that iss ass good ass a Board of Tred certuficate. Stop you till you're long enough on the *Fital Spark*, and you'll get your educaation. Hurricane Jeck was a chentleman. What money he had he would spend like the wave of the sea."

"It didna maitter wha's money it was, either," chimed in Macphail unsympathetically. "I kent him! Fine!"

"Like the wave of the sea," repeated the Captain, meeting the engineer's qualification with the silence of contempt. "Men like Jeck should never be oot of money, they distribute it with such a taste."

"I've seen chaps like that," remarked Sunny Jim, who was sympathetic to that kind of character. "When I was on the Cluthas — "

"When you was on the Cluthas, Jum, you were handlin' nothing but ha'pennies; Hurricane Jeck was a chentleman in pound notes, and that's the dufference."

"My Jove!" said Sunny Jim, "he must hae been weel aff!"

"There wass wan time yonder," proceeded the Captain, "when Jeck came into a lot o' money from a relative that died — fifty pounds if it wass a penny, and he spent it in a manner that was chust sublime. The very day he got it, he came down to the *Fital Spark* at Bowlin' for a consultation. 'You'll no' guess what's the trouble, Peter,' said he; 'I'm a chentleman of fortune,' and he spread the fifty notes fornent[2] him, with a bit of stone on each of them to keep them doon, the same as it wass a bleachin'-green. 'Fifty pounds and a fortnight to spend it in before we sail for China. Put bye your boat, put on your Sunday clothes, and you and me'll have a little recreaation.'

" 'I canna, Jeck,' says I — and Dougie himsel' 'll tell you — 'I canna, Jeck; the cargo's in, and we're sailin' in the mornin'.'

" 'That's the worst o' money," said Hurricane Jeck, 'there's never enough o't. If Uncle Willy had left me plenty I would buy your boat and no' let a cargo o' coals interfere wi' oor diversion.'

" 'Put it in the bank,' I said to him.

" 'I'm no' that daft,' he said. 'There's no' a worst place in the world for money than the banks; you never get the good o't.'

" 'Oh, there's plenty of other ways of gettin' rid of it,' I told him.

" 'Not of fifty pounds,' said Jeck. 'It's easy spendin' a pound or two, but you canna get rid o' a legacy withoot assistance.' Wassn't that the very words of him, Dougie?"

"Chust his own words!" said the mate; "your memory iss capital."

" 'There's a lot o' fun I used to think I would indulge in if I had the money,' said Hurricane Jeck, 'and now I have the opportunity if I only had a friend like yoursel' to see me doin' it. I'm goin' to spend it aal in trevellin'.' "

"And him a sailor!" commented the astonished Sunny Jim.

"He wass meanin' trevellin' on shore," said Para Handy. "Trains, and tramway cars, and things like that, and he had a brulliant notion. It wass aye a grief to Jeck that there wass so many things ashore you darena do withoot a prosecution. 'The land o' the Free!' he would say, 'and ye canna take a tack on a train the length o' Paisley withoot a bit of a pasteboard ticket!' He put in the rest of that day that I speak of trevellin' the Underground[3] till he wass dizzy and every other hour he had an altercaation wi' the railway folk aboot his ticket. 'Take it oot o' that' he would tell them, handin' them a pound or two, and he quite upset the traffic. On the next day he got a Gladstone bag, filled it with empty bottles, and took the train to Greenock. 'Don't throw bottles oot at the windows,' it says in the railway cairrages; Jeck opened the windows and slipped oot a bottle or two at every quarter mile, till the Caledonian system[4] looked like the mornin' efter a Good Templars' trip. They catched him doin' it at Pollokshields.

" 'What's the damage?' he asked them, hangin' his arm on the inside strap o' a first-class cairrage and smokin' a fine cigar. You never saw a fellow that could be more genteel.

" 'It might be a pound a bottle,' said the railway people; 'we have the law for it.'

" 'Any reduction on takin' a quantity?' said Jeck. 'I'm havin' the time o' my life; it's most refreshin'.'

"That day he took the train to Edinburgh — didn't he, Dougie?"

"He did that!" said Dougie. "You have the story exactly."

"He took the train to Edinburgh. It was an express and every noo and then he would pull the chain communication wi' the guard. The train would stop, and the guard would come and talk with Jeck. The first time he came along Jeck shook him by the hand, and said he only wanted to congratulate him.

" 'What aboot?' said the guard, no' lookin' very well pleased.

" 'On your cheneral ability,' said Hurricane Jeck. 'Your cairrages iss first-rate; your speed iss astonishin' quick; your telegraph communication iss workin' A1; and you stopped her in two lengths. I thocht I would chust like you to take my compliments to the owners.'

" 'It's five pounds o' a fine for pullin' the cord,' said the guard.

" 'That's only for the wan cord; I pulled the two o' them,' said Jeck, quite nice to him; 'first the port and then the starboard. You canna be too parteecular. There's the money and a shillin' extra for a dram.'

"The guard refused the money, and said he would see aboot it at Edinburgh, and the train went on. Jeck pulled the cords till he had them all in the cairrage wi' him, but the train never stopped till it came to Edinburgh, and then a score o' the offeecials came to the cairrage.

" 'What are you doin' with them cords?' they asked.

" 'Here they are, all coiled up and flemished-down,' said Jeck, lightin' another cigar. 'When does this train go back?' and he hands them over a bunch o' notes, and told them never to mind the change."

"Man! he was the comic!" exclaimed Sunny Jim. "Fair champion!"

"In Edinburgh," proceeded Pary Handy, "he waalked aboot till he came on a fire alarm where it said it would cost a heavy fine to work it unless there wass a fire. Jeck rung the bell, and waited whustlin' till the Fire Brigade came clatterin' up the street.

" 'Two meenutes and fifty seconds,' he says to them, holdin' his watch; 'they couldna do better in Gleska. I like your helmets. Noo that we're aal here, what iss it goin' to be, boys?'

" 'Are you drunk, or daft?' said the Captain o' the Fire Brigade, grippin' him by the collar.

" 'Not a drop since yesterday!' said Jeck. 'And I'm no' daft, but chust an honest Brutish sailor, puttin' bye the time and spreadin' aboot my money. There's me and there's Mr Carnegie[5]. His hobby is libraries; on the other hand I'm for Liberty. The Land of the Free and the Brave; it says on the fire alarm that I mustna break it, and I proved I could. Take your money oot o' that,' — and he hands the Captain the bundle of notes. 'If there iss any change left when you pay yoursel's for your bother, send home the enchines and we'll aal adjourn to a place.' "

"Capital!" exclaimed Dougie.

"It took three days for Jeck to get rid of his fortune in cheneral amusement of that kind, and then he came to see me before he joined his shup for China.

" 'I had a fine time, Peter, he said; couldna have better. You would wonder the way the week slipped by. But it's the Land of the Free, right enough; there's no' half enough o' laws a chentleman can break for his diversion; I hadna very mich of a selection.' "

35. *An Ocean Tragedy*

IT WAS a lovely afternoon at the end of May, and the *Vital Spark* was puffing down Kilbrannan Sound with a farmer's flitting. Macphail, the engineer, sat "with his feet among the enchines and his heid in the clouds," as Dougie put it — in other words, on the ladder of his engine-room, with his perspiring brow catching the cool breeze made by the vessel's progress, and his emotions rioting through the adventures of a governess in the 'Family Herald Supplement'. Peace breathed like an exhalation from the starboard hills; the sea was like a mirror, broken only by the wheel of a stray porpoise, and Sunny Jim indulged the Captain and the mate with a medley on his melodeon.

"You're a capital player, Jum," said the Captain in a pause of the entertainment. "Oh, yes, there's no doot you are cluver on it; it's a gift, but you havena the selection; no, you havena the selection, and if you havena the selection where are you?"

"He's doin' his best," said Dougie sympathetically, and then, in one of those flashes of philosophy that come to the most thoughtless of us at times — 'A man can do no more."

"Whit selections was ye wantin'?" asked the musician, with a little irritation; "if it's Gaelic sangs ye're meanin' I wad need a dram and the nicht aff."

"No, I wassna thinkin' aboot Gaalic sangs," explained Para Handy; "when we're consuderin' them we're consuderin' music; I wass taalkin' of the bits of things you put on the melodeon; did you ever hear 'Napoleon'?" and clearing his throat he warbled —

 "Wa-a-an night sad and dree-ary
    Ass I lay on my bed,
    And my head scarce reclined on the pillow;
    A vision surprisin' came into my head,
    And I dreamt I wass crossin' the billow.
    And ass my proud vessel she dashed o'er the deep — "

"It wasna the *Vital Spark*, onywye," remarked Macphail cynically; "afore I got her biler sorted she couldna dash doon a waterfall — "
 "I beheld a rude rock, it was craggy and steep,"
    (proceeded the vocalist, paying no attention),
 "'Twas the rock where the willow iss now seen to weep,
    O'er the grave of the once-famed Napo-o-o-ole-on!"

"I never heard better, Peter," said the mate approvingly. "Take your breath and give us another touch of it. There's nothing bates the old songs."

"Let me see, noo, what wass the second verse?" asked the Captain, with his vanity as an artist fully roused; "it was something like this —

 "And ass my proud vessel she near-ed the land,
    I beheld clad in green, his bold figure;
    The trumpet of fame clasped firm in his hand,
    On his brow there wass valour and vigour."

"Balloons! balloons!" cried Macphail, imitating some Glasgow street barrow-vendor. "Fine balloons for rags and banes."

"Fair do! gie the Captain a chance," expostulated Sunny Jim. "Ye're daein' fine, Captain; Macphail's jist chawed because he canna get readin'."

 "'Oh, stranger,' he cried, 'dost thou come unto me
    From the land of thy fathers who boast they are free;
    Then, if so, a true story I'll tell unto thee

Concerning myself — I'm Napo-o-o-ole-on,' "
proceeded the Captain, no way discouraged, and he had no sooner
concluded the final doleful note than a raucous voice from the
uncovered hold cried "Co-co-coals!'

Even Dougie sniggered; Macphail fell into convulsions of
laughter, and Sunny Jim showed symptoms of choking.

"I can stand MacPhail's umpudence, but I'll no stand that nonsense from a hoolit[1] on my own shup," exclaimed the outraged
vocalist, and, stretching over the coamings, he grabbed from the top
of a chest of drawers in the hold a cage with a cockatoo. "Come oot
like a man," said he, "and say't again."

"Toots! Peter, it's only a stupid animal; I wouldna put myself a bit
aboot," remarked Dougie soothingly. "It's weel enough known
them cockatoos have no ear for music. Forbye, he wassna meanin'
anything when he cried 'Coals!' he was chust in fun."

"Fun or no," said Macphail, "a bird wi' sense like that's no' canny.
Try him wi' another verse, Captain and see if he cries on the polis."

"If he says another word I'll throw him over the side," said Para
Handy. "It's nothing else but mutiny," and with a wary eye on the
unsuspecting cockatoo he sang another verse —

"'You remember that year so immortal,' he cried,

'When I crossed the rude Alps famed in story,

With the legions of France, for her sons were my pride,

And I led them to honour and glory — ' "

"Oh, crickey! Chase me, girls!" exclaimed the cockatoo, and the
next moment was swinging over the side of the *Vital Spark* to a
watery grave.

The fury of the outraged Captain lasted but a moment; he had the
vessel stopped and the punt out instantly for a rescue; but the
unhappy bird was irrecoverably gone, and the tea-hour on the *Vital
Spark* that afternoon was very melancholy. Macphail, particularly,
was inexpressibly galling in the way he over and over again brought
up the painful topic.

"I canna get it oot o' my heid," he said; "the look it gied when ye
were gaun to swing it roon' your heid and gie't the heave! I'll cairry
that cockatoo's last look to my grave."

"Whit kin' o' look was it?" asked Sunny Jim, eager for details; "I
missed it."

"It was a look that showed ye the puir bird kent his last oor was come," explained the engineer. "It wasna anger, and it wasna exactly fricht; it was — man! I canna picture it to ye, but efter this ye needna tell me beasts have nae sowls; it's a' my aunty. Yon bird — "

"I wish I hadna put a finger on him," said the Captain, sore stricken with remorse. "Change the subject."

"The puir bird didna mean ony hairm," remarked Sunny Jim, winking at the engineer. " 'Coals!' or 'Chase me, girls!' is jist a thing onybody would say if they heard a chap singin' a sang like yon; it's oot o' date. Fair do! ye shouldna hae murdered the beast; the man it belangs to 'll no' be awfu' weel pleased."

"Murdered the beast!" repeated the conscience-stricken Captain; "it's no' a human body you're talkin' aboot," and the engineer snorted his amazement.

"Michty! Captain, is that a' ye ken?" he exclaimed. "If it's no' murder, it's manslaughter; monkeys, cockatoos, and parrots a' come under the Act o' Parliament. A cockatoo's no' like a canary; it's able to speak the language and give an opeenion, and the man that wad kill a cockatoo wad kill a wean."

"That's right enough, Peter," said Dougie pathetically; "everybody kens it's manslaughter. I never saw a nicer cockatoo either; no' a better behaved bird; it's an awful peety. Perhaps the polis at Carradale will let the affair blow bye."

"I wassna meanin' to herm the bird," pleaded Para Handy. "It aggravated me. Here wass I standin' here singin' 'Napoleon', and the cockatoo wass yonder, and he hurt my feelin's twice; you would be angry yoursel' if it wass you. My nerves got the better o' me."

"If the polis cross-examine me," said the engineer emphatically, "I'll conceal naething. I'll no' turn King's evidence or onything like that, mind, but if I'm asked I'll tell the truth, for I don't want to be mixed up wi' a case o' manslaughter and risk my neck."

Thus were the feelings of the penitent Para Handy lacerated afresh every hour of the day, till he would have given everything he possessed in the world to restore the cockatoo to life. The owner's anger at the destruction of his bird was a trifle to be anticipated calmly; the thought that made Para Handy's heart like lead was that cockatoos DID speak, that this one even seemed to have the gift of irony, and that he had drowned a fellow-being; it was, in fact, he admitted to himself, a kind of manslaughter. His shipmates found a hundred ways of presenting his terrible deed to him in fresh aspects.

"Cockatoos iss mentioned in the Scruptures,"[2] said Dougie; "I don't exactly mind the place, but I've seen it."

"They live mair nor a hundred years if they're weel trated," was Sunny Jim's contribution to the natural history of the bird.

"Naebody ever saw a deid cockatoo," added the engineer.

"I wish you would talk aboot something else," said the Captain piteously; "I'm troubled enough in mind withoot you bringin' that accursed bird up over and over again," and they apologised, but always came back to the topic again.

"I wid plead guilty and throw mysel' on the mercy o' the coort," was Macphail's suggestion. "At the maist it'll no' be mair nor a sentence for life."

"Ye could say ye did it in self-defence," recommended Sunny Jim. "Thae cockatoos bites like onything."

"A great calamity!" moaned Dougie, shaking his head.

When the cargo of furniture was discharged and delivered, the farmer discovered the absence of his cockatoo, and came down to make inquiries.

"He fell over the side," was the Captain's explanation. "We had his cage hanging on the shrouds, and a gale struck us and blew it off. His last words wass, 'There's nobody to blame but mysel'.' "

"There was no gale aboot here," said the farmer, suspecting nothing. "I'm gey sorry to lose that cage. It was a kind o' a pity, too, the cockatoo bein' drooned."

"Say nothing aboot that," pleaded the Captain. "I have been mournin' about that cockatoo all week; you wouldna believe the worry it haas been for me, and when all iss said and done I consider the cockatoo had the best of it."

36. *The Return of the Tar*

A YACHTSMAN with "R.Y.S. *Dolphin*" blazoned on his guernsey came down Campbeltown quay and sentimentally regarded the *Vital Spark*, which had just completed the discharge of a cargo of coals under circumstances pleasing to her crew, since there had been a scarcity of carts, two days of idleness, and two days' demurrage. Para Handy saw him looking — "The smertest shup in the tred," he remarked to Sunny Jim; "you see the way she catches their eye! It's her lines, and cheneral appearance; stop you till I give her a touch of paint next month!"

"He'll ken us again when he sees us," said Sunny Jim, unpleasantly conscious of his own grimy aspect, due to eight hours of coal dust. "Hey, you wi' the sign-board, is't a job you're wantin'?" he cried to the yachtsman; and started to souse himself in a bucket of water.

The stranger pensively gazed at the Captain, and said, "Does your eyes deceive me or am I no' Colin?"

"Beg pardon!" replied the Captain cautiously.

"Colin," repeated the stranger. "Surely you must mind The Tar?"

"Holy smoke!" exclaimed Para Handy, "you're no' my old shupmate, surely; if you are, there's a desperate change on you. Pass me up my spy-gless, Dougie."

The yachtsman jumped on board, and barely escaped crashing into the tea-dishes with which Sunny Jim proposed to deal when his toilet was completed. "And there's Dougie himsel'," he genially remarked; " — and Macphail, too; it's chust like comin' home. Are ye aal in good condeetion?"

"We canna complain," said Dougie, shaking the proffered hand with some dubiety. "If you were The Tar we used to have you wouldna miss them plates so handy wi' your feet." They stood around and eyed him shrewdly; he certainly looked a little like The Tar if The Tar could be imagined wideawake, trim, cleanshaven, and devoid of diffidence. The engineer, with a fancy nourished on twenty years' study of novelettes, where fraudulent claimants[1] to fortunes and estates were continually turning up, concluded at once that this was really not The Tar at all, but a clever impersonator, and wondered what the game was. The Captain took up a position more non-committal; he believed he could easily test the bona-fides of the stranger.

"And how's your brother Charles?" he inquired innocently.

"Cherles," said the yachtsman, puzzled. "I never had a brother Cherles."

"Neither you had, when I mind, now; my mistake!" said the

Captain; "I wass thinkin' on another hand we used to have that joined the yats. Wass I not at your mairrage over in Colintraive?"

"I wasna mairried in Colintraive at all!" exclaimed the puzzled visitor. "Man, Captain! but your memory's failin'."

"Neither you were," agreed the Captain, thinking for a moment. "It wass such a cheery weddin', I forgot."

"If you're the oreeginal Tar," broke in the engineer, "you'll maybe gie me back my knife: ye mind I gied ye a len' o't the day ye left, and I didna get it back frae ye," but this was an accusation the visitor emphatically denied.

"You'll maybe no' hae an anchor tattooed aboot you anywhere?" asked the mate. "It runs in my mind there wass an anchor."

"Two of them," said the visitor, promptly baring an arm, and revealing these interesting decorations.

"That's anchors right enough," said the Captain, closely examining them, and almost convinced. "I canna say mysel' I mind o' them, but there they are, Dougie."

"It's easy tattooin' anchors," said the engineer; "whaur's your strawberry mark?"

"What's a strawberry mark?" asked the baffled stranger.

"There!" exclaimed Macphail triumphantly. "Everybody kens ye need to hae a strawberry mark. Hoo are we to ken ye're the man ye say ye are if ye canna produce a strawberry mark?" And again the confidence of the Captain was obviously shaken.

"Pass me along that pail," said the mate suddenly to the stranger, who, with his hands in his pockets, slid the pail along the deck to the petitioner with a lazy thrust of his foot that was unmistakably familiar.

The Captain slapped him on the shoulder. "It's you yoursel', Colin!" he exclaimed. "There wass never another man at sea had the same agility wi' his feet; it's me that's gled to see you. Many a day we missed you. It's chust them fancy togs that makes the difference. That and your hair cut, and your face washed so parteecular."

"A chentleman's life," said The Tar, later, sitting on a hatch with his bona-fides now established to the satisfaction of all but the engineer, who couldn't so readily forget the teachings of romance. "A chentleman's life. That's oor yat oot there; she comes from Cowes, and I'm doin' fine on her. I knew the tarry old hooker here ass soon ass I saw her at the quay."

"You're maybe doin' fine on the yats," said the Captain coldly, "but it doesna improve the mainners. She wassna a tarry old hooker when you were earnin' your pound a-week on her."

"No offence!" said The Tar remorsefully. "I wass only in fun. I've seen a wheen o' vessels since I left her, but none that had her style nor nicer shupmates."

"That's the truth!" agreed the Captain, mollified immediately. "Come doon and I'll show you the same old bunk you did a lot o' sleepin' in," and The Tar agreeably followed him with this sentimental purpose. They were below ten minutes, during which time the engineer summed up the whole evidence for and against the identity of the claimant, and proclaimed his belief to Dougie that the visitor had come to the *Vital Spark* after no good. He was so righteously indignant at what he considered a deception that he even refused to join the party when it adjourned into the town to celebrate the occasion fittingly at the Captain's invitation.

The Tar retired to his yacht in due course; Para Handy, Dougie, and Sunny Jim returned, on their part, to the *Vital Spark*, exhilarated to the value of half-a-crown handsomely disbursed by the Captain, who had never before been seen with a shilling of his own so far on in the week. They were met on board by Macphail in a singularly sarcastic frame of mind, mingled with a certain degree of restrained indignation.

"I hope your frien' trated ye well," he said.

"Fine!" said the Captain. "Colin was aye the chentleman. He's doin' capital on the yats."

"He'll be daein' time oot o' the yats afore he's done," said the engineer. "I kent he was efter nae guid comin' here, and when ye had him doon below showin' him whaur The Tar bunked, he picked my Sunday pocket o' hauf-a-croon. The man's a fraud, ye're blin' no' to see't; he hadna even a strawberry mark."

"Whatever you say yoursel'," replied the Captain, with an expansive wink at the mate and Sunny Jim. "If he's not The Tar, and took your money, it was lucky you saw through him."

37. *The Fortune-teller*

TARBERT FAIR was in full swing; the crew of the *Vital Spark* had exhausted the delirious delights of the hobby-horses, the shooting-gallery, Aunt Sally, Archer's Lilliputian Circus, and the booth where, after ten, they got pink fizzing drinks that had "a fine, fine appearance, but not mich fun in them", as Para Handy put it, and Dougie stumbled upon a gipsy's cart on the outskirts of the Fair, where a woman was telling fortunes. Looking around to assure himself that he was unobserved by the others, he went behind the cart tilt and consulted the oracle, a proceeding which took ten minutes, at the end of which time he rejoined the Captain, betraying a curious mood of alternate elation and depression.

"Them high-art fizzy drinks iss not agreeing with you, Dougie," said the Captain sympathetically; "you're losing all your joviality, and it not near the mornin'. Could you not get your eye on Macphail? I'll wudger he'll have something sensible in a bottle!"

"Macphail!" exclaimed the mate emphatically, "I wouldna go for a drink to him if I wass dyin'; I wouldna be in his reverence."

"Holy smoke! but you're gettin' desperate independent," said the Captain; "you had more than wan refreshment with him the day already," and the mate admitting it remorsefully, relapsed into gloomy silence as they loitered about the Fair-ground.

"Peter," he said in a little, "did you ever try your fortune?"

"I never tried anything else," said the Captain; "but it's like the herrin' in Loch Fyne[1] the noo — it's no' in't."

"That's no' what I mean," said Dougie; "there's a cluver woman roond in a cairt yonder, workin' wi' cairds and tea-leaves and studyin' the palm o' the hand, and she'll tell you everything that happened past and future. I gave her a caal mysel' the noo, and she told me things that wass most astonishin'."

"What did it cost you?" asked Para Handy, with his interest immediately aroused.

"Ninepence."

"Holy smoke! she would need to be most extraordinar' astonishin' for ninepence; look at the chap in Archer's circus tying himself in knots for front sates threepence! Forbye, I don't believe in them spae-wifes; half the time they're only tellin' lies."

"This wan's right enough, I'll warrant you," said the mate; "she told me at once I wass a sailor and came through a lot of trouble."

"What did she predict? — that's the point, Dougie; they're no' mich use unless they can predict; I could tell myself by the look o' you that you had a lot o' trouble, the thing's quite common."

"No, no," said the mate cautiously; "pay ninepence for yoursel' if you want her to predict. She told me some eye-openers."

The Captain, with a passion for eye-openers, demanded to be led to the fortune-teller, and submitted himself to ninepence worth of divination, while Dougie waited outside on him. He, too, came forth, half elated, half depressed.

"What did she say to you?" asked the mate,

"She said I wass a sailor and seen a lot o' trouble" replied the Captain.

"Yes, but what did she predict?"

"Whatever it wass it cost me ninepence," said the Captain, "and I'm no' givin' away any birthday presents any more than yoursel'; it's time we were back noo on the vessel."

Getting on board the *Vital Spark* at the quay they found that Para Handy's guess at the engineer's possession of something sensible in a bottle was correct. He hospitably passed it round, and was astonished to find the Captain and mate, for the first time in his experience, refuse a drink. They not only refused but were nasty about it.

"A' richt," he said; "there'll be a' the mair in the morn for me an' Jim. I daursay ye ken best yersel's when ye've gane ower faur wi't. I aye believe, mysel', in moderation."

The manner of Para Handy and his mate for a week after this was so peculiar as to be the subject of unending speculation on the part of the engineer and Sunny Jim. The most obvious feature of it was that they both regarded the engineer with suspicion and animosity.

"I'm shair I never did them ony hairm," he protested to Suuny Jim, almost in tears; "I never get a ceevil word frae either o' them. Dougie's that doon on me, he wad raither gang withoot a smoke than ask a match aff me."

"It's cruel, that's whit it is!" said Sunny Jim, who had a feeling heart; "but they're aff the dot ever since the nicht we were at Tarbert.

Neither o' them'll eat fish, nor gang ashore efter it's dark. They baith took to their beds on Monday and wouldna steer oot o' their bunks a' day, pretendin' to be ill, but wonderfu' sherp in the appetite."

"I'll give them wan chance, and if they refuse it I'll wash my hands o' them," said Macphail decisively, and that evening after tea he produced a half-crown and extended a general invitation to the nearest tavern.

"Much obleeged, but I'm not in the need of anything," said the Captain. "Maybe Dougie — "

"No thanky," said the mate with equal emphasis; "I had a dram this week already" — a remark so ridiculous that it left the engineer speechless. He tapped his head significantly with a look at Sunny Jim, and the two of them went ashore to dispose of the half-crown without the desired assistance.

Next day there was an auction sale in the village, and Para Handy and his mate, without consulting each other, found themselves among the bidders.

"Were you fancyin' anything parteecular?" asked the Captain, who plainly had an interest in a battered old eight-day clock.

"No, nothing to mention," said the mate, with an eye likewise on the clock. "There's capital bargains here, I see, in crockery."

But the Captain seemed to have no need for crockery; he hung about an hour or two till the clock was put to the hammer, and offered fifteen shillings, thus completely discouraging a few of the natives who had concealed the hands and weights of the clock, and hoped to secure the article at the reasonable figure of about a crown. To the Captain's surprise and annoyance, be found his mate his only competitor, and between them they raised the price to thirty shillings, at which figure it was knocked down to the Captain, who had it promptly placed on a barrow and wheeled down to the quay.

"Were you desperate needin' a nock?" asked the mate, coming after him.

"I wass on the look-out for a nock like that for years," said the Captain, apparently charmed with his possession.

"I'll give you five-and-thirty shillings for't," said the mate, but Para Handy wasn't selling. He had the clock on board, and spent at least an hour investigating its interior, with results that from his aspect seemed thoroughly disappointing. He approached Dougie and informed him that he had changed his mind, and was willing to hand over the clock for five-and-thirty shillings. The bargain was eageriy seized by Dougie, who paid the money and submitted his purchase to an examination even more exhaustive than the Captain.

Half an hour later the engineer and Sunny Jim had to separate the Captain and the mate, who were at each other's throats, the latter frantically demanding back his money or a share of whatever the former had found inside the clock.

"The man's daft," protested Para Handy; "the only thing that was in the clock wass the works and an empty bottle."

"The Tarbert spae-wife said I would find a fortune in a clock like that," spluttered Dougie.

"Holy smoke! She said the same to me," confessed the Captain. "And did she say that eatin' fish wass dangerous?"

"She did that," said the mate. "Did she tell you to keep your bed on the first o' the month in case o' accidents?"

"Her very words!" said the Captain. "Did she tell you to beware o' a man wi' black whiskers that came from Australia?" and he looked at the engineer.

"She told me he was my bitterest enemy," said the mate.

"And that's the way ye had the pick at me!" exclaimed the engineer. "Ye're a couple o' Hielan' cuddies; man, I never wass nearer Australia than the River Plate."

On the following day a clock went cheap at the head of the quay for fifteen shillings, and the loss was amicably shared by Para Handy and his mate, but any allusion to Tarbert Fair and fortune-telling has ever since been bitterly resented by them both.

38. *The Hair Lotion*

DOUGIE, the mate, had so long referred to his family album as a proof of the real existence of old friends regarding whom he had marvellous stories to tell, that the crew finally demanded its production. He protested that it would be difficult to get it out of the house, as his wife had it fair in the middle of the parlour table, on top of the Family Bible.

"Ye can ask her for the len' o't, surely," said the Captain. "There's nobody goin' to pawn it on her. Tell her it's to show your shipmates what a tipper she wass hersel' when she wass in her prime."

"She's in her prime yet," said the mate, with some annoyance.

"Chust that!" said Para Handy. "A handsome gyurl, I'm sure of it; but every woman thinks she wass at her best before her husband mairried her. Let you on that you were bouncin' aboot her beauty, and tell her the enchineer wass dubious — "

"Don't drag me into 't," said the engineer. "You micht hae married Lily Langtry[1] for a' I care; put the blame on the Captain; he's what they ca' a connysure among the girls," a statement on which the Captain darkly brooded for several days after.

The mate ultimately rose to the occasion, and taking advantage of a visit by his wife to her good-sister, came on board one day with the album wrapped in his oilskin trousers. It created the greatest interest on the *Vital Spark*, and an admiration only marred by the discovery that the owner was attempting to pass off a lithograph portrait of the late John Bright[2] as that of his Uncle Sandy.

"My mistake!" he said politely, when the engineer corrected him; "I thocht it wass Uncle Sandy by the whuskers; when I look again I see he hasna the breadth across the shouthers."

"Wha's this chap like a body-snatcher?" asked the engineer, turning over another page of the album. "If I had a face like that I wad try and no' keep mind o't."

"You're a body-snatcher yoursel'," said the mate warmly, "and that's my advice to you. Buy specs Macphail; you're spoilin' your eyes wi' readin' them novelles."

"Holy smoke!" cried the Captain; "it's a picture o' yoursel', Dougie. Man! what a heid o' hair!"

"I had a fair quantity," said the mate, passing his hand sadly over a skull which was now as bare as a bollard. "I'm sure I don't ken what way I lost it."

"Short bunks for sleepin' in," suggested the Captain kindly; "that's the worst o' bein' a sailor."

"I tried everything, from paraffin oil to pumice-stone, but nothing did a bit of good; it came oot in handfuls."

"I wad hae left her," said the engineer. "When a wife tak's her hands to ye the law says ye can leave her and tak' the weans wi' ye."

"I see ye hae been consultin' the lawyers," retorted the mate readily; "what way's your ear keepin' efter your last argument wi' the flet-iron?" and Macphail retired in dudgeon to his engines.

Sunny Jim regarded Dougie's portrait thoughtfully. "Man!" he said, "if the Petroloid Lotion had been invented in them days ye could hae had your hair yet. That's the stuff! Fair champion! Rub it on the doorstep and ye didna need to keep a bass. The hair mak's a difference, richt enough; your face is jist the same's it used to be, but the hair in the photo mak's ye twenty years younger. It's as nice a photo as ever I seed; there's money in 't."

"None o' your dydoes noo!" said the mate, remembering how Sunny Jim had found money in the exploitation of the Tobermory whale. "If you think I would make an exhibeetion o' my photygraph — "

"Exhibeetion my aunty!" exclaimed Sunny Jim. "Ye're no' an Edna May[3]. But I'll tell ye whit we could dae. Thae Petroloid Lotion folks is keen on testimonials. A' ye hae to dae is to get Macphail to write a line for ye saying ye lost yer hair in a biler explosion, and tried Petroloid, and it brocht it back in a couple o' weeks. Get a photograph o' yersel' the way ye are the noo and send it, and this yin wi' the testimonial, lettin' on the new yin's the way ye looked immediately efter the explosion, and this yin's the way ye look since ye took to usin' the lotion."

"Capital!" cried the Captain, slapping his knees. "For ingenuity you're chust sublime, Jum."

"Sublime enough," said Dougie cautiously, "but I thocht you said there wass money in it."

"So there is," said Sunny Jim. "The Petroloid Lotion folk'll gie ye a pound or twa for the testimonial; I kent a chap that made his livin' oot o' curin' himsel' o' diseases he never had, wi' pills he never saw except in pictures. He was a fair don at describin' a buzzin' in the ear, a dizzy heid, or a pain alang the spine o' his back, and was dragged back frae the brink o' the grave a thoosand times, by his way o't, under a different name every time. Macphail couldna touch him at a testimonial for anything internal, but there's naething to hinder Macphail puttin' a bit thegither aboot the loss and restoration o' Dougie's hair. Are ye game, Dougie?"

The mate consented dubiously, and the engineer was called upon to indite the requisite document, which took him a couple of evenings, on one of which the mate was taken ashore at Rothesay and photographed in the Captain's best blue pilot pea-jacket. The portraits and the testimonial were duly sent to the address which was found in the advertisement of Petroloid's Lotion for the Hair, a gentle hint being included that some "recognition" would be looked for, the phrase being Sunny Jim's. Then the crew of the *Vital Spark* resigned themselves to a patient wait of several days for an acknowledgment.

Three weeks passed, and Sunny Jim's scheme was sadly confessed a failure, for nothing happened, and the cost of the Rothesay photograph, which had been jointly borne by the crew on the understanding that they were to share alike in the products of it, was a subject of frequent and unfeeling remarks from the engineer, who suggested that the mate had got a remittance and said nothing about it. But one afternoon the Captain picked up a newspaper, and turning, as was his wont, to the pictorial part of it, gave an exclamation on beholding the two portraits of his mate side by side in the midst of a Petroloid advertisement.

"Holy smoke! Dougie," he cried, "here you are ass large ass life like a futbaal player or a man on his trial for manslaughter."

"Michty! iss that me?" said the mate incredulously. "I had no notion they would put me in the papers. If I kent that I would never have gone in for the ploy."

"Ye look guilty," said the engineer, scrutinising the blurred lineaments of his shipmate in the newspaper. "Which is the explosion yin? The testimonial's a' richt onyway; it's fine," and he read his own composition with complete approval —

I unfortunately lost all my hair in a boiler explosion, and tried all the doctors, but none of them could bring it back. Then I heard of your wonderful Petroloid Lotion, and got a small bottle, which I rubbed in night and morning as described. In a week there was a distinct improvement. In a fortnight I had to have my head shorn twice, and now it is as thick as ever it was. I will recommend your Lotion to all my friends, and you are at liberty to make any use of this you like. — (Signed) Dougald Campbell, Captain, *Vital Spark.*

"What's that?" cried Para Handy, jumping up. "Captain! who said he was captain?"

"The advertisement," said the engineer guiltily. "I never wrote 'captain'; they've gone and shifted a lot o' things I wrote, and spiled the grammar and spellin'. Fancy the way they spell distinck!"

A few days later a box was delivered on the *Vital Spark* which at first was fondly supposed to be a case of whisky lost by somebody's mistake, but was found on examination to be directed to the mate. It was opened eagerly, and revealed a couple of dozen of the Petroloid specific, with a letter containing the grateful acknowledgments of the manufacturers, and expressing a generous hope that as the lotion had done so much to restore their correspondent's hair, he would distribute the accompanying consigninents among all his bald-headed friends.

"Jum," said the Captain sadly, "when you're in the trum for makin' money efter this, I'll advise you to tak' the thing in hand yoursel' and leave us oot of it."

Politics, International Affairs and the Crew of the Vital Spark

A steam-lighter, whether or not "the smertest boat in the tred", going about her routine business on the peaceful waters of the Clyde and in remote West Highland harbours would seem comfortably removed from the troubles of the wider world. However, as we shall see, the problems of the outside world increasingly impinge on the *Vital Spark* and her crew.

Nowhere does this happen more dramatically than in the next story "Para Handy and the Navy". The tale starts off with the crew being lectured by Macphail on the plight of the Royal Navy. This was a highly topical issue of the day. German–British naval rivalry, on the increase since the German Naval Act of 1898 had laid the foundations for a German battle fleet, came to a head in 1906.

In that year the Royal Navy launched the first of a new and powerful class of battleships, H.M.S. *Dreadnought*. This ship represented a major qualitative leap in warship design and mounting ten 12–inch guns was both more powerful, faster and better protected than any contemporary warship. Germany responded with the 1906 Naval Act which committed her to matching British battleship production both in quantity and quality. In 1909 British Naval Estimates were considerably increased and the new construction programme was publicly justified by reference to the German naval threat.

Feelings in Britain became raised, as this story indicates, and a popular Jingoistic slogan of the day was "We want eight and we won't wait!" The eight in question being battleships of the Dreadnought class.

A later story "The Stowaway" deals with the German spy scare. In the years before the First World War there was consisderable concern about German espionage, war plans and preparations. This led, among other things, to the passing of the Official Secrets Act in 1911. A substantial body of literature was published on the theme of a future war between Britain and Germany, the best known example of this genre being Erskine Childers' "The Riddle of the Sands", published in 1903.

As we have seen from "Pension Farms" the crew generally keep abreast of national politics and home affairs as well as being alert to the latest developments on the international scene. In "The Goat", Para's account of Wully Crawford, Tarbert's first "polisman", is initiated by a discussion of the conduct of the Metropolitan Police and Home Secretary Winston Churchill at the "Siege of Sidney Street" — the incident in Stepney in 1911 with a gang of Latvian anarchists and criminals led, it was thought, by the mysterious figure of Peter Piaktow, "Peter the Painter". While Para had nothing but praise for the Home Secretary (who Macphail the engineer, with a degree of exaggeration, describes as shaking 127 bullets out of his Astrakan coat) "Man, he must be a tough young fellow, Wunston! Them bullets give you an awfu' bang."; his view of the London police was not entirely complimentary "...the London polisman iss greatly wantin' in agility...". He suggests that they could take lessons from the Tarbert "polisman" who managed to keep law and order among the unruly Tarbert trawlermen by virtue of his agility.

39. *Para Handy and the Navy*

MACPHAIL the engineer sat on an upturned bucket reading the weekly paper, and full of patriotic alarm at the state of the British Navy.

"What are you groanin' and sniffin' at?" asked the Captain querulously. "I should think mysel' that by this time you would be tired o' Mrs Atherton. Whatna prank iss she up to this time?"

"It's no' Mrs Atherton," said the reader; "it's something mair important; it's the Germans."

"Holy smoke!" said Para Handy, "are they findin' them oot, noo? Wass I not convinced there wass something far, far wrong wi' them? Break the full parteeculars to me chently, Mac, and you, Jim, go and get the dinner ready; you're far too young to hear the truth aboot the Chermans. Which o' the Chermans iss it, Mac? Some wan in a good poseetion, I'll be bound! It's a mercy that we're sailors; you'll no' find mich aboot the wickedness o' sailors in the papers."

"The British Navy's a' to bleezes!" said Macphail emphatically. "Here's Germany buildin' Dreadnought men-o'-war as hard's she can, and us palaverin'[1] awa' oor time."

Para Handy looked a little disappointed. "It's politics you're on," said he; "and I wass thinkin' it wass maybe another aawful scandal in Society. That's the worst o' the newspapers — you never know where yuu are wi' them; a week ago it wass nothing but the high jeenks of the beauteous Mrs Atherton. Do you tell me the Brutish Navy's railly done?"

"Complete!" said the engineer.

"Weel, that's a peety!" said Para Handy sympathetically; "it'll put a lot o' smert young fellows oot o' jobs; I know a Tarbert man called Colin Kerr that had a good poseetion on the *Formidable*[2]. I'm aawful sorry aboot Colin."

The engineer resumed his paper, and the Vital Spark chug-chugged her sluggish way between the Gantocks[3] and the Cloch, with Dougie at the wheel, his nether garments hung precariously on the half of a pair of braces. "There's nothing but dull tred everywhere," said he. "They're stoppin' a lot o' the railway steamers, too."

"The state o' the British Navy's mair important than the stoppage o' a wheen passenger steamers," explained the engineer. "If you chaps read the papers ye would see this country's in a bad poseetion. We used to rule the sea — "

"We did that!" said the Captain heartily; "I've seen us doin' it! Brutain's hardy sons!"

"And noo the Germans is gettin' the upper hand o' us; they'll soon hae faur mair Dreadnoughts than we hae. We're only buildin' four. Fancy that! Four Dreadnoughts at a time like this, wi' nae work on the Clyde, and us wi' that few Territorials we hae to go to the fitba' matches and haul them oot to jine by the hair o' the heid. We've lost the two-Power standard."[4]

"Man, it's chust desperate!" said the Captain. "We'll likely advertise for 't. What's the — what's the specialty aboot the Dreadnoughts?"

"It's the only cless o' man-o'-war that's coonted noo," said the engineer; "a tip-top battle-winner. If ye havena Dreadnoughts ye micht as weel hae dredgers."

"Holy smoke! what a lot o' lumber aal the other men-o'-war must be!" remarked the Captain. "That'll be the way they're givin' them up and payin' off the hands."

"Wha said they were givin' them up?" asked the engineer snappishly.

"Beg pardon! beg pardon! I thocht I heard you mention it yon time I remarked on Colin Kerr. I thocht that maybe aal the other boats wass absolute, and we would see them next week lyin' in the Kyles o' Bute wi' washin's hung oot on them."

"There's gaun to be nae obsolete boats in the British Navy efter this," said the engineer; "we're needin' every man-o'-war that'll haud thegither. The Germans has their eye on us."

"Dougie," said the Captain firmly, with a glance at the deshabille of his mate, "go doon this instant and put on your jecket! The way you are, you're not a credit to the boat."

A terrific bang broke upon the silence of the Firth; the crew of the *Vital Spark* turned their gaze with one accord towards the neighbourhood of Kilcreggan, whence the report seemed to have proceeded, and were frightfully alarmed a second or two afterwards when a shell burst on the surface of the sea a few hundred yards or so from them, throwing an enormous column of water into the air.

"What did I tell ye!" cried Macphail, as he dived below to his engine-room.

"Holy smoke!" exclaimed Para Handy; "did ye notice anything, Dougie?"

"I think I did!" said the mate, considerably perturbed; "there must be some wan blastin'."

"Yon wassna a blast," said the Captain; "they're firin' cannons at us from Portkill."[5]

"There's a pant for ye!" exclaimed Sunny Jim, dodging behind the funnel.

"What for would they be firin' cannons at us?" asked the mate, with a ludicrous feeling that even the jacket advised a minute or two ago by the Captain would now be a most desirable protection.

Another explosion from the fort at Portkill postponed the Captain's answer, and this time the bursting shell seemed a little closer.

"Jim," said the mate appealingly, "would ye mind takin' haud o' this wheel till I go down below and get my jacket? If I'm to be shot, I'll be shot like a Hielan' chentleman and no' in my shirt-sleeves."

"You'll stay where you are!" exclaimed the Captain, greatly excited; "you'll stay where you are, and die at your post like a Brutish sailor. This iss WAR. Port her heid in for Macinroy's Point[6], Dougald, and you, Macphail, put on to her every pound of steam she'll cairry. I wish to Providence I had chust the wan wee Union Jeck."

"Whit would ye dae wi' a Union Jeck?" asked the engineer, putting up his head and ducking nervously as another shot boomed over the Firth.

"I would nail it to the mast!" said Para Handy buttoning his coat. "It would show them Cherman chentlemen we're the reg'lar he'rts of oak."

"Ye don't think it's Germans that's firin', dae ye?" asked the engineer, cautiously putting out his head again. "It's the Garrison Artillery that's firin' frae Portkill."

"Whit are the silly duvvles firin' at us for, then?" asked Para Handy; "I'm sure we never did them any herm."

"I ken whit for they're firin'," said the engineer maliciously; "they're takin' the *Vital Spark* for yin o' them German Dreadnoughts. Ye have nae idea o' the fear o' daith that's on the country since it lost the two-Power standard."

This notion greatly alarmed the Captain, being distinctly complimentary to his vessel; but his vanity was soon dispelled, for Sunny Jim pointed out that the last shot had fallen far behind them, in proximity to a floating target now for the first time seen. "They're jist at big-gun practice," he remarked with some relief, "and we're oot o' the line o' fire."

"Of course we are!" said Para Handy. "I kent that aal along. Man, Macphail, but you were tumid, tumid! You're losin' aal your nerve wi' readin' aboot the Chermans."

40. *Piracy in the Kyles*

"I'M GOIN' doon below to put on my sluppers," said the Captain, as the vessel puffed her leisured way round Buttock Point[1]; "keep your eye on the *Collingwood*[2], an' no' run into her; it would terribly vex the Admirality."

The mate, with a spoke of the wheel in the small of his back, and his hands in his trousers pockets, looked along the Kyles towards Colintraive, and remarked that he wasn't altogether blind.

"I didna say you were," said the Captain; "I wass chust advisin' caaution. You canna be too caautious, and if anything would happen it's mysel' would be the man responsible. Keep her heid a point away, an' no' be fallin' asleep till I get my sluppers on; you'll mind you were up last night pretty late in Tarbert."

Macphail, the engineer, projected a perspiring head from his engine-room, and wiped his brow with a wad of oily waste. "Whit's the argyment?" he asked. "Is this a coal-boat or a Convention o' Royal Burghs?[3] I'm in the middle o' a fine story in the *People's Frien'*[4], and I canna hear mysel' readin' for you chaps barkin' at each other. I wish ye would talk wee."

Para Handy looked at him with a contemptuous eye, turned his back on him, and confined his address to Dougie. "I'll never feel safe in the Kyles of Bute," he said, "till them men-o'-war iss oot o' here. I'm feared for a collusion."

"There's no' much chance of a collusion wi' a boat like that," said the mate, with a glance at the great sheer hulk of the discarded man-o'-war.

"You would wonder!" said Para Handy. "I haf seen a smert enough sailor before now come into a collusion wi' the whole o' Cowal. And he wassna tryin 't either! Keep her off yet, Dougald."

With his slippers substituted for his sea-boots, the Captain returned on deck, when the Collingwood was safely left astern; and, looking back, watched a couple of fishermen culling mussels off the lower plates of the obsolete ship of war. "They're a different cless of men aboot the Kyles from what there used to be," said he, "or it wouldn't be only bait they would be liftin' off a boat like that. If she wass there when Hurricane Jeck wass in his prime, he would have the very cannons off her, sellin' them for junk in Greenock. There's no' that hardy Brutish spirit in the boys that wass in't when Hurricane Jeck and me wass on the *Aggie*."

"Tell us the baur," pleaded Sunny Jim, seated on an upturned bucket, peeling the day's potatoes.

"It's not the only baur I could tell you about the same chentleman," said the Captain, "but it's wan that shows you his remarkable agility. Gie me a haud o' that wheel, Dougie; I may ass well be restin' my back ass you, and me the skipper. To let you ken, Jum, Hurricane Jeck wass a perfect chentleman, six feet two, ass broad in the back ass a shippin'-box, and the very duvvle for contrivance. He wass a man that wass namely in the clipper tred to China, and the Board o' Tred had never a hand on him; his navigation wass complete. You know that, Dougie, don't you?"

"Whatever you say yoursel'," replied the mate agreeably, cutting himself a generous plug of navy-blue tobacco. "I have nothing to say aginst the chap — except that he came from Campbeltown."[5]

"He sailed wi' me for three or four years on the *Aggie*," said the Captain, "and a nicer man on a boat you wouldna meet, if you didna contradict him. There wass nothing at aal against his moral character, except that he always shaved himsel' on Sunday, whether he wass needin' it or no'. And a duvvle for recreation! Six feet three, if he wass an inch, and a back like a shippin'-box!"

"Where does the British spirit come in?" inquired the engineer, who was forced to relinquish his story and join his mates.

"Hold you on, and I'll tell you that," said Para Handy. "We were lyin' wan winter night at Tighnabruaich wi' a cargo o' stones for a place they call Glen Caladh, that wass buildin' at the time, and we wanted a bit o' rope for something in parteecular — I think it wass a bit of a net. There wass lyin' at Tighnabruaich at the time a nice wee steamer yat belonging to a chentleman in Gleska that was busy at his business, and nobody wass near her. 'We'll borrow a rope for the night from that nice wee yat,' said Hurricane Jeck, as smert as anything, and when it wass dark he took the punt and went off and came back wi' a rope that did the business. 'They havena much sense o' ropes that moored that boat in the Kyles,' said he; 'they had it flemished down and nate for liftin'. They must be naval architects.' The very next night did Jeck no' take the punt again and go oot to the wee steam-yat, and come back wi' a couple o' india-rubber basses and a weather-gless?"

"Holy smoke!" said Dougie. "Wasn't that chust desperate?"

"We were back at Tighnabruaich a week efter that," continued Para Handy, "and Jeck made some inquiries. Nobody had been near the wee steam-yat, though the name o' her in the Gaalic was the *Eagle*, and Jeck made oot it wass a special dispensation. 'The man that owned her must be deid,' said he, 'or he hasna his wuts aboot him; I'll take a turn aboard the night wi' a screw-driver, and see that all's in order.' He came back that night wi' a bag o' cleats, a binnacle, half a dozen handy blocks, two dozen o' empty bottles, and a quite good water-breaker.

" 'They may call her the *Eagle* if they like,' says he, 'but I call her the *Silver Mine*. I wish they would put lights on her; I nearly broke my neck on the cabin stairs.'

" 'Mind you, Jeck,' I says to him, 'I don't ken anything aboot it. If you're no' comin' by aal them things honest, it'll give the *Aggie* a bad name.'

" 'It's aal right, Peter,' says he, quite kind. 'Flotsam and jetsam; if you left them there, you don't ken who might lift them!' Oh, a smert, smert sailor, Jeck! Six feet four in his stockin's soles, and a back like a couple o' shippin'-boxes."

"He's gettin' on!" remarked the engineer sarcastically. "I'm gled I wasna his tailor."

"The Glen Caladh job kept us comin' and goin' aal winter,"

pursued the Captain, paying no attention. "Next week we were back again, and Jeck had a talk with the polisman at Tighnabruaich aboot the lower clesses. Jeck said the lower clesses up in Gleska were the worst you ever saw; they would rob the wheels off a railway train. The polisman said he could weel believe it, judgin' from the papers, but, thank the Lord! there wass only honest folk in the Kyles of Bute. 'It's aal right yet,' said Jeck to me that night; 'the man that owns the *Silver Mine*'s in the Necropolis, and never said a word aboot the wee yat in his will.' In the mornin' I saw a clock, a couple o' North Sea charts, a trysail, a galley-stove, two kettles, and a nice decanter lyin' in the hold.

" 'Jeck,' I says, 'is this a flittin'?'

" 'I'll not deceive you, Peter,' he says, quite honest, 'it's a gift'; and he sold the lot on Setturday in Greenock."

"A man like that deserves the jyle," said the engineer indignantly.

"I wouldna caal it aalthegither fair horny," admitted the Captain, "parteecularly as the rest of us never got more than a schooner o' beer or the like o't oot of it; but, man! you must admit the chap's agility! He cairried the business oot single-handed, and there wass few wass better able; he wass six feet six, and had a back on him like a Broomielaw shed. The next time we were in the Kyles, and he went off wi' the punt at night, he came back from the *Silver Mine* wi' her bowsprit, twenty faddom o' chain, two doors, and half a dozen port-holes."

"Oh, to bleezes!" exclaimed Sunny Jim incredulously, "noo you're coddin'! What wye could he steal her port-holes?"

"Quite easy!" said Para Handy. "I didna say he took the holes themsel's, but he twisted off the windows and the brass aboot them. You must mind the chap's agility! And that wassna the end of it, for next time the *Aggie* left the Kyles she had on board a beautiful vernished dinghy, a couple o' masts, no' bad, and a fine brass steam-yat funnel."

"Holy smoke!" said Dougie; "it's a wonder he didna strip the lead off her."

"He had it in his mind," exclaimed the Captain, "but, mind, he never consulted me aboot anythin' and I only kent, as you might say, by accident, when he would be standin' me another schooner. It wass aalways a grief to Jeck that he didna take the boat the way she wass, and sail her where she would be properly appreciated. 'My mistake, chaps!' he would say; 'I might have kent they would miss the masts and funnel!' "

41. *Among the Yachts*

MACPHAIL was stoking carefully and often, like a mother feeding her first baby; keeping his steam at the highest pressure short of blowing off the safety valve, on which he had tied a pig-iron bar; and driving the *Vital Spark* for all she was worth past Cowal. The lighter's bluff bows were high out of water, for she was empty, and she left a wake astern of her like a liner.

"She hass a capital turn of speed when you put her to it," said the Captain, quite delighted; "it's easy seen it's Setturday, and you're in a hurry to be home, Macphail. You're passin' roond that oil-can there the same ass if it wass a tea-pairty you were at, and nobody there but women. It's easy seen it wass a cargo of coals we had the last trip, and there's more in your bunkers than the owner paid for. But it's none o' my business; please yoursel'!"

"We'll easy be at Bowlin' before ten," said Dougie, consulting his watch. "You needna be so desperate anxious."

The engineer mopped himself fretfully with a fistful of oily waste and shrugged his shoulders. "If you chaps like to palaver awa' your time," said he, "it's all the same to me, but I was wantin' to see the end o' the racin'."

"Whatna racin'?" asked the Captain.

"Yat-racin'," said the engineer, with irony. "Ye'll maybe hae heard o't. If ye havena, ye should read the papers. There's a club they ca' the Royal Clyde[1] at Hunter's Quay, and a couple o' boats they ca' the *Shamrock*[2] and the *White Heather*[3] are sailin' among a wheen o' ithers for a cup. I wouldna care if I saw the feenish; you chaps needna bother; just pull doon the skips o' your keps on your e'en when ye pass them, and ye'll no' see onything."

"I don't see much in aal their yat-racin'," said Para Handy.

"If I was you, then, I would try the Eye Infirmary," retorted the engineer, "or wan o' them double-breisted spy-glesses[4]. Yonder the

boats; we're in lots o' time — " and he dived again among his
engines, and they heard the hurried clatter of his shovel.

"Anything wi' Macphail for sport!" remarked the Captain sadly.
"You would think at his time o' life and the morn Sunday, that his
meditaations would be different. . . . Give her a point to starboard,
Dougie, and we'll see them better. Yonder's the *Ma'oona*[5]; if the
duvvle wass wise he would put aboot at wance or he'll hit that patch
o' calm."

"There's an aawful money in them yats!" said the mate, who was
at the wheel.

"I never could see the sense o't," remarked the Captain. . . .
"There's the *Hera*[6] tacking; man, she's smert! smert! Wan o' them
Coats's boats[7]; I wish she would win; I ken a chap that plays the pipes
on her."

Dougie steered as close as he could on the racing cutters with a
sportsman's scrupulous regard for wind and water. "What wan's
that?" he asked, as they passed a thirty-rater which had struck the
calm.

"That's the *Pallas*[8]," said the Captain, who had a curiously
copious knowledge of the craft he couldn't see the sense of.
"Another wan o' the Coats's; every other wan you see belongs to
Paisley. They buy them by the gross, the same ass they were pirns[9],
and distribute them every noo and then among the faimely. If you're
a Coats you lose a lot o' time makin' up your mind what boat you'll
sail to-morrow; the whole o' the Clyde below the Tail o' the Bank[10] is
chock-a-block wi' steamboat-yats and cutters the Coats's canna hail
a boat ashore from to get a sail, for they canna mind their names.
Still-and-on, there's nothing wrong wi' them — tip-top sportin'
chentlemen!"

"I sometimes wish, mysel', I had taken to the yats," said Dougie;
"it's a suit or two o' clothes in the year and a pleasant occupaation.
Most o' the time in canvas sluppers."

"You're better the way you are," said Para Handy; "there's
nothing bates the mercantile marine for makin' sailors. Brutain's
hardy sons! We could do withoot yats, but where would we be
withoot oor coalboats? Look at them chaps sprauchlin'[11] on the
deck; if they saw themsel's they would see they want another fut on
that main-sheet. I wass a season or two in the yats mysel' — the good

old *Marjory*[12]. No' a bad job at aal, but aawful hurried. Holy smoke! the way they kept you jumpin' here and there the time she would be racin'! I would chust as soon be in a lawyer's office. If you stopped to draw your breath a minute you got yon across the ear from a swingin' boom. It's a special breed o' sailor-men you need for racin'-yats, and the worst you'll get iss off the Islands."

"It's a cleaner job at any rate than carryin' coals," remarked the mate, with an envious eye on the spotless decks of a heeling twenty-tonner.

"Clean enough, I'll alloo, and that's the worst of it," said Para Handy. "You might ass weel be a chamber-maid — up in the mornin' scourin' brass and scrubbin' floors, and goin' ashore wi' a fancy can for sixpenceworth o' milk and a dozen o' syphon soda. Not much navigation there, my lad! ... If I wass that fellow I would gybe her there and set my spinnaker to starboard; what do you think yoursel', Macphail?"

"I thocht you werena interested," said the engineer, who had now reduced his speed.

"I'm not much interested, but I'm duvellish keen," said Para Handy. "Keep her goin' chust like that, Macphail; we'll soon be up wi' the *Shamrock* and the *Heather*; they're yonder off Loch Long."

A motor-boat regatta was going on at Dunoon; the *Vital Spark* seemed hardly to be moving as some of the competitors flashed past her, breathing petrol fumes.

"You canna do anything like that," said Dougie to the engineer, who snorted.

"No," said Macphail contemptuously, "I'm an engineer; I never was much o' a hand at the sewin'-machine. I couldna lower mysel' to handle engines ye could put in your waistcoat pocket."

"Whether you could or no'," said Para Handy "the times iss changin', and the motor-launch iss coming for to stop."

"That's whit she's aye daein'," retorted the engineer; "stoppin's her strong p'int; gie me a good substantial compound engine; nane o' your hurdy-gurdies! I wish the wind would fresh a bit, for there's the *Shamrock* and her mainsail shakin'." He dived below, and the *Vital Spark* in a little had her speed reduced to a crawl that kept her just abreast of the drifting racers.

"Paddy's hurricane — up and doon the mast," said Dougie in a tone of disappointment. "I would like, mysel', to see Sir Thomas Lipton[13] winnin', for it's there I get my tea."

Para Handy extracted a gully-knife from the depths of his trousers pockets, opened it, spat on the blade for luck, and, walking forward, stuck it in the mast, where he left it. "That's the way to get wind," said he; "many a time I tried it, and it never fails. Stop you, and you'll see a breeze immediately. Them English skippers, Sycamore and Bevis[14], havena the heid to think o't."

"Whit's the use o' hangin' on here?" said the engineer, with a wink at Dougie; "it's time we were up the river; I'll better get her under weigh again."

The Captain turned on him with a flashing eye. "You'll do nothing o' the kind, Macphail," said he, "we'll stand by here and watch the feenish, if it's any time before the Gleska Fair."

Shamrock, having split tacks off Kilcreggan, laid away to the west, while *White Heather* stood in for the Holy Loch, seeking the evening breeze that is apt to blow from the setting sun. It was the crisis of the day, and the crew of the *Vital Spark* watched speechlessly for a while the yachts manoeuvring. For an hour the cutter drifted on this starboard leg, and Sunny Jim, for reasons of his own, postponed the tea.

"It wants more knifes," said Para Handy; "have you wan, Dougie?" but Dougie had lost his pocket-knife a week ago, and the engineer had none either.

"If stickin' knifes in the mast would raise the wind," said Sunny Jim, "there would be gales by this time, for I stuck the tea-knife in an oor ago."

"Never kent it to fail before!" said Para Handy. … "By George! it's comin'. Yonder's Bevis staying!"

White Heather, catching the wind, reached for the closing lap of the race with a bone in her mouth, and Para Handy watched her, fascinated, twisting the buttons off his waistcoat in his intense excitement. With a turn or two of the wheel the mate put the *Vital Spark* about and headed for the mark; Macphail deserted his engine and ran forward to the bow.

"The *Heather* hass it, Dougald," said the Captain thankfully; "I'm vexed for you, considerin' the place you get your tea."

"Hold you on, Peter," said the mate; "there's the *Shamrock* fetchin'; a race is no' done till it's feenished." His hopes were justified. *Shamrock*, only a few lengths behind, got the same light puff of wind in her sails, and rattled home a winner by half a minute.

"Macphail!" bawled the Captain, "I'll be much obleeged if you'd take your place again at your bits of engines, and get under weigh; it's any excuse wi' you for a diversion, and it's time we werena here."

42. *Fog*

IN A silver-grey fog that was not unpleasant, the *Vital Spark* lay at Tarbert quay, and Dougie read a belated evening paper.

"Desperate fog on the Clyde!" he said to his shipmates; "we're the lucky chaps that's here and oot o't! It hasna lifted in Gleska for two days, and there's any amount o' boats amissin' between the Broomielaw and Bowlin'."

"Tck! tck! issn't that deplorable?" said the Captain. "Efter you wi' the paper, Dougald. It must be full o' accidents."

"The Campbeltown boat iss lost since Setturday, and they're lookin' for her wi' lanterns up and doon the river. I hope she hassna many passengers; the poor sowls 'll be stervin'."

"Duvvle the fear!" said Para Handy; "not on the Campbeltown boat ass long ass she has her usual cargo[1]. I would sooner be lost wi' a cargo o' Campbeltown for a week than spend a month in wan o' them hydropathics."

"Two sailors went ashore at Bowlin' from the *Benmore*, and they havena been heard of since," proceeded the mate; "they couldna find their way back t o the ship."

"And what happened then?" asked Para Handy.

"Nothing," replied the mate. "That's all; they couldna find their way back."

"Holy smoke!" reflected Para Handy, with genuine surprise; "they're surely ill off for news in the papers nooadays; or they must have a poor opeenion o' sailor-men. They'll be thinkin' they should aalways be teetotalers."

The Captain got the paper to read for himself a little later, and discovered that the missing *Benmore* men had not lost themselves in the orthodox sailor way, but were really victims of the fog, and his heart went out to them. "I've seen the same thing happen to mysel'," he remarked. "It wass the time that Hurricane Jeck and me wass on the *Julia*. There wass a fog come on us wan time there so thick you could almost cut it up and sell it for briquettes."

"Help!" exclaimed Macphail.

"Away, you, Macphail, and study your novelles; what way's Lady Fitzgerald gettin' on in the chapter you're at the noo? It's a wonder to me you're no' greetin'," retorted the Captain; and this allusion to the sentimental tears of the engineer sent him down, annoyed, among his engines.

"It wass a fog that lasted near a week, and we got into it on a Monday mornin' chust below the Cloch. We were makin' home for Gleska. We fastened up to the quay at Gourock, waitin' for a change, and the thing that vexed us most wass that Hurricane Jeck and me wass both invited for that very night to a smaal tea-perty oot in Kelvinside."[2]

"It's yoursel' wass stylish!" said the mate. "It must have been before you lost your money in the City Bank."[3]

"It wassna style at aal, but a Cowal gyurl we knew that wass cook to a chentleman in Kelvinside, and him away on business in Liverpool," explained the Captain. "Hurricane Jeck wass in love wi' the gyurl at the time, and her name wass Bella. 'This fog 'll last for a day or two,' said Jeck in the efternoon; 'it's a peety to lose the ploy at Bella's party.'

" 'What would you propose, yoursel'?" I asked him, though I wass the skipper. I had aye a great opeenion o' Hurricane Jeck's agility.

" 'What's to hinder us takin' the train to Gleska, and leavin' the *Julia* here?' said Jeck, ass smert ass anything. 'There's nobody goin' to run away wi' her.'

"Jeck and me took the train for Gleska, and left the enchineer — a chap Macnair — in full command o' the vessel. I never could trust a man o' the name o' Macnair from that day on.

"It wass a splendid perty, and Jeck wass chust sublime. I never partook in a finer perty — two or three hens, a pie the size o' a binnacle, and wine! — the wine was chust miraculous. Bella kept it comin' in in quantities. The coalman wass there, and the letter-carrier, and the man that came for the grocer's orders, and there wassna a gas in the hoose that wassna bleezin'. You could see that Hurricane Jeck had his he'rt on makin' everybody happy. It wass him that danced the hornpipe on the table, and mostly him that carried the piano doon the stair to the dinin'-room. He fastened a clothes-line aft on the legs o' her, laid doon a couple o' planks, and slided her. 'Tail on to the rope, my laads!' says he, 'and I'll go in front and steady her.' But the clothes-rope broke, and the piano landed on his back. He never had the least suspeecion, but cairried her doon the rest o' the stair himsel', and put her in poseetion. And efter a' oor bother there wass nobody could play. 'That's the worst o' them fore-and-aft pianos!' said Jeck, ass vexed ass anything; 'they're that much complicated!'

"We were chust in the middle o' the second supper and Bella wass bringin' in cigars, when her maister opened the door wi' his chubb, and dandered in! There wassna a train for Liverpool on account o' the fog!

" 'What's this?' says he, and Bella nearly fainted.

" 'It's Miss Maclachlan's birthday' — meanin' Bella — answered Jeck, ass nice ass possible. 'You're chust in the nick o' time,' and he wass goin' to introduce the chentleman, for Jeck wass a man that never forgot his mainners.

" 'What's that piano doin' there?' the chentleman asked, quite furious.

" 'You may weel ask that,' said Jeck, 'for aal the use it iss, we would be better wi' a concertina,' and Bella had to laugh.

" 'I've a good mind to send for the polis,' said her maister.

" 'You needna bother,' said Bella; 'he's comin' anyway, ass soon ass he's off his bate and shifted oot o' his uniform,' and that wass the only intimation and invitation Hurricane Jeck ever got that Bella wass goin' to mairry Macrae the polisman.

"We spent three days in the fog in Gleska, and aal oor money," proceeded Para Handy, "and then, 'It's time we were back on the hooker,' said Hurricane Jeck; 'I can mind her name; it's the *Julia*.'

" 'It's no' so much her name that bothers me,' says I; 'it's her latitude and longitude; where in aal the world did we leave her?'

" 'Them pink wines!' said Jeck. 'That's the rock we split on, Peter! The fog would never have lasted aal this time if we had taken Brutish spirits.'

"It wass chust luck we found the half o' a railway ticket in Jeck's pocket, and it put us in mind that we left the boat at Gourock. We took the last train doon, and landed there wi' the fog ass bad ass ever; ay, worse! it wass that thick noo, it wassna briquettes you would make wi't, but marble nocks and mantelpieces.

" 'We left the *Julia* chust fornenst this shippin'box,' said Jeck, on Gourock quay, and, sure enough there wass the boat below, and a handy ladder. Him and me went doon the ladder to the deck, and whustled on Macnair. He never paid the least attention.

" 'He'll be in his bed,' said Jeck; 'gie me a ha'ad o' a bit o' marlin'.'

"We went doon below and found him sleepin' in the dark; Jeck took a bit' o' the marlin', and tied him hands and feet, and the two o' us went to bed, ass tired ass anything, wi' oor boots on. You never, never, never saw such fog!

"Jeck wass the first to waken in the mornin', and he struck a match.

" 'Peter,' said he, quite solemn, when it went oot, 'have we a stove wi' the name Eureka printed on the door?'

" 'No, nor Myreeka,' says I; 'there's no' a door at aal on oor stove, and fine ye ken it!'

" He lay a while in the dark, sayin' nothing, and then he struck another match. 'Is Macnair redheided, do you mind?' says he when the match went oot.

" 'Ass black ass the ace o' spades!' says I."

" 'That wass what wass runnin' in my own mind,' said Jeck; 'but I thocht I maybe wass mistaken. WE'RE IN OOR BED IN THE WRONG BOAT!'

"And we were! We lowsed the chap and told him right enough it wass oor mistake, and gave him two or three o' Bella's best cigars, and then we went ashore to look for the *Julia*. You never saw such fog! And it wass Friday mornin'.

" 'Where's the *Julia*?' we asked the harbour-maister. 'Her!' says he; 'the enchineer got tired waitin' on ye, and got a couple o' quayheid chaps and went crawlin' up the river wi' the tide on We'nesday!'

" So Hurricane Jeck and me lost more than oorsel's in the fog; we lost oor jobs," concluded Para Handy. "Never put your trust in a man Macnair!"

43. *Christmas on the Vital Spark*

THERE WAS something, plainly, weighing on Dougie's mind; he let his tea get cold, and merely toyed with his kippered herring; at intervals he sighed — an unsailor-like proceeding which considerably annoyed the engineer, Macphail.

"Whit's the maitter wi' ye?" he querulously inquired. "Ye would think it was the Fast, to hear ye. Are you ruein' your misspent life?"

"Never you mind Macphail," advised the Captain; "a chentleman should aalways hev respect for another chentleman in tribulation. What way's the mustress, Dougald?" He held a large tablespoonful of marmalade suspended in his hand, while he put the question with genuine solicitude; Dougie's wife was the very woman, he knew, to have something seriously wrong with her just when other folk were getting into a nice and jovial spirit for New Year.

"Oh, she's fine, thanky, Peter," said the mate; "there's nothing spashial wrong wi' er except, noo and then, the rheumatism."

"She should always keep a raw potato in her pocket," said Para Handy; "it's the only cure."

"She micht as weel keep a nutmeg-grater in her coal-bunker," remarked the engineer. "Whit wye can a raw potato cure the rheumatism?"

"It's the — it's the influence," explained Para Handy vaguely. "Look at them Vibrators!¹ But you'll believe in nothing, Macphail, unless you read aboot it in wan o' them novelles; you're chust an unfidel!"

Dougie sighed again, and the engineer, protesting that his meal had been spoiled for him by his shipmate's melancholy, hurriedly finished his fifth cup of tea and went on deck. There were no indications that it was Christmas Eve; two men standing on the quay were strictly sober. Crarae is still a place where they thoroughly celebrate the Old New Year after a first rehearsal with the statutory one.

"If you're not feelin' very brusk you should go to your bed, Dougie," remarked the Captain sympathetically. "The time to stop trouble iss before it starts."

"There's nothing wrong wi' me," the mate assured him sadly; "we're weel off, livin' on the fat o' the land, and some folk stervin'."

"We are that!" agreed Para Handy, helping himself to Dougie's second kipper. "Were you thinkin' of any wan parteecular?"

"Did you know a quarryman here by the name o' Col Maclachlan?" asked the mate, and Para Handy, having carefully reflected, confessed he didn't.

"Neither did I," said Dougie; "but he died a year ago and left a weedow yonder, and the only thing that's for her iss the poorshouse at Lochgilpheid."

"Holy smoke!" exclaimed the Captain; "isn't that chust desperate! If it wass a cargo of coals we had this trip, we might be givin' her a pickle, but she couldna make mich wi' a bag o' whinstones."

"They tell me she's goin' to start and walk tomorrow mornin' to Lochgilpheid, and she's an old done woman. She says she would be affronted for to go in the *Cygnet* or the *Minard*[2], for every one on board would ken she was goin' to the poorshouse."

"Oh, to the muschief!" said Para Handy; "Macphail wass right — a body might ass weel be at a funeral ass in your company, and it comin' on to the New Year!' He fled on deck from this doleful atmosphere in the fo'c'sle, but came down again in a minute or two.

"I wass thinkin' to mysel'," he remarked with diffidence to the mate, "that if the poor old body would come wi' us, we could give her a lift to Ardrishaig; what do you say?"

"Whatever you say yoursel'," said the mate; "but we would need to be aawfu' careful o' her feelin's, and she wouldna like to come doon the quay unless it wass in the dark."

"We'll start at six o'clock, then," said the Captain, "if you'll go ashore the now and make arrangements, and you needna bother aboot her feelin's; we'll handle them like gless."

As an alternative to walking to the poorhouse, the sail to Lochgilphead by the Vital Spark was quite agreeable to the widow, who turned up at the quay in the morning quite alone, too proud even to take her neighbours into her confidence. Para Handy helped her on board and made her comfortable.

"You're goin' to get a splendid day!" he assured her cheerfully. "Dougie, iss it nearly time for oor cup o' tea?"

"It'll be ready in a meenute," said Dougie, with delightful promptness, and went down to rouse Sunny Jim.

"We aalways have a cup o' tea at six o'clock on the *Fital Spark*," the Captain informed the widow, with a fluency that astonished even the engineer. "And an egg; sometimes two. Jum 'll boil you an egg."

"I'm sure I'm an aawful bother to you!" protested the poor old widow feebly.

"Bother!" said Para Handy; "not the slightest! The tea's there anyway. And the eggs. Efter that we'll have oor breakfast."

"I'll be a terrible expense to you," said the unhappy widow; and Para Handy chuckled jovially.

"Expense! Nonsense, Mrs Maclachlan! Everything's paid for here by the owners; we're allooed more tea and eggs and things than we can eat. I'll be thinkin' mysel' it's a sin the way we hev to throw them sometimes over the side" — at which astounding effort of the imagination Macphail retired among his engines and relieved his feelings by a noisy application of the coaling shovel.

"I have the money for my ticket," said the widow, fumbling nervously for her purse.

"Ticket!" said Para Handy, with magnificent alarm. "If the Board o' Tred heard o' us chergin' money for a passage in the *Fital Spark*, we would never hear the end o't; it would cost us oor certuficate."

The widow enjoyed her tea intensely, and Para Handy talked incessantly about everything and every place but Lochgilphead, while the *Vital Spark* chugchugged on her fateful way down Loch Fyne to the poorhouse.

"Did you know my man?" the woman suddenly asked, in an interval which even Para Handy's wonderful eloquence couldn't fill up.

"Iss it Col Maclachlan?" he exclaimed. "Fine! me'm; fine! Col and me wass weel acquent; it wass that that made me take the liberty to ask you. There wass never a finer man in Argyllshire than poor Col — a regular chentleman! I mind o' him in the — in the quarry. So do you, Dougie, didn't you?"

"I mind o' him caapital!" said Dougie, without a moment's hesitation. "The last time I saw him he lent me half-a-croon, and I never had the chance to pay him't back."

"I think mysel', if I mind right, it wass five shullin's," suggested Para Handy, putting his hand in his trousers pocket, with a wink to his mate, and Dougie quickly corrected himself; it WAS five shillings, now that he thought of it. But having gone aside for a little and consulted the engineer and Sunny Jim, he came back and said it was really eight-and-sixpence.

"There wass other three-and-six I got the lend o' from him another time," he said; "I could show you the very place it happened, and I was nearly forgettin' aal aboot it."

"My! ye're an awfu' leear!" said the engineer in a whisper as they stood aside.

"Maybe I am," agreed the mate; "but did you ever, ever, ever hear such a caapital one ass the Captain?"

Sunny Jim had no sooner got the dishes cleaned from this informal meal than Para Handy went to him and commanded a speedy preparation of the breakfast.

"Right-oh!" said Sunny Jim; "I'll be able to tak' a job as a chef in yin o' thae Cunarders efter this. But I've naething else than tea and eggs."

"Weel, boil them!" said the Captain. "Keep on boilin' them! Things never look so black to a woman when she can get a cup o' tea, and an egg or two 'll no' go wrong wi' her. Efter that you'll maybe give us a tune on your melodeon — something nice and cheery, mind; none o' your laments; they're no' the thing at aal for a weedow woman goin' to the poorshouse."

It was a charming day; the sea was calm; the extraordinary high spirits of the crew of the *Vital Spark* appeared to be contagious, and the widow confessed she had never enjoyed a sail so much since the year she had gone with Col on a trip to Rothesay.

"It's five-and-thirty years ago, and I never wass there again," she added, just a little sadly.

"Faith, you should come wi' us to Ro'say," said the Captain genially, and then regretted it.

"I canna," said the poor old body; "I'll never see Ro'say again, for I'm goin' to Lochgilphead."

"And you couldna be goin' to a nicer place!" declared Para Handy. "Lochgilpheid's chust sublime! Dougie himsel' 'll tell you!"

"Salubrious!" said the mate. "And forbye, it's that healthy!"

"There wass nothing wrong wi' Crarae," said the widow pathetically, and Sunny Jim came to the rescue with another pot of tea.

"Many a time I'll be thinking to mysel' yonder that if I had a little money bye me, I would spend the rest o' my days in Lochgilpheid," said Para Handy. "You never saw a cheerier place — "

"Crarae wass very cheery, too — in the summer time — when Col wass livin'," said the widow.

"Oh, but there's an aawful lot to see aboot Lochgilpheid; that's the place for Life!" said Para Handy. "And such nice walks; there's — there's the road to Kilmartin, and Argyll Street, full o' splendid shops; and the steamers comin' to Ardrishaig, and every night the mail goes bye to Crarae and Inveraray" — here his knowledge of Lochgilphead's charms began to fail him.

"I didna think it would be so nice ass that," said the widow, less dispiritedly. "I forgot aboot the mail; I'll aye be seein' it passin' to Crarae."

"Of course you will!" said Para Handy gaily; "that's a thing I wouldna miss, mysel'. And any time you take the notion, you'll can take a drive in the mail to Crarae if the weather's suitable."

"I would like it fine!" said the widow; "but — but maybe they'll no' let me. You would hear — you would hear where I wass goin' in Lochgilpheid?"

"I never heard a word!" protested Para Handy. "That minds me — will you have another egg? Jum, boil another egg for Mrs Maclachlan!"

"You hev been very kind," said the widow gratefully, as the *Vital Spark* came into Ardrishaig pier; "you couldna hev been kinder."

"I'm sorry you have to waalk to Lochgilpheid," said the Captain.

"Oh, I'm no' that old but I can manage the waalk," she answered; "I'm only seventy."

"Seventy!" said Para Handy, with genuine surprise; "I didna think you would be anything like seventy."

"I'll be seventy next Thursday[3]," said the widow and Para Handy whistled.

"And what in the world are you goin' to Lochgilpheid for? — the last place on God's earth, next to London. Efter Thursday next you'll can get your five shillin's a week in Crarae."

"Five shillin's a week in Crarae!" said the widow mournfully; "I hope I'll be ass well off ass that when I get to heaven!"

"Then never mind aboot heaven the noo," said Para Handy,

clapping her on the back; "go back to Crarae wi' the *Minard*, and you'll get your pension regular every week — five shillin's."

"My pension," said the widow, with surprise. "Fancy me wi' a pension; I never wass in the Airmy."

"Did nobody ever tell you that you wass entitled to a pension when they knew you were needin' 't?" asked the Captain, and the widow bridled.

"Nobody knew that I wass needin' anything," she exclaimed; "I took good care o' that."

Late that evening Mrs Maclachlan arrived at Crarae in the *Minard Castle* with a full knowledge for the first time of her glorious rights as an aged British citizen, and the balance of 8*s*. 6*d*. forced upon her by the mate, who had so opportunely remembered that he was due that sum to the lamented Col.

44. *The Maids of Bute*

EVEN the captain of a steam lighter may feel the cheerful, exhilarating influence of spring, and Para Handy, sitting on an upturned pail, with his feet on a coil of rope, beiked[1] himself in the sun and sang like a lintie[2] — a rather croupy[3] lintie. The song he sang was:
"Blow ye winds aye-oh!
  For it's roving I will go,
  I'll stay no more on England's shore,
  So let the music play.
  I'm off by the morning train,
  Across the raging main,
  I have booked a trup wi' a Government shup,
  Ten thousand miles away."

"Who's that greetin'?" asked the engineer maliciously, sticking his head out of the engine-room.

The Captain looked at him with contempt. "Nobody's greetin'," he said. "It's a thing you don't know anything at aal about; it's music. Away and read your novelles. What way's Lady Fitzgerald gettin' on wi' her new man?"

The engineer hastily withdrew.

"That's the way to settle him," said the Captain to Dougie and Sunny Jim. "Short and sweet! I could sing him blin'. Do ye know the way it iss that steamboat enchineers is aalways doon in the mooth like that? It's the want o' nature. They never let themselves go. Poor duvvles, workin' away among their bits o' enchines, they never get the wind and the sun aboot them right the same ass us seamen. If I wass always doon in a hole like that place o' Macphail's dabbin' my face wi' an oily rag aal day, I would maybe be ass ugly ass himsel'. Man, I'm feelin' fine! There's nothing like the spring o' the year, when you can get it like this. It's chust sublime! I'm feelin' ass strong ass a lion. I could pull the mast oot o' the boat and bate Brussels carpets wi' it."

"We'll pay for this yet," said Sunny Jim. "Ye'll see it'll rain or snow before night. What do ye say, Dougie?"

"Whatever ye think yoursel'," said Dougie.

"At this time o' the year," said the Captain, "I wish I wass back in MacBrayne's boats. The *Fital Spark* iss a splendid shup, the best in the tred, but there's no diversion. I wass the first man that ever pented the Maids o' Bute."

"Ye don't tell me!" exclaimed Dougie incredulously.

"I wass that," said Para Handy, as modestly as possible. "I'm not sayin' it for a bounce; the job might have come anybody's way, but I wass the man that got it. I wass a hand on the *Inveraray Castle*[4] at the time. The Captain says to me wan day we were passin' the Maids — only they werena the Maids then — they hadna their clothes on — 'Peter, what do you think o' them two stones on the hull-side?'

" 'They'll be there a long while before they're small enough to pap at birds wi',' says I.

" 'But do they no' put ye desperate in mind o' a couple o' weemen?' said he.

" 'Not them!' say I. 'I have been passin' here for fifteen years, and I never heard them taalkin' yet. If they were like weemen what would they be sittin' waitin' there for so long, and no' a man on the whole o' this side o' Bute?'

" 'Ay, but it's the look o' them,' said the Captain. 'If ye stand here and shut wan eye, they'll put ye aawfu' in mind o' the two Mac-Fadyen gyurls up in Pennymore. I think we'll chust christen them the Maids o' Bute.'

"Well, we aalways caaled them the Maids o' Bute efter that, and pointed them oot to aal the passengers on the steamers. Some o' them said they were desperate like weemen, and others said they were chust like two big stones. The Captain o' the Inveraray Castle got quite wild at some passengers that said they werena a bit like weemen. 'That's the worst o' them English towerists,' he would say. 'They have no imachination. I could make myself believe them two stones wass a regiment o' sodgers if I put my mind to't. I'm sure the towerists might streetch a point the same ass other folk, and keep up the amusement.'

"Wan day the skipper came to me and says, 'Are ye on for a nice holiday, Peter?' It wass chust this time o' the year and weather like this, and I wass feelin' fine.

" 'No objections,' says I.

" 'Well,' he says, 'I wish you would go off at Tighnabruaich and take some pent wi' ye in a small boat over to the Maids, and give them a touch o' rud and white that'll make them more like weemen than ever.'

" 'I don't like,' said I.

" 'What way do ye no' like?' said the skipper. 'It's no' even what you would caal work; it's chust amusement!'

" 'But will it no' look droll for a sailor to be pentin' clothes on a couple o' stones, aal his lone by himsel' in the north end o' Bute, and no' a sowl to see him? Chust give it a think yersel', skipper; would it no' look awfu' daft?"

" 'I don't care if it looks daft enough for the Lochgilphead Asylum, ye'll have to do it,' said the skipper. 'I'll put ye off at Tighnabruaich this efternoon; ye can go over and do the chob, and take a night's ludgin's in the toon, and we'll pick you up to-morrow when we're comin' doon. See you and make the Maids as smert as ye can, and, by Chove, they'll give the towerists a start!'

"Weel, I wass put off at Tighnabruaich, and the rud and white pent wi' me. I got ludgin's, took my tea and a herrin' to't, and rowed mysel' over in a boat to Bute. Some of the boys aboot the quay wass askin' what I wass efter, but it wassna likely I would tell them I wass goin' to pent clothes on the Maids o' Bute; they would be sure to caal me the manta-maker efter it. So I chust said I wass going over to mark oot the place for a new quay MacBrayne wass buildin'. There's nothing like discretioncy.

"It wass a day that wass chust sublime! The watter wass that calm you could see your face in it, the birds were singing like hey-my-nanny, and the Kyles wass lovely. Two meenutes efter I started pentin' the Maids I wass singin' to mysel' like anything. Now I must let you ken I never had no education at drawin', and it's wonderful how fine I pented them. When you got close to them they were no more like rale maids than I am; ye wouldna take them for maids even in the dark, but before I wass done with them, ye would ask them up to dance. The only thing that vexed me wass that I had only the rud and white; if I had magenta and blue and yellow, and the like o' that, I could have made them far more stylish. I gave them white faces and rud frocks and bonnets, and man, man, it wass a splendid day!

"I took the notion in my heid that maybe the skipper o' the *Inveraray* wass right, and that they were maids at wan time, that looked back the same as Lot's wife in the Scruptures and got turned into stone. When I wassna singin', I would be speakin' away to them, and I'll assure ye it wass the first time maids never gave me any back chat. Wan o' them I called Mery efter — efter a gyurl I knew, and the other I called 'Lizabeth for she chust looked like it. And it wass a majestic day. 'There ye are, gyurls,' I says to them, 'and you never had clothes that fitted better. Stop you, and if I'm spared till next year, you'll have the magenta too.' The north end o' Bute iss a bleak, wild, lonely place, but when I wass done pentin' the Maids it looked like a lerge population. They looked that nate and cheery among the heather! Mery had a waist ye could get your arm roond, but 'Lizabeth wass a broad, broad gyurl. And I wassna a bad-lookin' chap mysel'."

Here Para Handy stopped and sighed.

"Go on wi' your baur," said Dougie.

"Old times! old times!" said the Captain. "By Chove! I wass in trum that day! I never saw finer weather, nor nicer gyurls. Och! but it wass chust imachination; when we pass the Maids o' Bute now, I know they're only stones, with rud and white pent on them. They're good enough for towerists."

45. *Herring — a Gossip*

"OF AAL the fish there iss in the sea," said Para Handy, "nothing
bates the herrin'; it's a providence they're plentiful and them so
cheap!"

"They're no' in Loch Fyne, wherever they are," said Dougie
sadly; "the only herrin' that they're gettin' there iss rud ones comin'
up in barrels wi' the *Cygnet* or the *Minard Castle*. For five years back
the trade wass desperate."

"I wouldna say but you're right," agreeably remarked the Captain. "The herrin' iss a great, great mystery. The more you will be
catchin' of them the more there iss; and when they're no' in't at aal
they're no' there" — a great philosophic truth which the crew
smoked over in silence for a few minutes.

"When I wass a hand on the gabberts," continued the Captain,
"the herrin' fishin' of Loch Fyne wass in its prime. You ken yoursel'
what I mean; if you don't believe me, Jum, there's Dougie himsel' 'll
tell you. Fortunes! chust simply fortunes! You couldna show your
face in Tarbert then but a lot of the laads would gaither round at
wance and make a jovial day of it. Wi' a barrel of nets in a skiff and a
handy wife at the guttin', a man of the least agility could make
enough in a month to build a land o' hooses, and the rale Loch Fyne
was terrible namely over aal the world."

"I mind o't mysel'," said Sunny Jim; "they never sold onything
else but the rale Loch Fyne in Gleska."

"They did that whether or no'," explained Para Handy, "for it
wass the herrin's of Loch Fyne that had the reputation."

"I've seen the Rooshians eatin' them raw in the Baltic," said
Macphail, the engineer, and Dougie shuddered. "Eating them raw!"
said he; "the dirty duvvles!"

"The herrin' wass that thick in Loch Fyne in them days," recalled
the Captain, "that you sometimes couldna get your anchor to the
ground, and the quality was chust sublime. It wassna a tred at aal so
much as an amusement; you went oot at night when the weans wass
in their beds, and you had a couple o' cran[1] on the road to Clyde in
time for Gleska's breakfast. The quays wass covered wi' John
O'Brian's boxes[2], and man alive! but the wine and spirit tred wass

busy. Loch Fyne wass the place for Life in them days – high jeenks and big hauls; you werena very smert if you werena into both o' them. If you don't believe me, Dougie himsel' 'll tell you."

"You have it exact, Peter," guaranteed the mate, who was thus appealed to; "I wass there mysel'."

"Of course I have it exact," said Para Handy; "I'll assure you it's no' a thing I read in the papers. To-day there's no a herrin' in Loch Fyne or I'm mistaken."

"If there's wan he'll be kind o' lonely," said the mate. "I wonder what in the muschief's wrong wi' them?"

"You might shot miles o' nets for a month and there's no' a herrin' will come near them."

"Man! aren't they the tumid, frightened idiots!" said Dougie, with disgust.

"If ye ask me, I think whit spoiled the herrin' fishing in Loch Fyne was the way they gaed on writin' aboot it in the papers," said Macphail. "It was enough to scunner[3] ony self respectin' fish. Wan day a chap would write that it was the trawlers that were daein' a' the damage; next day anither chap would say he was a liar, and that trawlin' was a thing the herrin' thrived on. Then a chap would write that there should be a close time so as to gie the herrin' time to draw their breaths for anither breenge[4] into the nets; and anither chap would write from Campbeltoon and say a close time would be takin' the bread oot o' the mooths o' his wife and weans. A scientific man said herrin' came on cycles — "

"He's a liar, anyway," said the Captain, with conviction. "They were in Loch Fyne afore the cycle was invented. Are you sure, Macphail, it's no' the cod he means?"

"He said the herrin' fishin' aye missed some years noo and then in a' the herrin' places in Europe as weel's in Loch Fyne, and the Gulf Stream had something to dae wi't."

"That's the worst o' science," said the Captain piously; "it takes aal the credit away from the Creator. Don't you pay attention to an unfidel like that; when the herrin' was in Loch Fyne they stayed there aal the time, and only maybe took a daunder[5] oot noo and then the length o' Ballantrae."

"If it's no the Gulf Stream, then ye'll maybe tell us whit it is?" said the engineer, with some annoyance.

"I'll soon do that," said Para Handy; "if you want to ken, it's what I said — the herrin iss a mystery, chust a mystery!"

"I'm awfu' gled ye told me," said the engineer ironically. "I aye wondered. Whit's parteecular mysteriousness aboot it?"

"It's a silly fish," replied the Captain; "it's fine for eatin', but it hasna the sagacity. If it had the sagacity it wouldna come lower than Otter Ferry, nor be gallivantin'[6] roond the Kyles o' Bute in daylight. It's them innovations that's the death o' herrin'. If the herrin' stayed in Loch Fyne attendin' to its business and givin' the drift-net crews encouragement, it would have a happier life and die respected.

"Whenever the herrin' of Loch Fyne puts his nose below Kilfinan, his character is gone. First the Tarbert trawlers take him oot to company and turn his heid; then there iss nothing for it for him but flying trips to the Kyles o' Bute, the Tail o' the Bank, and Gareloch. In Loch Fyne we never would touch the herrin' in the daytime, nor in winter; they need a rest, forbye we're none the worse o' one oorsel's; but the folk below Kilfinan have no regard for Chrustian principles, and they no sooner see an eye o' fish than they're roond aboot it with trawls, even if it's the middle o' the day or New-Year's mornin'. They never give the fish a chance; they keep it on the run till its fins get hot. If it ventures ass far ass the Tail o' the Bank, it gets that dizzy wi' the sight o' the shippin' trade that it loses the way and never comes back to Loch Fyne again. A silly fish! If it only had sagacity! Amn't I right, Dougie?"

"Whatever you say yoursel', Captain; there's wan thing sure, the herrin's scarce."

"The long and the short of it iss that they're a mystery," concluded Para Handy.

46. *To Campbeltown by Sea*

"MAN, it's hot[1]; most desperate hot!" said Para Handy, using his hand like a squeegee to remove the perspiration from his brow. "Life in weather like thiss iss a burden; a body might ass weel be burnin' lime or at the bakin'. I wish I wass a fush."

The *Vital Spark* was lying at Skipness[2], the tar boiling between her seams in unusually ardent weather, and Macphail on deck, with a horror of his own engine-room.

"Bein' a fush wouldna be bad," said Dougie, "if it wass not for the constant watter. The only thing you can say for watter iss that it's wet and fine for sailin' boats on. If you were a fush, Captain, you would die of thirst."

"Watter, watter everywhere,
  And not a single drop of drink,"
quoted the engineer, who was literary.[3]

The Captain looked at him with some annoyance. "It's bad enough, Macphail," said he, "withoot you harpin', harpin' on the thing. You have no consuderation! I never mentioned drink. I wass thinkin' of us plowterin' doon in weather like this to Campbeltown, and wishin' I could swim."

"Can you no' swim?" asked Sunny Jim with some surprise.

"I daresay I could, but I never tried," said Para Handy. "I had never the time, havin' aye to attend to my business."

"Swimmin's aal the rage chust now,"[4] remarked Dougie, who occasionally read a newspaper. "Look at the Thames in London — there's men and women swimmin' it in droves; they'll do six or seven miles before their breakfast. And the Straits o' Dover's busy wi' splendid swimmers makin' their way to France."

"What are they wantin' to France for?" asked Para Handy. "Did they do anything?"

"I wouldna say," replied the mate; "it's like enough the polis iss efter them, but the story they have themsel's iss that they're swimmin' for a wudger. The best this season iss a Gleska man caaled Wolffe[5]; he swam that close to France the other day he could hear the natives taalkin'."

"What for did he no' land?" asked Sunny Jim.

"I canna tell," said Dougie, "but it's likely it would be wan o' the places where they charge a penny at the quay[6]. Him bein' a Gleska man, he would see them d — d first, so he chust came back to Dover."

"I don't see the fun of it, mysel'," said Para Handy reflectively. "But of course, if it's a wudger — "

"That's what I'm throng tellin' you," said the mate. "It looks a terrible task, but it's simple enough for any man with the agility. First you put off your clo'es and leave them in the shippin'-box at Dover if you have the confidence. Then you oil yoursel' wi' oil, put on a pair o' goggles, and get your photygraph. When the crood's big enough you kiss the wife good-bye and start swimmin' like anything."

"Whit wife?" asked the engineer, whose profound knowledge of life as depicted in penny novelettes had rendered him dubious of all adventures designed to end in France.

"Your own wife, of course," said Para Handy impatiently. "What other wife would a chap want to leave and go to France for? Go on wi' your story, Dougie."

"Three steamers loaded wi' beef tea, champagne, chocolate, and pipers follows you aal the way — "

"Beef tea and chocolate!" exclaimed the Captain, with astonishment. "What's the sense o' that? Are you sure it's beef tea, Dougie?"

"I read it mysel' in the papers," the mate assured him. "You strike out aalways wi' a firm, powerful, over-hand stroke, and whenever you're past the heid o' Dover quay you turn on your back, take your luncheon oot of a bottle, and tell the folk on the steamers that you're feelin' fine."

"You might well be feelin' fine, wi' a luncheon oot o' a bottle," said Para Handy. "It's the beef tea that bothers me."

"Aal the time the pipers iss standin' on the paiddleboxes o' the steamers playin' 'Hielan' Laddie' and 'The Campbells iss Comin'.'"

"Aal the time!" repeated Para Handy. "I don't believe wan word of it! Not aboot pipers; take my word for it, Dougie, they'll be doon below noo and then; there's nothing in this world thirstier than music."

"Do they no' get ony prizes for soomin' a' that distance?" asked Sunny Jim.

"I'll warrant you there must be money in it some way," said the engineer. "Whatever side they land on, they'll put roond the hat. There's naething the public 'll pay you quicker or better for, than for daein' wi' your legs what an engine 'll dae faur better."

"I could soom ony o' them blin'!" said Sunny Jim. "I was the natest wee soomer ever Geordie Geddes[7] dragged by the hair o' the heid frae the Clyde at Jenny's Burn[8]. Fair champion! Could we no' get up a soom frae here to Campbeltown the morn, and mak' a trifle at the start and feenish?"

"Man! you couldna swim aal that distance," said the Captain. "It would take you a week and a tug to tow you."

"I'm no' daft," explained Sunny Jim; "the hale thing's in the startin', for seemin'ly naebody ever feeniṣhes soomin' ower to France. A' I hae to dae is to ile mysel' and dive, and the *Vital Spark* can keep me company into Kilbrannan Sound."

"There's the photygraphs, and the beef tea, and the pipers," said the engineer; "unless ye hae them ye micht as well jist walk to Campbeltown."

"Dougie can play his trump, and that'll dae instead o' the pipers," said Sunny Jim. "It's a' in the start. See? I'll jump in at the quay, and you'll collect the money from the Skipness folk, and pick me up whenever they're oot o' sicht. I'll dae the dive again afore we come into Campbeltown, and Dougie'll haud the watch and gie a guarantee I swam the hale length o' Kintyre in four oors and five-and-twenty minutes. Then — bizz! — bang! — roon' the folk in Campbeltown wi' the bonny wee hat again! See?"

"Man! your cluverness is chust sublime!" said Para Handy; "we'll have the demonstration in the mornin'."

The intelligence that the cook of the *Vital Spark* was to swim to Campbeltown found Skipness curiously indifferent. "If he had been swimming FROM Campbeltown it might be different," said the natives; so the attempts to collect a subscription in recognition of the gallant feat were poorly recognised and Sunny Jim, disgusted, quitted the water, and resumed his clothes on the deck of the vessel less than a hundred yards from the shore. The *Vital Spark* next day came into Campbeltown, and the intrepid swimmer, having quietly dropped over the side at not too great a distance, swam in the direction of the quay, at which he arrived with no demonstration of excitement on the part of the population.

"Swam aal the way from Skipness," Para Handy informed the curious; "we're raisin' a little money to encourage him; he's none of your Dover Frenchmen, but wan of Brutain's hardy sons. Whatever you think yoursel's in silver, chentlemen."

"Wass he in the watter aal the time?" asked a native fisherman, copiously perspiring under a couple of guernseys and an enormous woollen comforter.

"He wass that!" Para Handy assured him. "If you don't believe me, Dougie himsel' 'll tell you."

"Then he wass the lucky chap!" said the native enviously. "It must have been fine and cool. What's he goin' to stand?"

47. *How to Buy a Boat*

It was shown in a former escapade[1] of Para Handy's that he wasn't averse from a little sea-trout poaching. He justified this sport in Gaelic, always quoting a proverb that a switch from the forest, a bird from the hill, or a fish from the river were the natural right of every Highland gentleman. Sunny Jim approved the principle most heartily, and proposed to insert a clause including dogs, of which he confessed he had been a great admirer and collector in his Clutha days. Ostensibly the Captain never fished for anything but flounders, and his astonishment when he came on seatrout or grilse[2] in his net after an hour's assiduous splashing with it at the mouth of a burn was charming to witness.

"Holy smoke!" he would exclaim, scratching his ears, "here's a wheen o' the white fellows, and us chust desperate for cod. It's likely they're the Duke's or Mr Younger's, and they lost their way to Bullingsgate. Stop you! Dougie, a meenute and hand me up a fut-spar.... I'm sure and I wassna wantin' them, but there they are, and what can you make of it? They might be saithe; it's desperate dark the night; what a peety we didna bring a lantern. Look and see if you divna think they're saithe, Dougie."

"Whatever you say yoursel'," was the mate's unvarying decision, and it could never be properly made out whether the fish were saithe or salmon till the crew had eaten them.

There was one favourite fishing bank of the Captain's inconveniently close to the county police station. The constable was very apt to find a grilse on the inside handle of his coal-cellar door on mornings when the *Vital Spark* was in the harbour, and he, also, was much surprised, but never mentioned it, except in a roundabout way, to Para Handy.

"You must be makin' less noise oot in the bay at night," he would say to him. "By Chove! I could hear you mysel' last night quite plain; if you're not more caatious I'll have to display my activity and find a clue."

It was most unfortunate that the men of the *Vital Spark* should have come on a shoal of the "white fellows" one early morning when the river-watchers were in straits to justify their job. The lighter's punt with an excellent net and its contents, had hurriedly to be abandoned, and before breakfast the Captain had lodged a charge of larceny against parties unknown at the police station. Some one had stolen his punt, he said, cutting the painter of her during the calm and virtuous sleep of self and mates. He identified the boat in the possession of the river-bailiffs; he was horrified to learn of the nefarious purpose to which it had been applied, but had to submit with curious equanimity to its confiscation. Local sympathy was aroused — fostered unostentatiously by the policeman; a subscription sheet was passed round the village philanthropists — also on the discreet suggestion of the policeman; and the sum of two pounds ten and tenpence was collected — the tenpence being in ha'pence ingeniously abstracted by means of a table-knife from a tin bank in the possession of the policeman's only boy.

"You will go at wance to Tighnabruaich and buy yourself another boat, Peter," said the policeman, when informally handing over the money. "If you are circumspect and caautious you'll pick up a smert one chape that will serve for your requirements."

"I wouldna touch a penny," protested Para Handy "if it wass not for my vessel's reputation; she needs a punt to give her an appearance."

A few days later the *Vital Spark* came into Tighnabruaich, and the Captain, by apparent accident, fell into converse with a hirer of rowing-boats.

"Man, you must be coinin' money," he said innocently; "you have a lot of boats."

"Coinin' money!" growled the boat-hirer; "no' wi' weather like this. I micht be makin' mair at hirin' umbrellas."

"Dear me!" said the Captain sympathetically, "that's a peety. A tidy lot o' boats, the most o' them — it's a wonder you would keep so many, and tred so bad."

"You werena thinkin' maybe o' buyin', were ye?" asked the

boat-hirer suspiciously, with a look at the stern of the *Vital Spark*, where the absence of a punt was manifest.

"No," said the Captain blandly, "boats iss a luxury them days; they're lucky that doesna need them. Terrible weather! And it's goin' to be a dirty summer; there's a man yonder in America that prophesies we'll have rain even-on till Martinmas. Rowin'-boats iss goin' chape at Millport."

"If that's the look-out, they'll be goin' chape everywhere," incautiously remarked the boat-hirer.

"Chust that," said Para Handy, and made as if to move away. Then he stopped, and, with his hand, in his pockets, pointed with a contemptuous foot at a dinghy he had had an eye on from the start of the conversation. "There's wan I aalways wondered at you keepin', Dan," said he; "she's a prutty old stager, I'll be bound you."

"That!" exclaimed the boat-hirer. "That's the tidiest boat on the shore; she 's a genuine Erchie Smith."

"Iss she, iss she?" said the Captain. "I mind her the year o' the Jubilee; it's wonderful the way they hold thegither. A bad crack in her bottom strake; you wouldna be askin' much for her if a buyer wass here wi' ready money?"

"Are ye wantin' a boat?" asked the boat-hirer curtly, coming to the point.

"Not what you would caal exactly," said the Captain, "but if she's in the market I might maybe hear aboot a customer. What did you say wass the figure?

"Three pound ten, and a thief's bargain," said the boat-hirer promptly, and Para Handy dropped at his feet the pipe he was filling.

"Excuse me startin'!" he remarked sarcastically, "you gave me a fright. It wass not about a schooner yat I was inquirin'."

"She's worth every penny o't, and a guid deal mair," said the boat-hirer, and Para Handy lit his pipe deliberately and changed the subject.

"There's a great run on them motors," he remarked, indicating one of the launches in the bay. "My friend that iss wantin' a boat iss — "

"I thocht ye said ye werena wantin' ony kind o' boat at a'," interjected the boat-hirer.

"Chust that; but there wass a chentleman that spoke to me aboot a notion he had for a smaal boat; he will likely take a motor wan;

they're aal the go. That swuft! They're tellin' me they're doin' aal the hirin' tred in Ro'sa' and Dunoon; there'll soon no' but a rowin'-boat left. If I wass you I would clear oot aal the trash and start a wheen o' motors."

"A motor wad be nae use for the *Vital Spark*," said the boat-hirer, who had no doubt now he had met a buyer. "Hoo much are ye prepared to offer?"

"What for?" said Para Handy innocently, spitting on the desirable dinghy, and then apologetically wiping it with his hand.

"For this boat. Say three pounds. It's a bargain."

"Oh, for this wan! I wouldna hurt your feelings, but if I wass wantin' a boat I wouldna take this wan in a gift. Still and on, a boat iss a handy thing for them that needs it; I'm not denyin' it. I'll mention it to the other chentleman."

"Wha is he?" asked the boat-hirer, and Para Handy screwed up his eyes, and was rapt in admiration of the scenery of the Kyles.

"What you don't know you don't ken," he replied mysteriously.

"Ye couldna get a better punt for the money if ye searched the Clyde," said the boat-hirer.

"I'm no' in any hurry; I'll take a look aboot for something aboot two pound ten," said Para Handy. "Ye canna get a first-class boat a penny cheaper. I got the offer of a topper for the forty shillings, and I'm consuderin' it." He had now thrown off all disguise, and come out in the open frankly as a buyer.

"Ye shouldna consider ower lang, then," said the boat-hirer; "there's a lot o' men in the market the noo for handy boats o' this cless; I have an offer mysel' o' two pounds fifteen for this very boat no later gone than yesterday, and I'm hangin' oot for the three pounds. I believe I'll get it; he's comin' back this afternoon."

"Chust that!" said Para Handy, winking to himself. "I'm sure and I wish him weel wi' his bargain. She looks as if she would be terrible cogly."[3]

"Is Tighnabruaich quay cogly?" asked the boat hirer indignantly. "Ye couldna put her over if ye tried."

"And they tell me she has a rowth," continued Para Handy, meaning thereby a bias under oars.

"They're liars, then," said the boat-hirer; "I'll sell ye her for two pound twelve to prove it."

The Captain buttoned up his jacket, and said it was time he was back to business.

"A fine boat," pleaded the boat-hirer. "Two pairs o' oars, a pair o' galvanised rowlocks, a bailin' dish and a painter — dirt chape! take it or leave it."

"Would ye no' be chenerous and throw in the plug?" said the Captain, with his finest irony.

"I'll dae better than that," said the boat-hirer. "I'll fling in a nice bit hand-line."

"For two pound ten, I think you said."

"Two pound twelve," corrected the boat-hirer. "Come now, don't be stickin'."

"At two pounds twelve I'll have to consult my frien' the chentleman I mentioned," said the Captain; "and I'll no' be able to let you know for a week or two. At two pounds ten I would risk it, and it's chust the money I have on me."

"Done, then!" said the boat-hirer. "The boat's yours," and they went to the hotel to seal the bargain.

The boat-hirer was going home with his money when he heard the Captain stumping hurriedly after. "Stop a meenute, Dan," he said; "I forgot to ask if you haven't a bit of a net you might throw in, chust for the sake o' frien'ship?"

The boat-hirer confessed to his wife that he had made ten shillings profit on the sale of a boat he had bought for forty shillings and had three seasons out of.

Para Handy swopped the dinghy a fortnight later in Tarbert for a punt that suited the *Vital Spark* much better, and thirty shillings cash. With part of the thirty shillings he has bought another net. For flounders.

48. *The Stowaway*

"DID YOU ever, ever, in your born days, see such umpidence?" said the mate of the smartest boat in the coasting trade, looking up from his perusal of a scrap of newspaper in which the morning's kippers had been brought aboard by Sunny Jim.

"What iss't, Dougald?" asked the Captain, sitting down on a keg to put on his carpet slippers, a sign that the day of toil on deck officially was over. "You'll hurt your eyes, there, studyin' in the dark. You're gettin' chust ass bad ass the enchineer for readin'; we'll have to put in the electric light for you."

"Chermans!" said Dougie. "The country's crooded wi' them. They're goin' aboot disguised ass towerists[1], drawin' plans o' forts and brudges."

"Now, issn't that most desperate!" said Para Handy, poking up the fo'c'sle stove, by whose light his mate had been reading this disquieting intelligence. "That's the way that British tred iss ruined. First it wass Cherman clocks, and then it wass jumpin' jecks, and noo it's picture post-cairds."[2]

"Criftens!" said Sunny Jim, who had come hurriedly down to put on a second waistcoat, for the night was cold: "Whit dae ye think they're makin' the drawin's for?"

"Iss't no' for post-cairds?" asked the Captain innocently, and the cook uproariously laughed. "Post-cairds my auntie!" he vulgarly exclaimed. "It's for the German Airmy. As soon's they can get their bits o' things thegither, they're comin' ower here to fght us afore the Boy Scouts[3] gets ony bigger. They hae spies a' ower Britain makin' maps; I'll lay ye there's no' a beer-shop in the country that they havena dotted doon."

"Holy smoke!" said Para Handy.

He watched the very deliberate toilet of Sunny Jim with some impatience. "Who's supposed to be at the wheel at this parteecular meenute?" he asked, with apparent unconcern.

"Me," said Sunny Jim. "There's naething in sicht, and I left it a meenute just to put on this waistcoat. Ye're gettin' awfu' pernicketty wi' your wheel; it's no' the *Lusitania*."[4]

"I'm no' findin' faault at aal, at aal, Jum, but I'm chust

considerin'," said the Captain meekly. "Take your time. Don't
hurry, Jum. Would you no' give your hands a wash and put on a
collar? It's always nice to have a collar on and be looking spruce if
you're drooned in a collusion. Give a kind of a roar when you get up
on deck if you see we're runnin' into anything."

"Collusion!" said Sunny Jim contemptuously. "Wi' a' the speed
this boat can dae, she couldna run into a pend close[5] if it started
rainin'," and he swung himself on deck.

"He hasna the least respect for the vessel," said the Captain sadly.
"She might be a common gaabert for aal the pride that Jum hass in
her."

The *Vital Spark* had left Loch Ranza an hour ago, and was
puffing across the Sound of Bute for the Garroch Head on her way
to Glasgow. A pitch-black night, not even a star to be seen, and
Sunny Jim at the wheel had occasionally a feeling that the
Cumbrae Light for which he steered was floating about in space,
detached from everything like a fire-balloon that winked every
thirty seconds at the sheer delight of being free. He whistled softly
to himself, and still very cold, in spite of his second waistcoat,
envied Macphail the engineer, whom he could see in the grateful
warmth of the furnace-door reading a penny novelette. Except for
the wheeze and hammer of the engine, the propeller's churning,
and the wash of the calm sea at the snub nose of the vessel, the
night was absolutely still.

The silence was broken suddenly by sounds of vituperation from
the fo'c'sle: the angry voices of the Captain and the mate, and a
moment later they were on deck pushing a figure aft in front of them.
"Sling us up a lamp, Macphail, to see what iss't we have a haad o'
here," said the Captain hurriedly, with a grasp on the stranger's
coat-collar, and the engineer produced the light. It shone on a burly
foreigner with coal-black hair, a bronze complexion, and a sack of
onions[6] to which he clung with desperate tenacity.

"Got him in Dougie's bunk, sound sleepin'," explained the
Captain breathlessly, with the tone of an entomologist who has
found a surprising moth. "I saw him dandering aboot Loch Ranza
in the mornin'. A stowaway! He wants to steal a trip to Gleska."

"I'll bate ye he's gaun to the Scottish Exhibeetion"[7] said Sunny
Jim. "We'll be there in time, but his onions 'll gang wrang on him

afore we get to Bowlin'. Whit dae they ca' ye for your Christian name, M'Callum?"

"Onions," replied the stranger. "Cheap onions. No Ingles."

"Oh, come aff it! come aff it! We're no' such neds as to think that ony man could hae a Christian name like Onions," said Sunny Jim. "Try again, and tell us it's Clarence."

"And what iss't your wantin' on my boat?" asked Para Handy sternly.

The foreigner looked from one to the other of them with large pathetic eyes from under a broad Basque bonnet. "Onions. Cheap onions," he repeated, extracting a bunch of them hastily from the bag. "Two bob. Onions."

"Gie the chap a chance," said Sunny Jim ironically. "Maybe he gie'd his ticket up to the purser comin' in."

"He hasna a word o' English in his heid," said Dougie. "There's something at the bottom o't; stop you, and you'll see! It's no' for his health he's traivellin' aboot Arran wi' a bag o' onions, and hidin' himsel' on board a Christian boat. I'll wudger that he's Cherman."

"It's no a German kep he's wearin' onyway," said Macphail, with the confidence of a man who has travelled extensively and observed.

"That's a disguise," said Dougie, no less confidently. "You can see for yoursel' he hass even washed himsel'. Try him wi' a bit of the Cherman lingo, Macphail, and you'll see the start he'll get."

Macphail, whose boast had always been that he could converse with fluency in any language used in any port in either hemisphere, cleared his throat and hesitatingly said, "Parly voo Francis?"

"Onions. Cheap onions," agreeably replied the stranger.

"Francis! Francis! Parly voo?" repeated the engineer, testily and loudly, as if the man were deaf.

"Maybe his name's no' Francis," suggested Sunny Jim. "Try him wi' Will Helm, or Alphonso; there's lots o' them no' called Francis."

"He understands me fine, I can see by his eye," said the engineer, determined to preserve his reputation as a linguist. "But, man! he's cunnin'."

"It's the wrong shup he hass come to if he thinks he iss cunnin' enough for us!" said the Captain firmly. "It's the jyle in Greenock that we'll clap him in for breakin' on board of a well-known steamboat and spoilin' Dougald's bunk wi' onions."

The stowaway sat nonchalantly down on a bucket, produced a knife and a hunk of bread, and proceeded to make a meal of it with onions. Immediately the crew was constituted into a court-martial, and treated the presence of their captive as if he were a deaf-mute or a harmless species of gorilla.

"What wass I tellin' you, Captain, at the very meenute I saw his feet stickin' oot o' my bunk?" inquired the mate. "The country's overrun wi' Chermans. I wass readin' yonder that there's two hunder and fifty thousand o' them in Brutain."

"What a lot!" said Para Handy. "I never set eyes on wan o' them to my knowledge. What are they like, the silly duvvles?"

"They're chust like men that would be sellin' onions," said Dougie. "Lerge, big, heavy fellows like oor frien' here; and they never say nothing to nobody. You've seen hunders o' them though you maybe didna ken. They're Chermans that plays the bands on the river steamers."[8]

"Are they? are they?" said Para Handy with surprise; "I always thought yon chaps wass riveters, or brassfeenishers, that chust made a chump on board the boat wi' their instruments when she wass passin' Yoker and the purser's back wass turned."

"Germans to a man!" said Sunny Jim. "There's no' a Scotchman among them; ye never saw yin o' them yet the worse o' drink."

"Ye needna tell me yon chaps playin' awa' on the steamers iss makin' maps," said Para Handy. "Their eyes iss aalways glued on their cornucopias."[9]

"They're goin' aboot ports and forts and battleships drawin' plans," said the engineer. "Whit did the Royal Horse Artillery find the ither day at Portsmouth? Yin o' them crawlin' up a gun to mak' a drawin' o't, and they had to drag him oot by the feet."

"Chust that!" said Para Handy, regarding their captive with greater interest. "I can see mysel' noo; he looks desperate like a Cherman. Do you think he was makin' plans o' the *Vital Spark*?"

"That's what I was askin him in German." said Macphail, "and ye saw yersel's the suspicious way he never answered."

"Jum," said the Captain, taking the wheel himself, "away like a smert laad and make up a cup o tea for the chap; it's maybe the last he'll ever get if we put him in the jyle[10] in Greenock or in Gleska."

"Right-oh!" said Sunny Jim, gladly relinquishing the wheel. "Will

I set the table oot in the fore saloon? Ye'll excuse us bein' short o' floral decorations, Francis? Is there onything special ye would like in the way o' black breid or horse-flesh, and I'll order't frae the steward?"

"Onions," said the stranger.

The foreigner spent the night imprisoned in the hold with the hatches down, and wakened with an excellent appetite for breakfast, while the vessel lay at a wharf on the upper river.

"There's money in 't; it's like salvage," Dougie said to Para Handy, as they hurried ashore for a policeman.

"I canna see't," said the Captain dubiously. "What's the good o' a Cherman? If he wass a neegur bleck, you could sell him to the shows for swallowin' swords, but I doot that this chap hassna got the right agility."

"Stop, you!" said the mate with confidence. "The Government is desperate keen to get a haad o' them, and here's Mackay the polisman."

"We have a kind o' a Cherman spy on board," he informed the constable, who seemed quite uninterested.

"The Sanitary Depairtment iss up in John Street," said the constable. "It's not on my bate." But he consented to come to the *Vital Spark* and see her stowaway.

"Toots, man! he's no' a Cherman, and he's no' a spy," he informed them at a glance.

"And what iss he then?" asked the Captain.

"I don't ken what he iss, but he's duvvelish like a man that would be sellin' onions," said Mackay, and on his advice the suspect was released.

It was somewhat later in the day that Dougie missed his silver watch, which had been hanging in the fo'c'sle.

49. *Confidence*

THE CAPTAIN of the *Vital Spark* and his mate were solemnly drinking beer in a Greenock public-house, clad in their best shore-going togs, for it was Saturday. Another customer came in –

a bluff, high-coloured, English-spoken individual with an enormous watch-chain made of what appeared to be mainly golden nuggets in their natural state, and a ring with a diamond bulging out so far in it that he could hardly get his hand into his trousers pocket. He produced a wad of bank-notes, peeled one off, put it down on the counter with a slap, and demanded gin and ginger.

"A perfect chentleman!" said Para Handy to his mate in a whisper; "you can aalways tell them! He'll likely have a business somewhere."

The opulent gentleman took his glass of gin and ginger to a table and sat down, lit a cigar, and proceeded to make notes in a pocket-book.

"That's the worst of wealth," said Dougie philosophically; "you have to be aalways tottin' it up in case you forget you have it. Would you care for chust another, Peter? I think I have a shullin'."

Another customer came in — apparently a seaman, with a badge of a well-known shipping line on his cap.

"Hello, bully boys!" he said heartily. "Gather around; there's a letter from home! What are we going to have? In with your pannikins, lively now; and give it a name," and he ordered glasses round, excluding the auriferous gentleman who was taking notes behind.

"Looks like a bloomin' Duke!" he remarked in an undertone to Para Handy. "One of them shipowners, likely; cracker-hash and dandy-funk for Jack, and chicken and champagne wine for Mister Bloomin' Owner! Ours is a dog's life, sonnies, but I don't care now, I'm home from Callao!"

"Had you a good trup?" asked Para Handy, with polite anxiety.

"Rotten!" said the seaman tersely. "What's your line? Longshore, eh?" and he scrutinised the crew of the *Vital Spark*.

"Chust that!" said Para Nandy mildly. "Perusin' aboot the Clyde wi' coals and doin' the best we can."

"Then I hope the hooker's your own, my boy, for there's not much bloomin' money in it otherwise," said the seaman; and Para Handy, not for the first time, fell a victim to his vanity.

"Exactly," he said, with a pressure on the toe of Dougie's boot; "I'm captain and owner too; the smertest boat in the tred," and he jingled a little change he had in his pocket.

"My name's Tom Wilson," volunteered the seaman. "First mate

of the *Wallaby*, with an extra master's papers, d — n your eyes! And I've got five-and-twenty bloomin' quids in my pocket this very moment, look at that!" He flourished a wad of notes that was almost as substantial as the one displayed a little before by the gentleman with the nugget watch-chain.

"It's a handy thing to have aboot ye," said Para Handy sagely, jingling his coppers eloquently. "But I aalways believe in gold mysel'; you're not so ready to lose it."

"I've noticed that mysel'," said Dougie solemnly.

Tom Wilson ordered another round, and produced a watch which he confidently assured them was the finest watch of its kind that money could buy. It had an alarm bell, and luminous paint on the hands and dial permitted you to see the time on the darkest night without a light.

"Well, well! issn't that cluver!" exclaimed Para Handy. "They'll be makin' them next to boil a cup o' tea. It would cost a lot o' money? I'm no' askin', mind you; I wass chust remarkin'."

"Look here!" cried Tom Wilson impulsively; "I'll give the bloomin' clock to the very first man who can guess what I paid for it."

"Excuse me, gentlemen," said the man with the nugget watch-chain, putting away his note-book and pencil. "I'd like to see that watch," and they joined him at the table, where he generously ordered another round. He gravely examined the watch, and guessed that it cost about twenty pounds.

"Yes, but you must mention the exact figure," said its owner.

"Well, I guess two-and-twenty sovereigns," said the other, and Tom Wilson hastily proceeded to divest himself of the chain to which it had been originally attached. "It's yours!" he said; "you've guessed it and you may as well have the bloomin' chain as well. That's the sort of sunny boy I am!" and he beamed upon the company with the warmth of one whose chief delight in life was to go round distributing costly watches.

"Wass I not chust goin' to say twenty-two pounds!" said Para Handy with some chagrin.

"I knew it wass aboot that," said Dougie; "chenuine gold!"

The lucky winner of the watch laughed, put it into his pocket, and took out the wad of notes, from which he carefully counted out twenty-two pounds, which he thrust upon Tom Wilson.

"There you are!" he said; "I wouldn't take your watch for nothing, and it happens to be the very kind of watch I've been looking for."

"But you have only got my word for it, Mister, that it's worth that money," protested Mr Wilson.

The stranger smiled. "My name's Denovan," he remarked; "I'm up here from Woolwich[1] on behalf of the Admiralty to arrange for housin' the torpedo workers[2] in first-rate cottage homes with small back gardens. What does the Lords o' the Admiralty say to me? The Lords o' the Admiralty says to me, 'Mr Denovan, you go and fix up them cottage homes, and treat the people of Greenock with confidence.' I'm a judge of men, I am, bein' what I am, and the principle I go on is to trust my fellow-men. If you say two-and-twenty pounds is the value of this watch, I say two-and-twenty it is, and there's an end of it!"

Mr Wilson reluctantly put the notes in his pocket, with an expression of the highest admiration for Mr Denovan's principles, and Para Handy experienced the moral stimulation of being in an atmosphere of exceptional integrity and unlimited wealth. "Any wan could see you were the perfect chentleman," he confessed to Mr Denovan, ducking his head at him. "What way are they aal keepin' in Woolwich?"

"I took you for a bloomin' ship-owner at first," said Mr Wilson. "I didn't think you had anything to do with the Admiralty."

"I'm its right-hand man," replied Mr Denovan modestly. "If you're thinkin' of a nice cottage home round here with front plot and small back garden, I can put you in, as a friend, for one at less than half what anybody else would pay."

"I haven't any use for a bloomin' house unless there was a licence to it," said Mr Wilson cheerfully.

Mr Denovan looked at him critically. "I like the look of you," he remarked impressively. "I'm a judge of men, and just to back my own opinion of you, I'll put you down right off for the first of the Admiralty houses. You needn't take it; you could sell it at a profit of a hundred pounds to-morrow; I don't ask you to give me a single penny till you have made your profit," and Mr Denovan, producing his pocket-book, made a careful note of the transaction lest he might forget it. " 'Treat the people of Greenock with confidence,' says the Lords of the Admiralty to me; now, just to show my confidence in you, I'll hand you back your watch, and my own watch, and you can go away with them for twenty minutes."

"All right, then; just for a bloomin' lark," agreed Tom Wilson, and with both watches and the colossal nugget-chain, he disappeared out of the public-house.

"That's a fine, smart, honest-lookin', manly fellow!" remarked Mr Denovan admiringly.

"Do you think he'll come back wi' the watches?" said Dougie dubiously.

"Of course he will," replied Mr Denovan. "Trust men, and they'll trust you. I'll lay you a dollar he would come back if he had twenty watches and all my money as well."

This opinion was justified. Mr Wilson returned in less than five minutes, and restored the watches to their owner.

"Well, I'm jeegered!" said Para Handy, and ordered another round out of admiration for such astounding honesty.

"Would you trust me?" Mr Denovan now asked Tom Wilson.

"I would," said the seaman heartily. "Look here; I've five-and-twenty bloomin' quid, and I'll let you go out and walk the length of the railway station with them."

"Done!" said Mr Denovan, and possessed of Wilson's roll of notes, went out of the public-house.

"Peter," said Dougie to the Captain, "do you no' think one of us should go efter him chust in case there's a train for Gleska at the railway station?"

But Tom Wilson assured them he had the utmost confidence in Mr Denovan, who was plainly a tip-top gentleman of unlimited financial resources, and his confidence was justified, for Mr Denovan not only returned with the money, but insisted on adding a couple of pounds to it as a recognition of Mr Wilson's sporting spirit.

"I suppose you Scotch chaps don't have any confidence?" said Mr Denovan to the Captain.

"Any amount!" said Para Handy.

"Well, just to prove it," said Mr Denovan, "would you be willin' to let our friend Wilson here, or me, go out with a five-pound note of yours?"

"I havena the five pounds here, but I have it in the boat," said the

Captain. "If Dougie 'll wait here, I'll go down for it. Stop you, Dougie, with the chentlemen."

Some hours later Dougie turned up on the *Vital Spark* to find the Captain in his bunk, and sound asleep.

"I thocht you were comin' wi' a five-pound note?" he remarked on wakening him. "The chentlemen waited, and better waited, yonder on you, and they werena pleased at aal, at aal. They said you surely hadna confidence."

"Dougie," said the Captain, "I have the greatèst confidence, but I have the five pounds, too. And if you had any money in your pocket it's no' with Mr Denovan I would leave you."

50. *The Goat*

PARA HANDY, having listened with amazement to the story of the Stepney battle[1] read by the engineer, remarked, "If it wassna in print, Macphail, I wouldna believe it! They must be desperate powerful men, them Rooshian burgulars. Give us yon bit again aboot Sir Wunston Churchill."[2]

" 'The Right Honourable gentleman, at the close of the engagement, went up a close and shook 127 bullets out of his Astrakan coat,' " repeated Macphail, who always added a few picturesque details of his own invention to any newspaper narrative.

"It was 125 you said last time," Para Handy pointed out suspiciously.

"My mistake!" said Macphail frankly; "I thocht it was a five at first, but I see noo it's a seven. A couple o' bullets more or less if it's anyway over the hundred doesna make much odds on an Astrakan coat."

"Man, he must be a tough young fellow, Wunston!" said the Captain, genuinely admiring. "Them bullets give you an awfu' bang. But I think the London polisman iss greatly wantin' in agility; they would be none the worse o' a lesson from Wully Crawford, him that wass the polisman in Tarbert when I wass at the school. Wully wouldna throw chuckies at the window to waken up the Rooshians; he wass far too caautious. He would pause and consuder. Wully wass never frightened for a bad man in a hoose: 'It's when they're goin' lowse aboot the town they're dangerous,' he would say; 'they're chust ass safe in there ass in my lock-up, and they're no' so weel attended.'

"Wully wass the first polisman ever they had in Tarbert. He wassna like the chob at aal, at aal, but they couldna get another man to take it. He wass a wee small man wi' a heid like a butter-firkin, full to the eyes wi' natural agility, and when he would put the snitchers[3] on you, yuu would think it wass a shillin' he wass slippin' in your hand. If you were up to any muschief — poachin' a bit o' fish or makin' a demonstration — Wully would come up wi' his heid to the side and rubbing his hands thegither, and say a kindly word. I've seen great big massive fellows walkin' doon the street wi' Wully, thinkin' they were goin' to a Christmas pairty, and before they knew where they were they were lyin' on a plank in his lock-up. You never saw a man wi' nicer mainners; he wass the perfect chentleman!

" 'Stop you there, lads, and I'll be back in a meenute wi' a cup o' tea,' he would say when he wass lockin' the door of the cell on them. 'Iss there anything you would like to't?' The silly idiots sometimes thocht they were in a temperance hotel by Wully's mainners, and they got a terrible start in the mornin' when they found they had to pay a fine. You mind o' Wully Crawford, Dougie?"

"Fine!" said Dougie. "He was the duvvle's own!"

" 'Caaution and consuderation iss the chief planks in the armour of the Brutish constable,' Wully used to say, rubbin' his hands. 'There iss no need for anybody to be hurt.'

"It wass the time when Tarbert herrin'-trawlers wass at their best and money goin'. It wass then, my laads, there wass Life in Tarbert! The whole o' Scotland and a regiment o' arteelery couldna have kept the Tarbert fishermen in order, but Wully Crawford held them in the hollow o' his hand."

"It's a' very weel," said Macphail, "but they didna go aboot wi' automatic pistols."

"No, they didna have aromatic pistols," admitted Para Handy, "but they had aawfully aromatic fists. And you never saw smerter chaps wi' a foot-spar or a boat-hook. The wildest of the lot wass a lad M'Vicar that belonged to Tarbert and wass called The Goat for his sagacity. He could punch his heid through a millstone and wear it round his neck the rest o' the day instead o' a collar. When The Goat wass extra lucky at the trawlin' the Tarbert merchants didna take the

shutters off their sloops and the steamboat agents had to put a ton or
two o' ballast in their shippin'-boxes. Not a bad chap at aal, The
Goat — only wicked, wicked! The only wan that could stand up to
him in Tarbert wass three Macdougall brothers wi' a skiff from
Minard; him and them wass at variance.

"The Goat would be going through the toun wi' his gallowses
ootside his guernsey and his bonnet on three hairs, spreading devastation, when the Free Church minister would send for Wully Crawford.

" 'You must do your duty, Wullium,' he would say, wi' his heid
stickin' oot at a garret window and the front door barred. 'There's
M'Vicar lowse again, and the whole o' Tarbert in commotion. Take
care that ye divna hurt him.'

" 'There's nobody needs to be hurt at aal, wi' a little deeliberation,'
Wully would say wi' his heid to the side, and it most dreadful like a
butter-firkin. 'I'll chust paause and cousuder, Mr Cameron, and
M'Vicar'll be in the cell in twenty meenutes. Terrible stormy
weather, Mr Cameron. What way's the mustress keepin'?'

"Then Wully would put off his uniform coat and on wi' a wee
pea-jecket, and go up to where The Goat wass roarin' like a bull in
the streets of Tarbert, swingin' a top-boot full o' stones aboot his heid
— clean daft wi' fair defiance.

" 'John,' Wully would say to him, rubbin' his hands and lookin'
kindly at him, 'it's a wonder to me you would be carryin' on here, and
them Macdougalls upon the quay swearin' they'll knock the heid off
you.'

"The Goat would start for the quay, but Wully wass there before
him, and would say to the Macdougalls, 'In to your boat, my laads,
and on wi' the hatch; M'Vicar's vowing vengeance on you. Here he
comes!' He knew very well it wass the last thing they would do; five
minutes later and the three Macdougalls and The Goat would be in
grips.

" 'Pick oot whatever bits belong to yoursel's, and I'll collect what's
left of poor M'Vicar,' Wully would say to the Macdougalls when the
fight wass done, and then he would hurl The Goat to the lock-up in
a barrow.

"But that wass only wan of Wully's schemes; his agility was
sublime! There wass wan time yonder when The Goat took a fancy
for high jeenks, and carried a smaal-boat up from the shore at night

and threw it into the banker's lobby. It wass a way they had in Tarbert at the time o' celebratin' Hallowe'en, for they were gettin' splendid fishin's, and were up to aal diversions.

"Wully went roond in the mornin' to M'Vicar's house, and ass sure ass daith he hadna the weight or body o' a string o' fish, but a heid on him like a firkin. If The Goat had kent what he came for, he would have heaved him through the window.

" 'You werena quarrellin' wi' Mackerracher last night and threw him ower the quay?' asked Wully, rubbin' his hands.

" 'I never set eyes on Mackerracher in the last fortnight!' said The Goat, puttin' doon a potato-beetle, as you might say disappointed.

" 'Tuts! wassn't I sure of it!' said Wully, clappin' him on the back. 'Mackerracher's missin', and there's a man at the office yonder says he thocht he saw you wi' him. It's chust a case of alibi; come awa' across to the office for a meenute; he's waitin' there, and he'll see his mistake at wance.'

"The Goat went over quite joco to the polis-office, knowin' himsel' he wass innocent of any herm to poor Mackerracher, and wass fined in thirty shullin's for puttin' a boat in the banker's lobby. Oh, a cluver fellow, Wullium! A heid like a butter-firkin!

"You would think The Goat would never be got to the polis-office any more wi' such contrivances o' Wully Crawford. 'If that wee duvvle wants me again, he'll have to come for me wi' the Princess Louisa's[4] Own Argyll and Sutherland Highlanders and a timber-junker,' he swore, and Wully only laughed when he heard it. 'Us constables would be havin' a sorry time wi' the like of John M'Vicar if we hadna the Laaw o' the Land and oor wuts at the back o' us,' he said, wi' his heid on the side, and his belt a couple o' feet too big for him.

"Two or three weeks efter that, when the fishin' wass splendid, and The Goat in finest trum, he wakened one morning in his boat and found that some one had taken away a couple o' barrels o' nets, a pair o' oars, and a good pump-handle on him.

" 'I'll have the Laaw on them, whoever it wass!' he says. 'Tarbert will soon be a place where a dacent man canna leave his boat withoot a watch-dog; where's Wully Crawford, the polisman?'

"He went lookin' up and doon the toon for Wully, but Wully wasna to be seen at aal, at aal, and some wan said he wass over at the polis-office. The Goat went over to the polis-office and chapped like a chentlemen at the door withoot a meenute's prevarication.

" 'Some wan stole on me through the night, a couple o' barrel o' nets, a pair o' oars, and a good pump-handle, and I want you to do your duty!' says The Goat to the polis-constable, and the head of him chust desperate like a butter-firkin!

" 'Did you lose them, John?' said Wully, rubbin' his hands. 'Man! I think I have a clue to the depridaation; I have some of the very articles you're lookin' for in here,' and he opened the cell door, and sure enough there was a couple o' barrels o' nets in a corner. What did the silly idiot, John M'Vicar, no' do, but go into the cell to look at them, and the next meenute the door was locked on him!

" 'A couple o' barrel o' nets and a pair o' oars or the like o' that can be taken in charge withoot assistance from the Princess Louisa's Own Argyll and Sutherland Highlanders,' said bold Wully through the keyhole. 'Iss there anything I could get for your breakfast to-morrow, John? You'll need to keep up your strength. You're to be tried for yon assault last Saturday on the Rechabite Lodge.'

"The Goat lay in the cell aal day and roared like a bull, but it didna make any odds to Wully Crawford; he went aboot the toon wi' his heid more like a firkin than ever, and a kindly smile. But when The Goat begood at night to kick the door o' his cell for oors on end and shake the polis-office to its foundations, Wully couldna get his naitural sleep. He rose at last and went to the door o' the cell, and says, says he, 'John, ye didna leave oot your boots; if you'll hand them oot to me I'll gie them a brush for the mornin'.'

"M'Vicar put oot the boots like a lamb.

" 'There now,' said Wully, lockin' the door again, ye can kick away till you're black in the face. Would you like them oiled or bleckened?' And you never saw a man wi' a heid more like a firkin o' Irish butter!"

51. *Para Handy's Vote*

PARA HANDY had finished tea on Saturday night, and was ruefully contemplating the urgent need for his weekly shave, when Mary, his wife, was called to the outer door. She came back to the kitchen to inform her husband that a gentleman wished to see him.

"A chentleman!" said Para Handy, with surprise and even incredulity. "What in the world will he be wantin'?"

"He didna say," replied Mrs Macfarlane. "He said he wanted to see you most particular, and wouldna keep you a meenute. Whatever you do, don't go and buy another o' thae Histories uf the Scottish Clans."

"Could you not tell him I'm away on the boat, or that I'm busy?" asked her husband, nervously putting on his jacket.

"I'm no' goin' to tell any lies aboot you," said Mrs Macfarlane. "It's nobody for money anyway, for we're no' in anybody's reverence a single penny."

"What the duvvle can the man be wantin'? What kind o' look did you get at him? Do you think he's angry?"

"Not a bit of him; he spoke quite civil to mysel', and he has a book wi' a 'lastic band on't, the same as if it was the meter he was comin' for."

"A book!" said Para Handy, alarmed. "Go you out, Mary, like a cluver gyurl, and tell him that I slipped away to my bed when you werena lookin'. Tell him to come back on Monday."

"But you'll be away wi' the boat on Monday."

"Chust that; but he'll be none the wiser. There's many a sailor caaled away in a hurry. Don't be a frightened coward, Mary. Man, but you're tumid, tumid! The chentleman's no' goin' to eat you."

"He's no' goin' to eat you either," said Mrs Macfarlane. "He's standin' there at the door, and you'll just have to go and see him."

"I wish I wass back on the boat," said Para Handy in despair. "There's no' much fun in a hoose o' your own if you'll no' get a meenute's peace in't. What in the mischief iss he wantin' wi' his book and his 'lastic bands?"

He went to the door and found an exceedingly suave young gentleman there, who said, "I'm delighted to find you at home, Captain Macfarlane; my business won't take five minutes."

"If it's a History o' the Clans, we have it already," said Para Handy with his shoulder against the door. "I ken the clans by he'rt."

"You have a vote in the College Division,"[1] said the visitor briskly, paying no attention to the suggestion that he was a book-canvasser. "I'm canvassing for your old friend, tried and true, Harry Watt."[2]

"Chust that!" said Para Handy. "What way iss he keepin', Harry? I hope he's in good trum?"

"Never was better, or more confident, but he looks to you to do your best for him on this occasion."

"That's nice," said Para Handy. "It's a blessin' the health; and there's lots o' trouble goin' aboot. Watch your feet on the stair goin' down; there's a nesty dark bit at the bottom landin'."

"Mr Watt will be delighted to know that he can depend on you," said the canvasser, opening up his book and preparing to record one more adherent to the glorious principles of Reform. "He'll be sure to come round and give you a call himself."

"Any time on Monday," said Para Handy. "I'll be prood to see him. What did you say again the chentleman's name wass?"

"Mr Harry Watt," said the canvasser, no way surprised to find that the voter was in ignorance on this point, an absolute indifference to the identity of its M.P.s being not unusual in the College Division.

"Yes, yes, of course; I mind now, Harry Watt. A fine chentleman. Tip-top! He wass aalways for the workin' man. It's a fine open wunter we're havin' this wunter, if it wassna for the fogs."

"What do you think of the House of Lords now?" asked the canvasser, desirous to find exactly what his victim's colour was, and Para Handy shifted his weight on another leg and scratched his ear.

"It's still to the fore," he answered cautiously. "There's a lot of fine big chentlemen in it. Me bein' on the boat, I don't see much of them, except noo and then their pictures in the papers. Iss there any Bills goin' on the noo?"

"I think we're going to clip their wings this time," said the canvasser with emphasis; and the Captain shifted hurriedly back to his former leg and scratched his other ear.

"Capital!" he exclaimed, apparently with the utmost sympathy. "Ye canna clup them quick enough. They're playin' the very muschief over yonder in Ireland. There's wan thing, certain sure — I never could stand the Irish."[3]

"Yes, yes; but you'll admit a safe measure of Home Rule — "[4] began the canvasser; and the Captain found the other leg was the better one after all.

"I'll admit that!" he agreed hurriedly. "Whatever you say yoursel'."

"See and be round at the poll early," said the canvasser. "It's on Thursday."

"I'm making aal arrangements," said the Captain cordially. "Never mind aboot a motor-car; I can walk the distance. Give my best respects to Mr Harry; tell him I'll stand firm. A Macfarlane never flinched! He's no' in the shippin' line, Mr Harry, iss he? No? chust that! I wass only askin' for curiosity. A brulliant chentleman! He hass the wonderful agility, they tell me. Us workin' men must stand thegither and aye be bringin' in a bill."

"Of course the question before the electors is the Veto,"[5] said the canvasser.

"You never said a truer word!" said the Captain heartily. "It's what I said mysel' years ago; if my mate Dougie wass here he would tell you. Everything's goin' up in price, even the very blecknin'."

"See and not be carried away by any of their Referendum arguments," counselled the canvasser, slipping the elastic band on his book. "It's only a red herring dragged across the track."

"I never could stand red herring," said the Captain.

"And remember Thursday, early — the earlier the better!" was the visitor's final word as he went downstairs.

"I'm chust goin' in this very meenute to make a note of it in case I should forget," said Para Handy, ducking his head reassuringly at him.

"A smert young fellow!" he told his wife when he got back to the kitchen. "He took my name doon yonder chust as nate's you like!" and he explained the object of the caller's visit.

"It's the like o' me that should have the vote," said Mrs Macfarlane humorously. "I have a better heid for politics than you."

"Mery," said her husband warmly, "you're taalkin' like wan of them unfidel Suffragettes.[6] If I see you goin' oot wi' a flag and standin' on a lorry, there'll be trouble in the College Diveesion!"

The Captain had hardly started to his shaving when Mrs Macfarlane found herself called to the door again, and returned with the annoying intelligence that another gentleman desired a moment's interview.

"Holy smoke!" said Para Handy. "Do they think this hoose iss the

Argyle Arcade? It must be an aawful wet night outside when they're
aal crowdin' here for shelter. Could you no' tell him to leave his name
and address and say I would caal on him mysel' on Monday?"

On going to the door he found an even more insinuative canvasser
than the first one — a gentleman who shook him by the hand several
times during the interview, and even went the length of addressing
him like an old friend as Peter.

"I'm lucky to find you at home," he said. "You are that!" said the
Captain curtly, with his shoulder against the door. "What iss't?"

"I'm canvassing for our friend — "

"It's no' ten meenutes since another wan wass here afore," broke
in the Captain. "You should take stair aboot, the way they lift the
tickets in the trains, and no' be comin' twice to the same door. I made
aal arrangements for the Thursday wi' the other chap."

"Think it over again," said the canvasser, no way crestfallen, with
an affectionate hand on the Captain's shoulder. "Don't be misled by
plausible stories. I have your name down here since last election as a
staunch upholder of the Constitution. You must support Carr-
Glyn."[7]

"There's not a man in Gleska stauncher than mysel'," said the
Captain. "What did you say the chentleman's name wass?"

"Mr Carr-Glyn," said the canvasser. "One of the good old sort;
one of ourselves, as you might say; a nephew of the Duke of
Argyll's."

"The very man for the job! I'll be there on Thursday; keep your
mind easy on that. My mother wass a Campbell. The Duke iss a
splendid chentleman. Tremendous agility!"

"The whole situation has changed in the last few days. You see, the
Referendum practically puts the final decision upon every new
constitutional change in the hands of the individual elector, and the
Lords are gone."[8]

"Cot bless me! you don't say so?" said the Captain with genuine
surprise. "Where are they away to?"

The canvasser rapidly sketched the decline and fall of the
hereditary principle in the Upper House.

"Holy smoke! iss the Duke goin' to lose his job, then?" asked Para
Handy with sincere alarm; and the visitor hastened to reassure him.

"If you like, I'll send round a motor-car on Thursday," said the canvasser, when he had satisfied himself that the vote of Para Handy was likely to go to the side which had his ear last.

"Don't put yoursel' to any bother aboot a car; I would sooner walk: it's the least a body could do for Mr Glyn," said the Captain. "Tell him that I'll stand firm, and that I'm terrible weel acquainted wi' his uncle."

"Thank you," said the canvasser. "Mr Carr-Glyn will be highly pleased."

"You'll not answer the door the night again if a hundred chentlemen comes to it," said Para Handy when he got back to his wife. "A man might as weel be livin' in a restaurant."

"What day's the pollin[9] on?" said Mary.

"On Thursday," said her husband. "Thank Cot! I'll no' be within a hundred miles o't. I'll be on the *Fital Spark* in Tobermory."

Hurricane Jack of the Vital Spark

Para and the War

The third collection of Para stories, *Hurricane Jack of the Vital Spark,* is set in a world changed by the Great War. Some of the stories give the crew opportunities to tell highly coloured tales of deeds of daring to innocent "towerists".

Other tales afford the opportunity for reflection on the changed ways which the War brought about. We learn of women wearing trousers ("Land Girls"); of the restrictions on the crew's natural instincts brought about by the legislation banning "treating" in Clydeside pubs (a measure introduced to improve production in the shipyards and munitions works, and not Lloyd George's most popular enactment); of the horror of "munition ale" a weak wartime brew made, Para surmised, on the premises after the last washing-day ("The Mystery Ship"); of the inevitable confusion caused by the government "tamperin' wi' the time o' day the way God made it" ("Summer-Time on the *Vital Spark*").

However despite the problems of war, with anti-submarine nets across the Clyde and Macphail being called up to join the Scottish Fusiliers (though Sunny Jim in the end goes in his place), the *Vital Spark* sails on its traditional routes and many of the stories could have been written at any point in the saga. Such tales include the splendid "An Ocean Tragedy" (oddly enough the second time this title was used) which enables Para's vivid

imagination to be displayed to best advantage. The only
remotely military part of this story is Para's reference to his deck
cargo of feather bonnets for the Territorials.

Seemingly unaffected by war is the classic "Mudges" —
perhaps the pick of the entire collection, with its account of the
particular horrors of the Tighnabruaich midge — which can
bite through corrugated iron roofs; the well-educated Gareloch
midges "...ye'll see the old ones leadin' roond the young ones,
learnin' them the proper grips" and the ferocious midges of
Colonsay and their vicious attack on a "chenuine English
towerist". Perhaps on reflection "Mudges" is not an entirely
un-warlike story!

53. *Hurricane Jack*

"STOP YOU!" said Para Handy, looking at his watch, "and I will give
you a trate; I will introduce you to the finest sailor ever sailed the
seas. He's comin' aboard the vessel in a little to say good-bye to us
before he joins a kind o' a boat that's bound for Valapariza. Am I
right or am I wrong, Dougie?"

"That's what he said himsel', at any rate," said Dougie dubiously.
"But ye canna put your trust in Jeck. He meant it right enough at the
time, but that wass yesterday, and Jeck hass wan o' them memories
for mindin' things that's no' to be depended on — ass short and
foggy ass a winter day!"

"You'll see he'll come!" said Para Handy confidently. "Jeck's a
man o' his word, a perfect chentleman! Forbye, I have the lend o' his
topcoat."

"Who is the consummate and accomplished mariner?" I asked,
delaying my departure from the *Vital Spark*.

"There's only wan in all the cope and canopy[1] o' British
shippin'," said the Captain. " 'John Maclachlan' in the books,
but 'Hurricane Jeck' in every port from here to Callao. You
have heard me speak of him? An arm like a spar and the he'rt of a
child!'

"I'll assure you there iss nothing wrong wi' his arm whatever," said the mate; "it's like a davit." But he offered no comment on the heart of the illustrious seaman.

"He'll be here in a chiffy," Para Handy assured me eagerly. "It's worth your while waitin' to meet him when you have the chance. You'll find him most agreeable; no pride nor palavers about him; chust like any common sailor. A full-rigged ship tattooed on his chest, and his hat wi' a list to starboard. A night wi' Jeck iss ass good ass a college education. You never saw such nerve!"

"I'll wait a little," I said; "life offers so few opportunities for seeing the really great."

Five minutes later, and a lanky weather-beaten person with a tightly buttoned blue serge suit, a brown paper parcel in his hand, and a very low-crowned bowler hat at an angle of forty-five, dropped on to the deck of the *Vital Spark*.

"Peter," he said to the Captain anxiously, without preamble, "what did ye do wi' my portmanta?"

"I never saw it, Jeck," said Para Handy. "Iss it runnin' in your mind ye lost it?"

"Not exactly lost," said Hurricane Jack, "but it's been adrift in this old town since Friday, and I'm tackin' round my friends to see if any of them's wearin' a good Crimea shirt I had in it. No reflections upon anybody, mind — that was an A1 shirt," and he looked with some suspicion at the turned-up collar of my coat.

"Nobody here hass your shirt, Jeck, I'll assure you," protested the Captain. "What kind of a portmanta wass it?"

"It was a small tin canister," said Hurricane Jack quite frankly, and, having said so, cheered up magically, unburdened his mind of his loss, and was quite affable when I was formally presented to his distinguished notice by the Captain. He had a hybrid accent, half Scotch and half American, and I flatter myself he seemed to take to me from the very first.

"Put it there!" he exclaimed fervently, thrusting out a hand in which, on my response to the invitation, he almost crushed my fingers into pulp. "I'm nothin' but an old sailor-man, but if I can do anything for anybody at any time between now and my ship sailin', say the word, sunny boys!"

I assured him there was nothing pressing that I wanted done at the moment.

"I told ye!" exclaimed the Captain triumphantly. "Always the perfect chentleman! He thinks of everything!" He beamed upon the visitor with a pride and gratification it was delightful to witness.

"We havena anything on the boat," remarked Dougie, with what, to stupid people, might seem irrelevance. Hurricane Jack, however, with marvellous intuition, knew exactly what was indicated, looked at me with some expectancy, and I had not the slightest difficulty in inducing them all to join me in a visit to the Ferry Inn.

The bright particular star of the British mercantile marine having given the toast, "A fair slant!" three minutes later, addressed himself to the disposal of the largest quantity of malt liquor I have ever seen consumed at one breath, put down the empty vessel with unnecessary ostentation, and informed all whom it might concern that it was the first to-day.

"The chentleman," said Para Handy, alluding to me, "would take it ass a special trate, Jeck, to hear some specimens of your agility."

I did my best to assume an aspect of the most eager curiosity.

"In the old clipper tred," Para Handy informed me in a stage whisper. "Wan of the very best! Namely in all the shuppin' offices! Took a barque they called the *Port Jackson*[2] from Sydney to San Francisco in nine-and-thirty day; Look at the shouthers o' him!"

"If a bit of a song, now — an old come-all-ye, or a short-pull shanty like 'Missouri River,' — would be any good to the gentleman," said Hurricane Jack agreeably, "I'll do my best endeavours as soon as I've scoffed this off. Here's salue!"

Para Handy looked a little apprehensive. "What wass runnin' in my mind," said he, "wass no' so mich a song, though there's none can touch you at the singin, Jeck, but some of our diversions in foreign parts. Take your time, Jeck; whatever you like yoursel'!" He turned again to me with a glance that challenged my closest and most admiring attention for the performance about to take place, and whispered, "Stop you, and you'll hear Mr Maclachlan!"

The gifted tar was apparently reluctant to abandon the idea of a song, and rather at a loss which of the stirring incidents of his life to begin with.

"Vino," he remarked, and then, lest there should be any mistake about the word, he spelled it. "V-i-n-o, that's wine in the Dago lingo. Wherever there's land there's liquor, and down away in the Dago countries you take a wide sheer in, see, to a place like Montevidio. Montevidio's like here, see — " and he drew some lines on the counter with spilt ale; "and down about here's Bahia, and round the Horn, say just right here, there's Valaparisa. Well, as I say, you tack into any o' them odd places, it might be for a cargo o' beef, and you're right up against the vino. That's Dago for wine, sunny boys! V-i-n-o."

"Didn't I tell ye!" exclaimed Para Handy ecstatically, looking at me. "Jeck hass been everywhere. Speaks aal their languages like a native. Yes, Jeck; go on, Jeck; you're doin' capital, Jeck!"

"Extremely interesting!" I said to the fascinating child of the sea. "Valparaiso now; it's pretty liable to earthquake, isn't it?"

"Take your time, Jeck; don't be in a hurry," said Para Handy anxiously, as if I had been a K.C. trying to trap a witness.

"Never saw the bloomin' place but it was pitchin' like a Cardiff tramp," said Hurricane Jack. "It's the vino. V-i-n-o. Silly thing, the Dago lingo; I know it fine, all the knots and splices of it, but it's the silliest lingo between Hell and Honolulu. Good enough, I guess, for them Johnny Dagoes. What this country wants is genuine British sailormen, to sail genuine British ships, and where are they? A lot o' ruddy Dutchmen! None o' the old stuff that was in the Black Ball Line[3] wi' me; it wasn't blood we had in our veins in them days, sunny boys, but Riga balsam and good Stockholm tar."

He suddenly put his hand into a pocket, dragged out a leather bag, and poured a considerable quantity of silver coinage on the counter.

"Set her up again, sunny boy!" he said to the barman; "and don't vast heavin' till this little pot o'money's earned."

"Always the perfect chentleman!" said Para Handy with emotion. "Money is nothing to Jeck; he will spend it like the wave of the sea." But he gathered it up and returned it, all but a shilling or two, to the leather bag, which was by force restored to its owner's pocket.

"What," I asked, "is the strangest port you have seen?"

Hurricane Jack reflected. "You wouldn't believe me, suuny boys," said he, "if I told you."

"Yes, yes, Jeck; the chentleman 'll believe anything," said Para Handy.

"The rummest port I've struck," said Hurricane Jack, "is Glasgow. The hooker I was on came into the dock last week, the first time

I've been home for three years, and I goes up the quay for a tot o' rum wi' a shipmate, Jerry Sloan, that comes out o' Sligo. It wasn't twelve o'clock — "

"At night?" asked Dougie.

"Certainly! Who wants rum in the middle o' the day? I'd been so long away, perusin' up and down the South America coasts and over to Australia, I'd clean forgot the Glasgow habits, and I tell you I got a start when I found the rum-shops battened doum. There wasn't even a shebeen![4] They tell me shebeenin's against the law in Glasgow now. They'll soon be shuttin' up the churches!

" 'This is the worst place ever I scoffed!' says Jerry, and he's a lad that's been a bit about the world. Next day Jerry and me takes a slant up-town to buy a knife, and blamed if there was a cutlery shop or an ironmonger's open in the whole village!

" 'The man that makes the knives in Sheffield's dead and they're celebratin' his funeral, or this is the slowest town on the Western Hemisphere,' says Jerry.

"Next day we took another slant to buy boiled ham, and went into a shop that was full of ham, but the son-of-a-gun who kept it said he daren't sell us anything but oranges! So the both of us went back like billy-oh to the waterside and signed for Valaparisa. That's where the vino is, sunny boys, and don't you forget it! V-i-n-o."

"Capital!" said Para Handy, and, turning again to me, remarked: "It's wonderful the things you see in traivellin'. If you'll come over to the vessel now, we'll maybe get Jeck to give a stave o' 'Paddy came round'."

But I tore myself away on the plea of urgent business.

53. *The Mystery Ship*

UP AT the bar of the inn the crew of the Vital Spark mildly regaled themselves with munition ale[1] which the Captain audibly surmised had been made on the premises after the last washing-day.

It seemed good enough, however, for a gang of young Glasgow Fair lads who were also in the bar, and made as much noise as if the liquor legislation[2] of the past five years had been abandoned.

"They're only lettin' on," said Para Handy sadly. "Just play-actin'! It's no' on ale o' this dimensions that they're keepin' up the frolic. A barrel o' that wouldna rouse a song in a Templar lodge."

He cut himself a plug of thick black twist, and chewed it to remove as speedily as possible the flavour of Macalister's still undemobilised beer.

"I say, old chap," said the cheekiest of the Glasgow youths, "what do ye chew tobacco for?"

"Just to get oot the juice," said Para Handy. "Iss everybody weel aboot Barlinnie?"[3]

The trippers came surging boisterously up to his end of the counter; there was about them an infectious jollity that slightly thawed even the saturnine Macphail.

"Is that your vessel at the quay?" said one of the strangers after a while. "She looks a bit battered. Needin' paintin' an' that — "

Para Handy sighed.

"Ye may weel say it!" he responded. "It would be droll if she wassna lookin' battered. Ye would read in the papers aboot the 'Mystery Ship'?"

"Often," said the Glasgow man.

"That's her," whispered Para Handy. "Q Boat 21[4] — the chenuine article! The cammyflage iss off her, and her cannons iss back at Beardmore's[5], but if ye had seen her a year ago ye would call her the gem o' the sea. Am I right or am I wrong, Dougie?"

"Ye chust took the word oot o' my mooth" responded the mate with impressive alacrity. "The gem o' the ocean."

Macphail merely snorted.

"What was she for?" asked one of the trippers, quite impressed.

"That's just the very words I asked the Admirality when they took her over," said Para Handy, "and they wouldna tell me. 'Ye'll fin' oot soon enough,' says they; 'she's the very packet we're lookin' for to play a prank on Jerry. She looks like a boat that would have agility.'

"They painted her streakum-strokum[6] like the batters o' a book I have at home called John Bunyan's 'Holy War', so that ye couldna make her oot a hundred yerds off if ye shut your eyes; they put a wireless instrument doon her funnel, and a couple o' nice wee guns at her stern, wi' a crate on the top o' them the same ass they were chickens, and put on board her an old frien' o' my own by the name o' Hurricane Jeck that's weel acquent wi' the ocean tred, and another chap for a gunner. The hold was packed wi' ammunition."

"Where did ye a' sleep?" asked one of the Glasgow company.

"It wassna a place to sleep in that wass botherin' us," explained the Captain; "the trouble wass to find a place to put doon the pail in when Dougie and me and Macphail and Jeck was takin' oor baths in the morning."

"Oh, Jerusalem!" exclaimed Macphail to himself, with his face in another mug of munition ale. "Baths!"

"Had ye navy uniforms?" asked one of the intensely interested strangers.

"The very latest!" Para Handy assured him. "I'll assure you they did it handsome."

" 'Q21' on the guernsey in red, red letters," added Dougie. "Tasty!"

"Every man a telescope and a heavily mounted blue pea-jacket," added Macphail, with an ironic humour that went over the heads of the audience.

"But whit was the mystery bit?" inquired an impatient listener. "Did ye sink onything?"

"Did we sink onything?" repeated Para Handy in an impressive whisper, after looking round the bar, to assure himself no person of German sympathies might be present. "When I tell you, chentlemen, that Hurricane Jeck wass the Admirality's man on board my boat, there iss no need to go into the question aboot sinkin'."

"Perhaps the gentleman never heard o' Hurricane Jeck," suggested the engineer maliciously.

"Perhaps not by that name," said Para Handy briskly, "but they would hear o' John Maclachlan, V.C., and that's the same chentleman."

"I mind o' readin' the name o' a V.C. like that in the papers," said an intelligent Glasgow man.

"There iss no more namely sailor in the Western Ocean tred," said Para Handy, "and no man livin' that did more to win the war than my old friend Jeck. Yon old fellow Tirpitz[7] had a great respect for Jeck; he gave orders to aal the German submarines to beware of Jeck in parteecular. But, mind ye — Jeck Maclachlan iss aalways the perfect chentleman! He would sink your boat on ye the way ye would think it wass a favour."

"What sort o' lookin' chap is he?" asked a Glasgow man.

"A great big copious kind o' fellow wi' fur in his ears and the he'rt of a child," said Para Handy with fervour. "He wass on the China clippers in his time; there's not a quirk of navigation that Jeck iss not acquent wi', nor a British sailor that hass seen more life. Am I no' right, Dougie?"

"Chust exactly what I would say myself," responded the mate. "Jeck's a clinker! I never met a more soothin' man — very soothin'!"

"Puts ye in mind o' Steedman's Powders,"[8] interpolated Macphail in a confidential whisper to Macalister, the publican. "Whit is it ye put in that beer? It has a queer effect."

"Where did ye sail to?" asked one of the strangers, eager to get on with what gave promise of being amost thrilling narrative.

Para Handy shook his head, and had another glass under pressure. "If I had a bit o' a map and two or three days wi' ye," he said, "I could show ye where we sailed. But it wouldna be fair to Jeck. Ye'll mind this was the Mystery Ship, and though I wass in command of her, Jeck wass for the Admirality. Would I dare put it any clearer, Dougie?"

"Ye'll have to be caautious, Captain," said the mate anxiously. "Keep mind o' the regulations!"

"Don't get into trouble, whitever you do!" advised the engineer with a sardonic air.

Para Handy paid no heed to the engineer. He had sized up the Glasgow visitors as a most agreeable and vivacious party of fine young gentlemen whose acquaintance was well worth cultivating in the absence of more exhilarating elements in John Macalister's bar.

"Where are ye bidin'?" he asked them abruptly, and was informed that the bell-tent round the point, on the shore, was to be their residence for another week.

"Capital!" said Para Handy. "A tent's the very place for speakin' your mind; ye never ken who's aboot ye in a bar. Dougie and me'll go roond to the tent at supper-time and tell ye things aboot the Mystery Ship that'll make your blood run cold."

"Right-ho!" said the Glasgow gentlemen with one accord.

"Mind ye!" warned the Captain, "strictly between oorsel's! If the

Admirality thocht that we wass blabbin' the way we won the war, there would be trouble. We're no' a bit feared for oorsel's — Dougie and me — but we must consuder Jeck. It wass me that wass in command o' Q Boat 21, but it wass Jeck that had the agility. Jest to let ye ken — we would be sailin' oot each trip wi' oor life in oor hands, and comin' back wi — "

"Caautious, Captain! Caautious!" implored Dougie, with his eye on the clock.

"Half-past two; bar's closed, gentlemen!" announced Macalister, and his guests streamed out.

"Be round at the tent at six," said one of the Glasgow fellows.

"Ye can depend on it!" the Captain assured him. "And just to show ye the kind o' man he wass, I'll bring Hurricane Jeck's photygraf."

54. *Under Sealed Orders*

"The first time the *Vital Spark* and us took up the line o' mystery shippin'," said Para Handy, settling down to his yarn, "she wasna cammyflaged at aal, but in her naitural colour. I wass thinkin' to spruce her up a bit for the occasion wi' a yellow bead aboot her, and the least wee touch o' red aboot her funnel, but Hurricane Jeck, wi' the Admirality's orders, made us sail the way we were.

" 'This boat, my sunny boys,' says he, 'iss ta look like any ordinar' packet that would be carryin' coals, or wud, or gravel,' and he wouldna let Dougie even wash his face for fear the enemy would have suspeecions she wass some vessel oot o' the usual. Indeed, I wass black affronted the way she took to sea — aal rust and tar, the deck reel-rall wi' buckets and boxes, a washin' o' clothes on the riggin', and everywhere Irish pennants[1]. Am I right or am I wrong, Dougie?"

"Ye have it exact, Captain," promptly agreed the mate; "I have seen a bonnier boat on a valentine."

" 'The thing is to look naitural,' says Jeck, and his notion aboot lookin' naitural wass to have us like a boat in a pantomime, and a crew like a wheen o' showmen. He wouldna even let me put on my jecket! And, oh, but Macphail wass the angry man! Jeck's orders wass that we were to keep her at four or five knots, but make her funnel smoke like bleezes. Macphail had to burn up all his novelettes; if he wass here himsel' he would tell ye."

"Where did ye start frae?" asked one of the Glasgow men.

"I'll tell ye that withoot wan word o' devagation," said Para Handy. "We started from Bowling, under sealed orders that Jeck had at his finger-ends, and a lot o' unpudent brats o' boys on the quay cryin' 'Three cheers for the *Aquitania!*' "[2]

"Oor lives in oor hands!" remarked Dougie solemnly. "We didna know but every minute would be oor next."

"There wass a lot o' talk at the time aboot submarines roond Arran, and we made oor course first for Loch Ranza," continued the Captain. "We never came on nothing — not a thing! Jeck and me and Dougie put oot the punt at Loch Ranza, and went ashore to see the polisman. We took Jenkins wi' us — he wass the English chentleman in cherge of the guns, and he would aye be scoorin' them wi' soft soap — fair made pets o' them! The polisman assured us Kilbrannan Sound wass hotchin' wi' submarines the week before, and he wass of opeenion they were shifted up Loch Fyne, for a whale wass seen at Tarbert on the Friday.

"We carried on to Tarbert, and by good luck it wass Tarbert Fair. Jeck threw open the boat for visitors, considerin' the occasion. They came on boardin droves to see a mystery ship, and Jeck put roond a hat in the aid of Brutain's hardy sons. He gaithered seventeen shillin's, and we stayed three days."

"Seventeen and ninepence ha'penny," said Dougie, apparently determined on absolute accuracy.

"I stand corrected, Dougald; it wass seventeen and ninepence ha'penny," admitted the Captain, on reflection.

"It wass a chentleman's life under Jeck; ye never saw a better hand for navigaation! Duvvle the place did we go into but there was sport — a displenishin' sale at Skipness that lasted a couple o' days; a marriage at Carradale wi' fifteen hens on the table, and everybody hearty — "

"Kind, kind people in Carradale!" enthusiastically testified the mate. "That homely! Ye had just to stretch your hand, and somebody would put something in it. It wass wi' us bein' in the Navy."

"But did ye no' see ony submarines?" impatiently inquired one of the Glasgow men.

The narrator refused to be hurried. "Jeck jaloosed,"[3] he proceeded, "that the Blackwaterfoot wass the kind of a place where the Chermans might be lurkin'; we went ashore and scoured aal roond the inn, ootside and in, and up as far as Shisken, lookin' at night for signals. We followed a light for an oor, and tracked it to Shisken Inn; it wass only a man wi' a lantern.

" 'My goodness! aren't they cunnin'?' said Jeck at the end of the week, when there wassna ony sign o' the Chermans. 'We'll have to go roond the Mull and see if they're no' in Islay.' Ye'll mind o' him lookin' the book, Dougie?"

"Fine!" said the mate, without a moment's hesitation, but with a questioning look in his eye for Para Handy.

"It wass an almanac, and Jeck wass studyin' it like a book o' Gaelic songs.

" 'What are ye studyin', Jeck?' I asked him. 'Iss it the tides ye're lookin'?'

" 'The tides iss aal right,' says Jeck; 'I'm lookin' to see what day the wool market's on in Port Ellen.' Man! ye couldna keep step to Jeck; he wass chokeful o' naitural agility. We got into Port Ellen chust when the market started, and they couldna trate us better than they did. The English chentleman in charge o' oor guns said he had traivelled the world, and never seen the like o't. For a couple o' days his cannons got little scourin', I'll assure you!

"Jeck looked the map on Monday, and gave a start. 'Holy sailors!' says he, 'we forgot to caal on Campbeltown, and I have fifteen cousins there!'

"We were chust goin' roond by Sanda[4], and it wass desperate dark, when a boat pops up and hails us. We couldna mak' oot wan word they were sayin'!

" 'Now we're into the midst of it!' said Jeck, quite cool, puttin' oot the light and takin' off his slippers. 'Heave oot the punt and start the panic party!' "

"Whit was the panic party?" asked one of the Glasgow men.

"Chust me and Dougie and Macphail. I assure you we were well put through oor drills at Bowling! Whenever a U-boat hailed ye, ye understand, we were to get in the punt in a desperate confusion, and

leave the English chentleman and Jeck on the vessel, below the crate
where the guns wass.

"Macphail wass first in the punt, wi' his clock and a canister he
kept his clothes in; Dougie fell into the water, and wass nearly
drooned, and I wass chust goin' to jump in when I minded and went
back to get my papers — "

" 'John Bull' and the 'Oban Times'," explained the mate with
unnecessary and misunderstanding minuteness.

"When we put off in the punt, the gallant Jeck, wi' his gunner
below the crate, was usin' terrible language, bawlin' oot to the
Chermans to egg them to come on. A stiff bit breeze wass blowin'
from the south'ard. We waited to hear the battle and pick up Jeck and
the English chentleman when it wass feenished — "

"Ye mind we were driftin', Captain," remarked the mate.

"As dark ass the inside o' a coo," pursued Para Handy, "and, as
Dougie tells ye, we were driftin'. Believe it or no', but in oor hurry wi'
the panic, we clean forgot the oars!"

"Oor lives in oor hands!" said Dougie lugubriously. "And me at
the bailin' dish. The chentlemen's gettin' tired listenin', Peter."

"Aal night we drifted in the punt, and it wass desperate dark, but
a trawler towed us in to Campbeltown in the mornin'. There wass a
demonstration when we landed, us bein' in the Navy, but it wass
kind o' spoiled at first for me and Dougie, wonderin' aboot the
vessel. And there she wass, lyin' at the quay!"

"Criftens!" said a Glasgow man, with an air of frank disappointment; "I thocht she would be sunk by that time!"

"Not under Hurricane Jeck!" said Para Handy. "Ye'll mind o'
Jeck's agility. He had sunk the other fellow, him and Jenkins, and
that's the way he got the Victoria Cross. And it wassna fifteen
cousins he had in Campbeltown, when the story went aboot; the half
o' aal the folk in Kintyre wass cousins to him."

"I have a bit here o' the Cherman boat," said Dougie, taking a
fragment of a herring-box from below his guernsey. "Jeck picked it
up for a sample. Any of you chentlemen that would like
souveneer — "

55. *A Search for Salvage*

"HURRICANE JECK got a great, great name wi' the Admirality for his cheneral agility, efter we sunk the Cherman submarine off Sanda," said Para Handy, "and they would be sendin' him letters every other day, but not an article in the way o' money, and Jeck got vexed. Ye never, never in your life saw a man in such a bad trum; I declare the sparks would fly from him if ye rubbed his whiskers. He wass chust wicked! Am I right or am I wrong, Dougie?"

"Ye have it chust exact, Captain," chimed in the mate promptly. "His language wass deplorable for a Christian vessel."

"And, indeed, I wassna in tremendous good trum mysel' efter a fortnight or two o' danderin' roond the islands in the search o' Mr Tirptiz, wi' my boat pented in aal the colours o' a sixpenny kahouchy ball — "

"Chust makin' a bauchle o' the boat!" said Dougie, with feeling.

"I had no money neither, and if it wass not that Jeck had a fine brass-braided deep-sea kep in the bottom o' his kist, we would be stervin'. Every noo and then he would go ashore wi' a Western Ocean chart rolled up under his oxter and the kep weel cocked, and come back wi' a dozen o' eggs, a pound or two o' poothered butter, and a hen. They're silly folk aboot them islands — chust ass Hielan' ass Mull! — and when Jeck would cock his deep-sea kep at them, and wave the chart, and say he wass offeecial forger for the Navy, they would give him the very blankets!

"We went one day for water to a creek o' a place that was called Baghmohr[1], and spent the efternoon in pausin' and consuderin'. There iss a trig[2] wee cotter hoose at Baghmohr, and a lot o' ducks aboot it; Jeck went in to caal wi' his kep on, efter studying the ducks to see which wass the fattest, and all that wass at home wass a woman and a cat.

"Jeck is aye the chentleman; he took off his kep and asked the woman in Gaelic where wass her husband.

" 'I don't ken where in the world he iss,' said the wife, 'but he left this mornin' wi' an empty keg on his shouther, and him singin'.'

" 'Chust that!' said Jeck. 'It's a bonny place ye have here; iss there chust the two o' ye?'

" 'Bonny enough,' said the wife. 'There's only me and my man and the cat and the ducks, but it iss a terrible place for scandal!'

" When Jeck came back withoot a duck I was dumfoondered. 'Surely ye hadna the right cock on your bonnet?' I says to him. 'I'm sure ye never saw finer ducks.'

"It wass then he told me aboot the keg. 'When a man goes away in them parts wi' an empty keg on his shouther, and him singin',' says Jeck, 'it's no' for holy water. We'll chust wait, Peter, till he comes back!' Oh, man! Ye couldna be up to Jeck! He iss chust a perfect duvvle for contrivance! Am I right or am I wrong, Dougie?"

"Oh, he's smert enough wi' his heid," frankly admitted the mate.

"We watched for the man comin' back wi' the keg till it was nearly dark," continued Para Handy, "and when he came, he hadna a keg at aal wi' him, but wass singin' that lood it put the fear o' daith on the very ducks.

" 'Whatever he went away for, it wassna in the keg he put it,' says Hurricane Jeck, 'but I'll bate ye anything he'll go back in the mornin', and Jenkins and me 'll follow him up for fear that anything happens.'

"It wass hardly daylight when the man of Baghmohr wass out wi' a bowl at the well, and cold spring water didna please him, for before breakfast-time he wass leapin' like a hare across the island.

" 'Put by your polishin' paste and put on your Sunday garments,' said Jeck to Jenkins, 'and the two o' us 'll find oot where that fellow goes for the hair o' the dog that bit him.'

"Jenkins stopped scourin' his cannon, and they started off in chase o' the Baghmohr man, for Jenkins had the greatest respect for Jeck and his agility.

"Ye'll maybe no' believe me, but they tramped six miles till they came to a clachan where everybody wass singin' like a Sunday School choir, and it a Tuesday mornin'! Every man in the place that had his wits aboot him wass doon on the shore aboot a cave wi' a great big puncheon o' rum in it. It had drifted ashore on the Sunday, but nobody put a hand on it till the Monday mornin'.[3]

"They were singin' like hey-my-nanny when Jeck and Jenkins came in the midst o' them — Jeck wi' a terrible cock on his kep, and the North Sea chart as weel as the Western Ocean wan in his oxter, Jenkins wi' bell-moothed troosers and a white string wi' a whustle on't.

" 'Birl your whustle!' commanded Jeck, and him throng buttonin' up his jecket.

"Jenkins birled his whustle the same's it wass for a British battle; Jeck cocked his kep on three hairs, turned up wan side o' his moustache, and steps in front o' the biggest man in the company. What wass it he said, Dougald?"

"Whatever ye say yoursel', Captain," replied the mate with deference.

"I canna mind the words exactly, but Jeck assured them it wass the jyle for them. 'You are fair pollutin' the island wi' the King's rum,' said Jeck, and him sniffin'. 'Ye ken ass weel ass I do that every article that drifts ashore belongs to the Admirality. Gie me a tinny, and I'll see what will require for to be done.'

"They passed him a tinny — Jeck filled it at the spigot-hole that they had made in the puncheon, took a good sup, and said, 'Chust what I wass jalousin' — Jamaica rum. Iss that not desperate, Jenkins? Chust you taste it, to make sure.'

"Jenkins tasted near a pint, shut his eyes wan efter the other, and said it wass rum, withoot a question.

" 'What ye'll do iss this,' says Jeck to the crofters, 'ye'll drive that spigot in again, put the puncheon on a cairt, and hurl it over to Baghmohr, where ye'll find oor gunboat lyin', and if ye're slippy aboot it I'll maybe let the thing blow by.'

"Jeck and Jenkins wass back at the boat by dinner-time, lookin' fine, and full o' capers, but the cairt wi' the puncheon in it didn't come till late in the efternoon. They said they had to travel seven miles to get a horse and cairt.

"We slung the goods aboard wi' the winch, and the men wass wantin' something for the salvage.

" 'I daurna do it,' said Jeck, 'it's against the regulations; forbye, ye didna bring your tinnies,' and in a few meenutes we had up the anchor, and were off to sea again.

"It would be near ten o'clock at night when Macphail the engineer took ill of a sudden, and nothin' would do him but a drop o' spurits. Jeck took a gimlet and bored a couple o' holes in the puncheon. He filled a cup for Macphail, and the silly fool had it swallowed before he found it wass nothing but a sample o' the Sound o' Sleat[4]. Weren't they the black-guards! They had emptied the cask in their kegs and filled it up again wi' plain sea water! Oh, my! but Jeck wass angry."

56. *The Wonderful Cheese*

"WE WERE, wan time yonder, perusin' up and doon the Long Isle[1] looking for mines," said Para Handy. "We looked high, and we looked low, on sea and land; many a droll thing we found drifting, but never came on nothing more infernal[2] than oorsel's. Hurricane Jeck had a terrible skill for mines. At night he would take the punt, wi' a bit o' a net in her, and splash the mooths o' the burns for oors on end in search a' them. Not wan iota! The only thing he would get in the net would be a grilse or two, or a string o' troot; Uist is fair infested wi' them.

"But wan night yonder he came back wi' a whupper o' a cheese; he got it on the high-water mark.

" 'Capital!' I says to him; 'that's something wise-like!' for I wass chust fair sick o' salmon — salmon — salmon, even-on.

"Jeck rolled the cheese on board; sixty pounds wass in it if there wass an ounce! I never saw a cheese that better pleased the eye. Wi' a cheese like yon and a poke o' meal, ye could trevel the world.

"But Jeck wass dubious. 'She looks aal right,' he says, 'but ye canna be up to them Cherman blackguards. We'll be better to trate that cheese wi' caaution. I didna put a hand on her mysel' till I walked three times roond her lookin' for horns, and when I lifted her it wass wi' my he'rt in my mooth and a word o' prayer.'

" 'Hoots, man, but ye're tumid, tumid!' I says to him. 'What harm's in a Cheddar cheese? Take her aft and put your knife in her.'

"He took oot his knife at that, and made to hand me 't. 'Open her up yoursel', Peter,' says he, 'but first let me and the rest o' the crew get off a bit in the punt. I would be black affronted to be blown up wi' a Cherman cheese wi' a bomb inside o't.'

"I looked at the cheese, and, my goodness, it wass a whupper! Ye could feed an airmy on't! And I never wass as hungry in my life! There iss something aboot a cheese on board a ship that grows on ye! But I didna like the look o' Jeck, at aal, at aal, for he aye took care that the cheese wass on wan side o' the funnel, and he had a startled eye.

" 'I don't care a docken for cheese,' I says to him at last, 'but Dougie's fond o't. Gie the knife to Dougie.' By this time Dougie wass in the hold wi' a tarp'lain over his heid, but he heard me fine.

" 'Take it away and sink it,' he bawls; 'cheese never agreed wi' me; I promised my wife I would never taste it.'

"Jeck looked roond for Macphail, but he was off like a moose among his engines, and meh'in' like a sheep.

"The only man on the ship that wass quite cool and composed wass Jenkins, and he wass under the crate where his gun wass, and him sound sleepin'.

" 'Mind ye, I'm no' sayin' there is anything wrong wi' the cheese,' says Jeck. 'She may be a topper o' a cheese for aal I ken, but chust you put your ear doon close to her, Peter, and tell me if you don't hear something tickin'.'

"I made wan jump for the punt, and rowed away like fury!

" 'Heave that cursed cheese o' Satan over the side this instant, or there'll be the duvvle's own devastation!' I roared to Hurricane Jeck. 'Ye were surely oot o' yer mind to meddle w'it.'

"I came back in twenty meenutes, and found Jeck and the gunner Jenkins had the cheese below a barrel.

" 'It's all right,' said Jeck; 'it wass my mistake aboot the tickin'; Jenkins couldna hear it. But aal the same, we'll better keep her at a distance till we come to some place where there's folk that is keener on cheese than we are.'

"For near a month — ay, more than a month — we pursued oor devagations roond the islands seekin' mines, and aye the cheese was in below the barrel. Nobody would touch it. Dougie had his Book oot every night, and indeed I wasna in the best o' trum mysel', wi' my ear aye cocked for clockwork and the boots never on my feet.

"Every other day Jeck would tilt the barrel up, and we could see that cursed cheese ass like a cheese ass anything, but lookin' duvelish glum. I couldna have worse nightmares if I ate it. We gave it, between us, the name o' Jerry.

"It wass the time o' the plewin' matches. The night before a plewin' match we came into Portree and a wheen o' chentlemen were gatherin' prizes. Ye ken yoursel' the kind o' prizes they have at a plewin' match — a smoked ham for the best start-and-finish; a trooser-length o' tweed cloth from J. & A. Mackay, the merchants, for the best oots-and-ins; a gigot o' black-faced mutton for the best-groomed horse; a silver chain and pendulum for the largest faimily plewman; and a pair o' gallowses for the best-dressed senior plewman at his own expense.

"The chentleman at the store had a fine collection o' prizes when Jeck and me went in to look at them, and Jeck's eye lighted up when he saw the gallowses. For months his breeks wass hingin' on him wi' a lump o' string.

" 'What ye're needin' to complete them prizes,' say she, 'iss a fine big sonsy Cheddar cheese. I'll make a bargain wi' ye. If ye'll let me into the plewin' competition, I'll gie ye a prize o' the bonniest biggest keppuck between Barra Heid and the Butt o' Lewis.'

"The man in charge o' the prizes looked hard at Jeck, who had a gless in him, but not wan drop more than he could cairry like a chentleman, and he says quite sharp, 'What's wrong wi' the cheese?'

" 'There's nothing wrong wi' the cheese,' says Jeck; 'she's a chenuine Thomas Lipton, but my mates and me iss desperate keen on the agricultooral tred, and we'll gie the cheese to promote the cheneral hilarity.'

" 'Are ye sure ye can plew?' asks the other one, dubious.

" 'I've been plewin' all my days,' says Jeck, quite smert; 'chust look at the boots o' me!'

"They agreed that Jeck would get into the competition, and sent doon to the vessel to fetch the cheese, and all the time they were away for 't I wass in the nerves, for fear they might jolt it. 'God help the harbour o' Portree this night,' says I to Jeck, 'if they start to sample Jerry!'

"The plewin' match wass a great success. Jeck dressed himsel' in his Sunday clothes, and his Navy kep, and his hair was oiled magnificent. Ye never saw a more becomin' man between the stilts. He had got the lend o' a horse and plew from a cousin o' his on the ootskirts o' Portree.

"His plewin' wass lamentable, but he got the gallowses for bein' the best-dressed senior plewman at his own expense.

"A young man by the name o' Patrick Sinclair won the cheese, and Jeck and me helped him to hurl it in a barrow to his hoose. The whole time we were helpin' him home wi't my he'rt wass in my mooth for fear it would go off, and we laid it on the kitchen bed the same's it wass a baby!

"We got two good drams apiece from Sinclair's wife, and were no sooner oot o' the hoose than Jeck began to run for the ship ass fast as he could shift his legs, me efter him.

" 'It's time we were oot o' Portree,' says he, when we got on board; 'there's likely to be trouble.'

" 'Do ye think that cheese 'll burst before we're started?' I asked him, busy lowsing the ropes.

" 'It's no' the cheese I'm frightened for,' says Jeck, 'but it's Patrick Sinclair. I'm no' a bit vexed for him: a fine strong young man like that should be in the Navy when the land's at war, and no' idlin' his time away at plewin'. But when he opens up that cheese there'll be a desperate explosion.'

" 'What do ye think'll be in it, Jeck? Will it be dunnymite?'

" 'Duvvle the dunnymite!' says Jeck; 'chust chucky-stones! Jenkins an' me scooped oot the inside o' the cheese between us in the last four weeks. We sliced the top off first, and used it for a lid. Three days ago, when you and the rest wass sleepin', we filled her up to the proper weight wi' stones and tacked the top on.' "

57. *The Phantom Horse and Cart*

THE *Vital Spark*, with the labours of the day completed, dozed in her berth inside the harbour, enveloped in an atmosphere of peace and frying mackerel. From the stove-pipe rose the pale blue smoke of pine-wood: she had been loading timber. A couple of shirts were drying on a string; the Captain felt them. "Duvvle a drop o' drouth iss in it, Dougie," he remarked to the mate impatiently; "they'll no' be dry till Monday!"

"My goodness!" said the mate. "I wish I wass a shirt! I'm that dry you could use me for a blot-sheet! And there iss Jum again wi' his mackerel for the tea; the fellow has no contrivance at the cookin' — mackerel even-on since we came roond Ardlamont! Ye would think he was stockin' an aquarium. Fried mackerel iss the thirstiest fish that ever swam the sea!"

"All right, chaps!" Sunny Jim cried from the stove; "to-morrow ye'll get boiled yins!"

Dougie cast a pathetic look at the engineer.

"Issn't that the ruffian?" said he. "Many a man that caals himself a cook would put his mind into the business noo and then and think o' something else than mackerel. It iss my opinion Jum goes doon to the slips wi' a pail at night and picks them up where the fishermen threw them over the quay in the mornin'. Man, I never, never, never wass so thirsty."

Macphail, the engineer, who was rather bored with mackerel himself, was in a nasty humour. "It's my opeenion," he remarked, "that that's no' a mackerel thirst at a', but the thirst ye started wi' last Setturday when ye got yer pay. There's naething 'll cure it for ye, Dougie; it would tak' far mair money than ye earn, and it's worse noo that tratin's no permitted¹ on the Clyde."

The mate was so indignant at the suggestion that trouble seemed impending, when Para Handy hurried to the restoration of a more peaceful humour with a defence of Dougie which, to subtler instincts, would have rather appeared an added insult.

"Never you mind him, Dougie!" said he; "Macphail iss aalways jibing. And he's aal wrong aal thegither; the worst man in the world can be turned from drink if his friends go aboot the thing wi' kindness. It's aal in the kindly word! That puts me in mind o' wan time yonder my old frien', Hurricane Jeck, made a Rechabite for life o' a man in Campbeltown that up till then wass keepin' the distilleries goin' till his wife, poor body, wass near demented. It wass aal in the kindly word, and Jeck's agility.

"It wass long afore Jeck sailed on the clippers and made his reputation. Me and him and a bit o' a boy wass on the *Margaret Ann*, a gaabert that made money for a man in Tarbert. At that time, even, Jeck wass a perfect chentleman; his manners wass complete. To see him stavin' up the quay ye would think he wass off a steamboat, and 'twas him, I'll assure you, had the gallant eye! 'Peter,' he would say to me, and his bonnet cocked, 'I'm goin' for a perusal up the village, chust to show them the kind o' men we breed in Kinlochaline.' My Chove! he had the step!

"There wass wan the yonder, we were puttin' oot coals in Campbeltown, and a cairter wi' the bye-name o' the Twister wass a perfect he'rtbreak to us wi' drink. He couped ower the side o' the cairt the best part o' the coals we slung to him, and came back from every rake² wi' another gill in him. The cargo was nearly oot, and him no' over the side o' the quay yet wi' his horse and cairt, when his wife came doon and yoked on us³ for leadin' her man astray.

"Mrs MacCallum,' Jeck said to her, calm and gentle, 'there iss not a man on board this boat the day hass drunk ass much ass would wet the inside o' a flute; when wass the good-man sober last?

" 'The year they took the lifeboat over the Machrihanish; he was at the cairtin' o't,' says she, and her near greetin'.

" 'It iss high time he wass comin' to a conclusion wi't!' said Hurricane Jeck. 'Away you home, and I'll send your husband back to ye a dufferent character. For the next three months have in a good supply of buttermilk!'

"The woman went away. Her man came back to the boat ten meenutes efter, worse than ever. 'No more the night,' said Hurricane Jeck; 'we'll put the rest oot in the mornin',' and the Twister made a course at wance wi' his horse and cairt for the nearest public-hoose.

"Jeck and me and the boy went efter him, and found the horse tied to a ring at the mooth o' a close. The Twister wass in the next door in the public-hoose, and so wass the rest o' Campbeltown, perhaps, for the street was like a Sunday mornin'.

" 'There's goin' to be a cairt amissin' here,' said Jeck, quite blithe wi' us, and made a proposeetion. We took the horse oot o' the trams and led it through the close to a washin'-green that wass at the back. We then took off the wheels o' the cairt and rolled them in beside the horse. Between us we lifted the body o' the cart on its side and through the close wi't, too, like hey-ma-nanny, and back on the green we put on the wheels again and yoked the horse.

" 'There you are!' said Jeck. 'The first time ever a cairt wass here since they built the tenement! Stop ye till ye hear what the Twister says when he finds it!'

"Oh, man! man! I tell you it wass Jeck had the agility! He wass chust sublime!

"It took nearly half an oor for the Twister to find where his cairt wass, and we gave him twenty meenutes to himsel' before we went up to the close to see what he wass doin'.

"He had a bit o' string. First he would measure the width o' the close and then the cairt, and he was greetin' sore, sore!

" 'What iss't?' says Hurricane Jeck, quite kindly.

" 'Issn't this the fearful calamity that's happened?' said the cairter. 'I canna get my cairt oot.'

" 'What cairt?' said Hurricane Jeck, quite cool — oh, man, he was a genius!

" 'What cairt but this wan,' said the Twister. 'The horse in some way that I canna fathom broucht it in, and noo I canna get it oot!'

" 'Willyum,' said Jeck, and clapped his shouther, 'that's no' a horse and cairt at all; it's just imaginaation! Hoo on earth could a cairt get in here? Chust you go home like a decent lad, and stop the drinkin' or ye'll see far worse than cairts!'

"We got him home. 'Mind what I said aboot the buttermilk!' said Jeck to the Twister's wife; 'he's fairly in the horrors!' And thcn we went back, took doon the cairt again and through the close, and to the yaird where it belonged, and stabled the horse as nate as ninepence.

"From that day on the Twister never tasted drink. I can tell you he got the start! It wass ten years efter that before he found oot it wass railly his cairt wass up the close, and no' a hallucinaation. And by that time it wass hardly worth while to start drinkin' again."

58. *Hurricane Jack's Luck-bird*

PARA HANDY, with his arms plunged elbow-deep inside the waist-band of his trousers, and his back against a stanchion, conveniently for scratching, touched the animal misgivingly with the toe of his boot, and expressed an opinion that any kind of pet was unnecessary on the *Vital Spark* so long as they had Macphail. "Forbye," said he, "you would have to pay a licence for the beast, and the thing's no' worth it."

"Your aunty!" retorted Sunny Jim, lifting the hedgehog in his cap; "it's no' a dug. Ye divna need a licence for a hedgehog ony mair nor for a mangle. There's no' a better thing for killin' clocks[1]; a' the foreign-goin' boats hae hedgehogs. Forbye, they're lucky."

But the Captain still looked with disapproval on the animal which Sunny Jim had picked up in a ditch along the shore that morning and brought aboard in a handkerchief.

"There wass never a beast on board this boat," said he, "but brought bad luck. I once had desperate trouble with a cockatoo[2]; Dougie himsel' 'll tell you; and you mind yoursel' yon dog caaled Biler[3] that you brought, that kept me ashore till the break o' day because it didna know me in my Sunday clothes? You never can tell the meenute you would get an aawful start from a hedgehog; you don't know when you might be sittin' doon on't suddenly. It might be worse than Col Macdougall's tortoise."

"What happened wi' it?" asked Sunny Jim.

"It wass the time o' the big Tarbert fishin's," said Para Handy, "and Hurricane Jeck wass home from sea and workin' a net wi' cousins that had a skiff caaled the *Welcome Back*. There never wass another boat that season had the luck o' the *Welcome Back* — she wass coinin' fortunes. She had only to dander over in the cool o' the evening to the Skate or Ealan Buie, and pick up an eye o' fish that would load her to the gunnel, and the others would be slashin' at it on the other side o' Otter and not a bloomin' tail.

"The other Tarbert boats wass desperate. They were sure there wass something in't, and one Sunday night they asked at Hurricane Jeck for an explanation. Jeck was a man that never took a mean advantage; he wass ass open ass the day.

"'I'll not deceive you, sunny boys,' says he. 'If the *Welcome Back* iss gettin' fishin's, it's because she carries a luck-bird,' and he took a tortoise out o' his top-coat pocket.

"'She's no' a bird at aal!' said one o' the MacCallums.

"'Perhaps you'll tell me what she iss, then,' said Hurricane Jeck, quite patient, and without a word o' divagaation. 'You can see for yoursel' she's no' an animal.'

"'I would say she was an insect,' says MacCallum, and Jeck put the tortoise back in his top-coat pocket."

"'If it wassna the Sabbath evenin',' says he, 'and me wi' my reputation to consider, I would give you a lesson in naitural history that would keep you studyin' in your bed for a day or two.'

"There wass no doubt after that in Tarbert that the *Welcome Back* got her luck fram Jeck's tortoise, and many a crew in Tarbert tried to buy her. But Jeck was terribly attached to her, and money wouldna tempt him. The beast had wonderful agility — not nimble, if you understand, but terrible sagacity. When Jeek would whustle to her she would come and put her heid oot to be scratched, and she knew his very step when he wass comin' doon the quay. My own he'rt never warmed to them tortoises; for aal the sport that's in them you would be better wi' a partan[4], but Jeck aye said she grew on you. There's beasts in nature I never could see the use o' — lollipin' about wi' neither meat nor music in them, chust like polismen; and of aal the pets a man could make a hobby of, I think the tortoise iss the most rideeculus. You might ass well be friendly wi' a floo'er-pot.

"Jeck caaled her Sarah efter an aunt he had in Stirling. He wass never very sure aboot her sect, but he said he had a feelin' in his mind that the name o' Sarah suited. When he would be chirpin' to her and caalin' her Sarah, it made my blood run cold; he couldna be more respectful if she had a sowl, and still-and-on he only bought her off a barrow in Stockwell[5]. I think mysel' it wass the great big he'rt o' him; Jeck must aye have something to be kindly to. Isn't that so, Dougie?"

"The very man," said Dougie. "If he wassna puttin' the fear o' daith on his fellow-bein's, he wass lookin' aboot for people to give money to."

"He wass ass chentle ass a child. He would be clappin' Sarah on the back, and her wi' no more sense o' kindness than a blecknin' bottle. He could feed her from the hand. They said she would trot roond the deck behind him, cheepin' like an English curate, and when he went ashore he aalways had her in his pocket, feared the Tarbert men would steal her.

"Many a time I heard him comin' doon the quay at night, and him throng taalkin' away to Sarah in his pocket. If she had lived I don't believe he ever would have mairried. 'The best o' a tortoise,' he would say, 'iss that she never gives you any back chat.'

"There wass never a man more downed than Jeck when Sarah went and died on him. It wass the start o' the winter-time, and he said she took a chill. The *Welcome Back* wass at the long-line fishin', and from the day that Sarah slipped away the luck wass clean against them.

"Col Macdougall, a fisherman in Kilfinnan, wass a chentleman that offered a bonny penny for the luck-bird when she wass in life, and her eye was hardly closed in daith when Jeck wass over at Macdougall's boat wi' her remains in a pocket-naipkin.

" 'If ye're on,' says he, 'for Sarah noo, you can have her at a bargain,' says Jeck, and he clapped her doon on a thwart.

" 'She doesna seem to have much vivacity. What's wrong wi' her?' said Col, and he wass a man that played the bagpipes.

" 'Not one article iss the matter wi' the poor wee cratur, except that she's kind o' deid,' said Hurricane Jeck. He wass, in all respects, the perfect chentleman and would never take advantage.

" 'Dear me,' said Col, 'isn't that a peety! She wass worth her weight in gold when she wass livin'.'

" 'And she's worth her weight in silver noo she's deid,' said Jeck. He proved to Col that the luck-bird wass ass good ass ever, and went away wi' seven-and-sixpence in his pocket, leavin' Sarah's mortal elements behind him.

" 'I wouldna part wi' her,' said he, 'unless to a comfortable home.' There wass nothing wrong wi' Jeck; he had the finest feelin's.

"Col put the late lamented in behind the stove o' his skiff, and started out for splendid fishin's. They werna in't. There didna seem to be a single cod or whitin' left in aal Loch Fyne. He would go doon to the den o' his skiff and turn poor Sarah over on her back, and give her the worst abuse because she didna came to his assistance, but Sarah was no more concerned than a smoothin'-iron.

"He used her for breakin' coal, and he used her for a toaster, and the winter slipped away. It wass a period namely still in Tarbert ass the Big New Year, money bein' rife, and Col wass oot wi' his bagpipes every evening till the month o' March. He wass over wi' his boat one night at Tarbert at a horo-yally[6], and came back on board, himsel', wi' his bagpipes aal reel-rall below his oxter, greatly put aboot because o' the barren fishin's.

"Doon to the den o' the boat he went, and struck a match, and turned up Sarah, who wass lyin' on her back.

" 'You're there,' said he, 'and the name to you of bein' lucky, but duvvle the tail iss Col Macdougall in your reverence. Paid good money for you, and there you are like a lump of stick, and the white fish laughin' at you!'

"The next meenute and Sarah put oot her heid and started walkin'!

"He wass the valiant laad, wass Col, like aal the folk he came off, but at that he started squealin', for to see a deid tortoise wi' such agility, and took his feet from the skiff the same ass if the duvvle wass efter him. He fell and staved his arm on the quay, but still had the sense to throw his bagpipes into the middle o' Loch Tarbert.

"The parish minister, Macrae, wass gettin' ready for his bed wi' a drop o' toddy, when a ring came to the door, and a meenute efter Col Macdougall grabbed him by the elbow in the lobby.

" 'Oh, Mr Macrae,' said he, 'isn't this the visitaation? Yonder's Sarah skippin' aboot the boat, and her a corpse since Martinmas. I'll assure you this'll be the bonny lesson for me!'

" 'Whatna Sarah?' said the munister.

" 'Hurricane Jeck's tortoise,' said Col Macdougall, trumblin' all over. 'Her ghost iss crawlin' through my boat, so I want to lead a better life, and I've drooned my bagpipes.'

" 'A tortoise,' said the munister, lookin' droll at Col Macdougall, who wass lamentably known to him for a musician. 'Are you sure it wass an actual tortoise?'

" 'If you heard her bark!' said Col. 'She wass bitin' at the heels o' me, and her, as you might say, poor Jeck's relict since last Martinmas. I'll never touch the pipes again. Excuse me caalin', but I came to give a pound for the Foreign Missions.'

" 'What you want,' said the munister, 'iss to take the temperance pledge. You have been keepin' the New Year too long.

" 'It's no' so bad as that,' said Col. 'I only saw but one o' them.'

"But Macrae took him into his study-room, and told him there wass nothing that would keep away tortoises but the temperance pledge. Col must keep teetotal for a twelvemonth, and put his promise doon in black and white.

" 'And what aboot yoursel'?' said Col Macdougall, wi' his eye on the gless o' toddy.

" 'I'll sign it too if you want,' said the munister with much acceptance; and Col agreed. The munister wrote out a line and said, 'I, Col Macdougall, promise to abstain from all intoxicatin' liquors for a twelvemonth,' and Col put his name to it.

" 'That's aal richt,' said the munister. 'Now for me,' and he signed at the bottom, 'George Macrae, M.A., witness.'

" That shows you," said Para Handy, "that it's no' aalways lucky to have any kind of beast aboot the boat. Col staved his arm, and lost his pipes, and a pound for the Foreign Missions, and his liberty for a twelvemonth."

"He must have been an awful idiot that didna ken a tortoise sleeps a' winter," said Macphail, the engineer.

59. *A Rowdy Visitor*

THE ONLY man of the crew who dared to go ashore at Bunessan[1] was Hurricane Jack. He had joined the *Vital Spark* again for a season, fed up with "going foreign". It was subsequent to the deplorable incident of the minister's hens, when Para Handy and his men had to fight their way to their vessel through an infuriated populace, and the *Vital Spark*, for the Ross of Mull, got the unpleasant reputation of being nothing better than a buccaneer.

It was nightfall when she came grunting into Loch Lathaich, and lay-to, while Jack went ashore in the punt on an urgent search for milk and butter.

The Captain gave him money to pay for these provisions. "Take a good big can wi' ye, and don't bring less than two or three prints o' butter," he instructed Jack. "Don't let on what boat ye're off, or they'll twist the neck off ye. And for God's sake, never let your eye light on a hen!"

"Anything at aal but hens!" implored Dougie. "They watch their hens like hawks. A body might lift a horse in Bunessan, and no' much said aboot it, but the loss o' a hen makes them fair demented."

"Right-oh! sunny boys," said Hurricane Jack, and rowed off into the darkness.

He was gone for hours, and in the absence of the punt nobody could get ashore to look for him.

"I doot Jeck's in trouble," said Para Handy about midnight. "He has too flippant a style wi' him aaltogether! After yon calamity we had wi' the Bunessan folk last Candlemas they're no' to be trifled wi'. We'll chust need to go roond to Tobermory and look for him in the polis-office. Wassn't I stupid to gie him the half croon?"

It was the early hours of the morning, and the crew were sound asleep on the *Vital Spark* when Jack came aboard again with a clatter to wake the dead, and apparently with some companion who required assistance.

"Bless my sowl!" said the Captain, sitting up on the edge of his bunk. "Who on aal the earth hass he wi' him here? He's far too flippant, Jeck, for a coastin' sailor!"

"No consideration! Not the least!" said Macphail the engineer, bitterly. "There's my sleep sp'iled for the night!"

"Perhaps it's a chentleman he hass wi' him," said Dougie hopefully, listening to some terrific bangin' up on deck. "It sounds like a chentleman from the hotel, that would have a gless or two in him. Jeck wouldna bring him unless he had something wi' him in his pocket. Light you the lamp, Peter."

The Captain was fumbling at the lamp when a shout of "Stand from under!" came from Hurricane Jack on deck, and some frantic object, kicking wildly, landed between the bunks.

"Holy smoke!" exclaimed Para Handy, and the next moment he was doubled up on the floor from a violent impact in the pit of the stomach.

For ten minutes pandemonium reigned in the sailors' narrow quarters, without its occupants being able to form any idea of the nature of this alarming visitation. The wooden sides of the bunks resounded with blows; a galvanised pail and a box of potatoes were flung back and forward with the wildest racketing; seaboots were flying; it looked as if the visitor meant to batter the *Vital Spark* to pieces.

Para Handy had gathered himself together and gone under the blankets again. "I'm done for!" he proclaimed, gasping. "Whoever Jeck's friend iss, he iss no chentleman."

"It's an Englishman," said Dougie, sniffing, his nose the only part of him uncovered as he cowered in his bunk. "Ye can feel the smell o' him, he's in the horrors. Light you the lamp, Peter. Man! don't be tumid!"

There was an interval of silence, broken only by the Captain's groans and the visitor's noisy breathing. Macphail cautiously put out a leg, with the idea of rising to light the lamp himself, slipped on the potatoes with which the floor was strewn, and fell on the top of the Captain, who, putting up his hands to clear himself, seized an unmistakable frantic pair of horns!

"It's no' an Englishman at aal!" he yelled in terror; "it's the duvvle! He has on a wincey shirt, and I have him by the horns!"

Dougie's instant and vociferous praying was interrupted by the descent of Hurricane Jack with a lantern he had lit on deck, which revealed the mysterious and turbulent visitor as a shaggy yellow goat.

"What iss all the commotion?" angrily demanded the Captain, skipping briskly out of his bunk. "Ye're far too flippant, Jeck! Did ye get my butter and my milk?"

"I had the milk, right enough," said Hurricane Jack, "but I put the can down at my feet till I would talk wi' the fellow that had the goats, and this one emptied it before I noticed. It was milk I went for, and milk I was bound to bring, and the only way I could do it was to bring her ladyship here, the goat. Isn't she a topper?"

The goat, as if calmed by the presence of light on the subject, was lying down, peaceably chewing the top of a sea-boot with the utmost gusto.

"But did ye bring the butter?" pursued the Captain.

"There's no' an ounce of butter in Bunessan," said Hurricane Jack. "That's another reason for me bringin' ye the goat. If we're wantin' butter we must make it oorsel's. A coo's oot o' the question on the *Vital Spark*, for we havena the accommodation, but a goat can pick up its livin' anywhere, and it's far more hyginkic than a coo."

"I'm warnin' ye it's no' me that'll milk it, I wou'dna lower mysel'!" loudly declared Dougie. "I'll leave the vessel first!"

"Where's my half croon?" inquired the Captain, having rescued half a boot from the still unsatiated visitor.

"It's cost me more than half-a-croon to get that valuable goat," said Hurricane Jack. "There's a swab o' an Irishman yonder on the roadside wi' a herd o' thirty goats he's takin' aboot the country, but I couldna go away wi' wan as long as he could coont them. It took me more than half-a-croon, but I left him yonder thinkin' he had a herd o' fifty."

"It's no' me that'll milk that brute!" again protested Dougie. "I wadna be in the same boat wi't. Look at its eye! Fierce! Fair wicked! Forbye, ye canna make butter wi' a goat's milk."

"Ye can!" said the Captain; "it's ass easy ass anything. The best o' butter!" He was looking now with more friendly eyes on the visitor, who was finishing off supper with a sock of the engineer's. The odd thing was that the engineer seemed in no way worried about his sock; he was in a helpless paroxysm of laughter, lying in his bunk.

A violent altercation rose between the Captain, Jack, and Dougie — first, as to whether goat's milk would make butter, and second, as to which of the crew should be what the Captain called the "dairy-maid". It came to wrestling. Pandemonium prevailed again, and the goat, apparently much refreshed by its meal, leapt into the fray with strict impartiality butting at anything soft or hard that lay in the way of its lowered horns. Though seriously handicapped by the narrowness of the fo'c'sle limits, it had all the honours of the battle, and the three men ignominiously rushed on deck.

Macphail was still convulsed in his bunk, safe out of the conflict, and the goat turned joyfully to a change of diet in the form of raw potatoes.

Para Handy's head appeared in the companion.

"Macphail," he said coaxingly, "we forgot to bring her ladyship up wi' us. Slip you that piece o' marlin' roond her neck, and take her up on deck till we'll consuder who iss to be the master of this vessel."

"Come doon and get the beast yoursel'," retorted the engineer. "The dairy's no' in my depairtment."

"At least ye'll put up oor clothes," implored the Captain; "Dougie and me'll get oor daith o' cold." And now the mate's head appeared at the top of the companion. "Don't be stickin', Macphail," he pleaded piteously. "It's a cold east wind, and I want my garments. The Captain and me hass compromised the situation. I'm willing to do the milkin' and Jeck'll churn."

"Good luck to the churnin' then!" shouted the engineer. "The whole lot o' ye's a lot o' Hielan' stots. Your goat's a billy!"

60. *The Fenian Goat*

A WHITE elephant would have been no more awkward a gift to the *Vital Spark* than the yellow goat which Hurricane Jack purloined from the Irish goat-herd in Bunessan. It had apparently been nurtured in the principles of Sinn Fein[1], and was utterly unamenable to restraint, law, order, or the chastening influence of a stiff rope's end. From dawn to dark it was up to mischief, and gave as much trouble as a cargo of rattlesnakes.

On account of its incorrigible bad character and its presumable origin, they called it Michael, and Hurricane Jack professed to have great expectations of the luck that would go with it as a mascot. But this consideration weighed less with the rest of the crew than the possibility of selling it at a pleasing price at some port of call remote from Mull.

"A capital goat!" said Para Handy. "Everything's complete! There's money in him! A fine big strappin' goat like that would be worth a pound."

"Ay, and more nor a pound!" calculated Dougie. "We would get far more than that even if we were selling his remains for venison."

"Naebody in their senses wants a billy-goat," said Macphail, the engineer, unfeelingly. "But perhaps ye could pass him off for a she if ye shaved him."

Michael really might have been shaved on the strength of the ironical suggestion; but already it was manifest that he was a goat to take no liberties with. He had broken away through the night from the stanchion to which they had tethered him, and roamed about the vessel, haughty and truculent, his eye for ever cocked for anything to butt at, and his appetite unappeasable.

The Captain had put his trousers over the stove to dry the night before; in the morning all that was left of them was the blade of a pocket-knife, and Michael chewed his cud with an air of magnificent detachment.

Dougie was sent ashore on Oronsay[2] for a bag of grass, and came back with withered bog hay, which Michael refused to put a tooth to, and strewed about the deck until it looked like the Moor of Rannoch in a droughty spring.

Two or three turnips that were in the bag seemed more to the passenger's fancy: they quickly disappeared, with the most stimulating effect on the consumer, who caught the Captain bending twice to tap his pipe on his boot, and on each occasion butted him clean across the hatches.

"I'll have his he'rt's blood!" roared Para Handy, dancing with rage. "It iss not a Fenian[3] goat will be the master of my boat, and, affront me behind my back! Get me a coal-slice or a shovel, Macphail, and I'll give him a bit o' Boyne Water!"[4]

But Macphail, discretion itself, refused to involve himself in any way in a vulgar brawl, and retired among his engines.

For the rest of the day Michael was content to keep the ship's company interned abaft the funnel. Even Hurricane Jack, with a wonderful reputation for encounters with all sorts of wild forest animals in his voyages with the China clippers and the Black Ball Line, showed the utmost respect for Michael's lowered horns.

They threw lumps of coal at him till Macphail rebelled, finding himself in danger of being left with insufficient fuel to keep up a head of steam: the goat was no more affected than if it had been hailstones.

It was Dougie who had at last discovered that even an Irish goat has some human susceptibilities.

"There's no use o' batterin' away at that duvvle o' a beast," he said, "we should try kindness. I wonder would he take a lozenger?" Since he had stopped smoking a month before, the mate incessantly devoured pan drops of a highly peppermint nature; he never sailed from the Clyde without a half-stone of them.

Pan drops appeared to be a passion with Michael; he devoured them readily from Dougie's hand, and became the most friendly goat in Britain, following the mate about the ship continually with his nose in the pocket where the sweets were.

In the Sound of Islay, Dougie's store of imperial pan drops went done, and Michael became more wicked than ever. He would tolerate no sound or movement of any kind on board his vessel. If timbers creaked — and creaking was a feature of the *Vital Spark* — he laid out with horns and hoofs at the nearest part of the bulkwark; if the man at the helm altered the course, the goat swept down on him at fifty knots.

The Captain positively wept! "I don't believe that's a human goat at aal!" he declared. "It's something super-canny. Iss it the will o' Providence that we're to be gybin' and yawin' aboot the Atlantic Ocean aal the rest o' oor days because a brute like that'll no' let us steer for harbour?"

"We could trap him," suggested Hurricane Jack. "I've seen them trappin' the elephants in India."

"What way would ye trap him?" inquired the Cantain eagerly.

"We would need a pit, but the hold would do if we could get the hatches off — and then — and then we would need some cable, and a lot o' trees," explained Jack weakly.

"And whar the bleezes are ye gaun to get the trees?" asked the engineer indignantly. "Are ye gaun to grow them? I'll be clean oot o' coal to-morrow mornin', and ye daurna touch the sails."

"There iss nothing for it but abandon the ship and take to the punt," said Dougie lugubriously. "We're no far from Port Askaig."[5]

"We'll do better than that!" said the Captain, with an inspiration; "ye'll row ashore yoursel' and bring back a poke o' sweeties. That'll maybe keep that cratur in trim till we reach Port Ellen."

Dougie succeeded in getting into the punt with difficulty, for Michael objected to having the only source of pan drops desert him. Half an hour later, a further supply of his favourite provender quite restored him to amiability, and they were able, at Port Ellen, to lead him ashore on a string.

"If we'll no' sell him we can wander him," was the Captain's idea. "Many a wan would be gled to have him."

"He would look fine in a great big park," remarked Hurricane Jack. "I've seen goats just like that one on the River Plate. They make wineskins o' them. Exactly the same in Bilbao."

"Watch you his eye. I don't like the look o't," said Macphail, as they went up the quay.

At that very moment Dougie's second supply of sweets was finished, and Michael, with the old Fenian ferocity aroused again, escaped from his halter, and proceeded to give animation to the scenery and populace of Port Ellen.

The first thing he altered was the structure of a shipping-box, whose vivid red colour apparently displeased him. A man who emerged from it was instantly butted back among its debris. The goat put its head through a large framed map of the Royal Route, and, thus embellished, swept up the town with the proud and lofty gait of a stag.

"I'm gaun to clear oot o' this for wan thing!" cried Macphail, and bolted back to the vessel.

The others would have liked to follow him, but were irresistibly compelled to follow their property as he strewed terror and havoc in his track. Port Ellen shops hastily put up their shutters, unable to rescue barrels and boxes of goods displayed at their doors; into the only one too late of closing its door the goat went bounding furiously, but calmed down instantly at the odour of peppermint.

Dougie went immediately after him.

"A pound of imperial pan drops!" he gasped to the shopkeeper, who proceeded to weigh them out, all unsuspicious of the commotion in the street.

There was a woman customer at the counter.

"Do ye care for lozengers?" Dougie asked her calmly patting Michael.

"I whiles take them," she admitted.

"Then here's a present for ye," said Dougie, hurriedly thrusting the sweets in her hand. "Give wan or two to the goat; he's desperate fond o' them."

"Come away oot o' this!" he commanded his shipmates, as he hurriedly quitted the shop. "I have Michael planted on a wife, and he'll bide wi' her ass lang ass her poke holds oot."

"Whatna cairry on! It iss chust lamentable!" panted Para Handy, as they sped for their vessel.

The *Vital Spark* was leaving the quay when an infuriated carter ran up and bawled, "Stop you a meenute till I talk to ye!"

"What are ye wantin'?" asked the Captain.

"I'm wantin' a word wi' a bowly-legged man ye have there wi' whiskers on him, that tried to come roond my wife wi' a poke o' lozengers," roared the jealous carter.

"No offence at aal, at aal!" cried Dougie, answering for himself. "I wassna flirtin' wi' her; tell her to keep the sweeties for the goat. He's quite a good goat, and answers to the name of Michael."

"Take oot the chart and score oot Port Ellen," said the Captain a little later; "that's another place we daurna enter in the Western Isles!"

61. *Land Girls*[1]

ON THE morning of Hallowe'en the *Vital Spark* puffed into the little creek where the cargo of timber was already waiting for her. The Land Girls who had felled, and snedded[2], and sawn the trees in the forest two miles off, and driven the logs down to the water's edge, completed their job by wading knee-deep in Loch Fyne, leading the horses that dragged the logs from the beach right out to the vessel's quarter, where the steam-winch picked them up and lowered them into the hold.

Amazing young women! It was the first time Para Handy and his crew had seen their kind. Those girls, in their corduroy breeches, leggings, strong boots and smocks, with their bobbed hair, and Englified accent, made as much sensation as if they had been pantomime princesses.

They were not unconscious of the impression they created. They put, accordingly, a lot of sheer swank into their handling and hauling of the timber; one or two boldly smoked cigarettes; a little plump one, apparently known as Podger, who had come from a Midlothian Manse, actually stammered out a timid "d-d-damn!" in the hearing of the crew, and blushed furiously as she did so.

"My goodness! chust look at them! Aren't they smert?" said Para Handy. "If they were in Gleska they would make money at the dancin'."

Dougie could not keep his gaze off them.

"I wish my wife could see them!" he remarked regretfully. "She never gets over the door to see anything. I'll wudger ye it would open her eyes. Chust fancy them wi' troosers!"

"That's the latest style, sunny boys," intimated Hurricane Jack, with all the assurance of a man of the world, up to date in all new movements. "First the vote and then the breeches. Ye can see them's no common carteresses-born ladies!"

Jack's natural gallantry, even at the age of fifty-five, had made him oil his hair, put on his best pea-jacket, and borrow a pair of misfit boots which Dougie had bought a week or two before in Greenock, found far too small for him, and intended to take back to the vendor. They fitted Hurricane Jack like a glove.

"If my wife wass to go aboot in troosers wi' her hair cowed, I would bring her before the Session,"[3] said the Captain. "It's not naiture! There is not wan word aboot women wearin' breeches between the two boards o' the Bible."

"You look the Book o' Hezekiah!" said Hurricane Jack. "In the fifteenth chapter ye'll see there that a time would come, accordin' to the prophets, when women would arise in Babylon and put their husband's garments on, and the men go forth in frocks."

The Captain was plainly staggered. He had overlooked that bit. "Go you doon, Dougie," he said, "and look your Bible to see if Jeck iss right. I thocht I knew every word o' Hezekiah by he'rt."

Twenty minutes later the mate came back with the Bible and his specs on. "I canna put my hand on Hezekiah at aal, at aal," he admitted. "What way do ye spell it?"

Hurricane Jack took the Bible from him and hurriedly flicked through its pages; then he turned to the dedication to "The Most High and Mighty Prince James by the Grace of God, King of Britain, France, Ireland, Defender of the Faith."

"Tach!" he said; "no wonder ye canna find it! You might as well look a last year's almanac for the Battle o' Waterloo, as look in a Bible that's oot o' date completely for the Prophet Hezekiah."

"Anyway," said Dougie fervently, "ye'll never in aal your life see me in a frock. I never thocht much o' Hezekiah. He wass a waverer."

"I'll bate ye a pound to your pair o' boots ye'll wear a frock this winter," challenged Hurricane Jack.

"Done wi' ye!" said Dougie. "Ye may as weel hand over the money."

By the time the vessel was loaded, her crew and the surprising ladies were on terms of the utmost cordiality. Old Macphail stood off reserved and cynical. He knew about women, all they were up to, all they were capable of: for twenty years he had been studying them in novelettes. The profound impression created on his shipmates by these bob-haired, be-breeched huzzies merely amused him.

That was why he was not invited to the Hallowe'en party.

It was to take place that night at the forest huts, two miles off, where the girls lived and worked. The Captain and Hurricane Jack were to come in their Sunday clothes; Dougie's despair was that his Sunday clothes were in Glasgow.

"That's all right!" said the girls, languishing round him till his shyness made his very whiskers tickle him. "The wood manager is from home; he's just your build of a man — with a suit in his wardrobe to fit you like a halo. We'll parcel it up and send it down to you in an hour."

"Nothing fancy, I hope?" said Dougie nervously. "I canna stand knicker-bockers. I never had them on my person."

"It's quite all right!" Podger assured him. "Mr Taylor's taste is chaste. You can turn up the foot of the legs a little — that will be more convenient for the dancing."

"But I'm no' goin' to dance!" protested Dougie in alarm. "The only dance I ken iss Paddy O'Rafferty."

"Then we'll have it every now and then," said Podger, beaming on him. "But you needn't join in anything else. You can sit out on the doorstep and hold our hands."

"My gracious!" said the mate to himself, "we're seein' life!"

In Mr Taylor's morning coat and a pair of shepherd-tartan[4] trousers, Dougie was unmistakably the most conspicuous guest at the Land Girls' party. The garments were obviously made for an ampler person, but by the time the borrower had worked his way through several plates of mashed potatoes, which, he was assured, were full of threepenny-bits, but found loaded with nothing but buttons, and had consumed apples, nuts, cold ham, and tea till he perspired, there was not a single crease in the waistcoat.

"Mind, I'm no' goin' to dance wan step!" he confided to Hurricane Jack and the Captain. "It iss twenty years since I shook a foot at a pairty, and the only dance I ken iss Paddy O'Rafferty."

"I doot it's oot o' date; I'm no' goin' to dance mysel'," said Para Handy.

"Wi' a splendid pair o' shepherd-tartan troosers like that," said Hurricane Jack, "the thing for you to do, Dougie, is to drape yoursel' over the stern o' the piano and turn the music. Be up an' doin', man! Cairry yoursel' like a sailor!"

To Dougie's horror Podger came up at this stage with a partner for him.

"Here's a lady who is dying to dance with you," she announced. "Her Sunday name is Miss Mathilde Vavasour MacKinlay, but you can call her 'Tilda. In the Greek that means 'very choice'."

"I can see that," said Dougie gallantly, "but if it's dancin' she wants, she'll better take the Captain. Wi' aal them buttons I swallowed, I'm no' in trum at aal and the Captain's a fine strong dancer."

"Me!" cried Para Handy, horrified. "I daurna dance a step for palpitation! Jeck's the chentleman for 'Tulda! He hass great experience in Australia, and the boots for't. There's no a man on the roarin' deep more flippant on his feet."

Hurricane Jack's performance for the rest of the evening justified this testimony; he went through the country dances like a full-rigged ship among the lugsail young lads who were in the party, and refrained from the waltzes and fox-trots only on the grounds of moral disapproval.

It was shortly after midnight when Podger, all in a tremble, pale with apparent alarm, though really from more application of powder than usual, came in to intimate that Mr Taylor had unexpectedly returned, and was to join the party as soon as he had had supper.

"And he'll want to wear these very clothes!" she said to Dougie; "what on earth are we to do?"

"I'll go back to the boat and shift," said Dougie agreeably; he had discovered a very obvious defect in the trousers. The pockets had been sewn up by Podger, and he had nowhere to put his hands.

"There's no time for that. He'll want them in fifteen minutes," said Podger. "We could loan you quite a good waterproof. He'd bring down the house if he found we had meddled with his wardrobe."

" 'Dalmighty! What am I to do?" bleated Dougie. "This iss a bonny habble! And there iss not a pair of breeches in the company will fit me."

"Ye'll no' get mine, whatever!" firmly declared Para Handy.

"Ye havena, by any chance, a kind o' kilt?" inquired Hurricane Jack, who took contretemps of this sort with amazing calmness and resource.

"The very thing!" cried Podger. "There's 'Tilda's tartan skirt! It's good enough for a kilt. Go out to the hut at the back and we'll throw it in to you."

Twenty minutes later, attired, with the aid of Jack and the Captain, in a tartan skirt and a knitted jumper of a vivid yellow, Dougie was coaxed back to the ballroom.

A roar of uncontrollable laughter greeted his appearance. He stood for a moment, blinking and confused, in the middle of the room, in a nether garment much too short for a skirt and yet too long for a kilt, to which in other respects it bore no earthly resemblance.

"Dougie will now oblige wi' the Reel o' Hullichan for the sake of the cheneral hilarity," announced the Captain.

"I'll see you aal to the duvvle first!" cried the mate; "I didna come here for guisin'."[5]

He bolted from the company, and an hour or two later, when Para Handy and Jack got back to their ship, they found him in bed still painfully conscious that he had been made to look ridiculous.

"Hoots, man!" said Hurricane Jack, "what for did ye run away? It wass chenerally admitted that ye were the belle o' the ball. Didn't I tell ye frocks wass goin' to be aal the go for men this winter, accordin' to the Prophet Hezekiah? I never, never, in aal my life got a better bargain in a pair o' boots!"

62. *Leap Year on The Vital Spark*

THE LAST cart of coals was no sooner out of the *Vital Spark* than the crew were up at the Ferry Inn with a bright new tin can Para Handy had bought three days before from a tinker in Ardrishaig. It would hold a gallon. To carry a gallon of ale from the Ferry Inn to the quay obviously did not require two sturdy sailormen and an engineer, but it was thought best that all of them should accompany the can to obviate any chance of accident.

"I have seen a can couped[1] before noo," the Captain had remarked, with his eye on the engineer, who had offered to go alone; "it takes a steady hand and a good conscience to cairry a gallon o' ale withoot spillin'."

"Wha are ye yappin' at noo?" asked the engineer truculently.

"I am not yappin' at nobody," replied the Captain calmly. "I wass chust mindin' some droll things that happened in the way o' short measure wi' the last can that we had. Keep you calm, Macphail, and don't put on a bonnet that your heid doesna fit!"

They went into the back room of the public-house and, sitting down, carefully sampled a schooner[2] each before presenting the wholesale order for a canful.

"What way did Jeck no' come?" inquired Dougie. "I thocht he wass at oor back."

"Ye'll no' see Jeck for an oor or two," replied Para Handy. "He's away gallivantin'. I'm sure ye saw him washin' his face? If ye were to go over twenty minutes efter this to Mary Maclachlan's delf and sweetie-shop, I'll wudger ye'll get Hurricane Jeck languishin' on the lady wi' his hench on the coonter and smellin' like a valenteen wi' hair-oil. The last time we were here she made a great impression on Jeck wi' her conversation lozenges. He's no much o' a hand at flirtin' by word o' mooth, but he's desperate darin' when it comes to swappin' sweeties."

"I havena seen a conversation lozenger since the war," said Dougie. "They'll no' be printin' them."

"If they're no'," said Para Handy, "it's a blue look-oot the night for Jeck! There wass never a gallanter man in oilskins, but he's tumid, tumid among women. It's my belief that Jeck would make a match of it wi' his namesake Mary Maclachlan if only he could summons up his nerve to ask her."

Macphail gave a sardonic laugh. "If bounce would dae, Jeck would be the champion lady-killer," he remarked unkindly. "The man's no' thinkin' o' merrage, in my belief; he has nerve enough to sample, every noo and then, the sweetie boxes on the coonter."

There was genuine indignation in the Captain's reception of a remark so unflattering to the absent shipmate. He had to call in another schooner for himself and Dougie; Macphail this time he overlooked.

"Amn't I the forlorn poor skipper o' a boat to have an enchineer like you, Macphail, that's aalways makin' light o' other people!" he retorted. "Ye have chust been sailin' dubs aal your days, when Jeck wass makin' his name in the Black Ball Line and the China clippers. He wass sailin' roond the Horn before ye learned your tred in the gasfitter's shop in Paisley — that's where ye came from, and all ye ever learned aboot engines, or I'm mistaken!"

"I'm no' sayin' onything against the chap," said the engineer, "except that I don't think ony wise-like woman would ever mairry him. The man's fifty if he's a day!"

"He iss not a brat o' a boy, I admit," said the Captain, "but he's in the prime o' life and cheneral agility."

"It's time he wass married, anyway," chimed in Dougie. "It's a poor life, ludgin's. Are ye sure Peter, he has a chenuine fancy for Miss Maclachlan?"

"She has him that tame he would eat oot o' her hand and jump through girrs," said the Captain. "Did he no' tell me himsel'? It's costin' him half his wages for hair-oil, pan drops, and 'Present-for-a-good-Boy' mugs every time he's in Loch Fyne and goes to see her, but he canna, for his life, screw up his nerve to ask her."

"It's Leap Year[3]; maybe she'll ask hersel'," suggested the engineer.

Para Handy's visage glowed at the suggestion. He banged the table.

"For a low-country man," he exclaimed, "ye have sometimes a wonderful sagacity, Macphail. If Mary Maclachlan would only put the word to Jeck and save him from confusion, it would be capital!"

"We could give her a bit o' a hint," proposed Dougie. "Break it to her gently that Jeck is bashful."

"I have a wonderful lot o' nerve mysel'," said the Captain, "but I'm no' wan' o' them gladiators to risk my life in a delf shop. Perhaps Macphail would venture to put the position to Miss Maclachlan."

"Seein' it wass his idea — " said Dougie.

"I'll dae better than that," said the engineer; "if ye ring the bell for ink and a pen and paper, I'll write a nice wee letter for Jeck frae Miss Maclachlan that'll bring things to a heid and show if he's in earnest."

Macphail's forged Leap Year letter was a masterpiece of tact. It indicated that the ostensible writer was fully aware of the difficulty a sensitive gentleman might have in expressing his feelings to a young lady as sensitive as himself, and pointed out that as this was Leap Year, she was justified in making the first overtures. She remarked that Jack was no longer a youth, and was arriving at that period of life when he required some one to look after him. It was a position she felt thoroughly qualified to occupy. Though he might be of the impression that she was happy in her present position, it was far from being the case, and she was willing to change her condition on the slightest encouragement from him.

"Capital!" exclaimed the Captain when the note was finished. "Chust the way a girl like Miss Maclachlan would put it. If I wass not a married man and got a letter like that I would merry the girl, even if she was a bleck from South Australia."

"It should save a desperate lot o' hair-oil, that!" was Dougie's view. "I wonder where they'll get a hoose?"

A discreet boy, with instructions to say the letter was given him by a girl, was sent with it to the vessel, and the can and its convoy an hour or two later got on board.

Hurricane Jack was invisible. More remarkable was the fact that his dunnage bag and all his belongings were gone too. Inquiries on the quay brought out the information that he had left with the *Minard Castle* an hour ago, having got, as he explained to one informant, an unexpected letter which made his instant departure imperative.

"Holy sailors!" exclaimed Para Handy, "isn't thus the bonny caper? Do ye think we scared him?"

Para Handy and Macphail went down to the delf and sweetie-shop to make inquiries, and found it in charge of Miss Maclachlan's sister.

"Did ye see any word o' Hurricane Jeck the night?" he inquired.

"He was here two hours or more ago, and only stopped a minute," said the girl.

"Did he see your sister Mary?" asked the Captain.

"Hoo could he see Mary?" replied the girl. "She was married a week ago to Peter Campbell, and she's left the shop."

63. *Bonnie Ann*

IT WAS Macphail the engineer who first discovered the fame of Bonnie Ann, and the little shop, half dairy, half greengrocery, where that gifted lady had far more young customers for her occult powers than for her excellent potted-head[1] and home-made soda scones. The occult department of her thriving business was carried on behind the shop, in a room where she read tea-cups, disclosed the future vicissitudes of any love affair with the aid of a pack of cards, or — for a somewhat larger fee — took cataleptic fits, in the course of which she held communication with the dead.

Nor even then was Bonnie Ann's versatility exhausted; she called this chamber of hers a "Beauty Parlour and Séance Saloon", and could guarantee the most ravishing complexions, busts of an agreeable contour, lustrous long hair, fascinating eyelashes, finger-nails to do credit to any lady, and an infallible cure for chilblains, corns, and cuticular blotches.

The notorious Madame Blavatsky[2] was a bungling amateur in the magic arts compared with the shy, almost morbidly unostentatious Ann, who never advertised.

Macphail, having gone to Bonnie Ann for treatment of an ingrowing toe-nail, had been privileged to witness a trance performance, in which she conversed fluently with Mary Queen of Scots, and he returned to the *Vital Spark* immensely impressed.

"I'm tellin' ye, there's something in't!" he declared to his shipmates. "She had Bloody Mary[3] to the life, and I ken, for I've read history. Ye can get it a' in 'The Scottish Chiefs'."

"Did she read the palm o' your hand?" inquired Para Handy, his interest wakened.

"There's nane o' that hanky-panky about Bonnie Ann," replied the engineer. "Pure science! She throws hersel' into a trance till ye only see the whites o' her eyes, and then ye hear the depairted jist the same's they were in the room. She's weel in wi' the Duke o' Wellington; he tell't her three years ago we would win the war."

Dougie, the mate, was not surprised to hear of these wonderful manifestations. "The papers iss full o' them," he said. "It's aal the go wi' the titled gentry and Epuscopalian munisters. I heard mysel', wan night, a noise I couldna understand inside a kitchen dresser."

"I'm no' sayin' whether I believe in the spirits or no'," remarked Para Handy cautiously. "There iss spirits in the Scruptures, though they were different in the Holy Land, and no' up to capers — shiftin' sideboards, spillin' oil on the ceilin', rappin' in coal scuttles. But if Bonnie Ann hass the gift, we should give her a trial to see what she can make o' Hurricane Jeck."

Three weeks before, Hurricane Jack, alarmed at the apparent intentions of a lady who wished to take advantage of her Leap Year privilege and propose to him, had disappeared. He had left the *Vital Spark* without warning, and never been heard of since. Convinced — or almost convinced — that Jack had drowned himself for they knew the lady — his three shipmates proceeded to Bonnie Ann's shop at night, and began negotiations diplomatically with an order for turnips and cabbages.

"Could we hae a word wi' ye at the back?" inquired Macphail in a husky whisper over the counter. "I wass tellin' my mates aboot Bloody Mary."

Bonnie Ann, who apparently had got the adjective to her name from an ironic customer, looked at her watch, and intimated that it was shutting-up time.

"Forbye," she added, "if it's Mary Queen o' Scots ye're wantin', it's no her nicht oot; I couldna get her. A lot o' you sailor chaps thinks a beauty parlour and séance saloon is jist like a shebeen that ye can come intae ony oor o' the day or nicht and ring for the depairted the same's it was a schooner o' beer."

"It's no' Bloody Mary we're wantin'," explained Para Handy soothingly. "We'll no' put ye to the slightest bother. To let ye ken — a shipmate o' oors, Jeck Maclachlan, went missin' three weeks ago. He's no' in the polis-office, he's no' in his uncle's hoose in Polmadie[4], and he must be deid, fair play or foul. Could ye help us, Ann, to find oot something aboot Jeck?"

He bent upon Bonnie Ann a gaze of compelling languishment.

"Awa' into the back," she said, "and I'll put up the shutters and jine ye in a meenute."

They were seated in the beauty parlour and séance saloon when she joined them.

She lit the gas and turned it down to a peep, after first having lowered the blind. Picking up, and gazing intently at, a crystal ball, the size of a satisfactory Seville orange, she muttered, "There's a man missin'. He has a tattoo mark on his airm — it's blue. He's been missin' three weeks; his friends is anxious to hear aboot him."

"And that's the God's truth," exclaimed Dougie awestruck by this swift, unerring comprehension of the situation. "He had a lend o' my pocket- naipkin."

"He's a sailor," continued Bonnie Ann. "The initials o' his name is J. M'L., and he's a Scotchman. He traivelled a lot on boats. He wasna a teetotaller and whiles his language was coorse — "

"Holy Frost! Jeck to the life!" exclaimed Para Handy. "I doot he iss done for; he never even came for his pay. Iss he on deck or under hatches, Annie?"

"Did I no' tell ye!" cried Macphail triumphantly. "Never mind the glessy Annie; throw us a trance, and get in touch wi' somebody that was in the sea tred when he was in the body. There's nae use botherin' Bonnie Mary o' Argyll[5] to ask for Jack: if he's in the Better Land, he'll be doon aboot the quay, or in a beershop whaur she wouldna care to venture."

"I could try the Duke o' Wellington," suggested Bonnie Ann. "Mind, I'm no' guaranteein' ony communication; the Duke, whiles, tak's a lot o' humourin'."

Para Handy looked dubious. "Is there no' a wee chape skipper chap could do the job? His Grace would be an expensive pairty. If Jeck iss there at aal, I'll wudger he's weel kent."

"In life he wass a toppin' singer, and he could play the trump," remarked Dougie helpfully.

Bonnie Ann put the crystal ball back on the chimney-piece, and pulled out a little table to the middle of the room.

"Ye'll hae to help yoursel's," she intimated, having placed chairs for them round the table. "Draw in."

"Don't put yoursel' to any bother, Annie," huskily implored the Captain, under a misapprehension. "We're chust efter a splendid tea."

"I wasna gaun to offer ye onything," said Bonnie Ann. "Ye needna be sae smert! A' put your baith hands flet on the table wi' me and concentrate your minds on — what did ye say the chap's name was — Maclachlan?"

"Better kent as Hurricane Jeck," explained Macphail, who entered into the ceremony with absolute enthusiasm. "If ye put some tumblers on the table he'll be wi' us in a jiffy."

This suggestion that the spirit of their departed shipmate was to join the company alarmed Para Handy, who hastily withdrew his hands.

"Bless my sowl!" he exclaimed, "are ye thinkin' to bring Jeck here in the spirit?"

"I thocht that was whit ye wanted," answered Bonnie Ann peevishly. "It's shairly no' to play catch-the-ten we're gaithered here!"

"And it's no' to see the ghost o' Jeck Maclachlan, I'll assure ye!" exclaimed Para Handy. "Take my advice, and don't you bother him, Annie. He wass a tricky lad in life, and dear knows what he would be up to in the spirit! Am I no' right, Dougie?"

"Ye're quite right, Captain," agreed the mate emphatically. "We're no' wantin' to see himsel' at aal, but just to get the news o' him. Let him keep his distance! Could ye no' get him, Annie, to do something in the air wi' a tambourine?"

"As shair's daith I canna come the tambourine the nicht," pleaded Bonnie Ann; "I'm deid tired — bakin' a' the aifternoon. There's naething for't but to ask the Duke o' Wellington for your frien'."

"I don't believe the Duke's a bit o' good; he'll go on haverin' aboot the battle o' Waterloo, and that's the wan battle Jeck wass never in," declared the Captain.

Macphail looked at the skipper with disgust. "Ye're makin' a fair cod o' the thing," he exclaimed. "Gie the woman a chance! Fling us a trance, Annie, and see whit the Duke says."

Bonnie Ann sat back in her chair, shut her eyes, and in a minute or two was in wireless communication with the Iron Dukc, who, in a falsetto baritone through her lips, conveyed the information that he had seen John Maclachlan in the last two days.

"What happened to Jeck?" inquired Para Handy, in an awestruck whisper.

The unfortunate seaman, it appeared, had fallen over the side of a ship in a storm, swam three days, and perished within sight of land.

"That's Jeck, sure enough!" exclaimed Dougie. "He was a capital sweemer!"

"Iss he happy, Annie?" whispered Para Handy. "Ask His Grace what sort o' trum he's in."

"The life and soul o' the place!" replied the Duke of Wellington. "As happy's the day's long. He sends his best respects to all concerned."

Having recovered from her trance, Bonnie Ann briskly collected a fee of five shillings which the crew of the *Vital Spark* made up with difficulty between them; saw her clients off the premises as quickly as possible, shut up her shop, and retired to the beauty parlour to make herself some supper.

The crew made for the quay in a state of considerable mental excitement, solemnised by the knowledge of their shipmate's fate, and were staggered to find Hurricane Jack himself on board the *Vital Spark*! He had arrived by the *Minard Castle*.

"'Dalmighty! where were ye, Jeck?" inquired Para Handy, who was first to recover himself

"Oh, jist perusin' about the docks o' Gleska," said Jack airily. "I fell in wi' a lot o' fellows."

"Of aal the liars ever I heard," said the Captain viciously, "the worst iss the Duke o' Wellington!"

64. *The Leap-year Ball*

SUNNY JIM, back again on one of his periodical short spells of
long-shore sailoring, went ashore on Friday morning with a can for
milk, and an old potato-sack for bread, and, such is the morning
charm of Appin[1], that he made no attempt to get either of them filled
until he reached the inn at Duror. He wasn't a fellow who drank at
any time excessively, but, Glasgow-born, he felt always homesick in
foreign parts unless he could be, as Para Handy said, "convenient
and adjaacent to a licensed premise." In a shop beside the inn he got
his bread, and he might have got the milk a mile or two nearer
Kintallen quay, from which he had come, but a sailor never goes to
a farm for milk so long as he can get it at an inn.

"A quart," he said to the girl at the bar, and pushed the can across
the counter. As she measured out and filled his can with ale, he
sternly kept an averted eye on a bill on the wall which spoke in the
highest terms of Robertson's Sheep Dips.

"What in the world do ye ca' this?" he exclaimed, regarding the
can's contents with what to an unsophisticated child would look like
genuine surprise. "Michty! what thick cream! If the Gleska coos
gave milk like that, the dairies would mak' their fortunes."

"Was it not beer you wanted?" asked the girl, with sleeves rolled
up on a pair of arms worth all the rest of the Venus de Medici, and a
roguish eye.

"Nut at all!" said he emphaticaliy. "Milk. What ye sometimes put
in tea."

"Then it's the back of the house you should go to," said the girl.
"This is not the milk department," and she was about to empty the
can again, but not with unreasonable celerity, lest the customer
should maybe change his mind.

"Hold on!" said Sunny Jim, with a grasp at it. "Seein' it's there, I'll
maybe can make use o't. See's a tumbler, Flora."

For twenty minutes he leaned upon the counter and fleeted the
time delightfully as in the golden world. He said he was off a yacht,
and, if not officially, in every other sense the skipper. True, it was not
exactly what might be called the yachting season, but the owners of
the yacht were whimsical. Incidentally, he referred to his melodeon,

and at that the girl declared he was the very man she had been looking for.

"Oh, come aff it, come aff it!" said Sunny Jim, with proper modesty, but yet with an approving glance at his reflection which was in the mirror behind her. "I'm naething patent, but I'll admit there's no' a cheerier wee chap from here to Ballachulish."

"Ye would be an awful handy man at a ball," said the girl, "with your melodeon. We're having a leap year dance to-night, and only a pair of pipers. What's a pair of pipers?"

"Two," said Sunny Jim promptly.

"You're quite mistaken," replied the girl with equal promptness; "it's only two till the first reel's by, and then it's a pair o' bauchles no' able to keep their feet. You come with your melodeon, and I'll be your partner."

He went back to the *Vital Spark* delighted, looked out his Sunday clothes and his melodeon, and chagrined his shipmates hugely by the narrative of his good fortune.

"What's a leap-year baal?" asked Para Handy. "Iss there a night or two extra in it? No Chrustian baal should last over the week-end."

"It's a baal where the women hae a' the say," explained Macphail, the engineer, whose knowledge was encyclopaedic.

"Iss that it?" said Para Handy. "It's chust like bein' at home! It's me that's gled I'm not invited. Take you something wise-like wi' ye in your pocket, Jim; I wouldna be in their reverence."[2]

"I would like to see it," said Dougie. "Does the lady come in a kind of a cab for you?"

"It's only young chaps that's invited," explained Sunny Jim, with brutal candour.

The Captain looked at him reproachfully. "You shouldna say the like o' that to Dougie," he remonstrated. "Dougie's no' that terrible old."

"I was sayin' it to baith o' you," said Sunny Jim. "It's no' a mothers' meetin' this, it's dancin'."

"There's no man in the shippin' tred wi' more agility than mysel'," declared the indignant skipper. "I can stot[3] through the middle o' a dance like a tuppenny kahoochy ball. Dougie himsel' 'll tell you!"

"Yes, I've often seen you stottin'," agreed the mate, with great solemnity. Para Handy looked at him with some suspicion, but he presented every appearance of a man with no intention to say anything offensive.

"You havena an extra collar and a bit o' a stud on you?" was the astonishing inquiry made by Dougie less than twenty minutes after Sunny Jun had departed for the Duror ball. "I wass thinkin' to mysel' we might take a turn along the road to look at the life and gaiety."

"Dougie, you're beyond redemption!" said Para Handy."A married man and nine or ten o' a family, and there you're up to all diversions like a young one!"

"I wassna going by the door o' the ball," the mate exclaimed indignantly. "You aye take me up wrong."

"Oh, ye should baith gang," suggested the engineer, with malicious irony. "A couple o' fine young chaps! Gie the girls o' Appin a treat. Never let on you're mairried. They'll never suspect as lang's ye keep on your bonnets."

"I think mysel' we should go, Dougie, and we might be able to buy a penny novelle for Macphail to read on Sunday," said the Captain. "Anything fresh about Lady Audley, Macphail?"

Macphail ignored the innuendo. "Noo's your chance," he proceeded. "Everything's done for ye by the fair sect: a lady M.C. to find ye pairtners; the women themsel's comin' up to see if your programme's full, and askin' every noo and then if ye care for a gless o' clairet-cup on draught. I wouldna say but ye would be better to hae a fan and a Shetland shawl to put ower your heids when you're comin' hame; everything's reversed at a leap-year ball."

He would simply have goaded the Captain into going if the Captain had not made up his mind as soon as Dougie himself that he was going in any case.

"Two-and-six apiece for the tickets," said the man at the door when Para Handy and his mate came drifting out of the bar and made a tentative attempt at slipping in unostentatiously.

"Not for a leap-year dance, Johnny," said the Captain mildly. "Everything is left to the ladies."

"Except the payin'; that's ass usual," said the doorkeeper, and the Captain and his mate regretfully paid for entrance. The room was crowded, and the masculine predominated to the extent that it looked as if every lady had provided herself with half-a-dozen partners that she might be assured of sufiicient dancing. One of the pipers had already lapsed into the state so picturesquely anticipated by the girl whom Sunny Jim ca!led Flora; the other leant on a window-sill, and looked with Celtic ferocity and disdain upon Sunny Jim, who was playing his melodeon for the Flowers of Edinburgh.

"You're playin' tip-top, Jum. I never heard you better," said the Captain to him at the first interval and the musician was so pleased that he introduced his shipmates to Flora.

"We're no' here for the baal at aal, at aal, but chust to put bye the time," the Captain explained to her. "I see you're no' slack for pairtners."

"Not at present," she replied; "but just you wait till the supper's bye and you'll see a bonny difference."

She was right, too. The masculine did certainly not predominate after midnight, being otherwise engaged. The fact that Flora was a wallflower seemed to distress Sunny Jim, who would gladly now relinquish his office of musician to the piper.

"That's a charmin' gyurl, and a desperate sober piper," said the Captain to his mate, who spent most of the time looking for what he called the "commytee," and had finally discovered, if not the thing itself, at all events what was as good. "Jum's doin' capital at the melodeon, and it would be a peety if the piper took his job."

They took out the piper, and by half an hour's intelligent administration of the committee's refreshments rendered him quite incapable of contributing any further music to the dancers.

"Now that's aal right," said the Captain cheerfully, returning to the hall. "A piper's aal right if ye take him the proper way, but I never saw one wi' a more durable heid than yon fellow. Man, Jum's doin' capital! Hasn't he got the touch! It's a peety he's such a strong musician, for, noo that the pipers hass lost their reeds, he's likely to be kept at it till the feenish."

"Lost their reeds!" said Dougie.

"Chust that!" replied the Captain calmly. "I took them oot o' their drones, and I have them in my pocket. It's every man for himsel' in Duror of Appin. You and me'll dance with Flora."

Nothing could exceed the obvious annoyance of Sunny Jim when he saw his shipmates dance with Flora to the music of his own providing. Again and again he glanced with impatient expectancy towards the door for the relieving piper.

"The piper 'll be back in a jiffy, Jum," said Para Handy to him, sweeping past with Flora in a polka or a schottische. "He's chust oot at the back takin' a drop of lemonade, and said he would be in immediately."

"You're doing magnificent," he said, coming round to the musician again as Dougie took the floor with Flora for the Haymakers. "Ye put me awful in mind of yon chap, Paddy Roosky[4], him that's namely for the fiddle. Man, if ye chust had a velvet jecket! Flora says she never danced to more becomin' music."

"That's a' richt," said the disgusted musician; "but I'm gettin' fed up wi' playin' awa' here. I cam' here for dancin', and I wish the piper would look slippy."

"He'll be in in wan meenute," said Para Handy, with the utmost confidence, turning over the pipe reeds in his trousers pocket. "It's a reel next time, Jum; you might have given us 'Monymusk' and 'Alister wears a cock't bonnet'; I'm engaged for it to Flora."

Dance after dance went on, and, of course, there was no relieving piper. The melodeonist was sustained by the flattering comments of his shipmates on his playing and an occasional smile from Flora, who was that kind of girl who didn't care whom she danced with so long as she got dancing.

"Special request from Flora — would ye give us 'The Full-Rigged Ship' the next one? That's a topper," said the Captain to him. Or, "Compliments of Flora, and would you mind the Garaka Waltz and Circassian Circle for the next, Jum? She says she likes my style o' dancin'."

"I wish to goodness I'd never learned to play a bloomin' note," said Sunny Jim.

But he played without cessation till the ball was ended, the fickle Flora dancing more often with his shipmates than with anybody else.

As they took the road to Kintallen quay at six o'clock in the morning, Para Handy took some chanter reeds from his pocket and handed them to Sunny Jim.

"You should learn the pipes, Jum," he remarked. "They're no' so sore on you ass a melodeon. Man, but she wass a lovely dancer, Flora! Chust sublime! Am I no' right, Dougie?"

"A fair gazelle! The steps o' her!" said the mate poetically.

"And we were pretty smert on oor feet oorsel's," said Para Handy. "It doesna do to have aal your agility in your fingers."

65. *The Bottle King*

THE *Vital Spark* at nightfall put into the little bay where her cargo of timber was assembled. On an ingenuous excuse of "takin' the air", Hurricane Jack who had not been there before, went ashore at the earliest possible moment in the dark, and, trusting to an instinct usually unerring, searched for some place of cheer.

He came on the inn through a back yard, where were several vans and dogcarts, and a curious sort of chariot, highly ornamental to the feel, that puzzled him considerably, till he struck a match, and found it was a hearse.

The hearse, however, engaged his attention less intently than the enormous array of empty bottles which were piled up all round the yard. Crates were full of them, barrels were brimming over with them; they were in layers ten deep under the stable eaves, and tinkling with the water that fell through them from a broken rhone.

"Whatever they are in this place," said Jack to himself, "they're no' nerrow-minded. They must have a fine cheery winter of it! If they drank all that, there must have been great tred wi' the hearse."

He opened that solemn vehicle, looked inside, and found it too was filled with the relics of conviviality, mostly wine-bottles.

"English gentlemen. Towerists. Shooters. The money them folk waste!"

He shook some of the bottles, to make certain they were empty. "No fears o' them!" he reflected cynically. "It makes me sad. Puttin' bottles in a hearse — it's no respectable; I wonder what the ministers would say!"

There was no access to the inn from the yard that he could find, so to save time he climbed a wall, and found himself on the other side of it, by that marvellous intuition of his, exactly at the door of the bar where all the winter business of the inn was done.

Nobody was inside but the innkeeper, who was washing tumblers in the light of a hanging paraffin -lamp, and was suspiciously flushed.

"A wet night," said Hurricane Jack, taking off his soaking cap and slapping it against the skirt of his oilskin coat to get rid of part of its moisture. "I'll take a small sensation."

The landlord looked surprised. "I thought you were from Balliemeanach," said he, "to order the hearse. Where in the world did ye come from?"

"From the boundin' deep," said Hurricane Jack. "My ship's outside there, as ye might say, on the doorstep."

The landlord looked immensely relieved.

"As sure as death," said he, "I thought ye were from Balliemeanach. Maclean the wudman had a couple o' glesses o' Cream de Mong here yesterday, and I havena slept a wink since, wonderin' would he get over it."

"Cream de Mong," said Hurricane Jack, with genuine interest; "if it's anything like that, I'll try it."

The landlord produced a bottle of green liqueur from below the counter. "Mind ye," he said, "it's at your own risk. I don't fancy the look o't mysel'. It was in the cellar when I came here three years ago, and I hadna the nerve to offer it to any one till Maclean was here in desperation yesterday, and me withoot a drop o' spirits in the hoose."

Hurricane Jack picked up the bottle, looked at it, and put it down again. "Starboard Light," he remarked. "I've seen it. They take it in cabins. I wouldn't use it to oil my hair. What I'm wantin's something to drink."

A bottle of beer was promptly uncorked and put before him. "Ninepence," said the landlord.

"Holy sailors!" exclaimed Hurricane Jack. "I could buy wine for that on the Rio Grande."

"There's a penny for the bottle," said the landlord. "Eightpence if ye bring back the bottle."

Jack, two seconds after, handed him back the empty bottle and eightpence.

Inveraray – Neil Munro's birthplace (Authors' collection)

P.S. Columba at Ardrishaig (Authors' collection)

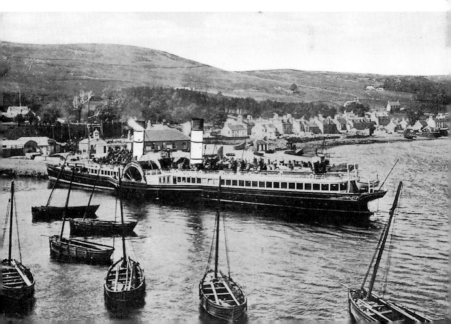

der.

"Take Clynder . . . or any other place in the Gareloch" (*Mudges*)
(Authors' collection)

"They're jist at big-gun practice" (*Para and the Navy*)
(Argyll & Bute Libraries)

"Where were they bound for? Was't Kirkintilloch?" (*Queer Cargoes*)
(East Dunbartonshire Libraries)

"I'll bate ye he's gaun to the Scottish Exhibeetion" (*The Stowaway*)
(Mitchell Library, Glasgow)

"I will go over and see my good-sister at Helensburgh"
(*Para Handy Master Mariner*) (West Dunbartonshire Libraries)

"There's no much fun in Tobermory in the summer time"
(*Treasure Trove*) (Argyll & Bute Libraries)

Lochgoilhead (Argyll & Bute Libraries)

The Pier, Dunoon (Argyll & Bute Libraries)

Brodick Pier and Goat Fell (Argyll & Bute Libraries)

"High jeenks and big hauls" (*Herring: a gossip*) (Argyll & Bute Libraries)

"A handy wife at the guttin'" (*Herring: a gossip*) (Argyll & Bute Libraries)

"Jack went ashore . . . on an urgent search for milk and butter"
(*A Rowdy Visitor*) (Argyll & Bute Libraries)

"The place for life in them days" (*Herring: a gossip*)
(Argyll & Bute Libraries)

"It was Glasgow Fair Saturday" (*Wee Teeny*)
(Argyll & Bute Libraries)

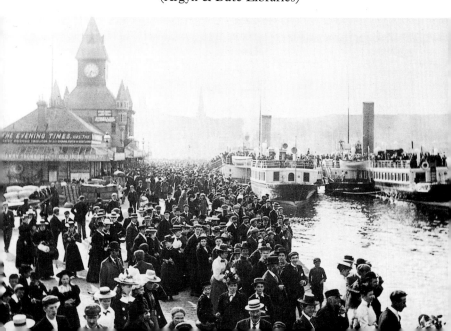

"Ye're surely keen on empty bottles," he remarked. "A penny apiece, and glad to get as many as I can; they call me the Bottle King," said the landlord. "But someway, this while back, my mind's a' reel-rall."

Para Handy and Dougie were going to bed, and Macphail was there already, when Hurricane Jack gat back to the ship and excitedly demanded a large spale basket.[1]

"What on earth are ye goin' to do wi' a spale basket Jeck?" inquired the Captain. "Were ye fishin'?"

"No, nor fishin'!" retorted Jack; "but there's a man up yonder at the inn that calls himsel' the Bottle King, and payin' a penny apiece for them. I think I can put a lot o' tred in his way." He had already found a basket.

Para Handy looked at him uneasily. "Iss it Peter Grant?" he asked. "Ye'll no' get roond Peter wi' aal your agility. If it's buyin' bottles he is, ye'll no' put him off wi' jeely jars. Where in the name o' fortune are ye goin' to get the bottles? There iss not wan bottle in this boat, unless it's under Macphail's pillow."

"Hoots, man!" said Dougie, remonstrative; "give Jeck a chance! Jeck never yet put oot his hand farther than he could streetch his arm."

"Come on the pair o' ye, and see a pant!" said Hurricane Jack. "We'll have to look slippy afore Grant shuts his shop."

"I hope it's nothing that'll be found oot," said Para Handy, still uneasy. "Ye're a duvvle for quirks, Jeck, and I wouldna like the ship to get into trouble."

Ten minutes later they all trailed up to the inn with the empty basket.

The innkeeper was still washing tumblers when the Captain and Dougie, carrying a spale basket of empty bottles between them, came into his bar, and Hurricane Jack behind them.

"Three pints o' ale," said Jack, with the utmost confidence, "and here's two dozen bottles. We're glad to get rid o' them."

The Bottle King was frankly surprised at such a consignment from such a quarter.

"Wherever ye got them bottles, it wasna here," he said. "At least, as far as I can mind. My heid's a' reel-rall, but it doesna maitter. I'm willin' to tak' them," and, having emptied the basket, he produced the beer for his customers.

"Are ye sure they're no' worth more than a penny the piece?" inquired Para Handy. "We were gettin' tuppence for them in Port Askaig. Am I right, Dougie, or am I wrong?"

"It wass tuppence in Port Askaig, and tuppence ha'penny in Port Ellen," replied the mate, with unhesitating assurance. "Bottles is scarce[2]. They're no' makin' them. And ye never in your life saw bonnier bottles than them; they're the chenuine gless."

"Pure plate-gless," said Hurricane Jack. "Look at the labels — 'Sherry Wine' — I'll wager there's a lot o' money in them."

"We have a ship-load yonder o' them," said the Captain. "Could ye be doin' wi' a gross or two? Chust for the turnover. We must aal put oor hand to the plew to help the government, Mr Grant."

The Bottle King for a moment suspended his washing of tumblers, with tremulous hands put on a pair of spectacles, and looked more closely at his purchase.

"God bless me!" he exclaimed; "them's my own wine bottles! Where did ye get them?"

"We got them in a hearse behind the hoose here," frankly admitted Hurricane Jack. "There's a thoosand deid men yonder, if there's wan."

"My Chove! aren't you the ruffians?" cried Peter Grant. "Sellin' me my own bottles! I never could mind where I put them, and me lookin' for them high and low since the Old New Year. But tach! it doesna maitter; they caal me the Bottle King."

66. *"Mudges"*[1]

"By chove! but they're bad the night!" said Dougie, running a grimy paw across his forehead.

"Perfectly ferocious!" said Para Handy, slapping his neck. "This fair beats Bowmore[2], and Bowmore iss namely for its mudges. I never saw the brutes more desperate! You would actually think they were whustlin' on wan another, cryin', 'Here's a clean sailor, and he hasna a collar on; gather ahout, boys!'

"Oh, criftens!" whimpered Sunny Jim, in agony, dabbing his face incessantly with what looked suspiciously like a dish-cloth; "I've see'd midges afore this, but they never had spurs on their feet afore. Yah-h-h! I wish I was back in Gleska! They can say what they like aboot the Clyde, but anywhere above Bowlin' I'll guarantee ye'll no' be eaten alive. If they found a midge in Gleska, they would put it in the Kelvingrove Museum."

Macphail, his face well lubricated, came up from among the engines, and jeered. "Midges never bothered me," said he contemptuously. "If ye had been wi' me on the West Coast o' Africa, and felt the mosquitoes, it wouldna be aboot a wheen[3] o' gnats ye would mak' a sang. It's a' a hallucination aboot midges; I can only speak aboot them the way I find them, and they never did me ony harm. Perhaps it's no midges that's botherin' ye efter a'."

"Perhaps no'," said Para Handy, with great acidity. "Perhaps it's hummin'-birds, but the effect iss chust the same. Ye'll read in the Scruptures yonder aboot the ant goin' for the sluggard[4], but the ant iss a perfect chentleman compared wi' the mudge. And from aal I ever heard o' the mosquito, it'll no' stab ye behind your back withoot a word o' warnin'. Look at them on Dougie's face — quite black! Ye would never think it waas the Sunday."

It was certainly pretty bad at the quay of Arrochar. With the evening air had come out, as it seemed, the midges of all the Highlands. They hung in clouds above the *Vital Spark*, and battened gluttonously on her distracted crew.

"When I was at the mooth o' the Congo River — " began the engineer; but Para Handy throttled the reminiscence.

"The Congo's no' to be compared wi' the West o' Scotland when ye come to insects," said Para Handy. "There's places here that's chust deplorable whenever the weather's the least bit warm. Look at Tighnabruaich! — they're that bad there, they'll bite their way through corrugated iron roofs to get at ye! Take Clynder, again, or any other place in the Gareloch, and ye'll see the old ones leadin' roond the young ones, learnin' them the proper grips. There iss a spachial kind of mudge in Dervaig, in the Isle of Mull, that hass aal the points o' a Poltalloch terrier[5], even to the black nose and the cocked lugs, and sits up and barks at you. I wass once gatherin' cockles in Colonsay — "

"I could be daein' wi' some cockles," said Sunny Jim. "I aye feel like a cockle when it comes near the Gleska Fair."

"The best cockles in the country iss in Colonsay," said the Captain. "But the people in Colonsay iss that slow they canna catch them. I wass wance gatherin' cockles there, and the mudges were that large and bold, I had to throw stones at them."

"It was a pity ye hadna a gun," remarked Macphail, with sarcasm.

"A gun would be no' much use wi' the mudges of Colonsay," replied the Captain; "nothing would discourage yon fellows but a blast o' dynamite. What wass there on the island at the time but a chenuine English towerist, wi' a capital red kilt, and, man! but he wass green! He was that green, the coos of Colonsay would go mooin' along the road efter him, thinkin' he wass gress. He wass wan of them English chentlemen that'll be drinkin' chinger-beer on aal occasions, even when they're dry, and him bein' English, he had seen next to nothing aal his days till he took the boat from West Loch Tarbert. The first night on the island he went oot in his kilt, and came back in half an oor to the inns wi' his legs fair peetiful! There iss nothing that the mudges likes to see among them better than an English towerist with a kilt: the very tops wass eaten off his stockin's."

"That's a fair streetcher, Peter!" exclaimed the incredulous engineer.

"It's ass true ass I'm tellin' you," said Para Handy. "Any one in Colonsay will tell you. He had wan of them names shed in the middle like Fitz-Gerald or Seton-Kerr; that'll prove it to ye. When he came in to the inns wi' his legs chust fair beyond redemption, he didna even know the cause of it.

" 'It's the chinger-beer that's comin' oot on you,' says John Macdermott, that had the inns at the time. 'There iss not a thing you can drink that iss more deliteerious in Colonsay. Nobody takes it here.'

" 'And what in all the world do they take?' said the English chentleman.

" 'The water o' the mountain well,' said John, 'and whiles a drop of wholesome Brutish spirits. There's some that doesna care for water.'

"But the English chentleman was eccentric, and nothing would do for him to drink but chinger, an' they took him doon to a shed where the fishermen were barkin' nets[6], and they got him to bark his legs wi' catechu[7]. If it's green he wass before, he wass now ass brown's a trammel net[8]. But it never made a bit o' odds to the mudges oot in Colonsay! I tell you they're no' slack!"

"They're no' slack here neithers!" wailed Sunny Jim, whose face was fairly wealed by the assailants. "Oh, michty! I think we would be faur better ashore."

"Not a bit!" said Dougie, furiously puffing a pipe of the strongest tobacco, in whose fumes the midges appeared to take the most exquisite pleasure. "There's no' a place ashore where ye could take shelter from them — it being Sunday," he significantly addcd.

"I'm gaun ashore anyway," said Macphail, removing all superfluous lubricant from his countenance with a piece of waste. "It wouldna be midges that would keep me lollin' aboot this auld hooker on a fine nicht. If ye had some experience o' mosquitoes! Them's the chaps for ye. It's mosquitoes that spreads the malaria fever."

They watched him go jauntily up the quay, accompanied by a cloud of insects which seemed to be of the impression that he was leading them to an even better feeding-ground than the *Vital Spark*. He had hardly gone a hundred yards when he turned and came hurriedly back, beating the air.

"Holy frost!" he exclaimed, jumping on deck, "I never felt midges like that in a' my days afore; they're in billions o' billions!"

"Tut, tut!" said Para Handy. "Ye're surely getting awfu' tumid, Macphail. You that's so weel acquent wi' them mosquitoes! If I wass a trevelled man like you, I wouldna be bate wi' a wheen o' Hielan' mudges. They're no' in't anyway. Chust imagination! Chust a hallucination! Ye mind ye told us?"

"There's no hallucination aboot them chaps," said Macphail, smacking himself viciously.

"Nut at all!" said Sunny Jim. "Nut at all! If there's ony hallucination aboot them, they have it sherpened. G-r-r-r! It's cruel; that's whit it is; fair cruel!"

"I promised I would go and see Macrae the nicht," said the engineer. "But it's no' safe to gang up that quay. This is yin o' the times I wish I was a smoker; that tobacco o' yours, Dougie, would shairly fricht awa' the midges."

"Not wan bit of it!" said Dougie peevishly, rubbing the back of his neck, on which his tormentors were thickly clustered. "I'm beginning to think mysel' they're partial to tobacco; it maybe stimulates the appetite. My! aren't they the brutes! Look at them on Jim!"

With a howl of anguish Sunny Jim dashed down the fo'c'sle hatch, the back of his coat pulled over his ears.

"Is there naething at a' a chap could dae to his face to keep them aff?" asked the engineer, still solicitous about his promised visit to Macrae.

"Some people 'll be sayin' paraffin-oil iss a good thing," suggested the Captain. "But that's only for Ro'sa' mudges; I'm thinkin' the Arrochar mudges would maybe consuder paraffine a trate. And I've heard o' others tryin' whusky — I mean rubbed on ootside. I never had enough to experiment wi't mysel'. Forbye, there's none."

"I wadna care to gang up to Macrae's on a Sunday smellin' o' either paraffine-oil or whisky," said Macphail.

"Of course not!" said Para Handy. "What was I thinkin' of? Macrae's sister wouldna like it," and he winked broadly at Dougie. "Ye'll be takin' a bit of a daunder wi' her efter the church goes in. Give her my best respects, will ye? A fine, big, bouncin' gyurl! A splendid form!"

"You shut up!" said Macphail to his commander, blushing. "I think I'll gie my face anither syne wi' plenty o' saft soap for it, and mak' a breenge across to Macrae's afore the effect wears aff "

He dragged a pail over to the water-beaker, half filled it with water, added a generous proportion of soft soap from a tin can, and proceeded to wash himself without taking off his coat.

"Ye needna mind to keep on your kep," said the Captain, grimacing to Dougie. "Mima 'll no' see ye. He's been callin' on Macrae a score o' times, Dougie, and the sister hasna found oot yet he's bald. Mercy on us! Did ye ever in your life see such mudges!"

"I'm past speakin' aboot them!" said the mate with hopeless resignation. "What iss he keepin' on his bonnet for?"

"He's that bald that unless he keeps it on when he's washin' his face he doesna know where to stop," said Para Handy. "The want o' the hair's an aawful depredaation!"

But even these drastic measures failed to render Macphail inviolate from the attack of the insects, whose prowess he had underestimated. For the second time he came running back from the head of the quay pursued by them, to be greeted afresh by the irony of his Captain.

"There's a solid wall o' them up there," he declared, rubbing his eyes.

"Isn't it annoyin'?" said the Captain, with fallacious sympathy. "Mima will be weary waitin' on ye. If there wass a druggist's open, ye might get something in a bottle to rub on. Or if it wassna the Sabbath, ye might get a can o' syrup in the grocer's."

"Syrup?" said the engineer inquiringly, and Para Handy slyly kicked Dougie on the shin.

"There's nothin' better for keepin' awa' the mudges," he explained. "Ye rub it on your face and leave it on. It's a peety we havena any syrup on the boat."

"Sunny Jim had a tin o' syrup last night at his tea," said the engineer hopefully.

"But it must be the chenuine golden syrup," said Para Handy. "No other kind 'll do."

Sunny Jim was routed out from under the blankets in his bunk to produce syrup, which proved to be of the requisite golden character, as Para Handy knew very well it was, and five minutes later Macphail, with a shining countenance, went up the quay a third time attended by midges in greater myriads than ever. This time he beat no retreat.

"Stop you!" said Para Handy. "When Mima Macrae comes to the door, she'll think it's no' an enchineer she has to caal on her, but a fly cemetery."[9]

67. *An Ocean Tragedy*

GEORGE IV, being a sovereign of imagination, was so much impressed by stories of Waterloo that he began to say he had been there himself, and had taken part in it. He brought so much imagination to the narrative that he ended by believing it — an interesting example of the strange psychology of the liar. Quite as remarkable is the case of Para Handy, whose singular delusion of Sunday fortnight last is the subject of much hilarity now among seamen of the minor coasting-trade.

The first of the storm on Saturday night found the *Vital Spark* off Toward[1] on her way up-channel, timber-laden, and without a single light, for Sunny Jim, who had been sent ashore for oil at Tarbert, had brought back a jar of beer instead by an error that might naturally occur with any honest seaman.

When the lights of other ships were showing dangerously close the mate stood at the bow and lit matches, which, of course, were blown out instantly.

"It's not what might be called a cheneral illumination," he remarked, "but it's an imitataation of the Gantock Light, and it no' workin' proper, and you'll see them big fellows will give us plenty o' elbow-room."

Thanks to the matches and a bar of iron which Macphail had hung on the lever of the steam-whistle, so that it lamented ceaselessly through the tempest like a soul in pain, the *Vital Spark* escaped collision, and some time after midnight got into Cardwell Bay[2] with nothing lost except the jar, a bucket, and the mate's sou'-wester.

"A dirty night! It's us that iss weel out of it," said Para Handy gratefully, when he had got his anchor down.

The storm was at its worst when the Captain went ashore on Sunday[3] to get the train for Glasgow on a visit to his wife, the farther progress of his vessel up the river for another day at least being obviously impossible. It was only then he realised that he had weathered one of the great gales that make history. At Gourock pierhead[4] shellbacks[5] of experience swore they had never seen the like of it; there were solemn bodings about the fate of vessels that had to face it. Para Handy, as a ship's commander who had struggled through it, found himself regarded as a hero, and was plied with the most flattering inquiries. On any other day the homage of the shellbacks might have aroused suspicion, but its disinterested nature could not be called in question, seeing all the public-houses were shut.

"Never saw anything like it in aal my born days," he said. "I wass the length wan time of puttin' off my sluppers and windin' up my watch for the Day of Chudgment. Wan moment the boat wass up in the air like a flyin'-machine, and the next she wass scrapin' the cockles off the bottom o' the deep. Mountains high — chust mountains high! And no' wee mountains neither, but the very bens of Skye! The seas was wearin' through us fore and aft like yon mysterious river rides that used to be at the Scenic Exhibeetion, and the noise o' the cups and saucers clatterin' doon below wass terrible, terrible! If Dougie wass here he could tell you."

"A dog's life, boys!" said the shellbacks. "He would be ill-advised that would sell a farm and go to sea. Anything carried away, Captain?"

A jar, a bucket, and a sou'-wester seemed too trivial a loss for such a great occasion. Para Handy hurriedly sketched a vision of bursting hatches, shattered bulwarks, a mate with a broken leg, and himself for hours lashed to the wheel.

It was annoying to find that these experiences were not regarded by the shellbacks as impressive. They seemed to think that nothing short of tragedy would do justice to a storm of such unusual magnitude.

Para Handy got into the train, and found himself in the company of some Paisley people, who seemed as proud of the superior nature of the storm as if they had themselves arranged it.

"Nothing like it in history, chentlemen," said Para Handy, after borrowing a match. "It's me that should ken, for I wass in it, ten mortal hours, battlin' wi' the tempest. A small boat carried away and a cargo o' feather bonnets on the deck we were carryin' for the Territorials. My boat was shaved clean doon to the water-line till she looked like wan o' them timber ponds at the Port[6] — not an article left standin'! A crank-shaft smashed on us, and the helm wass jammed. The enchineer — a man Macphail belongin' to Motherwell — had a couple of ribs stove in, and the mate got a pair o' broken legs; at least there's wan o' them broken and the other's a nesty stave. I kept her on her coorse mysel' for five hours, and the watter up to my very muddle. Every sea was smashin' on me, but I never mudged. My George, no! Macfarlane never mudged!"

The Paisley passengers were intensely moved, and produced a consoling bottle.

"Best respects, chentlemen!" said Para Handy. "It's me that would give a lot for the like o' that at three o'clock this mornin'. I'm sittin' here withoot a rag but what I have on me. A fine sea-kist, split new, wi' fancy grommets, all my clothes, my whole month's wages, and presents for the wife in't — it's lyin' yonder somewhere off Innellan. . . . It's a terrible thing the sea."

At Greenock two other passengers came into the compartment, brimful of admiration for a storm they seemed to think peculiarly British in its devastating character — a kind of vindication of the island's imperial pride.

"They've naething like it on the Continent," said one of them. "They're a' richt there wi' their volcanic eruptions and earthquakes and the like, but when it comes to the naitural elements — " He was incapable of expressing exactly what he thought of British dominance in respect of the natural elements.

"Here's a poor chap that was oot in his ship in the worst o't," said the Paisley passengers. Para Handy ducked his head in polite acknowledgment of the newcomers' flattering scrutiny, and was induced to repeat his story, to which he added some fresh sensational details.

He gave a vivid picture of the *Vital Spark* wallowing helplessly on the very edge of the Gantock rocks; of the fallen mast beating against the vessel's side and driving holes in her; of the funnel flying through the air, with cases of feather bonnets ("cost ten pounds apiece, chentlemen, to the War Office"); of Sunny Jim incessantly toiling at the pump; the engineer unconscious and delirious; himself, tenacious and unconquered, at the wheel, lashed to it with innumerable strands of the best Manila cordage.

"I have seen storms in every part of the world," he said; "I have even seen yon terrible monsoons that's namely oot about Australia, but never in my born life did I come through what I came through last night."

Another application of the consolatory bottle seemed to brighten his recollection of details.

"I had a lot o' sky-rockets," he explained. "We always have them on the best ships, and I fired them off wi' the wan hand, holdin' the wheel wi' the other. Signals o' distress, chentlemen. Some use cannons, but I aye believe in the sky-rockets: you can both hear and see them. It makes a dufference."

"I kent a chap that did that for a day and a nicht aff the Mull o' Kintyre, and it never brung oot a single lifeboat," said one of the Paisley men.

It was obvious to Para Handy that his tragedy of the sea was pitched on too low a key to stir some people; he breathed deeply and shook a melancholy head.

"You'll never get lifeboats when you want them chentlemen," he remarked. "They keep them aal laid up in Gleska for them Lifeboat Setturday processions. But it was too late for the lifeboat anyway for the *Vital Spark*. The smertest boat in the tred, too."

"Good Lord! She didna sink?" said the Paisley men, unprepared for such a *dénouement*.

"Nothing above the water at three o'clock this mornin' but the winch," said the Captain. "We managed to make our way ashore on a couple o' herrin'-boxes. . . . Poor Macphail! A great man for perusin' them novelles, but still-and-on a fellow of much agility. The very last words he said when he heaved his breath — and him, poor sowl, withoot a word o' Gaelic in his heid — wass, 'There's nobody can say but what you did your duty, Peter.' That wass me."

"Do ye mean to say he was drooned?" asked the Paisley men with genuine emotion.

"Not drooned," said Para Handy; "he simply passed away."

"Isn't that deplorable! And whit came over the mate?"

"His name wass Dougald," said the Captain sadly, "a native of Lochaline, and ass cheery a man ass ever you met across a dram. Chust that very mornin' he said to me, 'The 5th of November, Peter; this hass been a terrible New Year, and the next wan will be on us in a chiffy.' "

By the time the consolatory bottle was finished the loss of the *Vital Spark* had assumed the importance of the loss of the *Royal George*[7], and the Paisley men suggested that the obvious thing to do was to start a small subscription for the sole survivor.

For a moment the conscience-stricken Captain hesitated. He had scarcely thought his story quite so moving, but a moment of reflection found him quite incapable of recalling what was true and what imaginary of the tale he told them. With seven-and-sixpence in his pocket, wrung by the charm of pure imagination from his fellow-passengers, he arrived in Glasgow and went home.

He went in with a haggard countenance.

"What's the matter wi' ye, Peter?" asked his wife.

"Desperate news for you, Mery. Desperate news! The Vital Spark is sunk."

"As long's the crew o' her are right that doesna matter," said the plucky little woman.

"Every mortal man o' them drooned except mysel'," said Para Handy, and the tears streaming down his cheeks. "Nothing but her winch above the water. They died like Brutain's hardy sons."

"And what are you doing here?" said his indignant wife. "As lang as the winch is standin' there ye should be on her. Call yoursel' a sailor and a Hielan'man!"

For a moment he was staggered.

"Perhaps there's no' a word o' truth in it," he suggested. "Maybe the thing's exaggerated. Anything could happen in such a desperate storm."

"Whether it's exaggerated or no' ye'll go back the night and stick beside the boat. I'll make a cup o' tea and boil an egg for ye. A bonny-like thing for me to go up and tell Dougie's wife her husband's deid and my man snug at home at a tousy tea! ... forbye, they'll maybe salve the boat, and she'll be needin' a captain."

With a train that left the Central some hours later Para Handy returned in great anxiety to Gourock. The tragedy of his imagination was now exceedingly real to him. He took a boat and rowed out to the *Vital Spark*, which he was astonished to see intact at anchor, not a feature of her changed.

Dougie was on deck to receive him.

"Holy smoke, Dougie, iss that yoursel'?" the Captain asked incredulously. "What way are you keepin'?"

"Fine," said Dougie. "What way's the mistress?"

The Captain seized him by the arm and felt it carefully.

"Chust yoursel', Dougie, and nobody else. It's me that's prood to see you. I hope there's nothing wrong wi' your legs?"

"Not a drop," said Dougie.

"And what way's Macphail?" inquired the Captain anxiously.

"He's in his bed wi' 'Lady Audley',"[8] said the mate.

"Still deleerious?" said the Captain with apprehension.

"The duvvle was never anything else," said Dougie.

"Did we lose anything in the storm last night?" asked Para Handy.

"A jar, and a bucket, and your own sou'-wester," answered Dougie.

"My Chove!" said Para Handy, much relieved. "Things iss terribly exaggerated up in Gleska."

68. *Freights of Fancy*

DURING several days on which the *Vital Spark* lay idle at Lochgoilhead, the crew spring-cleaned her. "My goodness! ye wouldna think she would take such a desperate lot o' tar!" said Para Handy, watching the final strokes of Dougie's brush on the vessel's quarter. There seemed, however, to be as much of the tar on the person and clothing of himself and his shipmates as on the boat.

"Ye're a bonny-lookin' lot!" said Macphail, the engineer, who never took any part in the painting operations. "If ye just had a tambourine apiece, and could sing 'The Swanee River', ye would do for Christy Minstrels."[1]

But all the same, in spite of such tar as missed her when they slung it on, the *Vital Spark* looked beautiful and shiny, and the air for half a mile round had the odour of Archangel[2], where the Russians come from.

With his own good hand, and at his own expense, her proud commander had freshened up her yellow bead and given her funnel a coat of red as gorgeous as a Gourock sunset[3]. He stood on one leg, in a favourite attitude of his when anything appealed to his emotions, and scratched his shin with the heel of his other boot.

"Man! it's chust a trate to see her lookin' so smert!" he said with admiration. "The sauciest boat in the coastin' tred! If ye shut wan eye and glance end-on, ye would think she wass the *Grenadier*. Chust you look at the lines of her — that sweet! I'm tellin' you he wassna slack the man that made her."

Sunny Jim wiped his brow with the cuff of his jacket, and made a new smear on his countenance which left him with a striking resemblance to the White-Eyed Kaffir. His comparatively clean eye twinkled mischievously at Macphail.

"What I say is this," said he; "there's no' much sense in bein' so fancy wi' a boat that's only gaun to cairry coals and timber inside the Cumbraes. Noo that we're blockaded[4], do ye no' think, Macphail, she should be cairryin' passengers?"

"Holy smoke!" ejaculated Dougie, with genuine surprise. "Ye might chust ass well say that the Admirality should put some guns on her and send her to the Dardanelles."[5]

Sunny Jim, with his back to the Captain, winked.

"There's maybe something in't," added Dougie hurriedly. "There's boats no' better carryin' passengers aal winter, and I'll warrant ye there's money in't."

"It's the chance o' a lifetime!" broke in the engineer, warming up to the play. "Half the regular steamers will be aff the Clyde for months takin' Gleska breid and the sodgers' washin's to the Bosphorus and thereabouts; if you have ony say at a' wi' the owners, Peter, you advise them to let oot the *Vital Spark* for trips."

"Trups!" said Para Handy, beaming. "Man, Jum, ye hit the very thing! It wass aalways my ambeetion to get oot o' the common cairryin' tred and be a chentleman. I aalways said a boat like this wass thrown awa on coal, and wud, and herrin'; if she had chust a caibin and a place for sellin' tickets, I wouldna feel ashamed to sail her on the Royal Rowt."

Again his eye swept fondly over her bulging hull, with the tar still wet and glistening on it; the bright new yellow stripe which made her so coquettish; the crimson funnel.

"Of course, ye would need a band if ye went in for trips," suggested Macphail in a ruminating way. "Yin o' thae bands that can feenish a' thegither even if they're playin' different tunes, or drap the piccolo oot every noo and then to go roond and lift the pennies."

"Ach! I wouldna bother wi' a band," said Para Handy. "A band's no use unless ye want to chase the passengers below to take refreshments, and we havena the accommodation. We maybe might get haud o' a kind o' fiddler. I mind when the tippiest[6] boats on the Clyde had chust wan decent fiddler or a poor man wantin' the eysight, wi' a concerteena. Tiptop!"

He took a piece of twine from his trousers pocket and measured the standing room between the wheel and the engines; Sunny Jim was in a transport of delight at a joke which went so smoothly.

"Two and a half," said Para Handy firmly, like a land surveyor. "I think there would be room for a no' too broad-built fiddler, if he didna bate the time wi' his feet. Stop you till we make a calculaation for the passenger accommodation. We'll need to rnake it cubic."

"There's only forty cubic feet[7] allo'ed for every lodger in the Garscube Road," said Sunny Jim. "That's the Act o' Parliament. Ye can easy get the cubic space if ye coont it longways up in the air, and there's naething to prevent it."

Para Handy stood on one leg again and scratched a shin, with a look of the profoundest calculation.

"Ye couldna have cabin passengers," suggested Dougie, snatching up an oil-can of Macphail's and pouring some of its contents into his hands to clean the tar off.

"There's no' goin' to be no caibin in this boat," said the Captain quickly. "Short runs and ready money! Gourock and Dunoon, maybe, and perhaps a Setturday to Ardentinny. I could get a dozen or two o' nice wee herrin' firkins[8] doon at Tarbert for passengers to sit on roond the hatch."

"Do ye no' think it would look droll?" asked Dougie, a little remorseful to have awakened such ecstatic visions.

"What way would it be droll?" retorted his Captain sharply. "I'm thinkin' ye havena much o' a heid for business, Dougie. If you would just consider — a shillin' a heid to Hunter's Quay — "

"Ye would need a purser," suggested Suuny Jim.

"Allooin' I did!" replied the Captain. "Aal a purser needs is a pocket-naipkin, a fancy tie, a flooer in his jaicket, and a pleasant smile. There iss not a man on the Clyde would make a better purser than yoursel' if ye showed the right agility. I'm tellin' you there's money in't! The people 'll chust come in and pay their tickets. Look at the way they crood doon at the Gleska Fair! We could put their wee tin boxes in the howld."

"Of course, we would have moonlight cruises," said Macphail. "It's just found money — no extra cost for the engineer and crew."

On the prospect of moonlight cruises the Captain pondered for a moment. "No," he said. "I'm aal for daylight sailin'; they slip in past ye in the dark withoot a ticket, or give ye a Golden Text from the Sunday School that looks like the chenuine article, and then where are ye? Forbye, it's no' that easy to watch a purser on the moonlight cruises; he would make his fortune."

He looked at his bright new funnel; imaginatively peopled the narrow deck with summer trippers; smelled the pervading odour of paint and tar, and glowed all over at the thought of his beloved vessel taking the quay at Dunoon on a Saturday afternoon with a crowd of the genteelest passengers seated on herring firkins, and a fiddle aft.

"I'll speak my mind aboot it to the owners whenever I get to Gleska!" he declared emphatically. "It's no' a chance they should let slip. They might could put up a bit o' a deck-house where a body could get a cup o' tea and a penny thing at tuppence."

"And wha would serve the tea, like?" asked Sunny Jim.

"There's nobody could do it cluverer than yoursel', Jum," said Para Handy. "You would wash your hands and put on a brattie[9], and every noo and then a chentleman would slup a penny in below his plate for a testimonial."

"That puts the feenish on it then!" said Sunny Jim, with emphasis. "I jined this ship for a sailorman, and no' to hand roond cookies and lift the tickets."

"And the mate would need to wear a collar," said Dougie. "It's no' a thing I fancy at aal, at aal."

"A bonny-like skipper ye would look withoot a bridge to stand on," wound up the engineer. "Besides, ye would need a Board o' Tred certificate."

The Captain's visage fell. His dream dispelled. "Perhaps ye're right," said he. "It would look a little droll. But, man, I aalways had the notion that the *Vital Spark* wass meant for something better than for cairryin' coals."

69. *Summer-time on The Vital Spark*

PARA HANDY, on Saturday night, wound up the ship's Kew-tested 2s. 11d. tin alarm chronometer with more than usual solemnity. It stopped as usual in the process, and he had to restore it to animation, after the customary fashion, by tapping it vigorously on the toe of his boot.

"If it wassna the law o' the land,"[1] he remarked, "I would see them at the muschief afore I would be tamperin' wi' the time o' day the way God made it. We'll have to come up the quay to our beds next Setturday in broad daylight; there's no consuderation for the sailor's reputaation."

"Science!" said the mate, with bitterness. "Goodness knows what prank them fellows 'll be up to next! There wass nothing wrong wi' the time the way it wass, except that it wass aalways slippin' past when ye werena thinkin'."

"There's the nock for ye, Jim," said Para Handy. "Ye'll stay up till two o'clock, and do the needful."

"What'll I stay up for?" asked Sunny Jim indignantly. "Ye can shift the handles noo; it's a' the same."

"But it's no' aal the same! If you would read the papers instead o' wastin' your time gallivanting, ye would see the Daylight Ack says two o'clock's the oor for shifting nocks. Ye daurna do it a meenute sooner."

Sunny Jim laughed. "Right-oh, Captain!" he agreed. "I'll sit up and dae the shiftin' for ye. You and Dougie better leave me your watches, too; it'll be a' the yin operation."

"Can ye see the nock, Dougie? What time iss't by the Daylight Ack?" the Captain sleepily asked next morning without turning out of his bunk.

The mate unhooked the olock, and incredulously surveyed its face. "Stop you till I get my watch," he said, crawling out of his bunk. "Them German nocks iss not dependable; ye couldna boil an egg wi' them."

A rich resonant snore came from the bunk of Sunny Jim.

"Holy sailor!" exclaimed Dougie, having consulted his watch; "it's half-past ten o'clock! No wonder I wass hungry! That's your science for you!"

"Half-past ten o'clock!" said the Captain. "And chust you listen at the way that fellow iss snorin'! Up this meenute, Jum, and make the breakfast!"

It was with difficulty Sunny Jun was wakened, and then he proved of the most mutinous temper. "Ye can mak' your breakfast for yoursel's!" he protested. "If I'm to sit up till twa o'clock in the mornin' to shift the time, I'm no' gaun to rise till my sleep's made up."

Two seconds later he was snoring more resonantly than ever, in syncopated time with MacPhail, the engineer, who had volunteered to sit up till two o'clock with him, and who had a snore of an intermittent gurgling character like one of his own steam pipes.

Between them the Captain and the mate made breakfast.

A blissful Sabbath calm was on loch and land when Para Handy put his head up through the hatch. The *Vital Spark* was bumping softly against her fenders at a deserted quay; the smoke of morning fires was rising in the village. The tide was ebbing, but not yet far from full.

"I didna think they could do't," said the Captain.

"Do what?" asked Dougie, finishing off the last of the marmalade.

"The tide," said Para Handy, "it's no' near where it wass at this time yesterday. It's shifted too."

"Chust what I told ye — science! The ruffians'll do anything! Do you no' think, Peter, we'll get punished some day for all this schemin' and contrivance? Chust the work of unfidels! What way iss a man to ken noo whether it's Setturday night or Sunday morning? Many a wan 'll go wrong at twelve o'clock on the Setturday night and start whistling. Noo that they're startin' takin' liberties wi' clocks and tides, ye'll see they'll cairry it further and play havoc wi' the almanacs. If they can rob us o' an oor they can steal a fortnight."

"Chust that!" agreed the Captain. "I could spare them a day or two at the Whitsunday term; that's the sort o' thing they should abolish." He sighed. "Indeed, it's a solemn thing, Dougie, to see the way they're flyin' aal round to new human devices; do ye no' think me and you should go to the church this mornin'?"

"Whatever you say yoursel'," said Dougie.

The bell was ringing as they went up the street, and had ceased when they reached the church. No other worshippers were visible.

"This place needs a great upliftin'," said Para Handy piously. "On a day like this, with the things of time upset and shifted, ye would think they would be croodin' in to hear Mr M'Queen. Have ye any losengers?"

"Not wan!" said Dougie, "but maybe he'll no' be long."

The beadle was shutting the door of the church as they approached to enter. "Where are ye goin'?" he asked, with a curious look at them.

"Where would we be goin' but to hear my good frien', John M'Queen," said the Captain fervently.

"Then ye'll better come back at half-past eleven," said the beadle dryly." This is no' the place for you at all; it's the Sunday School."

"Holy sailors!" exclaimed the Captain; "what o'clock iss't?"

"Exactly half past nine by the summer time," said the beadle, "but it's only half past eight by naiture."

The Captain looked at Dougie. "Aren't we," said he, "the fools to be leavin' nocks and watches to fellows like Sunny Jim and Macphail! The tricky duvvles! There's no' an inch o' a chentleman between them. It's no' wan oor but three they put us forrit and they're still snore-snorin' yonder!"

70. *Eggs Uncontrolled*

SUNNY JIM, with his sleeves rolled up, a sweat-rag stuck in the waistband of his trousers, and his face much streaked with soot, clapped down a bowl of eggs before the Captain, rinsed his hands in a pail of water, dried them on his waistcoat, and sat down on the edge of his bunk to enjoy his breakfast.

A gloomy silence fell upon the crew when they saw the eggs. They were just plain ordinary eggs of oval shape, and no more soiled on the shells than usual, but their presence seemed momentous. Para Handy looked at them like one entranced; Dougie put a finger out and touched them gingerly; Macphail withdrew his incredulous gaze from them with a muttered exclamation, and starting furiously spreading bread with marmalade.

"Iss that eggs?" said the Captain, like one who was uncertain whether they were eggs or curling-stones.

"Oh no! Not at all!" cried Macphail, with bitter irony; "it's the best Devonshire bacon, fried kidneys, kippered herring, finnan haddies, omelets, pork sausages. Jim would never shove us off wi' eggs!"

"They're duvvelish like eggs!" said Dougie lugubriously. "I never saw a better imitation. The look o' them fairly makes me grue."[1]

"What way's the wind, Jum?" said Para Handy mildly. "I don't feel the smell o' ham. Hurry you up, like a good laad, and bring us doon a wise-like[2] breakfast."

"That's a' the breakfast that's gaun," said Sunny Jim. "There's no a bit o' ham in Tarbert."

"But, bless my he'rt! there's many another thing than ham a body could enjoy!" said Para Handy. "There's things like — fush, and — sausages, and — fush, that a man could eat wi' some diversion. You're awfu' nerrow, Jum! You havena no variety. Even-on it's eggs wi' you; you havena had a thing but eggs since we left Bowling."

"Tak' them or leave them!" said the cook; "the day 'll come ye'll be gled to get them. I'm no' a Grand Hotel nor an Italian Warehouse[3]; I can only gie ye what I can get, and there's dashed all left to eat in Tarbert since the Fair, unless it's rhubarb."

The Captain chipped an egg with no enthusiasm. "Goodness knows," said he, "what this country would come to withoot the hens! Everybody in the land is eatin' eggs — eggs — eggs! Half the year there's nothing in the morning for ye but an egg. What, in aal the world, iss in an egg?"

"That's what I'm aye wonderin' when I start yin," said the engineer.

"There's nothing patent in an egg; it's chust a thing ye would expect from hens. If it wassna for the salt, ye might ass weel be eatin' blot-sheet. Did ye ever see any dufference between wan egg and another?"

"Some o' them's bigger," suggested Dougie, scooping out his own, apparently without much interest in the contents.

"That's the thing that angers me aboot an egg!" continued the Captain. "It never makes ye gled to see it on the table; ye know at wance the thing's a mere put-by because your wife or Jum could not be bothered makin' something tasty."

"We'll hae to get the hens to put their heids thegither, and invent a new kind o' fancy egg for sailors," said Sunny Jim, consuming his with ostentatious relish. "Ye can say whit ye like — there's naething bates a country egg; and I can tell ye this, the lot o' ye, it's eggs ye're gaun to get for dinner tae; there's no' a bit o' butcher meat in Tarbert!"

"Holy smoke!" exclaimed the Captain. "Eggs for dinner! Not a morsel more will I be eating; you have spoiled my breakfast on me!"

The *Vital Spark* had her coals discharged by noon, and the Captain went ashore to a public-house for a change of diet. The very idea of eggs again for dinner was repugnant to him, and several schooners of beer intensified his inward feelings of revolt against monotony of cuisine. There came into the bar a man he thought he knew; he said, "Hallo, Macdougall!" to him, "hoo's the fishin'?" and they had a glass together.

"What way's hersel' — the mustress keepin'?" Para Handy asked. "I hope she's splendid?"

"She's no bad at aal," said the other, with a little hesitation.

"Tell her I was askin' kindly for her health. I'm fine mysel'. Yon's a nice bit hoose ye have, Johnny; it's very creditable to aal coucerned."

"It's no' that bad at aal!" replied the other, thinking for a moment. "What way do ye no' come up some night and see us?"

"Nobody would be better pleased!" said Para Handy. "Iss your mother-in-law still wi' ye?"

"Aye, she's yonder yet, but ach! ye needna mind for her; come up some night, and have your supper. . . Bring the boys!" Macdougall added with effusive hospitality. So far, he had not suggested another.

"If I go up, I'll better go mysel'; there's four of us on board," said Para Handy.

"Bring them all! This very night at seven o'clock, and, I assure you, you'll have supper."

"Hoots! That would be puttin' the wife to bother," said the Captain, with polite solicitude. "We would chust be goin' to have a crack."

"Ye'll have a crack, and ye'll have your supper too!" said Macdougall firmly. "Mind and bring the boys! Sharp at seven, mind, and take your music."

The Captain hurried on board his vessel, watched his crew disgustedly eat eggs, which he professed disdain for, and when they had finished, told them of his invitation.

"Ye micht hae tell't us sooner!" said Macphail, with genuine vexation. "There's a supper spoiled!"

"A capital cook, Mrs Macdougall! — namely, in the place for cooking," callously said Para Handy. "I'm chust in trum mysel' for something else than eggs."

They dressed in their Sunday clothes, and went up at night to the house of John Macdougall.

"He's not at home, he's at the fishin'!" said a lady whom the Captain shook warmly by the hand, and addressed as Katrin.

"I met him in the toon at twelve the day, and he asked us to be sure and come to supper," said the Captain, much surprised.

"What was he like?" said she, with some amusement.

"A burly wise-like man, wi' a tartan kep; I ken him fine!

She laughed; she was a cheerful body. "That's no' my man at all, Captain," said she; "but I'll tell ye who it was — his brother Peter; they're as like as peas!"

"Isn't this the bonny caper!" said Dougie, with distress. They stood like sheep.

"It's no' the first time Peter played that trick," said the woman; "he's a rascal! If he had a house and a wife of his own, I would just advise ye to go up, and take him at his word, but seein' ye're here, ye'll just come in and have your supper."

They went in, with mingled hope and diffidence, and she boiled them eggs!

71. *Commandeered*

"STOP YOU! We'll have a fine pant[1] oot of Dougie; he's ass timid ass a mountain hare," said Para Handy in the absence of his mate, who was ashore on one of the missions the crew of the *Vital Spark* entirely disapproved often to buy some special and exclusive "kitchen" for his tea. He had an unpleasantly ostentatious way of eating ham or kippered herrings when the rest had nothing more piquant or interesting than jam.

As a consequence of some deliberation and rehearsal, when Dougie came back to the boat with his parcel he found an unusual bustle at an hour when, waiting for the tide to get her off at flood, the crew of the *Vital Spark* were apt to be yawning their heads off. The Captain was peeling his guernsey off, preparatory to washing himself — a proceeding in itself unusual enough to be surprising. Macphail, the engineer, was studying a map of the North Sea cut from some recent newspaper, and flourishing a one-legged compass. Sunny Jim was oiling the parts of a telescope he had won once in a raffle.

Such signs of unaccustomed activity could not but impress

Dougie. "What's wrong wi' ye?" he asked; "ye're duvvelish busy!"

"We'll be busier yet before we're done!" said the Captain, gravely and mysteriously, and turned his back to look over the shoulder of Macphail at the North Sea map. "Did ye find the place, Macphail?" he asked anxiously.

"Ay!" said the engineer. "It's just aboot whaur I said it was — a dangerous place, fair hotchin'[2] full o' mines."[3]

"Chust that!" said Para Handy. "It's chust what I wass thinkin' to myself. Well, well; we canna help it when the King and country caals. I'm only vexed aboot the boat." He stifled a sigh, bent over the enamelled basin, and hurriedly damped himself: it must be admitted the afternoon was cold.

"There's no' even the chance o' a medal on the job," said Sunny Jim. "That's what gives me the needle!"

They behaved as if Dougie with his irritating groceries had no existence. He determined to show no curiosity.

"It might be sweepin' mines they mean," said Para Handy in a little, drying his face. "Whatever it iss, it iss goin' to be a time of trial."

"It's me that's gled I can swim," said Sunny Jim. "The very first bang, and aff goes my galoshes! It's no' sae bad for me, as if I had a wife and family."

Dougie pricked his ears.

"It's no' sweepin' mines," said the engineer emphatically. "If it was to sweep mines they wanted us they would put steel plates roond the bows and leave her light; there wouldna be any sense in stuffin' her hold wi' cement and stones. Tak' you my word for it — she's gaun to jam the Kiel Canal.[4] It's a risky job we're on, I'll warrant ye!"

"I wouldna care so much if it wasna for my aunty," said Sunny Jim in a doleful accent, with a wink to the engineer. "I aye made up her rent. Perhaps it's to cairry troops we're needed."

"Not at aal!" said Para Handy. "Where would ye put troops on the *Vital Spark*, and her hold filled up wi' causey and cement?"

Dougie's curiosity could no further be restrained. "What in aal the earth are ye palaverin' at?" he asked impatiently, and with some forebodings.

"I'm sorry to tell ye that, Dougald," said the Captain feelingly, "for it's a serious, serious business for us aal; the boat is commandeered. I have a kind o' letter here from the Admirality" — he produced it with a flourish from his trousers pocket. "Chust a line in their usual way: — 'Report at Renfrew; get an extra dummy funnel and some wuden guns; fill up wi' causey and cement, and take the North Sea for it. To Captain Peter C. Macfarlane.'"

" 'Peter C. Macfarlane,' " Dougie said, surprised. "I never heard o' the 'C' before; where did ye get the title?"

"They must have kent my mother was a Cameron," said Para Handy; "and they're always for the stylish thing in the Admirality. Never you mind aboot the title, Dougald; have ye an extra shirt or two and a pair o' mittens? Ye'll need them yonder."

"Where?" asked the mate, alarmed.

"In the North Sea. Amn't I tellin' ye we're comandeered!"

"I'll see them to the muschief first!" said Dougie warmly. "If I'm to do the British Navy's work, it's no' in a cockle-shell!" But his heart was in his boots.

For once his meal had no attractions for him, and the others, for the first time, shared his private ham with surprising appetite and relish, considering the tragic possibilities they discussed. So perfectly did they sustain their parts as previously arranged among them that it never occurred to him to doubt the story.

"Of course, ye'll break the news to your mustress the best way that ye can," said the Captain, spreading jam on the bread with a soup spoon; "ye needna put the worst face on the job; chust say it's an East Coast cargo, and ye'll send a postcaird home. I hope and trust ye kept up your insurance!"

"Of course, there's aye a chance they micht take us prisoners," said Sunny Jim. "That wouldna be sae bad."

"I ken a man that's no' goin'," said Dougie with profound conviction.

"There's nane o' us can get oot o't," said the engineer, finishing the last of the ham in an absent-minded way. "I think your letter makes that quite plain, Peter?"

"It does that," said Para Handy, having scrutinised the document again, and shoved it under his plate for further reference if necessary. Dougie eyed it slyly, unobserved.

"The dashed thing is there's no' a uniform," said Sunny Jim. "I wouldna mind sae much if we wore a blue pea-jaicket wi' brass buttons, and the name o' the boat on oor keps; if I'm to be drooned for my country I would like to be a wee bit tasty."

"There's a man I ken, and he's no' goin', whatever o't!" again said Dougie firmly.

The Captain had another inspiration. "Of course" said he, "they're goin' to change the name o' the boat. There's a cruiser caaled the *Vital Spark*, and if we were sunk it would make confusion. The Chermans would be sayin' we were the big one."

"There's one thing I can tell ye, and it's this — the man that iss not goin' on this ploy iss me!" said Dougie, and slapped his knee.

"Toots, man! ye shouldna be so tumid!" said Para Handy; "Brutain's hardy sons!"

The rule of the vessel was that a man who indulged in extras to his tea had to wash the dishes, and Dougie was left behind when the others went on deck. He lost no time in reading the document the Captain had forgetfully left below his plate, and a great illumination came to him when he found it was nothing more than a second and final notice demanding the Captain's poor-rates.

"My goodness! wass there ever such a lot o' liars?" said their victim. "Spoiled my tea on me! Stop you!"

By and by he went up on deck, and found his shipmates solemnly discussing the purpose of the dummy funnel and the wooden guns.

"It's to draw their torpedo fire," the engineer suggested. "When they're bangin' awa' at us the cruiser'll slip by."

"And then it's domino wi' us!" said Sunny Jim lugubriously.

"There's wan thing I can say," said Para Handy unctuously, "and it's this — that my affairs is aal in the best condeetion; quite complete. There's no' a penny that I'm owin'."

"Except your poor-rates," broke in Dougie witheringly. "There's your letter from the Admirality. It's in Berlin the whole o' ye should be, and writin' Cherman telegrams."

72. *Sunny Jim Rejected*

WHEN tea was finished, Sunny Jim put on his Sunday clothes, turned up the foot of his trousers, oiled his boots, put his cap on carefully, with a saucy tilt to it, and then spent several minutes violently brushing what was left below it of his hair. Thus only could his curl be coaxed into that tasty wave above the forehead, and complete his fatal beauty for the girls.

"Capital!" said Para Handy. "Never saw ye nicer, Jum; chust a regular Napoleon! Don't you shift another hair, or ye'll spoil yersel'!"

"The only other thing I could recommend," said Macphail, "is to put some soap and water on a brush and gie a flourish aboot the ears."

Sunny Jim paid no attention. From the small tin box that held his dunnage he produced his mouth harmonium and a tin of Glasgow toffee, which he stowed in his jacket pockets.

"My goodness!" said Dougie, the mate, "it's a desperate thing this love; there's such expense in it! There's a sixpence away on sweeties for another fellow's dochter!"

"Of course, we'll have a bite o' something ready for ye, Jum, when ye come back," remarked the Captain with magnificent sarcasm. "Dougie'll sit up. Will a bit of cold roast chucken do, or would ye like an omelet?

"Best respects to Liza," said the engineer rudely. "I think it's specs she's needin' if you're her fancy."

Sunny Jim calmly lighted a cigarette and buttoned up his jacket. "So long, chaps!" he said. "It's a pity ye're a' that old! Just a lot o' bloomin' fossils from the Fossil Grove[1], Whiteinch. Mak' yoursel's some gruel in a while, and awa' to your beds."

He was back to the *Vital Spark* in less than an hour in an obviously agitated state of mind.

"Bless me!" said Para Handy, starting up; "iss it that time o' night? The way time has o' slippin' past when ye're a fossil! Set you the table, Dougie, and put oot a chucken for his lordship. Maybe ye would like a drop o' something, Jum? To start wi', like. What way iss Liza keepin' in her health! My Chove! But yon's the beautious gyurl!"

"Shut up!" said Sunny Jim disgustedly. "I'm done wi' her, onywey! I wouldna trust a woman like yon the length that I could throw her!"

"That's no far," said Macphail reflectively. "Sixteen stone, if she's an ounce. Tell me this — is she wearin' specs at last?"

"It would need to be some sort o' specs she was wearin' to see onything in yon chap o' Mackay's she's awa' for a walk wi'," said Sunny Jim with feeling. "Naething at a' to recommend him but a kilt and a hack on his heel!"

Dougie, who never lost his head even in the most exciting circumstances, asked the despondent lover abruptly if he had brought the tin of toffee back. In a moment of aberration Sunny Jim produced it, and put it down on the top of a barrel, and it sped so quickly round them several times that wheu his turn came there were only two sticky bits left in the bottom. He sucked them like one for whom toffee had no greater taste than gas-work cinders. Such is the effect of unrequited love.

He was too profoundly grieved to be reticent. "I had a tryst wi' her, right enough, chaps. Eight o'clock she said, at the factor's corner, and just at that very meenute she went sailin' past wi' Dan Mackay, that's hame frae the Territorials at Dunoon, lettin' on he's wounded, and a' the time, I'll bate ye, t's only a hack on his heel.

" 'It's eight o'clock, Liza,' says I, and gied her the wink.

" 'Fancy that!' says she, as nippy 's onything. 'But ye've loads o' time; they're signin' on recruits in the armoury up till ten. Did ye hear aboot the war?' says she afore I could get my breath. 'It's fairly ragin'! Corporal Mackay's gaun oot to the front as soon as his feet get better.'

"And aff she went wi' Mackay, and left me standin' like a dummy! Yon's no gentleman! He hadna a word to say for himsel'. Naething to tak' the eye aboot him but a kilt and a hack on his heel!"

"Holy smoke!" said Para Handy sympathetically. "Isn't that the desperate pity? There's nothing noo in the heids o' the gyurls but sodgers. But ye canna blame the craturs! There's something smert aboot the kilt and the coat bonnet."

"If I wassna one o' them old fossils from Whiteinch," remarked Dougie, with rancorous deliberation, "it wouldna be the like o' Liza Cameron, the tyler's dochter, could cast up to me a war wass ragin' and go off wi' another man — aye, even if he had a hack on every heel inside his boots."

Sunny Jim was distressed almost to the verge of tears. "I'm fair sick o' this!" said he. "I'm gaun to 'list! Every quay this boat comes in to somebody's shair to chip in something aboot my age and me no' bein' married, and whitna regiment I'm gaun to. The last trip we cam' up Loch Fyne I got as mony feathers[2] as would stuff a bolster."

"I wass aye wonderin' what for so many feathers got into the porridge," said Dougie. "Did I no' say to the Captain yesterday, 'I'm fond o' porridge and I'm fond o' chicken, but I never cared to get them both mixed'?"

"Mind ye, it's no' that I'm feared to 'list," said Sunny Jim. "I never seen a German yet I couldna knock the napper[3] aff, and it couldna be worse in the trenches than in the howld o' this old vessel shovellin' coal. But I'm feared they wouldna tak' me for a recruit — "

"If it's the bowly legs ye're thinkin' o'," said Macphail, "that's no ony obstacle; ye're just the very make o' a horse marine."

Para Handy measured the disconsolate lover with a calculating eye. "I doot," says he, "Jum hassna got the length for a horse marine unless they put him through a mangle first. The regiment for you, Jum, is the Bantams."[4]

"I doot they wouldna pass me," said Sunny Jim. "But to show that woman I'm game enough, although I'm no' bloodthirsty, I'll go up this very meenute and put in my name."

"You be fly and stand on your tiptoes!" Macphail cried after him as he climbed up on the quay from the vessel's rail.

He came back in half an hour a little more disconsolate than ever. "I tell't ye!" said he, "they wouldna sign me on," and stood with his back close to a glowing stove.

"No wonder," said the engineer. "Warpin' your legs still worse wi' standin' against the fire! Did I no' tell ye to get on the tips o' your taes?"

"You're a disgrace to the boat," said Para Handy, with genuine vexation. "I'm black affronted! If Dougald and me wass a trifle younger, it's no' wi' troosers on we would be puttin' past the time. Just bringin' a bad name on the boat — that's what ye are! What way would they no' take ye?"

"Just look at the legs o' him!" said the engineer, as if they made the question quite ridiculous.

"It would likely be his character," suggested Dougie sadly. "They're duvvelish parteecular noo aboot the character; it's no like the old Milishia."

"It's no' my legs at a'; there's naething wrang wi' my legs," said the disappointed candidate. "And they never asked aboot my character. But I kent fine a' alang they wouldna tak' me."

"What for?" asked Para Handy. "Ye have all your faculties aboot ye, and ye're in your prime."

"It was this e'e o' mine," explained Sunny Jim, and indicated his dexter optic, which had always a singularly stern expression even in his amorous hours.

"That wan?" exclaimed the Captain. "That's the best o' the pair, to my opeenion, it's aye that steady. What's wrong wi't?"

"It's gless," said Sunny Jim, blushing; "they found it oot at the first go-aff."

"Holy frost!" said Para Handy. "Five years in this boat wi' us, and we never kent it. Did I no' think ye were chust plain skeely!"

73. *How Jim joined the Army*

"JUMPIN' JEHOSOPHAT!" said Para Handy. "Here's Macphail. I doot they havena lifted him."

Dougie's visage fell. He had been confident that the want of an engineer would keep them idle in Tarbert for at least a week. "Isn't that the trash!" he said lugubriously. "Ye never could put dependence on him. Look you, has he any badge in his coat lapel? He iss chust the man would let on a enchineer on the *Vital Spark* was a special tred. Ye canna be up to the quirks o' him."

"There is nothing on his coat lapel that I can see but a patch o' egg," said Para Handy, "and he had that when he started to go to Stirling. Ye'll see we'll no' get rid o' Macphail so easy; they're gettin' gey parteecular in the airmy, and he never could keep the step."

"Oh, man! if I had jist the ither eye!" said Sunny Jim in a passionate outburst of yearning.

Macphail came down to the quay with the biscuit tin which fulfilled the function of a suitcase when he travelled. His gait was most dejected, and his general air of infestivity was accentuated by the fact that he wore his Sunday clothes and a hat that, having been picked up casually some years before at the close of a ball in Crarae, had never fitted.

"See's your canister in case ye break the bottle," suggested the Captain politely as his engineer stood on the edge of the quay and prepared to jump on board.

"We werena expectin' to see ye again withoot your kilt," said Dougie maliciously. Macphail's anatomical defects had been considered to render kilts so absurdly out of the question that his shipmates always insisted General Haig[1] would instantly pick him for the Gordons.[2]

Without a word the engineer sat down on his biscuit tin and burst into tears.

"Man, Macphail, I'm wonderin' at ye!" exclaimed the Captain. "Your system's chust run doon wi' travellin'; a little drop o' Brutish spirits — have ye much left in the canister?"

"Stand back and gie the chap breath!" implored Sunny Jim. "I'll bate a pound they found there was something wrang wi' him internal. I wouldna bother, Mac, if it's checked in time ye'll maybe linger on for years."

"Tach!" said Para Handy sympathetically. "I wouldna heed them doctors, Mac; it's only guesswork wi' them. But to tell ye the truth I didna like yon chrechlin'[3] cough ye had since ye went afore the Tribunal.[4] The only hope I had wass ye were puttin' 't on. If I had chust a wee small drop o' spurrits wi' some sugar in't — will ye no' sit on this bucket? — a cannister iss cold."

"Ye may be glad they wouldna take ye!" said Dougie consolingly. "Even if it wass only for the sake o' yer wife and pickle children."

"That's the dashed thing!" sobbed Macphail shamelessly; "they're takin' me richt enough. I've passed the doctors at Stirling, and I have a ticket here to jine a regiment to-morrow at Fort Matilda."[5]

"Oh, michty!" exclaimed Sunny Jim with envy. "Whit regiment?"

"I canna mind its name," said the engineer, drying his eyes with a piece of waste; "but it starts wi' an F, and I'm to be a private. And me! — I don't ken the least wee thing aboot the way to be a private! I was bred an engineer."

In proof of these lamentable tidings he produced an official document which declared he was physically fit in every respect, and a card with which to present himself to the office for recruits.

"Man alive! Did ye no' cough at them?" asked Para Handy. "Yon chrechlin' cough wass chust a masterpiece."

"Cough!" exclaimed Macphail. "I coughed till ye would think it was the Cloch on a foggy night, but yon chaps never heeded. They put a tape aboot my chest, and chapped me between the shoulders, and listened could they hear my circulation. I was stripped stark naked — "

"My Chove! issn't that chust desperate!" said the Captain, horrified.

"I don't care!" cried Macphail in an excess of indignation. "I'm no' gaun to go, and that's a' aboot it!" He incautiously rose from his seat and stamped the deck.

"Wi' a little wee drop sugar in't, there's nothing better for a cough," said the Captain, hurriedly opening the biscuit tin. He looked disappointed. "Tach!" he said. "There's only an empty gill bottle and wan other garment. That iss not the way a chentleman would be travellin' from Stirling."

"See here!" said Sunny Jim with some eagerness. "Did they tak' your photograph?"

"No," said the melancholy engineer.

"Then gie me your tickets and I'll go to Fort Matilda in the name o' Dan Macphail. They'll never ken the difference. If it wasna this e'e o' mine was gless, I would hae 'listed a year ago. I've tried, and I've better tried to jine, but they'll no' iet ye jine wi' a glessy yin unless ye have lots o' influence."

"Ye canna hide that eye on them; it looks that flippant!" said the Captain incredulously.

Macphail hurriedly handed over his documents lest any debate should diminish the young man's ardour.

"They canna go back on the doctor's line!" said Sunny Jim. "It says here Dan Macphail is medically fit — that's me, and I'm faur better value for the British Airmy wi' my glessy than Macphail would be wi' a full set o' een and his Sunday specs and his he'rt no' in it. It's the chance o' my life!"

"I wash my hands of it!" said Dougie, who had not yet recovered from his disappointment at the engineer's return. "It is against the Defence o' the Realm[6] to pass gless eyes on the British Airmy, and ye'll get this boat in trouble."

"I jist have time to catch the boat for Greenock," said Sunny Jim. He put the documents in his pocket, buttoned his jacket, and climbed ashore.

74. *The Fusilier*

Two weeks after Sunny Jim stole into the Scottish Fusiliers[1] under false pretences with the name and papers of Macphail, the engineer, and a glass eye he had previously made a dozen vain attempts to foist on recruiting officers as the natural article, he turned up in his uniform on the *Vital Spark*. He carried himself so erect that he had a rake aft like a steamer's funnel, his chest preceding him by about nine inches, and his glengarry bonnet cocked on three hairs. Every button glinted.

"Jumpin' Jehosophat!" exclaimed the Captain. "It's on you they've made the dufference! Wi' a step like that ye would make a toppin' piper. Ye're far more copious aboot the body than ye were."

"Broader in every direction!" said Dougie, with genuine admiration. "By the time they're done wi' ye, ye'll be a fair Goliath."

Macphail looked sourly on his substitute, but even he could not restrain surprise. "I take the credit," said he, "for the makin' o' ye; if it wasna for my testimonials ye wouldna be in the airmy yet."

Sunny Jim saluted his old shipmates with a rapid movement that threw his bonnet on to two hairs and an eyebrow, then cut away the right hand smartly.

"Cheer up, chaps!" he said; "the war's near by; I'm gaun oot wi' the very next draft to put the feenisher on it."

"Did they no' say nothin' aboot your eye?" aslsed Para Handy, intently regarding that notorious organ.

"Oh, they just passed the remark that it was a fair bummer for the shootin'- ranges, seein' I wouldna need to shut it," said Sunny Jim. "But we had a kind o' a pant wi't the first day I was on parade. I was daein' the Swedish exercise, and sweatin' that much the glessy yin near slipped oot. I put up my hand to kep it, and the sergeant-major says, 'Whit's wrang wi' your eye, Macphail?

" 'There's something in it,' says I.

" 'Then fall to the rear three paces and tak' it oot,' says he, 'and no' mak' a bloomin' demonstration o' the squad; the folk that's lookin' on'll think ye're greetin'.'

"I took it oot and slips it into my pocket, and when I steps into the ranks again the sergeant-major nearly fainted.

" 'Gless!' said he, when I explained it was a fancy yin. 'Man, it's no' a sodger you should be, but a war correspondent; ye have half the full equipment for the job!'"

"And whit kind o' a situation hae ye?" asked Macphail.

"Oh, I'm a cook," said Sunny Jim. "It's really a chef's job, for ye hae to be parteecular."

"Oh, my goodness!" cried Macphail. "The Scottish Fusiliers is gaun to suffer."

"No fears!" said Sunny Jim; "cookin' in a camp is no' like cookin' in a coal-boat; it's no' a pound o' boiled beef ham and a quarter loaf that's yonder; the place is fair infested wi' the best o' butcher meat."

"Still-and-on it must be a hard life, James," suggested Para Handy. "Everything by word o' command, and no time for to pause and to consuder."

"It's a gentleman's life," declared the young recruit. "Naething hard aboot it, except that ye have to keep your teeth brushed. I don't think I could think o' goin' back to follow the sea when the war's past; sodgerin' puts ye aff the notion o' a sedimentary life. I'm thinkin' o' gaun in for bein' a major; the best yins does it, and ye get a horse."

They gave the ambitious son of Mars a cup of tea, and two boiled eggs to it; he politely disposed of them, though it was evident such fare was rather homely for a chef. His new fastidiousness only came out when he asked for a saucer; he forgot that the only one on board was used for the engineer's black soap.

"The only thing that's wrang wi' the Fusiliers is that they spoil ye," he explained apologetically. "Every other day there's a duff ."

"Whit like iss the other chentlemen in the business wi' ye?" inquired Dougie.

"The very best!" said Sunny Jim, with enthusiasm. "It's yonder ye meet wi' genteel society; regular gentlemen, tip-top toffs right enough. The chap that's lyin' next to me in the hut's in a capital business o' his ain aboot Dalry[2]; I think it's linen drapery, for every sleeve he has is filled to the brim wi' hankies."

"Jehosophat!" said Para Handy. "Dougie will boil another egg for ye this meenute."

"I hope," said Macphail, "that ye'll no' mak' a Ned o' yoursel' in ony way in the airmy, seein' ye're there in the name o' Dan Macphail.

The Macphails was aye respectable, and I wouldna care to have my reputation spoiled."

Dougie laughed derisively. "The Macphails!" he exciaimed. "Everybody kens they came from Ireland — Fenians and Sinn Feiners."

"Your reputation," said Sunny Jim indignantly. "Ye're aye takin' oot your reputation and polishin' it up the same's it was a trombone or a cornet; no' much o' a reputation, and ye needna bother. To tell ye the truth, I found your reputation was the worst thing I could tak' wi' me to the Fusiliers. By George, they had your history in their books!"

"It's a lie!" shouted the engineer, reddening.

"It's as true as I'm tellin' ye! I wasna jined a week when I went to my officer and tellt him straight I wasna Macphail at a'; and wasna gaun to stand the brunt o' bein' Dan Macphail. For the recruitin' officer had Dan Macphail doon in his books for a married man wi' five o' a family, and they were gaun to tak' so much aff my pay every week for your wife's allooance!"

75. *Para Handy, M.D.*

THE rain came down on Tarbert in a torrent. Dougie, while the cards were being shuffled and dealt again, put his head out by the scuttle, and looked up the deserted quay at the blurred lights of the village.

"What in the wide world are ye doin' there?" querulously demanded Para Handy. "If ye keep that scuttle open any longer we'll be swamped! Come in and take your hand; it's no' ke-hoi[1] we're playin'."

"It's a desperate night," said Dougie, shivering in an atmosphere that, now the hatch was closed, was stuffier than that of an oven. "Rain even-on; ass black ass the Earl o' Mansfield's waistcoat, and nothin' stirrin' in the place but the smell o' frying herrin'."

"Herrin'!" exclaimed the Captain, starting to his feet, and slamming down his cards. "That puts me in mind I wass to caal the night on Eddie Macvean, the carter. I clean forgot! I'm sorry to leave ye, laads, but ye'll get your revenge to-morrow, maybe."

A minute later, and he was off the *Vital Spark*, with two-and-ninepence in his pocket, the total amount of gambling currency on the boat, not counting Dougie's lucky sixpence.

It was discovered by his shipmates, left behind, that the cards he had abandoned were "rags" without exception.

Macvean was apparently alone in his house when the Captain entered, sitting quite disconsolately by his fire, smoking.

"I wass up the toon for a message, Eddie," explained the visitor, "and I thocht I would gie ye a roar in the passin'. What way are ye keepin', this weather?"

"I canna compleen," replied the carter in a doleful tone, as if he bitterly regretted his obviously robust condition of health. "Are ye fine yoursel'?"

"What way iss the mustress?" politely continued the Captain. "I hope she's keepin' muddlin' weel."

Eddie Macvean sighed profoundly. "That's the trouble in this hoose," he remarked; "there's no come and go in her. She's that dour! I got the finest offer o' a wee coal business in Lochgilphead, but she's that taken up wi' Tarbert for gaiety and the like, she'll no' hear tell o' flittin'."

"Chust that!" commented Para Handy sympathetically. "Did ye no' try coaxin' her?"

"It's no' the poker I would try wi' Liza Walker, you may be sure, Peter! I have been throng[2] coaxin' her aal this week wi' that much patience ye would think I wass coortin', but she'll no budge! She says if I'm goin' to take her to Lochgilphead, it'll be in her coffin. Nothin' for her but gaiety! It's them Young Women's Guilds that's leadin' them off their feet!"

"Iss she oot at the Guild the night?" inquired the Captain, with a well- simulated air of regret at the lady's absence.

"No," said the husband sadly, "she's away to her bed wi' a tirravee of a temper."

There was a loud banging on the wall which divided the room of Macvean's house from the kitchen; he darted next door with significant alacrity, and was gone ten minutes.

"I canna make her oot at aal, at aal!" he remarked on returning. "She's tellin' me where I'll get clean stockin's for mysel', and to send oot a pair o' sheets she has in the bottom of the kist for manglin'."

"Iss she angry" inquired Para Handy.

"That's the duvvelish thing aboot her noo," replied the distracted husband. "She's quite composed, and caalin' me Edward. She says I wass a good man to her nearly aal the time we were togither."

"God bless me!" exclaimed Para Handy, staggered. "Ye should get the doctor. Never let the like o' that go too far! It might be somcthing inward!"

There was another banging on the wall; Macvean went out again, and came back more confounded than ever.

"I never saw Liza in my life like that before!" he said. "She says she's quite resigned, and the only account against her iss a gallon of paraffin oil she got last Tuesday in the merchant's. I think she's kind o' dazed. She's wantin' a drink o' water."

"If I was you, Eddie, I would get the doctor," advised the Captain firmly. "Ye would be vexed if anything happened to her, and she died on ye in weather like this."

The carter returned from his wife's bedside with the empty cup and a look of greater anxiety.

"She says there's nothing wrong wi' her; no pain nor nothing, except that when she dovers over she dreams she's in Lochgilphead poorhouse, and wakens wi' a start. Her voice is aal away to a whisper. When I spoke aboot the doctor she said I wassna to let him in the door ass long ass she had aal her faculties. I'm to gie ye her best respects, and tell ye her faith wass aye in the Protestant releegion. 'Tell Captain Macfarlane,' she says, 'to be a sober man, and be good to his family.' "

"It's the munister she's needin', Eddie, or a drop o' spirits," said the Captain gravely, though a little annoyed at the imputation. "Slip you oot and rouse the munister; he'll be in his bed. Or, do ye think yoursel' ye would try the spirits first?"

But another knocking summoncd the carter, who returned to the kitchen, weeping.

"There's something desperate wrong wi' Liza!" he blubbered; "she wants me to go round to the baker's shop and order a seed-cake."

"What for?" asked Para Handy, astonished.

"Goodness knows!" said Macvean; "the only seed-cake ever I saw wass at New Year or a funeral. I'm vexed I ever spoke about Lochgilphead! Do ye think yoursel' there is any danger, Peter?"

The Captain had no time to answer, for another knocking had called away his host, who returned in a little wringing his hands.

"There iss nothing for it but to go for the doctor," he said. "She's ramblin'; she says I'm to try and keep the hoose together, and no' pairt wi' her mother's sofa."

"I'll go ben and see her," said Para Handy.

An oil-lamp on the chimney-piece lit up the room where Mrs Macvean was lying. The Captain was surprised to find her looking remarkably well, with the hue of health on her face, though a little embarrassed by his unexpected appearance. She whipped off her nightcap.

"What way are ye keepin', Mrs Macvean?" he asked, in sympathetic tones.

The patient paid no heed to him, beyond putting up her hands to feel if her hair was tidy. In a feeble voice she remarked to her husband, "Edward, ye'll give my Sunday frock to Aunty Jennet, and my rings to Mary MacMillan; she wass kind, kind to me!"

" 'Dalmighty!" said the Captain, scratching his ear. "Do ye no' think the least wee drop o' spirits would lift ye, Liza?"

"Nothing 'll lift me noo but John Mackay, the joiner," sobbed the patient. "Tell him to keep my heid away from them M'Callums when he's carryin' me doon the stairs. . . . And oh, Edward!" she continued, "I hope ye'll be happy in Lochgilphead, though it's a place I never cared for."

Her husband by now was prostrate with emotion, incapable of speech.

"Did ye order the seed-cake?" she asked.

"It's aal right aboot the seed-cake," broke in Para Handy. "Mrs Cleghorn, the baker's widow, iss takin' it in hand. I wudger ye she'll make a topper! She's terrible vexed to hear ye're poorly, and says ye're no' to bother. She's comin' in in the mornin' to make Eddie's breakfast."

Mrs Macvean at this sat up in bed with an amazing recovery of strength and speech, her visage purple with indignation.

"Comin' here!" she cried. "She'll no' put a leg inside this door if I can help it! I can see, noo, Edward, what ye're plottin' — to get me oot o' the road and mairry the bakehoose, but I'm no deid yet! It's only you and your Lochgilphead — "

"It's aal right aboot Lochgilphead, Liza," said the Captain soothingly. "Edward's changed his mind; he's goin' to cairry on in Tarbert."

"Cairry on!" exclaimed the wife. "He'll no' cairry on wi' Susan Cleghorn anyway, and I'm goin' wi' him to Lochgilphead. If he had chust asked me the right way, I would be quite agreeable from the start. Away oot o' this, the pair o' ye, till I get on my garments!"

76. *A Double Life*

"PHILANDERIN'; what in the world's philanderin'?" inquired Dougie, honestly eager for the definition of a word which Macphail the engineer had recently learned from a Blue Bell novelette, and was apt to drag into every conversation about the female sex.

"It's the same as flirtin', but fancier, if ye follow me," replied Macphail. "Many a chap starts flirtin' jist to pass the time and get the name o' being a regular teaser, and finds himsel' married withoot knowin' hoo the devil it happened to him. A philanderer's different. He has a' his wits aboot him and doesna mak' a pet o' any woman in particular. He'll have half a dozen o' them knittin' socks for him at the same time in different localities, but the last thing he would think o' wastin' money on would be a bride's-cake. There's no philanderers in lodgin's; they're all supportin' poor old mothers."

"The best philanderer I ever kent," said Para Handy, "wass Hurricane Jeck. He wass a don at it when he wass younger. He would cairry on wi' a whole Dorcas[1] meetin' if they didna crood roond him aal at wance. Ye never saw a more nimble fellow, and there he iss — no' married yet, nor showin' any signs o't."

"Hurricane Jeck's no' my notion o' a proper philanderer," commented the engineer with some acidity. "He hasna the knowledge for 't — a chap that never opens a book!"

"There's no books needed," retorted the Captain.

"Jeck had the gift by nature. I'm speakin' o' the time before he went sailin' foreign, when he had his whuskers. We were on the *Mary*

Jane thegither, and faith I wasna slack mysel', though I never had his agility. He wass ass smert ass salt on a sore finger. There wassna a port inside o' Paddy's Milestone² where Jeck wass not ass welcome wi' the girls ass Royal Cherlie! But I can tell ye it took some management!

"I mind that wan time Jeck got into a nesty habble wi' a couple o' girls in Gleska.

"He wass very chief³ at the time wi' a young weedow wife in Oban that had a pickle money o' her own. If Jeck wass not a rover he would have married her, for she was a fine big bouncin' woman quite suitable for a sailor, but he couldna make up his mind between her and a girl called Lucy Cameron he wass walkin' oot wi' any time the vessel wass in Gleska.

"Wan time yonder when the *Mary Jane* wass in Oban the weedow trysted Jeck to take her to the Mull and Iona Soirée, Concert, and Ball in the Waterloo Rooms⁴ in Gleska. Jeck wass always the perfect chentleman; he would promise anything if it wassna that week.

"The night o' the Mull and Iona Gaitherin' came on, and Jeck clean forgot his engagement wi' Mrs Maclachlan. That very night he was booked for Hengler's Circus⁵ wi' Lucy Cameron. It wassna till the weedow came to his lodgin's in a cab, wi' a fine new pair o' white kid gloves for him and a flooer for his button-hole, that the poor chap minded o' his promise.

"A lad less nimble in his wits would have thocht the poseetion hopeless, but Jeck wassna so easy daunted. Though he wass dressed aal ready for the Circus, he went to the Mull and Iona, clapped Mrs Maclachlan doon among a wheen o' freen's o' hers from Tobermory chust before the soirée started; took a bloodin' nose, by his way of it, and wass oot in the street again in a jeffy, skelpin' it for Lucy Cameron's."

"Wasn't that the rogue?" exclaimed Dougie admiringly.

"When the Mull and Iona wass singin' the chorus o' Farewell to Fuinary, or maybe aboot the time the orangers wass passin' roond in the Waterloo Rooms, Jeck wass sittin' across the street in Hengler's wi' Lucy Cameron, clappin' his hands at my namesake, Handy Andy the clown.

"Every noo and then he would take oot his watch when Lucy wassna lookin', and calculate hoo far the Mull and Iona folk would be in their programme, and in twenty meenutes his nose began to blood again.

" 'Beg pardon!' says Jeck — for he was aalways the perfect chentleman — 'but I'll have to go oot a meenute for a key to put doon my back.' And away he went like the wind across the street to the Waterloo Rooms.

"He was chust in time for the start o' the Grand March.

" 'Are ye better?' asked the weedow, quite anxious, never jalousin' Jeck wass a fair deceiver.

" 'Tip-top!' says Jeck, and into the Grand March wi' her like a trumpeter. It wass chenerally allooed there wassna a handsomer couple on the floor. He feenished Triumph wi' the weedow, saw her settled wi' another partner for Petronella, and then skipped like a goat across to Hengler's. Little did Lucy Cameron ken her lad wass at the dancin'!

"Every twenty meenutes Jeck wass oot o' the circus on some excuse or other, and puttin' in a dance wi' the Oban weedow, then back again to Lucy. He wass so busy between the two o' them he couldna even get a drink, and at the Mull and Iona his condeetion was noticed. At the circus Lucy wass wonderin' too, for he aye came back wi' an oranger, or a poke o' sweeties from the baal, and a smell o' lavender, but as right as a Rechabite.

"For four mortal oors Jeck ran the ferry this way; when the circus wass feenished he took Miss Cameron home, and then back to the Waterloo Rooms, where he made a night o't.

"He told me aal aboot it himsel' next day. 'If I hadna my health, Peter,' he said, 'I couldna do it. And the dash thing iss they're both fine girls! I wass nearly poppin' the question to Lucy, and Mrs Maclachlan wass most attractive.'

"The thing would have passed aal right if it wassna that the 'Oban Times' next week gave an account o' the Mull and Iona, wi' Jeck's name among the chentlemen that wass present, and Lucy saw it. She wass desperate angry!

"Jeck denied it; said it wass aalthegither a mistake; that somebody must have been tradin' on his reputation; but Lucy's mother had a lodger in the polis force that made an investigation, and it wass all up wi' poor Jeck and the Cameron family.

"And it didna stop there neither, for the polisman informed the

Oban weedow the way Jeck had been cairryin' on, and the next time Jeck made a caal on her in Oban to clinch things for a merrage, Mrs Maclachlan wouldna speak to him."

"That shows ye," said the engineer, "that he wasna a rale philanderer; a philanderer's never found oot."

77. *The Wet Man of Muscadale*[1]

"TALKIN' aboot the health," said Para Handy, "the drollest man I ever saw that made a hobby o' his health wass a pairty in Muscadale caaled the Wet Man."

"What in the name o' goodness did they caal him that for?" asked the mate.

"Chust because he wass never dry," replied the Captain. "He went aboot damp for forty years, and would be livin' yet if it wassna for the doctors. They took him to a cottage hospital in Campbeltoon, dried his clo'es on him, and packed him in a bed wi' hotwater bottles. He drank every drop that wass in the bottles before the mornin', and efter that they wouldna gie him any more, so he withered like the rose o' Sharon[2] in the Scruptures. Died o' drooth, like a geranium in a flooer-pot! He wass over ninety years o' age, wi' aal his faculties aboot him till the end, and never used a towel."

"My goodness!" exclaimed the mate.

"Many a time I'll be thinkin'," said Para Handy, "that the man in Muscadale wass born a bit before his time. If he wass spared another fifty years the world would see there iss a lot o' nonsense aboot science and the droggists' shops, and that long life iss aal a maitter o' moisture."

"If bein' wet would keep us healthy," interjected Macphail the engineer, "we would never dee at a' in the West Coast shippin' tred."

"There iss a lot o' rubbidge talked regairdin' damp," continued the Captain. "Colin MacClure in Muscadale proved it. He wass fifty years o' age when he took a desperate cold that he couldna get rid o' till he fell wan day in the watter in the Sound o' Jura, and when they fished him oot he hadna a vestige. A chrechlin' cough he had wass gone completely.

"From that day he wass a changed man, and pinned his faith in watter, ootside and in. He couldna pass a pump-well withoot a swig at it, and when any other fisherman would be takin' a Chrustian dram in moderation wi' his frien's, nothin' but a barrel and a bailin'-dish would serve the Wet Man o' Muscadale."

"Issn't that chust duvvelish!" exclaimed Dougie. "I would say there iss nothing worse for a man's inside than watter; look at the way it rots your boots!"

"He got heavy, heavy on the watter; aye nip-nippin' at it whcn he thocht that nobody wass lookin'. Many a time his wife — poor body! — had to go and look for him at the river-side and bring him home."

"I can take a little watter in moderation," said the mate; "a drop o't in your tea does herm to nobody, but it's ruinaation to be always tipplin' at it."

"It would be diabetes,"[3] suggested the engineer.

"There wassna a diabete in Colin's composeetion," said the Captain. "His constitution wass grand. He could eat tackets[4] and sleep like a babe on a slab o' granite. A big bold healthy fisherman wi' a noble whusker on him! — wan o' the chenuine old MacClures that's in the 'History o' the Clans'. If there wass any germs o' any kind in the Wet Man o' Muscadale they would nced to wear life-belts. The only time that Colin wass in danger for his health was in frosty weather; he would get ass hard then ass a curlin'-stone, and the least bit jar against the corner o' a hoose would knock a chip off him.

" 'Be wet and ye'll be weel!' wass Colin's motto; he could prove it wi' the Bible. 'Noah,' he would say, 'made a fair hash o' the business in landin' on Ben Ararat; if it wassna for that, we would be sweemin' aboot the deep the day like fishes, in the best o' health and trum, and no need for your panel doctors. Ye never heard o' a herrin' yet that had lumbago.'

"From the day that he wass picked oot o' the Sound o' Jura, he never let his clo'es dry on his back for fear o' trouble, and the very sight o' a dry shirt on a washin'-green would make him shiver. He wass the wan man in Scotland ye would find lamentin' if it wassna rainin'. Colin's notion o' comfort wass a good big hole in the roof o' the hoose, a dub on the hearth, a thin alpaca jecket stickin' to his ribs, all splashin', and his sea-boots full o' watter."

"Did he no' get rheumatism?" inquired the mate, astounded.

"Not him! He wass ass flippant on his feet ass an Irish ragman, and never spent a penny on his health till the day they buried him. He cairried his notion to a redeeculous degree, for he was staunch teetotal."

"If he was livin' the day he would get a' the watter he needed in half a mutchkin,"[5] suggested the engineer cynically.

"That wouldna do for the Wet Man o' Muscadale," said the Captain. "Ye see, he had to be wet ootside ass well ass in. Many a sore trauchle his wife had wettin' him wi' a watterin'-can in the summer, the same's he wass a bed o' syboes.[6] She wass a poor wee cricket o' a low-country woman, and darena even dry the blankets efter washin' them for fear that Colin would get a cold. On their golden weddin' day she said to a neebour, 'Bonny on the golden weddin'! My man's yonder sittin' on the ebb and steepin' like a lump o' dulse.'[7]

"The Wet Man thrived so weel on the watter treatment that a lot o' the folk in the countryside aboot began to follow his example, and then nothin' would do for Colin but to start a new releegion. At first he thocht, himsel', o' joinin' the Baptists, thinkin' that the Baptist churches had a pond in them the same ass the Greenheid Baths in Gleska, but when he heard that the Baptists only got a splash in a kind o' boyne and then came oot and dried themsel's, he wass fair disgusted.

" 'They're chust a lot o' back-sliders,' he says; 'they havena the fundamentals o' releegion in them!' So he started a body o' his own they caaled the MacClurites. The other denominations gave them the by-name o' the Muscadale Dookers, and they suffered a lot o' persecution, them bein' so close on Campbeltoon. The MacClurites never used oilskins nor umberellas; they're tellin' me the second cheneration o' them had web feet and feathers on them chust like jucks.

"The MacClurites quarrelled among themsel's aboot the doctrine; some sayin' salt watter wasna the naitural element o' salvaation, and others that ye werena proper wet unless ye fell in the Sound o' Jura. It clean broke up the MacClurites, and they aal went back to the Wee Free Church ass dry ass anything, and died in the prime o' life at seventy or eighty.

"But Colin MacClure never flinched nor bowed the knee to Ramoth-Gilead.[8] When the laird put rhones and a galvanised roof on his dwellin', he took his abode below high-water mark in a skiff turned upside doon that wass aalways flooded at every tide."

"He would be a' mildew," said the engineer.

"Fair blue-moulded!" said the Captain.

"For fifty years the clo'es wass never dry on him; ye would think it wass gress wass growin' in his back, but he went aboot to the very last wi' wonderful agility. It is from scenes like them that Scotia's grandeur springs."[9]

Para and the 'Scruptures'

THE late-twentieth century reader can hardly have failed to notice the frequent references to churches, religious life and religious controversy contained in these stories. From the first story, "Para Handy, Master Mariner" with its reference to the minister's glebe through to the somewhat unorthodox religious views of "The Wet Man of Muscadale", churches, clergymen and religion play a significant part in the life of the crew of the *Vital Spark*, as indeed they did in the life of the Scottish nation as a whole.

Perhaps even more interestingly from the point of view of cultural history are the very many quotations, or mis-quotations from Holy Scripture used in the stories. Para's frequent recourse to a Biblical text is an interesting indication of a common culture and betokens a significant level of familiarity with the Bible on the part of his readers. A reference such as "I am going up and down like yon fellow in the Scruptures — whatt wass his name? Sampson — seeking what I may devour." with its confusion of two separate Biblical texts relies for its humorous effect on the reader knowing that Para has got it wrong. Similarly the reference in "A Lost Man" to "the eagle that knew the youth", a garbled version of metrical psalm 103:

"So that, ev'n as the eagle's age
    renewed is thy youth."

totally fails to amuse if the reader has not a more than passing familiarity with the Psalter.

The original context of these stories must be remembered. They were almost all originally published in a popular daily newspaper and it is only reasonable to assume that their first audience found these scriptural references no more alien or obscure than the allusions to Clyde steamers or the activities of politicians such as Churchill and Lloyd George. Munro, as an experienced and talented journalist, could well judge what his readers would know and what had to be explained. It is also worth remembering that although Munro was a member of the Church of Scotland there is no evidence to show that he was more than usually devout or indeed particularly interested in religious matters. He was however, like his audience, a participant in a common culture which had, as one of its main components, a sound knowledge, inculcated at school and church, of Scripture.

It is very clear that no modern writer of similar humorous short stories could or would today make such extensive use of Scripture. The existence, in the general population, of a reasonably detailed knowledge of the Bible, which Munro could take for granted, has largely vanished. The decline in Church membership from the period in which these stories first appeared has of course been very marked, but it is doubtful if, even among late twentieth-century churchgoers, one could count on the detailed knowledge of the Bible which Munro was able to rely on to give point to so many of his references. Whatever religious opinions one may hold, this loss of what was a significant shared cultural heritage must be regrettable. If today we were to come on a whale at Tobermory could we, like Dougie, know enough to remark "It was right enough, I can see, Peter, aboot yon fellow Jonah: chust look at the accommodation" and would anyone know what we were talking about?

78. *Initiation*

THERE was absolutely nothing to do to pass the time till six o'clock, and Hurricane Jack, whose capacity for sleep under any circumstances and at any hour of the day or night was the envy of his shipmates, stretched himself out on the hatches with a fragment of tarpaulin over him. In about two seconds he was apparently dreaming of old days in the China clipper trade, and giving a most realistic imitation of a regular snorter of a gale off the Ramariz.

"There's some people iss born lucky," remarkcd the Captain pathetically. "Jeck could go to sleep inside a pair o' bagpipes and a man playin' on them. It's the innocent mind o' him."

"It's no' the innocent mind o' him, whatever it iss," retorted Dougie with some acidity. "It's chust fair laziness; he canna be bothered standin' up and keepin' his eyes open. Ye're chust spoilin' him. That's what I'm tellin' ye!"

Para Handy flushed with annoyance. "Ye think I'm slack," he remarked; "but I'm firm enough wi' Jeck when there's any occasion. I sent him pretty smert for the milk this mornin', and him wantin' me to go mysel'. I let him see who wass skipper on this boat. A body would think you wass brocht up on a man-o'-war; ye would like to see me aye bullyin' the fellow. There's no herm in Jeck Maclachlan, and there iss not a nimbler sailor under the cope and canopy, in any shape or form!"

Dougie made no reply. He sat on an upturned bucket sewing a patch on the salient part of a pair of trousers with a sail-maker's needle.

"There ye are!" resumed the Captain. "Darnin' away at your clothes and them beyond redemption! Ye're losin' aal taste o' yoursel'; what ye're needin's new garments aalthegither. Could ye no', for goodness sake, buy a web o' homespun somewhere in the islands and make a bargain wi' a tyler?"

"Tylers!" exclaimed Dougie. "I might as weel put mysel' in the hands o' Rob Roy Macgregor![1] They're askin' £6 10s. the suit, and it's extra for the trooser linin'."

Para Handy was staggered. He had bought no clothes himself

since his marriage, and had failed to observe the extraordinary elevation in the cost of men's apparel.

"Holy Frost!" he cried. "That's a rent in itsel'! If that's the way o't, keep you on plyin' the needle, Dougie. It's terrible the price o' everything nooadays. I think, mysel', it's a sign o' something goin' to happen. It runs in my mind there wass something aboot that in the Book o' Revelations. I only paid £2 10s. for a capital pilot suit the year I joined the Rechabites."

The mate suspended his sewing, and looked up suspiciously at the skipper.

"It's the first time ever I heard ye were in the Rechabites," he remarked significantly. "Hoo long were ye in them?"

"Nearly a week," replied Para Handy, "and I came oot o' them wi' flyin' colours at the start o' the Tarbert Fair. It wass aal a mistake, Dougie; the tyler at the time in Tarbert took advantage o' me. A fisherman by the name o' Colin Macleod from Minard and me wass very chief at that time, and he wass a Freemason. He would aye he givin' grips and makin' signs to ye. By his way o't a sailor that had the grip could trevel the world and find good company wherever he went, even if he didna ken the language.

"Colin wass high up in the Freemasons; when he had all his medals and brooches on he looked like a champion Hielan' dancer.

"He wass keen, keen for me to join the craft and be a reg'lar chentleman, and at last I thocht to mysel' it would be a great advantage.

" 'Where will I join?' I asked him.

" 'Ye'll join in Tarbert; there's no' a Lodge in the realm o' Scotland more complete,' says Colin. 'And the first thing ye'll do, ye'll go up and see my cousin the tyler; he'll gie ye a lot o' preluminary instruction.'

"The very next time I wass in Tarbert I went to the tyler right enough for the preluminaries.

" 'I wass thinkin' o' joinin' the Lodge,' I says to him, 'and Colin Macleod iss tellin' me ye're in a poseetion to gie me a lot o' tips to start wi'. What clothes will I need the night o' the meetin'?'

"He was a big soft-lookin' lump o' a man, the tyler, wi' a smell o' singed cloth aboot him, and the front o' his jecket aal stuck over wi' pins; and I'll assure ye he gave me the he'rty welcome.

" 'Ye couldna come to a better quarter!' he says to me, 'and it'll no' take me long to put ye through your facin's. There's a Lodge on Friday, and by that time ye'll be perfect. Of course, ye'll have the proper garments?

" 'What kind o' garments?' says I. 'I have nothing at aal but what I'm wearin'; my Sabbath clothes iss all in Gleska.'

" 'Tut! tut!' says he, quite vexed. 'Ye couldna get into a Lodge wi' clothes like that; ye'll need a wise-like suit if ye're to join the brethren in Tarbert. But I can put ye right in half a jiffy.'

"He jumped the counter like a hare, made a grab at a pile o' cloth that wass behind me, hauled oot a web o' blue-pilot stuff, and slapped it on a chair.

" 'There's the very ticket for ye!' he says, triumphant. 'Wi' a suit o' that ye'll be the perfect chentleman!'

"I wassna needin' clothes at aal, but before I could open my mouth to say Jeck Robe'son he had the tape on me. Noo there's something aboot a tyler's tape that aye puts me in a commotion, and I lose my wits.

"He had the measure o' my chest in the time ye wud gut a herrin', and wass roond at my back before I could turn mysel' to see what he wass up to. 'Forty-two; twenty-three,' he bawls, and puts it in a ledger.

"He wass on to me again wi' his tape, like a flash o' lightnin'; pulled the jecket nearly off my back and took the length o' my waistcoat, and oh! my goodness, but he smelt o' Harris tweed, and it damp, singein'!

" 'Hold up your arm!' says he, and he took the sleeve-length wi' a flourish, and aal the time he wass tellin' me what a capital Lodge was the Tarbert one, and aboot the staunchness o' the brethren.

" 'Ye'll find us a lot o' cheery chaps,' he says; 'there's often singin'. But ye'll have to come at first deid sober, for they're duvvelish particular.'

"By this time he wass doon aboot my legs, and the tape wass whippin' aal aboot me like an Irish halyard. I wass that vexed I had entered his shop withoot a dram, for if I had a dram it wasna a tyler's tape that Peter Macfarlane would flinch for.

"By the time he had aal my dimensions, fore and aft, in his wee bit ledger, I wass in a perspiration, and I didna care if he measured me for a lady's dolman.[2]

" 'Do ye need to do this every time?' I asked him, put aboot tremendous.

" 'Do what?' says the tyler.

" 'Go over me wi' a tape,' says I.

" 'Not at aal,' he says, quite he'rty, laughin'. 'It's only for the first initiation that ye need consider your appearance. Later on, no doot, ye'll need regalia, and I can put ye richt there too.'

" 'It's only the first degree I'm wantin' to start wi'' I says to him; 'I want to see if my health 'll stand it.'

" 'Tach!' says the tyler; 'ye'll get aal that's goin' at the wan go-off There's no shilly-shallyin' about oor Lodge in Tarbert. Come up to the shop to-morrow, and I'll gie the first fit on.'

"I went to him next day in the afternoon, and ye never in aal your life saw such a performance! The tape wass nothin' to't! He put on me bits o' jeckets and weskits tacked thegither, withoot any sign o' sleeves or buttons on them; filled his mooth to the brim wi' pins, and started jaggin' them into me.

" 'Mind it's only the first degree!' I cries to him. 'Ye maybe think I'm strong, but I'm no' that strong!'

"Him bein' full o' pins, I couldna make oot wan word he wass mumblin', but I gaithered he wass tellin' me something aboot the grips and password. And then he fair lost his heid! He took a lump of chalk and began to make a regular cod o' my jecket and weskit.

" 'Stop! Stop!' I cries to him. 'I wass aye kind o' dubious aboot Freemasons, and if I'm to wear a parapharnalia o' this kind, all made up o' patches pinned thegither, and chalked aal o'er like the start o' a game o' peever, I'm no' goin' to join!'

"The tyler gave a start. 'My goodness!' he says, 'it's no' the Freemasons ye were wantin' to join?'

" 'That wass my intention,' I told him. 'And Colin said his cousin the tyler in Tarbert wass the very man to help me. That's the way I'm here.'

" 'Isn't that chust deplorable!' says the tyler, scratchin' his heid. 'Ye're in the wrong shop aalthegither! The tyler o' the Mason's Lodge in Tarbert's another man aalthegither, that stands at the door o' his Lodge to get the password. I'm no' a Mason at aal; I'm the treasurer o' the Rechabites.'

" 'The Rechabites!' says I, horror-struck. 'Aren't they teetotal?

" 'Strict!' he says. 'Ye canna get over that — to start wi'. And ye're chust ass good ass a full-blown Rechabite noo, for I've given ye aal I ken in the way o' secrets.'

"So that's the way I wass a Rechabite, Dougie. wass staunch to the brethren for seven days, and then I fair put an end to't. I never went near their Lodge, but the suit o' clothes came doon to the vessel for me wi' a wee boy for the money. It wass £2. 10s., and I have the weskit yet."

"£2. 10s. and aal that sport!" said Dougie ruefully. "Them wass the happy days!"

79. *The End of the World*

"WHEN MEN gets up in years — say aboot eighty or ninety — there should be something done wi' them," said Para Handy.

"What in the world would ye do wi' them?" asked Dougie. "Ye darena wander them."

"Ye canna wander them nooadays; the Government iss watchin' them like hawks, and, anyway, they'll never venture half a mile from the Post Office where they get their Old Age Pensions. I would put them aal oot on the island o' St Kilda[1], wi' a man in cherge. Any old man of ninety that wass dour and dismal I would ship him yonder wi' aal his parapharnalia. I'm no sayin' but here and there ye'll find an old chap worth his keep — chust as jolly and full o' mischief as if he wass a young man, but most o' them's a tribulation to their frien's, and always interferin'. Hurrcane Jeck could tell ye."

The Captain's startling scheme for dealing with nonagenarians originated in a conversation on longevity among the people of Arran.

"Jeck," he continued, "had his life fair spoiled on him wi' an uncle he had in Govan. He wass ninetytwo if he wass a day, but wasna pleased wi' that; he would aye be braggin' that he wass a hundred. He lived by himsel' in a but-and-ben[2], and he made poor Hurricane's life a torment.

"Jeck at the time wass in his prime, and sailin' back and forrit, slipper o' a nice wee boat they caaled the *Jenet*. It wass years before he started goin' foreign. A more becomin' man on a quay ye never clapped an eye on — ass trig's a shippin'-box, and always wi' a nate wee roond broon hat.

"His Uncle Wilyum wass a tyrant. In his time he wass a landscape gairdner —"

"What iss a landscape gairdner?" asked Dougie.

"A landscape gairdner iss a man that scapes gairdens. . . . But for twenty years old Wilyum lived on his money and spent his time contrivin' what way he would make his nephew Jeck a credit to the Second Comin' and the family o' Maclachlan.

"He had every failin' that a man could have, Uncle Wilyum — he wass lame wi' rheumatism, as deaf's a post, teetotal to the worst degree, and never went to church but made a patent kind o' releegion o' his own oot o' the 'Christian Herald' and the 'Gospel Trumpet'. Chust an old pagan! Ye would be sick listenin' to him on the prophet Jeremiah and the Second Comin' and the opening o' Baxter's Seven Phials."[3]

"Whatna man was Baxter?" inquired the mate.

"Chust Baxter!" replied Para Handy petulantly. "The man that wass a prophet and wrote the 'Christian Herald'.

"Nobody could be nicer to an uncle up in years than Jeck. Many a firkin o' herrin' and scores o' eggs he brocht from the Hielan's for the old chap. He wass his only livin' relative except a sister o' his that lived in Colonsay, and any money that the old man left wass likely to be Jeck's.

"Money wass the last thing Jeck at the time had his mind on; he wass a born rover that asked for nothing better than to dodge aboot the Western Hielan's in his own dacent boat, or go percolatin' roond the Broomielaw wi' a cheery frien' or two when his vessel wass in Clyde.

"There wass no more harm in Jeck than in a goldfish, but the silly old body thocht he was a limb o' Satan, and never missed a chance to board him wi' a bundle o' tracts. Jeck had no sooner his foot on shore in Gleska than Uncle Wilyum, wi' his sticks, would hirple up and follow him every place he went to keep him oot o' temptation.

"He put the peter on't at last wan time he went efter Jeck to the Oban and Lorn Soirée and Ball in the Waterloo Rooms, and found him wi' a clove hitch round the waist o' a bouncin' girl and them throng waltzin'.

"I can tell you Jeck got Jeremiah from his Uncle Wilyum that night!

" 'The like o' you dancin' there wi' a wanton woman, and us on the verge!' says the old chap, groanin'.

" 'What verge?' says Jeck.

" 'Did ye no' hear?' says his uncle, lookin' fearful unsatisfactory.

" 'No,' says Jeck,

" 'That's what I wass thinkin',' says his uncle, whippin' oot a 'Christian Herald', and showin' him a bit o' Baxter that said the end o' the worid wass fixed for that day fortnight.

" 'Chust that!' says Jeck. 'I heard a kind o' rumour aboot it doon at Greenock; but I'm no' botherin', for I'm goin' to take the boat for't when the time comes.'

"My goodness, but the old man wass staggered! It had never entered his head to take to the sea for't when the end o' the world came, and he cocked his ears when he heard that Jeck wass goin' to get the better o' the Prophet Baxter wi' the *Jenet*.

" 'Will ye take me wi' ye?' he says to his nephew."

" 'Wi' aal the pleesure in the worid,' says Jeck, who wass aye the perfect chentleman. 'Get you your bits o' sticks collected; we'll put them in the hold for broken stowage, and ye'll come wi' me on Wednesday. We'll be roond the Mull before the trouble breaks oot.'

"Jeck wass only in fun, and you can imagine his consternation when a lorry came doon to his boat next day wi' aal Uncle Wilyum's plenishin'[4], and the old man on the top o' a chest o' drawers wi' a bundle o' Baxter's prophecies!

"There's one thing aboot Jeck-he's never bate!"

He took the old man on board wi' all his dunnage, and started oot for Colonsay, where he wass takin' coals.

"It was the dreariest trip he ever made in aal his life; for when the old man wassna takin' his meat or sleepin', he wass greetin' aboot the end o' aal things and swabbin' his heid-lights even-on wi' a red bandana hanky, or groanin' over the 'Christian Herald'.

" 'Tach! I wouldna bother aboot the Prophet Baxter,' says Jeck to him at last. 'Perhaps he wass workin' wi' a last year's almanack, and fairly oot o't wi' his calculations.'

"But Uncle Wilyum said that wass blasphemy, and kept on reelin' oot fathoms o' Jeremiah, till poor Jeck wass near demented.

" 'What place iss this?' says Uncle Wilyum when they came to Colonsay, and Jeck began dischairgin' coal.

" 'It's the end o' the world,' says Jeck', quite blithe. 'Away you ashore and see your sister Mary, and I'll send up your furniture ass soon ass the coals iss done.'

" 'For aal the time we have thegither,' wailed his Uncle Wilyum, 'is it worth my while?'

" 'Worth your while!" cried Jeck. 'Of course it's worth your while! I'll bate ye Baxter never heard o' the Isle o' Colonsay. It's forty years since ye saw your sister. Away and spend your money on her like a chentleman.'

"Uncle Wilyum went ashore wi' his bundle o' the prophets, and settled down wi' his sister, waitin' for the day o' tribulation. He lingered seven years, and shaved himsel' every mornin', so as to be ready; but Baxter failed him at the last, and he died o' influenza, leavin' his pickle money to his sister."

"That wass a pity for Jeck," said Dougie.

"Tach! Jeck didna care a docken! He wass enjoyin' life."

80. *The Captured Cannon*

As soon as it grew dark, when the quay was quite deserted and the village seemed wholly asleep, the crew of the *Vital Spark* set briskly about getting the gun ashore.

They passed two unrailed gang-planks between the vessel and the slip, took the tarpaulins off the mysterious mass of inert material at the bow and revealed a German 18-pounder, without its breech-block, exceedingly battered and rusty. Hurricane Jack fastened a stout rope to the gun itself, and going behind lifted up the trail of the carriage with an effort.

"Tail you on to the rope and pull like bleezes," he cried to Dougie; "Macphail and Peter 'll shove roond the wheels o' her, and I'll hold up this cursed contrivance. . . . Aalthegither, boys; heave!"

Para Handy took up the task allotted to him, almost weeping. "Holy Frost!" he wailed; "isn't this the bonny habble we're in? I wish we had never seen the blasted thing; it's aal your fault, Jeck."

"There'll be trouble aboot this, you'll see!" said Macphail, putting all his propulsive vigour into a wheel spoke. "I knew from the beginnin'. But ye wouldna listen to me!"

"Shut up; and haul like Horse Artillery!" growled Hurricane Jack. "Ye're no' in the Milishy."

By almost superhuman efforts they got the gun onto the slip, and up to the level of the wharf.

"What are we to do noo?" panted the Captain. "We canna leave it here; mind you, it's no' Crarae; there's a polisman in the place."

"We'll hurl it doon the quay and oot on the ebb," said Hurricane Jack with confidence and alacrity. "Ye can put anything ye like under high-water-mark, there's no law against it. If we get it oot on the ebb noo it'll be covered wi' the tide afore the mornin'," and he picked up the trail again.

They trundled the piece noisily over the granite pier, perspiring at the task; the weapon had never heard such lurid language in the process since it left the Hindenburg Line.[1]

"If anybody catches us at this!" moaned Dougie apprehensively, blowing like a whale.

They were just on the verge of the sand when Macnaughton appeared in his official glazed tippet, but without his helmet. He had just been making his last round for the night.

"What in the name o' goodness are ye doin' here?" he inquired sternly. "Whose cairt have ye there?"

"It's no' a cairt," said Hurricane Jack, letting down the trail. "It's a quite good cannon the War Office sent for a War Memorial for the place. We're jist dischargin' it."

"Dischargin' it!" exclaimed the constable, horrified; "ye'll waken the whole community!" He came closer, peered in the dark at the weapon, and had a sudden inspiration.

"I know your capers fine!" he exclaimed, throwing back his tippet to show his metal buttons. "We're no' that far behind in this place but we ken aboot that gun; it's the hue and cry o' the county."

"What did ye hear aboot it?" asked Hurricane Jack, coolly taking a seat on the carriage.

"I have it aal here in my book," said the constable, slapping his tail-pocket. "I might have ken't when I saw your boat come in this efternoon wi' a tarp'lin over the bows o' her, that you were up to some o' your dydoes. Ye got the gun from a hawker in Lochgilphead."

"Right enough!" acknowledged the Captain soothingly. "But it wass his own gun; the burgh that got it from the War Office for a souvineer got sick o't, and gave him't for old metal."

"We took it for a speculation," added Hurricane Jack. "Ye would think there's many a place in Loch Fyne would like a chenuine German cannon."

"We were goin' to make oor fortune wi't," said Macphail, with bitter sarcasm. "Jeck assured us there was money in't."

"I ken aal aboot it," said the constable, with an air of profound omniscience. "Ye've been cairryin' that lumber up and doon the loch for the last three weeks tryin' to palm it off on His Majesty's lieges. It's aal in my book! Ye offered it for a pound in Cairndow; the price wass down to ten shillin's at Strachur; ye couldna sell't for a shillin' in Crarae, and ye left it on the quay there, but they made ye shift it."

"It's the God's truth — every word o't," confessed Hurricane Jack. "A German cannon's worse than a drunken reputation; ye canna get rid o't."

The crew of the *Vital Spark* stood in the rain and dark round the degraded and rejected relic of Imperial power, and violently abused Jack.

"A bloomin' eediot! I told him it would be left on oor hands!" cried Macphail. "Whit could onybody dae wi' a cannon?"

"There might be another war at any time," suggested Hurricane Jack defensively.

"I never wass ass black affronted in my life," bleated Para Handy. "The whole loch-side iss laughin' at us. The very turbine steamers blows their whistles when they pass and cry '*Hood*, ahoy!'[2] It's no' like a thing ye could break in bits and burn in Macphail's furnace; it's solid iron in every pairt. Nobody hass a kind word for it; we tried to get a minister to put it in his glebe, or fornent the door o' his manse, and he put his dog on us."

"Ye'll take it oot o' here anyway," said the constable firmly. "We have plenty o' trash o' oor own. It's a mercy I came on ye tryin' to leave it here and spoil the navigation!"

"I never dreamt that a gun wass so ill to manoeuvre," remarked the imperturbable Jack. "Do ye no' think sergeant, there's anybody in the place would care for it for an orniment? Anybody wi' a bit o' a gairden: they could cover it wi' fuchsias."

"No expense at aal!" added Para Handy eagerly. "We would put it in poseetion. Many a wan would be gled to have it if it wass in London or in Gleska. It's a splendid cannon! Captured by the Australian Airmy. Cost the British Government £50 to take to Loch Fyne."

"I don't care if it cost £100," said the constable fiercely; "it's no' goin' to be palmed off on this community that suffered plenty wi' the war. Get it back on board your ship at wance, like dacent lads, and don't make any trouble."

"'Dalmighty!" cried the Captain, wringing his hands, "are we goin' to have this Cherman abomination on oor decks the rest o' oor naitural lifes? . . . It's all your fault, Jeck, ye said there wass a fortune in it."

"My mistake!" admitted Hurricane Jack, most handsomely. "I wash my hands noo o' the whole concern."

"I would wash my hands too, if they werena aal blistered," said Dougie piteously. "What are we to do wi' the cursed thing? There iss no place we dare leave it."

"Could ye no' put it over the side o' the boat somewhere doon about Kilbrannan?" suggested the constable.

They stared at one another, utterly astounded.

"My Chove!" said Para Handy. "We never thocht o' that! Aren't you the born eediot, Jeck, that would have us cairtin' it up and doon the ocean for the last three weeks!"

"I didna want to see a good gun wasted," explained Hurricane Jack, rather lamely, and he picked up the trail again. "But maybe that's the best way oot o' the difficulty; get a ha'd o' the rope again, and pull, Dougie."

81. *An Ideal Job*

As the *Vital Spark*, outrageously belching sparks and cinders from fuel eked out by wood purloined some days before from a cargo of pit-props, swept round the point of Row[1], Para Handy gazed with wonder and adoration at the Gareloch, full of idle ships.[2]

"My word!" he exclaimed, "isn't that the splendid sight! Puts ye in mind o' a Royal Review!"

"I don't see onything Royal aboot it," growled the misanthropic engineer, Macphail. "It's a sign o' the terrible times we're livin' in. If there was freights for them boats, they wouldna be there, but dashin' roond the Horn and makin' work for people."

"Of course! Of course! You must aye be contrary," said the Captain peevishly. "Nothing on earth 'll please you; ye're that parteecular. It's the way they chenerally make work for people that spoils ships for me. I like them best when they're at their moorin's. What more could ye want in the way o' a bonny spectacle than the sight o' aal them gallant vessels and them no' sailin'?"

Macphail snorted as he ducked his head and withdrew among his engines. "There's enough bonny spectacles on board this boat to do me for my lifetime," he said in a parting shot before he disappeared.

Para Handy turned sadly to the mate. "Macphail must aye have the last word," he said. "The man's no' worth payin' heed to. Greasin' bits o' enchines cvery day o' your life makes ye awfu' coorse. I'm sure that's a fine sight, them ships, Dougie? There must be nearly half a hundred there, and no' a lum reekin'."

"They're no bad," answered Dougie cautiously. "But some o' them's terrible in need o' a stroke o' paint. Will there be anybody stayin' on them?"

"Ye may depend on that!" the Captain assured him. "There iss a man or two in cherge o' every vessel, and maybe a wife and femily. The British Mercantile Marine iss no' leavin' ocean liners lyin' aboot Garelochheid wi' nobody watchin' them. A chentleman's life! It would suit me fine, instead o' plowterin' up and doon Loch Fyne wi' coals and timber. Did I no' tell ye the way Hurricane Jeck spent a twelvemonth on a boat laid up in the Gareloch when tred was dull aboot twenty years ago?"

"Ye did not!" said Dougie.

"She wass a great big whupper o' a barquenteen[3] caaled the *Jean and Mary*, wi' a caibin the size o' a Wee Free Church, and fitted up like a pleesure yacht. She had even a pianna."

"God bless me!" gasped the mate, half incredulous.

"Jeck had the influence in them days, and he got the job to look efter her in the Gareloch till the times got better. The times wass good enough the way they were for Jeck, wance he had his dunnage on board. 'Never had a job to bate it!' he says; 'I wouldna swap wi' the polisman in the Kelvingrove Museum.' "[4]

"I would think he would be lonely," said Dougie dubiously. "A great big boat wi' nobody but yersel' in it at night would be awfu' eerie."

The Captain laughed uproariously. "Eerie!" he repeated. "There iss nothin' eerie any place where Hurricane Jeck iss; he had the time o' his life in the *Jean and Mary.*

"Wance they got their boat clapped doon in the Gareloch and Jeck in charge o' her, the chentlemen in Cardiff she belonged to forgot aal aboot her. At least they never bothered Jeck except wi' a postal-order every now and then for wages.

"The wages wassna desperate big, and Jeck put his brains in steep to think oot some contrivance for makin' a wee bit extra money.

"It came near the Gleska Fair, and there wassna a but-and-ben in Garelochheid that wassna packed wi' ludgers like a herrin'-firkin. When Jeck would be ashore for paraffin-oil or anything, he would aye be comin' on poor craturs wantin' ludgin's, so he filled the *Jean and Mary* wi' a fine selection. For three or four weeks the barquenteen wass like an hotel, or wan o' them hydropathics.[5] Jeck swithered aboot puttin' up a sign to save him from goin' ashore to look for customers.

"Ye never saw a ship like it in aal your life! It wass hung from end to end wi' washin's aal July, and Jeck gave ludgin's free to a man wi' a cornacopia that he played on the deck from mornin' till night."

"Wass it no' a terrible risk?" asked Dougie.

"No risk o' any kind, at aal, at aal. The owners wass in Cardiff spendin' their money, and they never saw the Gareloch in their lifes but in the map. Jeck kent he wass doin' a noble work for the health o' the community — far better than the Fresh Air Fortnight![6]

"When the Fair wass feenished, and his ludgers went away, I'll assure ye they left a bonny penny wi' the landlord o' the *Jean and Mary.* He thocht the season wass done, but it wasna a week till he wass throng again wi' a lot o' genteel young divinity students that came from Edinburgh wi' a banjo.

" 'Gie me a bottle o' beer and a banjo playin', and it's wonderful the way the time slips by,' says Jeck. He learned them a lot o' sailor songs like 'Ranza, Boys!' and 'Rollin' doon to Rio', and the folk in Garelochheid that couldna get their night's sleep came oot at last in a fury to the ship and asked him who she belonged to.

" 'Ye can look Lloyd's List,' says Jeck to them, quite the chentleman, 'and ye'll see the name o' the owners. But she's under

charter wi' a man that's aal for high jinks and the cheneral hilarity —
and his name iss John Maclachlan. If there iss any o' ye needin'
ludgin's, say the word and I'll put past a fine wee caibin for ye, wi' a
southern exposure.'

"They went away wi' their heids in the air. 'I ken what's wrong wi'
them,' says Jeck. 'Oh, man! if I chust had the spirit licence!'

"That wass his only tribulation: he had ass good an hotel below his
feet as any in the country, but he daurna open a bar.

"The summer slipped by like a night at a weddin'; the cornacopia
man went back to his work, but Jeck fell in wi' an old pianna-tuner that
could play the pianna like a minister's wife, and aal the autumn Jeck
gave smokin' concerts on the *Jean and Mary*, where all the folk in
cherge o' the other vessels paid sixpence apiece and got a lot o' pleesure.

" 'If I had chust a brass band!' says Jeck, 'and a wise-like[7] man I
could trust for a purser, I would run moonlight trips. But it would be
an awful bother liftin' the anchor; perhaps I'm better the way I am;
there's no' the responsibility wi' a boat at moorin's.'

"But the time he showed the best agility wass when he had a
weddin' on the ship. The mate o' another vessel was gettin' spliced in
his good-mother's[8] hoose in Clynder, where there wasna room for
dancin'.

"Jeck hired the *Jean and Mary* to them; the company came oot in
boats from aal ends o' the Gareloch, wi' a couple o' pipers and that
many roasted hens ye couldna get eggs in the shire for months efter
it. They kept it up till the followin' efternoon, wi' the anchor lamp still
burnin' and aal the buntin' in the vessel flyin'.

"A well-put-on[9] young Englishman from Cardiff came alongside
in a motor-lench in an awfu' fury, and bawled at Jeck what aal this
carry-on meant. There wass sixty people on board if there wass a
dozen.

" 'Some frien's o' my own,' says Jeck, quite nimble, and aye the
chentleman. 'I have chust come into a lot o' money, and I'm givin'
them a trate.'

"But that was the last o' Jeck's command in the *Jean and Mary*; the
poor duvvle had to go back and work at sailorin'."

Uncollected Stories
1905–1924

82. Para Handy's Shipwreck[1]

ONE OF Para Handy's favourite stories is about the wreck of the *Sarah*. It is only to be got from him under certain circumstances. First of all the audience must be congenial; then Dougie must be present for purposes of corroboration, and the Captain himself must be in trum. If you show the slightest glint of incredulity in your eye as the story progresses, the narrator will miss out all the most thrilling details, and give you a story with no more excitement in it than there is in a temperance tract; if Dougie is absent the Captain's story completely fails him; if he is not in trum, he prefers to borrow your tobacco and listen quietly to any lies you yourself may have to tell.

I never heard him tell it with such dramatic effect as on the night they put in the cries for Dougie's wedding.[2] Two very innocent drovers were in the company at the Ferry House, and at nine o'clock Para Handy buttoned his pea-jacket tightly, tied a firm knot in his muffler, and announced that he was in the best of trum.

"I'm feeling chust sublime," he said. "If I had my old ear for music I would sing aalmost anything, and then you would see the fun. It's not drink, mind ye; it's chust youth. Youth! youth! man, there's nothing like it! If I wass on board of the boat I would put the peter on that silly cratur, Macphail the enchineer."

"You have as fine an ear for music ass any man ever I heard at your time of life," said Dougie.

"Well, I'll alloo I'm consudered not bad at times, but I have wan of them ears that comes and goes, and this iss one of the nights I would be going off the tune here and there."

"It's me that would like fine to hear you singin', Captain Macfarlane," said one of the drovers. "If another dram wass — eh — what do you say yoursel?"

"Och, there's no occasion for another dram," said the Captain. "I'm no' needin' it; but maybe Dougie would be none the worse, poor fellow."

Dougie graciously signified his acceptance of the drover's further hospitality on behalf of the company, and then proposed that, as the Captain was not prepared to sing, he might tell about the wreck of the *Sarah*.

"It's not every place I would tell it," said the Captain, clearing his throat, "for I'm wan of these men that hates to be taalkin' and braggin' aboot themsels, but seein' we're all together, and it's a solemn occasion for Dougie, I'll tell you."

"It wass a kind of gabbard I had called the *Sarah* before I got command of the *Fital Spark*; she wass the smertest gabbard ever you saw, built by a man of the name of Macnab, and his with one eye, that's mairried to a cousin of my own. Her rale name was the *Sarah Elizabeth*, but och! we chust called her *Sarah* for a short cut. Dougie and me wass six years on her together, were we no', Dougie?"

"We were that!" said Dougie. "Go on, Captain, fine, Captain!"

"I canna stand bouncin', but as sure as daith the *Sarah*, when she had a wind on her quarter and her sails mended, would go like a man-o'-war, and I made passages between Bowling and Campbeltown that was the taalk of the country at the time. We were that smert with her there wass some notion of us carryin' the mails; you'll mind of that yoursel' Dougie?"

"Fine," said Dougie.

"The place where the *Sarah* wass wrecked wass up aboot Loch Hourn way;[3] if I had wan of them maps I would show you. We were carryin' a cargo of salt for the herrin'-curers. It wass blowin' a gale of wind that would frighten any man but a Macfarlane, but I kept her at it in a way that was chust sublime. I forgot to tell you I wass the smertest sailor sailin' oot of the Clyde at that time, though I wass only three-over-twenty years of age. Isn't that so, Dougie?"

"Quite right, Captain." said the mate, promptly. "You were splendid aalthegither."

"It would be aboot half-past ten o'clock in the forenoon, or maybe twenty-five meenutes to eleven, when Dougie, my friend here, wass struck on the small of the back by a nasty kind of a wave, and washed over the side. He made a duvvle of a splash! There wass me left in the boat mysel', for there wass only the two of us to start with; I can tell you it wass a sore predicament! I put her nose roond into the wind and brought here to, and threw off my boots and jumped over the side efter Dougie. I forgot to tell you I was acknowledged the best swimmer in Scotland at that time. I think you'll guarantee that, Dougie?"

"Ay, or England, too," said Dougie. "You could sweem like a dooker."[4]

"Well, Dougie would be two-and-a-half miles, or maybe two-and-three-quarters, from the *Sarah* when I came up to him, and aal he had to keep him afloat wass a match-box. He wass ass wet ass he could be. I kept him up with the wan hand, and swam with the other back to the vessel, and he wass that exhausted he had to go to his bunk. But that wass only the start of our tribulation, for when we were sweemin' back to the *Sarah* she gybed hersel', and the mast wass blown over the side. I wassna mich put aboot for the mast, for it wass an old wan anyway, but she wass driftin' ass hard ass she wass able in the direction of some terrible rocks yonder, and if she wass to be saved at aal I had to do something pretty slippy. I forgot to tell you I wass the strongest man in Britain at the time. Donald Dinnie's[5] wass chust a child to me; are ye hearin', Dougie?"

"You were a terrible strong man," said the mate, "Sampson wass a mudge compared to you."

"Well, I wouldna say Sampson mysel'," said the Captain with modest depreciation. "I hate bouncin', so I'll no' say I wass stronger than Sampson, but I wass pretty vigorous. So what did I do but get oot the oars and keep her from going ashore on the rocks. I wass rowing yonder the best part of six oors, and got her past the worst of it, but wan of the oars broke, and she went on a rock that wass not marked on the chart aboot sixty fathoms from the shore. She gave an awful dunt!

"I forgot to tell you that at that time I wass the best jumper in the world. I wass truly sublime ass a jumper; Dougie 'll tell you himsel'."

"There was nothing to touch you at the jumping," said the mate. "It's my belief you could have jumped higher than Ben Nevis at that time."

"Not at aal, not at aal; but I wass a bonny jumper at the same time. So what did I do when the *Sarah* went aground on the rock, but jump ashore with my mate here on my back, and we were not two meenutes off the *Sarah* when she went to bits no' the size of waistcoat buttons. So there wass me and Dougie in a strange country where they havena the right Gaalic at aal, and live on nothing but herring and potatoes. We lost everything; aal except tuppence ha'penny I had in my pocket. It wass the day of a cattle market. 'If we have oor wits aboot us, we'll ma be make something to be going on with,' I said to Dougie, and we made a bit of a plan. If Dougie had his trump it wouldna be so bad, but the trump went doon in the vessel, and so we had to fall back on mysel'. I wass to go into the middle of the market and sing, and Dougie was to come up in a wee while among the crood, the same ass if he didn't know me, and put roond the hat for a collection for a poor ship-wrecked mariner, efter puttin' in the tuppence ha'penny I had. Wassn't that the way of it, Dougie?"

"That wass exactly the way of it, ass sure ass I'm sittin' here," said Dougie. "You're doin' beautiful, Peter, go on."

"I forgot to tell you that there wass not a better singer in Scotland than myself at that time. I wass namely everywhere. When I started singin' at the market, the folk gathered roond in hundreds and listened. I wass doing tremendously fine at

‘ Up the back and doon the muddle
   te deedlum, te tadalum.'

but there wass no word of Dougie wi' the hat and the tuppence ha'penny. At last I saw him comin' oot of the inn, and I at that time I knew I wass a stupid man to trust him with so mich money aal at once. But fortunately he did not spend more than the tuppence; he came up and stood wi' the crood, and efter a while he said, ass smert ass you like, 'Is that you, Peter Macfarlane?' 'It' s me, sure enough,' said I, 'who are you?' 'Do you no mind your old shipmate?' said Dougie, winkin' at me. Then we shook hands, and Dougie told the crood that I wass the Captain of an Atlantic liner that went ashore, and the only wan saved. 'Let us make up a collection for the poor fellow,' said Dougie, 'and I'll be the first to put something in the hat.' Wi' that he put the ha'penny and the tin top of a lemonade bottle in his kep, and went roond the crood wavin' the kep in front of them. There wassna a man there that didn't come to the rescue of the poor shipwrecked mariner, and some of them, thinking the tin top of a lemonade bottle wass a shillin', put in silver and — hoo mich did we make Dougie?"

"Hoo mich do you say yoursel'?" asked Dougie, cautiously.

"Fifteen shillings and eightpence."

"That wass it exactly," agreed the mate. "It was a good thing I had the sense to go into the inn, for it wass there I got the tin top of the lemonade bottle."

"It wass salt wass the cargo," said Para Handy, reflectively. "I sometimes think I have it in my system yet; I'm that thirsty."

83. *The Vital Spark's Collision*[1]

THERE WAS a haze, that almost amounted to a fog, on the river. The long, unending wharves on either hand, and the crane-jibs, derricks, masts, hulls, and sheds looked as if they had all been painted in various tones of smoky grey. From the vague banks came the sound of rivet-hammers, the rumble of wheels, and once, quite distinctly, from out of the reek that hung about a tar-boiler at the foot of Finnieston Street, The Tar, who was standing by the Captain at the wheel, heard a gigantic voice cry, "Awa', or I'll put my finger in your e'e!"

"We'll soon be home noo," said The Tar. "Man, it's a fine cheery place, Gleska, too."

Para Handy gave one knock as a signal to the engineer, then bent down and said to that functionary, who was really within whispering distance, "I think you can give her another kick ahead, Macphail, there iss nothing in the road, and I would be aawful sorry if you lost the wife's tea-pairty."

"There's no' another kick in the old tinker," said Macphail, viciously, wiping his perspiring brow with a wad of waste, and spitting on his engine.

" 'Tinker' 's no' a name for any boat under my cherge," said Para Handy, indignantly "She's the smertest in the tred, if she chust had a wise-like enchineer that kent the way to coax her."

As he spoke there loomed out of the haze ahead the big hull of a steamer going much more cautiously in the same direction up the river, and threatening to block, for a little at least, the progress of the *Vital Spark*.

"Keep on her port and you'll clear her," said Dougie.

"Do you think yoursel' we can risk it?" asked the Captain, dubiously.

"We'll chust have to risk it," said Dougie, "if Macphail's going to get to his wife's tea-pairty this night."

And so the accident happened.

The case was tried at the Marine Court before River Bailie[2] Weir, the charge being that, on the afternoon of the 3rd inst., Captain Peter Macfarlane, of the steam lighter *Vital Spark*, had, between Lancefieid Quay and Anderston Quay, while going in the same direction as the steamer *Dolores*, of Havre, and at a greater rate of speed (1) caused the *Vital Spark* to pass the Dolores on the port side; (2) failed to signal to the master of the Dolores that he was approaching; and (3) attempting to cause the *Vital Spark* to pass the Dolores before she had given the *Vital Spark* sufficient room to pass.

The Captain of the French boat, who gave his evidence through an interpreter, said, in the course of it, that the *Vital Spark* was steering very badly.

Para Handy, the accused, interrupting — "Holy smoke! and me at the wheel mysel'!"

Witness, resuming, testified that he saw the skipper of the *Vital Spark* once leaving the wheel altogether, with the result that she took a sheer away and could not recover herself. More than once the crew of the *Vital Spark* shouted to him, and gesticulated wildly, but he did not understand their language. So far as he could guess, it was not English.

Para Handy, violently — "Not English! There iss not a man on my boat that hass wan word of any other language than English."

The Magistrate — "with a Scotch or Hielan' accent, of course." (Laughter.)

Para Handy — "Hielan' or Scotch is chust a kind of superior English."

Witness went on to say he told accused to come up on the starboard side, and he would try to make room for him to pass. But the *Vital Spark* came in on the port quarter and kept there, boring in under the *Dolores'* belting, with the result that there was a collision, and the *Dolores* had a plate bent, some stanchions broken at the aft port gangway, and pipes damaged.

The first witness for the defence was the mate of the *Vital Spark*, Dugald Cameron.[3] On being requested by the agent for the defence to tell his story in his own way, Dougie coughed, cleared his throat, took in his waist-belt two holes, rubbed the palms of his hands together till they creaked, and said — "We were comin' up the ruver at a medium speed, not sayin' a word to nobody, and the Captain himsel' at the wheel, when the French boat backed doon on the top of us and twisted two of her port-holes against the bow of oor boat. I cried to the French boat — "

The Magistrate — "What did you cry?"

Witness, addressing the accused — "What wass it I cried, Peter?" (Laughter.)

The Magistrate — "You must answer the question yourself."

Witness — "Ay, but the Captain helped me at the crying."

The Magistrate — "Never mind if he did; what did you shout to the *Dolores*?"

Witness, bashfully — "I would rather no' say; would it do to write it on a piece of paper?" (Renewed Laughter.)

The witness, being allowed to proceed without the question being pressed, said — "The *Fital Spark* at the time wass going with consuderable caaution, not more than three knots or maybe two-and-a-half, and everybody on board keeping a smert look-oot."

The Assessor — "Did the Captain leave the wheel at any time before the collision occurred?"

"Iss it Peter? Not him! he wass doing splendid where he wass if it wass a Chrustian he had to do with in front and not wan of them foreigners."

"Did you blow your steam-whistle?"

"Hoo could we blow the steam-whustle and the Captain's jecket hanging on it? Forby, there wass no time, and Macphail needed aal his steam for his enchines anyway. There wass not mich need for a whustle wi' The Tar and me roarin' to them to keep oot of the road.

Anybody would think to see them that they owned the whole ruver, and them makin' a collusion without wan word of English! They chust made a breenge down[4] on the top of us."

Colin Dewar (The Tar) was the next witness for the defence. He deponed[5] that he was standing close beside the Captain of the *Vital Spark* when the collision took place. The *Vital Spark* was hardly more than moving when the French steamer suddenly canted to the left and came up against the lighter's bow. She gave a good hard knock. Just before the collision the Captain and the Mate cried out to the Frenchman.

The Magistrate — "What did they cry?"

The Tar, after a moment's deliberation, "I don't mind very weel, but I think they said, 'Please, will you kindly let us past?' "

The accused — "Holy smoke! Colin; the chentleman that's tryin' the case will think we're a bonny lot of dummies." (Great laughter.)

The Tar, continuing his evidence, said there was a sort of fog on the river at the time. They had come up from Greenock to Govan at a pretty fair speed for the *Vital Spark* because the engineer was particularly anxious to get to his house early in the evening, but above Govan they slowed down a good deal. Could not say what rate of speed they were travelling at when the collision with the *Dolores* took place. Might be six knots; on the other hand, might be two or three knots; he was not a good counter, and would not care to say.

The Assessor — "Do you know the rules of the road at sea?"

The Tar — "What? Beg pardon, eh?"

"The rules of the road at sea?"

"It wass not in my depairtment; I am only the cook and the winch; the Captain and Dougie attends to the fancy work. It iss likely the Captain would know aal aboot rules of the road."

The accused — "I ken them fine —
    Green to green and rud to rud
    Perfect safety, go aheid!"

The Magistrate — "Did the Captain of the *Dolores* say anything when he found you butting under his port quarter?"

The Tar — "He jabbered away at us in French the same ass if we were pickpockets."

"You're sure it wass French?"

"Yes. If you don't believe me, ask Captain Macfarlane. And the very worst kind of French."

The Assessor, humorously — "What was he saying in French?"

The Tar — "Excuse me. I wouldna care to repeat it. I wish you saw his jaw workin'."

The charge was found not proven,[6] and the accused was dismissed from the bar. The crew of the *Vital Spark* promptly transferred themselves to a judicious hostelry near the police court, and in the gratitude of his heart at having got off so well, Para Handy sent The Tar out to look for the French captain to invite him to a little mild refreshment. "There's no doot," he said, "we damaged the poor fellow's boat, and it wass aal Macphail's fault cracking on speed to get up in time for his wife's tea-pairty."

Macphail, looking very uncomfortable in his Sunday shore clothes, sat gloomily apart, contemplating a schooner of beer.

"It's a waarnin'," said Para Handy, "no' to obleege onybody, far less an enchineer. All the thanks I got for it wass a bad name for the *Vital Spark*. She'll be namely aal over the country now."

"Ach! it wass only a — Frenchman!" said Dougie.

"Still and on a Frenchman hass feelings chust the same's a Chrustian," said Para Handy. "Here's The Tar; did you get him, Colin?"

"He wouldna come," said The Tar, "and I gave him every chance in the two languages."

"Weel, chust let him stay then," said the Captain. "Seein' we got Macphail into Gleska in time for his wife's tea-pairty at the cost o' the *Vital Spark*'s good name in the shipping world, perhaps he'll stand us another round."

Whereupon Macphail looked gloomier than ever, and contributed the first remark he had made all day.

"To the mischief wi' the tea-pairty," he said. "I was a' wrang wi' the date; it's no till the next Friday, and when I got hame my wife was in the middle o' a washin."

84. *Para Handy at the Poll*[1]

A LIBERAL canvasser, with two red rosettes displayed on his person, came down Campbeltown quay on Friday, and, with a hand on the standing rigging of the *Vital Spark*, asked which of the men on deck was Captain Macfarlane.

"That's the man they put the blame on," said the engineer Macphail, nastily, indicating Para Handy. "Him wi' the no' waistcoat."

"What is't?" asked the Captain, suspiciously eyeing the canvasser. His mother's house in Campbeltown was rented in his name, and he was a voter[2], though the fact had quite escaped his attention. He feared the man with the rosettes might be a committee man of some sort wanting to sell him tickets for a soirée, concert, and ball. Either that or a Rechabite looking for converts.

"I called about this election,"[3] said the canvasser, stepping on board. "Bein' a kind of a workin' man, I suppose ye'll be votin' for Mr. Dobbie?"[4]

"Holy smoke! have I a vote?" asked the Captain, really surprised.

"You have that," said the canvasser, briskly producing a burgh register, and sticking the stump of a lead pencil in his mouth preparatory to chalking off another adherent of Campbell-Bannerman's[5] and the cause of Chinese liberty.[6] "Here's your name as nate' as ye like in print — 'Peter Macfarlane, Master Mariner'; and it's lucky you're here anyway the day to put in your vote."

"I'm not much of a scholar," said Para Handy, scratching his head.

"It doesn't matter about that," said the canvasser. "It's only a scart[7] of a pen, but the whole nation's dependin' on't. It's men like you that's the the bulwark of Britain — "

"You said it!" agreed the Captain: "Brutain's hardy son; that's what I am; am I no', Dougie?"

"Whiles," said Dougie.

"Ye ken what the Tories is?" proceeded the canvasser. "Livin' on the fat o' the land, and the like o' you and me workin' our fingers to the bone for poor wages."

"I wouldna say but you're right," said the Captain.

"Then you're game for Dobbie?" said the canvasser, who was in a hurry to secure his man and pass on to the next on his list.

"Dobbie," said Para Handy, reflectively, "what way do you spell Dobbie?"

"Ye don't need to spell anything about it," said the canvasser. "It's spelt for ye; all ye have to do is to put a cross in front of his name, and that'll be all right."

"What's the other man's name?" asked the Captain.

"It's — it's — let me see now — oh, aye, it's Younger[8], but, tuts! never mind about him; he's all wrong. He's no use for the like o' you and me. If it's a cheap loaf[9] ye're wantin' and a Bill[10] for the workin'-man, stick you by Dobbie."

"That's what I wass thinkin' myself." said Para Handy, who as a matter of fact had never given the subject a thought before this moment. "He's no' in the shuppin' tred, Dobbie, is he? There's a lot o' new boats buildin' that skippers iss needed for."

"No," said the canvasser, diplomatically, "but he's acquent wi' a whole jing-bang o' folk that's in that line. It's the Liberal party that keeps up the shippin' trade. Give the chaps a chance; the Tories had it all their own way for nearly twenty years. And now what are they wantin'? To put up the price o' the loaf — "

"It's seldom I eat it," said Para Handy; "there's nothing like cakes and scones."

"It comes to the same thing," explained the canvasser. "They're goin' to tax everything. And just look at what they're doin' wi' the poor Chinese."

"What are they doin' wi' them?" asked Para Handy, who was determined even at the last hour to bring himself up-to-date with modern politics.

"They're — they're — makin' them work in mines and wash themselves every day," said the canvasser, who was a little vague on this subject himself.

"Holy smoke!" said Para Handy. "Poor craturs!'

"That'll be all right, then; you'll come up to the pollin'-booth as soon as ye can and back Dobbie?" said the canvasser, shutting up his book.

"Och, aye," said the Captain; "it's likely I'll take a daunder up and do the best I can."

The Liberal canvasser had scarcely reached the end of the quay when a gentleman with two blue rosettes swung himself airily on board the *Vital Spark* and button-holed her commander.

"Captain Macfarlane," he said, "I knew you at once. There's no smarter steam lighter comes into Campbeltown Loch than the *Vital Spark*, and I always said it. How's trade? Well, well, I suppose you're for the old flag. Not a word! Pity about Dobbie, isn't it? — nice sort of chap and all that but on the wrong side, the wrong side completely. You're for Younger, of course?" And he whipped out his section of the register, and damped his stump o' lead pencil as the other man had done.

"Younger," said the Captain, agreeably. "A smert chap. I hope and trust he's keepin' fine?"

"Oh, splendid!" said the canvasser. "Game for anything. By Jove, and he'll show them! Just fancy the way the Liberals are letting trade slip out of our hands! They say, you know, that what we import has to be paid for by what we export."

"What I said myself; if you don't believe me, ask Dougie," said the Captain.

"Of course. Well, it' s like this — there's the Irish; you don't want Home Rule for Ireland?"[11]

"The Irish!" said Para Handy. "They're aal wrong except Divverty, him that keeps the shippin' box at Greenock, and he's wan of the best. Divverty's chust sublime."

"Then look at the herring trade," said the canvasser. "The Norwegians dump their cheap herring on us and spoil the real Loch Fyne — that's Free Trade for you!"

"Ye're quite right," said Para Handy. "What sort of a man iss he this Mr. Dobbie I hear them speakin' aboot?"

"I could tell you lots about him," said the canvasser, darkly, "but I'm not the man to carry stories. Stick you by Mr. Younger and you'll be all right. It means bigger wages, and the Union, and a whole lot of other things you know as well as I do without my telling you. It's on the like of you the country's depending to — to — to see things put right. Will you come away up and vote now?"

"I'll be up efter my dinner," said Para Handy.

The Captain washed himself after dinner, put on his hard-felt hat, and went to do his duty as a citizen. When he returned more than an hour later he told the Mate all about it.

"It's no' an easy job yon," said he, "and ye get no thanks for it, not wan drop. You would think at a time like this there would be something goin', but it's a good thing we can do withoot it."

"Who did ye vote for?" asked the Mate.

"When I went up," said Para Handy, paying no attention to the question, "the polis sercheant showed me into a room where there wass two or three men and wan black tin box. 'What's your name?' said wan of the chaps. 'Peter Macfarlane,' said I, and he handed me a ticket. I wass goin' to put it in my pocket and come away when the sercheant lifts up a screen[12] and pushes me into a kind of a cell with no furniture in it but a bit of lead pencil, and it chained. I waited in for a while, thinkin' he was goin' to bring something, and at last he pulled the screen, and said, 'Hurry up, Peter; what's keepin' ye?'

" 'Nothing's keepin' me,' said I; 'it wass yoursel' put me here.'

" 'Tuts!' he said, 'it's in there ye vote. Put your cross on the paper ye got, and then come oot here and put the paper in this box,' and then he drew the screen again.

"I took oot the paper and looked at it, and, faith, it didna give me much help, for there wass chust two names on it. 'Peter,' I says to mysel', 'this iss a great responsibility. Ye must pause and consuder, and no' put in the wrong man.'

"I was thinkin' away to mysel' ass hard ass I could when the sercheant tugged back the screen again, and said, 'For the love of Moses, are ye sleepin' in there, Peter, or writing' a book, or what? Mind there's a lot o' other voters oot here waitin' a chance o' the keelivine[13]. Finish the chob, and come away oot.'

" 'Campbell,' I said to him, 'it's not every day Peter Macfarlane puts a man in Parliament and he's not goin' to be hurried over the chob by you or anybody else.'

" 'I'll have to bring the Sheriff to ye if ye don't come oot pretty sherp,' and the sercheant quite nesty, and went away.

"I started thinkin' again of what a responsibility it wass, and whether I would give the chob to Dougie or Younger, and in other ten meenutes back comes the polis sercheant wi' a chentleman.

" 'Come, come,' said the chentleman. 'what's all this aboot? It's no' a bathin'-machine ye're in, my good man. If you have filled up your paper, come out and put it into the ballot-box, and give others a chance. If ye're not ready in three minutes, oot ye come, whether ye vote or no'.'

"I saw there wass no use puttin' off any longer, so I made my mark on the paper and came oot and put it in the box and settled the thing."

"But who did ye vote for?" asked Dougie.

"The right man, of course," said Para Handy, cautiously.

"And who is the right man?" asked the Mate.

"The man I voted for,"[14] said Para Handy, and went below to hang up his hard hat.

85. *The Vital Spark at the Celebration*[1]

WHEN THE Patrol Boat *Clyde*[2] had got all the shipping dressed in lines off the Tail of the Bank on Saturday forenoon[3], and the fairway clear for the stately passage of the *Columba*[4], the Pilot Master who was in command cast a final approving glance upon the result of his organisation, consulted his watch, and said "Now, we're ready for them!"

The *Columba* was due in twenty minutes.

"Where the mischief is that chap goin'?" asked a seaman, pointing to a small steam-puffer, which, defiant of all advertised regulations for the day, had suddenly come round the stern of H.M.S. *Colossus*[5], and was deliberately coughing her way up-channel between the lines, right in the path of the expected inspecting vessel.

"Well, by Jove! that's nerve for you!" exclaimed the Pilot Master. "I'll jolly soon shift him! Chase him up full speed till I have a talk with him."

The saucy intruder upon the orderly ranked display of British shipping (at all events as much or as little of it as was at leisure for the day) was a bluff-bowed, red-bottomed craft with a yellow bead, fresh-painted, and a funnel on which crimson was scarcely dry. She flew a tattered Union Jack for ensign, unfortunately upside-down, and carried a string of bunting which, had it been washed, would probably have revealed itself as portions of the signal code.

The Pilot Master failed to catch the name on her stern as the Clyde came surging up to her.

"Who the devil are you?" said he, "and where do you think you're going?"

"*Vital Spark*," responded a figure at the wheel. "Smertest ship in the coastin' tred and homeward bound. What wey's the manoeuvres goin'."

"You know you shouldn't be in here at all," bawled the Pilot Master, hanging to a stanchion. "Sheer off to starboard now, and don't go spoiling the procession."

"I told ye that ye were wrong!" said Macphail, the engineer of the *Vital Spark*, to her commander, peevishly. "Ye havena got a ticket. Ye need a ticket for your moorin's, the same's a soiree and ball, and here were makin' a bloomin' cod o' oorsel's, a' fankled up wi' a wheen of men-o'-war and Liners. I'm black affronted."[6]

"Is this the demonstration?" inquired the Captain, with a supercilious eye upon the shipping, his inquiry addressed to the Pilot Master, with speed reduced, now steaming close beside him.

"Of course it is!" said the Pilot Master. "What did you think it was? – The Carter's Trip?"

"It's no at aal what I expeckit," said Para Handy, in a tone of undisguised disapproval. "You should have been up earlier in the mornin' and gathered a few more boats."

"You clear out of here!" shouted the Pilot Master. "You're right in the track of the *Columba*," and the *Clyde* fairly jostled the puffer out of the open lane between the lines and beyond the outmost fringe of the assembled fleet.

It was distinctly galling. The *Vital Spark*, as her paint and bunting demonstrated, had loyally done her best for the memory of Henry Bell[7], and had steamed all night from Carradale to join in the display. Para Handy had had the most grandiose idea of what the occasion should be like; he had promised the crew the spectacle of their lives – a Firth close-packed with ships from shore to shore, the roar of cannon, and the continuous crash of a myriad brass bands. The actual scene fell horribly short of his expectations.

"The best place to see this Great Demonstration," said he with disgust, "iss in the newspapers. I think we should be dodgin' up the river."

"Ye canna dodge up the river till this is over," Macphail pointed out. "The river's full o' steamers comin' doon to the celebration.

Noo that we're here, we'll ha'e to wait. And we're no even whit ye
micht ca' in the procession; we havenae ony locust standeye. Got the
dirty heave! Pushed! I told ye that ye would need to ha'e a ticket."

"The thing iss spoiled!" said the Captain, bitterly, "fair spoiled!
There's millions of people ashore there lookin' oot for us and the
Lusitania, and we're no' in't. What exactly was he, this Henry Bell?"

"Is that a' ye ken aboot it?" asked Sunny Jim. "Invented steam-
navigation; four horse-power, three miles an hour, and a stove-pipe
funnel rigged wi' sails. If there hadna been a *Comet* there wouldna
ha'e been a *Vital Spark.*"

"Did he build her?" asked Para Handy.

"Not him!" said Sunny Jim.

"Then he would sail her?"

"No, nor sail her! She just belonged to him, and he ran a
soomin'-pond in Helensburgh."[8]

"Chust an owner!" exclaimed Para Handy with contempt. "I
thought he wass wan of Brutain's hardy sons."

There was now a decided air of animation throughout the assembled fleet. Lascars[9] in snow white garments lined the sides of
two Clan liners[10], a pipe band played on the *Partridge*[11], a
hydroplane skimmed round the anchored boats at a speed which
made Macphail shudder; the *Columba* steamed down the lane, with
a tail of less important but fussy craft behind her[12], trying to look like
a flagship of the super-Dreadnought class, but only succeeding in
suggesting a special run to Ardrishaig with the Trades House[13] or
the Govan Weavers. Each vessel which she passed in her stately
progress dipped a perfunctory ensign.

"Tak' a kick or two oot of that cannister of yours you call an engine,"
said Sunny Jim to Macphail with impudent assurance, "and we'll be
richt in the middle o' the show whether we have a ticket or no."

Para Handy was agreeable; the *Vital Spark,* unauthorised and
irresponsible, drifted between the crowded Atlantic liners into the
lane again, and dipped her Union Jack with the best of them.

Immediately the Pilot Master's craft pounced down upon her.
"Take that washing-boyne o' yours to blazes out of this or I'll cut you
down to the water's-edge," was roared from the *Clyde.*

"Did my ears mislead me, or did ye say washin'-boyne?" asked
Para Handy, hurt beyond expression.

"That wass the very words he used," said Dougie. "washing-boyne. You made a terrible mistake to paint her, Peter, for the occasion."

"That settles it!" said the Captain, with a gloomy emphasis. "I wash my hands of their demonstraation. Put her aboot, Jum, and heid for Bowlin'. Take doon them flags, Dougall, and put them back in the barrel."

Para Handy got home to his wife at night to find her devouring all the graphic accounts of the evening press regarding the great display at the Tail of the Bank.

"Did ye see't?" she asked him, envious of his opportunities.

"I have a sore eye chust wi' lookin' at it," he declared. "We were fair in the muddle of it. 'Where is the *Vital Spark*?' says the Admiral in charge. 'She iss a namely boat, and must be in a good poseetion.' If Dougie wass here he would tell you. I came up the muddle line like the 'Floo'ers o' Edinburgh'[14], and you never, never heard such cheerin'! It was chenerally allo'd to be the event o' the day. The occasion was majestic."

"Was there many boats," asked Mrs Macfarlane.

"Like the sands of the sea!" said her husband. "You could walk from Cowal shore to the Cloch on the decks of them. Never the like of it in British history!"

"What did ye do?" asked his wife.

"Everything!" said Para Handy, with effusion. "I painted her funnel red, and blew the whustle, and kept on dippin' my flag, and –"

"I daresay it wouldna be oot o' the need o't," said his wife. "The last time I saw it, it was badly wantin' boilin'."

86. *War-Time on the Vital Spark*[1]

THE *Vital Spark* is now quite used to war conditions on the Firth, and when the patrol-boat *Flying Cormorant* fusses up off Gourock to demand the grip and password[2], so to speak, Para Handy, no longer awed by War Office or Admiralty, puts on his jacket and gives his cap a saucy cock to the side before responding to the challenges of the megaphone.

"Nothing at aal but timber, Captain Jellicoe[3]," he explains, though they haven't asked the nature of the cargo. "From Carradale; homeward bound. Everything's quite quate in Carradale; nothin' doin' yonder but knit-knit-knittin', and the Old-Age Pensions. What wey's the War? And hoo is Wullym[4] keepin'? They're tellin' me in Carradale that he was takin' fits."

But the blue and khaki-clad gentlemen of the Clyde patrol do not profess to supply war news or bulletins of the Kaiser's health; they contemptuously drop the *Vital Spark* like an empty sardine-can and turn their official attention to a liner coming round the Cloch.

Macphail the engineer begins to snigger. "Man, Peter, that's no Jellicoe," he says. "It's no on a tugboat Jellicoe's puttin' past his time; he's awa' in the North Sea on a whupper o' a vessel cheepin' and chirpin' on the Germans to come out and get a biscuit."

"I ken that fine, but nobody never lost anything in this world bein' nice and cuvil," says Para Handy. "Them poor chentlemen's needin' aal the cheerin' up a body can gie them – traikin' up and doon here day and night since the month of August last[5], and duvvel the thing to draw their swords at; they might as weel be in the Corn Exchange or in the Polis."

Though maritime life still remains quite uneventful on the Firth of Clyde, the coast continually resounds with sensational rumours, which may be nearly all traced to Para Handy. He plunged the whole of Dunoon one night in darkness by bringing in a story of a naval battle raging near the Cumbraes.

"Heard them wi' my own ears – every now and then a smash! I'll warrant ye there's cannon goin' yonder! Dougie himsel' 'll tell ye; he wass listenin'."

"I heard them right enough," said the mate. "A kind of a clatter. If it wassna cannon, it was somebody breakin' bottles on the shore at Inverkip."

But before this extremely plausible alternative had been suggested, the gas-works of Dunoon, with commendable promptitude, had turned off the town's supply at the main.

It was the *Vital Spark*, moreover, which came on the first and only mine as yet discovered inside of Ailsa Craig. They tenderly passed a bight of a tow-rope round it, and took it into Tarbert.

"There she iss for you," said Para Handy to the constable on the quay. "Aren't they the perfect ruffians? If it wassna I had aal my wuts aboot me, me and my boat was blown ass high's Ben Nevis."

"Bless me! where did you get her, Peter?" asked the constable, taking out his note-book, with shrewd official eye on the sinister-looking iron object floating in the harbour at the end of a mooring Dougie had hurriedly extemporised.

"On the other side o' the Skate," said Para Handy. "She wass plowterin' away her lone, the same ass she hadna any more mischief in her heid than a catechist or an empty herrin'-box, but I jaloused, and Dougie put a loop on her."

"It is not every man that would do it, either," said the mate, solemnly. "The whole time I wass near her, I wass thinking even-on of my wife and family."

"Chust that!" said the constable. "It is a ticklish business this to handle, Captain. You see, by Section 6 of the law, she's flotsam and she's jetsam; it iss only the Croon hass any right to her[6], and the thing you should have done if you were up in the law was to whustle for a man-o'-war. The sooner ye take her oot o' here the better. My goodness! Tarbert is bad enough on a Setterday night withoot explosions."

"But you're the constabulary; you'll have to take charge of her," Para Handy protested with indignation.

"No, no! Mich obliged! I hae nothing to do with nothing below high-water mark. If you will take my advice, you'll tow her to Dunoon, and hand her over to the Sheriff or the Depute-Fiscal.[7] There's one thing certain sure, you're no' goin' to leave her here to be a nuisance, and to make confusion. Chust you clear oot o' here, like a clever fellow, and I'll go up the toon this instant and tell the shops to put on their shutters in case what happens when ye start."

For three days more the *Vital Spark* was towing an empty sheep-dip drum about Loch Fyne and making vain attempts to get rid of it at every port where there was a constable. Its innocent character was only found out when Sunny Jim took in hand to get rid of it by sinking it. But since then, to all the coast, Para Handy, to save his reputation, declared his ship has been engaged by the Admiralty to sweep up mines. "A dangerous, dangerous job, but the money's big!" he says.

Similarly, the submarines whose mysterious appearance in the basin of the Clyde you will find the whole coast population swear to, owe their first discovery to the *Vital Spark*. The fault was Macphail the engineer's; he had read to the crew from day to day of submarines and periscopes till every breaking wave on a sunny day concealed a menace.

"You'll put a graavit[8] aboot your neck for the cold and keep a sharp look-oot, Dougald," Para Handy told his mate. "And if you'll see a fushin'-rod on end skooshin' through the loch, gie me a roar, no matter though I'm sleepin'.'"

"What on earth would ye dae if he did?" asked the engineer.

"Me!" said the Captain. "I would take a firm poseetion."

"There's no much use in a firm poseetion if a submarine's gawn below ye, and gie a lifter on the bottom," said Macphail.

"He'rts of oak! Brutain's hardy sons!" was the Captain's vague retort. "The meenute she shows her back it's me that'll ram her. Nothing but egg-shells at the best!"

After that Sunny Jim, with a spirit of humour, was seeing periscopes at every hour of the day, and able to convince the Captain and the mate of their existence, though his own more close examination proved them nothing more than porpoise fins.

It was his spell at the tiller one evening coming down Loch Fyne in dusk and a shower of sleet when a drifted log from a raft of timber moored along the shore came athwart his bows with a little shock and went scraping along the vessel's quarter. The others were below, about the stove; he gave a shout, and Para Handy, half-asleep, came tumbling up.

"What iss't, Jum?" he asked anxiously.

"My never-tae! if I havena struck a soup-tureen!" said Sunny Jim with masterly evidence of genuine agitation. "I just got a keek o' her periscope in front o' me, gaun at the rate o' a mile a meenute, and I let bang."

"Are ye sure?" asked Para Handy, peering into the vacant dusk behind them. "I heard a dunt and I felt a scrape, and did I no' think ye were on the Otter?"

"Otter my aunty! I'm no' that daft!" protested Sunny Jim. "It was yin o' them right enough. I could hear them playin' a concertina doon below afore the periscope came up, and I could whustle ye the tune, for it's yin I've heard a thousand times on the German bands.[9]

She's nicked onyway! I could hear the watter jaupin'[10] in the hole I made; dae ye no smell petrol ile?"

Para Handy sniffed, in which occupation he was intelligently and actively assisted by the mate. "I feel it," he said with what was virtually conviction. "Do ye no' feel it, Dougie?"

"Ay, fine!" said Dougie, without a moment's hesitation: Macphail retired among the enginery and snorted.

"Poor sowls!" said Para Handy, feelingly. "But it's a mercy they were only Chermans! I hope and trust they havena bashed my boat on me."

It was the next day the whole coast knew for the first time that the Clyde was swarming with submarines.

87. *The Three Macfadyens*[1]

ON ALL the coast along which the *Vital Spark* has traffic, the fishing hamlet of Kilbride alone has the unpleasant notoriety of having failed to provide a single recruit to the Army or the Navy. For two weeks Kilbride was able to hold its head up with any other district in the County, for its three Macfadyens figured in the 'Roll of Honour' in the *Oban Times*, where it was pointed out that they represented four per cent of the male population of military age, but now Kilbride is more in disrepute than ever. Letters to the natives come addressed to 'Jellyfish Terrace', 'Trafalgar Square', or 'Waterloo Avenue'. The few skiff-crews who come out of it have been lately christened the 'Royal Horse Marines', and as such are known to Kilbrannan Sound. When luggage boats or lighters pass Kilbride they hoot significantly and show a half-mast flag. But the worst insult, so far, to Kilbride was the delivery at Christmas of a bundle of Shetland shawls. They came from some unknown quarter to the minister, with an anonymous request that they should be distributed to his Young Men's Guild.[2]

Nobody feels the shameful position of Kilbride more than the mate of the *Vital Spark*, for his wife belongs to it,[3] and the rest of the crew make the most of the connection.

"That's Kilbride," Para Handy remarks in the most innocent way, when passing its score of low-thatched houses.

"I'm no blin'!" Dougie is sure to retort with much acidity. "I wasna imaginin', mysel', it wass Campbeltown."

"They're thinkin' o' changin' the name to Killwilliam," continued the Captain, with deadly irony. "The Kaiser took a stroke and nearly died when the news came to him that Kilbride was sendin' the Macfadyens...What way's the mustress keepin', Dougie? She'll be put about, poor body, her wi' aa' her cousins at the Front."

"If there's onybody from Kilbride at the Front," chips in Macphail the engineer, "it's wi' a label sayin', 'Fragile. With Great Care.' The men in Kilbride is no goin' to list till they get the hobble kilts and the feather bonnets. It's no 'Tipperary'[4] they'll be singin', but 'Put me among the Girls'."

To such satirical reflections on his wife's native place, Dougie is incapable of retort; he turns his back on Kilbride and on his shipmates, and peels potatoes.

"Poor Dougald! he's feelin' it sore!" the Captain confides to the others in a husky whisper quite audible to their victim. "But maybe his mustress wasna born there efter all, she would chust be there a whilie, when she wass a lassie, for her schoolin'."

But even that is too much for Dougie. "The first man who will cast up Kilbride to me or my wife," he roars, "I will strew his intervals over the deck."

For a fortnight, however, as has been said, the odium of being unpatriotic was removed from Kilbride, and indeed the hamlet was widely confessed to have a peculiar and enviable lustre attracted to it as the home of the three Macfadyens. They came for the first time into prominence after a recruiting party of the county Territorials had come to the place and failed to lift a single man.

The reputation of Kilbride was thus at its lowest ebb when the news leaked out that its manhood was already adequately represented in the Army by John Macfadyen's sons.

Dougie was fortunate in hearing about them first. He came back to the ship one day, elated.

"Let me not hear a word aboot Kilbride again!" he said. "It hass done nobly – my own three wife's cousins yonder at the Front, and not a cheep aboot it!"

"That's the finish!" said Macphail, "If that's the case, the War's as good as ended!"

"Whatna three wife's cousins are ye meanin'?" asked Para Handy "and when did they list?"

"John Macfadyen's family, my own wife's cousin, three of the finest laads that ever walked on leather."

"You're meanin' Pinny the merchant?" said the captain. "I never knew that sons of his wass in the Airmy."

"Ay, for seven years!" said Dougie, "and a credit to Kilbride. John iss not the man to make a blow aboot it, but they're yonder, and I'm tellin' you the same three laads'll not be slack among the Germans. Good laads too! – a pound a week their father gets between them. The eldest wan's a General."

"Are ye sure it's no a Corporal?" Macphail asked, dubiously.

"It's a 'ral of some sort anyway," said Dougie; "ten men under him, and never got a scratch. Came off a fightin' family, wherever there wass wars there wass Macfadyens. And what iss more, their father says if he had chust the leg he would be wi' them, too!"

"There's naething wrang wi' his leg," said Macphail, "a pin leg would be just the thing for trenches, if he could stand on it, and lift the other oot the watter."

"Well, well!" said Para Handy. "I am glad to find that all the heroes of Kilbride are not below the heidstones, and it iss a great credit to John Macfadyen, though I'm not acquent wi him. Many a gallant spirit goes wi' a wooden leg."

For another fortnight the fame of Kilbride as the nursing ground for heroes was disseminated along every shore skirted by the *Vital Spark*. From being the most contemptuous commentators upon the nativity of Dougie's wife the crew suddenly became the trumpeters of its glory, proclaiming it as an example for every other clachan in the shire. Skipness, Carradale, Crarae and other ports became quite jealous of Kilbride's new reputation, and squeezed out a few new recruits among them in a vain attempt to maintain their former pre-eminence, but nothing short of a complete new battalion could compete with the fame secured so suddenly for Kilbride by the discovery of the three Macfadyens.

"Three of the very best!" was Para Handy's eloquent tribute to them, though he had never set eyes on them. "Cousins of my mate Dougald's wife. They're in aal the regiments yonder, keepin' up the flag, and sendin' their pound a week to their poor old father, John Macfadyen, a gallant spirit in a wooden leg."

"We have only Dougie's word for it," the engineer suggested once, in a moment of dubiety. "Are ye sure they's at the Front, Dougie?"

"At the Front!" said Dougie. "Ay, at the very Edge. Did John no' tell me? Every man o' them six feet three and feared for naething."

At the suggestion of Para Handy, socks and Balaclava helmets were collected for the three Macfadyens, and at the first opportunity Para Handy took a punt ashore at Kilbride with these comforts to be forwarded to the trenches by the father.

He found the sire of the heroes sitting at a stove poking up the coals with his timber member.

"You'll be John Macfadyen, Dougald's frien'?" he asked, putting down the parcel.

"I am that!" said the merchant, looking up expectantly. "Did he send me anything?"

"Best regards," said Para Handy "I have a kind of a parcel we gaithered for your boys."

"What's in't?" the merchant asked, and poked at it with his artificial limb.

"Chust a sock or two, and some o' them Balaclava bonnets. We gathered them among the leddies aal along the loch."

"Iss that aal?" said the merchant, obviously disappointed. "I thocht it micht be something wise-like; I'm no very sore on socks mysel'."

"It iss a great pleesure to get them for your laads, Mr Macfadyen," said Para Handy. "You are a namely man about the country this day, an' your three fine sons in the Airmy yonder – a credit to yoursel' and Dougie's wife, and Kilbride. If every place in Scotland would do ass well ass Kilbride, the war would soon be ended – Dougie wass sayin' –"

"I'm no caring mich what Dougie wass sayin', it iss time for Dougie to be doin'," broke in the merchant, stumping in front of the stove. "There was talk about a pound a week that he could get for me if I had three sons in the Airmy; but my frien' Dougald hass never come near me since he made the proposeetion, and I'm vexed that I went into't."

"But you're gettin' the money from your sons," said Para Handy. The merchant snorted and took a snuff. "Tach!" said he, "there's no sons in't at all. There's chust the wan I have, and he's an ironmonger oot in Airdrie[5]. It was Dougie's notion; he wass that sick o' hearin' people runnin' doon Kilbride, and said we must put our heids together. But it wasna socks he promised me – him and his pally socks – it wass a pound."

"My cootness! issn't that the rogue?" said Para Handy, suddenly illuminated, and picked up his bundle.

88. *Running the Blockade*[1]

SUNNY JIM had painted out the name of the *Vital Spark* on her stern, and she was now the *Maid of Norway*, Bergen, on Macphail's suggestion. They all stood on Loch Ranza quay, where she was lying with her steam up, and agreed the job was a credit to him. "Capital," said Para Handy. "Nobody would think but what she wass the chenuine article. It's pentin' pictures you should be for a livin', Jum; a signboard that I seen on a Setturday night was not wan half so straight. They didna spare ye in your education."

Dougie the Mate was alone a little dubious. He gloomily scratched his ear, looked out on the jabbled waters of the Kilbrannan Sound and for the hundredth time declared the enterprise was desperate.

"Ye may pent away at your fancy names," said he, "but she hassna the foreign look, a German would be blin' that couldna see at first go-off she's chust an old Clyde hooker. Forbye ye havena the naitural flags." [2]

His captain looked at him with grave reproof.

"Man, Dougal," he said "I never, never saw a sailor man wi' less respect for the boat he made his breid on. It ill becomes my mate to caal the *Vital Spark* an old Clyde hooker – the nameliest boat and the smertest in the tred! I'm feared you're tumid, Dougal."

"No, I'm no' the least bit timid, but I'm gey and frightened for them mines and soup-tureens; it's chust wan bang wi' them, and then poor Dougal among the mackerel. I canna sweem a stroke."

"Tach, man! you're the silly golan!"[3] said his captain; "there's no occasion for your sweemin'; we'll tow the punt behind wi' a pan-loaf in it. I wish my old friend Hurricane Jack was here; my goodness, Jack would be the hero!"

"I never wass a hero in my life," confessed the mate with manly candour, "and I never felt less like being wan than chust this very meenute wi' my whole week's pay in my trousers pocket, and maybe my wife'll never touch it. Them Germans should be put in jyle; there's nothing else will settle them."

Sunny Jim put his paint-pot down, drew the cuff of a greasy sleeve athwart his nostrils, and playfully jabbed his brush, still wet, into his shipmate's ear. "We're richt as rain!" said he. "Macphail has only to keep her on the zeeg-zag[4] like a fitba' if we see a perioscope and a mine's a' richt if ye divna touch it. We're no gaun to cross the briny ocean: it's only Islay."

Macphail jumped down on the vessel's deck. "The three o' ye'll stand there gabblin' awa' till it's dark; if I'm gaun to go at all, I'm gaun in God's ain daylight! It's no a sailor, Dougie, you should be; but batin' a drum in the Salvation Army. Ye're as frichtened for your life as if ye had a fortune in the bank."

They got on board; a hearty breakfast fortified the resolution of all the rest; but the mate made a doleful meal of it, the more particularly as the engineer with malice hinted at its being possibly the last they might share together.

"Never you mind Macphail," said Para Handy, with kindlier consideration, "he's only frightenin' ye. Ye'll be in Bowmore before it's ten o'clock, in time for a refreshment."

"I never ran the blockade in my life afore," said the mate, dejectedly. "I havena no experience o' the thing."

"Tach! there's nothing in't," said Para Handy. "Are we no a naitural boat, and flyin' the naitural flag o' Norway, if I could only get my hands on it in the caibin. There's no man on the sea that needs to be frightened for the foe if he has some agility and the kindly eye."

"A kindly eye disna gang far wi' a German; ye would only need to show him't yince, and he just would stick his finger in't," said Sunny Jim.

"Weel, maybe it's no so much the eye as the agility," conceded Para Handy. "But that was always what my old friend Hurricane Jack would say when he was in cheery trum and tellin' aboot the time he was runnin' the blockade away doon yonder in America.[5] Jeck, ass everybody kens, iss the perfect chentleman, his manners iss complete. Many a time Jeck said to me, 'Peter, a man that hass a kindly eye and some agility need fear no foe in any shape or form; a purser on the Clyde can work his way with a kindly eye and a rose in his jacket, but in the deep sea tred it needs besides the science of agility.'"

"What kind o' agility," asked Macphail. "Agility's no a noun; it doesna mean onything unless ye explain."

The captain with his fork made certain mystic passes in the air. "Agility's chust like that," he explained; "ye have it, or ye divna have it. It iss not education, for Jeck gave up the school when he got the length o' 'lastic in his knickerbockers, but my Jove he had the science! And aalways, mind ye, the perfect chentleman! Complete!"

"What did the perfect Hurricane dae that was sae patent?" asked Macphail with maddening scepticism.

"I'll tell ye that – he showed the kindly eye! And he ran the blockade two times oot yonder in America wi' nothing more at his back than a gallon or two o' rum and a water melon. If that iss not agility of the best, chust you gie me another name for it, Macphail! He wass running' a cargo o' fruit and pistols and the like, and it wassna night-time sailin' for him, the way it wass with the others at the business; bold Jeck would come in in daylight, smokin' a big cigar, and standin' on the bridge wi' his feet on a bass[6] and his kep cocked to the side – the perfect gentleman born! Ye wouldna find better mainners on a yat. He wass flyin' the naitural flag."

"The only naitural flag I ken's a shirt," said Macphail. "If he flew some shirts I've seen in this boat they would take him for a pirate."

"He was flyin' a naitural flag, and when they would be firing across his bows to make him stop he would wave his pocket-hankey. Then they would put oot a boat wi' the heid wans on it, and come up and ask to see his papers. The only papers Hurricane had was a last year's almanac, and his marriage lines, but he would hand the visitors aal cigars the same as himsel' wass smokin', and ask them doon into the caibin.

"Now ye never, never in your life saw a kindlier human eye than Jeck's; it fair got roond ye!"

"I've seen an eye like that exactly," broke in Sunny Jim. "It was a tyler had it. Fair lead ye aff yer feet as lang's there was a shilling and the pubs was open."

"Weel, Jeck had chust the same; he would gie them the kindly look and a baur they never heard before, and doon the chaps would step to the caibin, where the pruncipe ingredients wass the jar o' rum and the water melon. Before they would start to look at the cargo Jeck must give them some refreshment. 'Away you, quick, and off them fore-hold hatches,' he would say quite nate to his mate; 'them chentlemen will soon be ready wance they're done wi' their refreshment.'

"Jeck would put the melon in the muddle o' the table and the jar beside it, pass the glasses roon and work the kindly eye. I'll warrant ye that any man that found himsel' in Hurricane's company would find the time slip by: they wouldna be be a meenute in the caibin till they had their belts off so as to get the best o' the joviality. He would show them his merrage lines, quite impident; tell them another good wan; give them a wee bit touch on his concerteena; and keep spillin' oot the rum among the heid wans. They didna bother much wi' the water melon; it was chust a decoration.

"Them bein' foreigners, they never saw a perfect chentleman afore, and Jeck wass the boy to take their fancy. And aye the jar went roond and roond.

"In a whilie, more o' the heid wans would row over chust to see what kept their neebours, and afore night wass on, the *Juliet* (for that was Hurricane's boat) wass full o' Spaniards listening to Jeck's best baurs and singing the Marshalazy Hymn[7]. Whenever a belt and cutlash would come off, Jeck kicked it in ablow the table, where a hatch was open to the hold, and he kept busy flashin' roond his kindly eye. When they hadna a cutlash left, 'Stop you,' says he, 'and I'll get another melon,' and oot he whips on deck and snibs[8] them in. Believe me, or believe me not, he would run them into port, and hand them over prusoners wi' his cargo."

"Weren't they the silly Neds!" said Sunny Jim.

"Ay, but its aal in the power o' the kindly eye and the agility," said Para Handy. "And that shows you, Dougie, there's nothing very great in going to Bowmore."

89. *The Canister King*[1]

THE PATROL-BOAT came alongside the *Vital Spark* for fun rather than for official information. "Sound of Kilbrannan; slates," said Para Handy, and scratched his ear, a gesture he had invented for himself, as the most appropriate salute for merchant skippers in time of war.

"What have you on the hatch there?" asked the naval officer, indicating a mysterious looking pile of cargo covered with a tarpaulin.

"Chust nothing else but a wheen o' buscuit-boxes," said the Captain. "Yon nice wee tin wans – ginger snaps. Chust the very ticket for the boys!"

"All that ginger for Kilbrannan Sound!" said the astonished officer. "Are you recruiting, Peter?"

"Na, na!" said Para Handy. "Empty buscuit-boxes wi' nothin' in them," and he banged on the tarpaulin till the tins below it clattered. "It's this way of it, Admiral – every wife in Skipness, Carradale and Saddel has a boy or two away at the war she wants to send a parcel to. They send them every week, on Setturday whenever the pay comes in or the man's back from the fishin'. There's not as much broon paper in aal Kintyre as would burn to put a smell away, and everybody's wanting wee tin-boxes handy for the postin'. Me and Dougie's gaitherin' aal the buscuit-boxes we can get a ha'd o' any place there's buscuits goin' and the folk wi' their boys away come to the *Vital Spark* for canisters."

"They're callin' him the Canister King noo," said Macphail the engineer. "If he was chargin' for them he would mak' his fortune. When there's a jabble o' a sea on, this old hooker jingles nooadays like a tinker's cairt."

"Chust that Macphail!" said Para Handy. "But chust you think o' the boys that's waiting oot in the battlefield for me and Dougie's boxes! Ye needna be so nippy on't, it's yoursel' that steals the twine to tie them!"

At Carradale that evening the demand for empty biscuit-tins was such that when it was satisfied there were less than half- a-dozen left. So keen was the female population for canisters, and so glad to get them, that it showered on Para Handy and his crew the surplus of many things left over after the boxes had been packed. Next morning children came to the boat with hard-boiled eggs, black puddings, sweeties, cigarettes, tobacco, kippered herrings, raisins, almonds, socks and soap which couldn't be packed into the weekly parcels for the front. The den of the *Vital Spark* smelled like a grocer's store.

"It's no a buscuit-tin at aal would suit them if there wassna stamps to pay," said Para Handy, "they would load a trunk! 'They're surely makin' buscuit-boxes wee'er than they used to be,' Maclachlan's wife said to me – her that never saw a buscuit-box afore the war! She said it was rideeculous makin' buscuit-boxes that wouldna hold two shirts and as much proveesions ass would keep her son, Big Angus, for a week."

"It's a' richt," said Sunny Jim; "the stuff left over'll no go wrang wi' us," and picked up a packet of cigarettes.

The Captain grabbed it from him. "Put you that doon!" he said commandingly. "Ye'll not touch wan iota o' the stuff that's there. It was bocht for the boys that's fightin' and it's them'll get it."

"That's chust what I wass thinkin' to mysel'," said Dougie, and returned to the stock of offerings a plug of tobacco he had slipped unobserved in his pocket a minute before.

"It's this that's botherin' me," said the Captain. "There's only six tins left, and six'll no' go far in Skipness, I'll assure ye! By the time this boat's dischairged and we go to Skipness for the wud, they'll have ready stuff to fill a hundred canisters. I'm black affronted to go near them wi' my six wee boxes. Man, they're awfu' wee, wee boxes too, when ye look at them!"

"People's no eatin' half enough ginger snaps!" said Dougie. "If I wass in the way o' buyin' snaps, it's no a silly wee box that size I would buy them in, but a big substantial, sonsy² size a woman could take some pleasure packin' for her son. And I would shift them snaps pretty sherp."

"It's a pity ye canna send mair in the parcels than eleven pounds," suggested Sunny Jim, "there shouldna be ony limit."

"If there wassna any limit," said Para Handy, "there's no a herrin'-box would be left in Tarbert, and where would the herrin' tred be then? But, man, I must alloo them wee tin boxes is smaal, smaal!"

"Tach! it's no' the size that counts wi' the chaps that gets them," said Sunny Jim, "it's the nice intention. Ony box at a' from hame must be a great relief to thae 'coal-boxes' that they're gettin' a' time from the Germans."

"But what am I to do wi' the folk in Skipness?" said the Captain. "Only six boxes and the stuff to fill a hundred wantin'! There's no as much broon paper in Skipness as would cover a mutchkin bottle[3], and there they'll be on the quay for canisters! You'll divide them, Dougie."

"Duvill the bit! Yoursel'll do it, Captain. It's you that has the right agility. Pick the six that's to get the boxes, and tell the rest we'll come back again wi' a cargo o' nothing else but empty canisters. I CAN NOT understand the way folk wi' money doesna eat more ginger snaps! I'm sure they're fine and wholesome! If I had the money I would be eatin' snaps aal the time for King and country, and constantly sluppin' out the canisters for mothers to send to the boys in Flanders."

Para Handy ranged out the six empty tins on the floor and took off the lids. "I have it noo!" said he; "we'll fill them aal oorsel's wi' this stuff here they couldna find room for in the parcel from Carradale."

"Whatever you say yoursel'," said Dougie. "I'm sure I'm quite agreeable."

"By the look o't, I would say that there's just enough to stow six canisters, and I'll be stevedore," said the Captain, and began to load the boxes. He gave each a bottom layer of kippered herrings, then a pair of socks, a stratum of sweeties followed; black-puddings, cigarettes, tobacco, raisins and soap promiscuously filled up what space was left. He finished off by tying the boxes up with marlin.[4]

"What are ye gaun to dae wi' them?" asked Sunny Jim. "Is't gaun to be a raffle?"

"Nothing of the kind!" replied the Captain. "They'll go to Skipness men in France that hasna frien's[5] to mind them; that's the way I'll do wi' my six wee boxes, and nobody needs to be offended. Many a poor lad yonder never gets a parcel, him no' havin' a mother, or a sister, or a lass."

"My Chove!" said Dougie with admiration, "it's you that hass the schoolin'!"

Two days later Skipness was chagrined to find the *Vital Spark* so short of empty tins, it had been counting on her.

"Hoo many were ye needin'?" asked Para Handy.

"If we had chust the six we were complete," a disappointed woman answered with her eye on the six packed boxes at his feet.

The Captain reluctantly picked them up one by one and passed them over. "Weel, there ye are," said he, "aal loaded to the muzzle. It's a kind of a new society that's started to give boxes for the boys that havena frien's –"

"There's no a boy o' that kind oot o' Skipness," she hastily assured him. "There's far too many second cousins, it's no a box a week we could send them each, but twenty. We'll chust be takin' these, and thanky."

"They're packed already," said the Captain, and she looked distressed, as did the other woman.

"Packed!" she said; "what are they packed wi'?"

"Everything o' the best," said Para Handy, and gave an offhand inventory.

"That's chust what we were goin' to send oorsels."

"It'll save ye the trouble then," said Para Handy.

"It'll save nothin' o' the kind," they told him bluntly: "where would be the pleesure o' sendin' parcels if we didnae pack them for oorsels?"

Five minutes later Sunny Jim was lighting a cigarette, and six women with empty tins were hurrying home in Skipness.

90. *Thrift on the Vital Spark*[1]

No SOONER had the *Vital Spark* got her rope ashore and fastened on the pawls than the *Kate* came round the head of the quay and rang her bell petulantly on finding her usual berth engaged.

"We canna shift her noo," said Macphail the engineer; "the steam's aff her, Macrae can go to bleezes!"

"Don't let on you see him!" said Para Handy. "Him and his bell! Macrae has no regard for sense or anything. He thinks because he carries a bag o' letters ye could put in a Sunday hat, he's like a fire brigade, and everything must clear the way for him. Little does he know I kent his folk before he wass captain of the *Kate*, and what were they but crofters out in Gigha! As Hielan ass a peat!"

The bows of the *Kate* were close up the stern of the *Vital Spark*, and her bell was rattling furiously. Yet the crew of the lighter paid no heed, and Sunny Jim nonchalantly filled up a kettle from a cask for tea, so Macrae backed out his launch with its imposing legend "Royal Mails" in blue paint amidships, and had to content himself with a quite inferior place along the quay. He jumped ashore as soon as he had landed his passengers – there were two – and came in a towering rage towards Para Handy.

"Iss it chust a stot ye are that you will take my berth from me?" he shouted. "Did you no' hear me ring-ring-ringin' at my bell?"

"My goodness, wass it you wass ringin'?" said Para Handy, with an aspect in which surprise, incredulity, and apology were finely blended; "I thought it wass the bell o' Mackinnon's milk cairt, and I wass chust goin' to look for the can."[2]

The altercation which followed was pretty tart and animated, but Para Handy got the best of it with a final and unanswerable allusion to the *Kate* as a "jeely-jar" on which no self-respecting sailor-man would sign, and sat down to his tea with an appetite pleasantly stimulated by the episode.

"Sling over the butter, Jum," he said, with a hunk of bread in one hand and knife in the other.

"There's no butter in this boat!" said Sunny Jim. "Ye mind yoursel' last night ye agreed we should start bein' thrifty."

The face of the Captain fell lugubriously. "Mercy on me!" he exclaimed, "did ye start already? And wi' butter, too? Ye're duvelish smert! Away you go this meenute up the town, and buy a pound."

"No use!" said Sunny Jim; "I think ye're losin' your memory for mindin' things! The shops is shut this efternoon; it's Wednesday."[3]

"Holy smoke!" said Para Handy. "Issn't that most desperate? I didn't say wan word aboot the butter; it's the last thing I would think o' savin', for ye need it wi' your breid. There's mony a thing ye could be thrifty on afore the butter. A body shouldna trifle wi' his health for the sake o' a bit o' butter."

He stuck his knife in the marmalade jar and scooped out butter's substitute which he laid on thickly.

"Stop you Peter!" said Dougie; "a knife is no use for you wi' the marmalade; Macphail'll get a shovel or a coal-claut [4] for ye. Ye were taalkin' away last night about the wastry that wass in this boat, and noo ye're the only wan that's greetin' about the butter, and layin' on the marmalade the same ass it wass wreck."[5] Macphail snorted, and addressed himself to the last speaker in a tone of reproof. "I wonder, Dougie, ye would be argyin' wi' him!" he remarked. "When he was talkin' aboot thrift he was thinkin' aboot his wife – "

"She gets the best o' everything!" hotly cried the Captain.

"I daresay that, when ye're at hame; she kens fine there's naething less'll please ye. It was yoursel' last nicht that made the proposeetion that we should start bein' thrifty."

"It wassna me that started it at aal," said Para Handy. "It wass yon fellow McKenna,[6] ye would see't yoursel' if you would read the papers. He said that folk wass takin' far too many luxuries for a time o' war."

"Whit kind o' luxuries?" inquired Sunny Jim, innocently; "there hasna been a chicken on board this boat since I came on her!"

"Meat, and drink, and clo'es, and recreaation," said the Captain. "Nothin' else but riotous livin' high and low. Last week ye had a dumplin', and ye ken fine it's a thing I canna stand!"

"Well, jist for the sake o' the argyfication," said Macphail, "what would ye start by bein' thrifty wi'?"

"A man that went away last week and spent a shillin' on a lookin'-gless!" said Dougie. "Pride! Chust pride!"

"It wassna a shillin', it wass only tenpence ha'penny!" the Captain corrected him; "and I never got your thruppence for it yet, Dougie. Before I got that gless ye could never tell on this boat if your face wass clean or no', it wass only guess- work."

"Surely to goodness ye could ask!" said Dougie. "And anyway it's no' every day ye're goin' to a party. You answer Macphail noo; what would ye save on?"

"I wouldna start wi' butter, anyway," said Para Handy, scooping again at the marmalade jar. "I would start wi' clo'es, they're a great extravagance."

Sunny Jim laughed. "If I'm to save ony mair money on cla'es than I'm daein'" said he, "I'll hae to get galvanised yins, I'm wearin' a Sunday suit I got at the Coronation."[7]

"It's no wi' sittin' on the kirk sates that ye're wearin' it," said Para Handy. "It would have lasted ye twice as long if it wissnae for your gallivantin' every Setturday and Sunday on the roads wi' the country lasses. Many a penny ye could save on choker collars, washin' them and ironin' them, if ye were chust like me and Dougie and put on a muffler."

"And what would I be savin' on," asked Dougie.

"Many a thing!" replied the Captain. "There iss time ye throw away your money like the green sea wave! Look at Friday last in Tarbert, when the merchant bocht a dram for us, ye wouldna be content wi' that, but must be the jolly tar and stand another at oor own expense. There is not much thrift in that and it's McKenna himsel' would tell ye if ye would ask him. Every time ye buy a dram yoursel' it's a silver bullet wasted. But you have no conception, Dougald – not the least!"

They had watched him finish the marmalade and his allotted share of bread and tea, themselves on various pretexts holding back till his appetite seemed reasonably satisfied. Macphail put his hand on a biscuit tin, and produced a little packet.

"What could I be thrifty on?" he asked.

"Many a thing," said the Captain, "if ye would chust get your wife to send ye parcels wance a week, the same ass ye were a soldier at the front. I'm goin' to do't mysel' if Jum's no' goin' to get us butter."

"The only way to save on butter is to mak' it margarine," said the engineer, and opened up his parcel.

"What's that?" Para Handy asked suspiciously.

"Margarine," said Sunny Jim. "Made oot o' genuine coco-nuts. It's a peety ye didna wait till Macphail had mind we had it."

"I wouldna use it for my boots!" said the Captain with sublime contempt.

They divided it between them, and evidently found it thoroughly satisfactory. A piece the size of a hazel nut was left, and the captain picked it up on the point of his knife and tasted; it was excellent Irish butter!

"There's no another man in Scotland sails the seas wi' such a lot o' liars!" he exclaimed. "That never came from the coco-nut but the coo! And I'm put off my tea wi' a jar o' marmalade."

91. *Difficulties in the Dry Area*[1]

"THE ONLY human place in Scotland now where there is liberty, and a man is not a mice, iss up Lochfyne," said Para Handy, looking at his watch with some anxiety and hurriedly leading the way up West Street[2] to the nearest pub. "If I had my way o't, I would never come up past Cloch ass long ass the war durated."

"Ye never in aal your life said a truer word, Peter!" said Dougie the mate. "A body might ass weel be in Tiree or a Band o' Hope ass in Gleska, them days, for aal the satisfaction."

Macphail the engineer, who had brought the *Vital Spark* up-river in the quickest time on record for her class, and was parched with thirst, mopped the back of his neck with cotton waste, and remarked with bitterness that the day was coming when the only place a man could kill the time would be in a dairy. "What this country needs," he added, "is Dr Bottomley [3] at the heid, and an independent parliament o' business men."

"Whit this country needs," said Sunny Jim, "is a bigger output o' penny fillers. The wee tin filler's the key to the situation. I'll bate ye there's no ony shortage o' them in Germany, and I scoured the hale of Anderston for yin last Setturday."

"Ye may weel say it, Jum!" said Para Handy.

The captain had another look at his watch as they turned into the public-house. "We'll have to be lookin' slippy," he remarked; "it's either a quarter-to-two or twenty-past; my watch iss slack in the hands and ye canna coont on her." They lined up at the counter, and he clapped down a pound note on it with a request for four full-rigged schooners. "Keep them up to the wind," he added: "I don't like too mich froth aboot the bows."[4]

"No schooners and no treatin'!"[5] said the barman, serving out one glass of beer only. "Have ye no' got smaller change!"

"Holy frost! iss that no' desperate! I have chust the tuppence nate," said Para Handy, counting the coppers down and putting the pound in his pocket. He disposed of the beer himself with great celerity, and meanwhile the barman waited expectant of the others' order.

They hadn't enough to pay for a glass between them!

"Stop you, laads!" said the Captain, "we'll go oot and take a dander."

They went out to the street considerably annoyed and stood in a group while the Captain looked at his watch again. "Did I no' clean forget aboot the tratin'!" he remarked in accents of regret. "I wass thinkin' aal the time it wass the same as Tarbert, only the bars was different. Ye're sure ye havena nothin', none o' ye?"

"No' a roost!"[6] said Dougie sadly.

"It's chust what I told ye," said the Captain. "Whenever ye come past the Cloch, ye're in trouble. It's no a boom[7] they should have doon yonder, but a dry-stone dyke, and us ootside of it aal the time doin' tred in wyse localities like Campbeltown and Tarbert. Man, if I had chust a shillin' or two! A pound is a great incumbrance!"

The engineer was flushed with indignation. "It's the silliest thing I ever saw!" he said. "It fair puts the hems on the geniality o' the gentality. Ye'll no' convince me it's no' just a dodge to confuse the customers. Half-a-dozen o' ye, like, puts doon your bob[8] or a half-crown[9] each; the man comes back wi' a fist-full o' change, does a jugglin' trick wi't on the coonter, and ye're left there standin' dizzy, wonderin' whether ye're a sixpence short or ninepence up. I'll wudger he comes oot o't rich himsel' at onyrate. I'll bate there's hundreds o' pounds lost that way every day in the muneetions area, and they talk aboot economy for the workin' man!"

"Ach, well, I have many a time seen better beer than that fellow's," said the Captain in a fine spirit of consolation.

Dougie sighed, "And I wass that thirsty" he confessed.

Again the Captain looked at his watch, having shaken it to rouse it into intelligence. "I'll tell ye what," said he; "I'll go into this shop here and buy tobacco, and get change, and give ye each enough to pay the dram in Devlin's."

"That's chust what I wass thinkin' to mysel' would be the best way oot of it," said Dougie, cheering up, and the three of them waited outside on the pavement while the Captain made his purchase.

He came back with a face as long as ever. "Do ye ken what I'm goin' to tell ye, laads! I'm chust ass bad ass ever! The only change I could get wass a ten shillin' paper note, three half-croons, and a two shillin' bit. She hadna any smaller. It must be a street this, packed wi' gentry. She hadna change that would suit a sailor in her till."

"That's a' richt!" said Sunny Jim with cheerful alacrity; "sling us oot a half-croon each and we'll up to Devlin's."

"A half-croon each!" cried the Captain. "I'm no that daft! If any o' ye had a half-croon in your hands, it's no much good ye would be on the *Vital Spark* to-morrow mornin'. Forbye, I'm no right sure that it's no' against the law for men that's no' in business to be distributin' money in the street before goin' into a place for a refreshment. It sticks in my mind I have read in the papers of men that was jyled for't. It's a thing that aal depends on the Act o' Parliament, and ye canna be too caautious."

Macphail laughed cynically. "If that's what ye're feared for, Peter," said he, "put the change in your ootside jaicket pocket and come up a close wi' us: we'll get it for oorselves and ye'll no ha'e its distribution on your conscience."

"I never in aal my life felt more like a gless of beer," pathetically said Dougie.

Again the Captain consulted his chronometer. "I'll tell ye what I'll do," said he. "I'll go in my lone to Devlin's and get a half-croon changed, and then come oot and give ye share of it in the proper spirit."

"If ye mean it, then hurry up!" implored Sunny Jim, "For the sake o' Dougie: he's desperate dry," he added in a disinterested manner which did his feelings credit.

"Chust hing aboot the door till I come oot; I'll no' be a meenute," said Para Handy at Devlin's hospitable entrance.

"If we're no here waitin' when ye come oot," suggested the engineer ironically, "jist ring us up on the telephone. In a' my life, and I've lived a lot in my time, I never seen mair hummin' and hawin' aboot a gless o' beer. It's enough to mak' a man teetotal."

The Captain edged in sideways through Devlin's swing door, leant over the bar, and expressed a desire for a glass of British spirits, which he imbibed without a moment's hesitation. At his own request he got three sixpences in his change and started for the street.

"Take a ha'd o' that!" he whispered to his crew, and slipped them surreptitiously each a coin.

They all streamed into the bar, and Dougie at least had his mind made up it should be a quart.

"Too late, gents!" said the barman. "Nothin' doin'! It's half-past two o'clock," and started putting on his coat.

Three sixpences were already on the counter; the Captain hastily scooped them up and put them in his pocket.

"Holy smoke!" said he, "issn't that deplorable! I never can trust that watch o' mine a meenute!"

92. *Truth about the Push*[1]

SUNNY JIM came down to the boat on Friday, ostensibly to receive a razor he had left behind when he joined the Army[2], but really to see who had got the job he had so patriotically abandoned. There was still, however, what the mate poetically described as a vacant chair.

"We advertised," said Para Handy, "for a smert young laad to study the shippin' tred, two eyes preferred, but nobody paid any heed. I doot aal the smert wans iss in the Airmy like yoursel'."

"And who's cookin' for ye?" inquired the soldier.

Dougie showed some embarrassment.

"We're in a kind o' a syndicate for cookin' now," explained Macphail maliciously. "We a' tak' turn aboot. Dougie started right enough for a day or two, and then nearly had us in a state o' habeas corpus wi' a favourite hash o' his made up o' whit he ca's ingredients. So far as I can mak' oot, ingredients is onything left over aboot a ferm efter they feed the hens."

Para Handy sighed. "Man, James," said he "it wass you had the Nelson touch at makin' hash! I can tell ye ye're the man that's missed on board this boat. Ye're lookin' splendid! Are ye no' a Major yet?"

"I'm gaun across to France wi' the first draft," said Sunny Jim, pitching the average Tommy's[3] favourite fiction. "Noo that we've started pushin' we'll no' be lang."

"That's what a fellow from Glendaruel was tellin' us yesterday," said the Captain. "It wass Johnny Carmichael; he wass doon at Colintraive wi' a shrapnel in his ankle. For the rale agility ye canna do better than go to Glendaruel; Johnny's chust sublime! 'I see ye started the push at last,' I said to Johnny. 'It's no a push,' said Johnny, 'it's a haul.' And then he lets me into the secret o' the way they get the prisoners. It's weel enough kent the Germans iss in great stervation; the only time they see a meal o' meat iss in a magic lantern.

"The British Airmy wass workin' away wi' gas[4] when Johnny went oot. 'I don't believe in the gas at aal, at aal,' said Johnny to the man in cherge o' the proceedin's, 'it only irritates them, and it's wastin' gas.' It was him put General Haig up to the notion of fryin' herrin'.'"

"Fryin' herrin'!" repeated Sunny Jim, bewildered.

"Chust fryin' herrin'! My Chove, they have aal their faculties aboot them in Glendaruel. A cargo o' herrin' from Lochboisdale wass brung over and distributed among the Hielan' regiments along the line. 'Noo, start you fryin' them at breakfast time,' says Haig, 'and if the wind is westerly ye'll see a bonny demonstration.' They tried it first on a streetch o' the line where the Chermans iss not of any particular great quality, and at breakfast time, wi' the wind in the right direction, the smell o' France wass like the Fair at Rothesay. Whenever the Chermans felt the smell they put up their hands and gave in in droves. Our chaps chust took a daunder across and gaithered them like nuts.

"Johnny Carmichael says the General wass quite delighted. 'We were chust wastin' time and money wi' the gas,' says he; 'there's nothin' will bate the herrin'. It carries further on the mornin' breeze, and it's far more soothin' to the foe.'

"The Lochboisdale herrin' lasted near a week, and every mornin' at breakfast time, if the wind was right, Johnny himsel' wi' a fryin'-pan would cross to the German trenches and come back wi' a hunder or two of the Germans on a string. Ye would read aboot yon raids we were makin' every noo and then in the German trenches – that was Johnny and the pan."

"I don't believe wan word of it!" declared Dougie. "Carmichael wass only bouncin'.[5] Forby, they're no' acquent wi' herrin' in Germany the only thing they eat is sausages."

"There's no bounce aboot it!" insisted Para Handy. "It's no' in Glendaruel ye'll get them bouncin', and although it's gas they caal it in the papers it's well enough kent the British have a secret process. That's the secret for ye – fryin'-pans! Johnny said they tried the sausages too, at wan place, but it hardly had any effect."

"I'm no' goin' to say," continued the Captain, "that herrin' would do the trick wi' aal the Germans; Johnny admitted that the Prussian Guards wass stubborn duvvles, them never havin' any experience o' that fish except in sardine boxes. But they got the Prussians, too, ye would notice – instead o' herrin' wi' them, they used fried ham and eggs. It worked miraculous! The Prussians were ready waitin' for the gas, wi' divin' helmets on them, and desperate hungry, when the perfume o' ham and eggs came driftin' over.

"Nothing would ha'ad them in after that! They took off their helmets, sniffed the Sabbath breeze, threw away their guns, and came skelpin' across where the British were, cryin' 'Kamerade! kamerade!' – that's the German language for 'Halfers!' Johnny told me himsel'.

"That's the way Johnny says its no' a great push at aal, but a great haul. We're no goin' to bother any more wi' gas; the muneetion factories iss workin' night and day at turnin' oot fryin'-pans. There's a hundred for every regiment."

"It's maybe richt enough, but it's awfu' like a bawr," said Sunny Jim.

93. *Foraging for the Vital Spark*[1]

PARA HANDY sadly rose from dinner, contributed his legitimate share to the duty of "tidying-up" by throwing his fish-bones over the side of the vessel, and cleaning his plate by an expert rotary movement with the cuff of his guernsey.

"Man, Dougie," he said, "ye're no' much o' a cook at aal; ye havena the agility! Could ye no' lift your mind off mackerel, mackerel, and give us something different?"

"Ye're a liar!" retorted the mate, indignantly; "it wassna mackerel we had the day before yesterday; it wass a kind of a cod."

"It doesna make any odds, it wass fush, and if there iss wan man under the cope and canopy that iss ashamed to look a boiled fush in the face it iss me. Could ye no' put your mind into the thing, Dougie, and think o' something dufferent? It's no fush, fush, for ever Sunny Jim would be content to gie us when he wass cook; he would make a kind o' divagation noo and then in the way o' somethin' tasty. But ye have no agility at aal when it comes to foragin'; ye might as weel be a married woman! I'm ass dry wi' eatin' fush as a baker's pass-book wi' blot-sheet in every page!"[2]

Macphail, the engineer, in the absence of a fruit course, took a generous chew of tobacco and regarded the captain with compassion. "I wonder to hear ye argue wi' him!" he remarked, "Dougie's hopeless! He has nae experience o' what ye could ca' richt nourishment. He was brocht up in Kinlochaline. I tell't ye from the start there was nae use o' puttin' him into a poseetion o' responsibility."

The mate filled up a pannikin at the water butt and had a drink. "I'm sure I don't ken what I'm to do to please ye!" he retorted. "I'm doin' my best! It's no on what I get from the pair o' ye to keep the ship that I can feed ye on pope's-eye steak and wully-muckle buscuits.[3] Three times last week I had rabbits –"

"Rabbits!" groaned Para Handy. "Don't mention the name o' rabbits to me! Wi' them and mackerel this boat's polluted."

"Stop you till the twelfth of August, and we'll have grouse!"[4] said the mate with bitter irony. "Or maybe ye would prefer a hen?"

"Indeed and a hen would be very nice!" said Para Handy with approval. "And if you had your wits aboot ye the same as Sunny Jim, ye would have wan sometimes. Many a chucken Jim got roon the back o' the hotels where he would be wi' his Sunday clo'es on, whustlin' on the lassies, Jim took an interest aalways in his business. The time that ye would think he would only be gallivantin', he wass plannin' Sunday's dinner. That's the kind o' man 'll get on in the British Airmy! And him wi' a gless eye, mind ye!"

"Weel, I canna pamper ye, anyway, wi' aal I get," protested Dougie. "Chust look at the price o' everything."

"There ye go!" cried Macphail. "Ye're tryin' to change the subject! It's no the price o' things we're talking about; it's the need for mair wise-like dinners."

Para Handy sat down on an up-turned bucket, and proceeded to give his mate a paternal lecture. "It iss chust this way of it, Dougie," he said; "ye'll need to be far more copious in your way o' goin' aboot things. It's no the same ass we were in Gleska; we're here in a boat that' constant sailin' up and down through the gifts o' naiture; aal ye need to do iss to show a little agility like Sunny Jim and stretch your hand. Money's needful enough for buyin' matches, paraffin oil, and a puckle tea, for they're no growin' them in the Kyles o' Bute or Carradale, though they grow everything else there from carrots to carbuncles. Ye're no' like a wife; ye're gettin' your coals for nothin', and there's nothing for the laundry. We're no expectin' ye to feed us even on wi' fancy things, but mackerel has a limit. Look at the way that Jim did – he wass aye on the look-oot for hooses wi' big gairdens to them, and there's no a manse between here and Tobermory where he didna wave a hanky to the maid when we were passin'. Jim would walk them oot wi' his mooth harmonium in the gloamin', and come back to the boat wi' a pillowslip o' caulifloo'er and leeks. There wass a laad o' spirit and contrivance for ye!"

"I canna play the mooth harmonium," said Dougie. "I never tried."

"But it wasna aalthegethir the mooth harmonium," said the Captain; "it wass chust naitural agility and the kindly word. When we would be pickin' up for nothing more mackerel or herrin' at the quays than we had need for, Jim would put a dozen on a string and hie away to a Sheriff's or Doctor's hoose, and make a present o' them to the cook. 'Chust new oot o' the watter,' Jim would say wi' yon gless eye o' his so jovial, and I'm tellin' you it wass seldom he came back to the boat withoot something tasty for the supper. Noo, since ever you took up his job, ye never had a cabbage on board the *Vital Spark*! And they're growin' everywhere."

"If it's vegetables ye're wantin', I can get plenty," said Dougie.

"Vegetables would do for a start," said Para Handy. "The main thing iss that you must show some agility. It's aal in the kindly word. And talkin' aboot eggs, there wassna a hen on the shore that Jim would not have an interest in; it cost him nothing at aal for eggs nor milk so long ass he could play the mooth harmonium and cock his bonnet. One of Britain's regular hardy sons!"

Stimulated by this instruction in the art of foraging, Dougie went ashore that evening with an empty sack. He was gone for hours, and came back with the sack full, but in no great spirit of elation.

"What speed did ye come?" asked the Captain, anxiously. "Did ye get any eggs?"

"Eggs!" exclaimed Dougie. "There's no an egg in the parish; they're a' collected warm for the wounded soldiers."

"Weel, we'll chust have to do, this twist, wi' the vegetables; I hope ye got syboes,"[5] said the Captain.

The mate turned the sack upside down and emptied it on the deck; it contained about three stone of rhubarb, and nothing else.

"Cristopher!" cried Para Handy, "that's no vegetables!"

"Perhaps it's no'," admitted Dougie sorrowfully, "but it iss the only kind the folk wi' gairdens here would give to me for nothing."

"It's clear enough ye need a mooth harmonium for moochin'," declared the engineer. "Ye need more than that," said Para Handy; "ye need to be a smert young fellow, wi' the kindly word among the gyurls, and I doot Dougie, that you're too old o' startin'."

94. *Our Gallant Allies*[1]

"WHAT WAY'S the War the day?" asked the Captain when Dougie, the mate, had taken off his glasses, folded his newspaper tightly up in the smallest compass possible, and put it carefully in his trousers pocket for continued study during the rest of the week.

"The Rooshians iss still hurlin' them back aal along the front," replied the mate. "Whit I canna understand iss the way they aye hurl them back, instead o' makin' the duvvles walk. We're far too considerate wi' them! They wouldna hurl[2] us!"

"It just let ye shows ye the Rooshians iss chentlemen," said Para Handy. "It iss many a day since Hurricane Jeck told me we had the wrong notion aaltogether aboot the Rooshians. Jeck trevelled the world, and wass weel acquaint wi' them. The Rooshian iss a large and ferocious man when he iss angry, but if he's in good trum he'll eat oot o' your hand. They live up aboot the Baltic, and hae a lot o' fur aboot them – fine chaps, regular human bein's! Ye can aye tell a Cossack: a Cossack never cuts his hair, and chenerally goes on horse-back: the other kind goes on steam road-rollers in the summer and sledges in the winter. They drink a kind o' spirits and wear blucher boots.[3] Ye'll see them in the pictures. They make the chenuine Riga balsam and Archangel tar;[4] if Jeck himsel wass here he would tell ye."

"The Italians iss doin' capital too," remarked Dougie. "I aye had a great respect for the Italians, though they're dufferent from oursel's; ye never saw them blowin' trombones on the steamboats the same ass the Chermans."[5]

"I wan time kent a chenuine Italian," said the Captain. "A civiler man ye couldna speak to, and he had wonderful agility; he could turn his hand to anything. Hurricane Jeck had aye a good word for the Italians, and he sailed a lot among them. At haulin' cannons up the mountain-tops[6] there's no the bate o' them; they're up one side and doon the other the time that you and me would be consuderin'. It's a trate to see them. They're yonder aal along the banks o' the Mediterranean. Jeck said ye could easy understand their language if they spoke it slow and waved their hands. Of course, I'll admit they're Roman Catholics, but ye canna blame them, the way they were oppressed. Jeck told me there wass a sayin' aboot them that wass very true – 'Wance an Italian, aalways an Italian.' Their buildin's iss gey ramshackle, but their wines is most notorious. All the colours o' the rainbow!"

"Was Jeck acquainted wi' the French?" inquired Dougie, his interest aroused on the national characteristics of our Allies.

"On the other hand the French iss dufferent," answered the Captain, warming up by the spirit of instruction. "They speak the French language. Jeck kent it fine, but he admitted it was difficult. Bits of it wass chust the same as Gaelic, but we had to watch, for the same word didna mean the same thing in the two languages. The French iss born chentlemen, their manners iss complete. They start their work early in the mornin' and get through wi't before the heat o' the day. The heat is desperate; ye have to take your drink oot on the pavement. There's two kinds o' Frenchmen – them that's in the Airmy, and the others mantle makers and milliners. They follow the sea like oorsels; they're capital sailors, Jeck allooed, and they're aawfully fond o' home."

"They're doin' weel chust now in the papers," said Dougie.

"I'll warrant ye that! Jeck never had but a kindly word for their ability. A Frenchman will never give in and hates the Cherman crew like poison. They're maybe no' so broad in the back, ass the British, but man, they're copious!"

"I like the Belgians," said Dougie; "there's something aboot them."

"The Belgians iss tip-top too. The Belgian, to let ye understand, is a kind of Frenchman, but desperate gallant. His native place iss over aboot Antwerp; it will need to be fumigated when they get the Chermans oot. Jeck had aye a great opeenion aboot Belgium; he said it was flat but capital for crops. I think they drink wine, too, in Belgium; it'll be the climate that's against them. But aal the same, they're splendid sodgers. And then, again, there's the Serbians – it's likely that they're entirely dufferent. I never heard Hurricane Jeck say mich aboot them, but if he had, I'm sure they would get his approval, for they're game to the very heels. Ye can see for yoursel' in the papers – it's aalways 'Gallant Little Serbia'. There's not a great many of them, but they're weel picked."

"Was Jeck acquented wi' the Japanese?" asked Dougie.

"Nobody kent them better! He came across them often when he wass sailin' in the clippers. It's years since Jeck first said to me the Japs wass a nation that he could see wass certain to get on, and weel deserved it. He had aalways a kindly word for the way they did in cheneral."

95. *Para Handy's Spectacles*[1]

MACPHAIL, THE engineer, being the only man on the *Vital Spark* with comparatively perfect vision, always reads the newspaper to his mates, and with fiendish malignancy often adds sensational details of his own imagining to the latest intelligence from the seats of war. On three successive days last week he craftily worked up a revival of intense interest in the health of the Kaiser. On Wednesday Para Handy and Dougie heard with no surprise that the All-Highest was so depressed by recent events that he was confined to bed. On Thursday they learned with Christian resignation that he was in a very low condition, and unable to swallow anything. On Friday Macphail had the august invalid surrounded by all the members of his family, hastily summoned to his bedside.

"Man! but there'll be a bonny scramble among them when he iss gone!" said the Captain with emotion. "That young fellow o his iss a great hand for gaitherin' clocks and watches."[2]

"I hope in providence his father'll no' slip away on them before Monday," said Dougie anxiously, "for when we leave Tarbert to-morrow we'll no' see a paper till we get to Greenock. Do ye think, yoursel', Macphail, he'll linger?"

"I wouldna be a bit surprised if he's deid already," said Macphail.[3]

"Didn't I tell ye!" he exclaimed with triumph on Saturday morning after a momentary scrutiny of the latest newspaper. "God bless me, is he gone?" squeaked Dougie, dropping his pipe.

"Died last night, at six o'clock," said Macphail with another glance at the paper. "The Bulgarians[4] is gaun into mournin's. 'We understand,' says our Berlin correspondent, that the Croon Prince will take up the business.'"

"Gie me a ha'ad o' that paper!" gasped the Captain, pulling it out of Macphail's hands. Dougie at the same time made a frantic grab, and secured a half that was practically all advertisements. He held it at arm's-length and screwed up his face.

"I canna make oot the least wee thing except the pictures," said he. "Oh man if I chust had a pair of tongs! I could read her fine at a distance."

The Captain hastily produced a pair of spectacles, seldom used except on Sundays, and buried his head in a page of Commercial and Stock Market Intelligence.

"He's no that long depairted that ye need to use your nose," said Macphail. "There it's there!" and pointed to a paragraph of shipping news in the smallest type.

"Holy sailors!" cried the Captain in disgust. "Ye would think they would have the sense to put a thing like that in print ass big ass a signboard. I canna make oot wan word o't. I never, never, in my life before, felt what a terrible thing's the want o' eyesight!"

"I aye tell't ye them specs o' yours is no' ony mortal use at your time o' life," said Macphail, coolly. "If I was you I would buy a richt pair frae the Gleska chap that's testin' eyesight up next Macallum, the butcher's shop. I'm tell't he's sellin' tippers – fair champions – at a half-a-croon."

"This pair wass all right in their time, but the gless in them iss gettin' done," said the Captain. "I got them in a shop the year they built the Cheneral Post Office,[5] and they cost me wan-and-six. Ye could read anything at aal wi' them at that time – even the Gaelic language, but they're gettin' that weak noo I can hardly read the label on a bottle."

"Give me a twist o' them!" implored Dougie, and tried on the spectacles.

"I can make oot a word here and there," he said with anguish, "but nothing that I can dwell on; I might as weel be lookin' through bits o' a washin'-hoose window. In the name o' goodness, could they no' put news like that into a picture? I can see the pictures fine."

"It's my opeenion ye neither o' ye can read, and this aboot your eyesight's a' my aunty!" declared Macphail.

At these insulting words the Captain thrust the paper in his pocket, reached for his jacket, and went ashore. A Glasgow philanthropist, agonised by the thought that thousands of men and women in the country were suffering from defective eyesight, which prevents the full enjoyment of the beauties of nature and of art, had spent three days in his work of mercy in the vicinity of Para Handy's boat. He applied to all-comers the most searching eyesight tests known to modern science, such as asking if they smoked too much, what their age was, how much they earned a week, and if their grandparents had rheumatism. There was absolutely no charge for this. Prescriptions for spectacles and eyeglasses were given free, and it luckily happened that the prescribed glasses could always be bought on the spot at reasonable prices from the philanthropist.

It was to consu!t this public benefactor that the Captain had hurried ashore.

"It's as well ye came," said the oculist after a momentary glance at the Captain's right eyeball through a theodolite. "In another six months ye would need a dog on a string and a tinny. Did ye ever use specs?"

Para Handy produced his souvenir of the laying of the foundation-stone of the George Square Post Office, and the oculist examined it. If window-glass could be fused at anything lower than furnace temperature the lenses would have melted under the concentrated glare of contempt with which the expert regarded them.

"Made in Germany!" he said. "Ruination to the optic nerve or sclerotic; what could ye expect? It's a wonder to me ye're no' in the Blin' Asylum. Can ye play the fiddle?"

"No," said Para Handy, "nor I never tried."

"Then the sooner you get a dacent pair o' specs the better," said the oculist ominously. "Just by chance, I have the very pair here to fit ye. There they are – pure pebble – seven-and-six."

The Captain set them on his nose, took out his newspaper, and deliberately scanned the page Macphail had indicated. "I can see wi' them top, but I canna see anything here aboot the death o' the Kaiser," he remarked at last with sudden illumination.

"If ye could see that I would gie them for naething," said the philanthropist. "Somebody has been blawin' up your heid."

"That's what I wass thinkin' to mysel'," said Para Handy, putting down the spectacles. "If it's no' in the papers that he's deid, there's no mich need for me to be spendin' my money on specs; the pair I have'll do first rate," and the oculist lost his customer.

96. *Para Handy in the Egg Trade*[1]

ALL JULY and August the crew of the *Vital Spark*, in the course of successive trips with coal to Salen and Tobermory, augmented their weekly income with delightful ease by taking advantage of the human craze for country eggs. They bought them at 1s 3d to 1s 6d per dozen in Mull, and let favoured customers on the mainland have them for their Glasgow lodgers as a privilege at 2s to 2s 3d, or even 2s 6d.[2] The difference between 1s 6d and 2s 6d is what Political Economy calls Profit, and Profit is the Legitimate Reward of Intelligent Enterprise combined with Capital.

Para Handy, however, simply called it "skin".

One of their best customers was a boarding-house keeper who had real hygienic views on the subject of eggs, and a marked preference for the Mull variety as having a luscious flavour all their own.

"It'll be the peats," said the Captain, quite ready to encourage this harmless delusion. "Forbye there's the draff[3] from the distillery; they feed their hens on draff, and it gives the eggs a jovial sensation to the taste. I've noticed it mysel'."

The supply of island eggs at reasonable prices fell off, however, in the middle of September.

"To let ye ken," said Para Handy to his disconsolate lady customer, after a trip from which he had brought back none – "To let ye ken, the Mull hen's no' like them munition workers: there's no control, and it goes and takes its holidays chust at the very time when folk is clamourin' for shells. They're yonder chust puttin' past their time till the rain stops; if I wass keepin' hens it wouldna be through the winter, stuffin' themsels' wi' the best o' draff and doin' nothin'!"

"Hen's 'll be chape in Mull at this time o' the year?" said his customer.

"I don't know," said Para Handy, "I never had any tred in what ye would caal the raw material for eggs, but ye're maybe right."

"I wish ye would bring me a pair o' chickens next time ye're across," suggested the lady. "I would pay ye half-a-croon apiece for them. If I canna get eggs I must get something for my lodgers."

"Did ye never think o' tryin' fish?" inquired the Captain, with a sudden idea of transferring his attention to the saithe trade.

"I don't want fish," said she emphatically, "bring you the chickens!"

Accompanied by Dougie, the mate, his partner in the egg trade, Para Handy took the first opportunity of interviewing a gamekeeper's wife in Salen, who throughout the summer had been one source of their supplies.

"Ye needna come here!" she cried, whenever she saw them; "there's no' a dozen o' eggs between here and Loch Scridain. I never saw dourer hens in aal my chudgement!"

"Chust that!" said Para Handy. "Aren't they the tinkers! I wonders to me, Mrs Maclean, you would put up wi' them. Hens at this time o' the year iss nothin' better than lumber."

"Ye may weel say that!" agreed Mrs Maclean, "and look at the price o' Indian meal for them!"

"Chust fair desperate!" said Para Handy, who knew no more about the price of Indian meal than about the price of Indian amethysts. "We'll buy a pair o' cracks from ye for half-a-croon."

"A piece?" said the lady.

"Not at aal! – the pair!" said the Captain, and she laughed.

"It's surely no chickens ye're wantin' to buy; it's surely rabbits. There iss not a chicken in the Isle of Mull would lay down its life this year for less than half-a-croon."

The Captain had a little private consultation apart, and came back to her with the surprising confession that the fowls were wanted, not for provender, but for scientific purposes. "It's a chentleman," said he, "that's startin' a kind o' a hydropathic, and wants stuffed birds o' the various speshie for a glass case in the bar. We're no parteecular what kind o' birds they are so long's they're fresh. Anything at aal your man has in the game line would do capital."

"He's away on the hill himsel', but here's the very thing for ye," said Mrs Maclean, and, reaching behind her, brought down from a hook a pair of new-killed herons.

Para Handy felt them carefully, with a little disappointment that birds so bulky to look at should conceal beneath their feathers so little actual meat.

"They would maybe do for stuffin'" he said anxiously to Dougie, handing them to him. "What do ye think?"

"Whatever ye say yersel'," said Dougie, with a gloomy air of resignation.

They had been meant for the keeper's vermin larder, so they got them for nothing.[4]

Plucked, cleaned, and trussed, with their heads and legs cut off by Dougie, who had often made a careful study of fowls in poulterer's windows, the two herons, pleasant and beautiful in their lives, in death presented a remote resemblance to chickens that have succumbed to malnutrition.

The boarding-house keeper regarded them with manifest disappointment. "If that's what feedin' on draff does," she said, "the folk in Mull should be teetotal. I never saw skinnier hens in a' my puff!"

Para Handy coughed. "I'll aloo they're no terrible robust," he admitted, "but the woman I get them from gave her warrant they were tender, and ass fresh ass the mornin' breeze. Indeed, she wass sweart[5] to let me have them; if Dougie wass here he would tell ye the job I had gettin' them, for she had them plucked and ready for a merrage. Mrs Macrae, Dalbuie – ye'll maybe ken her?"

"Not me!" said the customer. "Ye're surely no' wantin' half a croon a piece for a bunch o' bones?"

"Four shillin's the pair," said the captain, reluctantly; "that's chust exactly what they cost us."

When the *Vital Spark* came in again from Mull, she had a pair of genuine chickens with which a slightly uneasy conscience sent Para Handy to the lady who had brought his strange sea-fowl. He had acquired them cheaply in a mysterious commercial transaction involving the landing of a barrel-load of coal exactly where coal was wanted without too much ostentation.

"That's wyse-like hens!" said the lady, feeling promptly for her purse. "Ye swindled me fine wi' the last yins: they werena hens at a' – they were jucks!"[6]

Para Handy blushed. "What way did ye ken?" he asked, contritely.

"By the taste of fish," said she; "they wouldna roast; they wouldna bile; so I had to fillet them and gie them to my lodgers, with white sauce for ling!"[7]

97. *Sunny Jim Returns*[1]

SUNNY JIM, who 'listed in the Army mainly for the glory by which he expected to be surrounded when the war was finished and he got home, was a sadly disappointed Corporal. His ideas of how he should come home were necessarily vague in parts, but during three months' training at Fort Matilda he had had a definite vision of himself returning scatheless from the field of war, being met by a brass band at the Broomielaw on a glorious summer day – preferably, Fair Saturday – and marching with his regiment through all the widest streets in Glasgow.

He could, in imagination, see every detail of that impressive scene, and distinctly hear the frenzied roar of cheering that went up from the populace of Glasgow, thickly crowding all the streets.

All the people who knew him, would, by chance, have grand positions in the very front of the crowd for recognising him, and would shout "Good old Jim!" or "Ye gi'ed them't in the neck, Jim!"

Probably he, himself, would be on a horse – not a very big horse, nor one inclined to those hurried jerky motions he observed with misgivings in the adjutant's animal, but one you could sit right up on and even let go of its hair if you wanted to wave your hand to any of the classy-looking girls at the first-storey windows.

What excuse he should have for being on horseback puzzled him, rather, but he felt certain it could be wangled. In his vision, Sunny Jim always allowed several days for this sort of processioning through Glasgow; beer would be free and copious for the troops ... fireworks... presentations of medals...trips...

What really happened was that seven hours after leaving the field of war at Stòbs[2], when Sunny Jim, demobilised, sole representative of the cadre of the famous Umptieth H.L.I.[3] (Reserve), got out at the Central Station at 6.25 a.m. and emerged into the street, the only manifestation of popular excitement was confined to a jobbing baker, whose eye brightened at the sight of him, and who expressed a desire to borrow a match.

"I don't see ony signs o' the demonsteration," said Jim, anxiously, looking along a deserted Argyle Street.

"There hasna been yin in Gleska since Shinwell[4] got nicked," replied the baker. "Man! ye fair missed yersel'! We had the Riot Ack! And hoo are they a' at the Front?"

He did not wait for an answer; having absent-mindedly put Jim's match-box in his pocket, he shuffled off, leaving behind him a faint aromatic odour of parley dough.[5]

"I wisht the British Airmy had been bate!" said Sunny Jim to himself, with bitterness.

It was two days before Jim realised the incredible self-restraint and calm of Glasgow, and that his arrival home had been unaccountably overlooked by the Lord Provost, Maryhill Barracks[6], the Salvage Corps, or whatever authoritative body was responsible.

The necessity of finding a job of work began to assume an urgent aspect, and having looked out his sea-going togs in his old lodgings, he went down to the riverside to seek for a ship.

In front of the Sailors' Home he was boisterously accosted by a middle-aged mariner, who wore a bowler hat very much on the side of his head.

"James," said the mariner, "I see you're home. Give me a grip o' your hand!"

It was Hurricane Jack. "I was just perusin' aboot to see what's left on the Clyde o' the British Merchant Shippin' when my eye fell on ye, James," he continued, effusively. "Para Handy told me ye were in the Airmy. Gie me your hand again, lad! Sons o' the free and the brave!"

He beamed upon Sunny Jim with an ardent admiration that almost made up to the latter for the absence of any civic reception on his arrival home.

"Whit hae you been daein', Jeck?" asked Jim, extracting his fingers with difficulty from the mariner's iron fist, and shaking them to restore the circulation.

"I'll tell ye that withoot one word of divagation, lad," said Hurricane Jack. "Carousin' around the ocean wi' my life in my hand. I can assure ye I was well acquent wi' them torpedoes! For three years back I never had my boots off, night nor day. What I'm lookin' for noo's a kind o' boat where I can loll aboot in carpet slippers."

"Were ye in the Navy?" asked Jim, with his interest roused.

Hurricane Jack gave a sardonic smile. "Was I in the Navy!" he retorted. "Ask you Admiral Beatty![7] Just you mention to him the name of John Maclachlan, and see what he'll say to ye! There wasn't a battle betwixt Rockall and 60 South that I didn't lose all my dunnage in. And I'm tired o't! For the rest o' my days I don't want to sail further away than the Garroch Heid nor sign on a boat that's bigger than an Arran gabbart... But tell me aboot yoursel', James; were ye badly wounded?"

Sunny Jim flushed. "If ye asked Sir Douglas Haig aboot me," he said, "he would have to look up his books, whaur the only battle honours against my name's the mumps I had at Gailes[8] and the time I cut my haund to the bone wi' a bottle in the Stobs canteen."

"Did they no' let ye oot to the Front?" enquired the mariner, incredulous.

"They started me fifteen times on a draft, and every time I landed somewhere on the British Isles. Ye'll ken aboot my eye?"

"What eye?" asked Hurricane Jack.

"The left yin," said Jim. "It was a glessy[9] when the war broke oot, and fair spoiled me for ony chance o' the V.C. They said wi' an eye like that I darena go oot o' the country."

"Red tape!" exclaimed Hurricane Jack indignantly. "It's the same all over! One eye to the genuine son of the brave is as good as a pair to a German, but you need the influence to prove it. Look at mysel'. Fed on cracker hash and marlin' all my days; sailed on the China clippers; man and boy for a year on the White Ball Line[10]; as well acquent wi' Callao as wi' the Cloch, but would they gie me a chance in the Admiralty? – Not them! The only men they would sign on for the Navy in the last five years was chaps wi' Communion tickets,[11] and what did they do wi' me but put me to shovellin' coal on a depot

ship! Not another hand's turn did I do in the past five years but
shovel coal!"

"Jerusalem crickets!" said Sunny Jim. "Ye're as bad's myself. Talk
aboot war – it's a delusion! I jined up thinkin' I would be oot in the
trenches afore ye could say 'knife' and back wi' a bunch o' medals
that would fill a barrow. It wasna altogether my glessy; the mistake I
made was showin' them at the War Office I was a don at peelin'
potatoes.

"There's a way o' peelin' potatoes. There's not wan man in ten can
shift their skins to please a quartermaster. I was the bloomin' ned,
Jack, and from the start put my hert into makin' an artistic job o' the
regiment's potatoes.

"I tell you I was vexed for't! Everybody else was gettin' a trip to
France but me. There's no' a camp between Nigg[12] and five miles
oot o' London where I havena peeled potatoes for the so-called
British Airmy. The Generals began to compete for me. I was no
sooner settled in a camp and daein' fine than some auld geezer wi' a
pull at the War Office got me shifted where his camp was in another
pairt o' the country, and when I wasna peelin' spuds the kit was
hardly ever aff my back.

"God knows where they potatoes came frae! I've peeled mair
potatoes than ever grew on British soil. I hate the very look o' a
potato! There's nae sense in a potato. It's just a blob! The very sight
o' a tottie field noo maks me angry."

"Put it there!" said Hurricane Jack, extending his hand again, but
Jim, this time, kept his in his pocket.

"You and me, Jim," said the mariner, "is needin' a job where a
man can be happy. When I gave ye the signal there, I was just on my
way to Port-Dundas, where they tell me the *Vital Spark* is loadin'.[13]
Come you on wi' me and we'll get a gentleman's job the piece[14] from
Para Handy."

The master of the s.s. *Vital Spark* welcomed them with a hearty
open hand. "Brutain's hardy sons!" he greeted them. "The
country's prood o' ye! Isn't that your opeenion too, Dougie?"

"Whatever ye say yoursel', Peter," said the mate in a saturnine
way. "I hope they're both the better o' their holiday."

"We're wantin' a job the piece," explained Hurricane Jack,
without circumlocution. "Anything doin'?"

"Ye couldna come at a better time, Jeck!" said the skipper, gladly. "There's a kind of a strike[15] among the men that was puttin' in my coal; get you a ha'd o' a shovel, Jeck, and start this instant."

Hurricane Jack groaned. "And whit aboot me?" asked Sunny Jim.

"The very man I'm wantin'. The last cook that I had is away to a restaurant. Put you off your jecket, Jim, and peel that bucket o' potatoes for the dinner."

98. Hurricane Jack's Shootings[1]

PARA HANDY stood on the quay with me, and with a characteristic air of amused detachment watched the passengers disembarking from the steamer. There was the customary sprinkling of determined sportsmen for the Twelfth, with guns, dogs, ammunition-boxes, and cases of The Only Possible Marmalade from the Army and Navy Stores. "That'll be the gentry for Kilmagachan," he remarked. "Ye can tell by their stockin's – the chenuine zig-and-fur[2] wi' tassells on them. Tomorrow ye'll see slaughter on the hill, or I'm mistaken. Every wan o' they chaps has tacketty boots and the right kind o' kep for grouse-shootin'. Brutain's hardy sons! I'll wudger they'll play havoc."

"Yes, they look pretty fit and keen," I admitted. "Do they not have kilts now?"

"Completely oot o' date," the Captain informed me. "Them comic papers codded them oot o' the kilts; they're frightened noo to wear them. And that's a great peety, for they were most amusin'; I've seen some would keep ye laughin' for weeks. No herm in them, poor craturs, but they were that droll! Never you mind; it's them that hass the money!" he added philosophically. "And a chentleman that's oot for chenuine sport'll pay anything. There wass wan time yonder, Hurricane Jeck did a good stroke o' business wi' them."

"How?" I ask him, scenting a happy reminiscence of his distinguished friend and shipmate.

"He let wan o' them a shootin'."

"I never heard of Jack in the character of landed proprietor," I remarked with unreasonable surprise, for the Captain's friend, at one time or another, has been everything conceivable.

"Neither he wass," said Para Handy, frankly, "but Jeck would sell ye a croft in the New Jerusalem if ye were silly enough to buy it. It wass wan occasion he wass takin' a rest from the sea, and makin' a kind o' a livin' hirin' boats at ninepence an oor at the wee slip there.

"Wan day a chentleman from the inns, wi' tremendous knicker-bockers, and a spy-gless, came doon the slip where Jeck was sittin' doverin' and waitin' for his dinner. It wass bad luck for the chentleman that Jeck wassna at aal at aal in trum that day for botherin' aboot puttin' oot and in his boats, and he wass cranky. 'Can I get a boat?' asked the chentleman at Jeck.

" 'Ye can that!' said Jeck puttin' his hand up to his kep – to put it on firmer. 'Were ye wantin' wan?'

" 'Is she cogly?'[3] asked the chentleman.

" 'No more cogly than the Gaelic Church,' said Jeck, annoyed. 'If it's a cogly wan ye're wantin', ye'll have to go to the other slip and get wan o' Duncan MacCallum's boats; they'll give ye sport.'

" 'Have ye hand-lines?' said the chentleman.

" 'I have that!' said Jeck – 'and good wans! I'll guarantee they'll take in anything, from a saithe to a sea-serpent. But I don't think it's a good day for the fishin'; I don't like the way the wind's blowin'. Maybe to-morrow – if ye came doon to-morrow' –

" 'Have ye bait?' said the chentleman, never noticin' that Jeck wassna in trum for haulin' doon a boat before his dinner-time.

"Jeck got nesty at that, and up to his feet like a whutterick[4], wi' a glint in his eye would warn off anybody that wassna blin' or an Englishman. 'I'll gie ye aal the bait ye're needin', says Jeck.

" 'And I'll need a cushion for the sate,' says the poor deluded cratur. 'My wife's comin' wi' me. And if ye had a kettle to boil tea – '

"Noo ye'll admit that wass pretty hard on Jeck. It wass boats at ninepence an oor he wass hirin', and no steam yats, and forby that, he wass tired, and thinkin' o' his dinner. But, man, he kept himsel' in hand capital!

" 'Would ye no' like a gun?' said Jeck, wi' a rasp in his voice that would frighten any man in his wits. 'What would be the good o' a gun to me?' says the English chentleman. 'I would like fine a try at the gun, but I havena any shootin's.' He was a poor sowl that never before wass in the Hielans; Jeck completely took his measure.

" 'Shootin's!' says Jeck. 'Ass much as ye want! Do ye no ken it's the Twelfth o' August? All the gentry's shootin'. There's aye a gun goes wi' this boat on the Twelfth o' August, but it's a shillin' an oor extra.'

"The chentleman brisked up. 'Whereaboots iss the shootin'?' he asked.

" 'Two miles up this side o' the loch there's a toppin' place,' said Jeck, ass bold ass brass. 'It goes wi' the boat, but it's a pound a day extra.'

" 'I don't care if it wass two pounds!' said the chentleman, pullin' up his stockin's. 'Hurry you up and get ready the boat and everything, and I'll be doon wi' the wife in fifteen meenutes.'"

"The poor duvvle o' an Englishman went away up to the inns for his wife, and Jeck went up the Quay Close to old McVicars and borrowed a gun McVicar's grandfaither had at Inkerman[5], a poother flask that he filled wi' sand and a bed-bowster.[6]

" 'Do you understand guns?' he asked the chentleman when he came back.

" 'Ye don't understand wan word o' them, Percival!' says the wife, and her near demented at the notion that her man wass goin' to shoot wi't. 'Keep mind ye have a young faimily in Birmin'ham!'

"But her man's blood wass up for bigger game than codlin'; he payed no heed to her, and Jeck showed him the way to load the gun by the stroup o' the flask and put on a kep on the nipple.[7]

" 'Shut wan eye tight and glower at the game wi' the other. Gie a good hard tug at the trigger and hold your breath,' said Jeck, 'and ye'll see a bonny scamperin' o' grouse. Maybe ye'll get a deer, for my shootin's fair hotchin' wi' them. But ye'll need to stalk them, for they're timid, timid! When ye're stalkin' ye aye take off your watchchain in case ye spoil it, and ye need a drop o' spirits, for it's hard, hard work. I hope ye have a wee drop wi' ye?'

"The chentleman took oot a brandy-flask and Jeck took a swig of it.

" 'That's the very ticket!' he says. 'Ye couldna have better stalkin'. Ye needna tell me ye havena been on the hill before! I could see at wance ye were the chenuine sportsman.' But still-and-on the wife wass dubious. 'Will that gun make a lood noise?' she asks Jeck.

" 'Tach!" says Jeck; 'no more than a Vezuvian match! Ye'll chust hear the crack o' the kep. I wouldna gie any man a gun that would make a noise to frighten a lady. If it makes a bang I'll gie ye back the rent.'

" 'What rent?' says the chentleman.

" 'The rent o' the shootin's for the day,' says Jeck, quite numble. 'That minds me – the pound's aye paid fore-handed.'

"The Englishman paid him the pound, and went off wi' his wife and the gun in the boat.

" 'This iss the finest Twelfth o' August I ever mind,' says Jeck to himsel', watchin' them from the shore. 'But I doot I let my shootin' far too chape, and I should have tell't him he needed a piper. I wass stupid no' to think aboot the piper; there's a Townsley tinker[8] was in the toon this meenute.'

"It wass late in the afternoon when the chentleman and his wife came back to the slip where Jeck wass waitin' on them.

" 'What luck had ye?' says Jeck, puttin' up his hand to his kep, and takin' it off this time to the lady, for Jeck was aye the perfect chentleman.

"The chentleman wass in desperate bad trum, and his face aal swelled wi' mudges. 'Not one iota!' says he. 'There's aal sorts o' birds up yonder, squealin' away like anything, but I couldna hit them. It's my belief this gun iss not a bit o' use.'

" 'Hoo often did ye load it?' says Jeck, takin' it oot o' his hands.

" 'I never loaded it at aal,' says the poor sowl, and him aal hoved up wi' the mudges. 'Ye mind ye loaded it yoursel' afore we started?'

" 'Bless me!' cried Jeck. 'Ye're a bonny-like man to come from Birmin'ham![9] Do ye no understand ye need to be aye load-load-loadin' at a gun if ye want to hit anything? Ye needna miscaal my gun; she's a gun that's namely in the parish; she wass at the battle o' Inkerman.'"

99. *Wireless on the Vital Spark: Intercourse with the Infinite*[1]

WHEN MACPHAIL'S bright young son, the apprentice engineer, came down to the *Vital Spark* at Bowling and fitted up an aerial, none of the crew save Macphail himself showed any great enthusiasm.

"What kind o' a contrivance is this?" Para Handy asked, when he came on board to discover the wires already stretched between the mast head and the funnel. As captain, he felt that the innovation, without any authority from him, verged a little too closely on the informal.

"Mind your feet!" said Macphail, irritably; "you're standin' on the cat's whiskers."[2] He was closely engrossed in the wiring up of the crystal set extemporised so ingeniously by Johnny, who had left an expansive blue print showing the whole lay-out for his father's guidance.

"I can see its goin' to be a wild New Year this," said the Captain, ominously. "There's no' a cat on the whole horizon. The sooner we're at sea the better."

Macphail paid no attention, but stuck a headphone over his ears, and assumed an intently listening aspect... Science! ... The newest marvel of human discovery!... All made by Johnny from workshop scrap! A glow of pride went through the latest listener-in. For a little he heard nothing. Then came a faint pulsating sound of wheezing, curiously accompanied by an odour of beer. He screwed up his face and strained his ears with eager expectancy, while Dougie, the mate, bent over him in an effort at eavesdropping on this communion with the infinite.

"Confound you and your asthma!" indignantly cried the scientist, plucking off the 'phones. "I thought I was on to the start o' a comic song frae Gleska!"[3]

It was the nearest approach to wireless intercourse they got that evening.

Para Handy, from the start, was dubious of the whole thing, though induced to countenance the aerial by its manifest adaptability for drying shirts. Too proud to ask Macphail for explanations, he consulted Dougie, who gave him a brief synopsis of the principles of wireless telephony, as gathered at first-hand from the engineer.

"The sounds comes through the air and hit the mast," said the mate; "then slide down the wire and into Macphail's wee box that catches them like a moose-trap."

"Where do they come from?" asked the Captain in incredulous tones.

"From the air," replied the mate; "it's chock-a-block wi' music and news aboot the weather."

"But who makes the noise?" inquired the Captain.

"There's men and women that's paid for't," patiently explained Dougie. "Most of the time they're in London[4] and they speak into a great big trumpet. The sound travels at the rate o' a hundred and fifty miles a minute, and lands on a bit o' crystal."

"Would Macphail no' be better wi' a lemonade bottle?" asked the Captain ironically. "When does the concert start?"

"Start!" exclaimed Dougie. "Man, it's goin' on aal the time! Stop you till Macphail gets his bits o' wires put right thegither, and ye'll think ye're at the Mull and Iona Soiree, Concert and Ball.[5] They tell me it's wonderful."

"Dougald," said the Captain, putting his hand on the other's shoulder, "don't you listen to Macphail's palavers. He's pullin' your leg for ye. If you're wantin' to study music, buy a pair o' bagpipes."

Even Dougie's confidence in the engineer was shaken ultimately. Macphail spent all next evening in alternate tinkering with his set and futile listening. The others jeered at him.

"If we all sat round in a circle and joined hands," suggested Para Handy, "we might get a word or two from the Duke o' Wellington. Do you hear any spirits knockin', Mac? Maybe ye'll need to put oot the light, they're fearful timid."

"I wouldna' say but your instrument's needin' boilin'," was Dougie's sardonic contribution to the criticism. "Did ye oil it plenty?"

"A body might ass weel be readin' a book for aal the fun that's in this new diversion," said the Captain. "It's me that's vexed for poor Mrs Macphail! Gie them a shout, Mac; maybe they divna know ye're listenin'."

"Would a gimlet be any use?" inquired Dougie helpfully. "It's maybe fresh air that's wanted. Ye should surely be hearin' something or other, and it so close on Hogmanay! Never mind aboot Gleska or London, turn it on to Kinlochaline. There's bound to be gaiety of some kind on at Kinlochaline."[6]

"I wish youse would shut up!" cried Macphail, exasperated. "I canna hear an article wi' your bletherin'."

"Isn't he the poor, deluded cratur!" sadly soliloquised the Captain, addressing nobody in particular. "Good enough schoolin', too, and seen a lot o' trevel in foreign steamers. Never wass the same man since Hurricane Jeck hit him over the heid wi' a spanner![7] I wonder what would give him the notion he could hear anything wi' them things on his ears. He would be far better wi' a couple o' bungs and a bit o' marlin."

"Stand aside and gie me a shot at it," said Dougie at last. "Ye were always dull o' hearin', Mac."

He put the 'phones on his ears and listened a moment or two with increasing hopelessness. Suddenly he gaped; his eyes goggled.

"Dalmighty!" he exclaimed and pulled the 'phones off hurriedly, pale with apprehension.

"Are ye hearin' them?" inquired the Captain. "What's the latest news from London?"

"Ass sure ass I'm livin' I heard a man sayin' 'Hallo! hallo! hallo!' as plain ass anything," panted Dougie. "A great big English chentleman wi' a whisker!"

"The Duke o' Wellington," suggested Para Handy, still incredulous. "Plug up your ears again and ye'll maybe hear him gie a stave o' a song. Ask him if he knows the Gaelic."

"If ye don't believe me try't yoursel'," said Dougie, proffering the 'phones with some anxiety to get rid of them as soon as possible. "Ye would think the man was standin' beside ye sayin' 'hallo, hallo!' Sounds like a chentleman that would have a yacht. Where would he be speakin' from, Macphail?"

"Might be anywhere," said Macphail, himself a little dubious of Dougie's bona-fides. "London, Cardiff, or perhaps America." He picked up the 'phones again and stuck them over his ears with no great expectation of hearing anything.

"America!" said the Captain with withering sarcasm. "There's great blow-hards in America, but I never thought they could blow the length o' Bowlin'. Tell me when you're on to China."

A look of ecstasy came over Macphail's countenance. His head sunk into his shoulders: every nerve and fibre of his being seemed all at once to concentrate on listening.

"As clear's a bell!" he exclaimed in a whisper. "Good for Johnny! I kent that boy had talent."

"Isn't this deplorable?" said the Captain, sadly. "It's his own son Johnny he hass in the moose-trap noo. I never heard the like o't since Hurricane Jeck wass in the horrors. I'll go away ashore and get a bottle o' something from the druggist."

"Wheesht!" implored the engineer with a hand up. "It's a band, and they're playin' music. Reel and Strathspey – ye can hear them hoochin'! Just you listen to this, Dougie."

"Is't from Kinlochaline?" inquired the mate. "If it's not, I'm goin' ashore wi' the Captain."

Two hours after, when Para Handy and his mate returned, they found Macphail had gone to bed.

"Did you really hear a chap cryin' oot 'hallo'?" asked the Captain.

"I thocht I did," said Dougie, "but maybe it wass chust imagination."

Para Handy put on the phones, and plucked them off in a minute or two impatiently.

"There iss no more music there than there iss in a blecknin'-bottle!" he declared; "Macphail and you iss a bonny pair o' liars!"[8]

100. *Para Handy on Yachting*[1]

"IF I wass a man wi' a pickle money by me there's no' a hobby I would sooner have than sailin' a bit yat for my own amusement," said Dougie, as the *Vital Spark* came puffing out of Rothesay Bay through the fleet of the C.C.C.[2]

"Sailin' yats for yoursel' iss no' an amusement; it's wan o' them contagious diseases," said Para Handy. "You're better to get bye wi't when you're young, and spend the rest o' your days in the bosom o' your femily listening to the mustress playin' the pianolio."

"It's a great sport," insisted Dougie, looking with envy at a young fellow out on the bobstay of a plunging little cutter trying to clear a ton or so of deep-sea vegetation from the flukes of her anchor.

"Chust that! And so's keeping white rabbits; but for a man that's up in years a yat o' his own's a terrible affliction. It's the ruination o' many a happy home. A chentleman that hass it iss not much use to his wife and femily; he's away on the heavin' billow every Saturday efternoon, wi' no address where they can send a telegraph to tell him that his warehoose iss on fire. It's worse than bein' a chenuine sailor on the Western Ocean tred, for a sailor will always be bringin' something home – a bottle of Florida Water,[3] a parrot, or pound or two o' sweet tobacco. A chentleman that hass a yat o' his own never takes anything home to his wife and femily, except a picture post-caird o' the inns at Hunter's Quay,[4] and a splash o' tar doon the front o' his week-end weskit."

"You wouldna see aal them chaps goin' roond in yats o' their own if there wassna some diversion in't," said the Mate.

"There's some people'll do anything; you'll even see them climbin' mountains, and not a drop o' anything to be got on the top when they get there. Mountains iss good enough to look at, or for grazing sheep; if they were meant for men to climb on they would be flet. My idea of a pleesant sail iss a caibin ticket to Ardrishaig, and two or three cheery laads in the fore-saloon. Where iss the fun of yattin'? You'll take your week-end bag wi' your pynjamahs and a bottle of Fruit Saline in't, doon to Cardwell Bay[5] on a Saturday and you'll likely find your *Jackeroo*[6] hass dragged her moorin's and done fifty pounds o' damage to a boat belonging to a Lloyd's surveyor. Before you get a dozen or two o' beer and some refreshments put on board, and have gaithered thegither two or three handy fellows that can haul a rope, it's three o'clock in the efternoon, and there's only a flan o' wind to take you doon the length o' Lunderston[7]. There you are, my laad, and where, then, are you? A deid flat calm and nothing to do but open a tin of Australian meat[8] and make the best you can o't wi' the wan knife and the two tumblers. Perhaps she's a weel-found ship and hass a Primus stove; then wan o' your friends will say, 'I'll make an omelette, sunny boys; chust you hold on a meenute and you'll see a toppin' omelette!' The principal ingredient of a Primus omelette is a taste of paraffine oil; and it's no' an omelette anyway, it's either a piece of flannelette or a thing like an embrocation. 'Put oot your heid, Johnnie, and see if you see a sign o' wind,' says you to wan o' the laads. 'It is blowin' an Irishman's hurricane – up and doon the mast,' says Johnnie; 'the next time I come oot for sport I'll take a parasol.' 'Then we'll anchor here and go to our beds,' says you; 'I like the way the sun's goin' doon, we're sure to have a nice bit breeze in the mornin'.' So you sleep on a plank, and you waken every twenty meenutes wonderin' whether it's the foghorn at the Cloch[9] or Johnnie snorin'. It's chenerally Johnnie. There's only enough o' wind next day to take you up the length o' Gourock, and the beer iss done. That's the worst of beer, when it's finished there's none left. You take the early train to Gleska on the Monday mornin', and go back wi' your face aal sun-burnt. 'Where have you been wi' that face of yours?" says the chentlemen in the Stock Exchange – where you make your money. 'Oh, chust for a bit of a trip on the *Jackeroo*,' says you; 'it's a splendid healthy life. The crops iss looking beautiful oot in the Western Islands. Buy a yat,' says you, 'it's the sport of kings.' 'Where can I get wan?' says your frien'. 'I'll sell you the *Jackeroo*,' says you: 'I'm thinkin' o' startin' a motor car – or a laundry'."

"Aal the same if I had time and money it's a yat I would have for my diversion," said Dougie. "It's a cleaner job to be a common sailor on a yat than the mate o' a coal-boat."

"Clean enough, I'll alloo, and that's the worst of it," said Para Handy. "You might as weel be a chambermaid – up in the mornin' scourin' brass and scrubbin' decks, and goin' ashore wi' a bass[10] for loafs, and a fancy can for sixpence worth o' milk and a dozen o' siphon soda. I've been there mysel', my laad: not much navigation!"

"Maybe no', but a suit or two o' clothes in the year and a pleesant occupation. Most o' the time in canvas sluppers."

"You're better the way you are," said Para Handy. "There's nothing bates the mercantile marine for makin' sailors, Brutain's hardy sons! We could do without yats, but where would we be without oor coal-boats?"

Dougie went forward to coil a rope, and the Captain watched him with some uneasiness and curiosity. "Iss there anything wrong wi' Dougie, do you ken?" he asked Macphail, the engineer.

"Naething extra that I ken," replied Macphail with his usual cynicism.

"Do you think he's no' pleased wi' his job?" asked the Captain anxiously.

"Pleased wi't!" said Macphail, wiping his face with a fistful of waste. "The only men that's pleased wi' their jobs is bank directors. There's no much gaiety about a sailor's life on the *Vital Spark*."

"I'm afraid," said Para Handy, "that we're goin' to lose him; he's taken an aawful fancy for the yats. And I would be sorry to see this ship without a man I could depend on like my old frien' Dougald Campbell."

"Yats!" exclaimed Macphail. "Ye needna frighten yoursel'; Dougie wouldna sail in a yat for a couple o' pounds a week; he kens quite weel that a yatsman has to wear a collar whiles, and hae all his faculties aboot him. No, there's nae chance of us shiftin' him oot o' the *Vital Spark* as lang's there's the heel o' a loaf left in her in, and nae richt place to wash your hands."

"I'm gled to hear it," said the Captain, much relieved. "I got a start, I can tell you, when I thought I might lose Dougie. And I wass rubbin' it into him yonder aboot the poor life that they had in yats. To hear me speakin' you would actually think it wass worse than linen-draping or bein' on the stage. 'Nothing in it but flet calms, tinned beef, and bottled beer,' I told him."

"Then there's whaur ye were wrang," said Macphail. "Naething to dae in a calm and plenty o' bottled beers would look like Paradise to Dougie."

"I wouldna say but you're right," said Para Handy. "I'll have to shift his mind for him later on. But between you and me, myself, Macphail, I always think that dacent coal-boat sailors, when they die and go to heaven, should be put in chairge o' a handy size o' nice wee cruisin' yats wi' all expenses, and no needcessity for puttin' them on the hard in winter.

Notes

1 Para Handy, Master Mariner
1 A shallow draught sailing vessel used in the Scottish coastal trade.
2 A small steam lighter. Puffers were extensively used as general cargo carriers along the Western seaboard of Scotland. The puffer originated in the 1880s and were built in three types suited to canal, estuarine and off-shore work. The *Vital Spark* which, as Para Handy will shortly reveal, had made the crossing to Londonderry (without lights) was of the largest type. The name "puffer" derives from the characteristic puffing sound made by the engine exhaust venting through the funnel.
3 A mooring post.
4 The grazing for a cow — the parish Minister's glebe.
5 Para, though ready with a Scriptural quotation, frequently gets things a little confused. He is here quoting, not from the Old Testament story of Samson, but from 1st Peter Ch. 5.v. 8 "Be sober, be vigilant; because your adversary the devil, as a roaring lion, walketh about, seeking whom he may devour."
6 New Year's Day according to the old or Julian calendar — still celebrated in parts of the Highlands and Islands.
7 A type of bread, popular in Scotland, with a smooth crust; baked in a tin or pan.
8 A stretch of Loch Fyne between Otter Point and Skate Island.
9 Rinsing.
10 A small measure of liquid; hence a drink. Usually used of whisky, or as Para will be frequently found to refer to it "Brutish spirits".
11 Paddle steamer built in 1885 by J.&.G. Thomson at Clydebank for Messrs. David MacBrayne. Normally used on the winter service to and from Loch Fyne.
12 Sister-in-law.

2 The Prize Canary
1 Continuously or persistency.
2 The popular nickname for the small part of the Free Church of Scotland which refused to enter into the Union with the United Presbyterian Church

in 1900. The Free Kirk itself had been formed in the great Disruption of 1843 when a third of the members of the Church of Scotland left the Established Church over the issue of state control and the right of congregations to appoint the ministers of their choice. After the Union of 1900 there was a long legal battle, ending in the House of Lords, over the ownership of the property of the Free Church. In the end the Wee Frees were held to be the rightful possessors of the property of the Church, not the much larger portion which had entered the Union.

3 Owl.
4 Stroll.
5 A figure of speech derived from haims or hems, the two pieces of wood forming the collar of a draught horse — thus to "put the hems" on is to bring under control.
6 Delftware, earthenware.
7 Para and Dougie have walked towards the centre of the City along Argyle Street, passing under the bridge formed by the railway lines leaving the Caledonian Railway Company's Central Station. This bridge covers the area between Hope Street and Jamaica Street and was commonly known as the "Highlandman's Umbrella" from its popularity as a place of meeting and resort for the City's large Highland population. Hence Para's ready ability to consult "several Celtic compatriots".
8 Situated in Oswald Street near the Central Station.
9 A Scots legal term: a guarantee of indemnity.
10 Moulting.

3 The Malingerer

1 It's unnatural or it's imprudent.
2 Pin.
3 Monkey Brand soap. The advertisements for this widely used household soap featured a monkey wearing a dress suit. The text of the advertisement normally incorporated the phrase "Won't wash clothes".

4 Wee Teeny

1 The start of the annual Glasgow Trades' Holiday in mid-July.
2 Seaweed.
3 A reflection of the growing economic strength of Germany and of the political rivalry between Britain and Germany in the pre-war period (see "Politics, International Affairs and the Crew of the *Vital Spark*").
4 A comforter or baby's dummy.
5 Rubber, a corruption of caoutchouc.

5 The Mate's Wife

1 Green linnets or greenfinches. *(Chloris chloris)*.
2 Glasgow.
3 A member of the total abstinence society "The Independent Order of Rechabites". The Rechabites were formed in 1835 and in addition to practising and advocating total abstinence they also operated as a major Friendly Society. By 1910 the total British membership exceeded 200,000. The name comes from Jeremiah Ch. 35, vv. 5–6: "And I set before the sons of the house of the Rechabites pots full of wine, and cups, and I said unto

them, Drink ye wine. But they said, we will drink no wine: for Jonadab the son of Rechab our Father commanded us, saying ye shall drink no wine, neither ye, nor your sons for ever."

4 *cf.* Oscar Wilde (1854–1900): "A gentleman is one who never hurts anyone's feelings unintentionally."

5 In the years before the 1914–18 War the Clyde pleasure steamers often carried a small group of German instrumentalists.

6 Cousin.

6 Para Handy – Poacher

1 A household removal.

2 A weekday preceding the cerebration of Holy Communion kept as a local holiday. A service of preparation for Communion was held on the Fast Day. At the time of the Para Handy stories Communion services were, in the Highlands, held at very infrequent intervals-typically twice a year. The emphasis that the Presbyterian reformers had put on the importance of the Sacrament and the need for preparation had led, somewhat paradoxically, to a decline in the frequency of celebration.

3 Landowner.

4 Dougie clearly believed in the old Gaelic doctrine that argued "Slat a coille, breac a linne, fiadh a frithinn-trì mearlaidh de nach do gabh na Gaidheil riamh nàire" or "A branch from the wood, a trout from the pool, a deer from the deer forest-three thefts of which Highlanders are never ashamed".

5 Blew a whistle.

6 A land agent acting for the estate owner.

7 The Sea Cook

1 More refined or polite.

2 A beating or assault (physical or, as here, verbal).

3 Finnan haddock: a cured haddock. The name is usually held to derive from the Kincardineshire village of Findon. The *Concise Scots Dictionary* also suggests that the form "Findram Haddie" may derive from an confusion with the Morayshire village of Findhorn.

4 This somewhat obscure remark is presumably a reference to the notorious Australian bushranger Ned Kelly (1855–1880) who carried out his depredations wearing armour made from sheet metal.

8 Lodgers on a House-Boat

1 The second Clyde steamer to bear this name. This magnificent paddle steamer was built in 1891 for the Glasgow and Inveraray Steamboat Coy. by D.& W. Henderson at their Meadowside, Partick, yard. Designed for the daily Glasgow to Inveraray service she was transferred in 1903 to the Lochgoil and Inveraray Steamboat Coy. Ltd., and in 1912 sold to Turbine Steamers Ltd. who employed her on the daily cruise from Glasgow round the Isle of Bute.

2 The world's first commercial turbine passenger steamer. Built by William Denny & Bros. at Dumbarton in 1901 for the Turbine Passenger Steamer Syndicate. This group comprised Parsons Marine Steam Turbine Coy. Ltd., the pioneers of marine turbine propulsion, who were to build the King Edward's engines; Denny Bros., and John Williamson, a well-established independent steamer operator on the lower reaches of the Clyde. *King*

Edward, a screw steamer, sailed on a service between Greenock, Dunoon, Rothesay and Campbeltown.

3 Accommodation.

4 Horse.

5 Spout.

6 Crarae was chiefly noted for its large granite quarries.

7 Mud.

8 Village on the north bank of the River Clyde. The western terminus of the Forth and Clyde Canal.

9 A Lost Man

1 Once extensively used as a source of pyroligneous acid for the textile industry.

2 Para is thinking of Psalm 103.v.5 "Who satisfieth thy mouth with good things; so that thy youth is renewed like the eagle's." In the familiar Scottish metrical version this runs:

" Who with abundance of good things
   doth satisfy thy mouth
   So that, ev'n as the eagle's age
   renewed is thy youth."

3 See "Pare Handy, Master Mariner" note 6.

4 Wash tub.

5 This steamer was built for Messrs. David MacBrayne's cargo service between Glasgow and Inveraray. Launched by A. & J. Inglis at their Pointhouse yard in 1904 she was also used by MacBraynes as a relief steamer on the Outer Isles run in the winter season.

6 What became the most famous name in the West Coast shipping world came into prominence in 1879 when David MacBrayne, a partner in the long established firm of Messrs. D Hutcheson & Bros, took over complete control of the firm and went into business under his own name. MacBraynes became particularly well known due to their brilliantly marketed "Royal Route" – the excursion from Glasgow to Oban via Ardrishaig and the Crinan Canal. The route gained its name from Queen Victoria's use of it in 1847 and there are several references to it in the Para Handy stories. Even after rationalisation and nationalisation today's West Highland ferries still sail under the name of Caledonian MacBrayne.

"Along the western sea-board...generations of young Highlanders have grown up with the idea that their very existence was more or less dependent on MacBrayne. But for MacBrayne, most of them would never have seen bananas or the white loaf of the lowlands; might still be burning coalfish oil in cruisies..." Neil Munro: *The Brave Days* p.59.

7 Unlike the other vessels mentioned in this story the *Columbia* was not on Clyde passenger service though for all that she was a regular and familiar sight on the river. The *Columbia* was the 8,497 ton flagship of the Anchor Line, launched in 1902 from D & W Henderson's yard at Meadowside, Glasgow. She was used on the company's service from Glasgow to New York and was a familiar sight to "them brats of boys" as she made her way down river from Yorkhill Quay.

10 Hurricane Jack

1 Matting; especially that made of coconut fibre.

2 A highly respectable suburb of Glasgow lying on the south side of the city.

3 Cowcaddens. A district of central Glasgow lying to the north of Sauchiehall
  Street. Now largely given over to multi-storey car parks and motorway flyovers.
4 Shake.
5 Peewit, green plover or lapwing *(Vanellus vanellus)*.

11 Para Handy's Apprentice
1 Braces.
2 Jam sandwiches.
3 A rugby-playing fee-paying school in the West-End of Glasgow popular
  with middle class parents such as the *Vital Spark's* owner.

12 Queer Cargoes
1 A Dumbartonshire town on the Forth and Clyde Canal with a small but
  vigorous shipbuilding industry, chiefly producing puffers like the *Vital Spark*.
2 Wading in a muddy pool.
3 Branch canal linking the Forth and Clyde Canal with Port Dundas in the
  north of Glasgow and connecting with the Monklands Canal.
4 Crates made of delftware or earthenware. Para is being ironic and
  expressing his usual contempt for owners who fail to recognise the singular
  merits of the *Vital Spark*.
5 Fortune telling: *cf.* Spaewife: a woman who tells fortunes.
6 A fit, tantrum or wild mood.

13 In Search of a Wife
1 Sheriff. A locally based judge with wide-ranging civil and criminal jurisdiction.
2 Martinmas–11 November–was one of the traditional Scottish Quarter Days
  or term days on which rents were payable and agricultural and domestic
  servants' wages paid. By the time of this story the date of the Martinmas
  Term had been changed to 28th November.
3 Shy.
4 A district of Argyllshire lying between Loch Fyne and Loch Sween.
5 A once popular type of sweetmeat printed with helpful messages such as "I
  Love You", "Be Mine", "Until Tomorrow" and intended to aid bashful
  lovers like The Tar.

14 Para Handy's Piper
1 Sheep's head was once a popular Scottish dish and as an obvious preliminary
  it was necessary to have the wool singed off. Neil Munro wrote elsewhere
      "Yet the fact that every Wednesday Glasgow solemnly goes through the
  curious rite of eating mutton-heads and trotters cannot fail to impress every
  stranger who brings within her gates the gift of observation and a fresh
  expectant eye. Why sheep's-head? Why in the name of heaven Wednesday."
  (Neil Munro, *The Looker On*, 1933, p.115)
      In a characteristically colourful piece of journalism Munro explores the
  history, tradition and personalities associated with sheep's-head eating but
  fails to explain its unique hold on Scottish taste or its dominance in the
  Glaswegian's Wednesday diet.
2 Pipe tune composed by A. MacKellar.
3 Armpit.
4 Bagpipe tune. The 93rd Foot, the Sutherlandshire Highlanders, were

united in 1881 with the 91st Argyllshire Highlanders to form the Argyll and Sutherland Highlanders (Princess Louise's Own).

15 The Sailors and the Sale

1 The delay of a cargo due to the failure of a ship to sail or load; or the penalty imposed for the same.
2 A sale by auction of goods and livestock held when a farmer moved or went out of business.
3 "A saline substance obtained by the calcination of saltwort." *(Oxford English Dictionary).* Hence lemon kali=lemon soda. Kali derives from kalium. Kalium (K) is the chemical symbol for potassium.
4 The driver clearly distinguishes between beer and spirits. "A refreshment" is a popular Scottish euphemism for a glass of spirits; as in the phrase "I don't really drink much, but I do take the occasional refreshment".
5 Bullocks.
6 Sale by auction.
7 An object without value or significance: hence "I didn't give a docken for the thing" = "I cared nothing for the thing".
8 Heifers.

16 A Night Alarm

1 An all purpose word which means, as the context indicates, a tale, joke, situation or exploit.
2 A plank in a ship's hull.
3 A cape or cloak.
4 Wheezy, asthmatic.
5 Busy, occupied.
6 A tautology. The whole jeeng-bang (or jing bang) = all or everyone. Para intends to dismiss the entire crew on reaching Bowling.
7 Village by Loch Tay, Perthshire. The implication is that, coming from such inland stock, the engineer is in reality a land-lubber and not the terrifying deep-sea-going killer of his tales.
8 Suffering from *delirium tremens*

17 A Desperate Character

1 Red-edged hymn books. The Free Church (v.s.) eschewed the use of hymns, confining its praise to the metrical versions of the Psalms of David and the Scottish Paraphrases.
2 The established Church of Scotland followed the custom of standing to sing and sitting to pray. The "Wee Frees" observed the opposite convention.
3 *cf.* Romans, Ch. 11.,v.4 "I have reserved to myself seven thousand men, who have not bowed the knee to the image of Baal." Note that this Baal-a false god or idol-should be clearly distinguished from the type of baal held at Furnace (v.s. A Lost Man).
4 A reference to the once common practice of using pipeclay to whiten doorsteps.
5 Rough.
6 The seat of the MacNeil of Barra. Situated on a rock in Castlebay harbour.
7 Member of a temperance order.

18 The Tar's Wedding
1 An indeterminate small quantity.
2 The calling of the banns.
3 A ship's store or sailor's outfitters.
4 It was the custom at Scottish weddings for coins to be thrown to on-looking children as a means of ensuring good luck and prosperity for the newly married couple. This distribution was variously known as "bowl money", a "pour out", a "scatter" or a "scramble".
5 Relict; i.e. a widow.
6 A formal visit to a church after a significant event such as a wedding. Newly elected local councils used to visit the parish church in a body on a Sunday soon after the election in a ceremony known as the "Kirking of the Council".

19 A Stroke of Luck
1 Saithe or coley.
2 Very Highland: i.e. very simple or unsophisticated. It is curious to note Captain Macfarlane using this characteristically Lowland epithet and speaking scornfully (by implication) of his fellow Highlanders. Indeed Para seems oddly perverse in this story. He later goes so far as to compare Loch Fyne, unfavourably, with the dock area of Glasgow: "There iss more life in wan day in the Broomielaw of Gleska clan there is in a fortnight in Loch Fyne." This may be true but it is scarcely typical of Para Handy's normal attitudes and opinions.
3 A coal dump, a coal merchant's store. Para is of course implying that Macphail is a mere stoker, "chust a fireman" and not a "rare enchineer".
4 MacBrayne's magnificent flagship-kept exclusively for use on the prestige summer sailings from the Broomielaw to Ardrishaig, "The Royal Route". Built in 1878 at J & G Thomson's yard at Clydebank she continued in service until 1935. Perhaps the most famous, and certainly the most impressive, Clyde steamer of all time.

20 Dougie's Family
1 A dockside district in Govan, Glasgow, on the south side of the River Clyde.
2 Now a district of west Glasgow on the north side of the Clyde. At the time of this story a separate burgh whose inhabitants, many of Highland origin, took pride in asserting their civic independence.
3 Move house.
4 A standard size of print approximately 6"x4".
5 A home for orphan children at Bridge of Weir, Renfrewshire, founded in the 1860s by William Quarrier.
6 Clay pipe.
7 Field, pastureland.
8 Upset or confusion.
9 Chimney.
10 Pinafore.

21 The Baker's Little Widow
1 Card game.
2 Havering: talking nonsense.
3 Say a word.

4 Suspect.
5 Precipitately.

22 **Three Dry Days**
1 Bet, wager.
2 The Glasgow Necropolis was one of the City's main burying places and from its establishment in 1833 was extensively used by the city's industrial and commercial elite.
3 Tricks.
4 2nd February. One of the Scottish Quarter Days. The others being Whitsunday (15th May), Lammas (1st August) and Martinmas (11th November).
5 A spree, a piece of fun.

23 **The Valentine That Missed Fire**
1 This story was first published on 19th February 1906–as close to St Valentine's Day as could be arranged.
2 Gas light fitting.
3 Tailors. A tyler was also a minor official of a Masonic Lodge. For more on this confusion see No. 78 "Initiation".

24 **The Disappointment of Erchie's Niece**
1 To which family of Mactaggarts is she related?
2 Deeply embarrassed.
3 From top to toe. The earing was the top corner of a square sail while the clew was the bottom corner.
4 Erchie MacPherson has been borrowed from another series of Neil Munro's tales: "Erchie; my droll friend". In addition to his Para Handy stories and the Erchie Macpherson tales, Munro also produced a set of stories about a commercial traveller "Jimmy Swan; the joy traveller".
5 Gas light.
6 Erchie means that his son is now employed by the local authority.
7 Kitchen sink
8 Further important evidence on the vexed question of Para's place of birth.
9 Church officer, sexton. Erchie is here using the word as a verb; to beadle: to perform the duties of a beadle.
10 Consciousness.

25 **Para Handy's Wedding**
1 Wedding cake.
2 A once popular method of selling works of art. Subscribers took part in what was in effect a raffle.
3 To haiver is to talk nonsense, thus a haiver is one who talks in a foolish manner
4 Jocose: happy, contented.

26 **A New Cook**
1 The first story from the second Para collection *In Highland Harbours with Para Handy, s.s. Vital Spark,* originally published in 1911.
2 The *Texa* was acquired by Messrs. David MacBrayne in 1889 and, like the *Cygnet,* was used on the Glasgow to Inveraray cargo service.

3 Small passenger ferries operating on the Clyde between Victoria Bridge and Whiteinch.

4 A reference to a well known contemporary advertisement for the breakfast cereal, Force.
"High o'er the hill leaps Sunny Jim
   Force is the stuff that raises him."

5 Common entrance to a block of tenement flats.

6 Crown Street, Gorbals, a working-class area of Glasgow on the south side of the Clyde.

7 Vehicular ferry across the Clyde in Glasgow.

8 A reference to the poem of this name by Sir Walter Scott which opens with the lines:
"Why weep ye by the tide, ladye?
   Why weep ye by the tide?
   I'll wed ye to my youngest son,
   And ye sall be his bride;
   And ye sall be his bride, ladye,
   Sae comely to be seen:
   But aye she loot the tears down fa'
   For Jock o'Hazeldean."

9 Wooden spoon.

27 Pension Farms

1 The 9,000 acres of the Ardgoil Estate were presented to the City of Glasgow by A. Cameron Corbett, M.P. for Glasgow Tradeston. In his letter to Lord Provost John Ure Primrose announcing the gift he wrote "My general object is to preserve a grand rugged region for the best use of those who love the freedom of the mountains and wild natural beauty...". The area is sometimes known as Argyll's Bowling Green, popularly thought to be an ironic reference to its extremely rugged terrain; however other sources claim Bowling Green as a corruption of the Gaelic Buaile na Greine–the Sunny Cattle Fold. The estate was used for country holidays for underprivileged children and was a popular destination for trips and excursions. In 1965 after a number of years of substantial financial losses it was feued to the Forestry Commission.

2 A fit or tantrum. Variant spelling of "tirrivee".

3 Smallholdings in the Highlands and Islands.

4 In 1908 David Lloyd George, as Chancellor of the Exchequer in Asquith's Liberal Government, introduced the first state Old Age Pension scheme into Britain. This paid the sum of five shillings (25 pence) per week to single people aged 70 and over and seven shillings and sixpence (37 pence) per week to married couples.

5 Sheep pens.

6 To keel: to put a painted mark of ownership on a sheep.

28 Para Handy's Pup

1 The *Vital Spark* is in Islay. Port Ellen is the main port on the south coast of the island.

2 The huge Singer sewing machine factory at Clydebank renowned for the clock tower with its four 26 foot diameter dials; a prominent local landmark until its demolition in 1961 and as Macphail indicates, visible from the river.

3 Lighthouse on the Renfrewshire coast South-West of Greenock.
4 The shipyard at Govan of the Fairfield Shipbuilding and Engineering
   Company Ltd. known among many other famous ships for the *Empresses*
   built for the Canadian Pacific Line.
5 One of the main shopping and commercial streets of Glasgow.
6 Willie Stevenson is a supporter, from the bar rather than the terracing, of
   Celtic Football Club.

29 Treasure Trove

1 Hoops.
2 Dougie is of course referring to the story of Jonah and the whale recounted
   in the Old Testament (Jonah Ch.i.v.17–Ch.2.v.10).
3 An area in the East End of Glasgow, near the Gallowgate, used by circuses
   and fairs.
4 The Band of Hope was a juvenile religious and temperance organisation.
5 An evening entertainment.
6 Panting, breathing heavily.
7 The Kilbrannan Sound lies between the Island of Arran and the peninsula
   of Kintyre.
8 A famous steamer built by William Denny & Bros. at Dumbarton in 1881
   for David MacBrayne's West Highland services. *Claymore* was famed, both
   for her striking looks and for her fifty years of service on the West Coast.

30 Luck

1 A settlement in Knapdale on the shore of West Loch Tarbert.

31 Salvage for the *Vital Spark*

1 A kitten.
2 The heart of a house factor–or property manager, proverbially
   unsympathetic to tenants.
3 Kelvingrove Park in the west end of Glasgow – home to the city's Art
   Gallery & Museum.

32 Para Handy has an Eye to Business

1 An isolated pier on Loch Riddon in the Kyles of Bute.
2 As this story comes after "Pension Farms" in the Para Handy canon and as
   Mr Lloyd George had moved on from the Board of Trade to be Chancellor
   of the Exchequer and creator of Old Age Pensions in 1908 we must assume
   that Macphail had not been keeping up with recent Cabinet changes.
3 Village on Loch Awe-side.
4 Sabbatarian and temperance pressures in Victorian Scotland had resulted in
   the passing of the Public Houses (Scotland) Act of 1853, the so-called
   Forbes Mackenzie Act. This not only introduced the novelty of an official
   closing time for public houses (11.00 p.m.) but completely shut pubs on a
   Sunday. However, hotels, like the Inn at Cladich in this story, were
   permitted to serve *bonafide* travellers. As a result the thirsty from one village
   went two or three miles to the next and thus qualified for the privilege.
5 Pony.

33 A Vegetarian Experiment

1 In the early twentieth century a great many Italians settled in Scotland and entered the catering trade, particularly in the coastal resorts.

2 Island in Lamlash Bay, Arran.

3 Quite how the Scribes and Sadduccees ate is obscure. Could Para have been thinking of Matthew 16.v.6 "Take heed and beware of the leaven of the Pharisees and Sadducees"? As the husband of the former owner of a baker's shop this may have struck him with some force. Unfortunately the leaven referred to is not yeast but the doctrine of the Pharisees and Sadducees.

34 The Complete Gentleman

1 The area at the head of Loch Aline in Morvern, Argyll.

2 In front of.

3 Glasgow underground railway–a circle line more usually known as the "subway" completed in 1896.

4 The Caledonian Railway operated the route between Glasgow Central Station and Greenock.

5 Andrew Carnegie (1835–1919) Scots born multi-millionaire and philanthropist. Among his many benefactions he endowed some 600 public libraries in the United Kingdom as well as many more in the United States, Canada and other countries.

35 An Ocean Tragedy

1 Owl. Captain Macfarlane's grasp of ornithology is clearly breaking down under the strain!

2 Sadly, but perhaps unsurprisingly, Dougie is mistaken. The cockatoo comes from Australia and New Guinea, not the Holy Land. What the mate is perhaps thinking of (if he is not simply persecuting the hapless skipper) is the cockatrice. This is a bird of a very different feather, being generally considered as some sort of venomous snake and there are indeed four references to this unpleasant beast in the "Scruptures".

36 The Return of the Tar

1 Not only Macphail's novelettes dealt with this topic. The real-life case of the Tichbourne claimant, in which an imposter claimed to be the heir to the Tichbourne baronetcy and estates, had been fought in the English courts in the 1870s and continued to surface in the press for many years afterwards. The identification of the supposed Sir Roger Tichbourne involved a physical deformity and a missing tattoo–the parallels with The Tar's identification problems are clear.

37 The Fortune Teller

1 For a full discussion of the vagaries of the Loch Fyne herring see no.45 "Herring: A Gossip".

38 The Hair Lotion

1 Lillie Langtry 1852–1929 "The Jersey Lily". Actress and socialite, mistress of Edward VII.

2 John Bright (1811–1889), Liberal M.P. and prominent radical politician

and orator. President of the Board of Trade 1866–71; Chancellor of the Duchy of Lancaster 1873–74, 1880–82.

3 Edna May (1878–1948) was an American actress and singer best known for her starring role in the musical "Belle of New York" in London in 1898. Described by one authority as a "statuesque beauty".

39 Para Handy and the Navy

1 Fussing or trifling.

2 Pre-Dreadnought battleship built in 1898 and torpedoed in the English Channel on 1st January 1915 with extensive loss of life.

3 A notoriously dangerous shelf of barely submerged rocks off Dunoon.

4 The two-Power standard was a well-established target for British naval strength. The aim was to have a fleet to match those of any two possible combined adversaries. As Macphail observes, in his somewhat unaccustomed role as naval strategist, the advent of the Dreadnought type in Britain and Germany had eroded Britain's naval superiority. "If ye havena Dreadnoughts ye micht as weel hae dredgers." While this is a somewhat extravagant way of expressing the matter the fact remains that the Dreadnought type so outperformed earlier capital ships as to make them of very limited utility.

5 Fort, manned by Territorials of the Royal Garrison Artillery, on Rosneath Point.

6 Our hero is, despite his bold words, steaming for the shelter of the Renfrewshire coast. Macinroy's Point is just beyond Gourock.

40 Piracy in the Kyles

1 The northernmost point of the Island of Bute.

2 H.M.S. *Collingwood* was a battleship built in 1882 and sold in 1909 for scrap. At the time of this story, she was evidently laid up in the Kyles of Bute, the picturesque stretch of water between Bute and the mainland of Cowal. Readers will recollect that in the previous story "Pare Handy and the Navy", Para comments on "absolute" battleships "lyin' in the Kyles o'Bute wi' washin's hung oot on them." The Kyles were a popular area for the Royal Navy to moor obsolete warships.

3 The Convention of Royal Burghs was an ancient gathering of representatives of the main towns in Scotland to discuss common problems and the affairs of the nation. Together with the General Assembly of the Church of Scotland the Convention did much to fill the place of a parliament after 1707. Known to have been in existence in the sixteenth century it was replaced in the 1975 reorganisation of local government, which abolished the old structure of burghs and counties, by the Convention of Scottish Local Authorities, more generally known by its acronym COSLA.

4 *People's Friend,* a weekly magazine founded in 1869. One of the main outlets for the "kailyard school" of Scottish popular writing, it aimed at a popular audience of women and puffer engineers. Part of the legendary D.C. Thomson publishing empire of Dundee.

5 An alarming inconsistency. We have already learned from Para (The Complete Gentleman, No.34) that the legendary Hurricane Jack "...came from Kinlochaline and that iss ass good ass a Board of Tred certuficate...". Why Dougie should presume to disagree with his skipper is unclear.

41 Among the Yachts

1 The Royal Clyde Yacht Club, with its base at Hunter's Quay, near Dunoon, was founded in 1871, though its origins go back to the Clyde Model Yacht Club of 1856. This was a club formed to cater for owners of smaller yachts, not model yachts in the modern sense, who were excluded from membership of the prestigious Royal Northern Yacht Club (founded in 1824) which had its headquarters at Rothesay. In recent years the two clubs have merged and have their Headquarters at Rhu on the Gareloch.

2 Sir Thomas Lipton's famous 23 metre cutter designed and built in 1908 by the famous Clyde yacht building firm of W. Fife & Son of Fairlie.

3 Another of the classic Fife designed yachts–this time a 151 tons (Thames Measurement) yawl built in 1904 in Southampton and owned at this time by Myles B. Kennedy.

4 The sardonic engineer is referring to binoculars or field-glasses, still at this period something of a novelty.

5 Almeric Paget M.P.'s 15 metre cutter, built in 1888 by R. McAllister & Son at Dumbarton.

6 A 12 metre cutter built in 1908 by McAllister and owned by J.H. Gubbins.

7 The Coats family of Paisley textile magnates were prominent in yacht racing circles.

8 A smallish (35.6'cutter) owned by A.H. Glen-Coats.

9 A bobbin or spool. The Coats, as thread-makers, would be large scale buyers of pirns–hence the point of Para's allusion. Some idea of the family interest in yachting may be gained from a perusal of the Lloyd's Register of Yachts which, in 1910, listed James Coats Jnr. of Ferguslie House, Paisley as the owner of six yachts, ranging in size from the 3-ton *Sprite* to the 498-ton *Gleniffer*. The same edition lists another six vessels owned by members of the Coats or Glen-Coats family.

10 Stretch of the Clyde off Greenock, used as an anchorage for trans-Atlantic liners or for ships waiting for appropriate conditions to pass further up-river.

11 Sprawling.

12 A popular yacht name and it is sadly impossible to establish which vessel Para crewed on.

13 Thomas Johnstone Lipton (1850–1931), born in humble circumstances in Glasgow (in fact in Crown Street, the home of Sunny Jim), established a chain of stores through an original and dynamic approach to food retailing–he made his first million by the age of 30. Noted for his gifts to charity he also spent a fortune on attempts to win back the America's Cup from the United States with a series of yachts called (in tribute to his Irish ancestry) Shamrock. Knighted in 1898, he was made a baronet in 1902 by King Edward VII–another keen yachtsman.

14 The professional skippers of the great rivals *Shamrock* (Sycamore) and *White Heather* (Bevis).

42 Fog

1 The usual cargo of the Campbeltown boat would be the output of the twenty odd distilleries producing the distinctive Campbeltown malt whisky.

2 A select residential district in the west of Glasgow.

3 A reference to the failure of the City of Glasgow Bank in 1878. The collapse of this bank had major repercussions on the industry and

commerce of the West of Scotland, the extent of which can be judged by
Dougie's jibe, still obviously comprehensible thirty years after the event.

43 Christmas on the *Vital Spark*

1 The use of vibrators for massage and cosmetic purposes is first recorded by
the *Oxford English Dictionary* in a quotation dated 1906.
2 The s.s. *Minard Castle*, a cargo steamer built in 1882 for the Lochfyne and
Glasgow Steam Packet Coy. Ltd., was for 46 years a familiar sight on the
Clyde and Loch Fyne. As the story suggests she also carried a few
passengers in addition to her main trade in freight and livestock.
3 Another story based on the introduction of old age pensions, the qualifying
age for which was seventy years. See also No. 27 "Pension Farms".

44 The Maids of Bute

1 Warmed himself, basked.
2 A linnet (*Carduelis cannabina*).
3 Hoarse, suffering from a respiratory infection.
4 The third Clyde steamer to bear this name was built by Tod & McGregor of
Partick in 1839 and sailed for 46 years under a variety of owners, but as Para
suggests, eventually under MacBrayne's flag, on the Glasgow–Ardrishaig run.

45 Herring – a Gossip

1 The unit of measurement of herring; a barrel of 37.5 gallons capacity.
2 John O'Brian was a well-known West Coast fish merchant. Munro
commented in *The Brave Days* p.62 on MacBrayne's & O'Brien's economic
dominance: "You could not...land at a quay but across red-painted
gangways. MacBrayne and John O'Brian clearly shared the whole West
Highland trade between them. Wherever was a gangway and a couple of
bollards, there was also a pile of John O'Brian's herring boxes."
3 Disgust.
4 Rush, plunge or dash.
5 Stroll.
6 Gadding about, roaming around in search of pleasure.

46 To Campbeltown by Sea

1 Originally published in July 1908 during a remarkable heatwave.
2 Village in Kintyre at the North end of the Kilbrannan Sound.
3 The literary engineer is misquoting Samuel Taylor Coleridge's frequency
misquoted lines from "The Rime of the Ancient Mariner". In the original
the couplet runs
"Water, water, everywhere
  Nor any drop to drink."
4 Captain Matthew Webb's first crossing of the Channel in 1875 had inspired
many others to follow in his wake.
5 Jabez Wolffe was a noted swimmer with a number of Channel attempts to
his credit around 1908–1911. Amongst his other long distance swims was
the Dunoon-Rothesay crossing in July 1911
6 Most of the Clyde piers were privately owned and were maintained by
charging pier dues on all goods and passengers landed, in the case of the
latter, typically a penny.

7 The legendary George Geddes II was the officer of the Glasgow Humane
   Society from 1889–1932. By 1917 Geddes had rescued 56 people from
   drowning.
8 A stream in Rutherglen.

47 How to Buy a Boat
1 See No.6 "Pare Handy, Poacher".
2 A young salmon on its first return from salt to fresh water.
3 Unstable.

48 The Stowaway
1 Tourists.
2 German manufacturers had won a very large share of the fast-growing
   market for picture post cards. Many of the most popular series of views of
   picturesque British beauty spots were in fact produced in Germany.
3 The Boy Scout movement was founded by Robert Baden-Powell in 1908.
   This story was first published in 1910.
4 A famous trans-Atlantic liner launched from John Brown's Clydebank yard in
   1906 for Cunard. The outrage caused by her sinking by a German submarine
   in May 1915 was one of the factors which created the climate of opinion
   which brought about the United States' intervention in the First World War.
5 A passage or entry leading from the street to the rear of a tenement property.
6 Each year large numbers of Breton "onion Johnnies" came on their bicycles
   to various parts of Britain selling strings of onions from door to door. Such
   travelling salesmen would have been perfectly familiar to Para and his crew
   and the obvious identification would have been made but for the spy
   hysteria of the Mate, Dougie.
7 Three major international exhibitions were held in Glasgow in 1888, 1901
   and 1911. This story was published in September 1910 when preparations
   for the 1911 Exhibition were under way and had evidently become a
   subject of conversation even among puffer crews.
8 See above: No. 5 "The Mate's Wife", note 5.
9 While the "Cherman bands" might well have included a cornet, a member
   of the trumpet family, there is no evidence chat their line-up included the
   cornucopia or horn of plenty.
10 Jail.

49 Confidence
1 Woolwich Arsenal, the Royal Navy's technical centre on the Thames.
2 Admiralty torpedo production transferred from Woolwich to Battery Park,
   Greenock in 1911.

50 The Goat
1 A reference to the so-called Siege of Sidney Street, in January 1911, in
   which a detachment of the Metropolitan Police, personally supervised by
   Home Secretary Winston Churchill, surrounded a house in Stepney
   occupied by an anarchist gang, led by one "Peter the Painter".
2 Para anticipated Churchill's knight/hood by a matter of 42 years.
3 Handcuffs.
4 See No.14 "Pare Handy's Piper".

51 Para Handy's Vote

1 One of Glasgow's electoral divisions. Like so many others this story was, when first published, highly topical, appearing in December 1910 during a General Election campaign.

2 The Liberal candidate in Glasgow, College.

3 Glasgow, with its large immigrant population of Irish Catholics, from time to time displayed a degree of ethnic and religious prejudice seemingly shared by Para.

4 Irish Home Rule was for the fifty years between 1870 and 1920 a major and divisive issue in British politics.

5 Local Veto polls on the restriction of public house licences were introduced following pressure by the strong temperance movement of the period.

6 The Women's Social and Political Union, founded in 1903 by Emmeline Pankhurst and her daughter Christabel, was in the forefront of the campaign for votes for women. The first extension of women's suffrage in parliamentary elections came in 1918.

7 Mr Carr-Glynn was the Unionist (Conservative) candidate in the College constituency.

8 One of the planks of the Liberal manifesto for the 1910 election was the reform of the House of Lords by removing from it powers to oppose finance bills and restricting it to limited delaying powers in other matters. These changes were introduced in the Parliament Act of 1911, which was passed by the House of Lords under the threat of the creation of a flood of new Liberal Peers sufficient in number to outvote the Conservative majority.

9 The election took place on Thursday 8th December. Perhaps Mr Carr-Glyn's being "one of the good old sort" was the reason for the Liberal, Mr Watt, winning by only 359 votes, the smallest Liberal majority in this seat for many years.

52 Hurricane Jack

1 Popular poetic terms for the over-arching vault of heaven. Compare with "This most excellent Canopy the Ayre..." (Shakespeare, *Hamlet* Act 2, Sc.2.) or "Without any other cover than the cope of heaven" (Tobias Smollett, *Humphrey Clinker.*)

2 One of the vessels of Crawford & Rowat's Port Line. Lost by enemy action in 1917.

3 The Black Ball Line established the first regular trans-Atlantic service in 1816 and later was prominent in the Australian emigrant trade.

4 Unlicensed drinking house.

53 Mystery Ship

1 Low gravity beer made in response to wartime conditions and shortages.

2 A variety of wartime measures controlled licensing hours and imposed state management of public houses in certain areas. Lloyd George, as Minister of Munitions is reported to have said "Drink is doing us more damage than all the German submarines put together."

3 Prison in the east end of Glasgow.

4 Small merchant ships with concealed cannon were used by the Royal Navy during the campaign against German U-Boats. The theory was that, rather than waste a torpedo, the U-Boat would surface to attack by gunfire the disguised ships at which point the Q ship would open fire and sink the submarine.

5 A major warship yard established at Dalmuir near Clydebank in 1905.
6 Merchant ships were frequently painted in dazzle-pattern camouflage.
7 Admiral Alfred von Tirpitz (1849–1930), Secretary of State for the Imperial
  Navy, founder of the German High Seas Fleet.
8 Medicine much advertised for its soothing effect on teething infants.

54 Under Sealed Orders
1 A piece of rigging hanging loose.
2 Para would seem to have been bothered by the ironic cries of "brats of
  boys" (v.s. No.9 "A Lost Man"). The Cunarder *Aquitania*, at 45,647 tons
  and considered to be one of the most beautiful products of John Brown's
  yard at Clydebank, somewhat outclassed a "coal boat".
3 Surmised.
4 Sanda Island, the site of this remarkable incident, is one and half miles
  south of Cove Point at the south end of the Kintyre Peninsula.

55 A Search for Salvage
1 One of the few topographical references which may be questionable. There
  are a number of Baghmohrs in the Outer Hebrides, but none in Skye.
2 Neat.
3 A tribute to the Sabbatarian practices of the islanders.
4 Stretch of sea dividing Skye from the mainland.

56 The Wonderful Cheese
1 Name often applied to the entire archipelago of the Outer Hebrides
  stretching some 130 miles from the Butt of Lewis to Barra Head.
2 Bombs and mines were frequently referred to as "infernal devices".

57 The Phantom Horse and Cart
1 Another of the wartime restrictions, this time banning the purchase of a "round".
2 Load.
3 Seized on us.

58 Hurricane Jack's Luck-bird
1 Beetles.
2 *cf*. "An Ocean Tragedy" no.35.
3 *cf*. "Pare Handy's Pup" no.28.
4 Crab.
5 Stockwell Street in Glasgow.
6 Ceilidh, party.

59 A Rowdy Visitor
1 The *Vital Spark* is in the south-west of Mull.

60 The Fenian Goat
1 The Irish Republican movement founded in 1905 and, during the First
  World War period of this story, actively struggling for Irish independence.
2 Half-tidal island adjacent to Colonsay. The *Vital Spark* is southward bound.
3 A member of a nineteenth century Irish independence movement. Often, as
  here, used pejoratively.

4 A reference to the victory, in 1690, at the River Boyne of the Protestant William of Orange over the deposed James II and his Irish Catholic supporters. An event marked in Ulster and Scotland by the Orange Order in processions on the anniversary date of 12th July.

5 A small port on the East side of Islay facing the neighbouring island of Jura.

61 Land Girls

1 The recruitment of women for agricultural and forestry work was encouraged by the creation of the Women's War Agricultural Committees in 1916 and by the formation of the Women's Land Army in 1917.

2 Trimmed off branches.

3 The Kirk Session, the lowest ecclesiastical court of the Church of Scotland, had a traditional responsibility for the spiritual oversight and care of the inhabitants of the parish. This, in the past, extended to investigating and punishing breaches of morality or conduct likely to provoke public scandal.

4 A non-clan tartan—in effect a grey and black check.

5 Going in disguise, especially at Hallowe'en.

62 Leap Year on the *Vital Spark*

1 Overturned.

2 A tall glass containg 14 fluid ounces.

3 This, and a later story "Leap Year on the *Vital Spark*", hinge on leap-year celebrations and may acordingly be dated to 1916.

63 Bonnie Ann

1 A delicacy made from the meat from a cow or pig's head, boiled, minced and served cold in jelly.

2 Elena Petrovkna Blavatsky (1831–91). A Russian theosophist whose doctrines were an eclectic mixture of Indian mysticism and psychic practices.

3 Macphail has confused his Marys. Bloody Mary was Mary Tudor (1516–58), Queen Mary I of England, while Bonnie Ann's contact on the other side was Mary Queen of Scots (1542–87).

4 A southern suburb of Glasgow.

5 Macphail is becoming seriously confused. Bonny Mary o'Argyll or Mary Campbell was celebrated in verse by Robert Burns and died as she and the poet were planning to emigrate to the West Indies. Her statue in Dunoon would be a familiar sight to the crew.

64 The Leap-year Ball

1 The *Vital Spark* is in distant waters. Duror in Appin lies on Loch Linnhe to the north of Oban.

2 Indebted to them.

3 Bounce. Stotting (in the sense that Dougie uses it in the next paragraph) can also mean being in an intoxicated condition.

4 Para's familiarity with the world of classical music is somewhat suspect. Paddy Roosky (or somewhat more conventionally Ignace Jan Paderewski [1860–1941]) was a well-known Polish piano virtuoso, who became Prime Minister of Poland in 1919. He was, however, not in the least "namely for the fiddle".

65 The Bottle King
1 A basket made from strips of wood.
2 Another reflection of wartime shortages in this group of stories.

66 "Mudges"
1 Midges. "Almost everywhere in the Highlands below 2,000 feet there are vast hordes of midges *(Chironomidae)* which affect the movements of mammalian life, including man, to a considerable extent ... The place of the midge in human ecology is such that a greatly increased tourist industry to the West Highlands could be encouraged if the midge could be controlled." F. Fraser Darling & J. Morton Boyd: *The Highlands and islands*, London, Collins, 1964.
2 Port on the island of Islay.
3 An unspecified large number.
4 Proverbs Ch. 6.v.6 "Go to the ant, thou sluggard; consider her ways and be wise."
5 An ancestor of the West Highland White Terrier, the Poltalloch terrier had a whitish coat, black-tipped ears and often a black nose. Poltalloch is in the heartland of the "Para country", near Crinan.
6 Coating nets with preservative.
7 A resin derived from a species of Acacia used in tanning and dyeing.
8 A type of fishing net.
9 A popular type of cake, a pastry slice made with dried fruit, is commonly known in Scotland as a "fly cemetery" from the supposed resemblance of the filling of currants, raisins, etc. to an accumulation of dead insects.

67 An Ocean Tragedy
1 Toward Point, on the Cowal Peninsula south of Dunoon.
2 Part of Gourock Bay.
3 Compare—
"With chose who have been born and bred upon the coast there is nearly always to be found a curious illusion that the greatest storms invariably take place on Sundays." Neil Munro, *The Looker-On*, p. 137.
   This piece first appeared in the *News* on Monday 6th November 1911, the day after the fiercest storm for twenty years. The Para story inspired by the storm appeared a fortnight later on 20th November.
4 Gourock railway station, built by the Caledonian Railway Coy. opened to passenger traffic in June 1889.
5 Old or experienced sailors.
6 Along the Renfrewshire side of the Clyde, including the Port Glasgow area (the "Port" of Para's description) were a series of timberponds, areas of shallow water enclosed by wooden palisades, where logs lay seasoning.
7 The *Royal George*, a hundred gun ship of the line, capsized while under repair at Spithead in 1772 with the loss of 900 lives.
8 Not a case for concern or reflection on the engineer's morals – Lady Audley is of course the heroine of one of Macphail's beloved "penny novellas".

68 Freights of Fancy
1 "Black-face" minstrel ensemble popularised by Edwin R Christy (1815–62). Christy's company of white musicians caricaturing the music and

manners of negro slaves was formed around 1842 and had many imitators.

2 As well as Russians coming from Archangel the port on the Arctic Ocean was, as Para might say "namely for tar".

3 Gourock, a coastal town in Renfrewshire, has a commanding Westward view of the Clyde estuary and the Dumbartonshire and Argyllshire hills and accordingly enjoys splendid sunsets.

4 An anti-submarine boom was in place on the outer Firth and restricted shipping movements.

5 The Allied landing at Gallipoli in April 1915, intended to assist Russia and relieve pressure on the Western Front.

6 Smartest, neatest.

7 Sunny Jim is alluding to the practice, introduced into Glasgow after the passing of the Public Health (Scotland) Act of 1867, of "ticketing" slum properties to show their size and the maximum number of residents permitted to reside within.

8 A small wooden barrel of 9 gallons capacity.

9 Apron.

69 Summer-time on the *Vital Spark*

1 In 1916 the idea of Summer Time or Daylight Saving was introduced to assist in the war effort and during the summer months clocks were to be advanced one hour beyond Greenwich Mean Time.

70 Eggs Uncontrolled

1 Revolts me.

2 Sensible.

3 Many traditional Scottish grocers and provision merchants advertised themselves as Italian Warehousemen indicating that they sold wines and the more exotic products to be found nowadays in a delicatessen counter.

71 Commandeered

1 Joke.

2 Infested.

3 Large minefields were laid in the North Sea by both Britain and Germany.

4 An important strategic waterway linking the Baltic with the North Sea and capable of taking the largest battleships. The notion of blockading the Canal was not confined to Para and the Admiralty planners, early in the war, produced plans for an assault on the lock gates at the western end of the Canal.

72 Sunny Jim Rejected

1 One of Glasgow's noted sights, the remains of fossilised trees preserved in Victoria Park, Whiteinch.

2 During the First World War aggressively patriotic women made a practice of presenting white feathers to men whom they considered should have enlisted in the forces.

3 Head.

4 Among the units recruited during the Great War were battalions of Bantams-men of modest size who would have looked out of place among formations of taller comrades.

73 How Jim joined the Army
1 Douglas Haig (1861–1928). British Commander-in-Chief on the Western Front from 1915. Created Earl Haig 1919.
2 The Gordon Highlanders, formed in 1794 and recruiting from North East Scotland.
3 Wheezy.
4 Medical Board set up to examine recruits.
5 Barracks at Greenock.
6 The Defence of the Realm Acts of 1914 and 1915 controlled a wide number of aspects of national life. Whether this included the passing off of glass eyes on the Army is unclear.

74 The Fusilier
1 One assumes that Jim had entered the Royal Scots Fusiliers, a regiment which recruited from Ayrshire and South West Scotland as well as from Sunny Jim's native Glasgow. The 6th Battalion of the Regiment was briefly commanded by Winston Churchill after his resignation from the Government over the Dardanelles debacle.
2 Small town in Ayrshire six miles north of Irvine, a centre of the textile industry.

75 Para Handy, M.D.
1 Hide and seek.
2 Busy.

76 A Double Life
1 A church-based organisation of women dedicated to the provision of clothing for the poor. Named after Dorcas, a charitable woman of Joppa – see Acts Ch. 9:vv.36–39.
2 Ailsa Craig, the rocky islet in the outer Firth of Clyde.
3 Very close to or friendly.
4 Popular assembly rooms in Glasgow. On the site of the later Alhambra Theatre in Wellington Street.
5 The Hengler family were prominent in British entertainment from the 18th Century. Among the family's enterprises were permanent circuses in London, Dublin, Hull and Glasgow. The Glasgow establishment, patronised by Hurricane Jack, was opened in Wellington Street by Charles Hengler in November 1885 and operated there until 1903. From 1904 Hengler's Cirque performed in the Hippodrome building in Sauchiehall Street, a much less convenient location for philanderers attending the Mull and Iona Gathering in the Waterloo Rooms.

77 The Wet Man of Muscadale
1 We later read that Muscadale is close to Campbeltown. Unfortunately no Muscadale appears to be known to the Ordnance Survey.
2 The rose of Sharon which may wither is the shrub *Hypericum calycinum* also known as Aaron's beard. The Rose of Sharon in "Scruptures" is to be found in The Song of Solomon 2.: "I am the rose of Sharon, and the lily of the valleys. As the lily among thorns, so is my love among daughters. As the apple tree among the trees of the wood, so is my beloved among the sons. I

sat down under his shadow with great delight, and his fruit was sweet to my taste. And is of an obviously different nature."

3 One of the diagnostic indications of diabetes mellitus is an abnormal thirst. Diabetes had been identified by the 18th century, but was incurable until Banting, Best & MacLeod discovered the insulin treatment in 1922.

4 Nails for boot or shoe soles.

5 A measure approximating to half an imperial pint. A half mutchkin was a traditional measure by which whisky was bought in bulk and the cynical engineer is suggesting that post-war whisky was a weaker and more dilute spirit clan the pre-war product.

6 Spring onions.

7 Seaweed.

8 An Israeli town in Gilead near the Syrian border. Among other incidents it was the site of Jehu's annointing as King of Israel (II Kings ch.9 v. 1). Quite why, apart from the euphony of the name, Colin MacClure should have considered bending the knee to Ramoth-Gilead is not clear. Readers will recollect the bowing of the knee to Baal (No. 17 "A Desperate Character").

9 Para is quoting from Burns's "The Cotter's Saturday Night":
   From scenes like these, old SCOTIA's grandeur springs,
   That makes her lov'd at home, revered abroad:
   Princes and lords are but the breach of kings
   'An honest man's the noblest work of GOD.'

78 Initiation

1 Rob Roy Macgregor (1671–1734) was a notorious Highland outlaw and freebooter. He figures prominently in the novel "Rob Roy" by Sir Walter Scott.

2 A type of cloak with large cape-like sleeves.

79 The End of the World

1 Isolated group of islands 110 miles west of the mainland of Scotland. The remaining population was evacuated in 1930.

2 A two roomed cottage dwelling.

3 The details of this particular chiliastic prophecy are sadly unavailable. Similarities to Joanna Southcott's Box may occur to the alert reader.

4 Furniture and household effects.

80 The Captured Cannon

1 German defensive position on the Western Front. Named after Field Marshal Paul von Hindenburg (1847-1934) the German Army's chief-of-staff from 1916–18.

2 The battle cruiser H.M.S. *Hood* was completed in 1920 at John Brown's yard in Clydebank. Sunk by the *Bismarck* in May 1941 with the loss of 1416 men.

81 An Ideal Job

1 Row (a village on the Gareloch) was officially re-named Rhu in 1927 to avoid mispronunciation and to get closer to the original Gaelic source of the village's name-rudha-a promontory.

2 In the depressed trade conditions which prevailed after the First World War the sheltered waters of the Gareloch were used as moorings for surplus shipping.

3 Barquentine, a sailing vessel with square sails on the fore-mast and the main and mizzen rigged with fore and aft sails.
4 Glasgow's Museum and Art Gallery in Kelvingrove Park was opened in 1901.
5 A spa hotel specialising in the treatment of minor disorders by one form or another of water treatment-sea bathing, medicinal springs etc. One of the Clyde's leading establishments of this type-Shandon Hydro on Garelochside- was in sight of Para as he tells this tale.
6 A movement to give city dwellers holidays by the sea or in the countryside.
7 Sensible, reliable.
8 Mother-in-law.
9 Well spoken, of good manner.

82 Para Handy's Shipwreck
1 This previously uncollected story was published in the *Glasgow Evening News* of 21st August 1905.
2 Made arrangements for calling the banns for Dougie's wedding. The attentive reader will have noted that in "Dougie's Family" the mate had ten children. The time of this re-telling of the tale of Para's shipwreck must therefore be set at an early period.
3 A sea loch on the northern side of the Knoydart peninsula. This was presumably one of the times Para was "...wrecked in the North at places that's not on the maps" ("A Night Alarm").
4 Loch Fyne-side dialect name for the cormorant *(Phalocrocorax carbo)*.
5 Donald Dinnie (1837-1916): a noted strong man and athlete with 11,000 victories to his credit in Highland Games and other events.

83 The *Vital Spark's* Collision
1 This previously uncollected story appeared m the *Glasgow Evening News* of 20th November 1905.
2 Scottish burghs and cities appointed senior councillors to the office of Bailie to act as local magistrates. In addition to the other local courts Glasgow also had a River Bailie Court sitting daily in McAlpine Street to try minor cases originating on the river.
3 A salutary reminder to us not to trust the court reporting of even such a reliable journal as the *Glasgow Evening News*. All our other evidence points to Dougie's surname being Campbell. His testimonial to the benefits of the Petroloid Lotion (see "The Hair Lotion") is signed "Dougald Campbell". This is not however the only vexed issue affecting Dougie. Just like his skipper his very place of birth is a mystery. In "A New Cook" he is described as "a Cowal laad" while later in "An Ocean Tragedy" Para tells his audience that the mate was "a native of Lochaline". Lochaline is in Morvern on the Sound of Mull and many miles north of Cowal–the area around Dunoon on the Firth of Clyde. Could he have been confusing Dougie with Hurricane Jack, the redoubtable native of Kinlochaline?
4 A precipitate descent.
5 Declared on oath. One may compare The Tar's not entirely credible evidence with Munro's comment in *The Clyde River and Firth* about "the loyal lies of witnesses in a Board of Trade examination"!
6 The unique third verdict available to Scottish courts in addition to guilty or not guilty.

84 Para Handy at the Poll

1 This previously uncollected story was published in the *Glasgow Evening News* on 22nd January 1906, just days after the General Election which had resulted in the victory of the Liberal party.

2 Universal male suffrage was only introduced with the 1918 Reform Act. The provisions of the series of Reform Acts culminating in that of 1884/5 had extended the franchise to a widening range of householders. Thus Para enjoyed the right to vote by virtue of his mother's home being registered in his name.

3 Campbeltown, with Ayr, Irvine, Inveraray and Oban, formed part of the Ayr Burghs constituency. The total electorate, on the limited franchise of the period, was only 8,031.

4 Joseph Dobbie, an Edinburgh solicitor, was, in reality as well as in Munro's story, the Liberal candidate at the 1906 election. He was indeed the sitting member, having won the seat at a by-election in 1904.

5 Henry Campbell-Bannerman (1836–1908). Leader of the Liberal Party from 1899 Prime Minister from 1905 until his death. Knighted 1895. Born Glasgow. M.P. for Stirling Burghs 1868–1908.

6 The importation of indentured Chinese labourers into the Transvaal and the support of Balfour's Conservative Government for this measure was bitterly attacked by Campbell- Bannerman and the Liberals as the reintroduction of slavery.

7 Scratch.

8 George Younger was in fact the Conservative candidate for Ayr Burghs in 1906 and had stood against Dobbie at the 1904 by-election-when he had been defeated by the narrow margin of 44 votes.

9 Free trade, protectionism and the implications of these policies on prices were key issues in the 1906 election.

10 Universal manhood suffrage. Campbell-Bannerman was also an advocate of female suffrage.

11 Irish Home Rule had been a dominant issue in British politics from the 1870s. The Liberal party split on the issue in 1885 with the so-called Liberal Unionists voting against Gladstone. Campbell-Bannerman favoured granting Home Rule at a suitable time.

12 The Ballot Act of 1872 introduced the secret ballot into British Parliamentary elections.

13 Lead pencil.

14 Whether with Para's help or not the Conservative candidate, George Younger, won Ayr Burghs with a majority of 261 votes against the Liberal tide and continued to represent the constituency until 1922. A member of the well-known brewing family, Younger received a Baronetcy in 1911 and was created Viscount Younger of Leckie in 1929. He died in 1929.

85 The *Vital Spark* at the Celebration

1 This uncollected story was published in the *Glasgow Evening News* of 2nd September 1912.

2 A tug owned by the Clyde Navigation Trust.

3 Saturday 31st August saw the celebration of the centenary of the first Clyde steamer *Comet* being marked by a review of naval and merchant shipping in the Firth of Clyde.

4 MacBrayne's flagship R.M.S. *Columba* was used for the official party which sailed from Glasgow to inspect the review of shipping.

5 The flagship of Vice-Admiral Sir John R Jellicoe, commanding the detachment of the Home Fleet at the review.

6 embarrassed

7 Henry Bell, 1767–1830, Scottish engineer and owner and designer of the *Comet*, Europe's first practical ocean-going steamship.

8 Bell, in addition to his work as an engineer, and his ship-owning activities, was a hotelier in the Clydeside resort of Helensburgh. His hotel, the Baths Inn, did indeed boast hot and cold baths for the use of those who wished to take the sea-water cure.

9 Asian seamen

10 The Clan Line was one of the major Scottish international shipping lines.

11 Steamer employed on G &J Burns' Glasgow to Belfast service.

12 Following the *Columba* on her inspection were the Glasgow Corporation's sewage sludge boat *Shieldhall* carrying representative workers from the shipbuilding and engineering industries and the new Clyde steamer *Queen Empress* chartered by the Navy League.

13 The organisation uniting the various incorporated trade guilds of the City of Glasgow.

14 Scottish country dance.

86 War-Time on the *Vital Spark*

1 This uncollected story was published in the *Glasgow Evening News* of 14th December 1914, following Munro's return from a period spent in France as a Special Correspondent for the *News*.

2 A reference to Masonic identification rituals.

3 Admiral Sir John R Jellicoe, Commander in Chief of the Grand Fleet, was, as Macphail will shortly observe, unlikely to be serving on a Clyde patrol boat.

4 His Imperial Majesty, Kaiser Wilhelm II.

5 The First World War started in august 1914

6 *cf.* No. 29 "Treasure Trove"

7 The Procurator Fiscal is a Scottish legal official charged with responsibility for investigating and prosecuting criminal cases. Depute Fiscals were appointed as required.

8 Cravat or scarf

9 *cf.* reference to German bands in No. 5 "The Mate's Wife" and No. 48 "The Stowaway".

10 splashing

87 The Three Macfadyens

1 This uncollected story appeared in the *Glasgow Evening News* of 4th January 1915.

2 Before the introduction of conscription in 1916 considerable pressure was put, both officially and privately, on men to enlist in the forces; for example by women presenting white feathers, as symbols of cowardice, to men they considered should be in the armed forces. Men rejected by the forces on medical grounds were entitled to wear a khaki armband to distinguish them from those who had not tried to enlist.

3 Previously ("The Mate's Wife" No.5) we have been told that Dougie's wife

was "...a low-country woman, wi' no' a word o' Gaalic..." Quite how this
squares with this evidence of her birth in Kintyre is, at present, obscure.
4 The great marching song of the First World War
5 An industrial town in North Lanarkshire.

88 **Running the Blockade**
1 This uncollected story appeared in the *Glasgow Evening News* of 1st March 1915.
2 Neutral flags. Norway was neutral during the First World War.
3 Obscure. The Concise Scots Dictionary offers "gollan" a corn-marigold.
4 Shipping convoys, to reduce losses from submarine attack, adopted a
zig-zag course.
5 A previously unreported incident in the varied career of the redoubtable
Hurricane Jack. From a later reference to Spaniards one may perhaps surmise
that this blockade running took place during the Spanish American war of 1898.
6 *cf.* "Hurricane Jack" no. 10 "...you would see a man that's chust sublime,
and that careful about his 'lastic sided boots he would never stand at the
wheel unless there wass a bass below his feet."
7 Quite why the singing of the Marseillaise was appropriate is unclear – but
doubtless it was all due to the kindly eye.
8 locks

89 **The Canister King**
1 This uncollected story appeared in the *Glasgow Evening News* of 7th June 1915.
2 generously proportioned
3 a pint bottle
4 thin tarred rope
5 The thoughtful Para is using the word "friends" in its Scots meaning of
relations or kinsfolk.

90 **Thrift on the *Vital Spark***
1 This uncollected story appeared in the *Glasgow Evening News* of 19th July 1915.
2 A reminder that at this time, and for many years afterwards, milk was sold
in bulk from milk carts, rather than in bottles.
3 The most popular day for country towns to take their half-holiday was a
Wednesday and most, if not all shops, closed on the afternoon of this day.
4 coal-rake
5 Sea-weed, often spread in large quantifies on fields as a fertiliser.
6 Reginald McKenna (1863–1943) Liberal politician. McKenna, a former
First Lord of the Admiralty and Home Secretary, was appointed Chancellor
of the Exchequer in the Coalition Government formed in May 1915. In this
role he advocated economy and introduced a considerable range of
additional taxation to finance the war effort.
7 One assumes that Sunny Jim is referring to the Coronation of George V in
June 1911 rather than that of Edward VII in August 1902.

91 **Difficulties in the Dry Area**
1 This uncollected story first appeared in the *Glasgow Evening News* on
February 7th 1916.
2 The *Vital Spark* is in Glasgow. West Street is on the South Side of the
Clyde, opposite the Broomielaw.

3 Presumably the engineer is referring the controversial figure of Horatio William Bottomley (1860–1933) financier, company promoter, Liberal politician, founder of *John Bull* and bankrupt. During the War he regained something of his former reputation and restored his fortunes. After the war he was charged with fraud, convicted and expelled from Parliament.

4 Para Handy's instructions were for large glasses of beer with not too large a head of froth.

5 *cf.* "Para and the War" for comments on laws designed to reduce alcohol consumption in ports and munitions areas.

6 Not a penny, not a brass farthing.

7 Anti-submarine boom across the Clyde.

8 shilling

9 two shillings and sixpence

92 Truth about the Push

1 This uncollected story first appeared in the *Glasgow Evening News* on July 10th 1916.

2 See No. 73 "How Jim Joined the Army" in which the fact of Jim's glass eye was revealed.

3 Popular term for a British soldier. Derived from the specimen name, "Tommy Atkins", used in an Army paybook.

4 Poison gas was used by both armies in the First World War.

5 boasting

93 Foraging for the *Vital Spark*

1 This uncollected story first appeared in the *Glasgow Evening News* on August 7th 1916

2 Many country workers were only paid half yearly or quarterly. In consequence food was bought on credit and such transactions were recorded in account or pass-books interleaved with blotting paper. (Information from Peter Robertson of West Kilbride.)

3 A type of oatcake or bannock made with the addition of potato and served with meat dishes.

4 Twelfth of August – start of grouse-shooting season.

5 spring onions

94 Our Gallant Allies

1 This uncollected story appeared in the *Glasgow Evening News* on August 28th 1916.

2 Dougie is using "hurl" in its Scottish sense of a free ride.

3 A type of boot or high shoe named after the Prussian Marshal Blücher (1742–1819), joint victor with the Duke of Wellington (also namely for boots) of the battle of Waterloo (1815).

4 Marine stores which would be familiar to the crew – Archangel tar was frequency applied to the *Vital Spark* to keep her "the smertest boat in the coastin' tred".

5 *cf.* many previous references to German bands on Clyde steamers.

6 The Italians had much experience of hauling of cannon up the mountain-tops in their campaign against the Austrians. On the day that this story appeared the news also appeared that Italy had declared war on Germany, having then been at war with Austro-Hungary for over a year.

95 Para Handy's Spectacles

1 This uncollected story appeared in the *Glasgow Evening News* of September 18th 1916.

2 Crown Prince Wilhelm (1882–1951), known to the British wartime popular press as "Little Willy"; at this time commanding the German 5th Army on the Western Front.

3 Macphail was somewhat premature. Kaiser Wilhelm II survived until 1941.

4 Bulgaria; under a German-born King, Ferdinand of Saxe-Coburg; was an ally of Germany and Austria during the First World War.

5 The General Post Office in Glasgow's George Square was built between 1875 and 1878 A later reference in this story ties the date of Para's acquisition of his spectacles to the laying of the foundation stone: the spectacles must thus be assumed to be 41 years old. As Para admits to being "nine and two twenties of years old, no' countin' the year I wass workin' in the sawmill" in the story "In Search of a Wife", first published in 1905, he presumably bought these spectacles at the early age of 20.

96 Para Handy in the Egg Trade

1 This uncollected story appeared in the *Glasgow Evening News* on October 9th 1916

2 Para Handy's prices were hardly excessive. In late August a Glasgow poulterer advertised a sale of Irish Eggs at 2s 2d per dozen "same as priced all over Glasgow at 2s 6d and 2s 8d per Dozen."

3 The spent grain left after the malt and grain has been soaked in a distillery mash-tub. The dried residue was sold as cattle feed.

4 In a period when game preservation was treated with obsessive energy the heron was persecuted as a predator on trout and salmon streams. A gamekeeper's larder was a fence or dyke on which the corpses of "vermin" were displayed as evidence of his zeal.

5 reluctant

6 ducks

7 Sea-fish normally preserved by salting.

97 Sunny Jim Returns

1 This uncollected story appeared in the *Glasgow Evening News* on July 14th 1919.

2 Stobs is in Roxburghshire, some 4 miles south of Hawick. Sunny Jim would presumably have taken a train along the North British Railway's "Waverley Line" from Stobs Station to Edinburgh before travelling to Glasgow. The obvious route for this leg of the journey would have been from Edinburgh Waverley to Glasgow Queen Street. Quite why he arrived at Central Station is a mystery.

3 The Highland Light Infantry. However Sunny Jim, as we are told in "The Fusilier" (no. 74) enrolled in the Royal Scots Fusiliers. For a possible explanation of this apparent inconsistency the reader is asked to note Jim's tale of his culinary adventures around Britain's military installations.

4 Emmanuel Shinwell (1884–1986) Labour politician and activist, normally categorised as one of the "Red Clydesiders". A leader of the 1919 strike in favour of a 40 hour week which brought troops and tanks into Glasgow's George Square on 'Black Friday', 31st January. Shinwell was elected to Parliament in 1921 and served as Minister of Fuel and Power and as

Secretary of State for War and later as Minister of Defence in the 1945–51 Attlee administrations. Awarded a life peerage in 1970.

5 A rich dough used for baking pancakes.
6 The home depot in Glasgow of the Highland Light Infantry.
7 Admiral Sir David Beatty commanded the 1st Battle Cruiser Squadron at the outbreak of the 1914–18 War and played a central part in the Battle of Jutland. He succeeded Jellicoe as commander-in-chief of the Grand Fleet in 1916 and became First Sea Lord in 1919. Created Earl Beatty in 1919.
8 The site of an Army camp on the Ayrshire coast between Troon and Irvine.
9 It will be recollected that Sunny Jim had a glass eye – a "glessy" – which he successfully concealed from the military authorities when he volunteered.
10 The White Star Line and the Black Ball Line are familiar enough to maritime historians; however Hurricane Jack's erstwhile employer has escaped their attention.
11 Hurricane Jack is referring disdainfully to an officer's certificate of competence – a master's or mate's ticket – the comparison is with the Communion Card which admitted a communicant member of the Church to the Sacrament.
12 Nigg is on the Cromarty Firth in Easter Ross.
13 Port-Dundas in the north of Glasgow is on the Glasgow branch of the Forth and Clyde Canal. Curiously enough, although the *Vital Spark* was in all probability built on the Forth and Clyde Canal at Kirkintilloch and although there are a number of references to the Canal in the Para Handy stories this is the only time we find the *Vital Spark* actually working on the Canal.
14 each
15 Doubtless a reflection of the political and industrial unrest referred to in note above.

98 Hurricane Jack's Shootings
1 This uncollected story appeared in the *Glasgow Evening News* on 16th August 1920.
2 Probably a reference to the shooters' Argyle-pattern stockings.
3 unstable
4 ferret
5 The Battle of Inkerman, 5th November 1854, was part of the siege of Sebastopol during the Crimean War.
6 A bolster or pillow.
7 Hurricane Jack's gun was a muzzle-loader primed by an explosive cap.
8 A member of a notable Scottish family of tinkers.
9 Birmingham was, of course, the centre of the English gun-trade.

99 Wireless on the *Vital Spark*
1 This uncollected story appeared in the *Glasgow Evening News* on 7th January 1924.
2 The popular term for the fine wire used with the crystal detector in the early radios.
3 The British Broadcasting Company's Glasgow station (call sign 5SC) went on the air in March 1923.
4 National radio broadcasting from the London station (2L0) had commenced in November 1922.

5 Readers will recollect Hurricane Jack's adventures as a philanderer in "The Double Life" at a Mull and Iona Soiree, Concert and Ball at the Waterloo Rooms.
6 Unaccountably, Kinlochaline in Morvern, despite being the birth-place of Hurricane Jack, has still not been favoured with a BBC radio station.
7 A previously unrecorded incident.
8 It is appropriate that this, the last of the Para Handy stories to appear in the *Glasgow Evening News* before Neil Munro's final retirement, should look forward to the new and wonderful medium of radio. During the nineteen years in which these stories had delighted the newspaper's readers the world in which they were set had experienced many changes; changes which Munro had faithfully recorded through their impact on the crew of the *Vital Spark*. As we have seen, the ninety nine stories in this collection owe much of their inspiration to an astonishingly wide range of contemporary events and concerns, ranging from German spies to Clyde gales and General Elections, all of which were able to provide Para and his crew with the raw material for an enjoyable baur. It is thus fitting that this, the final tale, about the crew's "Intercourse with the Infinite", was, in its day, equally topical.

100 Para Handy on Yachting

1 This story, unlike the others in this collection, did not appear in the *Glasgow Evening News* but was written specially by Munro for the *Clyde Cruising Club Journal* in 1910. It was very kindly brought to our attention by Sheena Mowat of Clarkston, Glasgow through the good offices of Dorothy Paterson of Inveraray. The story "Among the Yachts" – no. 41 in this edition – has some passages in common with this story.
2 Clyde Crusing Club. The Club was formed in 1909 with the object of encouraging cruising, cruising races and the social side of sailing. Its first club-rooms were in the Royal Hotel, Rothesay.
3 It will be recollected that Para Handy courted Mary Crawford with a bottle of this exotic perfume (see "The Baker's Little Widow" – no. 21 in this edition.)
4 Hunter's Quay, near Dunoon, was the headquarters of the Royal Clyde Yacht Club
5 An anchorage on the Clyde between Greenock and Gourock
6 There is no *Jackeroo* listed in *Lloyd's Register of Yachts* for 1910/11
7 A bay on the Renfrewshire coast between Gourock and Inverkip
8 Corned beef or mutton
9 The Cloch Lighthouse between Gourock and Lunderston Bay
10 A bass generally means a door mat but the *Concise Scots Dictionary* notes as alternative meanings a workman's toolbasket or bag, or a fish-basket